"What the world needs is more books by
Susan Elizabeth Phillips."
—Elizabeth Lowell

"Next to Tracy and Hepburn, no one does romantic
comedy better than Susan Elizabeth Phillips."
—*Minneapolis Star-Tribune*

"She makes you laugh, makes you cry
—makes you feel good."
—Jayne Ann Krentz

PRAISE FOR
SUSAN ELIZABETH PHILLIPS AND
HONEY MOON

"If you read only one mainstream novel this summer, let this
be it."

—*Affaire de Coeur*

"Excellent reading."

—*Rendezvous*

HOT SHOT

"Fun and lively."

—*Publishers Weekly*

"Fascinating. . . . A crackerjack tale about the birth of the
high-tech industry."

—*Rave Reviews*

Also by Susan Elizabeth Phillips

Fancy Pants
Glitter Baby
Honey Moon
Hot Shot

Susan Elizabeth Phillips

Honey Moon
&
Hot Shot

POCKET BOOKS

New York London Toronto Sydney

POCKET BOOKS, a division of Simon & Schuster, Inc.
1230 Avenue of the Americas, New York, NY 10020

This book is a work of fiction. Names, characters, places and incidents are products of the author's imagination or are used fictitiously. Any resemblance to actual events or locales or persons, living or dead, is entirely coincidental.

Hot Shot copyright © 1991 by Susan Elizabeth Phillips
Honey Moon copyright © 1993 by Susan Elizabeth Phillips

ISBN-13: 978-1-4165-0741-3
ISBN-10:   1-4165-0741-8

This Pocket Books trade paperback edition November 2005

10 9 8 7 6 5 4 3 2

POCKET and colophon are registered trademarks of Simon & Schuster, Inc.

Manufactured in the United States of America

For information regarding special discounts for bulk purchases, please contact Simon & Schuster Special Sales at 1-800-456-6798 or business@simonandschuster.com

These titles were previously published individually by Pocket Books.

Honey Moon

Susan Elizabeth Phillips

In memory of my father

A great roller coaster makes you find God when you ride it.

—Anonymous

The
Lift Hill

1980–1982

1

All that spring Honey prayed to Walt Disney. From her bedroom in the rear of the rusty old trailer that sat in a clump of pines behind the third hill of the Black Thunder roller coaster, she prayed to God and Walt and sometimes even Jesus in hopes that one of those powerful heavenly figures would help her out. With her arms resting on the bent track that held the room's only window, she gazed out through the sagging screen at the patch of night sky just visible over the tops of the pines.

"Mr. Disney, it's Honey again. I know that the Silver Lake Amusement Park doesn't look like much right now with the water level down so far you can see all the stumps and with the *Bobby Lee* sitting on the bottom of the lake right at the end of the dock. Maybe we haven't had more than a hundred people through the park in the past week, but that doesn't mean things have to stay this way."

Ever since the Paxawatchie County *Democrat* had printed the rumor that the Walt Disney people were thinking about buying the Silver Lake Amusement Park as a location for a South Carolina version of Disney World, Honey hadn't been able to think of anything else. She was sixteen years old, and she knew that praying to Mr. Disney was a childish thing to do (not to mention questionable theology for a Southern Baptist), but circumstances had made her desperate.

Now she ticked off the advantages she wanted Mr. Disney to consider. "We're only an hour from the interstate. And with some good directional signs, everybody on their way to Myrtle Beach would be sure to stop here with their kids. If you don't count the mosquitoes and the humidity, the climate is good. The lake could be real pretty if your employees made the Purlex Paint Company stop dumping their toxics in it. And those people who are carrying on your business now that you're dead could buy it real cheap. Could you use your influence with them? Could you somehow make them understand that the Silver Lake Amusement Park is just what they're looking for?"

Her aunt's thin, listless voice interrupted Honey's combination of prayer and sales presentation. "Who're you talkin' to, Honey? You don't have a boy in that bedroom, do you?"

"Yeah, Sophie," Honey replied with a grin. "I got about a dozen in here. And one of 'em is gettin' ready to show me his dingdong."

"Oh, my, Honey. I don't think you should talk like that. It's not nice."

"Sorry." Honey knew she shouldn't bait Sophie, but she liked it when her aunt fussed over her. It didn't happen very often, and nothing ever came of it, but when Sophie fussed, Honey could almost pretend she was her real mother instead of her aunt.

A burst of laughter sounded from the next room as the *Tonight Show* audience responded to one of Johnny's jokes about peanuts and President Carter. Sophie always had the television on. She said it kept her from missing Uncle Earl's voice.

Earl Booker had died a year and a half ago, leaving Sophie the owner of the Silver Lake Amusement Park. She hadn't exactly been a ball of fire when he was alive, but it was even worse now that he was dead, and Honey was pretty much in charge of things. As she drew back from the window, she knew it wouldn't be much longer before Sophie fell asleep. She never lasted much past midnight even though she hardly ever got out of bed before noon.

Honey propped herself up against the pillows. The trailer was hot and airless. Despite the fact that she was wearing only an orange Budweiser T-shirt and a pair of underpants, she couldn't get comfortable. They used to have a window air conditioner, but it had broken down two summers ago just like everything else, and they couldn't afford to replace it.

Honey glanced at the dial on the clock sitting next to the bed she shared with Sophie's daughter, Chantal, and felt a twinge of alarm. Her cousin should have been home by now. It was Monday night, the park was closed, and there wasn't anything to do. Chantal was central to Honey's backup plan if Mr. Disney's employees didn't buy the park, and Honey couldn't afford to misplace her cousin, not even for an evening.

Swinging her feet down off the bed onto the cracked linoleum, she reached for the pair of faded red shorts she'd worn that day. She was small-boned, barely five feet tall, and the shorts were hand-me-downs from Chantal. They were too big for her hips and hung in baggy folds that made her toothpick legs seem even skinnier than they were. But vanity was one of the few faults Honey didn't possess, so she paid no attention.

Although Honey couldn't see it herself, she in fact had some cause for vanity. She had thickly lashed light blue eyes topped by dark slashes of brow. Her heart-shaped face held small cheekbones dusted with freckles and a pert little excuse for a nose. But she hadn't quite grown into her mouth, which was wide and framed by full lips that always reminded her of a big old sucker fish. For as long as she could remember, she had hated the way she looked, and not just because people had mistaken her for a boy until her small breasts had poked through, but because no one wanted to take a person seriously who looked so much like a child. Since Honey very much needed to be taken seriously, she had done her best to disguise every one of her physical assets with a perpetually hostile scowl and a generally belligerent attitude.

After slipping on a pair of flattened blue rubber flip-flops that had long ago conformed to the bottoms of her feet, she shoved her hands through her short, chewed hair. She performed this action not to straighten it but to scratch a mosquito bite on her scalp. Her hair was light brown, exactly the same color as her name. It liked to curl, but she seldom gave it the opportunity. Instead, she cut it whenever it got in her way, using whatever reasonably sharp implement happened to be handy: a pocketknife, a pair of pinking shears, and, on one unfortunate occasion, a fish scaler.

She closed the door behind her as she slipped out into a short, narrow hallway carpeted with an indoor-outdoor remnant patterned in brown and gold lozenges that also covered the uneven floor in the combination living and eating area. Just as she had predicted, Sophie had fallen asleep on an old couch upholstered in a worn tan fabric printed with faded tavern signs, American eagles, and thirteen-star flags. The perm Chantal had given her mother hadn't turned out too well, and Sophie's thin salt-and-pepper hair looked dry and vaguely electrified. She was overweight, and her knit top outlined breasts that had fallen like water balloons to opposite sides of her body.

Honey regarded her aunt with a familiar combination of exasperation and love. Sophie Moon Booker was the one who should have been worrying about her daughter's whereabouts, not Honey. She was the one who should have been thinking about how they were going to pay all those bills that were piling up and how they were going to keep their family together without falling into the peckerhead welfare system. But Honey knew that getting mad at Sophie was just like getting mad at Sophie's daughter, Chantal. It didn't do any good.

"I'm going out for a while."

Sophie snorted in her sleep.

The night air was heavy with humidity as Honey jumped down off the crumbling concrete step. The trailer's exterior was a particularly jarring shade of robin's-egg blue, improved only by the dulling film of age. Her flip-flops sank into the sand, and grit settled between her toes. As she moved away from the trailer, she sniffed. The June night smelled like pine, creosote, and the disinfectant they used in the toilets. All of those smells were overlaid by the distant, musty scent of Silver Lake.

As she passed beneath a series of weathered Southern yellow-pine support columns, she shoved her hands in the pockets of her shorts and told herself that this time she would keep going. This time she wouldn't stop and look. Looking made her think, and thinking made her feel like the inside of a week-old bait bucket. She moved doggedly ahead for another minute, but then she stopped anyway. Turning back the way she had come, she craned her neck and let her gaze move along the sweeping length of Black Thunder.

The roller coaster's massive wooden frame stood silhouetted against the night sky like the skeleton of a prehistoric dinosaur. Her eyes traveled up the steep incline of Black Thunder's mountainous lift hill and down that heart-stopping sixty-degree drop. She traced the slopes of the next two hills with their chilling dips all the way to the final spiral that twisted down in a nightmare whirlpool over Silver Lake itself. Her heart ached with an awful combination of yearning and bitterness as she took in the three hills and the steeply banked death spiral. Everything had begun to go wrong for them the summer Black Thunder had stopped running.

Even though the Silver Lake Amusement Park was small and old-fashioned compared to places like Busch Gardens and Six Flags over Georgia, it had something none of the others could claim. It had the last great wooden roller coaster in the South, a coaster some enthusiasts considered more thrilling than the legendary Coney Island Cyclone. Since it was built in the late 1920s, people had come from all over the country to ride Black Thunder. For legions of roller-coaster enthusiasts, the trip to Silver Lake had been a religious pilgrimage.

After a dozen rides on the legendary wooden coaster, they would visit the park's other more mundane attractions, including spending two dollars a person to take a cruise up and down Silver Lake on the paddle wheeler *Robert E. Lee*. But the *Bobby Lee* had fallen victim to disaster just like Black Thunder.

Almost two years ago, on Labor Day 1978, a wheel assembly had snapped off Black Thunder's rear car, separating it from the other cars and sending it hurtling over the side. Luckily no one had been hurt, but the State of South

Carolina had closed down the roller coaster that same day, and none of the banks would finance the expensive renovation the state required before the ride could be reopened. Without its famous attraction, the Silver Lake Amusement Park had been dying a slow and painful death.

Honey walked farther into the park. On her right a bug-encrusted light bulb illuminated the deserted interior of the Dodgem Hall, where the battered fiberglass cars sat in a sleeping herd waiting for the park to open at ten the next morning. She passed through Kiddieland, with its miniature motorcycles and fire trucks sitting motionless on their endless circular tracks. Further on, the Scrambler and Tilt-a-Whirl rested from their labors. She paused in front of the House of Horror, where a Day-Glo mural of a decapitated body gushing phosphorescent blood from its severed neck stretched over the entryway.

"Chantal?"

There was no answer.

Removing the flashlight from its hook behind the ticket booth, she walked purposefully up the ramp into the House of Horror. In the daytime the ramp vibrated and a loud-speaker emitted hollow groans and shrill screams, but now everything was quiet. She entered the Passageway of Death and shone her light on the seven-foot hooded executioner with his bloody ax.

"Chantal, you in here?"

She heard only silence. Brushing through the artificial cobwebs, she passed the chopping block on her way to the Rat Den. Once inside, she shone her flashlight around the small room. Scores of glowing red eyes looked back at her from the one hundred and six snarling gray rats that lurked in the rafters and hung from invisible wires over her head.

Honey regarded them with satisfaction. The Rat Den was the best part of the House of Horror, because the animals were real. They had been stuffed by a New Jersey taxidermist in 1952 for the spook house at Palisades Park in Fort Lee. In the late sixties her Uncle Earl had bought them thirdhand from a North Carolina man whose park near Forest City had gone bust.

"Chantal?" She called out her cousin's name one more time, and when she got no response left the House of Horror through the back fire exit. Dodging power cables, she cut behind the Roundup and headed for the midway.

Only a few of the colored light bulbs strung through the sagging pennants that zigzagged over the midway were still working. The hanky-panks were boarded up for the night: the milk-bottle pitch and the fish tank, the Crazy Ball game, and the Iron Claw with its glass case full of combs, dice, and Dukes of Hazzard key chains. The stale smell of popcorn, pizza, and rancid oil from the funnel cakes clung to everything.

It was the smell of Honey's rapidly vanishing childhood, and she breathed it deeply into her lungs. If the Disney people took over, the smell would disappear forever, right along with the hanky-panks, Kiddieland, and the House of Horror. She clasped her arms over her small chest and hugged herself, a habit she had developed over the years because no one else would do it.

Since her mother had died when she was six, this was the only home she'd known, and she loved it with all her heart. Writing the Disney people had been the worst thing she'd ever had to do. She had been forced to suppress all of her softer emotions in a desperate attempt to find the money she needed to keep her family together, the money that would keep them out of the welfare system and allow them to buy a small house in a clean neighborhood where they could maybe have some nice furniture and a garden. But as she stood in the middle of the deserted midway, she wished that she were old enough and smart enough to make things turn out differently. Because most of all, she couldn't bear the idea that she was losing Black Thunder, and if the coaster had still been running, nothing in the world could have made her give up this park.

The eerie night quiet and the smell of old popcorn brought back the memory of a small child huddled in the corner of the trailer, scabby knees drawn up to her chin, light blue eyes large and stunned. An angry voice from the past echoed in her mind.

"Get her out of here, Sophie! Goddamnit, she's givin' me the willies. She's hardly moved since she you brung her here last night. All she's done is sit in that corner and stare." She heard the crash of her Uncle Earl's meaty fist on the kitchen table, Sophie's monotonous whine.

"Where am I gonna put her, Earl?"

"I don't give a shit where you put her. It's not my fault your sister went and got herself drowned. Those Alabama welfare people had no right to make you go get her. I want to eat my lunch in goddamn peace without her spookin' me!"

Sophie came over to the corner of the trailer's living area and poked the sole of Honey's cheap canvas sneaker with the toe of her own red espadrille. "You stop actin' like that, Honey. You go on outside and find Chantal. You haven't seen the park yet. She'll show it to you."

"I want my mama," Honey whispered.

"Goddamnit! Get her out of here, Sophie!"

"Now see what you done," Sophie sighed. "You got your Uncle Earl all mad." She grasped Honey's upper arm and tugged on it. "Come on. Let's go get you some cotton candy."

She took Honey from the trailer and led her through the pines and out into the scorching sun of a Carolina afternoon. Honey moved like a tiny robot. She didn't want any cotton candy. Sophie'd made her eat some Captain Crunch that morning, and she'd thrown up.

Sophie dropped her arm. Honey already sensed that her aunt didn't like to touch people, not like Honey's mother, Carolann. Carolann was always picking Honey up and cuddling her and calling her sweetie pie, even when she was tired from working all day at the dry cleaners in Montgomery.

"I want my mama," Honey whispered as they stepped through the grass into a colonnade of great wooden posts.

"Your mama's dead. She's not—"

The rest of Sophie's reply was drowned out as a monster screamed above Honey's head.

Honey screamed then, too. All the grief and fear that had been building up inside her since her mother had died and

she was snatched away from everything familiar were released by the terror of that unexpected noise. Again and again she screamed.

She had a vague idea what a roller coaster was, but she had never ridden one, never seen one this size, and it didn't occur to her to connect the sound with the ride. She heard only a monster, the monster that hides in the closet and skulks under the bed and carries off little girls' mothers in fearsome fiery jaws.

The piercing screams spilled from her mouth. After being nearly catatonic for the six days since her mother had died, she couldn't stop, not even when Sophie began to shake her arm.

"Quit that! Quit that screamin', you hear?"

But Honey couldn't quit. Instead, she fought against Sophie until she broke away. Then she began running beneath the tracks, arms flailing, her small lungs heaving as over and over she screamed her sorrow and fear. When she came to a dip in the track too low for her to pass beneath, she grasped one of the wooden posts. Splinters dug into her arms as she held onto the thing she feared most in the confused belief that it couldn't devour her if she clasped it tightly enough.

She wasn't aware of the passage of time, only the sound of her screams, the sporadic roar of the monster as it rushed overhead, the rough splinters of the post digging into the baby-soft skin of her arms, and the fact that she wasn't ever going to see her mother again.

"Goddamnit, stop that noise!"

While Sophie stood helplessly watching, Uncle Earl came up behind them and dragged her off the post with a bellow. "What's wrong with her? What the hell is wrong with her now?"

"I don't know," Sophie whined. "She started doin' that when she heard Black Thunder. I think she's afraid of it."

"Well, that's just too goddamn bad. We're not coddling her, goddamnit."

He snatched Honey up by the waist and pulled her out from beneath the coaster. Walking with great loping strides, he carried her through the clusters of people visiting the park that day and up the ramp into the station house where Black Thunder loaded its riders.

A train sat empty, ready for its next group of passengers. Ignoring the protests of the people waiting in line, he pushed her beneath the lap bar in the first car. Her shrill screams echoed hollowly beneath the wooden roof. She struggled desperately to get out, but her uncle held her fast with one hairy arm.

"Earl, whatcha doin'?" Chester, the old man who ran Black Thunder, rushed up to him.

"She's goin' on a ride."

"She's too little, Earl. You know she's not tall enough for this coaster."

"That's too damn bad. Strap her in. And no goddamn brakes."

"But, Earl . . ."

"Do what I say, or pick up your paycheck."

She was vaguely aware of the loud objections of several of the adults waiting in line, but then the train began to move, and she realized that she was being delivered into the very stomach of the beast that had taken her mother.

"No!" she screamed. "No! *Mama!*"

Her fingers barely met at the tips as she clutched the lap bar in a death grip. Sobs ripped through her. "Mama . . . Mama . . ."

The structure creaked and groaned as the train crawled up the great lift hill that had helped create the legend of Black Thunder. It moved with sadistic slowness, giving her child's mind time to conjure ghastly visions of terrifying horror. She was six years old and alone in the universe with the beast of death. Utterly defenseless, she wasn't big enough, strong enough, old enough to protect herself, and there was no adult left on earth who would do it for her.

Fear clogged her throat and her tiny heart throbbed in her chest as the car climbed inexorably to the top of the great lift hill. Higher than the tallest mountain in the world. Beyond the comfort of clouds. Above the hot sky to a dark place where only devils lurked.

Her last scream ripped from her throat as the car cleared the top, and she had one glimpse of the terrifying descent before she was thrown into the stomach of the beast to be gobbled up and gnawed apart through the darkest night of her child's soul only to . . .

Rise again.

And then pitch back into hell.

And rise again.

She was plunged into hell and resurrected three times before she was hurled out over the lake and down into the devil's spiral. She slammed against the side of the car as she catapulted in a deadly whirlpool straight down into the water, only to level out at the last second, barely two feet above the surface, and be shot back to higher ground. The coaster slowed and gently delivered her to the station.

She was no longer crying.

The cars came to a stop. Her Uncle Earl had disappeared, but Chester, the ride operator, rushed up to lift her out. She shook her head, her eyes still tragic, her tiny face chalky.

"Again," she whispered.

She was too young to articulate the feelings the coaster had given her. She knew only that she had to experience them again—the sense that there was a force greater than herself, a force that could punish but would also rescue. The sense that somehow that force had allowed her to touch her mother.

She rode Black Thunder a dozen times that day and on through the rest of her childhood whenever she needed to experience hope in the protection of a higher power. The coaster confronted her with all the terrors of human existence, but then carried her safely to the other side.

Life with the Booker family gradually settled into a routine. Her Uncle Earl never liked her, but he put up with her because she became a much bigger help to him than either his wife or daughter. Sophie was as kind as it was possible for someone entirely self-absorbed to be. She made few demands other than to insist that Honey and Chantal go to Sunday school at least once a month.

But the great wooden coaster had taught Honey more

13

about God than the Baptist Church, and the coaster's theology was easier to understand. For someone who was small for her age, orphaned, and female to boot, she drew courage from the knowledge that a higher power existed, something strong and eternal that would watch over her.

A sound coming from inside the arcade jolted Honey back to the present. She reprimanded herself for getting distracted from her purpose. Before long, she was going to be as bad as her cousin. Walking forward, she stuck her head into the arcade. "Hey, Buck, have you seen Chantal?"

Buck Ochs looked up from the pinball machine he was trying to fix because she had told him that if he didn't get at least a few of the machines running she was going to kick his big old ugly butt right back to Georgia. His beer gut pushed against the buttons of his dirty plaid shirt as he shifted his weight and gave her his doltish grin.

"Chantal who?"

He laughed uproariously at his wit. She wished she could fire him right there on the spot, but she had lost too many men already because she couldn't always meet her payroll on time, and she knew she couldn't afford to lose another. Besides, Buck wasn't malicious, just stupid. He also had a disgusting habit of scratching himself right where he shouldn't when females were present.

"You're a real joker, aren't you, Buck? Has Chantal been around?"

"Naw, Honey. It's just been me, myself, and me."

"Well, let's see if one of you can get a couple of those damned machines working before morning."

With a quelling look, she left the arcade and continued to the end of the midway. The Bullpen, a run-down wooden building where the unmarried male employees bunked, sat in the trees behind the picnic grove. Only Buck and two others lived there now. She could see yellow light seeping from the windows, but she didn't go closer because she couldn't imagine Chantal visiting either Cliff or Rusty. Chantal wasn't one to sit and talk to people.

The uneasiness that had been growing inside her ever since she had realized how late it was settled deeper into her stomach. This was no time for Chantal to disappear. Something was definitely wrong. And Honey was afraid she knew exactly what it was.

She turned in a circle, taking in the dilapidated trailers, the midway, the rides. Dominating it all were the great hills of Black Thunder, stripped now of all their power to hurl a frightened young girl to a place where she could once again find hope in something eternal to protect her. Hesitating for only a moment, she began to head down the overgrown concrete walk that led to Silver Lake.

The night was deep and still. As the old pines closed over her head, shutting out the moonlight, the calliope sounds of "Dixie" began to drift through her memory.

Ladies and gentlemen. Children of all ages. Take a step back in time to those grand old days when cotton was king. Join us for a ride on the paddle wheeler Robert E. Lee *and see beautiful Silver Lake, the largest lake in Paxawatchie County, South Carolina. . . .*

The pines ended at a dilapidated dock. She stopped walking and shivered. At the end of the dock rose the ghostly hulk of the *Bobby Lee*.

The *Robert E. Lee* sat right where it had been anchored when it had sunk in a winter storm a few months after the Black Thunder disaster. Now its bottom rested in the polluted muddy ooze of Silver Lake fifteen feet down. All of its lower deck was underwater, along with the once-proud paddle wheel that had churned at its stern. Only the upper deck and pilothouse rose above the lake's surface. The *Bobby Lee* sat at the end of the dock, useless and half submerged, a phantom ship in the eerie moonlight.

Honey shivered again and crossed her arms over her chest. Watery moonlight etched ghostly fingers over the dying lake, and her nostrils twitched at the musty scent of decaying vegetation, dead fish, and rotting wood. She wasn't a chicken, but she didn't like being around the *Bobby Lee* at night. She curled her toes in her flip-flops so they wouldn't make any noise as she took first one and then another step along the dock. Some of the boards were broken, and she could see the stagnant waters of the lake below. She slid forward another step and stopped, opening her mouth to call out Chantal's name. But creepy-crawlies were strangling her voice box and nothing came out. She wished she'd stopped at the Bullpen and asked Cliff or Rusty to come with her.

Her cowardice made her angry. She was having a hard enough time as it was getting them to follow her orders. Men like that didn't respect women bosses, especially when they were only sixteen. If any of them ever found out she was afraid of something as foolish as an old dead boat, they'd never listen to her again.

A flutter of wings burst from behind her as an owl swooped out over the lake from the trees. She sucked in her breath. Just then, she heard the distant sound of a moan.

She didn't have any patience with superstition, but the menacing shape of the dead ship looming at the end of the dock had her spooked, and for a fraction of a second she thought the sound might be coming from a vampire or a succubus or some kind of zombie. Then the moon skidded out from beneath a wisp of cloud and common sense reasserted itself. She knew exactly what she had heard, and it didn't have anything to do with zombies.

She tore down the dock, her flip-flops spanking her heels as she sidestepped the rotted boards and dodged a pile of rope. The boat had sunk five feet from the end of the dock, and the upper deck railing, broken like a gap-toothed smile, loomed ahead of her above the water level. She raced toward the piece of plywood that served as a makeshift ramp and dashed up its incline. It sprang beneath her ninety pounds like a trampoline.

The bottoms of her feet stung as she landed hard on the upper deck. She clutched a piece of the railing to balance herself and then ran toward the staircase. It descended into the murky water. Even in the darkness, she could see the white belly of a dead fish floating near the submerged stair treads. Throwing her leg over the peeling wooden railing, she raced up the section of staircase that still rose above the surface of the water to the pilothouse.

A man and woman were sprawled near its door, their

bodies intertwined. They were too caught up in each other to hear the noise of Honey's approach.

"Let her go, you peckerhead!" Honey shouted as she reached the top.

The figures sprang apart. A bat flew out from the broken window of the pilothouse.

"Honey!" Chantal exclaimed. Her blouse was open, her nipples silver dollars in the moonlight.

The young man she was with sprang to his feet, jerking up the zipper of the cutoffs he wore with a University of South Carolina T-shirt that had "Gamecocks" written across the front. For a moment he looked dazed and disoriented, and then he took in Honey's chewed hair, tiny stature, and the hostile scowl that made her look more like an ill-tempered ten-year-old boy than a young girl.

"You go on, y'hear?" he said belligerently. "Y'all got no business here."

Chantal rose from the deck and lifted her hand to close the front of her blouse. The movement was slow and lazy, just like all her movements were. The boy draped his arm around her shoulders.

The familiar way he embraced Chantal, as if she belonged to him instead of to Honey, ignited her already simmering temper. Chantal was hers, along with Aunt Sophie and the ruins of the Silver Lake Amusement Park! Using her index finger as a weapon, she pointed down to the deck by her side. "You get over here, Chantal Booker. I mean it. You get over here right now."

Chantal stared at her sandals for a moment and then took a reluctant step forward.

The college boy grabbed her arm. "Wait a minute. Who is she? What's she doin' here, Chantal?"

"My cousin Honey," Chantal replied. "She runs things, I guess."

Once again Honey punched her finger toward the deck. "You bet I run things. Now you get over here this minute."

Chantal attempted to move forward, but the boy wouldn't release her. He curled his other hand over her arm. "Aw, she's just a kid. You don't have to listen to her." He gestured toward the shore. "You go on back where you came from, little girl."

Honey's eyes narrowed into slits. "Listen to me, college boy. If you know what's good for you, you'll pack that undersized pecker of yours right back in your dirty underwear and get off this boat before you make me mad."

He shook his head incredulously. "I think I might just throw you right over the side of this boat, baby face, and let the fish eat you."

"I wouldn't try it." Honey took a threatening step, her small chin jutted forward. She despised it when people made fun of the way she looked. "Maybe I better tell you that I got out of reform school just last week for knifing a man who was a lot bigger than you are. They would have give me the electric chair, but I was underage."

"Is that so? Well, I don't happen to believe you."

Chantal signed. "Honey, you gonna tell Mama?"

Honey ignored her and concentrated on the boy. "How old did Chantal tell you she was?"

"None of your beeswax."

"Did she tell you she was eighteen?"

He glanced at Chantal, and for the first time he looked uncertain.

"I might of known," Honey said with disgust. "That girl's only fifteen years old. Didn't they teach you anything about statutory rape at the University of South Carolina?"

The boy released Chantal as if she were radioactive. "Is that true, Chantal? You sure look older than fifteen."

Honey spoke before Chantal had the chance. "She matured early."

"Now, Honey . . ." Chantal protested.

He began easing away. "Maybe we better call it a night, Chantal." He sauntered toward the staircase. "I had a real good time. Maybe I'll see you again sometime, all right?"

"Sure, Chris. I'd like that."

He fled down the stairs. They could hear the *sprong* of the plywood plank and then a thump as he landed on the dock. Both girls watched him disappear into the pines.

Chantal sighed, eased down onto the deck, and leaned

back against the pilothouse. "You got any cigarettes on you?"

Honey pulled out a crushed pack of Salems and handed it over as she lowered herself next to her cousin. Chantal slipped the matches out from under the cellophane and lit the cigarette. She took a deep, easy drag. "Why'd you go and tell him I was only fifteen?"

"I didn't want to have to fight him."

"Honey, you weren't gonna fight him. You didn't even come up to his chin. And you know that I'm eighteen—two years older'n you are."

"I might have fought him." Honey took the cigarettes back but, after a moment's hesitation, decided not to light one. She'd been trying for months to learn how to smoke, but she just couldn't get the hang of it.

"And all that stuff about reform school and knifing a man. Nobody believes you."

"Some do."

"I don't think it's good to tell so many lies."

"It goes along with being a woman in the business world. Otherwise people take advantage of you."

Chantal's legs stretched bare and shapely from beneath her white shorts as she crossed her ankles. Honey studied her cousin's sandaled feet and polished toenails. She considered Chantal the prettiest woman she'd ever seen. It was hard to believe she was the daughter of Earl and Sophie Booker, neither of whom had ever won any prizes for good looks. Chantal had a cloud of curly dark hair, exotic eyes that tilted up at the corners, a small red mouth, and a soft, feminine figure. With her dark hair and olive skin, she looked like a Latin spitfire, a misleading impression since Chantal didn't have much more spirit than an old hound dog on a hot day in August. Honey loved her anyway.

Cigarette smoke ribboned from Chantal's top lip into her nostrils as she French-inhaled. "I'd give just about anything to be married to a movie star. I mean it, Honey. I'd give just about anything to be Mrs. Burt Reynolds."

In Honey's opinion, Burt Reynolds was about twenty years too old for Chantal, but she knew she could never convince her cousin of that fact so she played her trump card right off the top. "Mr. Burt Reynolds is a southern boy. Southern boys like to marry virgins."

"I'm still sort of a virgin."

"Thanks to me."

"I wasn't gonna let Chris go all the way."

"Chantal, you might not of been able to stop him once he got worked up. You know you're not real good at saying no to people."

"You gonna tell Mama?"

"A lot of good that'd do. She'd just change the channel and go back to sleep. This is the third time I've caught you with one of those college boys. They come sniffin' around you just like you're sending out some kind of radio signal or something. And what about that boy you were with in the House of Horror last month? When I found you, he had his hand right inside your shorts."

"It feels good when boys do that. And he was real nice."

Honey snorted in disgust. There was no talking to Chantal. She was sweet, but she wasn't too bright. Not that Honey had room to criticize. At least Chantal had made it through high school, which was more than Honey had been able to do.

Honey hadn't quit school because she was dumb—she was a voracious reader and she'd always been smart as a whip. She'd quit because she had better things to do than spend her time with a bunch of ignorant peckerhead girls who told everybody she was a lesbian just because they were afraid of her.

The memory still made her feel like crawling away somewhere and hiding. Honey wasn't pretty like the other girls. She didn't wear cute clothes or have a bubbly personality, but that didn't mean she was a lesbian, did it? The question bothered her because she wasn't absolutely sure of the answer. She certainly couldn't imagine letting a boy touch her under her shorts like Chantal did.

Chantal's voice interrupted the silence that had fallen between them. "Do you ever think about your mama?"

"Not so much anymore." Honey picked at a piece of

splintered wood on the deck. "But since you brought up the subject, it wouldn't do you any harm to think about what happened to my mama when she was even younger than you. She let a college boy come sniffin' around her, and it ruined her life."

"I don't follow you. If your mama hadn't slept with that college boy, you wouldn't of been born. Then where would you be?"

"That's not the point. The point is—college boys only want one thing from girls like you and my mama. They only want sex. And after they get it, they disappear. Do you want to end up all by yourself with a baby to take care of and nothing except the welfare system to support you?"

"Chris said I was prettier than any of the sorority girls he knows."

It was no use. Chantal always managed to get sidetracked when Honey was trying to make a point. At times like this, Honey despaired over Chantal. How could her cousin ever manage life if Honey weren't around to look after her? Even though Chantal was older, Honey had been taking care of her for years, trying to teach her right from wrong and how to get along in the world. Knowing about those things seemed to come naturally to Honey, but Chantal was a lot like Sophie. She didn't have much interest in anything that required effort.

"Honey, how come you don't fix yourself up a little bit so you could have some boyfriends, too?"

Honey leapt to her feet. "I'm not a damn lesbian, if that's what you're tryin' to say!"

"I'm not sayin' that at all." Chantal gazed thoughtfully at the smoke curling from the end of her cigarette. "I guess if you was a lesbian, I would of been the first one to know about it. We been sleepin' in the same bed ever since you came to live with us, and you never tried anything with me."

Vaguely mollified, Honey resumed her seat. "Did you practice your baton today?"

"Maybe . . . I don't remember."

"You didn't, did you?"

"Baton twirling is hard, Honey."

21

"It's not hard. You've just got to practice, that's all. You know I'm planning to put flames on it next week."

"Why'd you have to pick something hard like baton twirling?"

"You can't sing. You don't play any musical instrument or tap-dance. It was the only thing I could think of."

"I just don't see why it's so important for me to win the Miss Paxawatchie County Beauty Pageant. Not if the Walt Disney people are gonna buy the park."

"We don't know that, Chantal. It's just a rumor. I wrote them another letter, but we haven't heard anything, and we can't just sit back and wait."

"You didn't make me enter the contest last year. Why do I have to do it this year?"

"Because last year's prize was a hundred dollars and a beauty make-over at Dundee's Department Store. This year it's an all-expense-paid overnight trip to Charleston to audition for *The Dash Coogan Show.*"

"That's another thing, Honey," Chantal complained. "I think you got unrealistic expectations about all of this. I don't know anything about being on TV. I been thinking more along the lines of being a hairdresser. I like hair."

"You don't have to know anything about being on TV. They want a fresh face. I've explained it to you about a hundred times."

Honey reached into her pocket and pulled out the well-worn pamphlet that gave all the information about this year's Miss Paxawatchie County Beauty Pageant. She turned to the back page. The moonlight wasn't bright enough for her to read the small print, but she had studied it so many times she knew it by heart.

The winner of the Miss Paxawatchie County title will receive an all-expense-paid overnight trip to Charleston, compliments of the pageant's sponsor, Dundee's Department Store. While in Charleston, she will audition for *The Dash Coogan Show,* a much-anticipated new fall network television program that will be filmed in California.

The producers of *The Dash Coogan Show* are auditioning Southern lovelies in seven cities in search of an actress to play the part of Celeste, Mr. Coogan's daughter. She must be between eighteen and twenty-one years old, beautiful, and have a strong regional accent. In addition to visiting Charleston, the producers will also be auditioning actresses in Atlanta, New Orleans, Birmingham, Dallas, Houston, and San Antonio.

Honey frowned. That part bothered her. Those TV people were visiting three cities in Texas, but only one in the southern states. It didn't take much brain power to figure out that they would prefer a Texan, which she supposed wasn't surprising since Dash Coogan was the king of the cowboy movie stars, but she still didn't like it. As she gazed back down at the pamphlet, she comforted herself with the knowledge that there couldn't be a single woman in all of Texas who was prettier than Chantal Booker.

The final choices from the seven-city talent search will be flown to Los Angeles for a personal screen test with Mr. Coogan. Moviegoers will remember Dash Coogan for his many roles as the star of over 20 westerns including *Lariat* and *Alamo Sunset,* his most famous. This will be his first television show. All of us are hoping that our own Miss Paxawatchie County will be portraying his daughter.

Chantal interrupted her thoughts. "See, the thing of it is—I want to *marry* a movie star. Not *be* one."

Honey ignored her. "Right now what you want doesn't mean spit. We're pretty close to being desperate, and that means we have to make our own opportunities. Idleness is the beginning of a long slide into the welfare system, and that's where we're going to end up if we don't force things to happen." She hugged her knees, and her voice dropped nearly to a whisper. "I got this feeling way down deep in my stomach, Chantal. I can hardly explain it, but I just got this strong feeling that those TV people are going to take one look at you and they're going to make you a star."

Chantal's sigh was so prolonged it seemed to come from her toes. "Sometimes you make my head spin, Honey. You must take after that college boy who was your daddy because you sure don't take after any of us."

"We have to keep our family together," Honey said fiercely. "Sophie's useless, and I'm too young to get a decent job. You're our only hope, Chantal. Ever since you started modeling at Dundee's Department Store, it's been evident that you're the best chance this family's got. If the Disney people won't buy this park, we have to have another plan to fall back on. The three of us are a family. We can't let anything happen to our family."

But Chantal had gotten distracted by the night sky and dreams of marrying a movie star, and she wasn't listening.

2

"And our new Miss Paxawatchie County, 1980, is . . . Chantal Booker!"

Honey leapt to her feet with a bloodcurdling yell that rose above the applause of the audience. The loudspeaker blared out "Give My Regards to Broadway" and Laura Liskey, last year's Miss Paxawatchie County, placed the crown on Chantal's head. Chantal gave her vague smile. The crown slipped to the side, but she didn't notice.

Honey jumped up and down, clapping and hollering. This miserable week was having a happy ending after all. Chantal had won the title, despite the fact that her baton twirling was the worst talent routine anyone had seen since three years ago when Mary Ellen Ballinger had tap-danced to "Jesus Christ Superstar." Chantal had dropped the baton on every double reverse and left out half of her grand finale, but she had looked so pretty that nobody cared. And she had done better than Honey had expected during the question and answer part. When she had been asked about her plans for the future, she had dutifully announced that she wanted to be either a speech and hearing therapist or a missionary, just as Honey had told her to. Honey didn't suffer a single pang of conscience over insisting on the lie. It was a lot better than having Chantal announce to the world that what she really wanted out of life was to marry Burt Reynolds.

As Honey applauded, she breathed a silent prayer of thanksgiving that she had been smart enough to abandon the fire baton. Chantal would have done more damage to Paxawatchie County with those flames than William Tecumseh Sherman's entire army.

Ten minutes later, as she made her way through the crowd to the backstage area of the high school auditorium, she determinedly ignored the clusters of families gathered everywhere beaming at the girls in their filmy dresses: plump mothers and balding fathers, aunts and uncles, grandmothers and grandfathers. She never looked at families if she could avoid it. *Never.* Some things hurt too much to be borne.

She spotted Shep Watley, the county sheriff, with his daughter Amelia. Just the sight of him crimped the edges of her excitement over Chantal's victory. Yesterday Shep had nailed a foreclosure sign on the front gates, closing the park down forever and making her so scared about today that she hadn't been able to sleep. Now that Chantal had won the contest, Honey told herself it didn't matter about the foreclosure or the fact that the Disney people hadn't answered any of her letters. When those television casting agents saw Chantal, they were going to fall in love with her just as the judges had. Chantal would start making lots of money, and they'd be able to buy back the park.

Here her imagination faltered. If Chantal was going to be a movie star in California, how could they all be together again at the park?

Worrying was getting to be a bad habit with her lately, and she did her best to shake it off. Her heart swelled with pride as she saw Chantal talking with Miss Monica Waring, the pageant director. Chantal looked so beautiful standing there in the white gown she'd worn to her senior prom, with the rhinestone crown perched in her inky black curls, nodding and smiling at whatever Miss Waring was telling her. The television people wouldn't be able to resist her.

"That's fine, Miss Waring," Chantal was saying as Honey approached. "I don't mind the change at all."

"You're a darling girl for being so understanding." Monica Waring, the thin, stylish woman who was both the pageant director and the executive in charge of public relations for Dundee's Department Store, looked so relieved by Chantal's response that Honey immediately grew suspicious.

"What's this?" Honey stepped forward, her instincts twitching like a rabbit's nose at the hint of danger.

Chantal's eyes shifted nervously between the two women as she reluctantly introduced them. "Miss Waring, this is my cousin, Honey Moon."

Monica Waring looked startled, as people generally did when they heard her name for the first time. "What an unusual name."

According to Sophie, when Honey was born, the nurse had told Carolann that she had a little baby girl sweet as honey, and Carolann had decided right then that she liked the name. It wasn't until the birth certificate had arrived and Honey's mother saw the whole thing in print for the first time that she realized she might have made a mistake.

Since Honey didn't want anybody to think that her mother was stupid, she gave her usual response. "It's a family name. Oldest daughter to oldest daughter. One Honey Moon after another all the way back to the Revolutionary War."

"I see." If Monica Waring thought it was unusual that so many generations of childbearing women had never changed their last name, she gave no indication. Turning to Chantal, she patted her arm. "Congratulations again, dear. And I'll take care of the changes on Monday."

26

"What changes would those be?" Honey asked before Miss Waring could walk away.

"Uh—Jimmy McCully and his friends are waving at me," Chantal said nervously. "I'd better go say hi to them." Before Honey could stop her, she slipped away.

Miss Waring glanced past Honey. "I've explained our little mix-up to Chantal, but I did want to speak with Mrs. Booker personally."

"My Aunt Sophie isn't here. She's suffering from—uh— gall bladder, and what with the pain and everything, she has to stay at home. I'm sort of *in loco parentis,* if you know what I mean."

Miss Waring's skillfully penciled eyebrows shot up. "Aren't you a little young to be *in loco parentis?*"

"Nineteen on my last birthday," Honey replied.

Miss Waring looked skeptical but didn't press the issue. "I was explaining to Chantal that we've had to make a slight change in the prize for the winner. We're still offering the overnight trip to Charleston, but instead of the television show audition we're hiring a limousine to take the winner and a guest of her choice on a city tour followed by a marvelous dinner at a four-star restaurant. And of course Chantal will have the customary make-over at Dundee's Department Store."

The backstage area was hot from the press of people, but Honey felt cold chills racing through her bloodstream. "No! The first prize is an audition for *The Dash Coogan Show!*"

"I'm afraid that's no longer possible. Through no fault of Dundee's, I might add. Apparently the casting people have had to move up their schedule—although I do think they could have notified me earlier than yesterday afternoon. Instead of coming to Charleston next Wednesday as sched-uled, they're going to be in Los Angeles holding final auditions for the girls they've already picked."

"They're not coming to Charleston? They can't do that! How are they going to see Chantal?"

"I'm sorry, but they're not going to see Chantal. They found enough girls in Texas to call off the search."

"But you don't understand, Miss Waring. I know they would choose Chantal for the part if they just had a chance to see her."

"I'm afraid I'm not as confident as you. Chantal is quite beautiful, but the competition for the part has been enormous."

Honey immediately leapt to her cousin's defense. "Are you blaming her just because she dropped the baton? That was all my idea. She's a natural actress. I should have let her do that Quality of Mercy speech from *The Merchant of Venice* like she wanted, but, no, I had to make her twirl that stupid baton. Chantal's extremely talented. Katharine and Audrey Hepburn are her idols." She knew she was sounding frantic, but she couldn't help herself. Her fear was growing by the second. This contest was the last hope they had for a decent future, and she wouldn't let them snatch it away.

"I've spoken to the casting director several times. They've seen hundreds of girls just to weed out the final group they're auditioning in Los Angeles, and the chance of Chantal having actually been the one chosen is quite slim."

Honey set her jaw and tilted up on her toes until she was nearly on the same eye level as the pageant director. "You listen to me, Miss Waring, and you listen real good. I got the contest brochure right here in my pocket. It says in black and white that the winner of Miss Paxawatchie County gets to audition for *The Dash Coogan Show,* and I intend to hold you to that. I'm giving you until Monday afternoon to make sure Chantal gets her audition. Otherwise, I'm going to get me a lawyer, and that lawyer's going to sue you. Then he's going to sue Dundee's Department Store. And then he's going to sue every Paxawatchie County official who even came within a mile of this pageant."

"Honey—"

"I'll be at the store at four o'clock on Monday afternoon." She pointed her finger at Monica Waring's chest. "Unless you've got some positive news for me, that'll be the last time you see me without the meanest sonovabitch the courts of South Carolina have ever seen walking right by my side."

Honey's bravado collapsed on the ride home. She didn't

have the money to hire a lawyer. How could anyone at the store take her threat seriously?

But there was no place in her life for negative thinking, so she spent all day Sunday and most of Monday trying to convince herself that her bluff would work. Nothing made people more nervous than the threat of a lawsuit, and Dundee's Department Store wasn't going to want bad publicity. But no matter how much she tried to encourage herself, she felt as if her dreams for their future were sinking right along with the *Bobby Lee*.

Monday afternoon arrived. Despite her mental bravado, Honey was nearly sick with nervousness by the time she located Monica Waring's office on the third floor of Dundee's. As she stood in the doorway and peered in, she saw a small room dominated by a steel desk covered with neat stacks of paper. Promotional posters and store ads were lined up on a cork bulletin board that hung opposite the office's single window.

Honey cleared her throat, and the pageant director glanced up from her desk, which faced the door.

"Well, look who's arrived," she said, slipping off a pair of glasses with large black plastic frames and rising from her chair.

There was a smugness in her voice that Honey didn't like at all. The pageant director came around to the front of her desk. Leaning one hip against the edge, she crossed her arms.

"You're not nineteen, Honey," she said, obviously seeing no need to beat around the bush. "You're a sixteen-year-old high-school dropout with a reputation as a troublemaker. As a minor, you have no legal authority over your cousin."

Honey told herself that facing down Miss Waring shouldn't be any harder than facing down Uncle Earl when he had a few belts of whiskey in him. She walked over to the room's only window and, acting as if she didn't have a care in the world, gazed down at the drive-in lane of the First Carolina Bank across the street.

"You sure have been busy digging into my personal life,

Miss Waring," she drawled. "While you were doing that digging did you happen to discover that Chantal's mother, my aunt, Mrs. Sophie Moon Booker, is suffering from extreme craziness brought on by her sorrow over the death of her husband, Earl T. Booker?" Slowly, she turned back to the pageant director. "And did you also happen to find out that I've been running the family ever since he died? And that Mrs. Booker—who hasn't been a minor for a good twenty-five years—pretty much does whatever I tell her, up to and including slapping this candy-ass department store with the biggest lawsuit it's ever seen?"

To Honey's amazement and delight, that speech pretty much took the wind out of Monica Waring's sails. She hemmed and hawed around for a while longer, but Honey could tell it was mainly bluster. Obviously, she had been instructed by her superiors to protect the good name of Dundee's at any cost. She asked a secretary to bring Honey a Coke, then excused herself and bustled off down the hallway. Half an hour later, she returned with several pieces of paper stapled together.

"The producers of *The Dash Coogan Show* have very graciously agreed to give Chantal a short audition in Los Angeles with the other girls on Thursday," she said stiffly. "I've written down the address of the studio and have also included the information they sent me several months ago about the program. Chantal and her chaperon need to be in Los Angeles by eight o'clock Thursday morning."

"How's she supposed to get there?"

"I'm afraid that's your problem," she replied coldly as she passed the material she was holding over to Honey. "The pageant isn't responsible for transportation. I think you'll have to agree that we have been more than reasonable about this entire situation. Please wish Chantal good luck from all of us."

Honey took the papers as if she were doing Miss Waring a favor and sauntered out of the office. But once she reached the hallway, her bravado collapsed. She didn't have nearly enough money for plane tickets. How was she going to get Chantal to Los Angeles?

As she stepped onto the escalator, she tried to take courage from the lesson of Black Thunder. There was always hope.

"I think you have finally lost what's left of your mind, Honey Jane Moon," Chantal said. "That truck couldn't make it to the state line, let alone all the way to California."

The battered old pickup that stood near Sophie's trailer was the only vehicle left in the park. The body had once been red, but it had been patched with gray putty so many times that little of its original paint job remained. Because Honey was worried about exactly the same thing, she turned on Chantal.

"You're never gonna get anywhere in life if you keep being such a negative thinker. You've got to have a positive attitude toward the challenges life throws at you. Besides, Buck just put in a new alternator. Now load that suitcase in the back while I try one more time to talk to Sophie."

"But Honey, I don't want to go to California."

Honey ignored the whine in her cousin's voice. "That's just too bad, 'cause you're going. Get in that truck and wait for me."

Sophie was lying on the couch watching her Monday evening television shows. Honey knelt on the floor and touched her aunt's hand, running a gentle finger over the swollen knuckles. She knew that Sophie didn't like being touched, but sometimes she couldn't help herself.

"Sophie, you've got to change your mind and come with us. I don't want to leave you here by yourself. Besides, when those TV people offer Chantal that part on *The Dash Coogan Show,* they're gonna want to talk to her mama."

Sophie's eyes remained focused on the flickering screen. "I'm afraid I'm too tired to go anywhere, Honey. Besides, Cinnamon and Shade are getting married this week."

Honey could barely contain her frustration. "This is real life, Sophie, not a soap opera. We have to make plans for our future. The bank owns the park now, and you're not going to be able to go on living here much longer."

Sophie's lids formed saggy canopies over her small eyes as

she looked at Honey for the first time. Honey automatically searched her face for some small sign of affection, but, as usual, she saw nothing there except disinterest and weariness. "The bank didn't say anything about me moving out, so I think I'll just stay right where I am."

She attempted one final plea. "We need you, Sophie. You know how Chantal is. What if some boy tries to get fresh with her?"

"You'll take care of him," Sophie said wearily. "You'll take care of everything. You always do."

By early Wednesday afternoon, Honey was sick with fatigue. Her eyes were as dry as the Oklahoma prairie that stretched endlessly on both sides of the road, and her head had begun rolling forward without warning. A horn blared and her eyes snapped open. She jerked the wheel just before she slid over the double yellow line.

They had been on the road since Monday evening, but they hadn't even made it to Oklahoma City. They'd lost the muffler near Birmingham, sprung a leak in a water hose just past Shreveport, and had the same tire patched twice. Honey didn't believe in negative thinking, but her emergency cash supply was dwindling more rapidly than she had imagined it could, and she knew she couldn't drive much longer without sleep.

On the other side of the cab, Chantal slept like a baby, her cheeks flushed from the heat, strands of black hair whipping out the open window.

"Chantal, wake up."

Chantal's mouth puckered like an infant's in search of a nipple. Her breasts flattened under her white tank top as she stretched. "What's wrong?"

"You're going to have to drive for a while. I've got to get some sleep."

"Driving makes me nervous, Honey. Just pull off at one of the roadside stops and take a nap."

"We have to keep going or we'll never make it to Los Angeles by eight o'clock tomorrow morning. We're already way behind schedule."

"I don't want to drive, Honey. It makes me too nervous."

Honey considered pressing the issue and then decided against it. The last time she had made Chantal drive, her cousin had complained so much that Honey couldn't sleep anyway. Once again the truck wove toward the yellow line. She shook her head, trying to clear it, and then slammed on the brakes as she spotted the hitchhiker.

"Honey, what are you doing?"

"Never you mind."

She pulled over to the side and climbed out of the truck, leaving the motor running so she wouldn't have to go through all the work of starting it up again. She stepped over a torn rubber boot as she made her way down the shoulder of the interstate. The hitchhiker walked toward her carrying an old gray duffel bag.

She had no intention of endangering Chantal by picking up a pervert, so she studied him carefully. He was in his early twenties, a pleasant-faced boy with shaggy brown hair, a scraggly mustache, and sleepy eyes. His chin was a little weak, but she decided that she couldn't fault him for something that might be more of a reflection of his ancestors than his character.

She noted the fatigue pants he was wearing with his T-shirt and asked hopefully, "Are you military?"

"Naw. Not me."

Her eyes narrowed. "A college boy?"

"I spent a semester at Iowa State, but I flunked out."

She gave a small, approving nod. "Where are you on your way to?"

"Albuquerque, I guess."

He looked harmless, but so did all those serial killers she read about in Chantal's *National Enquirer.* "Did you ever drive a pickup?"

"Sure. Tractors, too. My folks are farmers. They got a place not far from Dubuque."

"My name's Honey Jane Moon."

He blinked his eyes. "Kind of a funny name."

"Yeah? Well, I didn't happen to choose it, so I'd appreciate it if you kept your opinions to yourself."

"Okay by me. I'm Gordon Delaweese."

She knew she had to make up her mind, and she couldn't afford a mistake. "You go to church, Gordon?"

"Naw. Not any more. I used to be Methodist, though."

Methodist wasn't as good as Baptist, but it would have to do. She shoved her thumb in the pocket of her jeans and glared at him, letting him see right off who was boss. "Me and my cousin Chantal are on our way to California so Chantal can get a part in a TV show. We're driving straight through and we've got to be there by eight o'clock tomorrow morning or we're going to miss what's looking like our last chance at self-respect. You try anything funny and I'll kick your ass right out of that truck. You understand me?"

Gordon nodded in a vague way that made her think he might not be any brighter than Chantal. She led him to the truck and when they got there told him he was driving.

He looked down at her and scratched his chest. "How old are you, anyway?"

"Almost twenty. And I just got out of prison last week for shooting a man in the head, so if you know what's good for you, you won't give me any trouble."

He didn't say anything after that, just tossed his duffel bag behind the seat and blinked a few times when he saw Chantal. Honey climbed in on the passenger side, putting Chantal in the middle. He worked the truck into gear and chugged out onto the highway. Honey was asleep within seconds.

Several hours later something woke her up, and when she saw the way Gordon Delaweese and Chantal Booker were making eyes at each other, she realized that she had made a big mistake.

"You sure are pretty," Gordon said, his skin taking on a rosy flush beneath his tan as he gazed over at Chantal.

Her elbow was propped up on the back of the seat and she was leaning toward him like a cottonwood in the wind. "I admire a man with a mustache."

"You do? I was thinking about shaving it off."

"Oh, no, don't. It makes you look just like Mr. Burt Reynolds."

Honey's eyelids sprang the rest of the way open.

Chantal's voice was breathless with admiration. "I think it's exciting how you're hitchhiking all over the country just so you can experience life."

"I figure you've got to see everything if you're going to be an artist," Gordon replied. He pulled into the left lane to pass an old clunker that was making nearly as much noise as their pickup.

"I never met a painter before."

Honey didn't like the soft, mushy quality in Chantal's voice. They didn't need any more complications. Why did her cousin have to fall for every boy she met? She decided the time had come to interrupt. "That's not true, Chantal. What about that man who came to the park to paint the mural over the House of Horror?"

"That's not real art," Chantal scoffed. "Gordon's a real artist."

Honey liked the mural over the House of Horror, but her tastes in art tended to be more catholic than most people's. Gordon sent another prurient glance in Chantal's direction, and Honey made up her mind to bring him down to size. "How many pictures have you painted, Gordon?"

"I don't know."

"More than a hundred?"

"Not that many."

"More than fifty?"

"Probably not."

Honey snorted. "I don't see how you can call yourself a painter if you haven't even painted fifty pictures."

"It's quality that counts," Chantal said. "Not how many."

"Since when did you turn into such a big art authority, Chantal Booker? I know for a fact that the only paintings you ever pay any attention to are ones of naked people."

"Don't let Honey hurt your feelings, Gordon. She gets moods sometimes."

Honey wanted to order him to pull over to the shoulder of

the road right that minute and get his weak chin out of her truck, but she knew that she needed him if she wanted to arrive in Los Angeles in time for that audition, so she held her tongue.

She wasn't anxious to take over the driving quite yet, but she couldn't stand watching the two of them drooling over each other so she pulled out the papers that Monica Waring had given her. They contained handwritten directions to the studio, as well as a short summary of *The Dash Coogan Show*. She studied it.

Rollicking laugh-a-minute humor results as ex-rodeo rider Dash Jones (Dash Coogan) marries beautiful East Coast socialite Eleanor Chadwick (Liz Castleberry) and they discover that love is funnier the second time around. He has a yen for country life, while she favors fancy cocktail parties. To complicate matters, his beautiful teenage daughter Celeste (to be cast) and Eleanor's almost-grown son Blake (Eric Dillon) form an attraction for each other. All of them discover that love is funnier the second time around.

Honey found herself wondering who wrote stuff like "rollicking laugh-a-minute humor." *The Dash Coogan Show* didn't sound all that funny to her, but since she couldn't afford to be critical, she told herself that Mr. Coogan wouldn't be part of something that was garbage.

She had never been enamored of movie stars, not like Chantal, but she had always cherished a secret admiration for Dash Coogan. Ever since she was a kid, she had watched his movies. Now that she thought about it, however, she realized it had been a long time since he'd made a new one. Cowboy movies didn't seem to be too popular anymore.

A sliver of excitement crept through her. She wasn't one to be impressed by movie stars, but wouldn't it be something if she actually got the chance to meet ol' Dash Coogan when she went to Hollywood? Now wouldn't that be something.

3

Honey shoved Chantal's best sundress through the partially opened door of the Shell station's rest room. "Hurry up, Chantal. It's almost eleven o'clock. The auditions started three hours ago."

Honey's old Myrtle Beach Fun in the Sun T-shirt was stuck to her chest with nervous sweat. She rubbed her damp palms on her shorts and nervously watched the traffic go by.

"Chantal, hurry up!" Her stomach was pumping bile. What if the auditions were already over? The truck had broken down on the San Bernardino Freeway, and then Chantal and Gordon had had a lover's quarrel right there on the shoulder of the road. Honey had begun to feel as if she were stuck in one of those nightmares where she was trying to get someplace but couldn't make it. "If you don't hurry up, Chantal, we're going to miss the audition."

"I feel like I'm getting ready to start my period," Chantal whined from the other side of the door.

"I'm sure they've got rest rooms where we're going."

"What if they don't have one of those Tampax machines? Then what am I going to do?"

"I'll go out and buy you some damned Tampax! Chantal, if you don't come out here right this minute . . ."

The door opened and Chantal came through, looking as fresh and pretty in her white sundress as if she'd just stepped out of a magazine ad for Tide laundry detergent. "You don't have to shout."

"I'm sorry. I'm just edgy." Honey grabbed her arm and dragged her toward the truck.

Gordon had followed Honey's orders and kept the pickup running. Honey pushed him out of the way and climbed behind the wheel herself. She peeled out of the parking lot and turned into the traffic, ignoring a light that was more red than yellow. She had never been in a city larger than Charleston, and the noise and bustle of Los Angeles was terrifying, but she didn't have time to give in to her fears. Another thirty minutes passed before she found the studio off one of Burbank's cross streets. She had expected something glamorous, but the high concrete walls made the place look like a prison. More time passed before the guard finally cleared them and they were permitted to drive inside.

Following the guard's instructions, Honey drove down a narrow street, then turned left toward another building with concrete walls and a few small windows near the entrance. As she climbed out of the truck, she was sweating so bad she looked like she'd just gotten out of the shower. She had hoped to get rid of Gordon back at the Shell station, but he wouldn't leave Chantal. He wasn't exactly an appetizing sight with his stubbly jaw and dirty clothes, and she told him he had to wait in the truck. Like her cousin, he was starting to get into the habit of following her orders, and he agreed.

The woman stationed inside the entrance told them that auditions were still going on, but that the last girl had already been called. For several terrifying moments, Honey was afraid the woman would tell them they were too late, but instead she directed them to a shabby waiting room with gray walls, mismatched furniture, and a litter of discarded magazines and diet-soda cans left behind by its former occupants.

As they walked into the empty room, Chantal began to make a whimpery noise at Honey's side. "I'm scared, Honey. Let's go. I don't want to do this."

In desperation Honey turned Chantal toward a smudged mirror hanging on the wall. "Look at yourself, Chantal Booker. Half the movie stars in Hollywood don't look as good as you. Now put your shoulders back and your chin up. Who knows? Burt Reynolds might walk through that door at any minute."

"But I can't do this, Honey. I'm too scared. Besides, since I met Gordon Delaweese, I don't think about Burt Reynolds so much anymore."

"You haven't even known Gordon for twenty-four hours, and you've been in love with Burt for two years. I don't think you should give up on him so fast. Now I don't want to hear another word, Chantal. Our whole damn future is resting on what happens here today."

The door opened behind her and a man's voice intruded on their privacy. "Tell her that I need to see Ross, will you?"

Honey automatically girded herself to do battle with whatever new enemy might have appeared to contest their right to be here. Setting her teeth, she spun around.

And her heart dropped through a gaping hole in the bottom of her stomach.

As he walked into the room, she felt as if she'd been hit by an eighteen-wheeler that had lost its brakes on a downhill curve. He was the handsomest young man she had ever seen: in his early twenties, tall and slender, dark brown hair falling in disarray over his forehead. His nose and jaw were strong and sunbrowned, just as a man's should be. Beneath thickly slashed eyebrows, his eyes were the same bright turquoise as the painted saddles on the park's carousel horses, and they speared right into her deepest female parts. In that moment, as she gazed into the depths of those turquoise eyes that seemed to burn right through her skin, womanhood paid her an unwelcome visit.

Her physical shortcomings gaped in her mind like festering wounds—her freckled little-boy's face, her mutilated hair and sucker-fish mouth. Her shorts were smeared with carburetor grease, she had spilled Orange Crush on her T-shirt, and her old blue rubber flip-flops had a piece missing from the heel. She agonized over her lack of height, her lack of breasts, her lack of any single redeeming feminine attribute.

He regarded Honey and Chantal steadily, not seeming to find it at all strange to be confronted with two speechless females. She tried and failed to manage the simple syllables of "hello." She waited for Chantal to step in—Chantal who was always so forward with boys—but her cousin had slipped behind her. When Chantal finally did speak, she addressed her remark to Honey and not to the gorgeous stranger.

"It's Jared Fairhaven," she whispered, sliding even farther behind Honey.

How did Chantal know who he was? "H—Hi, Mr. Fairhaven," Honey finally managed, her voice not much more than a little girl's quiver, certainly nothing at all like the profane bray she used to keep the employees at the park in line.

His eyes took in all the parts of Chantal that weren't hidden behind Honey's smaller body. He didn't smile—somehow his thin, hard mouth didn't seem to be made for that—but Honey's insides still twisted like a piece of hand laundry.

"My name is Eric Dillon. Jared Fairhaven is the part I used to play on *Destiny*."

Honey vaguely recalled that *Destiny* was one of Sophie's soap operas. She felt a pang as she saw the way he was gazing at her cousin. But then what did she expect? Did she really think he would notice her when Chantal was around?

Men were about the only thing that Chantal was good at, and Honey couldn't understand why she kept hovering behind her instead of stepping forward and taking over the conversation like she usually did. Unable to endure the indignity of appearing not only ugly but stupid, she swallowed hard.

"I'm Honey Jane Moon. This here's my cousin, Chantal Booker. We're from Paxawatchie County, South Carolina, and we're here to get Chantal a part on *The Dash Coogan Show*."

"Is that so?" His voice was deep-pitched and rich. He walked forward, ignoring Honey as he took in every inch of Chantal. "Hi there, Chantal Booker." He spoke in a soft, silky way that sent a shiver up Honey's spine.

To Honey's absolute and utter amazement, Chantal began pulling her toward the doorway. "Come on, Honey. We're gettin' out of here right now."

Honey tried to resist, but Chantal was determined. Sweet,

lazy Chantal who didn't have the gumption of a gnat was dragging her across the carpet!

Honey grabbed on to the soft-drink machine. "What's wrong with you? We're not going anywhere."

"Yes, we are. I'm not doing this. We're leavin' right now."

The waiting room door opened, and a frazzled-looking young woman with a clipboard appeared. When she saw Eric Dillon, she looked momentarily disconcerted, and then she turned to Chantal. "We're ready to see you now, Miss Booker."

This new arrival was one obstacle too many for Chantal to cope with and her momentary rebellion collapsed. She released Honey's arm and her bottom lip began to quiver. "Please, don't make me do this."

Honey was pricked with guilt, but she steeled herself against Chantal's distress. "You have to. We don't have anything else left."

"But . . . "

Eric Dillon stepped forward and took Chantal's arm. "Come on, I'll go in with you."

Honey thought she saw Chantal recoil from his touch, but she decided it was her imagination because Chantal had never recoiled from a man in her life. Chantal's shoulders slumped in resignation as she permitted Eric Dillon to lead her from the waiting room.

The door closed. She pressed the flat of her hand over her heart to keep it from jumping right out of her chest. Their entire future was riding on what happened now, but she was completely disoriented from her meeting with Eric Dillon. If only she were beautiful he might have noticed her. But who could blame him for ignoring an ugly little redneck girl who looked like a boy anyway.

She walked restlessly over to the room's single window look out on the parking lot. She heard the sound of ambulance in the distance. Her palms were damp. counted her breaths for a few minutes to calm herself, looked out. There wasn't much to see; some shrubbe few delivery trucks passing by.

The door opened and Chantal reappeared, this time alone. "They said I wasn't the right type."

Honey blinked.

Not even five minutes had passed.

They had driven all the way across the United States of America and these people hadn't even spent five minutes with Chantal.

All of her dreams crumbled like old yellow paper. She thought of the carefully hoarded money she had spent to get here. She thought of her hopes, her plans. The world spun around her, dangerous and out of her control. She was losing her home; she had no way to keep their family together. And they hadn't even given Chantal five minutes.

"No!"

She raced out through the door Chantal had just entered and ran into the hallway. Nobody was going to push her around like this! Not after all she'd been through. Somebody was going to pay!

Chantal called out her name, but Honey had spotted a set of metal doors with a glowing red light bulb above them at the end of the hallway, and her cousin's voice sounded a thousand miles away. Her heart pumping, Honey raced toward the doors. She shoved against them with all her strength and burst through into the studio.

"You sons of bitches!"

A half dozen heads turned in her direction. They were gathered in the rear of the studio behind pieces of equipment, a blur of male and female faces. A few of them were standing, others sat on folding chairs around a table littered with coffee cups and fast-food containers. Eric Dillon leaned against the wall and smoked a cigarette, but not even his magnetism was a powerful enough force to make her forget the horrible injustice that had been done her.

A women, tall and stern, shot up from her chair. "Now just a minute, young lady," she said, advancing on Honey. "You have no business in here."

"My cousin and me traveled all the way from South Carolina, you rotten sons of bitches," Honey shouted, pushing a folding chair out of the way to get to them. "We

blew out three tires, used up most of our money, and you didn't even spend five minutes with her!"

"Call security." The woman tossed the command over her shoulder.

Honey turned her rage on the woman. "Chantal's pretty and she's sweet, and you treated her like she was a stinking pile of dog shit . . . "

The woman snapped her fingers. "Richard, get her out of here!"

"You think just because you're some big Hollywood hotshot, you can treat her like dirt. Well you're the one who's dirt, you hear me? You and all those peckerheads sitting over there."

Several more people had risen to their feet. She turned on them, her eyes hot and burning, her throat clogged.

"You're all going to burn in hell. You're going to burn in the fires of everlasting hell, and—"

"Richard!" The woman's voice barked with command.

An overweight red-haired man with glasses had come forward, and now he grabbed Honey's arm. "You're leaving."

"Like hell." Drawing back her foot, she kicked him hard in the shin, then sucked in her breath as pain shot from her unprotected toes through her foot.

The man took advantage of her distraction to push her toward the door. "This is a private meeting. You can't come barging in here like this."

She struggled against him, trying futiley to escape from the bite of his fingers. "Let me go, you ignorant peckerhead! I killed a man! I killed three of them!"

"Did you call security?" This was a new voice, and it belonged to a man in a shirt and tie with silver hair and an air of authority.

"I called them, Ross," someone else replied. "They're on their way."

She was dragged past Eric Dillon. He looked at her with blank eyes. The man named Richard almost had her to the door. He was soft and flabby and wouldn't have presented much of a challenge to anyone with reasonable strength. But she was so little. If only she were bigger, stronger, more of a *man!* Then she'd show him. She'd show them all!

She punched him with her fists, blasting all of them with every curse she knew. They were so smug and self-righteous, these rich people with families waiting for them at home, beds to sleep in at night.

"Let her go."

The voice came from behind her. It was rough and tired, with a drawl that stretched from here to forever.

The stern-faced woman sucked in her breath indignantly. "Not until she's out of here."

Again the tired voice spoke. "I said to let her go."

The silver-haired man named Ross intervened. "I don't think that's wise."

"I don't care whether it's wise or not. Richard, get your hands off her."

Miraculously, Honey found herself free.

"Come here, honey," that rough, tired voice said.

How did he know her name? She turned toward her rescuer.

Creases like gullies bracketed his mouth, and a tan line from a hatband divided his forehead—pale skin above the line, sun-weathered skin below. He was lean and spare, and she didn't have to see him walk to know that he'd be bowlegged. Her first thought was that he should be on a billboard somewhere with a Stetson on his head and a Marlboro stuck in his mouth, except his face was a little too beat-up for billboards. His short, wiry hair was a combination of dusty blond, brown, and auburn. He looked like he was in his early forties, but his hazel eyes were a million years old.

"How'd you know my name?" she asked.

"I don't."

"You called me Honey."

"Is that your name?"

His eyes were kind, and so she nodded. "Honey Jane Moon."

"How about that."

She waited for him to make a crack about her name, but

44

he stood quietly, not asking anything of her, just letting her take him in. She liked his clothes: an old denim work shirt, nondescript pants, boots, everything comfortable and well-worn.

"Do you feel like coming over here and talking to me a little bit?" he said after a while. "It'll give you a chance to catch your breath."

She was starting to feel dizzy from yelling so much. Her stomach was upset, and her toes were hurting. "I guess that'd be okay."

As he led her toward a couple of chairs set up in front of some sort of light blue paper, she ignored the low conversation in the background.

"How about you sit right here, Honey," he said. "If you don't mind, I'm gonna ask these fellas to turn the cameras on while you and me talk."

The man named Ross stepped forward. "I don't see any need for this."

Honey's rescuer just looked at him with a cold, dead stare. "We've been doing it your way for weeks, Ross," he said in a hard voice. "I just ran out of patience."

Honey looked at the cameras suspiciously. "Why do you want to turn those cameras on? Are you trying to get me in trouble with the police?"

He chuckled. "The police would be more likely to come after me than you, little girl."

"Is that so? Why?"

"How about I ask the questions for a while?" He inclined his head toward the chair, not making her sit, but giving her a choice about it. She looked deeply into his eyes, but she couldn't see anything there that made her afraid, and so she sat.

It was a wise decision, because her legs wouldn't have held her up much longer.

"You mind telling me how old you are?"

He'd hit her with a stumper right off the top. She studied him, trying to position herself by reading his intent, but his face was closed up tighter than a Ziploc bag. "Sixteen," she finally volunteered, somewhat to her surprise.

"You look like you're about twelve or thirteen."

"I look like a boy, too, but I'm not."

"I don't think you look like a boy."

"You don't?"

"Nope. In fact, I think you're kind of a cute little thing."

Before she could ask him if he was being a male chauvinist pig patronizer, he hit her with another question.

"Where're you from?"

"Paxawatchie County, South Carolina. The Silver Lake Amusement Park. It's the home of the Black Thunder Roller Coaster. You might have heard of it. It's the most famous roller coaster in the South. Some say the whole country."

"I don't believe I knew that."

"Technically speaking, I guess maybe I'm not from the park any longer. The sheriff closed us down last week."

"I'm sorry to hear it."

His sympathy seemed so genuine that she began to tell him a little bit about what had happened. Because he was so undemanding and he always seemed to give her the choice not to answer his gentle questions, she found herself forgetting about the other people in the room, forgetting about the lights and cameras. Crossing her legs in her lap, she rubbed her sore toes and told him everything. She spoke of Uncle Earl's death, the *Bobby Lee*, and Mr. Disney's betrayal. The only thing she didn't tell him about was Sophie's mental condition, because she didn't want him to know she had a crazy person in her family.

After a while her toes stopped aching so bad, but when she began describing their trip across the country, her insides twisted up again. "Did you see my cousin?" she asked him.

He nodded.

"How could y'all only spend five minutes with her? How could anybody treat her like that? Don't you think she's beautiful?"

"Yeah, she's real pretty, all right. I can see why you're so proud of her."

"You bet I'm proud of her. She's pretty and sweet, and she came in here even though she was half scared to death."

"She looked like she was more than half scared, Honey.

46

She wouldn't even sit in front of the camera. Not everybody is cut out for a career in television."

"She could do it," Honey said stubbornly. "People can do anything they set their minds to."

"You've been going through life with your fists swinging for a long time, haven't you?"

"I do what I have to."

"Doesn't sound like you've had anybody looking after you."

"I look after myself. And I look after my family. I'm going to find us a house somewhere. A place where we can all be together. And we won't be on welfare, either."

"That's good. Nobody likes taking handouts."

"I think keeping your family together's the most important thing in the world."

Quiet fell between them. In the shadows beyond the lights, she saw an occasional movement. It was creepy having them watch her like this, not saying anything, just sitting there like a bunch of vultures.

"You ever cry, Honey?"

"Me? Hell, no."

"Why is that?"

"What good does crying do?"

"I'll bet you cried when you were a little kid."

"Only right after my mother died. From then on, whenever things got tough, I rode Black Thunder. I guess that's one of the best things about a roller coaster."

"How's that?"

She wasn't going to say that she felt close to God on the coaster, so she simply said, "A coaster gives you hope. You can pretty much ride a good one through the worst tragedy life throws at you. You can even ride it through somebody dying, I guess."

A noise distracted her. Beyond the cameras, she saw Eric Dillon slap the metal doors with the flat of one hand and stalk out.

The man sitting next to her shifted his weight. "I'm going to ask you to do something for me, Honey, and I don't think it'll be too hard. The way I look at it, these people here owe you a favor. You came all this way to see them, the least they can do is put you and your cousin up at a fine hotel for a few nights. You'll have plenty to eat and people to wait on you, and they'll pay for everything."

She eyed him suspiciously. "These people here don't think I'm any better than a maggot on spoiled meat. Why would they pay for me and Chantal to stay in some fancy hotel?"

"Because I'm gonna tell them they have to."

His absolute certainty filled her with a combination of envy and adoration. Someday she wanted to be powerful like him, to have people do exactly what she said. She thought over his offer and couldn't see any obvious hitch. Besides, she didn't think she could manage the drive back to South Carolina without some decent food and a night's sleep. Not to mention the fact that she'd just about run out of money.

"All right. I'll stay. But only until I decide I'm ready to go."

He nodded and everybody began to move at once. There was a whispered conference in the back of the studio, and then the frazzled-looking assistant who had originally taken Chantal to her audition came forward. After introducing herself as Maria, she told Honey she would help her get settled in a hotel. Maria pointed out some of the other people in the studio. The stern-faced woman was the casting director and Maria's boss. The man in the suit and tie with the silver hair was Ross Bachardy, one of the producers.

Maria led her to the studio doors. At the last minute, Honey turned back to address the man who had rescued her.

"I'm not ignorant, you know. I recognized you the moment I set eyes on you. I know exactly who you are."

Dash Coogan nodded. "I figured you did."

As the doors swung closed on Maria and Honey, Ross Bachardy slapped down his clipboard and shot up from the chair. "We need to talk, Dash. Let's go to my office."

Dash tapped his pockets until he came up with an

unopened pack of peppermint LifeSavers. He pulled on the red strip and then peeled away the coin of silver foil as he followed Ross out of the studio through a side door. They crossed a parking lot and entered a low stucco building that contained the production offices and editing rooms. Positioned at the end of a narrow hallway, Ross Bachardy's cluttered office was decorated with framed citations as well as autographed photos of the actors he had worked with over his twenty years as a television producer. A Lucite ice bucket half full of jelly beans sat on his desk.

"You were way out of line, Dash."

Dash slipped a LifeSaver in his mouth. "Seems to me that since this show is going right down the toilet, you shouldn't worry so much about the formalities."

"It isn't going down the toilet."

"I may not be a mental giant, Ross, but I can read, and that pilot script you told me was going to be so wonderful is the sorriest piece of horse crap I've ever seen. The relationship between my character and Eleanor is just plain silly. Why would the two of them ever get married? And that's not the only problem. Wet toilet paper is more interesting than that daughter, Celeste. It's amazing that people who call themselves writers could actually produce something like that."

"We're working with a preliminary draft," Ross said defensively. "Things are always a little rough at the beginning. The new version will be a big improvement."

Ross's reassurances sounded hollow even to his own ears. He walked over to a small bar and pulled out a bottle of Canadian Club. He wasn't much of a drinker, and certainly not this early in the day, but the strain of getting his troubled television series on the air had stretched his nerves to the breaking point. He had already splashed some into a glass before he remembered who he was with, and he hurriedly set down the tumbler.

"Oh, Christ. I'm sorry, Dash. I wasn't thinking."

Dash studied the bottle of whiskey for a few seconds, then tucked the LifeSavers into his shirt pocket. "You can drink around me. I've been sober for almost six years; I won't grab it away from you."

Ross took a sip, but he was clearly uncomfortable. Dash Coogan's old struggles with the bottle were as well known as his three marriages and his more recent battle with the Internal Revenue Service.

One of the technicians stuck his head in the office. "What do you want me to do with this videotape? The one of Mr. Coogan and the kid."

Dash was nearest the door, and he took the cassette. "You can give it to me."

The technician disappeared. Dash looked down at the cassette. "This is where your story lies," he said quietly. "Right here. Her and me."

"That's ridiculous. It would be an entirely different show if we used that kid."

"That's for sure. It might not be the piece of crap it is right now." He tossed the cassette on Ross's desk. "This little girl is what we've been looking for, the element that's been missing from the beginning. She's the catalyst that'll make this show work."

"Celeste is eighteen, for chrissake, and she's supposed to be beautiful. I don't care how old your girl says she is, she doesn't look more than twelve, and she sure as hell isn't beautiful."

"She may not be beautiful, but you can't fault her for personality."

"Her romance with Eric Dillon's character forms a major story line. She's hardly leading lady material for Dillon."

Coogan's lip curled at the mention of the young actor's name. He had made no secret of his antipathy toward Dillon, and Ross regretted introducing the subject.

"That's another point you and I happen to differ on," Dash said. "Instead of hiring somebody reliable, you had to find yourself a pretty boy with a talent for throwing temper tantrums and causing trouble."

For the first time since they'd entered his office, Ross felt as if he were on solid ground. "That pretty boy is the best young actor this town has seen in years. *Destiny* was the network's lowest-rated soap opera until he joined the cast, and within six months, it went to number one."

"Yeah, I watched it a couple of times. All he did was walk around with his shirt off."

"And he's going to have his shirt off on this show, too. We'd be fools not to take advantage of his sex appeal. But don't get that mixed up with his talent. He's intense, he's driven, and he's barely tapped the edges of what he can do."

"If he's so talented, he should be able to handle a more challenging story line than a romance with one of those Texas lingerie models you're trying to hire to play my daughter."

"The concept of the show—"

"The concept doesn't work. That cornball plot about a second marriage isn't cutting it because the audience is never going to understand why the stuck-up city lady and the cowboy got married in the first place. And nobody in the world will believe any of those beauty queens you brought in to audition is really my daughter. You know as well as I do that I'm no Lawrence Olivier. I play myself on the screen. It's what people expect. Those girls and I don't fit together."

"Dash, we didn't even have the kid read any lines. Look, if you're serious about this, I'll have her come back tomorrow and the two of you can do that opening scene between Dash and Celeste. Than you'll see how ridiculous this whole idea is."

"You still don't get it, do you, Ross? We're not reading that opening scene together. It's a piece of crap. That little girl isn't going to be playing Celeste. She's going to play herself. She's going to play Honey."

"It upsets the whole concept of the show!"

"The concept stinks."

"She came out of nowhere, and we don't know a damned thing about her."

"We know that she's part kid and part field commander. We know that she's years younger than her real age and a few decades older, both at the same time."

"She's not an actress, for chrissake."

"She may not be, but you look me in the eye and tell me you didn't feel some kind of excitement when you watched her talk to me."

Ross held out a hand, palm open, in a gesture of appeasement. "All right, she's quite a character, I'll give you that. And I'll even go so far as to admit that the two of you together had some interesting moments. But that's not what *The Dash Coogan Show* is about. You and Liz are supposed to be newlyweds with nearly grown children. Look, Dash, we both know the pilot script isn't what we hoped it would be, but the writing will improve. And even without a great opening script, the show's going to work because people will tune in to see you. America loves you. You're the best, Dash. You always have been, and nothing's going to change that."

"Yeah. That's right. Nobody plays Dash Coogan like I do. Now how about you stop grin-fuckin' this ol' boy and let those high-priced writers of yours see that videotape? Judging by their track records, they aren't half as stupid as they seem. Give them forty-eight hours to come up with a new concept."

"We can't change the concept of the show at this late date!"

"Why not? We don't start filming for six more weeks. The sets and locations don't have to change. Just give it a try. And tell them to forget the laugh track while they're at it."

"The show's a comedy, for chrissake!"

"Then let's make it funny."

"It *is* funny," Ross said defensively. "A lot of people think it's pretty goddamn funny."

Dash spoke with a core of sadness in his voice. "It's not funny, and it's not honest. How about asking the writers to try to make it at least a little bit honest this time?"

Ross gazed after Dash as he walked out of his office. The actor had a reputation for doing his job but ignoring the details. He had never heard of Dash Coogan worrying about a script.

Ross picked up his drink and took a long, thoughtful sip.

Maybe it wasn't so strange that Dash was taking more of an interest in this project than in others. The ravages of a hard life had stamped themselves on the actor's face, camouflaging the fact that he was barely forty years old. He was also the last of a proud breed of movie cowboys that had been given life in the early 1900s with William S. Hart and Tom Mix. A breed that had blazed into glory with Coop and the Duke in the fifties and then grown cynical with the times in the Eastwood spaghetti westerns of the seventies. Now Dash Coogan was an anachronism. The last of America's movie cowboy heroes was trapped in the eighties trying to fit on a screen much too small to contain a legend.

No wonder he was running scared.

4

Eric Dillon was the stuff of female fantasy. Dark, sullen, and gorgeous, he was Heathcliff gone supersonic and blasted through time into the nuclear age. People stared at him as he followed the two stuntmen through the crowd that jammed the Auto Plant, L.A.'s hot new night spot. The stuntmen were blond, with flashing smiles and party-animal demeanors, while Eric was grim and aloof. He wore a sports coat over a torn black T-shirt and faded jeans. His hair was brushed back from his forehead, and his turquoise eyes narrowly observed the world with a cynicism much too genuine for someone so young.

A hostess wearing a hard hat and short bib overalls that showed both breast and leg led them toward a table. He could tell by the way she looked at him that she recognized him, but she didn't say anything until he was seated.

"*Destiny*'s my favorite soap, and I think you're the greatest, Eric."

53

"Thanks." He wondered why he'd let Scotty and Tom talk him into coming with them tonight. He hated meat markets like this, and he wasn't overly fond of either one of the stuntmen.

"I'm going to UCLA during the day," the hostess said, "and I schedule all my classes so I don't miss it."

"No kidding." His eyes flicked to the dancers on the floor. He'd heard it a dozen times before. Sometimes he wondered why UCLA even bothered to hold classes between one and two in the afternoon.

"I can't believe you're leaving *Destiny,*" she pouted, her face girlish and surprisingly innocent beneath its veneer of professionally applied makeup. "It's going to ruin everything."

"The show's got a great cast. You won't even miss me." The cast was mediocre at best, made up of a bunch of has-beens and wanna-bes most of whom didn't even have enough respect for their profession to learn their lines.

The hostess was looking for an excuse to linger. He turned away from her and made a meaningless remark to Tom. Despite the girl's revealing outfit, there was a dewy freshness about her that attracted him, but as he lit a cigarette, he knew he wouldn't do anything about it. He never got involved with the innocents. Although he was only twenty-three himself, he had learned long ago that he hurt defenseless creatures with eager eyes and soft hearts, and so he stayed away from them.

As the hostess left, a waitress popped up at his elbow. "Hey, Mr. Dillon. I can't believe I got you at my table. I had Sylvester Stallone last week."

"How 'bout that."

"So how was he?" Scotty asked. The stuntmen collected movie-star gossip like other people collected stamps. He'd been trying to get work on a Stallone picture for months.

"Oh, he was real nice. And he left me a fifty-dollar tip."

Scotty laughed and shook his big blond head in admiration. "He can afford it, I guess. That Sly is some guy."

Eric ordered a beer. He cared too much about his body to

abuse it, and he never had more than two drinks when he went out. He didn't do drugs, either. He refused to turn into a burned-out zombie like so many other people in the business. Cigarettes were his only vice, and he was going to kick that habit as soon as things settled down.

For the next couple of hours, he tried to have a good time. Most of the girls in the place wanted to meet him, but he put up his invisible No Trespassing sign so that only the most aggressive bothered him. A guy with blow-dried hair offered him some coke that he guaranteed was pure, but Eric told him to fuck off.

He and Tom were shooting a game of pool in an alcove lined with metal lockers and time clocks when a busty blond in a sparkly blue dress came up to him. He saw right away that she was his kind of woman—stacked and gorgeous, four or five years older than he was, with good makeup and experienced eyes. One of the indestructibles. As she approached the pool table, he remembered why he had let Scotty and Tom talk him into coming along with them tonight. He wanted to get laid.

"Hi." She let her gaze travel from a dark lock of hair that had tumbled over his forehead all the way down to the crotch of his jeans. "My name's Cindy. I'm a big fan of yours."

He stuck his cigarette in the corner of his mouth and squinted at her through the smoke. "Is that so?"

"A *big* fan. My friends dared me to get your autograph."

He chalked his pool cue. "And you're not the kind of girl who's going to turn down a dare, are you?"

"No way."

He set down the pool cue and took the thick black marking pen she held out, then waited for her to pass over a piece of paper for the autograph. Instead, she sauntered closer toward him and slipped down the strap on her blue dress, exposing her shoulder for his signature.

He lightly scraped the clip of the pen over the flesh she had revealed. "If I'm going to autograph skin, how about I autograph something more interesting than a shoulder?"

"Maybe I'm shy."

"Why don't I believe that?"

Without bothering to raise the strap on her dress, she propped one hip up on the edge of the pool table and picked up his glass of 7-Up. She took a sip and then made a face when she realized it wasn't alcoholic.

"This girl I know said she slept with you."

"Could be." He flicked his cigarette to the floor and ground it out.

"You sleep with a lot of girls?"

"It's better than watching TV." He let his gaze drop to her breast. "So, do you want your autograph or not?"

The ice clicked in the tumbler as she set it back down. "Sure. Why not?" Grinning, she flipped over onto her stomach and offered him her buttocks. "Is this worth your time?"

Scotty and Tom snickered.

Eric hesitated for only a moment before he passed over his pool cue. Hell, if she didn't care, neither did he. "Definitely worth it."

Pushing her skirt up, he revealed a transparent pair of light blue panties. With one hand he slipped them down to the top of her thighs and uncapped the pen. The pool players at the next table caught sight of what was happening and stopped to watch. In bold script, he autographed her buttocks—"Eric" on the right side, "Dillon" on the left.

"Too bad you don't have a middle name," Scotty said with a leer.

Eric picked up his drink and took a sip. She didn't move, and he continued to gaze down at her. Condensation dripped from the glass onto her skin, trickling down over the rounded slope and into the valley. Her flesh pebbled with the sudden cold, and he could feel himself getting hard.

He slapped her lightly on the rear and hooked her panties with his index finger to pull them back up. "What do you say we get out of here, Cindy?"

Handing his glass over to Tom, he tossed Scotty a couple of twenties and headed toward the exit. It didn't occur to him to turn around and see if she was following. They always did.

"Let me come with you, Eric. Please."
"Get real, runt."
"But, Eric, I want to go with you. It's boring here."
"You'll miss Sesame Street.*"*
"I haven't watched Sesame Street *since I was a kid, you jerk."*
"When was that, Jase? Two weeks ago?"
"You think you're tough just because you're fifteen and I'm only ten. Come on, Eric. Please, Eric. Please."

Eric's eyes flew open. His pillow was soaked with sweat and his heart was thudding against his ribs. He gasped for air.

Jason. Oh, God, Jase, I'm sorry.

The sheet was clammy around his chest. At least he'd awakened before the dream got bad, before he heard that awful scream.

He sat up in bed, flicked on the light, and fumbled for his cigarettes. The woman beside him stirred.

"Eric?"

For a moment he couldn't remember who she was. And then it came back to him. The chick with the autographed ass. Dropping his feet over the side of the bed, he lit his cigarette with trembling hands and drew the smoke deep into his lungs. "Get out of here."

"What?"

"I said get out."

"It's three o'clock in the morning."

"You've got a car."

"But, Eric—"

"Get the fuck out!"

She jumped from the bed and snatched up her clothes. After scrambling into them, she walked over to the door. "You're a real asshole, you know that? And you're not even a good lay."

As the door slammed behind her, he sagged back down

into the pillows. Taking another drag on his cigarette, he stared up at the ceiling. If Jase were still alive, he'd be seventeen now. Eric tried to imagine a teenaged version of his half brother, with his chubby short-legged body, round face, and scholar's eyeglasses. Clumsy, nerdy, tender-hearted Jase, who had thought the sun rose and set on his big brother. God, how he'd loved that kid. More than he'd ever loved anybody.

The voices came back to him. The voices that were never far away.

"You're going to take Dad's car, aren't you?"

"Nib out, nerd-face."

"You shouldn't do it, Eric. If he finds out, he'll never let you get your license."

"He won't find out. Not unless somebody tells him."

"Take me with you and I won't tell. I promise."

"You won't tell anyway. 'Cause if you do, I'll beat the shit out of you."

"Liar. You always say you will, but you never do."

Eric squeezed his eyes shut. He remembered grabbing Jase in a good-natured headlock and giving him a Dutch rub, being careful not to hurt him—always so careful not to really hurt him—just to toughen him up a little. His stepmother, Elaine, who was Jason's mother, protected him too much. It made Eric worry about the little rodent. Jason was the kind of kid other kids automatically picked on, and they didn't know when to stop, not like Eric did. Sometimes Eric wanted to beat the shit out of all of them for picking on Jase, but he never did because he knew he'd only make it worse for his half brother.

"All right, runt. But if I take you with me tonight, you've got to promise me you won't bug me for the next two months."

"I promise. Promise, Eric."

And so he'd taken him. He'd let Jason climb into the passenger seat of his dad's Porsche 911, the car that was forbidden to him because he was only fifteen. The car that was too powerful for an inexperienced driver to handle.

He'd peeled from the driveway of their fashionable home

in the Philadelphia suburbs, a fifteen-year-old without a care in the world out for a joyride. His father was in Manhattan for the night on business and his stepmother was playing bridge with her friends. He hadn't worried about either of them finding out. He hadn't worried about the sleet that was beginning to fall. He hadn't worried about dying. At fifteen he was immortal.

But a nerdy pest of a little brother proved to be far more fragile.

Eric lost control of the car on a curve in a road that ran alongside the Schuylkill River. The Porsche spun like a top as it was tossed against a concrete abutment. Eric—too cool to wear a seat belt—was thrown free at the moment of impact, but law-abiding Jason had been trapped. He had died quickly, but not quickly enough. Not before Eric had heard him scream.

Tears trickled from the corners of Eric's eyes and slid down into his ears. *Jase, I'm sorry. I wish it had been me, Jase. I wish it had been me instead of you.*

Liz Castleberry's wardrobe fitting had taken longer than she'd planned. As a result, she was glancing down at her watch as she stepped into the hallway outside the studio's costume shop instead of watching where she was going. Just as she cleared the doorway, she found herself bumping against something solid.

She let out a soft exclamation. "Oh, excuse me. I'm sorry. I—" Her apology faded as she lifted her eyes and saw the man standing before her.

"Lizzie?"

His slow, deep drawl wrapped around her, drawing her back into the past. Hollywood wasn't as small a town as outsiders thought, and it had been over seventeen years since they had spoken. As she lifted her eyes, she experienced the dizzying sensation of being shot back through time to 1962 when she had arrived in Hollywood with a beautiful face and a spanking new degree from Vassar. Because she had been caught with her guard down, the words that slipped from her mouth were unexpected.

"Hello, Randy."

He chuckled. "It's been a long time since anybody in Hollywood has called me that. Nobody else remembers."

Each of them took a moment to study the other. Little was left of the Randolph Dashwell Coogan of those days, the wild young rodeo rider from Oklahoma who had been working as a stuntman when they met and had been so dangerously attractive to a well-bred young woman from Connecticut. His wiry blond-brown hair was shorter than it had been then. Although his body was still tall and spare, the passage of time had engraved unforgiving lines on the hard planes of his face.

His eyes weren't as critical as hers and they warmed with admiration. "You look beautiful, Liz. Those green eyes are as pretty as ever. I was real happy when Ross told me you were going to play Eleanor. It'll be great working together after all these years."

She lifted one dramatically curved eyebrow. "Did you read the same script I read?"

"Piece of crap, isn't it? But something interesting happened yesterday. We may see a few changes."

"I'm not going to hold my breath."

"Why did you take the job?"

"Tactless question, darling. I'm of a certain age, as they say. Work isn't as easy to find as it used to be, and my tastes are as expensive as ever."

"As I remember you're just about the same age I am."

"Just about the same age as Jimmy Caan and Nick Nolte, too. But while all of you forty-year-olds can still make screen whoopie with cute little ingenues, I'm reduced to playing a mother."

She said the last word with such distaste that Dash laughed. "You don't look much like any mother I ever saw."

Liz smiled. Despite her grumbling about her age and the career problems it was causing, she wasn't entirely displeased with being forty. Her long hair was the same rich shade of mahogany it had always been, and the green eyes that had first made her famous were still luminous. She hadn't put on weight, and her skin was only beginning to crease gently at the corners of her eyes. Being forty had its advantages. She was old enough to know exactly what she wanted out of life—enough money to maintain her Malibu beach house, buy the beautiful clothes she loved, and contribute generously to her favorite charity, the Humane Society. Her golden retriever, Mitzi, provided daytime fellowship and an assortment of discreet attractive men offered nighttime thrills. She truly enjoyed her life, which was more than many of her friends could say.

"How is your family?" she inquired.

"Which one?"

Once again, she smiled. There had always been something wonderfully self-effacing about Dash. "Take your pick."

"Well, you might have read that my last wife, Barbara, and I split a couple of years ago. She's doing real well for herself, though. Married a Denver banker. We still get together every once in a while. And Marietta started a chain of aerobics studios in San Diego. She always did have a good head for business."

"I seem to remember reading about that. She kept you in and out of the courtroom for years, didn't she?"

"I didn't mind the courtroom so much as the way she sicced the IRS on me six months ago. Those bastards don't have any sense of humor."

Seventeen years had passed since she had fallen in love with him, and she was no longer fooled by that easy cowboy charm. Dash Coogan was a complex man. She remembered him as a gentle, giving lover, generous to a fault with his money but unable to share anything of himself. Like the western heroes he played, he was a loner, a man who put up so many subtle barriers against intimacy that it was impossible to truly know him.

"My kids are doing real good," he went on. "Josh is in his junior year at the University of Oklahoma and Meredith's going to be a freshman at Oral Roberts."

"And Wanda?" After all these years there was still a slight sting to her voice. She and Dash had spent several weeks in bed together before he'd gotten around to mentioning the fact that he had a wife and two children tucked away in Tulsa. She thought too much of herself to be involved with another woman's husband, and that had been the end of the affair. But Dash Coogan wasn't the easiest man to get over, and it had taken her months to put her life back in order, something for which she had never quite forgiven him.

"Wanda's doing fine. She never changes."

Liz wondered if Wife Number Four was looming on the horizon. She also wondered what he would do if the show wasn't a success. Everyone knew that Dash had only agreed to do the show because he'd struck a deal with the IRS to pay off his debt. If he'd had a choice, she had no doubt that he would have stayed on his ranch with his horses.

A younger version of herself might have asked some of these questions, but the more mature Liz had learned to appreciate a life without messy personal entanglements, and so she made a play of looking at her watch. "Oh, dear. I'm late for my appointment with my masseuse, and my cellulite simply *hates* it when that happens."

He chuckled. "You and the second Mrs. Coogan would get along fine. Both of you enjoy all that fitness stuff, and you're both a lot smarter than you like to pretend. Of course, Marietta's degree came from the school of hard knocks, and yours came from Harvard or one of those places, didn't it?"

"Vassar, darling." Laughing, she gave him a brief wave.

He grinned and disappeared into the costume shop.

Several hours later, as Liz carried a glass of iced herbal tea and a small endive salad out onto the deck of her beach house, she found that she was still thinking about Dash. Mitzi, her golden retriever, trailed after her and plunked down across her feet. As Liz took a sip of her tea, she considered how much there was about Dash to admire.

He had fought a fierce battle with alcoholism and come out the winner. But he didn't seem to have taken his recovery for granted, and over the years she had heard stories of the ways in which he had helped other alcoholics.

The hero's white hat would have fit him perfectly, she decided, if it weren't for his womanizing.

In many ways he was an improbable Lothario, and if rumor were to be believed, he hadn't changed that much over the years. There had never been anything lecherous about his behavior. Quite the opposite. She remembered that he had always been shy around women, never directly seeking them out or trying to draw their attention. As much as she might want to rewrite her personal history, she knew that she had been the aggressor, setting her sights on the young stunt rider the moment they had been introduced on the set of her first picture. She had been drawn as so many women would be over the years by his overwhelming masculinity, made even more irresistible by a quiet, old-fashioned courtesy and deep sense of reserve.

No, Dash's flaw hadn't been lechery; it had been spinelessness. He couldn't seem to say no to an attractive woman, not even when he was wearing a wedding ring.

The afternoon was hot and breezy, and the faint sound of music came from the house next door. Liz glanced over to see Lilly Isabella sitting beneath an umbrella on her deck with several friends.

Lilly looked over and waved, her silvery-blond hair glistening in the sunlight. "Hi, Liz. Is the music too loud?"

"Not at all," Liz called back. "Enjoy yourselves."

Lilly was the twenty-year-old daughter of Guy Isabella, one of Liz's leading men in the seventies. He had bought the house several years ago, but his beautiful young daughter spent more time there than he did. Occasionally Liz invited the girl over, but she had grown selfish with her solitude and she didn't enjoy being around young people very much. All that desperate self-centeredness was too wearing.

As she sipped her tea, she reminded herself that she would be spending lots of time with young people for the next few months—the unknown actress Ross chose to play that silly part of Celeste, and Eric Dillon, of course. It pricked her vanity to be playing the mother of a twenty-three-year-old, even though Dillon's character was only supposed to be eighteen on the show. But more than that, she was worried about working with someone reputed to be difficult. Her hairdresser had been on the set of *Destiny* for a while, and Liz had heard stories that Dillon had a reputation for being surly and demanding.

He was also wildly talented. Her intuition about these things seldom failed her, and she had no doubt that he would one day be a big star. Those cruel good looks combined with a burning intensity that couldn't be taught in any acting class were going to catapult Eric Dillon to the very pinnacle. The question remained, would he be able to handle his fame or would he burn out as so many others had before him?

Eric had slept poorly, and he didn't get up until one in the afternoon. His head was aching and he felt like shit. Throwing his bare legs over the side of the bed, he reached for his cigarettes. A cigarette, a glass of high-protein breakfast drink, and then he'd work out for a couple of hours.

His clothes were strewn on the floor from the night before, and he thought about how much he liked sex. When he was in bed with a chick, he didn't have to think about anything —not who he was with, not anything. Life was reduced to the simple task of getting off. Once he'd heard a guy say he'd fucked some chick's brains out. Eric didn't think like that. He thought about fucking his own brains out.

As he got up, he spotted some black smudges soiling the bottom sheet. Puzzled, he made a closer inspection. It looked like writing, like script letters: ƆIЯƷ. His mouth curled as he remembered Cindy and her autographed ass. Just like a rubber stamp.

He pulled on a jock and a pair of running shorts, then walked out into the living room. The house was a small Benedict Canyon ranch, a perfect bachelor's quarters with its few pieces of comfortable furniture and big-screen television. He went into the kitchen and snatched a container of high-protein drink from the shelf. After dumping a couple of scoops into the blender, he added some milk and

hit the button. But the night dreams w
the sound filled the small kitchen like tl
drilled into his brain, bringing back th
the siren on the ambulance that had ca
body away. He jabbed at the blender
stared at the foamy contents.

*"Your stepmother feels—You have
that with Jason gone . . . You have to i
cult it is for Elaine to have you around*

Two weeks after Jason's funeral, Eric
father's drawn, handsome face and kr
Dillon couldn't stand to have him arou
own mother had died when he was a bal
for him to figure out what was going tc

He had ended up at an exclusive
Princeton where he had broken every r
out after six months. His father sen
schools before he managed to gradu
because he had discovered the school's
and learned that he could forget who he
into another person's body. He'd evei
years in college, but he'd missed so mai
the city for casting calls that he'd even

Two years ago one of the *Destiny*
spotted him in an Off-off Broadway pla
portray a character who was schedul
weeks. But viewer response had been
character had become a regular. Recent
the interest of the Coogan show produc

His agent wanted him to be a star, bu
an actor. He loved acting. Slipping insi
skin took away the pain. And sometir
ments, a look, a couple of lines of dial
really good.

He drank the protein mix straight fro
lit a cigarette while he wandered back
room. As he passed the couch, he caug
face in the oval wall mirror. For a mom

ion, wishing it were ordinary, wishing he were a
r guy with a funny nose and crooked teeth.
turned away from the face he hated, but he couldn't
way from what was inside himself. And he hated that
nore.

5

as Honey was concerned, the Beverly Hills Hotel was
k of pink-stucco heaven right on earth. The moment
epped into the small, flower-bedecked lobby, she
d that this was the place all good people should go the
l they died.

Iranian lady at the front desk explained how every-
in the hotel worked, and she wasn't the slightest bit
cending, although it had to be pretty obvious to her
either Honey nor Chantal had ever stayed at any place
han a ten-unit motel.

ey loved the wallpaper printed with fat banana
, the louvered doors, and the private patio that
l off their spacious, homey room. With the exception
uple of snooty peckerhead waiters in the Polo Lounge,
cided that the folks who ran the place were just about
est people on earth, not stuck-up at all. The maids
ll boys said hi to her even though they must have
ted that Gordon Delaweese was sneaking into their
and sleeping on the couch.

don looked up as she came out of the dressing room
urday afternoon. It was their second day in the hotel,
e had just changed into a bright red tank suit that one
maids had gotten for her so she could go swimming.
n and Chantal were curled up on the couch watching
of Fortune and trying to guess the puzzle.

y, Honey, why don't we order up some more food

hit the button. But the night dreams were still too near, and the sound filled the small kitchen like the whine of a siren. It drilled into his brain, bringing back the chilling memory of the siren on the ambulance that had carried Jason's broken body away. He jabbed at the blender to turn it off, then stared at the foamy contents.

"Your stepmother feels—You have to understand, Eric, that with Jason gone . . . You have to understand how difficult it is for Elaine to have you around."

Two weeks after Jason's funeral, Eric had looked into his father's drawn, handsome face and known that Lawrence Dillon couldn't stand to have him around, either. Since his own mother had died when he was a baby, it wasn't too hard for him to figure out what was going to happen to him.

He had ended up at an exclusive private school near Princeton where he had broken every rule and been kicked out after six months. His father sent him to two more schools before he managed to graduate, and then only because he had discovered the school's drama department and learned that he could forget who he was when he slipped into another person's body. He'd even spent a couple of years in college, but he'd missed so many classes going into the city for casting calls that he'd eventually flunked out.

Two years ago one of the *Destiny* casting agents had spotted him in an Off-off Broadway play and signed him to portray a character who was scheduled to die after six weeks. But viewer response had been so strong that his character had become a regular. Recently, he had attracted the interest of the Coogan show producers.

His agent wanted him to be a star, but Eric wanted to be an actor. He loved acting. Slipping inside another person's skin took away the pain. And sometimes, for a few moments, a look, a couple of lines of dialogue, he was good, really good.

He drank the protein mix straight from the blender, then lit a cigarette while he wandered back out into the living room. As he passed the couch, he caught a glimpse of his face in the oval wall mirror. For a moment he stared at his reflection, wishing it were ordinary, wishing he were a regular guy with a funny nose and crooked teeth.

He turned away from the face he hated, but he couldn't turn away from what was inside himself. And he hated that even more.

5

As far as Honey was concerned, the Beverly Hills Hotel was a chunk of pink-stucco heaven right on earth. The moment she stepped into the small, flower-bedecked lobby, she decided that this was the place all good people should go the second they died.

The Iranian lady at the front desk explained how everything in the hotel worked, and she wasn't the slightest bit condescending, although it had to be pretty obvious to her that neither Honey nor Chantal had ever stayed at any place nicer than a ten-unit motel.

Honey loved the wallpaper printed with fat banana fronds, the louvered doors, and the private patio that opened off their spacious, homey room. With the exception of a couple of snooty peckerhead waiters in the Polo Lounge, she decided that the folks who ran the place were just about the nicest people on earth, not stuck-up at all. The maids and bell boys said hi to her even though they must have suspected that Gordon Delaweese was sneaking into their room and sleeping on the couch.

Gordon looked up as she came out of the dressing room on Saturday afternoon. It was their second day in the hotel, and she had just changed into a bright red tank suit that one of the maids had gotten for her so she could go swimming. Gordon and Chantal were curled up on the couch watching *Wheel of Fortune* and trying to guess the puzzle.

"Hey, Honey, why don't we order up some more food

from room service?" he said, speaking through a mouthful of potato chips. "Those hamburgers sure were good."

"We just ate lunch an hour ago." Honey couldn't keep the disgust out of her voice. "When did you say you were leaving, Gordon? I know there's a lot of true life out there you still need to observe if you want to be a painter."

"I can't think of a better place for Gordon to observe real life than here at the Beverly Hills Hotel," Chantal commented, taking a sip of her Diet Pepsi. "This is a once in a lifetime opportunity for him."

Honey debated starting an argument, but every time she pressed the idea of Gordon leaving, Chantal began to cry. "I'm finished in the dressing room, Chantal. You can go change into your bathing suit now."

"I guess I'm too tired to swim. I think I'll stay here and watch TV."

"You said you'd come swimming with me! Come on, Chantal. It'll be fun."

"I'm feeling a little headachy. You go on."

"And leave the two of you alone in this hotel room? Do you think I'm crazy?"

"Some like it hot!" Gordon cried out, pointing to the television screen.

Chantal gazed at him with admiration. "Gordon, you are *so* smart. He's guessed every puzzle, Honey. Every single one."

Honey looked at the two of them curled up on that couch in the middle of the afternoon just like a couple of pieces of white trash. This would probably be their last day at the Beverly Hills Hotel, and she had been looking forward to swimming in that great big pool ever since she got here.

Inspiration seized her. Walking over to the small chest by the bed, she began opening the drawers. When she found what she wanted, she snatched it up and carried it over to Chantal.

"You put your hand right square in the middle of this Holy Bible and swear you won't do anything with Gordon Delaweese that you're not supposed to."

Chantal immediately looked guilty, which told Honey

everything she needed to know. "I want you to swear, Chantal Booker."

Chantal reluctantly swore. For good measure Honey made Gordon Delaweese swear, too, even though she wasn't sure exactly where his theology lay. As she left the room, she was relieved to see that both of them looked miserable.

The pool at the Beverly Hills Hotel was a wondrous place, bigger than most people's houses and inhabited by the most interesting group of human beings Honey had ever seen. As she stepped through the gate, she observed the women with thin, dark, oiled bodies and glimmering gold jewelry stretched out on the white lounges. Some of the men wore tiny bikinis and looked like Tarzan. One had straight white-blond hair that hung past his shoulders—either a WWF wrestler or a Norwegian. Some of the poolside loungers looked like ordinary rich men—paunchy bellies, thin slicked-back hair, and funny little canvas slippers.

Still, Honey felt sorry for them. None of them knew how to have real fun in a swimming pool. Occasionally, one of the men did a neat dive off the low board or swam a few slow laps. And a couple of women with diamonds in their ears squatted down in the water while they talked to each other, but they didn't even get their shoulders wet, let alone their hair.

What fun was it to be rich if you couldn't enjoy a swimming pool? Kicking off her flip-flops, she raced toward the water and, giving her best rebel yell, did a cannonball right into the deep end. The splash she sent up was one of her best. When she surfaced, she saw that everybody had turned to look at her. She called over to the people closest to her, a darkly tanned man and woman, both of whom had telephones pressed to their ears.

"Y'all should come in. The water's real nice."

They averted their eyes and went back to their phone conversations.

She dove beneath the water and swam along the bottom. The tank suit was too big and the nylon ballooned around her rear. She surfaced to catch her breath, then again dove for the bottom. As the peaceful underwater world engulfed her, she once again tried to sort out what was happening. Why had Dash Coogan wanted to videotape her? He had said he wasn't trying to get her into trouble with the police, but what if he'd been lying?

She came to the surface and flipped over onto her back. Water filled her ears and her chopped hair floated unevenly around her head. She thought about Eric Dillon and wondered if she would ever see him again. He was the handsomest man she had ever met. It was funny, though. When she'd casually mentioned his name, Chantal had gotten this strange look on her face and told Honey that Eric Dillon was scary. Honey had never heard Chantal say such a thing about a person in her life, and she figured her cousin must have gotten the real Eric Dillon mixed up with that character he played on the soap opera.

Half an hour later she was climbing out of the pool to do another cannonball off the diving board when she saw Ross Bachardy coming toward her. She nodded politely at the producer, but inside she felt like crying. She'd known their time in paradise had to come to an end, but she'd been hoping for one more day. She walked over to her lounge chair, retrieved her towel, and tucked it high into her armpits.

"Hello, Honey. Your cousin told me you were out here. Are you enjoying your stay?"

"It's about the best place I've ever been in my life."

"That's good. I'm glad you like it. Could we sit over here and talk?" He gestured toward a table tucked into the greenery.

She thought it was nice of him to show up personally to kick them out, but she wished he'd just get it over with. "It's your nickel." She followed him over to the table and pulled out a chair with her foot so she didn't lose the beach towel anchored under her arms. He looked hot in his taffy-colored sports coat, and she couldn't help feeling a little sorry for him.

"It's a shame you didn't bring your trunks along so you could take a swim. The water's real nice."

He smiled. "Maybe another time." A waiter appeared.

The producer ordered some kind of foreign beer for himself and an Orange Crush for her. Then he hit her with his bombshell.

"Honey, we want to cast you as the daughter in *The Dash Coogan Show.*"

She thought she must have pool water in her ears. "Beg your pardon?"

"We want you to play Dash Coogan's daughter."

She gaped at him. "You want *me* to play Celeste?"

"Not exactly. We're making some changes in the show, and we've gotten rid of that character. All of us liked that videotape you and Dash made together, and it gave us a few ideas that we're quite excited about. The details aren't worked out yet, but we think we have something special."

"You want me?"

"We certainly do. You'll be playing Janie, Dash's thirteen-year-old daughter. Dash and Eleanor won't be newlyweds anymore." He began to outline a story line for her, but she couldn't seem to take it in and eventually she interrupted in a voice that had a funny little squeak to it.

"No offense, Mr. Bachardy, but that's the craziest idea I've ever heard. I can't be an actress. I'm not the slightest bit pretty. Did you look close at my mouth—like a big old sucker fish? It's Chantal you should be casting in that part, not me."

"Why don't you let me be the judge of that."

Something he'd said earlier suddenly hit her. "Thirteen? But I'm sixteen years old."

"You're small, Honey. You can easily pass for thirteen."

Normally she wouldn't have swallowed such an insult, but she was too stunned to be offended.

Ross went on, giving her more details about the show and then talking about contracts and agents. Honey felt as if her head was spinning right off her neck, just like that poor little girl in *The Exorcist.* The breeze raised goose bumps on her skin as she realized how fiercely she wanted all this to be true. She was smart and ambitious. This was her chance to make something of herself instead of expending all of her

JANIE

to be a rodeo rider, Pop, but you're
re. You heard what the doc said. No
ncs unless you want to spend the rest
e in a wheelchair.

DASH

d have something underneath me that

JANIE

out that cocktail waitress in El Paso?

DASH

JANIE

p?

DASH

ne to tan your hide.

Q RANCH HOUSE FRONT PORCH

HADWICK steps out looking harried. She is
rfectly coiffed, and too stylishly dressed for
lings. She speaks to someone still in the

ELEANOR

are if we do have a horse foaling. Dusty
an obstetrician. I'm going into Goose
nd see if there's anyone in that godfor-
own who knows how to give a cucumber/
Marnier facial.

ash and Janie.

d, what now?

nie stop at the bottom of the stairs. Dash sets
e. He and Eleanor take each other in. He is a
man, and she can't help admiring him. On the

energy trying to prod Chantal. But a TV star? Not even in her wildest imagination could she have conjured up something like that.

Ross began to talk about salary, and the amounts he mentioned were so astronomical she could barely comprehend them. Her mind raced. This would change everything for them.

He pulled a small notebook from his suit-coat pocket. "You're a minor, so before we can go any farther with this, I'll need to meet with your legal guardian."

Honey fumbled with her glass of Orange Crush.

"You do have a guardian?"

"Of course I do. My Aunt Sophie. Mrs. Earl T. Booker."

"I'll need her phone number so I can call her to arrange for a meeting. Thursday at the latest. We'll fly her out at our expense, of course."

She tried to imagine Sophie getting on a plane, but she couldn't even imagine her getting up off the couch. "She's been sick lately. Uh—female trouble. I don't think she'll come to California. She's afraid to fly. Plus the female trouble."

He looked disturbed. "That's going to be a problem, but you'll have to get an agent to represent you anyway and he can take care of it. I'll give you a list of some of the better ones. We begin filming in six weeks, so you'll need to get it taken care of right away." The lines around his mouth grew deeper. "I have to tell you, Honey, that I think it was unwise of you to have come all the way to California without an adult."

"I came with an adult," Honey reminded him. "Chantal's eighteen."

He wasn't impressed.

After she returned to the room, she stumbled all over herself explaining what had happened, and Chantal and Gordon started whooping and hollering so much that before long they were all rolling around on the floor and acting crazy. When she settled down, she remembered what Mr. Bachardy had said about getting an agent and she pulled out the list of the names he had given her. She began to reach for the telephone, and then her eyes narrowed. She might be a redneck girl from South Carolina, and she certainly didn't know anything about agents or Hollywood, but she wasn't born yesterday either. Why should she trust Mr. Bachardy to give her a name? Wasn't that a little bit like trusting the fox to guard the chickens?

She considered the problem while she changed from her bathing suit back into her shorts. She didn't know anybody in Hollywood, so who could she turn to for advice? And then she smiled and picked up the phone.

The Beverly Hills Hotel prided itself on handling every emergency, even helping one of its guests find an agent, and by noon the next day the concierge had helped Honey hire Arthur Lockwood, an aggressive young lawyer who worked for one of the better-known talent agencies and promised to fly to South Carolina to meet with Aunt Sophie.

That night as Honey drifted off to sleep, she could hear the distant roar of Black Thunder in her ears. She smiled against her pillow. *There's always hope.*

6

THE DASH COOGAN SHOW
Episode One

EXTERIOR. TEXAS DIRT ROAD—LATE AFTERNOON. AS THEME MUSIC/CREDITS ROLL . . .

A battered pickup truck shudders to a stop, steam rising from the hood. CLOSE ON worn pair of cowboy boots emerging from cab. Boot kicks tire then walks around side to back and pulls out saddle. A second pair of boots emerges from the cab, this one small. Together, they

other hand, she hates everything about the West, including cowboys.

ELEANOR
My, my. If it isn't Wyatt Earp and Billy the
Kidette.

Eleanor's sarcasm doesn't go over well with Dash. Although he has a weakness for beautiful women, her
patronizing attitude sets his teeth on edge. Janie knows
her father too well and quickly intercedes.

JANIE
Howdy, ma'am. My name's Janie Jones. This
here is my pop, Mr. Dash Jones. He's your new
ranch manager.

DASH
I'll do my own talking, Jane Marie.

ELEANOR
(taking in Dash)
They certain do grow them big out here in the
West. It must be from smoking all that sage-
brush. You're late, by the way. You were supposed to be here yesterday. If you're going to
work for me, you'll have to be more reliable.

DASH
(resting one boot on the step)
Well, you see ma'am, that's just it. I'm not going
to be working for you. I just remembered that I
got a better offer from this fellow who runs a
rattlesnake ranch right off the interstate. All he
wants me to do is hand-feed those critters. The
way I figure it, the company'd be more polite.

ELEANOR
(indignantly)
Of all the gall. You're fired, do you hear me? I
wouldn't have you working for me if you were
the last ranch manager in Texas.

DASH

That's just fine with me, ma'am, because from
the looks of this place, you won't be in business
much longer.

Janie's eyes dart from her father to Eleanor and back
again. Realizing she has to do something, she clutches her
stomach and falls down on porch, groaning loudly.
Eleanor looks alarmed and runs to her side, fussing over
her.

ELEANOR

What's wrong? What's wrong with her?

DASH

(impervious to Janie's dramatic groans)
I'd watch yourself there, ma'am. When she gets
like this, she has a tendency to upchuck, and I
don't think the color scheme would coordinate
with those nice clothes of yours.

Janie's groans intensify. Eleanor becomes more alarmed.
She continues to fuss over Janie.

ELEANOR

Do something, will you! What kind of a father
are you to let your child suffer like this?

DASH

It's probably just another busted appendix. She
gets them all the time. I wouldn't trouble yourself.

With that, Dash picks Janie up and throws her over his
shoulder.

ANGLE TO SIDE OF HOUSE WITH BARN IN BACK-
GROUND

BLAKE CHADWICK comes running toward the house. A
handsome and charming young man, he's dressed in
jeans and a work shirt, both obviously new. But even

though he's a city slicker, Blake likes the PDQ Ranch, and he wants to make a go of it.

Janie's screams stop as she spots Blake. She stares at him open-mouthed. He's the handsomest man she's ever seen, and at the age of thirteen, she falls in love for the first time.

> **BLAKE**
> Mom, Dusty says the foal's not turned right. We're going to lose both the foal and the mare if that vet doesn't get here soon. And the trail party that left this morning should have been back hours ago. I'm going to have to go after them.

> **ELEANOR**
> That's impossible! You don't know the trails, and you'll get lost yourself. Where is that vet? How could he do something like this? If your father weren't already dead, I'd kill him for leaving me this awful ranch in his will. I swear, I'll sell it to the first person who makes me a decent offer. If it weren't for this horrid place, I could be lunching at the Russian Tea Room right now with Cissy and Pat and Caroline!

Pushing up the sleeves of her expensive suit, Eleanor sets off purposefully toward the barn, her head high, her spiked heels sinking deeply into the dirt.

Dash stares after her. Janie, still upside down over her father's shoulder, stares at Blake. Blake notices them and walks toward Dash, his hand extended.

> **BLAKE**
> Hi, there. I'm Blake Chadwick. Welcome to the PDQ.

> **DASH**
> Dash Jones.

BLAKE

The new ranch manager! Am I ever glad to see
you.

DASH

Ex-ranch manager. I'm afraid your ma and me
didn't hit it off too well.

JANIE
(still upside down)
Could I say something?

DASH

No.

Dash stares thoughtfully toward the barn.

Your ma doesn't look like she knows too much
about horses.

BLAKE
(fondly)
She's not too crazy about any animal that can't
be made into a coat. She tries, but this has been
hard on her.

A beautiful buxom female appears in the background
near the barn. She is dressed in jeans and a tight gingham
blouse and calls out Blake's name.

BLAKE

I'll be there in a minute, Dusty.

BLAKE turns back to Dash, who has picked up the saddle
with his other arm.

Are you sure you won't change your mind, Mr.
Jones? We could really use some help.

DASH

I'm afraid not, son.

BLAKE
(with resignation)
Yeah, you look like a man with good sense.

Blake heads toward the barn without having acknowledged Janie's presence.

Dash stares after Blake and slowly lowers Janie to the ground. Reluctantly, he puts down the saddle.

> DASH
>
> Janie?

> JANIE
>
> Yeah, Pop?

> DASH
>
> Remind me to tan your hide.

Grimly, he sets off toward the barn.

"And cut," the director called out. "Print it. Good work, everybody. Let's break for lunch."

It was the last week of July and their final day of shooting the pilot episode. They hadn't been filming the show in order, and they were just now doing the opening scenes. It was a confusing way to go about things as far as Honey was concerned, but then no one had asked her opinion. They didn't ask her about anything, in fact. They just told her what to do.

She gazed around her at the set for the PDQ ranch. They were filming all the exteriors at a former chicken ranch near the Tajunga Wash, an area in the San Gabriel Mountains north of Pasadena. The rugged slopes of the San Gabriels were covered by chaparral at the lower elevations, giving way to pine and fir as the peaks rose. Just that morning she had glimpsed desert bighorn sheep as well as a golden eagle soaring on the thermal updrafts. Most half-hour television shows were videotaped, she had learned, but since so much of *The Dash Coogan Show* took place outside, it was being filmed, instead, like a movie.

"Good job, Honey." Jack Swackhammer, the director, patted her on top of her head just as if she were some damn poodle dog. He was young and skinny, and he hopped around a lot. All week he had looked as if he was getting ready to have a nervous breakdown.

As he walked over to talk to his assistant, Honey looked after him with disgust. Everybody was treating her as if she were really thirteen. She shouldn't have been surprised, she supposed, considering the fact that those stupid writers kept taking her into their conference room and raping her mind.

The first time the writers had called her in, they'd been so nice, explaining the new concept for the show and asking her opinion about everything under the sun. Since there was nothing she enjoyed more than talking, she'd been pulled in like a fool. She had sat there sucking on the can of Orange Crush they'd offered her and talked, talked, talked—too stupid to figure out that all of her opinions would become Janie's opinions, that her feelings would become Janie's.

They had stuck her need for a home in the script, right along with all her secret feelings about Eric Dillon, although how they'd figured that out, she had no idea, since she certainly hadn't come out and told them. Maybe it wouldn't have been quite so humiliating if they had made Janie a mature, self-sufficient sixteen-year-old like herself, but instead they had turned her into a puny little thirteen-year-old retard. She still got indignant whenever she thought about it.

As the director ended his conversation with his assistant, she approached him. "Mr. Swackhammer—"

"Please, Honey. Call me Jack. We're all family here."

But they weren't her family. What should have been the most exciting time of her life was being ruined because Sophie refused to leave the park to come to California and Gordon Delaweese spent all his time at the new apartment she and Chantal had moved into. With Chantal paying so much attention to Gordon and with Sophie still in South Carolina, Honey was feeling all jangly, as if she didn't belong anywhere.

Working on the television show wasn't like she'd imagined it, either. After having been so nice to her the day they had met, Dash Coogan had gradually changed. He'd been real helpful to her at first, but then it seemed the friendlier she got, the more he backed off. Now he barely spoke to her unless they were on-camera together. And the only time Eric Dillon had sought her out was to ask her if Chantal would be coming around.

The director looked back down at his clipboard. She remembered her most pressing grievance. "I've got to talk to you about this haircut."

"Shoot."

"It's embarrassing."

"What do you mean?"

"It looks like somebody put a dog's dish on top of my head and cut right around it." The sides were cut high over her ears and the back formed a straight line two inches above her nape. Her bangs fell long and fine past her eyebrows, making the whole thing look off balance.

"It's great, Honey. Perfect for the part."

"I'm going to be seventeen in December. What kind of haircut is this for a girl who's almost seventeen?"

"Janie's thirteen. You have to get used to thinking younger."

"That's another thing. I saw that press kit you sent out, and it gives my *real* age as thirteen."

"That was Ross's idea. Audiences don't like it when they find out kid actors are lots older than the part they're playing. You're small, and you're an unknown. Ross wants to keep you away from the press for a while until you get your bearings, so it doesn't really make much difference, now, does it?"

Not to him, maybe. But it certainly did to her.

"Jacko! Honey! You're doing great, sweetheart. Just great."

One of the older network executives, a nervous-looking man in his late fifties, popped a little white pill in his mouth as he came up to them. She stepped back before he could chuck her under the chin as he'd done that morning.

"I think we've got a hit in the making here," he said with too much heartiness. Even without his eyelid twitching, she would have known that he didn't believe a word he was saying. The network was nervous because they said the new concept for *The Dash Coogan Show* wasn't really situation comedy but it wasn't quite drama either, and they were worried about confusing the audience.

Honey didn't see what the big deal was. The show was funny in some parts, sad in other parts, and pretty sentimental a lot of the time. What was so hard to understand about that? The American people might be getting ready to vote another Republican into the White House, but that didn't mean they were stupid about everything.

He smiled at her, displaying teeth too big and white to be real. "You've got star written all over you, sweetheart. She's the real thing, isn't she, Jacko?"

"Uh— Thanks, Mr. Evans."

"Call me Jeffrey, sweetheart. And I mean it. Really. You're going to be another Gary Coleman."

He started raving about all her natural talent and carrying on like she was the second coming. Her stomach began to feel queasy. She told herself it was from spending so much time upside down over Mr. Coogan's shoulder, but it was really because she didn't believe him. All of them knew that she didn't understand the first thing about acting. She was nothing more than a little redneck girl from South Carolina who had jumped into water that was way over her head.

The executive excused himself to corner Ross. Honey was getting ready to argue some more with Jack about her haircut when Eric Dillon appeared from behind them.

"Jack, I need to talk to you."

Honey hadn't heard him coming, and, at the sound of his voice, an achy sense of longing came over her. She was painfully conscious of her scruffy jeans and dog-dish hair. She wished she were beautiful and sophisticated like Liz Castleberry.

As Eric closed in on the director, his eyes darkened with an intensity that sent a shiver through Honey. "I'm not happy with the pacing, Jack. You're rushing me through lines where I need to take my time. I'm not driving a race car here."

Honey looked at him with admiration. Eric was a real actor, not a pretend one like herself. He studied with an acting coach, and he talked about things like sensory awareness. She, on the other hand, just did what people told her.

Jack glanced uncomfortably toward Honey. "Why don't we take this up in private, Eric? Tell you what. Give me five minutes, and then meet me in the production trailer."

Eric gave a curt nod. Jack walked off, and she tried to think of something intelligent to say before Eric left her side, too, but her tongue was paralyzed. The worst part of the way the writers had raped her mind was the fact they she had to act like a lovestruck ninny in all their scenes together. As a result, she had no idea how to act when they weren't on camera.

He pulled a cigarette from his shirt pocket and stared off into space as he lit it.

She stared off into space, too. "You—uh— You're real serious about acting, aren't you, Eric?"

"Yeah," he muttered, not bothering to look at her. "I'm real serious."

"I heard you talking about that sensory awareness stuff with Liz. Maybe sometime you could explain it to me."

"Yeah, maybe." He took off for the production trailer.

Feeling discouraged, she watched him go. As her spirits dipped lower, she told herself she was acting like a spoiled brat. In less than a month, she would have earned more money than the Silver Lake Amusement Park had made in gate receipts for the entire winter. She didn't have any reason to be unhappy. Still, she couldn't shake off the uneasy feeling that nothing was going right.

It was eight o'clock that evening before shooting was finished and Honey had climbed out of her costume jeans and into her own jeans. By the time she reached the apartment she shared with Chantal and parked the racy little fire-engine-red Trans Am her agent's secretary had helped her buy, she was so tired she could barely keep her eyes open.

The building was the nicest place Honey had ever lived—a vine-covered white stucco quadrangle with a red-tiled roof and a small courtyard in the center. The apartment itself boasted comfortable furniture, a little patio, and museum posters on the walls. It had everything she could want except Sophie. And one thing she didn't want—Gordon Delaweese.

As soon as she unlocked the front door and stepped into the foyer, she knew something was wrong. Usually when she came home, Gordon and Chantal were propped up in front of the television eating Hungry Man dinners, but now everything was dark.

A twinge of alarm shot through her. She flipped on the overhead light and dashed through the kitchen into the living room. Snack wrappers and ashtrays littered the coffee table. She rushed upstairs. Her heart pounding in her throat, she pushed open Chantal's bedroom door.

The two of them were lying naked in each other's arms, sound asleep. All the blood rushed from Honey's head. Her hand shook as she flipped on the overhead light. Chantal stirred and then blinked. Abruptly, she sat upright, pulling the sheet up over her breasts.

"Honey!"

"You Judas," she whispered.

Gordon struggled awake. A few strands of dark hair hung like ravelings at the center of his bony chest. He looked uneasily back and forth between the two women.

Honey shoved the words out through a small tight space in her throat. "You swore on the Holy Bible. How could you do this?"

"It's not what you think."

"I'm not blind, Chantal. I know what I see."

Chantal pushed her dark curls back from her face. Her red mouth grew soft and pouty. "You made it so hard on us, Honey. Maybe if you hadn't forced us to swear on the Bible, me and Gordon could have just done what came naturally and waited for the rest. But after you made us swear . . ."

"What are you talking about? What do you mean 'waited for the rest'?"

Chantal bit at her lip nervously. "Me and Gordon. We got married this afternoon."

"You did what?"

"It's not a sin now. We're married, so we can do whatever we want."

Honey stared at the two of them huddled in the bed, and she felt as if her whole life had just fallen apart around her. They were pressed together, already excluding her. Chantal, the person she loved most in the world, now loved somebody else more.

Chantal bit at her bottom lip. "Me and Gordon getting married doesn't make any difference, don't you see? Since you got the part on the TV show, we don't have to depend on me anymore. Now you're the one who can do great things, Honey. I can just be a regular person. Maybe learn how to do hair. I don't have to be anybody special."

Honey's jaw set into a hard line. "You Judas! I won't ever forgive you for this!"

She raced out of the room and down the steps. When she reached the front door, she threw it open and ran out into the night. She heard a roaring in her ears, the sound of Black Thunder hurling her through time and space. But Black Thunder was too far away for her to feel reassured that everything would be all right again.

She stayed in the courtyard by the fountain until she was shivering, as much from emotion as from the chill air. Then she went back inside and, sealing herself in her bedroom, called Sophie.

"Sophie, it's me."

"Who?"

Honey wanted to scream at her aunt, but she knew it wouldn't do any good. "Sophie, you can't put off coming to California any longer. I need you. Chantal married Gordon Delaweese, that boy I told you about. You got to come out and help me."

"Chantal got married?"

"This afternoon."

"I missed my baby's wedding?"

"I don't think it was much of a wedding. Now write this

down. I'm going to send you some airplane tickets for next week through that Federal Express mail. You're going to fly to L.A."

"I don't think so, Honey. The bank said I could live in the trailer for a while."

"Sophie, you can't stay there. It's not safe."

"It's safe. They hired Buck to stay around as caretaker and keep an eye on things."

"Buck can hardly keep an eye on himself, let alone you."

"I don't know why you're always so nasty about Buck. He gets my groceries and watches my soaps with me and everything."

Honey refused to let herself get sidetracked. "Listen to me, Sophie. Chantal just got married to a boy she hardly even knows. I need your help."

There was a long silence, and then the sound of Sophie's weary voice, no stronger than a sigh. "You don't need me, Honey. You'll take care of everything. Just like always."

7

Honey curled into Dash's lap. His shoulder was warm and solid against her cheek. She could feel the bite of his belt buckle at her waist and breathed in his particular scent. It was crisp and piney, overlaid with the hint of spearmint LifeSavers.

"I'm too old for cuddling," she whispered, cuddling closer.

His arm enfolded her more tightly, and his voice was husky with tenderness. "You're not too old until I say you're too old. I love you, Janie."

Silence fell between them, tender and good. His jaw rested on the top of her head, sheltering her. His arms and chest were a warm, snug harbor in a world that had grown too

dangerous. The camera pulled back for a wider angle. Honey closed her eyes, savoring every second. If only he were her dad, instead of Janie's. She had just celebrated her seventeenth birthday, and she knew she was too old to be taking pleasure in something so childish, but she couldn't help it. She had never had a father, but she had dreamed about it, and she wanted to stay in Dash Coogan's arms for the next thousand years.

He picked up her hand and enfolded it in his much larger one. "My sweet little Jane Marie."

"And cut! Print it. That looked good."

Dash dropped her hand. He stirred beneath her, and she rose reluctantly. As he stood, the big front-porch rocker they had been sitting in banged against the wall of the ranch house. Her body had been so warm seconds ago, but now her skin felt cold. He began to walk away, just as he always did when they were done, as if being in her presence for more than five minutes would contaminate him.

She rushed to the edge of the porch and spoke to his back as he walked down the steps. "I think that was a real good scene, don't you, Dash?

"It seemed to go okay."

"Better than okay." She hurried after him, jumping over a tangle of electrical cables on the way. "You were terrific. Really. I think you're a terrific actor. Maybe the best in the world. I think—"

"Sorry, Honey. I can't talk now. I've got things to do."

"But Dash—"

He picked up his stride, and before she knew it, he had left her behind. Lowering her head, she dragged her heels as she began walking toward the motor home they had given her to use when they were on location. Maybe her mind was playing tricks on her. Maybe her memory of that first day when he had treated her so kindly was a delusion. If only she knew what she had done to make him stop liking her.

From the very beginning she'd been just as friendly as she knew how to be. She'd run off all the time to get him coffee and donuts. She'd given him her chair. She'd told him how much she admired him and offered him back rubs. She entertained him with witty conversation during breaks and brought him newspapers. She'd even begged him to let her wash his shirt one day when he'd spilled coffee on it. Why had he turned on her?

When they were acting in a scene together, it seemed as if she really were his daughter and he truly did love her. Sometimes he looked at her so tenderly she felt as if a whole pitcher of warm wine was speeding through her blood veins. But then the camera stopped and the wine turned to ice water because she knew he'd do his best to get away from her.

She paused for a moment in the shade of one of the big sycamore trees, ignoring the fact that she had to finish her history assignment before her tutor arrived. They had asked her to go back to school, something she didn't mind too much even though the tutor they had given her was old and boring. Sitting down on the rope swing that hung from the branches, a prop they used from time to time, she pushed herself gently back and forth.

It was January now, and *The Dash Coogan Show* had turned into the biggest hit of the fall season. Reaching into the pocket of her flannel shirt, she pulled out a Xerox of an article that had just appeared in one of the most important news magazines in the country. Everyone had been given a copy that morning, but this was the first chance she'd had to look at it. She scanned it, but then slowed down as she came to the end.

The Dash Coogan Show has captured America's imagination in large part because of its superior acting. Liz Castleberry's intelligence shines through the stereotype of Eleanor, giving the spoiled socialite a delightfully ironic edge. Eric Dillon, an actor many critics thought to dismiss as another Hollywood hunk, plays her son Blake with the intensity and brooding melancholy of a young man still trying to discover his place in the world, adding layers of nuance to a character who would have been merely a piece of beefcake in the hands of someone less talented.

But most of all, America has fallen in love with the two leading characters. Dash Coogan has been looking for this part all his life, and he slips into the persona of the broken-down rodeo rider without a single misstep. And thirteen-year-old Honey Jane Moon as the feisty little girl who wants to settle down in a real home is the most winning child star in years. She's spunky without being precious, and so real it's hard to believe she's delivering a performance. The relationship between father and daughter as portrayed by Coogan and Moon is the way love between a parent and child should be—full of sharp edges, bristling with conflict, but deep and abiding.

She stared at the page, absorbing the painful irony of the final sentence. Not once since she was six years old had she known a deep and abiding love.

She sniffed and resolutely stuffed the article back in her pocket for Chantal to put in her shoe box along with the others. Some day when she got the time, her cousin planned to paste all of them in a scrapbook. There were a lot of articles in Chantal's shoe box, despite the fact that Ross wouldn't let any of the reporters who were clamoring to interview her get close. He said he wanted to shield her from public scrutiny until she grew more accustomed to the business, but she suspected his real reason for keeping her away from reporters was that he didn't trust her not to go on one of her talking jags and say things he didn't want made public, such as how old she really was.

She jumped up from the swing, and her heart started a rickety-rack clattering in her chest as she spotted Eric Dillon walking toward his trailer. He was wearing a pair of stone-washed jeans so tight that the outline of the wallet in his back pocket was visible, along with a black T-shirt that had the sleeves cut out.

He turned slightly and her mouth went cotton dry as she took in the clean lines of his profile. Her eyes traced the height of his forehead, the lean straight nose, that thin, strong mouth with its sharply chiseled bow. She loved his mouth and spent a lot of her spare time daydreaming about what it would be like to kiss it. But the only way that would happen was if the writers made it happen, and right now that didn't seem too likely.

Sometimes it gave her chills the way the writers kept calling her into that conference room and making her talk. In her old life, God had been in charge, but now that she had met the show's five writers, she understood real power.

"Eric!" His name spilled from her lips with embarrassing eagerness.

He turned toward her and she glimpsed something scary in his face, but then she decided it was only annoyance. People were after him all the time. Some of the crew members complained because Eric was sort of temperamental, but she couldn't find it in her heart to hold it against him. Not with all the pressures of stardom bearing down on him. She rushed toward him, telling herself to act casual, but he started walking away, so she had to move even faster.

"Would you like to run some lines, Eric? I've been working on those sensory-awareness exercises I heard you telling Liz about. We're filming the scene by the corral this afternoon. It's an important scene, and we need to be ready for it."

He began walking. "Sorry, kid. Not right now."

It was the dog-dish haircut. How could he ever think of her as a seventeen-year-old woman when she looked like somebody's little brother? She found herself moving faster, occasionally taking two steps to keep up.

"How about half an hour? Would half an hour be good for you?"

"I'm afraid not. I've got some business to attend to." He mounted the steps to his motor home and opened the door.

"But Eric—"

"Sorry, Honey. No time."

The door shut. As she stared at its unyielding surface, she realized that she'd done it again. Even though she kept telling herself to act mature and sophisticated, she ended up acting just like Janie.

She glanced around, hoping no one had witnessed what a fool she'd made of herself, but the only person nearby was Liz Castleberry, and she didn't seem to be paying attention. Honey slipped her hands back into her jeans pockets so she looked as if she were just wandering around with nothing particular on her mind.

On location, the four leading actors each had a small motor home. Liz's motor home was parked next to Eric's. She was sitting in a lawn chair near the door with Mitzi, her golden retriever, sprawled at her side. She had a sweater tossed over her shoulders and was studying her script through a pair of large sunglasses with clear pink rims.

From the beginning Honey had liked Liz's dog a lot better than she liked Liz. Liz was too glamorous for her to be comfortable in her presence. More than anyone else on the show, she acted like a real movie star, and since the first days of filming, Honey had been steering a wide berth around her. It hadn't been difficult to do. All the show's stars tended to keep to themselves.

Mitzi rose and trotted forward, her tail wagging. Honey was feeling bruised from her encounter with Eric and she wanted to be alone for a while, but it was hard to ignore a dog with a yen to play, especially one the size of Mitzi. She reached down and stroked the dog's large, handsome head. "Hi, girl."

Mitzi began circling her and nuzzling her knees, the rhythm of her tail moving from adagio to allegro. Honey sank down and pushed her fingers into the dog's soft, butterscotch fur. Leaning forward, she rested her cheek against Mitzi's neck, not minding the musty scent of dog breath. Mitzi's tongue scraped her cheek. Even though Mitzi was only a dog, Honey appreciated the affection.

It was getting harder all the time for her to blame other people for not wanting to be with her. There were so many things wrong with her. She was ugly and bossy. Other than the fact that she could cook and she was a good driver, she didn't have any particular talents. When she thought about it, she realized that there wasn't much to like, let alone love.

"Bad day?

Honey's head shot up at the sound of Liz's quiet voice. "Hell, no. I'm having a great day. A *great* one."

Releasing Mitzi, she sat back on her heels, taking in the actress's billowy chestnut hair and flawless skin and wishing she could look like her. Honey was beginning to think that she was the only ugly person in all of Southern California.

Liz slipped her sunglasses on top of her head. Her eyes were as green as Silver Lake before the water had gone bad. She nodded her head toward Eric's trailer. "You're way out of your league, kiddo. Be careful with that one."

Honey leaped to her feet. "I don't have the slightest idea what you're talking about. And I don't appreciate other people nibbing into my business."

Liz shrugged and pulled her glasses back down over her eyes.

Honey spun around and began to stomp away only to run into Lisa Harper, the actress who was playing Dusty. When she realized that Lisa was heading for Eric's trailer, she intercepted her.

"I wouldn't bother him if I were you, Lisa. Eric's got some business to attend to, and he doesn't want to be interrupted." She tried to conceal her resentment at the way Lisa's breasts stretched out the front of her purple knit top.

"You're a stitch, Honey." Lisa laughed. *"I'm* Eric's business." She climbed the steps to his trailer and disappeared inside.

An hour later she reappeared. Her purple knit top had been replaced with one of Eric's cropped-off T-shirts.

The conference room was dim, with only weak threads of late afternoon light seeping through the closed draperies. Honey sat before them like a sinner on judgment day called to the presence of the Almighty. Except there was only one of Him, and there were five of them.

A woman with burgundy fingernails gestured toward the can of Orange Crush they had set out for her. "Help yourself, Honey," she said quietly.

The man at the center of the table lit a cigarette and

leaned back in his chair. "You can start whenever you're ready."

Honey gazed stubbornly down at the floor. "I don't have anything to say."

"Look at us when you talk, please."

"I'm not saying anything. I mean it this time. I don't have a single thing on my mind."

Someone flicked a lighter. A chair creaked softly.

One of the men tapped a pencil on his notepad. "Why don't you tell us about Eric?"

"There's nothing to tell."

"We hear things."

She stiffened in her chair. "I'm not talking about him anymore."

"Don't hold out on us, Honey. That's not a good idea."

Honey's hand clamped tighter around the soda pop can. "Why should I tell you anything? I don't even know why I'm here. I don't like you people!"

Unmoved by her rebellion, they picked up their notepads. "Anytime you're ready."

And because she had no one else to talk to, she told the writers everything. . . .

EXTERIOR. THE LANDING OUTSIDE BLAKE'S APARTMENT OVER THE GARAGE—NIGHT.

Janie stands on the landing looking at the door of Blake's apartment. Nervously, she tucks her T-shirt into her pants and then tries to tidy her hair with her fingers, only to realize the task is hopeless and mess it up again. Finally, she loses her nerve and begins to go back down the stairs, then changes her mind and returns. Summoning her courage, she knocks on the door. When there is no answer, she knocks again.

JANIE
Blake? Blake, are you there?

BLAKE'S VOICE
What do you want, Janie?

JANIE

You—uh— You said you'd help me with my arithmetic homework one of these nights. The— uh—the fractions. Oh, man, those fractions are really hard.

Blake slowly opens the door. He is dressed in jeans, his chest bare. Janie stares at him and gulps.

BLAKE

I'm sorry, Janie, but tonight's not a real good night for me.

JANIE
(disappointed)
Oh . . . Well, maybe . . . You want to play some cards instead?

BLAKE

Not tonight, kid.

JANIE

How about some TV? The Cowboys are playing tonight.

DUSTY'S VOICE
(coming from inside the apartment)
Blake? Is something wrong?

Janie's face falls as she absorbs what is taking place.

BLAKE
(gives Janie a sympathetic smile)
Maybe some other time.

As he turns to go back inside, Janie's heartbreak changes to anger.

JANIE

You toad sucker! Dusty's in there. I heard her voice. You got Dusty in your apartment!

BLAKE

Now, Janie . . .

                    JANIE
                  (furiously)
Does your mama know about this? Because if
your mama knew, she'd kill you! I'm gonna tell
her! I'm going right down there and pound on
her door and tell her that her only son is a
low-life, scum-suckin' womanizer!

Dusty appears behind Blake's shoulder. She is wearing
Blake's robe and her hair is rumpled.

                    DUSTY
                (not unkindly)
Hey, Janie. What're you doin' here?

                    JANIE
And you! You should be ashamed of yourself! All
this time I thought you were a nice person! Now
it turns out you're nothing but a—a—*slut!*

                    BLAKE
                  (coldly)
I think you'd better calm down, Janie.

                    JANIE
                (hysterically)
I *am* calm. I am completely calm.

                    BLAKE
      (steps out on landing and shuts door)
Janie, you can't talk to Dusty like that. There are
things you don't understand. You're still a kid,
and—

                    JANIE
I'm not a kid! Don't ever say I'm a kid! I'm almost
fourteen and I'm—

Janie bursts into tears . . .

Silence fell over the set as they all waited.
    Dry-eyed and furious, Honey rounded on the cameras.
"This is stupid! I'm not doing this!"

"Cut!"

Eric slammed his hand down on the railing. "Aw, for chrissake. This is the ninth take."

The director stepped forward. Although the landing to Blake's apartment was supposed to be above the garage, the set rose just a few feet off the studio floor. While one of the wardrobe assistants handed Eric a shirt, the director gazed up at Honey.

"Do you need makeup to get the crystals?"

Honey had been working on the show for six months, long enough to know that he was talking about menthol crystals that could be blown into her eyes to make them tear. She shook her head, imagining Eric's disgust. Real actors didn't need menthol crystals. Not if they had prepared properly. Not if they'd done their sensory-awareness exercises. But doing this scene was like pulling at an open wound, and all she wanted was to get out of here.

Eric clenched his teeth. "For God's sake use the crystals. We don't have the time to wait for you to do it right."

His callousness destroyed the last vestige of her self-control. "Janie's not some damn crybaby! And she sure as hell wouldn't waste her time crying over a damn peckerhead like Blake!"

Lisa stuck her head out the door. "Are we going to take a break? Because I have to pee."

"No!" Eric shouted. "No goddamn break. It's six o'clock. If Honey doesn't get it right this time, I'm walking. I've got things to do."

"And everybody here knows exactly what kind of things!" Honey shouted.

"That's it. I'm out of here. I don't have to take this shit."

Eric vaulted over the railing to the studio floor. He worked out daily and there was no reason for him to be breathing so hard, but the panic that gripped him couldn't be cured by physical conditioning. From the beginning, he had hated working with her. He couldn't stand the way she looked at him, the way she followed him around. If he'd known about her in the beginning, he would never have signed the contract to do the show. Even his growing fame wasn't worth being forced to stare into those big, needy eyes, that face that begged for his attention.

"Hold it, everybody," the director exclaimed. "Things are getting a little out of control here. One more take, Eric. If Honey doesn't get it this time, we'll start fresh tomorrow. Come on, Eric, cut me some slack. It's late and everybody's nerves are shot. Makeup, get the menthol crystals."

Eric ground his teeth. He wanted to tell all of them to go to hell, but if he walked out now, he'd have to work with the little pest first thing tomorrow morning, and he had enough trouble sleeping as it was. Sometimes in his nightmares her voice was starting to get mixed up with Jason's.

Begrudgingly, he threw off his shirt and climbed back up the three steps. She stared at him, hurt and adoration making her light blue eyes huge. They wanted to suck him in, eat him up. He tried to distance himself from her by studying her face objectively. She was going to be a knock-out one of these days, when she stopped looking like a kid.

His small flash of objectivity faded, and all he could see was someone who reminded him far too much of his pain in the ass little brother.

He set his jaw and spoke in a nasty snarl, hoping to make her hate him. "Next time do your homework first. You're getting paid to be a professional. Start acting like one."

She sucked in her breath as if he'd hit her. Her eyes grew luminous with misery, and her bottom lip sagged with vulnerability. He felt the impact of her hurt in his own gut.

The director spoke up. "Let's take it from Janie's close-up. Positions, everybody."

The makeup man blew the crystals in her eyes, and they began to tear.

"Quiet, please. We're rolling. Marker. Action."

The camera came in for a close-up. One fat drop rolled over her bottom lashes and trickled down her cheek, but her expression remained mutinous.

Eric told himself that it was Blake who had to touch her. Blake. Not himself.

Stepping forward, he put his arms around her and pulled her to his chest. Her head didn't even reach his chin. She was just about Jason's height, and like his half brother, she only wanted his attention.

The squeal of brakes shrieked in his mind, the sound of a scream.

"Cut. Print it. Good. We can all go home."

"Asshole!" Honey shoved hard against his chest and ran from the set.

He stood at the top of the landing looking after her, his eyes dark and tormented.

Take me with you, Eric. Please.

8

Despite her determination to keep her head up, by lunch-time the next day Honey was in desperate need of a quiet place where she could go to lick her wounds. Everybody who hadn't been on the set the day before had heard about her fight with Eric, and she knew all of them were whispering behind her back. They were shooting on location today, but she rejected her motor home as a place to escape because her tutor was waiting there with a trigonometry lesson. Instead, she slipped behind the catering wagon to an outcrop of man-made rock. But as she stepped into the cool shadows, she realized that even here she couldn't be alone.

Thirty feet away, Dash Coogan leaned against one of the boulders with his hat pulled low over his eyes and one knee drawn up. She knew she should leave, but despite Dash's coolness toward her, she was enveloped with the sensation of having stumbled into a safe, secure place. If only she could crawl into his lap like Janie did. Knowing how impossible that was, she sank down in a shady spot about twelve feet away from him, drew up her knees, and dug the heels of her cowboy boots into the dirt. Maybe if she sat here for a little bit without talking, he wouldn't mind.

A minute ticked by, each second lasting forever. She tried to hold back, but the words spilled out anyway. "I hate people who don't have anything better to do than gossip about other people."

He didn't respond, even though he had to have heard about what had happened.

She told herself to keep quiet. She already knew that Dash didn't like talky women, but she was going to burst if she couldn't confide in someone other than that pack of jackal writers who took her deepest secrets and spread them out for all of America to see. And who better to confide in than this man who was sort of the closest thing she had to a father?

"Eric's a real peckerhead, if you ask me. Everybody thinks I've got a crush on him, but what kind of idiot would I be to have a crush on a conceited jerk like that?"

Coogan tilted up his hat with his thumb and stared at the horizon in the distance.

She waited for him to give her some advice like adults were supposed to give teenagers. Like a father might give his daughter.

She prodded him. "I guess I'm not stupid enough to think that somebody like him would look twice at a girl who looks like me."

Her muscles tense, she waited for him to respond. If only he would tell her there wasn't anything wrong with the way she looked. If only he'd tell her she was a late bloomer, just like he always told Janie.

But as silence ticked away between them, she decided she shouldn't expect him to read her mind.

"I know I'm not exactly pretty, but do you think—" She picked at a small hole on the knee of her jeans. "Do you think I might be—You know. Maybe a late bloomer?"

He turned to her with cold, dead eyes. "I came back here to be alone. I'd appreciate it if you'd take off."

She sprang to her feet. Why had she ever thought for a moment that he'd understand? That he cared enough about her to try to make her feel better? When was she ever going to admit that he didn't give a damn about her? Cocooned in her misery, she looked for a way to punch right back at him, to hurt him as he'd just hurt her.

Sucking in her breath, she glared at him, her voice crackling with hostility. "Who wants to be with you anyway, you old drunk?"

He didn't even flinch. He just sat there looking out toward the San Gabriels. The brim of his hat shaded his eyes so she couldn't see their expression, but his voice was as flat as the Oklahoma prairie.

"Then how about you leave this old drunk alone."

All her hurt turned to venom. Never again would she confess her true feelings to any of them. Beneath a black scowl that camouflaged her broken heart, she spun away from him and stalked back to her motor home.

Behind the outcrop of man-made rocks, Dash Coogan had sweated through his shirt. He squeezed his eyes shut, trying to block out the craving that had hit him so hard he felt as if his skin were being stripped from his bones. That little girl would never know how close her taunt had hit on the truth. He needed a drink.

With a trembling hand, he reached for the roll of LifeSavers he kept in his shirt pocket. These past few years, he'd begun to take his recovery for granted, but lately he'd realized that his complacency was a big mistake. As he shoved two of the spearmint candies into his mouth, he reminded himself that he'd long ago given up blaming his alcoholism on other people, and he wouldn't do it now. But it was an undeniable fact that every time that little girl came running after him expecting him to be her pa in real life, the urge to drink hit him like a slap in his face. He hadn't even been a decent parent to his real children, and he sure as hell couldn't be a parent to her.

Those first few days when they'd begun reading through the scripts and talking about the show, he'd been friendly, but it hadn't taken him long to see that he was making a big mistake. She followed him everywhere, not giving him an inch of breathing space. He had realized right then that he had to keep his distance. He had too many empty spaces inside himself to be able to fill up hers.

He knew how badly he was hurting her, but he told himself that she was a strong little cuss, just as he'd been when he was a kid, and she'd survive his rejection the same way he'd survived being shuttled from one foster home to another the whole time he was growing up. Maybe she'd even be stronger for it. She'd be better off learning right now that she shouldn't expect so much from other people, that she should stop wearing every one of her feelings right out in the open where anybody who came along could stomp all over them.

But damn, there was something about her that tore at his guts, and that, more than anything else, was the reason he had to stay away from her. Because when he felt vulnerable, he wanted to drink, and nothing on earth, not even that feisty little kid, was going to make him ruin six hard-earned years of sobriety.

Honey saw the house in early March, right before the show went on its four-month break, or hiatus, as all of them called it. They moved in a few weeks later, and she wandered outside the first evening just before the sun set to gaze at the whitewashed brick exterior. A network of bougainvillea vines climbed the walls and curled around the charcoal shutters that framed the mullioned windows. The small copper roof over the entrance had long ago formed the chalky-green patina of respectability. The shrubbery was well established and a small rose garden formed a crescent at the side. She had never imagined she would live in such a beautiful house. It was everything she had always dreamed of.

"Of course it's too close to Wilshire to be really fashionable," the realtor had told her. "But Beverly Hills is Beverly Hills."

Honey didn't care about what was fashionable. She didn't even care about living in Beverly Hills. The house was cozy and pretty, the perfect place for a family to live. Maybe things would start to get better for her now. She hugged herself, trying to take comfort in the house and forget everything else that was going wrong in her life: the conflicts on the set, the way people were talking behind her back. One of the directors had complained to Ross because she'd shown up late a few times and kept the cast waiting. But it hadn't been all the cast. Just Dash Coogan. And she had kept him waiting twice because she was sick of the way he ignored her, especially since the press had started treating him like Mr. Father of the Year.

The sound of a car pulling into the driveway distracted her. She turned to see her agent getting out of his BMW. Arthur Lockwood walked toward her, his wiry red hair and beard looking darker than normal in the fading light. She respected him, but the fact that he had two college degrees intimidated her, and she couldn't really warm up to his beard.

"Are you all settled?" he asked.

"We're getting there. One of the salesladies from this ritzy furniture store is arranging the furniture."

"It's a nice house."

"Let me show you the grapefruit tree." She led him toward the side, where he admired the tree, and then they entered the screened-in porch through the back door. The furniture saleslady hadn't gotten this far yet, so there was only an old folding chair, which Arthur declined. Honey looked out over the small backyard. She was going to string a hammock between two of the trees and buy a barbecue grill just like on all those TV commercials.

Arthur jiggled the change in the pocket of his chinos. "Honey, hiatus starts in a couple of weeks, and you won't have to report back to work until the end of July. It's not too late for you to accept the offer from TriStar."

The early evening air suddenly developed a chill. "I don't want to do any movies, Arthur. I already told you that. I want to finish up my high school courses during the break so I can graduate before we start filming again."

"You're working with a tutor. Another few months won't make any difference."

"It will to me."

"You're making a mistake. Even though the Coogan show is a huge hit now, it won't last forever, and you need to start planning for the future. You're a natural talent, Honey. The TriStar part will really showcase you."

"A fourteen-year-old girl dying of cancer. Just the thing to cheer America's heart."

"It's a great script."

"She's a rich girl, Arthur. I couldn't convince anybody in the world that I'm a rich girl." Playing a character other than Janie Jones scared her. No matter what the critics said, she knew she wasn't a real actress. All she did was play herself.

"You sell yourself short, Honey. You have real talent, and you'd be wonderful in this part."

"Forget it." She could imagine Eric's contemptuous reaction if he ever saw her trying to play a fourteen-year-old rich girl dying from cancer.

Just the thought of Eric made her ache. Unless they were doing a scene together, he acted as if she didn't exist. And Dash hadn't spoken to her off camera since that day three weeks ago when she'd tried to talk to him behind the rock. The only person who never seemed to avoid her was Liz Castleberry, and Honey figured that was just because of Mitzi. Liz's dog had become the closest thing Honey had to a best friend. She gazed out at her backyard, loneliness creeping all the way through her.

"You need a chance to stretch yourself," her agent said.

"I thought you worked for *me*, Arthur. I told you I don't want to do any movies, and I meant it."

His face tightened, and she knew he was angry with her, but she didn't care. He bossed her around too much, and sometimes she had to remind him who was in charge.

When he finally left, she went inside. She found Chantal in the living room, lying on their new gold and white brocade sectional couch and reading a magazine. Gordon sat across from her fiddling with his pocketknife.

"This room looks real pretty, Chantal. That saleslady did

a good job." Thick white carpet stretched from one wall to the next. In addition to the couch the room held fancy French chairs and amoeba-shaped glass tabletops sitting on thin brass legs. One of those tables held the remnants of a Hungry Man dinner.

"The plants come tomorrow."

"Plants'll be nice." Chantal stretched and set down her magazine. "Honey, me and Gordon have been talking. We think we might be takin' off in a couple of days."

Honey froze. "What do you mean?"

Chantal looked nervous. "Gordon, you tell her."

Gordon pocketed his knife. "We're thinking about driving around the country, Honey. Seeing more of America. Sort of making a life for ourselves."

Honey's heart slammed against her ribs.

"Gordon's got his career to think about," Chantal went on. "He needs inspiration if he's going to be a painter."

Honey tried to stem her panic. "Are both of you crazy? I just bought this house. I bought it for all of us. You can't take off now."

Chantal wouldn't look at her. "Gordon says Beverly Hills is suffocating him."

"We just moved in today!" Honey shouted. "How could it be suffocating him?"

"I knew you wouldn't understand. You always yell at people. You never try to understand." With a small, choked sob, Chantal fled from the room.

Honey spun on Gordon. "Just what the hell do you think you're doing, you stupid fool?"

Gordon stuck out his weak chin. "Don't call me that! I guess Chantal and me can take off if we want to."

"And how do you plan to support yourselves?"

"We'll find jobs. We've already talked about it. We're going to work our way around the country."

"*You* can work, maybe, but don't fool yourself about Chantal. Selling Ferris wheel tickets is the hardest thing she ever did, and she messed up the cash box so many times that she would have gotten fired if she hadn't been family."

"She might do hair. She's talked about it."

"She talked about marrying Burt Reynolds, too, but she didn't do that, either."

Gordon shoved his hands in his pockets, his frustration evident. "I can't keep going on like this. I've got to start painting."

"Then start!" Honey said desperately.

"I don't think I'm going to be able to paint here. This house. This neighborhood. Everything's too—"

"Just try it," she pleaded. "If it doesn't work out, we can always move." The idea of moving made her sick. They weren't even unpacked, and she loved this house, but she wasn't going to let him take Chantal away.

"I don't know. I—"

"What do you need? I'll buy you anything you need."

"I don't like taking your money all the time. I'm a man. I should—"

"I'll pay you two thousand dollars a month to stay right here."

Gordon stared at her.

"Two thousand dollars a month for as long as you stay. I'm already paying for the house and all the food. That's two thousand dollars just for spending money."

Gordon's breath made a soft, hissing sound. His face looked pinched, and when he spoke, his voice was soft and hoarse. "What gives you the right to try to run our lives like this?"

"I care about Chantal, that's all. I want to take care of her."

"I'm her husband. I'll take care of her."

But there wasn't much conviction left in his voice, and Honey knew that she had won.

The hiatus began. While Gordon and Chantal lay around the house eating the meals Honey cooked and watching television, Honey finished her high-school courses with straight As, except for physical science, which she hated. In June, the three of them flew to South Carolina to see Sophie. The park was even more depressing than she remembered. The rides had been sold off, and the *Bobby Lee* had finally

broken apart during a storm and sunk to the bottom of Silver Lake. Once again, Honey tried to talk her aunt into coming to L.A., but Sophie refused.

"This is my home, Honey. I don't want to live anyplace else."

"It's not safe, Sophie."

"Sure it is. Buck's here."

Honey drove into town the next day to meet with the lawyer she'd hired last December to negotiate the purchase of the park. By late afternoon, she had signed the final papers. The acquisition was going to wipe her out financially for a while, and she wouldn't be able to reopen the park, but at least she had it back.

"Honey, I asked you to walk past Dash and over to the window on the last line." Janice Stein, the show's only female director, pointed toward the correct position.

Hiatus was over. It was August, and they were in the studio working on their second show for the '81–'82 season. Honey had been in a foul mood ever since shooting had resumed. Dash hadn't acted as if he were the tiniest bit glad to see her again, and Eric had barely returned her greeting. Only Liz Castleberry, the Queen of the Bitches, had stopped to chat, and she was the last person Honey had wanted to talk to.

She splayed her hand on her hip and glared at Janice, who was standing in the middle of the ranch house living room set. "I don't want to move until I say, 'Calm down, Pop.' It'll work better there."

"That's too late," Janice said. "You should already be at the window by then."

"I don't want to do it that way."

"I'm the director, Honey."

Narrowing her eyes, Honey spoke in her snottiest voice. "And I'm an actress trying to do a decent job. If you don't like my work, maybe you should find another show to direct."

She flounced past Dash, who was standing next to the window with his script in one hand and a coffee cup in the

other, and walked off the set. Last year she had been intimidated by all of them, but this year would be different. She was tired of people pushing her around, tired of listening to Gordon's endless complaints about living in Beverly Hills, tired of Chantal's pouting. Nobody liked her anyway, so what difference did it make how she behaved?

She turned down the corridor that led to the dressing rooms and saw Eric at the end. Just the sight of him made her knees go weak. He had spent the summer filming his first feature role in a movie, and he looked so handsome it was hard for her to keep from staring.

Melanie Osborne, an attractive redhead who was one of the new assistant directors, was talking with him. They were standing just close enough for Honey to be certain the conversation wasn't about business. Melanie leaned toward him in a confident, sexy way that made Honey's toes curl with envy.

Eric looked up and saw her coming. He patted Melanie on the cheek and disappeared down the hallway into his dressing room.

Honey's mood grew uglier.

Melanie walked toward her, a friendly smile on her face. "Hi, Honey. I just overheard Ross say that he needs you as soon as you're free."

"Then he can come find me."

"Yes, ma'am," Melanie muttered as Honey swept past.

Honey stopped and spun around. "What did you say?"

"I didn't say anything."

Honey took in Melanie's long, wavy hair and generous breasts. Last week they'd cut her own hair in another dog's dish style. "You'd better watch yourself. I don't like smartasses."

"I apologize," Melanie said coldly. "I didn't mean to offend you."

"Well, you did."

"I'll try my best to avoid repeating the mistake."

"Try your best to stay out of my way."

Melanie clenched her teeth and began to move on, but something evil had taken possession of Honey. She wanted to punish Melanie for being pretty and feminine and for knowing how to talk to Eric. She wanted to punish Melanie for exchanging jokes with Dash and being popular with the crew and for having polished red fingernails the shape of almonds.

"Get me some coffee first," she snapped. "Bring it to my dressing room. And hurry it up."

Melanie stared at her for a moment. "What?"

"You heard me."

When the redhead didn't move, Honey planted her hand on her hip. "Well?"

"Go to hell."

Ross came around the corner just in time to hear the assistant director's words. He stopped in his tracks. Melanie spun around, saw who had approached, and paled.

Honey leapt forward. "Did you hear what she said?"

"What's your name?" Ross barked.

The assistant director looked sick. "Uh—Melanie Osborne."

"Well, Melanie Osborne, you've just joined the ranks of the unemployed. Pack up and get out."

"But—"

"Honey's a star," he said quietly. "Nobody talks to her like that."

Melanie turned back to Honey, waiting for her to say something, but it was as if a cadre of devils had speared her lips shut with their pitchforks. Her conscience screamed at her to set things right, but her pride was too strong.

As it became apparent that Honey wasn't going to speak, Melanie's eyes grew bitter. "Thanks for nothing." Straightening her spine, she turned and walked away.

"I'm sorry about that, Honey," Ross said, running one hand through his long, silver hair. "I'll make certain she doesn't work around here again."

A chill slithered along Honey's spine as she absorbed the awesome power of celebrity. He wasn't even going to ask her what had happened. She was important; Melanie wasn't. Nothing else mattered.

He began talking about a press conference for the new

season and the publicist who would accompany her on one of the few interviews he was permitting. Honey barely listened. She had done something terrible, but acknowledging that she was wrong stuck in her throat like a great lump of unchewed bread. She began the slow process of justifying her actions. She was hardly ever wrong about anything, she told herself. Maybe she wasn't wrong about this. Maybe Melanie was a troublemaker. She probably would have gotten herself fired anyway. But no matter how much she rationalized, she couldn't make the sick feeling inside her go away.

Ross left and she rushed toward her dressing room so she could be alone for a few minutes to think things over. But before she could get inside, she saw Liz Castleberry leaning in the open doorway of her own dressing room across the corridor. It was obvious from the disapproving expression on her face that her costar had heard everything.

"A word of advice, kiddo," she said quietly. "Don't screw people over. It'll come back to haunt you."

Honey felt as if she were being attacked from all sides, and she bristled. "Now isn't that funny. I can't seem to remember asking for your advice."

"Maybe you should."

"I suppose you're going to run to Ross."

"You're the one who should do that."

"Don't hold your breath."

"You're making a mistake," Liz replied. "I hope you figure that out before it's too late."

"Go to Ross," Honey said viciously. "But if Melanie shows up on this set, I'm walking!"

She went into her dressing room and slammed the door.

Melanie had a lot of friends on the set, and it didn't take long for word of her firing to spread. By the end of the week, Honey had become a pariah. The crew members only addressed her when they had to, and in retaliation Honey grew more demanding. She complained about her lines, her hair. She didn't like the lighting or the blocking.

The thought kept skittering through her mind that if she behaved badly enough, they'd have to pay attention to her, but Dash stopped talking to her completely, and Eric looked at her as if she were a slug leaving a slimy trail on the sidewalk of his life. Hatred joined the other complex feelings she held for him.

The following week, Arthur took her out to dinner. He'd heard about what had happened with Melanie, and he started giving her a big lecture about getting a reputation in the business for being difficult.

Instead of asking him to help her set things right, as she knew she should, she cut him off with a long recitation of all the slights she had suffered since her first day on the set. Then she told him that he could either take her side or she'd find another agent. He immediately backed off.

When she left the restaurant, she had the awful feeling that a devil had taken over her body. An internal voice whispered that she was turning into a spoiled Hollywood brat, just like a lot of the kid stars she had read about. She tried to repress it. Nobody understood her, and that was their problem, not hers. She told herself she should feel proud of the fact that she'd put her agent in his place, but as she got into her car, she was shaking, and she knew it wasn't pride she felt, but fear. Wasn't anybody going to stop her?

The next day she dropped by to see the writers. Not to talk to them. Hell, no, she wasn't going to talk to them. Just to sort of say hi.

9

The house sat all alone at the end of one of the murderously twisting narrow roads that wound through Topanga Canyon. The road had no guardrail, and the darkness, combined with a late November drizzle, made even as fearless a driver as Honey jumpy. She tried to work up some enthusiasm for her new house as it came into view around the final hairpin turn, but she hated its sweeping roof and stark contemporary lines as much as she hated its location.

Topanga Canyon was a far cry from Beverly Hills and the pretty little house she had loved so much. Every leftover hippie in Southern California lived here, along with packs of wild dogs that bred with the coyotes. But after seven months in Beverly Hills, Gordon still hadn't been able to paint, and so they had moved.

Honey was drooping with fatigue as she pulled into the drive. When they had lived in Beverly Hills, it had only taken her half an hour to get back and forth from the studio. Now she had to get up at five to be at work in time for a seven A.M. call, and at night, she rarely got home before eight.

Her stomach rumbled as she walked into the house. She wished that Chantal and Gordon would have dinner ready, but neither of them was good in the kitchen, and they usually waited till she came home to cook. She had hired four different housekeepers to take care of the cooking and cleaning, but they kept quitting.

She dragged herself into the great room that stretched across the back of the house, and as her eyes fell on Sophie and her new husband, the old adage about being careful what you wish for because you just might get it sprang into her mind.

"Mama's not feeling well," Chantal said, looking up from the issue of *Cosmo* she was thumbing through.

"Another one of my headaches." Sophie sighed from the couch. "And my throat is real scratchy. Buck, honey, could you turn down that TV?"

Buck Ochs, the amusement park's former handyman and Sophie's new spouse, was sprawled in the big recliner Honey had bought them for a wedding present, where he was eating Cheez Doodles and watching a swimsuit show on ESPN. He obediently reached for the remote control and pointed it toward the big-screen TV Honey had bought for them.

"Look at the busts on that one, Gordon. Man-oh-man."

Unlike Sophie, Buck had been more than willing to leave the decaying amusement park for the riches of LaLa Land, and the two of them had shown up on Honey's doorstep early in the fall, right after their marriage.

"Honey, would you mind going out and buying me some lozenges?" Sophie's voice rose weakly from the couch. "My throat's so dry I can barely swallow."

Buck zapped the volume back up. "Aw, Sophie, Honey can get those lozenges later. Right now what I'd like is a good steak dinner. How 'bout it, Honey?"

The expensive white furniture was grimy with stains. An overturned beer can lay on the rug. Honey was exhausted and heartsick, and she exploded.

"You're all pigs! Look at you, lolling around like white trash, not contributing one single thing to society. I'm sick of this. I'm sick of all of you!"

Buck tore his attention away from the television and looked around at the others, his expression befuddled. "Now what's wrong with her?"

Chantal slapped down her *Cosmo* and got up in a huff. "I don't appreciate being talked to like that, Honey. Thanks to you, I've lost my appetite for dinner."

Gordon unwound from the floor where he had been sitting with his eyes shut doing what he called his "mind painting." "I haven't lost my appetite. What's to eat, Honey?"

She opened her mouth to deliver a stinging retort, but then she checked it. No matter what, they were the only family she had. With a weary sigh, she went into the kitchen and began dinner.

In the three months since she had gotten Melanie fired, Honey's relationship with the crew and her coworkers had steadily deteriorated. One part of her couldn't blame them for hating her. How could anybody like somebody who was so horrible? But the other part of her—the scared part—couldn't back down.

The Monday after her unpleasant weekend with her

family, they began filming an episode in which Janie, jealous of Dusty's relationship with Blake, tries to get her fired. At the climax Dash was to rescue Janie from the roof of the barn while Dusty and Blake watched.

Dash ignored her as usual all week. Honey bided her time until the afternoon they were to shoot the final scene. She watched from her perch on top of the roof as Dash worked out the movements of the rigorous climb from the ground to the hayloft and then over two levels of roof. After almost an hour, they were finally ready to do the scene for real.

The cameras rolled. She waited until Dash had completed the climb. As he pulled himself up onto the top level of the barn roof, she stood and looked at the camera.

"I forgot my line."

"Cut! Give Janie her line." Jack Swackhammer was in charge of this episode. As the director who had been with them the longest, he had also had more than his share of run-ins with her. Honey hated him.

"Honey, this is a tough scene on Dash," he said. "Try to get it right the next time."

"Sure, Jack," she replied sweetly.

Dash gave her a warning glare.

During the next take, she managed to slip as she stood. On the following take, she flubbed her line. Then she didn't hit her mark. Dash had sweated through his shirt from the exertion and they had to stop while he changed. They began again, but once more she failed to hit her mark.

One hour later, after she had slipped again and ruined the shot for the fifth time, Dash exploded and walked off the set.

Jack immediately went to Ross to complain about Honey's increasingly disruptive behavior, but *The Dash Coogan Show* was a ratings giant, and Ross wouldn't risk antagonizing the actress that the newspapers were calling the most popular "child" star on television. Before the episode was over, Honey had gotten Jack Swackhammer fired.

When she heard the news, she felt sick. Why couldn't somebody care enough about her to make her stop?

* * *

The writers sat around the conference table and stared at the door Honey had just stamped out of and slammed shut. For several moments everything was silent, and then one of the women put down her yellow pad. "We can't let this go on any longer."

The man sitting to her left cleared his throat. "We said we wouldn't interfere."

"That's right," another agreed. "We promised to function as impartial observers."

"As writers we report reality; we don't alter it."

The woman shook her head. "I don't care what we promised. She's self-destructing, and we have to do something."

EXTERIOR. FRONT PORCH OF RANCH HOUSE—DAY.

Eleanor, dressed in a mud-spattered white designer suit, is filthy and furious. Dash is grim. Janie stands by the porch rocker looking guilty.

> DASH
>
> Is this true, Janie? Did you deliberately set that booby trap?

> JANIE
> (desperately)
>
> It was a mistake, Pop. Miz Chadwick wasn't supposed to fall into the trap. Old Man Winters was. I had to do something! She was getting ready to sell him the ranch.

> ELEANOR
> (wipes a clump of something organic from her cheek)
>
> That does it! I finally get a buyer for this miserable place, and what does your little hellion of a daughter do? She tries to kill him!

> JANIE
>
> I wasn't actually trying to kill him, Miz Chadwick.

Just slow him up until Pop got back from town. I'm
really sorry you fell into the trap instead.

ELEANOR

I'm afraid sorry isn't good enough this time. I've
overlooked a lot from your daughter, Mr. Jones,
but I'm not going to overlook this. I know you
think I'm spoiled and frivolous and possessed
of half a dozen other qualities of which you rugged cowboy types disapprove. But I will tell you
this. Never once have I not been a parent to my
son.

JANIE
(jumping forward)

Your son is a low-life, stinkin' womanizer who
should be struck right off the face of this earth!

DASH

That's enough Janie. If you're finished, Miz
Chadwick.

ELEANOR

I'm not finished. Not by a long shot. Never once
have I let my son harm other people, Mr. Jones.
Never once have I failed to point out to him the
difference between right and wrong. Perhaps
basic qualities of decency aren't fashionable
here in Texas, but I can assure you, they are
respected in the rest of this country.

DASH
(coldly)

When I need advice on how to raise my daughter, I'll ask for it.

ELEANOR

By that time, it may very well be too late.

Eleanor snatches up her purse and exits into the ranch
house.

JANIE
(smugly)
You sure told her, Pop.

DASH
Yeah, I told her, all right. And now I'm gonna tell
you. Miss Jane Marie Jones, your days as a
carefree child untouched by human hand are
about to come to an abrupt end.

He snatches up Janie by the waist and carries her
purposefully across the porch and down the steps toward
the barn.

"Cut it. Print it." The director looked down at his clip
board. "Janie and Dash, I need you back in fifteen minutes.
Liz, you're off till after lunch."

Before Dash could set her down, Honey began to struggle.
"You don't have to suffocate me, you clumsy sonovabitch!"
Dash dropped her like a rabid dog.

Liz came through the doorway back onto the porch,
wiping her face with a tissue. "Honey, you stepped on my
lines again. Give me a little space to work, all right?"

Liz's request had been mildly uttered, but Honey blew up.
"Why don't you both go straight to hell!" She stomped away
from them. As she passed one of the cameras, she slapped it
with all her force and launched her final verbal rocket.

"Fuckers!"

"Charming," Liz drawled.

The crew members looked away. Dash slowly shook his
head and mounted the porch steps toward Liz. "My biggest
regret is the fact that those fool writers chickened out and I
don't get to whale her butt this afternoon."

"Do it anyway."

"Yeah, right."

Liz spoke quietly. "I'm serious, Dash."

He scowled and pulled a pack of LifeSavers from his shirt
pocket. She scrupulously avoided personal entanglements
on the set, but the situation with Honey had grown so
impossible that Liz felt she could no longer ignore it.

She walked over to the far side of the porch out of earshot of the crew, hesitating for a moment before she spoke. "Honey's completely out of control."

"You're not telling me anything. She kept us waiting almost an hour this morning."

"Ross is useless, and the network's even worse. They're all so afraid she'll walk out on the show that they let her get away with murder. I'm really worried about her. For some perverse reason, I happen to be fond of the little monster."

"Well, believe me when I tell you the feeling isn't mutual. She doesn't make much secret of the fact that she hates your guts." Dash sank down into the rocker near where she was standing. "Every time I do a scene with that kid, I feel like she's going to stick a knife right through my back the minute it's turned. You'd think she'd show a little gratitude. If it weren't for me, she wouldn't even have a career."

"From the tone of this new script, the writers seem to be sending you a message to do something about her." Liz stopped trying to clean herself up and held the towel loosely in her hand. "You know what Honey wants from you. Everybody on the set knows it. Would it kill you to give it to her?"

His voice was flat. "I don't know what you're talking about."

"From the beginning, she's looked at you like you were God Almighty. She wants some attention, Dash. She wants you to care about her."

"I'm an actor, not a baby-sitter."

"But she's hurting. God knows how long she's been on her own. You've met that parasitic family of hers. It's obvious that she's raised herself."

"I was on my own when I was a kid, and I did all right."

"Sure you did," she said sarcastically. Anyone with three ex-wives, two children he hardly ever saw, and a long history of fighting the bottle could hardly brag about how well adjusted he was.

He got up from the chair. "If you're so worried about her, why don't *you* play mother hen?"

"Because she'd spit in my face. I'm more the wicked

stepmother type than a fairy godmother. This is a dangerous business for a young girl who doesn't have anyone watching out for her. She's looking for a father, Dash. She needs someone to put the reins on her." She tried to lighten the tension between them with a small smile. "Who better to do that than an old cowboy?"

"You're crazy," he said, turning away from her. "I don't know a damned thing about kids."

"You've got two of them. You must know something."

"Their mother has raised them. All I do is write the checks."

"And that's the way you like to keep it, isn't it? Just writing the checks." The words had slipped out of their own volition, and she wanted to bite off her tongue.

Dash turned back to her, his eyes narrowed. "Why don't you just come out and say whatever it is you've got on your mind."

She took a deep breath. "All right. I think Honey's identity has gotten all tangled up with Janie's. Maybe the writers are to blame, I don't know, but for whatever reason, the more you distance yourself from her, the more she resents it and the worse she behaves. I think you're the only person who can help her."

"I don't have the slightest intention of helping her. It's not my problem."

His coldness unearthed a fragment of old pain that Liz hadn't even known still existed. She was suddenly twenty-two again and in love with a stunt rider from Oklahoma who she had just learned was a married man.

"Honey's too needy for you, isn't she? That first month we filmed, she ran after you like a little puppy dog practically begging for some attention, and the more she begged, the colder you got. She was too needy, and you don't like needy women, do you, Dash?"

He gave her a dead, hard stare. "You don't know anything about me, so why don't you just mind your own goddamn business?"

Liz was silently berating herself for ever having begun this conversation. This show had enough problems without adding a conflict between Dash and herself. She shrugged and smiled brittlely. "But of course, darling. Why don't I do just that."

Without another word, she walked off the porch and headed for her motor home.

Dash stormed over to the catering wagon and got himself a cup of coffee. It burned his tongue as he swallowed, but he kept drinking it anyway. He was furiously angry with Liz. Where did she get the gall to act as if that little monster from hell was his responsibility? He had only one responsibility, and that was to keep himself sober, something that hadn't been requiring much effort on his part until Honey had stomped into his life.

He swallowed the last of his coffee and tossed away the cup. Ross was the person who should be keeping Honey in line, not himself. And from now on Miss Liz Castleberry could just mind her own goddamn business.

They called him for the next scene, a simple one in which he had to carry Honey across the yard and into the barn. The scene that followed in the barn would be trickier— what television people called the MOS, when the moral lesson for the episode was delivered. MOS stood for "Moral of Show," but all of them referred to it as the "Moment of Shit."

"Where's Honey?" the assistant director asked. "We're ready to shoot."

"I heard Jack Swackhammer took out a contract on her," one of the camera men said. "Maybe the hit man finally delivered."

"We should be so lucky," the AD murmured.

For ten more minutes, Dash cooled his heels while his temper burned. Someone located Honey with the horses, and one of the camera operators suggested that she spent so much time with the animals because they were the only ones who could stand being with her since they didn't have to worry about getting fired.

Bruce Rand was directing that week's episode. He had

been responsible for some of the best episodes of *M.A.S.H.*, and Ross had brought him in because he had a reputation for tact. But after working with Honey all week, even he was starting to show wear around the edges.

When she finally ambled onto the set, Bruce looked relieved and began blocking out the scene. "Dash, carry Janie from the bottom of the porch steps across the yard toward the barn. Janie, give the line about being opposed to violence when you reach the corner of the porch, then start to struggle when he ignores you."

He finished the blocking and called for a rehearsal. Dash and Honey climbed the porch steps to the open front door. The assistant director, whose job it was to maintain continuity from one shot to the next, looked down at her notes.

"You had her under your left arm, Dash. And Honey, you need your hat."

Several more minutes passed while one of the wardrobe people ran back over to the corral to retrieve the navy blue cap she had been wearing. When it was on her head with the bill turned up, Dash tucked her under his left arm and they walked through it.

They returned to the porch, but as Dash turned to pick her up, he saw something he didn't like in those light blue eyes of hers, a subtle air of calculation. He remembered the episode in November when she'd been stuck on the roof of the barn and had deliberately blown her lines so he had to keep climbing up after her. His back had bothered him for a week afterward.

"No tricks, Honey," he warned. "This is an easy scene. Let's get it over with."

"You just worry about yourself, old man," she sneered. "I'll take care of me."

He didn't like it when she called him that, and his anger settled in deeper. No matter what the mirror said, he was only forty-one. Not that damned old.

"Quiet, please," Bruce called.

Dash walked to the bottom of the porch steps and picked Honey up under his left arm.

"Stand by now. We're rolling. Marker. Action."

"No, Pop," Janie screamed, as he began to walk. "What are you doing? I said I was sorry."

He reached the corner of the porch.

"Don't forget you're opposed to unnecessary violence," she shrieked. "You can't turn your back on your principles."

She was giving it one hundred percent, just like always, and he had to clutch her more tightly as she struggled.

"No, Pop! Don't do this! I'm too old for this . . . "

She started to kick, and her knee caught him in the small of his back. He grunted and his arm tightened around her waist as he continued to move purposefully toward the barn. Without warning, she jabbed the sharp point of her elbow in his ribs. He gripped her even tighter, warning her without words that she was going too far.

Her teeth sank into the flesh of his arm.

"God damn it!" With a sharp exclamation of pain, he dropped her to the ground.

"Ow . . . " Her hat flew off, and she looked up at him, outrage stamped all over her small, furious face. "You dropped me, you fucker!"

Fireworks went off inside his brain. She was ruining his life, and he'd had enough. Reaching down, he snatched her up by the seat of her jeans and the collar of her shirt.

"Hey!" She cried out in a combination of surprise and indignation as she left the ground.

"You messed with me one too many times, little girl," he said, hauling her off to the barn, this time in earnest.

Her struggles before were merely a rehearsal for what she did now. He pinned her against his side, not giving a damn whether he hurt her or not.

Honey felt the painful pressure of hard muscles clamping her ribs and cutting off her breath. Apprehension ate away at her anger as she grew conscious of the fact that he was in deadly earnest. She'd been looking for her limits, and she'd finally found them.

The faces of the crew members flew by. She called out to them. "Help! Bruce, help! Ross! Somebody call Ross!"

No one moved.

And then she saw Eric standing on the side smoking a cigarette. "Eric, stop him!"

He took a drag and looked away.

"No! Put me down!"

He was carrying her into the barn. To her relief she spotted half a dozen crew members working there, adjusting the lights for the next scene. He couldn't do anything horrible to her with so many people standing around.

"Get out of here!" Dash barked. "Now!"

"No!" she screamed. "No, don't leave."

They scampered away like rats from a burning building. The last one out closed the barn door.

With a rough curse Dash sprawled down on a stack of hay bales that had been arranged for the next scene and threw her over his knees.

She'd read the script and she knew what happened next. He lifted his hand to spank her only to find out that he didn't have the heart. Then he told her a story about her mother, she started to cry, and everything was all right again.

The flat of his hand slammed down hard on her bottom. She screamed in surprise.

He hit her again, and her scream changed into a yelp of pain.

The next one hurt even worse.

And then he stopped. The flat of his hand cupped her bottom. "Here's the way it's going to be. From now on you've got one person to answer to, and that's me. If I'm happy, you don't have anything to worry about. But if I'm not happy, then you'd better start saying your prayers." He lifted his hand and slapped it down smartly on her rear. "And believe me. Right now, I'm not happy."

"You can't do this," she gasped.

He smacked her again. "Who says?"

Tears stung her eyes. "I'm a star! I'll quit the show!"

Smack. "Good."

"I'll sue you!" Smack. "Ouch!"

"You'll have to stand in line." Smack.

Her face was hot with pain and mortification, and her nose had started to run. A tear plopped down onto the floor of the barn and made a small dark stain on the wood. Her muscles screamed with tension as she waited for the next blow, but his hand had fallen still—as still as his voice.

"Now what I'm going to do is this. I'm going to start calling people in here that you've insulted. One by one, I'm going to call them in and hold you down and let each one of them take a whack at you."

A sob erupted from her throat. "This isn't the way it's supposed to be! This isn't the way it is in the script."

"Life isn't a script, little girl. You have to take responsibility for yourself."

"Please." The word slipped from her lips, small and lonely. "Please don't do this."

"Why shouldn't I?"

She tried to take a breath, but it hurt. "Because."

"I'm afraid you're going to have to do better than that."

Her bottom was burning and his big hand cupping over it seemed to hold in the heat and make it worse. But worse than the pain in her body was the pain in her heart. "Because . . . " she gasped. "Because I don't want to be like this."

He was quiet for a moment. "Are you crying?"

"Me? Hell, no. I—I never cry." Her voice broke.

He lifted his hand from her bottom. She scrambled up, pushing herself off his lap and trying to get to her feet. But the scattered hay on the barn floor was slippery and she lost her balance so that she sprawled awkwardly on the bale next to him. She immediately turned her back so he couldn't see her tear-smeared cheeks.

Everything was quiet for a moment. Her bottom burned, and she clenched her hands together to keep from rubbing it. "I—I didn't mean to hurt anybody," she said softly. "I just wanted people to like me."

"You sure have a strange way of going about it."

"Everybody hates me."

"You're a mean-tempered little bitch. Why shouldn't they?"

123

"I'm not a b-bitch! I'm a decent person. I'm a good Baptist with a-a strong moral code."

"Uh-huh," he replied skeptically.

She hunched her shoulder so she could use the sleeve of her T-shirt to catch her tears before he saw them drip off her jaw. "You're not—You're not really going to call all those people in here and—and let them take a whack at me, are you?"

"Since you're such a fine Baptist, you shouldn't mind a little public repentance."

She tried to stiffen her spine, but her misery was cramping her insides and keeping her bent forward. How had her life come to this? All she'd wanted was for them to like her, especially this man who held her in such contempt. There were too many tears to hold them back, and a few of them dripped onto her jeans. "I—I can't apologize. I can't embarrass myself like that."

"You've embarrassed yourself every other way. I don't see what difference it'd make."

She thought of Eric seeing her like this. "Please. Please, don't do it."

His boots shifted in the straw. There was a long silence. She hiccupped on a sob.

"I guess I could hold off for a while. Until I see if you've decided to mend your ways."

Her misery didn't ease. "You—you shouldn't have hit me. Do you know how old I am?"

"Well, Janie's thirteen, but I know you're older than that."

"She's sup—supposed to be fourteen this season, but the writers haven't changed her."

"Television time passes slow."

The tears kept leaking out like a faucet with an old washer, and her voice sounded all mushy. "Except on the s—soaps. My Aunt Sophie watched one show where a baby was born. Three—three years later, that baby was a pregnant teenager."

"The way I remember it, you're around sixteen."

Another sob squeezed through the narrow passageway in

her throat. "I'm eighteen. Eighteen years, o—one month and two weeks."

"I guess I hadn't realized. In a way that kind of makes it worse, doesn't it? Somebody who's eighteen should act more like a woman and less like a kid who has to be turned over somebody's knee."

Her voice broke. "I don't th—think I'm ever going to be a woman. I'm—I'm going to be caught in this kid's body forever."

"There's nothing wrong with your body. It's your mind that needs to grow up."

She crumpled forward, her arms squeezed between her chest and her legs, her body shivering. Self-hatred consumed her. She couldn't stand being herself anymore.

The brush of his fingers against her spine was so light that at first she didn't realize he was touching her. And then his hand opened and settled over the center of her back. The storehouse of emotions that she had locked away for so many years broke free. The feelings of abandonment, the loneliness, the need for love that was like an unmelting cone of ice at the center of her heart.

She twisted around and threw herself against his chest. Her arms wrapped around his neck, and she buried her face in his shirt collar. She could feel him stiffen and knew he hadn't meant to let her into his arms—nobody ever wanted her in their arms—but she couldn't help herself. She just took possession.

"I'm everything you said," she whispered into his shirt collar. "I'm hateful and selfish and a mean-tempered bitch."

"People change their ways all the time."

"You—you really think I should apologize, don't you?"

He held her awkwardly, neither pushing her away nor embracing her. "Let's just say I think you've reached a crossroads. You might not realize it now, but later on you'll look back at this moment and you'll know that you were forced to make a decision that affected how you were going to live the rest of your life."

She was quiet, pressing her cheek against his shoulder and thinking about what he had said. She'd gotten two people fired and insulted nearly everyone on the show. It was a lot to make up for.

Her breath caught on a small hiccup. "This is the real MOS, isn't it, Dash?"

There was a moment of silence.

"I guess it is, at that," he replied.

10

When she emerged from the barn, she found that the shooting schedule had been mysteriously rearranged while she was inside, and instead of filming her scenes with Dash, they were shooting a scene with Blake and Eleanor. Everyone was unnaturally busy, and nobody would meet her eyes, but she saw by their smug expressions that they all knew exactly what had happened inside. The sons of bitches had probably pressed their ears right up to the barn door.

Her eyes narrowed and her lips tightened. She wasn't going to let anybody laugh at her. She'd take care of all of them. She'd—

"I wouldn't advise it," Dash said softly at her side.

She looked up at him, eyes shadowed by the brim of his hat, mouth set in a firm line. She waited for the familiar resentment to bubble up inside of her, but she felt a peculiar sense of peace instead. Someone had finally drawn a line in the sand and told her she couldn't cross it.

"I suggest you make yourself an appointment to see Ross before you leave today. There are a few people you need to get un-fired."

She didn't really believe he'd hold her down and let everybody take a whack at her, but she wasn't going to take a chance, and she nodded.

"And don't even think about whining to anyone from the

network about what happened today. It's between you and me."

A small spark of spirit returned to her. "For your information, I didn't have any intention of whining to anybody."

The corner of his mouth twitched. "Good. You might have more brains than I've been giving you credit for." He touched the brim of his hat with his thumb and began to walk away.

She watched him for several seconds. Her shoulders drooped. By tomorrow, he wouldn't even speak to her. It would be just like always.

His steps slowed and then halted. He turned back to her, studying her for a moment before he spoke. "I know you like horses. If you want to drive out to my ranch some weekend, I'll show you a few I've got."

Her heart swelled in her chest until it seemed to fill every space. "Really?"

He nodded and once again began to walk toward his motor home.

"When?" She took several quick steps after him.

"Well . . . "

"This weekend? Would Saturday be all right? I mean, Saturday's good for me, and if it's good for you . . . "

He stuck his thumb in the pocket of his jeans and looked as if he regretted his invitation.

Please, she prayed. *Please don't take it back.*

"Well—This weekend isn't real good for me, but I guess next Saturday would be okay."

"That's great!" She could feel her grin stretching like Silly Putty over her face. "Next Saturday'd be just great."

"All right then. Let's make it around noon."

"Noon. Oh, that's great. Noon'll be fine."

Her heart floated like a baby's bath toy. It continued to float right through the rest of the day, allowing her to ignore the crew members' smirks and the satisfaction in Liz's eyes. Despite the blow to her pride, she was surprised at how good it felt not being bad any longer.

That evening she cornered Ross in his office and asked

him to rehire Melanie and Jack. He agreed with alacrity, and before she left the studio, she called both of them and apologized. Neither of them forced her to grovel, which made her feel even worse than she had before.

The next week dragged on forever as she waited for Saturday and her visit to the ranch. She bent over backward trying to be nice to everybody, and although most of the crew continued to keep her at a distance, a few of them began to warm up to her.

On Saturday she drove down a narrow dirt road in the rugged mountains north of Malibu and caught her first glimpse of Dash Coogan's ranch. It was tucked neatly into the hills amidst chaparral, oaks, and sycamore. A pair of red-tailed hawks circled in the sky overhead.

She pulled over to the side. The clock on the Trans Am's dash read 10:38 and she wasn't due at the ranch until noon. She flipped down the visor and studied her reflection, trying to decide if the lipstick she'd put on looked silly with her dog's dish haircut. It did. But then, everything looked silly with the haircut, so what difference did it make?

The clock read 10:40.

What if he had forgotten? Her palms were sweating, and she wiped them on her jeans. She tried to tell herself that he wouldn't forget something so important. Their day together was going to be everything she had dreamed about. He would show her around the place. They'd talk about horses, go riding, stop and talk some more. Maybe his housekeeper would have packed a picnic lunch. They'd spread a blanket next to a creek and share a few secrets. He'd smile at her just like he smiled at Janie and—

She pressed her eyes shut. She was getting too old for this kind of childish fantasy. She should be daydreaming about sex, instead. But whenever she did that, she imagined herself making love with Eric Dillon and that got her excited and upset all at the same time. Still, daydreaming about Dash Coogan treating her like Dash Jones treated his daughter Janie wasn't any better.

The clock read 10:43. One hour and seventeen minutes to go.

The hell with it. She turned the key in the ignition and pulled out on the road. She would just pretend she'd gotten the time mixed up.

The ranch house was a rambling one-story stone-and-cypress structure with green shutters at the windows and a front door painted charcoal gray. Considering the fact that Dash was a star, the place was relatively modest, probably the reason the IRS hadn't made him sell it. She got out of the Trans Am and walked up the steps to the front door. As she pushed the bell, she lectured herself about mature behavior. If she didn't want people to treat her as if she were fourteen, she shouldn't act that way. She needed to develop the gift of restraint. And she had to stop wearing her heart on her sleeve all the time.

She pushed the bell again. There were no signs of life. Her nervousness took a quantum leap into full anxiety, and she leaned on the bell. He couldn't have forgotten. This was too important. He—

The door swung open.

He had obviously just gotten out of bed. He wore only a pair of khaki pants, and he hadn't shaved. The wiry strands of his hair lay flat on one side of his head and stuck out on the other as if a herd of cattle had run a stampede right through it. Above all, he didn't look happy.

"You're early."

She swallowed hard. "Am I?"

"I said noon."

"Did you?"

"Yeah."

She didn't know what to do. "Do you want me to go for a walk or something?"

"As a matter of fact, I'd appreciate it."

"Dash?" A woman's voice called out from inside the house.

A look of displeasure came over his face. There was something familiar about the low husky tones of that female voice. Honey bit down on her lip. It was none of her business.

"Dash?" the woman called out again. "Where's your coffeepot?"

Honey's mouth gaped in outrage. *"Dusty!"*

Lisa Harper's familiar blond head appeared behind his shoulder. "Honey, is that you?"

"It's me all right," she replied through clenched teeth.

Lisa's eyes widened in baby-blue innocence. "Oops."

"She's sleeping with *you*, too?" Honey exclaimed, glaring at Dash.

"How about you go take that walk now?" he replied.

She ignored him and glared at Lisa. "You certainly do spread your favors around."

"Comparison shopping," Lisa replied sweetly. "And just between the two of us, the old cowboy leaves Eric Dillon way back at the starter's gate."

"I think that's just about enough," Dash said. "Honey, if one word of this gets to those writers, your butt is going to become public property. Do you hear me?"

"Yeah, I hear you," Honey replied sullenly.

Lisa, who was always looking for ways to expand Dusty's role, grinned at Honey behind Dash's back, obviously hoping she'd talk her head off.

"I'll go take that walk now," Honey said, before he could order her to leave. She fled down the walk, barely breathing until she heard the front door close behind her.

Later, as she stood over by the paddock admiring three of Dash's horses and breathing in the tang of eucalyptus overlaid with the faint scent of manure, she heard Lisa drive away. Envy gnawed at her as she thought of Lisa and Dash, Lisa and Eric—Lisa, who knew all the secrets of womanhood that were still mysteries to her.

Not long after, Dash appeared wearing a long-sleeved plaid shirt with a pair of jeans and worn cowboy boots. Beneath his Stetson, the sides of his hair were still damp from his shower. He extended one of the two mugs of coffee he carried toward her. After she took it, he put a foot up on the fence rail and gazed out at the horses.

She put a foot up, too.

"I'm sorry," she finally said. She was beginning to discover that it was less work to apologize than to defend herself when she was wrong. "I knew I wasn't supposed to show up until noon."

He sipped his coffee from the white ceramic mug. "I figured you did."

That was all. He didn't give her any big lectures or say anything more about it. Instead, he pointed toward the animals in the paddock.

"Those two are quarter horses, and the other's an Arabian. I'm boarding them for friends."

"They're not yours?"

"I wish they were, but I was forced to sell mine off."

"The IRS?"

"Yep."

"Scum suckers."

"You got that right."

"We were audited once, right before Uncle Earl died. Sometimes I think that's what killed him. Nobody except serial killers should have to deal with the IRS. It ended up that I had to handle most of it."

"How old were you?"

"Fourteen. But I was always good in math."

"There's a lot more than math involved when you're up against the IRS."

"I'm smart about people. That helps."

He shook his head and chuckled. "I've got to tell you, Honey, that in all my life I can't ever remember meeting anybody—male or female—who was a worse judge of character than you are."

She bristled. "That's a terrible thing to say. And it's not true."

"It's true all right. The most competent people on the crew are the ones you give the most trouble to, and it's not just the crew, either. You only seem to attach yourself to people with character faults a mile wide. The best people are the ones you turn your back on."

"Like who?" she inquired indignantly.

"Well, Liz for one. She's smart and she's got integrity. She also liked you right from the beginning, although I have no idea why."

"That's ridiculous. Liz Castleberry is the queen of the bitches. And she hates my guts. It seems to me that all you've proved is that I'm a better judge of character than you are."

He snorted.

Honey pressed her point. "I'll give you a perfect example of how vindictive she is. Last week I got back to my trailer and I found a package from her. There was a note with it that said she was sorry she'd missed my birthday, and she hoped I'd like her present even though it was late."

"That doesn't sound too vindictive to me."

"That's what I thought until I opened the present. You'll never guess what was inside."

"A hand grenade?"

"A *dress*."

"Imagine that. You should take her to court."

"No. Listen. Not just any dress, but this frilly little yellow thing with a ruffle. And these stupid-looking shoes. And *pearls*."

"Pearls? Well, now."

"Don't you see? She was making fun of me."

"I'm having a little trouble following you here, Honey."

"It looked like something a Barbie doll would wear, not a person like me. If I put an outfit like that on, everybody would fall on the floor laughing. It was so—"

"Feminine?"

"Yes. Exactly. Silly. You know. Frivolous."

"Instead of being made out of barbed wire and razor blades."

"That's not funny."

"So what did you do?"

"I bundled it right back up and returned it to her."

For the first time he looked irritated. "Now why did you have to go and do that? I thought we decided that you were going to mend you manners."

"I didn't *throw* it at her."

"That's a relief."

"I merely said that I appreciated the gesture, but I didn't feel right accepting a gift from her because I hadn't bought her a birthday present."

"And *then* you threw it at her."

She grinned at him. "I'm a reformed character, Dash. Emily Post would have been proud of me."

He smiled, then reached out, and for a moment she thought he was going to rumple her hair, just like he rumpled Jane Marie's. But his arm fell back to his side, and he walked over to talk to the stable hand who worked for him.

He picked out one of the quarter horses for her, a gentle mare since she wasn't an experienced rider, while he took the spirited Arabian. As they headed out into the hills, the sun felt warm on her head, and she couldn't remember the last time she had felt so happy. Dash sat in the saddle with the easy slouch of a man who was more at home on a horse than he was on the ground. They rode in companionable silence for some time before the compulsion to talk became too much for her.

"It's beautiful out here. How much of the land is yours?"

"All of it used to be mine, but the IRS took a lot of it. Pretty soon it'll be part of the Santa Monica National Recreation Area." He pointed off to a steep-walled canyon on their right. "That was the northern boundary of my property, and that creek up ahead marked the western edge. It dries up in the summer, but it's real pretty now."

"You've still got a lot left."

"It's all relative, I guess. I don't think a man can ever own too much land."

"Did you grow up on a ranch?"

"I grew up just about everywhere."

"Did your family move around a lot?"

"Not exactly."

"What do you mean?"

"I didn't mean anything."

"You moved around by yourself?" she asked.

"Just what I said."

"You didn't say anything."

"That's right."

He gazed out at the line of trees that grew near the creek bed. She studied his profile, taking in the deep-set eyes and strong nose, the high cheekbones and square jaw. He looked like a national monument.

Still staring into the distance, he finally spoke. "I'm a private man, Honey. I don't like the idea of my personal life being broadcast to the world."

She looked down at her hands where they rested on the pommel. "You think I'll talk to the writers, don't you?"

"You've been known to do it."

"I don't have to talk to them. It's just that things get bottled up inside me and I don't have anybody else to tell."

"What you do is up to you, but my business is my own."

"Like you and Lisa."

"Like that."

"Lisa's just praying I'll tell the writers that I found the two of you in a compromising situation."

"Lisa's ambitious."

She sighed. "I won't say anything."

"We'll see."

His lack of faith made her angry. Just because she'd told the writers a few things in the past didn't mean she was a blabbermouth. "Do you love her?" she asked.

"Hell, no, I don't love her."

"Then why—"

"Jesus, Honey, there's such a thing in this world as recreational sex." He looked away, and she wondered if she had actually managed to embarrass him.

"I understand that. I just thought—"

"You thought I was too *old*. Is that it? I'll have you know I'm only forty-one."

"That old?"

His head snapped around and she grinned at him. His irritation faded. She looked out over the rugged landscape. Her mare whinnied and tossed its head. "I promise you right now, Dash, that anything you tell me stays with me."

"I appreciate your sincerity, but—"

"But you don't think I can keep my word. I guess I deserve that. The thing is—if occassionally I had someone else to talk to, I wouldn't have to go spilling my guts to the writers all the time."

"This is starting to sound a lot like blackmail."

"I guess you can take it however you like."

Dash released a long, put-upon sigh. "See, from my viewpoint, you're a pretty big talker, and I'm a man with a definite attachment to silence."

"It must have been hard being married to all those women."

"They were mutes compared to you."

"Those writers sure are going to be interested to hear about you and Lisa."

"Honey?"

"Yeah?"

"Remind me to tan your hide."

"You already did. And don't think I've forgotten it."

It was nearly three when they got back to the barn. They cooled off the horses and then handed them over to the stable hand. Dash led her to her Trans Am, which was parked at the side of the house near a heating-oil tank that was partially camouflaged by a hedge of hydrangeas. Honey didn't want the afternoon to be over. She hated the idea of going home to her family's unending complaints. Her stomach rumbled, and she was struck with inspiration.

"Do you ever get hungry for homemade biscuits, Dash? The kind that are so thick and fluffy that when you split them open a big puff of steam comes out. And the butter melts in this golden yellow puddle right in the middle. Then you pour some warm maple syrup—"

"I knew you were ornery, Honey, but I didn't think you were sadistic." He came to a stop near the trunk of the car.

"I guess I never told you what a good cook I am. That's exactly the way my biscuits turn out."

He was clearly dubious. "You don't exactly look like the domesticated type."

"See. That just goes to prove what a poor judge of character you are. I've been cooking for my family for years.

My Aunt Sophie was always too tired to fix meals, and by the time I was ten, I started to develop this allergy to TV dinners, so I began experimenting, and before long, I became an excellent cook. No fancy stuff. Just plain home cooking."

She pulled the car keys from the pocket of her jeans and jiggled them casually in the palm of her hand. "Gosh, now that I've got my mind on biscuits, I think I'll go on home and make up a batch. Thanks a lot for inviting me, Dash. I had a real good time."

He stuck his thumb in the pocket of his jeans and looked down at the ground. She jingled her car keys. He poked at a rock with the toe of his boot. She passed her keys from her right hand to her left.

"I guess if you wanted to check out my kitchen pantry and see if you can find what you need, I wouldn't object."

She widened her eyes. "Are you sure? I don't want to wear out my welcome."

He grunted and headed toward the ranch house.

Grinning, she fell into step behind him.

The kitchen was old-fashioned and roomy, with oak cupboards and toasted-almond paint. She hummed as she gathered up the biscuit ingredients and dug a pound of bacon from the freezer. As she began measuring the flour into a speckled stoneware mixing bowl, she could hear a Sooners basketball game on television in the family room. Although she would have enjoyed Dash's company while she cooked, it was still nice being alone in his kitchen.

Forty-five minutes later, she called him in to take a chair at the antique oak table that sat in the kitchen's small bay. Uncle Earl hadn't liked talk with his meals, so she didn't have any trouble keeping quiet as she flipped back a clean blue tea towel to reveal a bowl full of steaming golden-brown biscuits. He took two of them and speared a half dozen bacon slices onto his plate.

As he broke open the first biscuit, the steam rose up, just as she'd described. She handed him the butter and a pitcher of syrup she had warmed. It wasn't pure maple, but it was all she'd been able to find. The pat of butter soaked into the biscuit and the syrup sluiced down over the sides. She served herself.

"Good," he murmured as he polished off the first one and began his attack on the second.

She took a sip from the fresh coffee she had brewed. It was a little strong for her, but she knew he liked it that way. As he finished his second biscuit, she surreptitiously pushed the basket forward so he could take another.

She wasn't a big eater and she was satisfied with one biscuit and her coffee. He ate a fourth.

"Good," he murmured for the second time.

His enjoyment of her food filled her with pride. She might not be pretty or flirtatious or know how to talk to men, but she definitely knew how to feed them.

He ate nine strips of bacon and half a dozen biscuits before he finally stopped. Looking over at her, he grinned. "You are one fine cook, little girl."

"You should try my fried chicken. Real golden crispy on the outside, but on the inside it's moist and—"

"Stop! You ever heard of cholesterol, Honey?"

"Sure. That's what Lisa uses to bleach her hair."

"I think that's Clairol."

"My mistake." She smiled innocently.

While he was eating, she had been thinking about something he had said earlier. As he stirred a heaping teaspoon of sugar into his coffee, she decided to ask him about it. "Name one person with a weak character that I've attached myself to."

"Pardon?"

"Earlier. You said the strongest people are the ones I turn my back on. You said I only attach myself to weak characters. Name one."

"Did I say that?"

"You said it. Who were you talking about?"

"Well . . ." He stirred his coffee. "How about Eric Dillon for starters?"

"I haven't *attached myself* to Eric Dillon. As a matter of fact, I hate his guts."

"Sure you do."

"He's rude and stuck on himself."

"You got that right."

"But he's very talented." She felt a perverse need to leap to his defense.

"You're right about that, too."

"I'd have to be crazy to care about Eric Dillon. There isn't any way in the world somebody like him would ever look twice at somebody like me—a runty little redneck girl with a big old sucker-fish mouth."

"What's this thing you've got about your mouth?"

"Just look at it." She puckered.

Amusement flickered in his eyes as he studied her lips. "Honey, a lot of males would consider a mouth like yours sexy. If it wasn't moving so much, that is."

She glared at him. "Just try to name someone other than Eric Dillon. I happen to know you won't be able to because I see right through people. I admire strength."

"Is that so?"

"Yes, that is so."

"Then why, Miss Great Judge of Human Nature, have you been so all-fired determined to attach yourself to me?"

She could see that he'd meant to say it as a joke, but it didn't come out that way. As soon as he spoke, his face stiffened and the warmth that had been growing between them dissolved.

Abruptly, he pushed his coffee cup away and stood. "I think it's about time you go on. I've got some things I have to do this afternoon."

She rose and followed him out through the kitchen and across the comfortable family room that stretched along the back of the ranch house. It was decorated with leather furniture and framed posters from his old movies. He led her toward the front door, his boots clicking on the terra-cotta tiles, the air heavy with tension.

She couldn't stand for their day to end like this. Reaching out, she touched his arm and spoke in a voice so gentle that it hardly seemed to belong to her. "You're just about the strongest person I know, Dash. I mean that."

He turned to face her, his eyes weary and defeated. "I remember one day when you called me a worn-out old drunk."

Shame filled her. "I apologize for that. It's like Satan has taken over my mouth this past year."

"You didn't do much more than speak the truth."

"Don't say that. It makes me feel even worse."

He rested his hand on his hip, stared down at the floor for a moment, and then looked back up at her. "Honey, I'm an alcoholic. Every day is a struggle for me, and a lot of the time I'm not sure it's worth it. The bottle isn't my only problem, either. I'm hard on women. My own kids hate my guts. I've got a hot temper and I don't care much about anybody except myself."

"I don't believe that."

"You'd better believe it," he said harshly. "I'm a selfish son of a bitch, and I don't have any intention of changing at this point in my life."

He stalked from the house, and she couldn't do anything more than follow after him to her car. Their beautiful day together had been ruined, and somehow, it was all her fault.

11

Monday morning Honey arrived on the set with three dozen Rice Krispies squares and a chocolate sheet cake. The crew was surprised, but delighted.

"Clever, darling," Liz Castleberry drawled as she licked a dab of frosting from her bottom lip. "Bribery by chocolate."

"I'm not trying to bribe anybody," Honey countered, not at all happy that the Queen of the Bitches had seen through her so clearly.

She waited two days, and then she brought in several

dozen homemade chocolate-chip cookies. Adding baking to her already exhausting work day had left her so weary that she kept falling asleep between scenes, but the crew members began to smile at her, so she decided it was worth the sacrifice. Dash chatted casually with her during the day, but he didn't invite her out to the ranch or mention the possibility of taking her riding again. She blamed herself.

February slipped by. The writers began sending her frantic notes to meet with them, but she tore them up. Maybe if she proved to Dash that she could keep her mouth shut, he'd invite her back. But as the weeks passed and he didn't make an overture, she began to despair. They would go on hiatus soon, and then she wouldn't see him for four months.

After spending the weekend with her family, listening to Sophie whine and Buck burp beer, she arrived at work on a Monday in mid-March to begin shooting the last show of the season.

Connie Evans, who did her makeup, studied her critically in the mirror. "Those circles under your eyes are getting worse, Honey. It's a good thing the season's over or I'd have to start using industrial-strength concealer on you."

As Connie dabbed away at the shadows, Honey picked up the manila envelope printed with her name that lay on the makeup table. She was supposed to receive her script for the week by messenger no later than Saturday afternoon, but more frequently, she didn't see it until she arrived at work on Monday. She wondered what the writers had in store for her this week. Since she continued to ignore their increasingly strident demands to come and talk to them, she hoped they hadn't decided to get even with her by making Janie fall into a beehive or something like that.

The last few scripts had spotlighted Blake. In one of them, he had a steamy romance with an older woman who was a friend of Eleanor's. The script had taken full advantage of Eric's dark sexuality, and Honey had gotten so upset watching it that she'd turned off the TV.

As Connie dabbed her with makeup, Honey drew the

current week's script from the envelope and stared down at the title. "Janie's Daydream." That didn't sound too bad.

Ten minutes later, she leapt up from her chair and raced out to find Ross.

Liz, wrapped in a pale pink terry-cloth robe, was emerging from her own dressing room when Honey came barreling down the hall. Liz took one look at Honey's face and lunged for her as she flew by. With a hard yank, Liz pulled her into her dressing room and shut the door with her hip.

"What do you think you're doing?" Honey snatched her arm away.

"Giving you a minute to calm down."

Honey's hands clenched into fists at her side. "I don't need to calm down. I'm perfectly calm. Now get out of my way."

Liz leaned against the jamb. "I'm not moving. Pour a cup of coffee, sit down on that sofa, and get yourself under control."

"I don't want coffee. I want—"

"Now!"

Even in a bathrobe, the Queen of the Bitches looked forbidding, and Honey hesitated. Maybe she did need a few minutes to get herself together. Stepping over Mitzi, who was sprawled on the floor, she filled one of the floral china cups Liz kept next to her stainless-steel German coffeemaker.

Liz edged away from the door and gestured toward her own copy of the script lying open on her dressing table. "Be grateful that it's a family show and you don't have to do the scene nude."

Honey's stomach did a flip-flop. "How do you know what I'm upset about?"

"It doesn't take a mind reader, darling."

She stared down into her coffee cup. "I'm not kissing him. I mean it. I'm not going to do it."

"Half the women in America would be glad to stand in for you."

"Everybody's going to think I've been talking to the

writers again, and I haven't. I haven't talked to them in weeks."

"It's just a kiss, Honey. It's perfectly believable that Janie would be having daydreams about kissing Blake."

"But nobody's going to think it's *Janie's* daydream. They're all going to think it's *mine.*"

"Isn't it?"

She jumped up, sloshing her coffee into the saucer. "No! I can't stand him. He's conceited and arrogant and mean."

"He's a lot more than that." Liz sat down on the dressing-table stool and began pulling on a pair of sheer pearl-gray nylons. "Forgive the theatrics, darling, but Eric Dillon is a walking danger zone." She shuddered delicately. "I just hope I'm not around when he finally explodes."

Honey placed her untasted coffee on the table. "I've got to wear a nightgown and a wig and dance around with him under a tree. What a stupid daydream. It's so embarrassing I can't even stand to think about it."

"It's a long dress, not a nightgown. And the wig will probably be beautiful. You'd look silly kissing Blake in those jeans with that awful hair. If you ask me, you're going to look a hundred times better than you usually do."

"Thanks a lot."

Liz drew the panty hose to her waist. Beneath them, Honey could glimpse a skimpy pair of black lace panties.

"With all those marvelous displays of temperament, I could never understand why you didn't throw one of your hissy fits over something important. That horrid haircut, for example."

"I'm not talking about my hair," Honey retorted. "I'm talking about kissing Eric Dillon. I'm going to Ross right now, and I'm—"

"If you throw one of your famous fits, you'll undo all those delicious high-calorie bribes you've been baking. Besides, we start shooting in half an hour, so it's a little late to get a script change. And, anyway, what would you say? Spending a morning dancing around outside and kissing Eric Dillon hardly qualifies as hazardous duty."

"But . . ."

"You've never kissed a man, have you, Honey?"

She drew herself up to her full five feet and one inch. "I'm eighteen years old. I kissed my first man when I was fifteen."

"Was he the one you knifed or the one you shot in the head?" Liz drawled.

"I might have lied about that, but I'm not lying about the kissing. I've had a few romances." She searched her mind for some details that would convince her. "There was this one boy. His name was Chris, and he went to the University of South Carolina. He had this T-shirt with Gamecocks written on it."

"I don't believe you."

"I don't happen to care."

Liz slipped off her robe and reached for the dress she was wearing in the first scene. Honey stared at her bra. It was nothing more than two black lace scallop shells.

"Eric will do all the work, Honey. God knows he has enough experience. Janie's not supposed to know anything about lovemaking, anyway."

"It's not lovemaking! It's only a kiss."

"Exactly. I checked the shooting schedule. Since it's an exterior, they're not filming the scene until Friday. You'll have all week to get yourself together. Now calm down and treat it like any other piece of business."

Honey held Liz's gaze for a few moments and then dropped her eyes. Absentmindedly, she stroked Mitzi's head. "I don't understand why you're trying to help me. You do it all the time, don't you?"

"I try."

"That's what Dash said. But I can't understand why."

"Women should help each other, Honey."

Honey looked up at Liz and smiled. It was nice to hear herself classified as a woman. Giving Mitzi a final pat, she rose and made her way to the door. "Thanks," she said, just before she let herself out.

That afternoon, Liz caught Dash alone. "You'd better keep an eye on your young charge, cowboy. She's a bit upset about this week's show, and you know as well as I do that when Honey gets upset, anything can happen."

"Honey's not my responsibility!"

"Once you smacked her, you made her yours for life."

"Damn it, Liz . . ."

"Ta-ta, darling." She wiggled her fingers and walked away, leaving a cloud of expensive fragrance behind.

Dash swore softly under his breath. He didn't want Honey in his private life, but it was getting harder and harder to keep her out. If only he hadn't gotten soft in the head that day he'd blistered her butt. He should never have invited her to his ranch. Not that he'd had a bad time. In fact, he'd had a damn good time with her, and he hadn't once thought about taking a drink.

She was surprisingly easy to be with for a female. Of course, she wasn't much of a female, which had been the major reason he had enjoyed their day together. No hidden sexual agenda had been percolating beneath the surface, and there had been something relaxing about being with someone who pretty much said whatever was on her mind. Besides, in a funny way, Honey saw a lot of things the same way he did. The IRS, for example.

As Honey came toward him and they took their places for the next scene, he realized that he liked Honey more than he liked his own daughter. Not that he didn't love Meredith, because he did, but even when she was a child he hadn't felt close to her. When she'd turned fifteen she'd gotten religion, and after that there'd been no stopping her. Just last week Wanda had called him with the news that Meredith had decided to drop out of Oral Roberts because the place was getting too liberal for her. As far as his son, Josh, was concerned, things weren't any better. Josh had always been pretty much a mama's boy, something a little more attention from his father might have prevented.

A light meter popped up in front of his face. Honey yawned next to him. Even wearing makeup she looked tired.

"Did you get any of those cookies I brought in last week?" she asked. "The ones with M & Ms in them?"

"I had a couple."

"I didn't think they were as good as those frosted brownies. What did you think?"

"Honey, are you doing any sleeping when you get home, or do you just stay up all night and bake cookies?"

"I sleep."

"Not enough. Look at you. You're getting all run down." He knew he should stop right there, but she looked so small and worn-out that his heart took possession of his brain. "Starting right now, your baking days are over, little girl."

Her eyes shot open in outrage. "What?"

"You heard me. People are going to have to start liking you for your sweet personality and not for your cookies. The next time you bring anything to eat on the set, I'm pitching it right in the garbage."

"You are not! This isn't any of your business!"

"It is if you want to come out to the ranch on Saturday and go riding."

Right before his eyes, he watched the war going on inside her, the battle between her desire to be with him and her independent nature. Her jaw set in that stubborn line he'd grown all too familiar with.

"You're manipulating me. You think you can go hot or cold on me whenever you feel like it, without the slightest regard for my feelings."

"I told you the kind of man I am, Honey."

"I just want to be your friend. Is that so terrible?"

"Not if that was all you wanted. But you make me nervous." He looked out beyond the cameras to the rear of the studio and decided to say what was on his mind. "You want a lot from people, Honey. I get this feeling that you'd suck out my last drop of blood if I let you. To be honest, I don't have any to spare."

"That's an awful thing to say. You make me sound like a vampire."

He didn't reply. Just gave her some time to sort out her options.

"All right," she said sullenly. "If I can come out to the ranch, I won't bake anymore."

A queer glow of pleasure warmed his insides at the idea

that she enjoyed being with him enough to compromise her pride. She was a great kid when she wasn't being a pain in the ass. "One more thing," he added. "You also have to get through this week with a little dignity. I'm specifically talking about Friday's shooting schedule."

Honey glared over at Liz, who was flirting with a new cameraman. "Somebody has a big mouth."

"You should be glad that particular somebody is watching out for you."

They were interrupted before she could reply, which was probably just as well.

Friday crept toward her like smog. When it finally arrived, she refused to look in the mirror as they fussed with her makeup and zipped her into a white lace dress that sloped down off her shoulders and brushed the floor. They fastened a lavender lace choker around her neck, then set the wig on top of her head. It was long and honey-colored, just like her real hair.

"Perfect," Evelyn, her newest hairdresser, said, standing back to admire Honey.

Connie, who had just finished her makeup, concurred. "Go on, Honey. Stop being a chicken. Take a look."

Honey braced herself and turned toward the mirror. She looked . . .

"Holy shit," she whispered softly under her breath.

"My sentiments exactly," Evelyn replied dryly.

Honey had been afraid she'd look like a boy in drag, but instead, the delicate young woman who stared back at her was a vision of femininity. There was a blurry, dreamlike quality about her features—from the light blue luminosity of her eyes to her soft pink mouth, which didn't look like it belonged on a sucker fish at all but on someone beautiful. Her hair curled softly around her face and fell in waves over the tops of her shoulders, just like a story-book princess.

The AD stuck his head in the trailer. "Show time, Honey. We need you on—Wow!"

Evelyn and Connie laughed, then escorted Honey from the trailer. She squinted slightly in the sunlight. The women walked on each side of her, picking up the hem of her dress to keep it off the grass and giving her last-minute instructions.

"Don't sit down, Honey. And don't eat anything."

"Stop licking your lips. I'll have to powder you again."

Eric was already on the set. Honey avoided looking at him. She felt excited and scared at the same time. It was one thing to have to kiss Eric Dillon when she looked like a horse's rear end. It was quite another when she looked like Sleeping Beauty. She pressed her hand to the pocket in the side seam of the dress and was reassured to feel the tiny tube of Binaca breath spray she had slipped there.

Eric adjusted the lavender sash at his waist. He was dressed like Prince Charming in a white shirt with billowy sleeves, tight-fitting purple trousers, and calf-hugging black leather boots. The costume was constrictive, but as he leaned down to wipe a smudge off his boots, he decided he'd worn worse.

At the sound of female laughter, he looked up. Honey was coming toward him, but several seconds passed before his brain registered what he was seeing. His mouth set in a grim line. He should have known. For two seasons he'd been looking at those tiny features and that incredible mouth, but he still hadn't realized quite how pretty she could be.

She drew closer and lifted her head. Light blue eyes, dewy and star-filled, drank him in, begging him to find her beautiful. His stomach clenched. If he wasn't very careful today, she would go off in another love spin.

"What do you think, Eric?" she asked softly. "How do I look?"

He shrugged, his face blank of any expression. "Okay, I guess. The wig's a little weird, though."

Her bubble burst.

Jack Swackhammer, who was directing his first episode since Honey had gotten him fired, stepped into the shade beneath the oak tree. "Honey, we're going to begin with you in the swing." He motioned her toward the rope swing, which had been embellished with corny purple satin ribbons and puffy lavender tulle bows.

Honey did as he asked, and they began blocking out the

first shot. Since there was no dialogue in the scene, all she had to do was let Eric push her, but she was so tense she felt as if she would break apart if he even touched her.

"We're laying in an orchestral track on top of the video— lots of strings and schmaltz," Jack said. "Ray'll play it for you while we're shooting to get you in the mood."

She wanted to die from embarrassment when one of the speakers began emitting a romantic orchestral score.

"Will you relax?" Eric grumbled from behind her as the cameras rolled and he began to push.

Her insides cramped as she realized that she knew how to be Janie but she didn't have the faintest idea how to be Janie's fantasy of herself. "I am relaxed," she hissed, finding it easier to talk to him since she didn't have to face him.

"Your back is like a board," Eric complained.

She had never felt more awkward, more at a loss. She knew exactly who she was when she was dressed in jeans with her dog's dish haircut, but who was the creature in the fairy-tale gown?

"You worry about yourself, and I'll worry about me," she retorted, the skin beneath her lace dress hot with embarrassment.

He gave the swing a hard push. "It's going to be a long afternoon if you don't take it easy."

"It's going to be a long one anyway, because I have to work with you."

"Cut! We don't look like we're having a good time," Jack drawled from his position next to the first camera. "And we seem to have forgotten that some of our viewers can read lips."

Because she was embarrassed and unsure of herself, she took refuge in hostility. Lifting her head, she spoke directly to the camera. "This is bullshit."

The swing jerked to a stop.

Jack ran his hands through his thinning hair. "Let's settle down and try it again."

But the next take didn't go any better, nor did the one after that. She simply couldn't relax, and Eric wasn't helping. Instead of acting romantic, he behaved as if he hated her guts, which he probably did, but he didn't have to be so obvious about it. She tried to remember if he had eaten any of her cookies.

At Jack's orders, Ray, the sound man, turned off the music. The director looked at his watch. They were already behind schedule, and it was all her fault. This time she wasn't causing trouble on purpose, but nobody would believe that.

"How about a break?" she suggested, jumping up from the swing as Jack approached them both.

The director shook his head. "Honey, I understand that you've never done anything like this before, and you're bound to feel awkward—"

"I don't feel the slightest bit awkward. I'm as comfortable as I can be."

He apparently decided it was a waste of time to argue with her because he turned on Eric. "We've done at least ten shows together, and this is the first time I've seen you do half-assed work. You're holding out. What's going on here?"

To Honey's surprise, Eric didn't try to defend himself. He stared down at a bare spot in the grass as if he were trying to make up his mind about something. Probably whether or not he could kiss her without throwing up.

When he looked up, his mouth had thinned into a grim line. "All right," he said slowly. "You're right. Give us a chance to improvise a little . . . work it through. Just start to roll and then leave us alone for a while."

"We're on a tight schedule," Jack replied. And then he threw up his hands in frustration. "Go ahead. It can't be any worse. Okay with you, Honey?"

She nodded stiffly. Anything was better than what they had been doing.

There was a sudden purposefulness about Eric, as if he'd made some sort of decision. "Have sound crank up the music a little so the two of us can talk without everybody on the crew listening in."

Jack nodded and returned to his position behind the

camera. Connie scampered over and touched up their makeup. Within moments, the lush sound of strings filled the set.

Honey's stomach clenched. The Binaca! She'd forgotten to spray her mouth. What if her breath was bad?

"We're rolling," Jack said, speaking just loudly enough to be heard over the music. "Marker. Action."

She turned to Eric for direction and saw that he was studying her. He looked deeply unhappy. And then, as she watched, he seemed to go inside himself. She had observed him do this when he was getting ready for a difficult scene, but she had never been standing quite so close. It was eerie. An absolute stillness came over him, a blankness of expression, as if he were emptying himself out.

And then his chest began to rise and fall in gentle rhythm. A transformation came over him, subtle at first but gradually becoming more visible. He seemed to come into focus before her eyes in a new form. The ice chips melted in those turquoise eyes and the furrows eased from his forehead. Her bones turned to gelatin as the hard lines around his mouth softened. Before her eyes, he became young and sweet. He reminded her of someone, but for a moment she couldn't think who it was. And then she knew.

He looked like all of her daydreams of him.

Picking up her hand, he drew her over by the tree. "You should wear dresses more often."

"I should?" Her voice came out like a small croak.

He smiled. "I'll bet you've got your jeans on underneath."

"I do not!" she exclaimed indignantly.

He settled his hand on the small of her back, just below her waist, and squeezed gently. "You're right. I don't feel any jeans."

A tremor passed through her. He was standing so close that the heat of his body warmed her through the lace of her dress. "Shouldn't I get on the swing?" she asked, stumbling slightly over the words.

"Do you want to?"

"No, I—" She started to dip her head, but he caught her chin with the tip of his finger, making her look at him.

"Don't be afraid."

"I'm—I'm not afraid."

"Aren't you?"

"This wasn't my daydream," she said miserably. "It was the writers. They—"

"Who cares? It's a beautiful daydream. Why don't we enjoy it?"

She caught her breath at the husky intimacy in his voice, as if they were the only people left in the world. The sunlight filtering through the leaves of the tree threw lavender shadows across his features. They played hide-and-seek with his eyes and the corners of his mouth. She couldn't have torn her gaze away from him if she'd had to.

"How do we enjoy it?" she asked breathlessly.

"Why don't you touch my face, and then I'll touch yours."

Her hand trembled. It tingled at her side. She wanted to lift it, but she couldn't.

He gently clasped her wrist and drew it upward between their bodies until she touched him. As she brushed the side of his jaw, he released her, leaving her on her own.

With the tips of her fingers, she felt the slight hollow in his cheek, right beneath the ridge of bone. Her hand moved on to the corner of his jaw, his chin. She touched him as if she were blind, memorizing every dip and rise. Unable to stop herself, she slid her fingertips to his bottom lip and explored its contours.

He smiled beneath her touch and lifted his own hand to her mouth. Under the touch of his fingers, her mouth became beautiful. His eyes bathed her with admiration, and hard knots unraveled inside her until all of her became beautiful.

"I'm going to kiss you now," he whispered.

Her lips parted, and her heart raced. His breath fell softly on her skin as his head dipped. He drew her against his body so tenderly she might have melted there from the warmth of the sunlight. She anticipated his lips for a fraction of a second before they brushed against her own. And then her senses sang as he kissed her.

Castles and flowers and milk-white steeds danced through

her mind. His mouth was gentle, his lips chastely closed. A spell of wonder and innocence enveloped her. The kiss was pure, unsullied by awkwardness or lust, a kiss to awaken a sleeping princess, a kiss that had been formed from the gilded web of daydreams.

When their lips finally parted, he continued to smile down at her. "Do you have any idea how beautiful you look?"

Mutely, she shook her head, her customary glibness deserting her. He drew her away from the trunk of the tree into a patch of sunlight and kissed her again. Then he reached up, pulled a leaf from the tree, and tickled her nose with it.

She giggled.

"I'll bet you don't weigh anything." Without giving her a chance to reply, he picked her up in his arms and swung her in a slow, looping circle. The skirt of her dress tangled in his fingers and the sleeves of his shirt billowed. Thousands of tiny bubbles rose inside her. She tossed back her head, and her laughter seemed to mingle with the breeze and the sunlight that lit sparks in his dark hair.

"Are you dizzy yet?" he asked, laughing back at her.

"No . . . Yes . . ."

He set her on her feet, keeping his arm behind her waist so she didn't fall. And then he twirled her again, dancing her in and out of the shadows. She felt light and graceful and achingly alive, an enchanted princess in a fairy-tale forest. Pulling her into his arms, he kissed her again.

She sighed when he eventually drew away. The music swirled around them, bathing them in its magic. He cupped her cheek as if he couldn't get enough of her. He turned her again and again. Her lips tingled, and the blood sang in her veins. Finally she thought she understood what it was to be a woman.

They stopped moving. He held her still in front of him and looked beyond her. "Do you have what you need?"

His voice jolted her. It sounded different, harder.

"Cut and print!" Jack exclaimed. "Fantastic! Great work,

both of you. I may need a couple more close-ups, but let me check the tape first."

Eric stepped away from her. She felt a chill as he transformed himself before her eyes. All the warmth disappeared. He looked edgy, restless, and hostile.

His name seemed to stick in her throat. "Eric?"

"Yeah?" The day wasn't warm, but beads of sweat had broken out on his forehead. He walked behind the cameras toward one of the director's chairs and snatched up the cigarettes he had left there.

She followed him, unable to hold herself back. "I—It—uh—it went pretty well, didn't it?"

"Yeah, I guess." He lit a cigarette and took a deep, uneven drag. "I hope we don't have to do a piece of shit like that again. From now on do us all a favor and keep your adolescent sexual fantasies to yourself."

Her daydream shattered. He had been acting. None of it was real. Not his kisses, his whispers, his gentle, loving touch. With a soft exclamation of pain, she turned into an ugly duckling again. Picking up her skirts, she raced for the solitude of her trailer.

Dash stood less than twenty feet away observing it all. He had seen how skillfully Dillon had maneuvered her so the cameras could photograph them from different angles, and he couldn't remember the last time he'd felt such an urge to hurt someone. He told himself it wasn't any of his business. Hell, he'd done worse to women in his life. But Honey wasn't a woman yet, and as Dillon bent over to retrieve his script, Dash found himself walking up to him.

"You're a genuine sonovabitch, aren't you, pretty boy?"

Eric's eyes narrowed. "I was doing my job."

"Is that so? And what job is that?"

"I'm an actor."

Dash opened and closed his fist at his side. "A bastard is more like it."

Eric's eyes narrowed and he tossed his cigarette to the ground. "Go ahead, old man. Take a swing." He braced himself, the muscles beneath his shirt tightening.

Dash wasn't intimidated. Dillon had Hollywood muscles, built on high-priced gym equipment instead of hard work and barroom brawls. They were cosmetic muscles, no more real than the kisses he had given Honey.

And then Dash saw the sweat glistening on Eric's forehead. He had seen men sweat from fear before, and they always looked wild in the eyes. Dillon just looked desperate.

He knew then that Eric wanted him to hit him, and as abruptly as it had seized him, he lost his desire to draw blood. For a moment he did nothing, and then he pushed his hat back on his head and gave Dillon a long, steady gaze.

"I guess I'll pass for now. I don't want a young stud like you humiliating me in front of everybody."

"No!" A vein began to throb in Eric's temple. "No! You can't do that. You—"

"So long, pretty boy."

"Don't—"

The plea stuck in Eric's throat as he watched Dash walk away. He fumbled for another cigarette, lit it, and drew the poisoned smoked into his lungs. Coogan didn't even respect him enough to fight him. At that moment he admitted to himself what he had refused to acknowledge before. How much he admired Dash Coogan—not as an actor, but as a man. Now that it was too late, he knew that he wanted Coogan's respect, just as he'd always wanted respect from his father. Dash was a real man, not a pretend one.

The smoke was choking him. He had to get out of here. Someplace where he could breathe. An image of needy, light blue eyes swam before him. He stalked from the set, pushing his way through the equipment and the crew, trying to escape those eyes. But they stayed with him. She was so desperate for love that she didn't have any sense of self-preservation. She hadn't even put up a fight, just let him throw her right over the edge of the cliff.

His lungs burned. Stupid. She was so goddamn stupid. She didn't understand the first rule of fairy tales. She didn't understand that little girls weren't ever supposed to fall in love with the evil prince.

Air Time

1983

12

Liz Castleberry's Fourth of July beach party was in full swing when Honey arrived. She wedged the silver Mercedes Benz 380 SL she had purchased after the show's third season onto the side of the road between a Jag and an Alfa Romeo. As she stepped down onto the sandy soil, she heard the bang of a firecracker exploding from the beach on the other side of the house. This was the first of Liz's party invitations Honey had accepted, and then only because it was informal and because Dash was going to be here.

Slinging the faded denim slouch bag that contained her bathing suit over her shoulder, she locked the car. Three years ago last month she had arrived in Los Angeles, but she felt decades older than that sixteen-year-old girl. Thinking back, she decided the horrible day toward the end of the second season when Eric Dillon had humiliated her in that phony fantasy love scene was what had finally forced her to grow up. At least the experience had put an end to the childish crush she'd had on him. No one, not even Dash, knew how much the memory of that day still made her cringe.

As she approached the beach house, she found herself wondering what the new season held in store for her. They would begin shooting at the end of the month for the show's fourth year, and the producers were finally going to permit Janie to turn fifteen. It was about time, since she would be twenty in December.

After the painful adjustments of the first two seasons, last season had been relatively uneventful. She had gotten along well with the crew, stayed away from Eric, and deepened her friendship with Liz Castleberry. But her relationship with Dash had been the most important change in her life.

She spent a lot of her spare time on the set with him, as well as nearly every Saturday at the ranch, doing chores and helping out with the horses. Not only did she love being with him, but the work gave her a convenient excuse to get away from the new house in Pasadena that Chantal had nagged her into buying because she insisted it would help Gordon get back to his painting. It hadn't helped, a fact that didn't surprise Honey at all. She liked the house much better than that awful place in Topanga Canyon, but it certainly didn't feel like home. For one thing, Buck Ochs was still in residence, and for another, her relationship with Sophie hadn't improved at all.

Shaking off depressing thoughts of her family, she approached the front entrance of Liz's beach house. The house was deeper than it was wide, with salt-weathered gray siding and salmon shutters. A small garden lay off to one side, along a low stone retaining wall that marked the boundary of the neighboring house, where Guy Isabella's daughter Lilly lived. The walk was tiled in a fish-scale pattern and edged with clusters of crimson and white impatiens.

As she approached the front door, she hesitated. After three years in L.A., she still hadn't been to that many parties. She wasn't comfortable at social functions because she was always afraid she'd use the wrong fork and because everyone seemed so sophisticated. Besides, Ross's lie about how old she was had taken hold, and the few times she had tried to convince people of her real age, they hadn't believed her.

She rang the bell, and a sunburned middle-aged man in bathing trunks let her in. The hairy patch on his chest looked like a map of Indiana.

He threw up his hands. "Honey! Hi, I'm Crandall. I love, love, love your show. It's absolutely the only thing I watch on television. You should have won last year."

"Thanks." She wished people would stop bringing up her Emmy nomination. She hadn't won—a fact her agent attributed to her continuing refusal to take any of the other acting parts that were offered her. Eric had won two years in a row. The movies he had filmed during the last few hiatuses were turning him into a major box-office star, and it was no secret that he was going to break his contract so he could make movies full time.

"Lizzie's out on the deck," Crandall said, leading her through a white-tiled entryway decorated with misty impressionistic paintings.

The living room was filled with people in various forms of casual wear, from bathing suits to slacks, everything stylish and expensive compared to her khaki shorts and Nike T-shirt. Liz had been nagging her to dress better, but Honey didn't have the talent for it. She moved past overstuffed sofas and chairs upholstered in baby blue and pale salmon toward a wall of windows that provided a panoramic view of the sea. The room smelled of barbecue, suntan lotion, and Chloè.

Liz came through a set of French doors that opened onto the deck and made her way toward Honey. Puckering her lips, she blew a kiss into the air somewhere near her costar's ear.

"You actually showed up. Happy Fourth of July, darling. Dash told me he'd ordered you to appear, but I didn't believe you'd really do it."

"Is he here yet?" Honey gazed hopefully through the sophisticated crowd, only a few members of which she recognized, but she didn't spot him.

"I imagine he'll be along." Liz stared at Honey's hair. "I can't believe that it's actually starting to curl. Evelyn told me you've been letting her work with it. You're beginning to look like a woman instead of a grade-school bully."

Honey had too much pride to let Liz see how much she liked her new hair. On the final day of shooting last March, Liz had ordered Evelyn to soften the blunt edges and feather back the bangs. At first, since the hair was so short, Honey hadn't seen much of an improvement, but as it had grown these past four months and Evelyn had continued to touch it up, it now curled softly around her face and brushed the slopes of her jaw.

"But you still look so young," Liz complained. "And you dress like an absolute infant. Look at those shorts. They're too big, and the color is putrid. You don't have any style at all."

Honey had grown used to Liz's blunt judgments, and she was merely annoyed instead of angry. "Why don't you give up, Liz? You'll never make me into a fashion plate. I don't have the talent for it."

"Well, I do, and I can't imagine why you won't let me take you shopping."

"I'm not interested in clothes."

"You should be." Before Honey could protest, Liz was whipping her through the crowd and up a narrow circular staircase into a pink and rose bedroom that reminded Honey of an expensive flower garden. Chintz draperies were tied back from the windows with tasseled cords, and sea-green carpeting covered the floor. One corner held a watered-silk chaise, another an ornate armoire made of bleached oak. A misty pastel fabric that looked as if it had been painted by Cézanne draped the double bed. Honey spotted a pair of masculine cuff links on the table next to it, but as much as she would have enjoyed hearing the details of Liz's love life, she had always restrained herself from asking.

Liz opened one of the louvered closet doors and began to dig around inside. "You'd have more confidence in yourself if you dressed your age."

"I have lots of confidence. I'm the most independent person I know. I take care of my family, and I—"

"Confidence in yourself as a woman, darling. It's the most amazing coincidence—" She pulled out a navy sack with crimson lettering. "I bought this for myself last week in a little boutique just off Rodeo, but when I got home, I realized I'd picked up the wrong size. I'll bet this would fit you perfectly."

"I brought a suit with me," Honey said stubbornly.

"And I can just imagine what it looks like."

Honey's hand clamped over the top of the slouch bag that

contained the old red tank suit the maid at the Beverly Hills Hotel had bought for her the week she'd arrived in L.A.

Liz shoved the sack at her and fluttered her hand toward the bathroom. "Try it on. You can always take it off if you don't like it."

Honey hesitated and then decided if she tried on the suit she could at least postpone going back downstairs for awhile. Maybe by then Dash would have arrived and she wouldn't have to face so many strangers by herself.

The bathroom looked like a tropical grotto complete with lush flowering plants, a sunken pink marble tub, and gold faucets shaped like dolphins. She peeked into the sack. Tucked inside the folds of tissue paper lay a skimpy bikini in a soft peach-and-white Hawaiian print along with a short wrap skirt in the same fabric. She pulled out the separate pieces. They were certainly prettier than her red tank suit, but she didn't like the idea of letting Liz manipulate her. She began to stuff the suit back into the sack, but hesitated. What was the harm in trying it on? Slipping out of her clothes, she donned the separate parts of the bikini and turned to assess herself in the beveled mirror that lined the wall behind the tub.

She hated to admit it, but Liz was right. The suit fit her perfectly. The under-wire top made the most of her small breasts by pushing them together just enough to give her a hint of cleavage. The bottom covered up everything important and was cut high enough on the sides to make her legs look longer. Still, she wasn't used to having so much of herself exposed. She opened the short, sarong-style skirt, looking for the clasp. When she found it, she wrapped it around her waist and fastened it on the left side. It fell low on her hips, just revealing her navel.

With the curling halo of her hair, her enhanced bust line, and her navel peeking out over the top of the skirt, even she had to admit she looked a little bit sexy.

"Knock, knock. I hope you're decent." The door swung open, and before Honey could respond, Liz had entered and clipped a pair of gold hoops to her earlobes. "You really need to get your ears pierced."

Honey touched the swaying hoops. "I can't go swimming with these on."

"Why on earth would you want to swim? I haven't been in the ocean in years. At least you're wearing a decent shade of lipstick, but I think a dab of mascara would be lovely."

Liz pushed her down onto a stool, whisked some pale peach blusher over her cheeks, and then dabbed at her lashes with light-brown mascara.

"There. Now you look your age. Whatever you do, don't go near the water."

Honey stared at the gold hoops shimmering through the honey-colored tendrils at her ears and studied the soft, flattering makeup. Even her mouth was sexy. She looked like herself, and yet not like herself. Older, more mature. Much prettier. Her reflection was disconcerting. She liked the way she looked, and yet the young woman in the mirror wasn't altogether a person she could respect. She was a bit too soft, too feminine, not nearly tough enough to fight life's battles.

Liz must have sensed her indecision because she spoke quietly. "It's time to grow up, Honey. You're nineteen years old. You need to come out of your cocoon and start discovering who you are."

Awareness hit her, and Honey jumped up from the stool. "You set me up, didn't you? You didn't buy that bathing suit for yourself. You bought it for me." She snatched up the tube of light-brown mascara. "And why would someone with lashes as dark as yours happen to have this lying around?"

Liz didn't even look guilty. "I've been bored lately, and I must admit the challenge of transforming you into a reasonable facsimile of a young woman has its appeal. Of course Ross is going to have a coronary when he sees you, but that's his problem. All this secrecy about your age is ridiculous."

Honey shook her head. "You're a complete fraud."

"Whatever do you mean?"

"That bitch-goddess act you put on."

"It's not an act. I'm ruthless and unscrupulous. Ask anyone."

Honey smiled. "Dash tells everybody you're a pussycat."

"Oh, he does, does he?" Liz laughed, but then gradually her amusement faded. "You've seen a lot of Dash this past year, haven't you?"

"I like the ranch. I go out there on weekends. We ride and talk, and I help out in the stable. That housekeeper of his doesn't know how to fix the kind of food he likes. Sometimes I cook for him."

"Honey, Dash is— He can be hard on people who care about him. I don't think he means to, but he can't seem to help it. Don't make up too many fatherly fantasies about him. He only lets people so close before he pushes them away."

"I know. I think it's because of his childhood."

"His childhood?"

"He spent a lot of time in foster homes. As soon as he got attached to somebody, they'd make him move someplace else. After a while, I guess he decided it was better not to get close to anybody."

Liz stared at her in astonishment. "He told you all that?"

"Not exactly. You know how he is. But he's said a few things here and there, and I've sort of drawn my own conclusions. When you're an orphan yourself, it's not too hard to recognize the symptoms in somebody else. Dash and I have handled our situations differently, though. He doesn't attach himself to anybody, and I attach myself to just about everybody."

She looked down at her hands, embarrassed to have said so much. "My mouth is getting away from me again. It's like a disease."

Liz studied her for a moment before linking her hand through Honey's arm. "We'd better get back to the party. I have the most wonderful young man I want you to meet. He's the son of an old friend—cute, smart, and only a little bit arrogant. The best part—he's not in the business."

"Oh, I don't think—"

"Don't be a baby. It's time to test your wings. Not to mention the effect of that sexy outfit."

Ignoring Honey's reluctance, Liz led her downstairs. Honey was disappointed to see that Dash hadn't yet arrived. Lately, he'd been getting a little too bossy with her, and she couldn't wait to see how he reacted to her appearance. It was about time she showed him that she wasn't a child anymore.

Liz began introducing her to the other guests, and people greeted her with varying degrees of surprise.

"You look a lot younger on television, Honey."

"I hardly recognized you."

"How old are you, anyway?"

Ross appeared next to her just as this blunt inquiry was being made and quickly whisked her away. He had gained a few pounds over the summer and his stomach, visible beneath an open terry-cloth wrap, was sunburned.

"What do you think you're doing?" he growled, his eyes skimming from her hair to her flat, bare midriff. "You shouldn't be in public looking like that."

Liz hadn't left Honey's side. "Leave her alone, Ross. And stop being such a worrywart. There's nothing in the world —not even her real age—that would make audiences stop loving her. Besides, she's here to have fun."

They greeted several more people, and then Liz steered her out onto the deck and toward a young man standing alone by one of the umbrella tables. He had light-brown hair cut short, square, blunt features, and an athlete's trim build. Sunglasses dangled from a short cord around his neck, and a gold watch glimmered at his wrist. Despite the rumpled and faded purple polo shirt that accompanied his swim trunks, the easy assurance of his stance made Honey suspect he came from money. As Liz led her relentlessly forward, she felt herself begin to panic. She didn't know anything about men like this.

"No, Liz. I—"

"Darling, I want you to meet Scott Carlton. Scott, would you make certain Honey gets something to eat and drink?"

"My pleasure."

Honey gazed up into a pair of warm brown eyes that were regarding her with obvious admiration. Some of her tension eased.

"What are you drinking?" he asked, as Liz left them alone.

She started to request an Orange Crush, but stopped herself just in time. "Whatever you're having. I'm not particular."

"Coors it is." He went over to an ice chest and pulled out a can of beer. Returning to her side, he popped the top and handed it over to her. She took a nervous sip.

"I must be the only person in America who hasn't watched your show. I've been taking classes in the evenings for my M.B.A. I've seen photos of you, of course, in magazines." His eyes dropped momentarily to the little swell of cleavage rising from the cups of her bikini and he smiled. "You look lots different in person."

"The camera puts on weight," she said inanely. Where was Dash? Why hadn't he shown up? She hoped he wouldn't bring a date. Watching him with other women bothered her.

"Not something you need to worry about. So how long have you been in L.A.?"

She told him. He asked her a few questions about her work, and then began to tell her about his job with a well-known market research firm. She realized to her amazement that he was trying to impress her. Imagine somebody like him trying to impress somebody like her. Gradually she became aware of the fact that several of the young men were giving her sidelong glances, and her self-confidence took a baby step forward.

"If you don't mind a personal question, how old are you, Honey?"

She resisted the urge to look over her shoulder and see if Ross was nearby. "Nineteen. Twenty in December."

"Really. I'm surprised. You look older. Even though you're small, there's something about your eyes. A maturity."

She decided that she definitely liked Scott Carlton.

He was joking with her about one of his coworkers when Dash came out on the deck and her heart gave a crazy jolt. All the men around him faded like old photographs. He was taller than most of them, but it was more than his physical stature that made the others seem diminished. He was a legend, while they were merely mortals.

A young woman approached him, and Honey realized it was Lilly Isabella, Liz's next-door neighbor. She had met her once last fall when she had visited Liz. Lilly was tall and beautiful, with full breasts and slim hips. Her silver-blond hair swept back from her face like liquid silk, displaying a finely chiseled classical profile.

The sight of Lilly sapped some of Honey's confidence. She was so sexy and sophisticated, obviously born to money and privilege. She wore a light blue raw-silk top tucked into a pair of darker blue slacks that set off her long legs. A silver slave bracelet encircled her upper arm and a matching belt cinched her waist. As Dash smiled at her, jealousy nipped at Honey. He never looked like that when he talked to her.

"Do you know Lilly?" Scott asked, following the direction of her eyes.

"Not really. We've met, but that's all. Why? Do you know her?"

"We dated for a while. But Lilly's complicated. It's hard for an ordinary guy to compete with her father. Besides, she doesn't stay with any guy for long if he's not an actor."

Honey waited, but he didn't elaborate. She watched as Dash tilted his head attentively, treating Lilly as a mature, desirable woman, even though she wasn't all that much older than Honey. Her resentment grew, and she decided it was time she showed him that Lilly Isabella wasn't the only desirable woman around. She gazed up at Scott through her lashes. "If Lilly walked away from someone as attractive as you, then she's definitely not as smart as she looks."

He grinned. "You want to go down to the beach?"

She glanced toward Dash and saw that he still hadn't noticed her. "I'd love to."

They had to pass Dash and Lilly to reach the steps. As she and Scott drew close, Dash spotted her for the first time. To Honey's delight, Scott slipped his arm around her waist. A flicker of surprised crossed Dash's features, but she couldn't tell whether it was from the change in her appearance or Scott's familiarity.

different kind of strength from what she experienced when she cussed at somebody. Flirting gave her another sort of power, one she didn't fully understand but that she was definitely enjoying. She hoped Dash was watching.

"I can't imagine someone as athletic as you ever being awkward." Her voice held just the right degree of admiration.

"You should have seen me when I was fourteen."

He pitched his beer can over her shoulder toward the trash container that sat in the sand behind her. It bounced off the rim. This was their second trip to the beach. After their earlier walk, they had eaten and chatted with some of the other guests. She had spotted Eric, looking gorgeous and unsavory with a week's worth of stubble on his chin, but her old fascination with him had been murdered that day under the oak tree.

Dash, however, was definitely distracting her. Every time she looked at him he had a woman hanging on his arm. In retaliation, she concentrated on Scott. Lovely Scott, who licked her with his eyes and treated her as if she were every inch a mature, desirable woman.

"I'll bet you were cute when you were fourteen," she said as they waded at the edge of the water.

"Not half as cute as you are right now."

Incredibly, she felt her mouth forming a coquettish pout. "You make me sound like a puppy dog."

"Believe me, you don't look anything like a puppy dog."

She had only a few seconds to enjoy his compliment before he slipped his arms around her body and drew her against him. Her bare midriff brushed against the soft knit fabric of his shirt. He lifted his hand and cupped the back of her neck. Then he lowered his head and kissed her.

His kiss wasn't anything like those lying kisses Eric had once given her. This one was real. He opened his mouth to encompass hers. A wave swirled around her calves, unbalancing her enough so that she leaned into him. He held her more tightly, and warmth spread through her body.

"God, you're really something," he whispered against her open lips. "I want to make love to you."

"Hi, Dash." She greeted him as if she had just noticed him, then introduced Scott and spoke to Lilly.

"Honey! I didn't recognize you. You look terrific." Lilly gave her a friendly smile and exchanged a few pleasantries with Scott.

Dash's eyes surveyed Honey's bare midriff, then locked on to her breasts. He was obviously displeased, and his scowl deepened as he spotted the beer can she still held in her hand. "Since when did you start drinking?"

"Since absolutely forever," she replied in her best Liz Castleberry imitation.

"Honey and I were just going for a walk on the beach," Scott said, taking her elbow. "We'll talk to you later."

She fancied she could feel Dash's eyes boring into her back as she walked away. The idea pleased her, and she added a defiant swing to her hips.

Eric regretted accepting the invitation to Liz's party before he'd stubbed out his first cigarette. He had been filming a movie since hiatus had begun, and this was his first day off in weeks. He should have spent it in bed. Rubbing the stubble on his jaw, he looked for a corner where he could hide out undisturbed. He'd have a drink and then slip away.

As he walked across the deck, a young woman in a red sundress shot him an admiring glance. He wondered why. He was unshaved and disreputable looking, in keeping with his role as a renegade cop on the run from the kingpin of a drug ring. The movie role was a far cry from Blake Chadwick, and exactly what Eric needed to flush the saccharin of *The Dash Coogan Show* from his veins.

Even though he had two years left on his contract, he'd decided he had to get out now. He didn't care how much it cost or what his lawyers had to do. From now on he was concentrating on his film career and putting television behind him.

He spotted Coogan on the other side of the deck and turned his back to look out at the ocean. He avoided his costar as much as possible, maybe because he had the uneasy sense that Dash saw right through him. Being with

Dash Coogan always made him feel inferior, the same way he used to feel with his own father. Eric didn't like to think about how much he wanted Dash's respect. Every time Dash called him "pretty boy," Eric felt sick.

Sunlight sparkled the tips of the waves and he thought about going for a swim, but it was too much trouble. A couple stood talking on the beach in front of him. He dismissed the man but his eyes lingered for a moment over the woman. Squinting against the glare from the sand, he saw that she was tiny but well proportioned, with small round breasts and good legs. From a distance, she looked a bit too fragile to appeal to him, but she was still tempting. Maybe he'd take a closer look when she came up on the deck. He didn't bother to consider what he would do if she weren't interested in him. That never happened.

The man reached out and touched her arm. She tossed her curls and her earrings sparked in the sun. Turning her head, she laughed.

With a shock he realized it was Honey. What had happened to the tomboy with the cropped hair and perpetual scowl? Occasionally last season, she had shown up in lipstick and a skirt. But she hadn't looked like this.

She stretched out her arm and made a sweeping gesture toward the water. The wind whipped her skirt, revealing the V of her thighs. His gaze settled there, and then he was disgusted with himself because his instinctive response seemed vaguely incestuous. No matter how much she might have changed, Honey still reminded him of Jase.

"Haven't I seen your face on a post-office wall somewhere?"

A woman's voice, rich and musical, came from behind him. He turned toward her and forgot all about Honey.

"An innocent man wrongly accused," he said.

She took a sip of wine from her glass and regarded him with a pair of widely spaced light gray eyes. A long lock of silvery hair blew across her face. She hooked it with her little finger and pushed it away.

The corners of her mouth twitched. "Why don't I believe that?"

"It's the truth. I swear."

"I can't imagine anyone describing you as innocent."

He feigned hurt. "I'm a choirboy. Really."

She laughed.

He held out his hand. "Eric Dillon."

She gave it a lazy glance. "I know."

And then she walked away.

He stared after her, intrigued as much by her aplomb as by her beauty. She walked over to a group of men and was quickly surrounded. He heard her musical laughter. The crowd parted and he saw one of the men offering her a shrimp speared on a toothpick. She took it from him, brushed it over her lips before she tasted it, then nibbled it slowly, as if she were savoring each bite.

Liz Castleberry came up behind him. "I wondered how long it would take you and Lilly to find each other."

"Is that her name?"

Liz nodded. "She's Guy Isabella's daughter."

"That turkey?" Eric gave a snort of disgust. Guy Isabella was a movie star, not an actor.

"Don't let Lilly hear you say that. She thinks he's perfect. Not even the fact that he's a lush tarnishes the halo she's put on him."

But Eric wasn't interested in Lilly Isabella's father. As he watched her with the men, he lit a cigarette. She definitely intrigued him. Maybe it was because she didn't look like the type of woman who could be easily hurt.

Not even by him.

"I don't believe you." Honey laughed. "Nobody could break his arm three times in one summer."

"I did."

As dusk fell, Scott showed no signs of losing interest in her, and her self-confidence had grown by leaps and bounds. Now she found herself extending her leg ever so slightly through the slit in her skirt and hanging onto Scott's words as if each one were shaped from precious metal. Once she'd gotten the hang of it, flirting hadn't proved to be difficult at all. In a queer way it made her feel strong, although it was a

"You do?" She suppressed the urge to look toward the deck and see if Dash was watching.

"Can't you feel how hard I am?"

He pressed his hips against her stomach. A delicious heat spread through her, along with a new sense of power. She had done that to him.

One of his hands slipped down from the small of her back to cup her bottom. He gave it a gentle squeeze. "You're terrific. Has anybody ever told you that?"

"Everybody." She gazed up at him. "Has anybody ever told you that you're a wonderful kisser?"

"You're not so bad yourself."

She smiled and he kissed her again. This time his lips parted and he slipped his tongue into her mouth. She received the intimacy with curiosity and decided kissing was definitely something she wanted to learn more about. An image of who she wanted her teacher to be flashed through her mind so quickly that she couldn't grab hold of it.

She pushed against his hips to make certain she hadn't lost her effect on him and discovered that she hadn't. His hand slid between their bodies and closed around her breast. She tensed, not wanting so much intimacy so quickly. He slipped his thumb inside the bikini bra and found her nipple. She began to pull away.

"Just what in the goddamn hell do you think you're doing?"

She sucked in her breath at the sound of the gruff, familiar voice coming from behind her.

Scott released her slowly, removing his hand from her breast and frowning at the interloper over the top of her head. "Do you have a problem?"

Turning slowly, she confronted a furious Dash Coogan, his face as dark as a thundercloud, invisible six-shooters riding on his hips. He was paying no attention to Scott, but was glaring at her instead, and he looked as if he were ready to take on all of Dodge City.

"You're drunk," he accused.

Lifting her chin, she returned his stare glare for glare. "I've had two beers. Not that it's any of your business."

"What's this all about, Mr. Coogan?"

Scott's respectful form of address seemed to make Dash even angrier, and the corner of his mouth curled unpleasantly. "I'll tell you what it's about, sonny. You're getting a little too free with your hands."

Scott looked puzzled. "I'm sorry, but I don't see what this has to do with you. She's a consenting adult."

"Not even close." Lifting his arm, he jabbed his hand toward the house. "You get your butt back there right this minute, little girl. That is if you're sober enough to walk that far."

She drew herself up to her full height. "Go to hell."

"What did you say to me?"

"You heard me. I'm not a *little girl,* and I have no intention of letting you order me around. Scott and I are leaving right now for his apartment."

He took a step closer, his eyes narrowing to slits. "I wouldn't bet on it."

She had to tilt her head all the way back so she could stare him down. A dangerous excitement had taken hold of her, a need to dance on the edge of a perilous cliff. "We're going to his apartment, and I'm going to spend the night there."

"Is that so?"

Scott was growing increasingly uncomfortable. "Honey, I don't know what kind of relationship you have with Mr. Coogan, but—"

"We don't have any relationship at all," she said, daring Dash to contradict her.

His voice was low and flat as he addressed Scott. "She's just a kid, and I'm not going to have you taking advantage of that. The party's over for tonight."

"Mr. Coogan—"

Ignoring him, Dash grasped Honey's arm and began steering her across the sand toward the house, just as if she were a disobedient five-year-old.

"Don't you do this to me," she hissed between her teeth. "I'm not a child, and you're ruining everything."

"That's exactly what I had in mind."

"You have no right to interfere."

"You don't even know that boy."

"I know that he's a great kisser." She tossed her head, deliberately making her curls fly. "And I imagine he'll be an even better lover. He'll probably be the best lover I ever had."

He didn't slacken his pace. Her shorter legs were having a difficult time keeping up with his longer ones, and she stumbled slightly in the sand. His grip tightened on her arm. "That wouldn't be too hard, would it?"

"You don't think I've had lovers before? That just goes to show what you know. I've had three lovers just this summer. No, four. I forgot about Lance."

Instead of taking her back up on the deck, he drew her around the side of the house. "Oh, I know you've had lovers. All the men on the crew talk about how easy you are."

She came to a dead stop. "They do not! I never did anything with a single person on the crew."

He pulled her forward. "That's not what I hear."

"You heard wrong."

"They told me you'll undress for anything in pants."

She was outraged. "I will not! I never undressed for a man in my life. I—" She clamped her mouth shut, realizing too late that he'd trapped her.

He shot her a triumphant look. "You're damned right, you haven't. And we're going to keep it that way for a while."

They had reached his car, a four-year-old Cadillac Eldorado. He opened the door and pushed her inside. "Just in case you're lying to me about how many beers you've had, I'm driving you home."

"I'm not lying. And you're not my father, so stop acting like one."

"I'm the closest thing you've got to a father." He slammed the door.

As he stalked around the front of the car, she remembered a time in her life not all that long ago when she would have given anything to hear him speak those words. But something inside her had changed. She didn't know when it had happened or why. She only knew that she didn't want him to act like a father any longer.

When he got behind the wheel, she confronted him, turning her head so swiftly that one of the gold hoops swung forward and bounced against her cheek. "You can't lock me up, Dash. I'm not a kid anymore. I like Scott, and I've decided to go to bed with him. If not tonight, then another night."

He pulled out onto the road, tires spinning in the gravel. He didn't speak until they had passed the guardhouse at the entrance of the private compound and were out on the highway. As the headlights of a passing car cast slanted shadows over his face, he said softly, "Don't give it away cheap, Honey. Make it mean something."

"Like *your* affairs?"

He snapped his head back to the road. She waited. When he didn't say anything in his own defense, her anger grew. "You make me sick. You'll go to bed with any woman who throws herself at you, but you still have the nerve to give me lectures on morality."

He hit the button on the radio, blasting George Jones through the car and drowning out any further conversation.

13

A light flicked on inside the house. Eric had been dozing, but his head snapped up. Music and muted conversation still drifted over from Liz's party next door. He glanced down at the illuminated dial on his watch and saw that it was nearly two o'clock. He had to be on the set in five hours. He should be home in bed instead of skulking in the shadows of Lilly Isabella's deck, waiting for her to return from the party.

Another light went on. Unzipping the dark green windbreaker he had slipped into earlier, he wandered over to the sliding doors that led from the deck into the house and lit a cigarette. There were no curtains on the windows, and he could see the room inside. It held low contemporary furniture in neutral tones that served as a background for the wall of enlarged color photographs that dominated the room. Some of them were portraits of Guy Isabella in various roles he'd played, others artistically posed male nudes. He rapped on the glass.

She appeared almost immediately. Her upper arm held a faint red mark from the silver slave bracelet she had just removed, and her feet were bare. When she saw who was standing on her deck, she gave him a mischievous grin and shook her head. He grabbed the back of one of the tubular deck chairs, turned it so it was facing the doors, and sank down into it.

She slid the door open and regarded him steadily for several seconds. "What do you want?"

"Bad question, sweetheart."

"You're a real tough guy, aren't you?"

"Not me. I'm gentle as a lamb."

"I'll bet. Listen, I'm tired and you're trouble. That's a bad combination, so why don't we just call it a night?"

He stood and flicked his cigarette over the rail into the sand. "Sounds like a good idea." Stepping past her, he entered the house.

She splayed one hand on the hip of her dark blue slacks. He saw that her fingernails were unpainted and bitten nearly to the quick. The flaw intrigued him.

"That's funny. I can't remember inviting you in."

He gestured toward several of the nude male photographs. "Friends of yours?"

"The Hall of Fame of my old lovers."

"I'll bet."

"You don't believe me?"

"Let's just say that most of them look like they'd be more comfortable in a steam bath than in bed with a woman."

She sank down on the couch and stretched like a cat who had gone too long without stroking. "Funniest thing. That's what I've heard about you."

"Is that so?"

"You know how rumors fly about good-looking actors. You're all supposed to be gay."

He laughed, then took his time enjoying the generous lines of her body.

She had enough self-confidence to be amused instead of insulted by his perusal. "Is this where I'm supposed to surrender to your mesmerizing sexuality and take off my clothes?"

"I don't know if I'm ready to give up the pleasures of those steam baths."

She laughed, a rich, throaty sound. "Why do I have the feeling my guardian angel was looking the other way when I let you in the door?" She stood and yawned, this time lifting her silken blond hair from her neck. "You want a nightcap before you leave?"

He shook his head. "I have an early call."

"I'll tell you what, Mr. Dillon. If you want to stop by some time next week, I might be persuaded to open a bottle of Château Latour and play my Charlie Parker tapes for you."

He had no intention of making it that easy for her. "Sorry, I'm going on location."

"Oh?"

Flipping up the collar on his windbreaker, he walked over to the patio doors. "Maybe I'll call you when I get back."

Her head shot up. "And maybe I won't be available."

"I guess I'll have to take my chances." He let himself out, then grinned and lit a cigarette.

Dash was in the paddock inspecting the fetlock of one of the three Arabians he was now boarding along with four other horses when Honey arrived at the ranch. She got out of her car and walked toward him, her full prairie skirt whipping around her legs, the eyelet trim at the hem playing peek-a-boo with the hot afternoon breeze.

She wore the skirt with a white knit tank top, powder-blue sandals, and tiny gold balls in her just-pierced earlobes. In the week and a half that had passed since the party, Liz had taken her on two shopping trips, and she now had a new wardrobe of flouncy little dresses, slacks and tops that had cost a fortune, designer jeans, silk T-shirts, belts and bangles and shoes in every style and color. These past few nights she had found herself standing in her closet simply staring at the beautiful fabrics. It was as if she had spent years suffering from a particularly acute form of malnutrition, only to be confronted by a banquet table laden with food that was irresistible. No matter how much she looked, she couldn't get her fill.

Some of the clothes even seemed to be taking on a life of their own. A few hours ago she had fingered a shimmery little ice-blue evening gown, an updated version of a flapper's dress, and had fought a nearly irresistible urge to put it on, even though she was planning to drive out to see Dash. The gown was hardly designed for a casual afternoon visit to a dusty ranch, but she'd barely been able to resist. *Slip me on,* the shimmery blue gown seemed to say. *If he sees you wearing me, he won't be able to resist you.*

Her hand felt clumsy as she lifted it to wave at him. "Hi!"

He nodded but didn't stop what he was doing. She gripped the top rail of the fence and watched. The sun felt good on her back and arms, but it didn't ease her tension. They hadn't spoken since the night of the party.

He finally finished inspecting the horse and walked over to her, all sweaty and smelling of the stable. He took in her feminine attire but didn't comment on the absence of her customary baggy jeans and faded T-shirt. One part of her wished that she had worn the blue evening gown after all.

"Nice of you to tell me you were stopping by," he said sarcastically.

"I called, but nobody answered." She slipped her foot off the bottom rail. "Why don't I go inside and make you some lemonade? You look hot."

"Don't bother. I don't have time to be sociable today."

She gazed at him steadily. "You're really mad at me, aren't you? You've given me the deep freeze ever since Liz's party."

"Is there any particular reason why I shouldn't?"

"Dash, I'm not Janie. There wasn't any reason for you to turn into Father Avenger."

She had uttered the statement mildly, but his temper immediately flared. "I turned into your friend is what I did. You were smearing yourself all over that boy like a bitch in heat. It was one of the most disgusting things I ever saw in my life. And I don't even know why I bothered to stop you. I'll bet he was on the phone to you that same night, and you were in bed with him by morning."

"It was a little later than that."

He cursed softly, and an emotion that almost seemed like pain furrowed his forehead. "Well, you got what you wanted, didn't you? I just hope you're ready to live with yourself knowing you gave it away so cheap."

"That's not what I meant. I meant that he didn't call me that night. He called me the next day. But I haven't gone out with him."

"Now why is that? I'm surprised that somebody so anxious to explore life's mysteries didn't just get right down to it."

"Please. Don't be so mad." She tried to curb her tongue, but a devil inside prodded her on. "I wanted to talk to you about it first."

He snatched off his hat and slapped it against the side of his jeans, sending up a puff of dust. "No. Uh-uh. I'm not going to turn into your damn sex therapist."

As if she had moved outside her body and was standing on the side observing, she heard herself say, "Liz told me I should go to bed with him."

His eyes narrowed and he slammed his hat back on his head. "Oh, she did, did she? Now why am I not surprised? The way I remember it, she was pretty free with her favors, too."

"What a rotten thing to say. As if you weren't?"

"That doesn't have the slightest thing to do with it."

"You make me sick." Turning on her heel, she stomped away.

He grabbed her arm before she'd taken two steps. "Don't you walk away from me when I'm talking to you."

"Mount Rushmore finally wants to talk," she scoffed. "Well, forgive me very much, but I'm no longer in the mood to listen."

The stable hand was watching them curiously, so Dash pulled her toward the house. The moment they were out of sight of the paddock, he lit into her.

"I never thought I'd see the day when you'd misplace your integrity, but that's just what you're about to do. You seem to be losing all sight of who you are. There's right and there's wrong, and you're not the kind of person who should be jumping into bed with somebody you don't love."

He spoke so fiercely that some of her anger faded. No one except Dash Coogan had ever given a damn about what she did. As she saw the lines concern had drawn in his face, her temper dwindled into a warm, cozy flame. Without thinking about what she was doing, she lifted her hand and flattened her palm against his shirt where she could feel his heart thudding beneath the damp cotton.

"I'm sorry, Dash."

He jerked away from her. "You should be. Start thinking before you jump into things. Think about the conse- quences."

The way he recoiled from her touch made her angry all over again. "I'm going to the doctor for birth control pills," she shot back at him.

"You're what? You're doing what?" Before she could respond, he launched into a tirade about young people and sexual promiscuity and was so obviously outraged that she almost wished she hadn't baited him. Even so, she couldn't stop herself from prodding him further.

"I'm ready to have sex, Dash. And I'm not going to be casual about protecting myself."

"You're not ready, dammit!"

"How do you know? I think about it all the time. I'm—edgy."

"Edgy isn't the same thing as being in love, and that's the question you have to ask yourself. Are you in love?"

She gazed into those hazel eyes that had seen it all and the word *yes* sprang to her lips, only to be bitten back before it could escape. The truth she had been trying so hard to shut out of her conscious mind refused to be contained any longer. At some point along the way, without knowing exactly when it had happened, her child's love for Dash Coogan had changed into a woman's love. The knowledge was new and old, wonderful and terrible. She couldn't meet his eyes so she gazed at the brim of his Stetson, just above his ear.

"I'm not in love with Scott," she said carefully, her voice sounding thin to her own ears.

"Then that should settle the issue."

"Were you in love with Lisa when you slept with her? Do you love those women who leave makeup smears in your bathroom sink?"

"That's different."

Heartsick, she turned away from him. "I'm going home."

"Honey, it really *is* different."

She looked back at him, but this time he was the one who wouldn't meet her eyes. He cleared his throat. "I'm sort of worn out when it comes to women. But it's not the same with you. You're young. Everything's new for you."

Her response was flat. "I haven't been young since I was six years old and I lost the only person who ever loved me."

"You're not going to find love in some stranger's bed."

"Since I haven't been able to find it anyplace else, I guess I might as well give it a try." She shoved her hand in her pocket and pulled out her car keys, angry with herself for sounding so self-pitying.

"Honey—"

"Forget it." She began walking to her car.

"If you'd still like to make some lemonade, I wouldn't object."

She looked down at the keys in her palm and wanted to cry. "I'd better go. I've got some things to do."

It was the first time since they'd known each other that

she was the one to walk away. As she looked back up, she saw that she had surprised him.

"You bought some new clothes."

"Liz and I have gone shopping a couple of times. She's making me over."

For some reason this seemed to reignite his anger, and his hazel eyes grew as hard as flints. "There wasn't anything wrong with the way you were."

"It was time, that's all."

As she climbed behind the wheel of the car, he held on to the top of the door so she couldn't close it. "You want to drive over to Barstow with me on Friday? A friend of mine wants to show me some quarter horses he's raising."

"Liz and I are going to the Golden Door for a week."

He looked at her blankly.

"It's a spa."

A muscle ticked in his jaw, and he released his hold on the door. "Well, now. I sure wouldn't want you to miss an intellectual experience like that."

She started the car. Her tires spit gravel as she sped down the drive.

He stood in front of the house and watched until the rooster tail of dust grew too small to see. A spa. What in the goddamn hell had gotten into Liz, taking Honey to someplace like that? She was just a kid. Smaller than a peanut. Not even as old as his daughter.

And the thought of her in bed with some good-looking young stud fill him with rage.

He turned his back to the road and stalked toward the stable. He told himself it was natural to feel protective toward her. For the past three years, he had been the closest thing she'd had to a father, and he didn't want to see her get hurt.

That was the reason he was upset. He cared about her. She was tough and fragile and funny. She had a conscience as big as all outdoors, and she was the most generous person he knew. Look at the way she treated that band of parasites she called a family. She was smart, too. Damn, she was smart. Good-hearted and optimistic, always certain there were at least three pots of gold at the end of every rainbow. But her optimistic nature made her vulnerable. He hadn't forgotten the crush she'd had on that bastard Eric Dillon, which was exactly why he didn't want to see her jumping into bed with the first young stud who caught her eye.

Now if the boy were somebody decent, someone who really cared about her and wasn't just looking to put a celebrity notch on his bedpost, he'd feel different. If she fell in love with somebody decent who would be good to her and not hurt her, he'd—

Smash the sonovabitch's face in.

The craving for a drink hit him hard. He pulled off his hat and wiped the sweat from his forehead with his shirtsleeve. He had just turned forty-three. He had three ex-wives and two kids. Already in his lifetime he'd lost more money than most people ever dreamed of making. Life had thrown him a second chance when he'd stopped drinking, but when it came to women there was an empty place inside him that had been formed when he was a child being moved from one family to another. He couldn't love the same way other men loved. Women wanted intimacy and fidelity from a man, qualities he had proven time and again that he couldn't give.

Disgusted, he slammed his hat back on. She was just like a pesky little termite, gnawing her way bit by bit through his different layers. But he couldn't deny that she made him feel young again. She made him believe that life still held possibilities. And he wanted her. Damn did he want her. But he'd put a bullet right through his brain before he'd let himself hurt that little girl.

"Lilly, sweetheart."

Eric watched Guy Isabella weaving through a rain forest of long silver streamers trailing from the huge crimson and black helium balloons that bobbed at the vaulted ceiling of his Bel Air home. Impeccably dressed in formal wear, he smiled at Lilly and then looked at Eric with distaste. Obviously, Eric's tuxedo didn't make up for his stubbly jaw.

Everything about Lilly seemed to glow at the sight of her

roughly parallel to the house, her silver-blond hair flying, her skirt swirling around her long legs. He grew aroused just watching her. She was beautiful, but not fragile. And definitely not an innocent.

Recessed lights hidden in the landscaping softly illuminated the leafy branches of the magnolia and olive trees they passed. As the slope grew steeper and the red-tiled roof of the house slipped out of sight, she turned back and took his arm. They rounded a curve and another house came into view—a tiny replica of Snow White's cottage.

He laughed softly. "I don't believe it. Was this yours?"

"The perfect playhouse for a Hollywood kid. Dad had it built for me when he and Mother got divorced. I guess it was my consolation prize."

The story-book cottage was half-timbered and made of stucco with rustic patches of brick showing through. A small chimney rose from one end of a mock thatched roof. The front held a set of diamond-paned windows framed by wooden shutters.

"The window box used to be filled with geraniums," she said, letting go of his arm and walking up to the cottage. "Daddy and I planted them together every year." She pushed the latch on the wooden double door, and the hinges creaked as it opened. "Most of the original furnishings are gone now, and the place is mainly used for pool storage. You'll have to duck."

Eric took one last drag on his cigarette before he tossed it away. Bending, he entered the cottage. The ceiling was just above his head even though he wasn't standing completely upright.

"Give me your matches."

He passed them over and heard her moving about. A few seconds ticked by and then the interior was filled with flickering amber light as she lit a pair of candles on the mantelpiece of a miniature stone fireplace.

He shook his head in wonder as he looked around. "I don't believe this place."

"Isn't it wonderful?"

The ceiling of the playhouse cottage was beamed and

father. She hugged him and kissed his cheek. "Hi, Daddy. Happy birthday."

"Thank you, angel." Although he was speaking to his daughter, his attention was still on Eric.

"Daddy, this is Eric Dillon. Eric, my father."

"Sir." Eric carefully concealed his contempt as he shook Isabella's hand. Blond and boyishly handsome, both Guy Isabella and Ryan O'Neal had spent most of the seventies competing for many of the same roles. But O'Neal was a better actor, and from what Eric had heard, Guy had hated his guts ever since *Love Story*.

Guy Isabella represented everything Eric detested about motion picture actors. He was a pretty face, nothing more. He was also said to have a problem with alcohol, although that might not be anything more than rumor since Eric had also heard that he was a health nut. His worst sin in Eric's eyes was professional laziness. Apparently Isabella didn't think it was important to work at his craft, and now that he was pushing fifty and no longer capable of playing male ingenues, the parts were getting more difficult to come by.

"I saw that spy movie you made," Isabella said to him. "It was a little too gritty for my taste, but you did some fairly good work. I understand you're filming something new now."

Isabella's condescension set his teeth on edge. What right did an aging male bimbo have to pass judgment on his performance? Still, for Lilly's sake, he tempered his reply. "We finish shooting next week. It's gritty, too."

"Too bad."

Eric turned away to study the house. It was built in the style of a Mediterranean villa, but with a heavy Moorish influence that indicated it had been constructed in the twenties. The interior was dark and opulent. He could imagine one of the old silent-screen vamps being at home with the narrow stained-glass windows, arched doorways, and wrought-iron grillwork. The living room had priceless Persian rugs on the floor, custom-made chairs with leopard-skin upholstery, and an antique samovar over the fireplace. A perfect place for a man with a Valentino complex.

Isabella was still regarding Eric's unshaven jaw with disapproval. His cologne smelled heavily of musk, which mingled with the aroma of the whiskey in the heavy crystal tumbler he was carrying.

"I'll tell you what I like, Dillon. Your TV show. My people are trying to put together something like that for me, but you've got to have a special kid."

"Honey's hard to duplicate."

"Damn cute. She gets you right here, you know what I mean. Right in the heart."

"I know what you mean."

Isabella finally turned his attention to Lilly, who was dressed in pale raspberry silk and asymmetrical silver jewelry. "So how's your mother, kitten?"

Lilly filled him in on the latest news from Montevideo, where her stepfather was ambassador, while Eric surveyed the gathering. It was an old Hollywood crowd made up of megastars from the fifties and sixties, former studio heads, agents. Everyone eminently respectable. He wouldn't have been caught dead here if it weren't for Lilly.

Tonight marked their third date, and he hadn't even kissed her. Not because he didn't desire her or because he was bored with her, but because he liked being with her so much. It was a new experience for him to be both physically and mentally attracted to a woman.

He and Lilly had so many things in common. Both of them had been raised in affluence. She knew art and literature, and she understood his passion for acting. She was an irresistible combination of beauty and brains, aloofness and sensuality. Even more important, she had an air of worldliness that allowed him to relax when he was with her instead of worrying that somehow he would hurt her.

"Isn't he wonderful?" she said as her father left to greet a guest.

"He's something, all right."

"Most divorced men would have passed their daughters off onto their ex-wives, but my mother was never very maternal and he was the one who raised me. It's the funniest thing, but in a way you remind me of him."

Eric reached for his cigarettes without comment. [H]er relationship with her father was her one drawback, b[ut he] had to admire her filial loyalty.

"Of course, you're dark and he's blond," she went [on.] "But both of you belong in the Greek god category." S[he] lifted a champagne glass from the tray of a passing wait[er] and gave him a mischievous smile. "Don't let this go to tha[t] swelled head of yours, but each of you has a certain—I don't know—an aura or something." She dipped the tip of her index finger into her champagne glass and then brought it to her lips, where she sucked it. "Oh, sorry, you can't smoke in here."

He gazed around with irritation and saw that no one else was smoking. He remembered that Isabella was supposed to be a health nut. "Let's go outside then. I need a cigarette."

She began leading him along the limestone paved foyer to the back of the house. "You smoke too much."

"I'm quitting as soon as this movie's over."

"And the check's in the mail." She lifted one of her expressive eyebrows at him. He smiled. She never let him get away with bullshit, another thing he liked about being with her.

He gazed up at the coffered ceiling. "How long has your father lived here?"

"He bought the house right after he and my mother were married. Louis B. Mayer used to own it, or King Vidor. Neither of them remembers which one."

"Sort of a weird place to grow up."

"I guess."

She led him into the kitchen where she nodded absentmindedly at the help before she took him out through a service door. The grounds, lush with mature vegetation, sloped sharply in the back. Water splashed gently in a hexagonal-shaped fountain covered in blue-and-yellow patterned tiles. He caught the scent of eucalyptus, roses, an[d] chlorine.

"I want to show you something." Lilly was whisperi[ng] even though the grounds were deserted. He lit his cigar[ette.] She danced ahead of him down along a curved path tha[t]

sloping, high enough for him to stand upright at the center
but falling off at the sides. A muted but still colorful mural
of elves, fairies, and forest creatures frolicked across the
walls. The muralist had painted rustic cracks along with
several patches of bricks, as if the plaster had broken away in
places. Even the cans of pool chemicals and the neatly
stacked pile of lounge cushions didn't spoil the cottage's
enchantment.

"It's a little musty, but Dad keeps the place maintained.
He knows I'd kill him if he let anything happen to it."

He couldn't tear his eyes away from her. In her pale
raspberry gown with her silver-blond hair and exquisite
features, she looked as enchanted as the figures in the mural.

She moved a cushion from the top of the stack to the floor.
Sinking down on it, she leaned back against the others.
"You're too big for the place. The boys I used to bring here
were a lot smaller."

He lowered himself onto the cushion next to her, prop-
ping up one knee and loosening his tie. "Were there lots of
them?"

"Only two. One lived in the next house, and he was
boring. All he wanted to do was move the chairs around and
make forts."

There was a husky, seductive quality in her voice that
intrigued him. He turned her hand over in the lap of her
gown and traced a circle in her palm with his fingernail.
"And the other?"

"Uhm. That would have been Paulo." She leaned her
head back against the cushions, her eyes drifting shut. "His
father was our gardener."

"I see."

"He came here whenever he could." She drew her hand to
the bodice of her gown and laid the tips of her fingers across
her full breast.

His mouth went dry, and he knew he could no longer hold
out against her. "What did the two of you do?"

"Use your imagination."

"I think"—he toyed with her fingers—"that you were
naughty."

"We played"—she caught her breath as he stroked the center of her palm— "pretend games."

Leaning forward, he brushed his lips over the corner of her mouth. "What kind of games?"

The small, pointed tip of her tongue flicked out to lick the place he had kissed. "Uhmm . . . The usual ones children play."

"Such as?" He slid his finger over her wrist and along her inner arm.

"I was afraid of getting a shot. Paulo told me he could fix me up so I wouldn't have to go to the doctor."

"I like the kid's style."

"I knew what he was doing, of course, but I pretended I didn't." Her breath caught as his hand slipped down along her leg and crept under the hem of her dress. "It was all pretty comic."

"But exciting, too."

"Definitely exciting."

He rubbed her leg through her shimmery stocking, gradually moving higher until his thumb rested in the small cave at the back of her knee. "I like to play games, too."

"Yes, I know."

He stroked her lower thigh and then tensed with excitement as her stockings came to an end and he touched bare skin. He should have known that she wouldn't wear anything as ordinary as panty hose.

"And do you still hate going to the doctor?" he asked.

"It's not my favorite thing." At the slight pressure he was exerting, she eased her legs apart. The insides of her thighs were firm and warm where he stroked them.

"But what if you're sick?"

"I—I'm hardly ever sick."

She gasped as his thumb brushed her through her panties. "I don't know about that," he said. "You feel warm."

"Do I?" she asked breathlessly.

"You might have a fever. I'd better check." He slipped his finger inside the leg opening. She made a small, moaning sound.

"Just as I thought."

"What?"

"You're hot."

"Yes." She squirmed beneath his intimate touch.

In the candlelight her lips were parted and her face flushed. His own excitement burned more fiercely as he saw how the sweet perversion of this fantasy had aroused her. Women had never been anything more than medicine to him, an over-the-counter drug to be taken at night in hopes that he'd feel better in the morning. He had never cared about his partner's satisfaction, only his own, but now he wanted to watch Lilly shatter beneath his touch, and he knew his own satisfaction wouldn't be complete without hers.

"I'm afraid I'll have to take these off." He met no resistance as he slipped the panties down over her hips. When they were off, he reached up and touched her breast through her dress. She moaned, and her forehead puckered in a frown, as if she were upset about something, but she pushed her breast against his hand, so he didn't stop.

"Your heart rate is fast," he said.

She didn't reply.

He found the zipper at the back of her dress. Sliding it down, he lowered the bodice and then removed her bra.

She lay, half sitting, half reclining in front of him, naked except for her shimmering stockings and the pale raspberry gown bunched at her waist, knees raised, legs open, wanton. He touched her breast and then gently squeezed on her nipple. She made an animal sound deep in her throat, almost a sound of distress, while at the same time she arched against his more intimate caress below, inviting him to touch more deeply.

The mixture of conflicting emotions she was exhibiting bothered him but at the same time aroused him so fiercely he could hardly hold himself back. Her moans grew guttural in her throat, and tears began to leak from beneath her eyelids.

Alarmed, he drew back, only to have her sink her fingers into the muscles of his forearms and pull him closer. He continued his caresses, sweat dampening his shirt. As his body demanded its own release, he held back to watch the disturbing fusion of emotions that played across her face: pleasure and pain, feverish arousal and a disturbing anguish. Her passion dewed his hand, and his breathing echoed harshly in the enchanted interior of the cottage as she splintered beneath his touch.

He moaned and held her through the aftershocks. "Lilly, what's wrong?" He'd never seen a woman react with so much distress to lovemaking. When she didn't answer, he crooned softly to her. "It's all right. Everything's all right."

And then he decided he had imagined her distress because her quick hands began working at the zipper on his trousers. When she had freed him, she grasped the loose ends of his bow tie in her fists and drew his mouth to hers, giving him her tongue. She stroked him until he lost all reason.

He fumbled in the pocket of his trousers for the foil packet he never went anywhere without and drew it to his teeth to rip it open with a shaking hand. She brushed it away. "No. I want to feel you."

Shifting her weight, she lowered herself upon him.

He was too far gone to heed the alarms that clanged in his brain, and only after he had spilled himself inside her did he feel a chill of foreboding. He had been attracted to her because she seemed so strong, but now he wasn't sure.

She began nibbling his ear and then she insisted on running back to the house to steal some food from the kitchen for them. Before long they were laughing together over lobster and petits fours, and his forebodings had evaporated.

The next day they went to a Wynton Marsalis concert together, and after that he continued to see her several times a week. Her beauty fascinated him, and they never ran out of conversation. They argued about art, shared a mutual passion for jazz, and could talk for hours about the theater. It was only when they climbed into bed that something was very wrong. Even as Lilly demanded that he bring her to orgasm, she almost seemed to hate him for doing it. He knew it was his fault. He was a bad lover. He had used women for so long that he had no idea how to be unselfish.

He redoubled his efforts to make certain that she was satisfied, giving her back rubs, kissing every part of her, caressing her until she begged him for release, but her distress continued unabated. He wanted to talk to her about the problem, but he didn't know how, and he realized that he could converse with Lilly on any topic except those intimate ones that mattered. As summer slipped into fall and nothing improved, he knew he had to put an end to it.

While he was making up his mind how to do it, she appeared unexpectedly at his house one night in early October just after he'd gotten back from the studio. He poured two glasses of wine and held one of them out to her. She took a sip. Once again he noticed her fingernails, bitten nearly to the quick.

"Eric, I'm pregnant."

He stared at her as a cold sense of dread crept through him. "Is this a joke?"

"I wish it were," she said bitterly.

He remembered that first night in the playhouse two months earlier when he hadn't used anything, and his gut tightened. Fool. What a goddamned fool.

She stared into the depths of her wineglass. "I've— Tomorrow I have an appointment for an abortion."

As quickly as her words sank in, rage exploded inside him. "No!"

"Eric—"

"No, goddamnit!" The stem of his wineglass cracked in his hand.

She gazed at him miserably, her light gray eyes swimming with tears. "There isn't any other way. I don't want a baby."

"Well, you have one!" He pitched the glass into the corner where it shattered, splattering its contents everywhere. *"We* have one, and there won't be any abortion."

"But—"

He could see that he was scaring her, and he tried to calm his breathing. Setting aside her glass, he grasped her hands. "We'll get married, Lilly. It happens all the time."

"I—I care about you, Eric, but I don't think I'd be a very good wife."

He attempted a shaky laugh. "That's another thing we have in common, then. I don't think I'll be a very good husband, either."

She smiled tremulously. He drew her into his arms and squeezed his eyes shut while he began to make promises to her, promises of roses and sunshine, daffodils and moonbeams, everything he could think of. He didn't mean any of it, but that made no difference. She had to marry him, because no matter what, he wouldn't be responsible for the death of another innocent.

14

INTERIOR. RANCH HOUSE LIVING ROOM—DAY.

Dash and Eleanor stand in the middle of the floor, their expressions combative.

ELEANOR
I have no respect for you. You know that, don't you?

DASH
I believe I've heard you mention it before.

ELEANOR
I admire men of education and refinement. True gentlemen.

DASH
Don't forget the necktie part.

ELEANOR
What are you talking about?

DASH
The last time we had this conversation, you said

you couldn't respect a man who wasn't wearing
a suit and tie at the exact moment he died.

ELEANOR
I most certainly did not say that. I simply pointed
out that I could never respect a man who doesn't
even own a necktie, much less wear one.

DASH
I do so own one.

ELEANOR
It has a hula girl painted on it.

DASH
Only when you look at it straight on. From the
side, it's more of a flamingo.

ELEANOR
I rest my case.

DASH
So what you're saying is that we've got a
doomed relationship, is that it?

ELEANOR
Absolutely.

DASH
No hope.

ELEANOR
Not a bit.

DASH
Because we're too different.

ELEANOR
Polar opposites.

DASH
(taking a step closer)
So how's come I'm getting ready to kiss you?

ELEANOR
Because you're a crude, unprincipled cowboy.

DASH
Is that so? Then how's come you're going to kiss
me right back.

ELEANOR
Because—Because I'm crazy about you.

They move into each other's arms and exchange a long,
satisfying kiss. The door bangs open and Janie rushes in.

JANIE
I knew it! You're doing it again. Stop it! Stop that!

DASH
(still holding Eleanor in his arms)
I thought you were off polishing your fingernails
for that Bobby character.

JANIE
His name is Robert and you should be ashamed
of yourselves.

DASH
I don't see why.

JANIE
She's just using you. Ever since Blake went off to
join the air force, she's been hanging onto you
like a burr. She's afraid of getting old and
ending up alone. She's afraid—

DASH
(moving away from Eleanor to confront Janie)
That's enough, Jane Marie.

JANIE
The minute your back is turned, she laughs at
you. I've heard her, Pop. She makes fun of you
on the telephone to all her New York City
friends.

<pre>
                   ELEANOR
                  (together)
     Janie, that's not true.

                    DASH
                  (together)
     You go back to the house.
</pre>

Janie regards them mutinously and then runs from the
house.
Dash and Eleanor stare at the door.

<pre>
                   ELEANOR
                  (quietly)
     And there goes the biggest reason of all why
     this relationship doesn't stand a chance.
</pre>

When the scene ended, Honey walked behind the cameras
to retrieve her script, tugging at the rubber band that held
back her ponytail and rubbing her scalp with her fingers. She
had refused to let them cut her hair, and the producers had
finally agreed to let Janie wear a ponytail, but they made
Evelyn scrape her hair back so tightly that Honey sometimes
got a headache. Even so, it was worth it. In the five months
that had passed since Liz's beach party, her hair had grown
long enough that it brushed the tops of her shoulders.

As she fluffed it with her fingertips, she watched Liz and
Dash, who were still on the set talking quietly with each
other. Jealousy gnawed at her. They were the same age, and
they had once been lovers. What if the two people to whom
she was the closest were slipping back into their old relationship?

One of the assistants broke up their tête-à-tête by telling
Dash he had a phone call. Liz walked over to her, and
Honey noticed that her lipstick was smeared slightly at one
corner. She looked away.

"Have you seen that boutique catalogue I put in your
dressing room this morning?" Liz asked as she picked up a
bottle of mineral water. "They have the most marvelous
belts."

Liz was the best female friend she had, and Honey determinedly repressed her jealousy. "I wish you'd stop tempting me. You're turning me into a shopoholic."

"Nonsense. You're just making up for lost time." Liz took a drink, holding the neck of the bottle so gracefully she might have been sipping from Baccarat.

"Clothes are starting to be an obsession," Honey sighed. "For months I've been reading every fashion magazine I can get my hands on. Last night I fell asleep dreaming about that new coral silk I bought." She grinned ruefully. "I read *Ms.* magazine, and I know that femininity is a trap, but I can't seem to help myself."

"You're just trying to find some balance."

"Balance! This is the most unbalanced thing I've ever done. For the first time in my life, I can't respect myself."

"Honey, regardless of the body parts you were born with, you grew up more as a boy than a girl. Now you're simply trying to discover yourself as a woman. Sooner or later you'll be able to bring all the different parts of yourself together. You're just not ready yet. And until you are . . ." She lifted the mineral water bottle in a toast. "Shop till you drop." With a grin, she set off for her dressing room.

Honey picked up her script and stuffed it in a tote bag silk-screened with splashy red poppies. She knew her obsession with her physical appearance was because of Dash, but her attempts to make him look at her as a woman were failing dismally. If anything, he had become more paternal, huffing and puffing and frowning at everything she did. No matter how hard she tried, she couldn't seem to please him. And playing Janie Jones five days a week didn't help. The role that had once fit so comfortably had begun to chafe.

She turned to leave the soundstage just as a pair of fingers jabbed her ribs from behind. "Damn it, Todd!"

"Hey, gorgeous. You want to run some lines with me?"

Honey glared at Todd Myers, the sixteen-year-old actor who was playing Janie's new boyfriend, Robert. He had been chosen for his well-scrubbed, all-American looks— brown eyes and hair, round cheeks, small build so he didn't overpower her. Beneath all that apple pie, however, he was an egotistical brat. Still, in light of her own past behavior problems, she hadn't quite had the heart to rip into him.

"I wasn't planning on eating lunch today. I've got a psych paper due, and I'm going to my dressing room to finish it."

"I don't see why anybody who's making as much money as you should be wasting your time with college."

"Just a correspondence course. I've been taking them on and off ever since I finished high school. I like to learn things. It wouldn't hurt you to spend a little more time with the books."

"You sound like my old lady," he said with disgust.

"You should listen to her."

"Yeah, sure." He stuck out his arms and wiggled his hips. "So, are you ready for our big love scene this afternoon?"

"It's not a love scene. It's just a kiss. And I swear to God, Todd, if you try to French me again—" She let her threat hang in the air.

"I won't French you if you promise to go out with me this weekend. One of my friends is having a Christmas party. There'll be plenty of grass and maybe even some coke. Have you ever had a coco-puff? You take a cigarette and sprinkle it with—"

"I don't do drugs, and I'm not going out with you."

"You're still stuck on that asshole Eric Dillon, aren't you? I heard all about the way you used to hang around him. I'll bet you cry yourself to sleep every night now that he's married and he knocked up his old lady"

She gave him a silky smile. "Has anybody ever told you that you're a wonderful argument for mercy killing?"

His face grew sulky. "You should be nice to me, Honey. Otherwise I might be tempted to tell everybody the birthday you're going to celebrate tomorrow is your eighteenth instead of your seventeenth like everybody thinks."

"It's my twentieth, Todd."

"Yeah, right," he scoffed.

She gave up. Ross's lie had become so commonly accepted that few people believed the truth, not even when she flashed her driver's license. For the past six months, her face had been plastered on the covers of half the teen magazines in the country celebrating the fact that Janie had turned fifteen. The event was receiving nearly as much press as Michael Jackson's new *Thriller* album.

Leaving Todd behind, she headed back to her dressing room to work on her psych paper. Two of the women writers broke up a whispered conversation as she came into view and then gave her mischievous grins. At one time she would have suspected that they were plotting against her, but now she knew it was more likely that they were part of the birthday surprise the cast and crew were planning for her. She chatted with them for a few minutes, and as she left, she remembered those early days when the writers had seemed like gods to her. That had ended when she and Dash had become friends.

Unlike her family, the cast and crew wouldn't forget her birthday. Last year they had surprised her with a leather-bound set of all the scripts of *The Dash Coogan Show*. She had been deeply touched, but she couldn't help wishing her family would remember the occasion just once. Even if they only gave her a card, she would appreciate the gesture.

Dash came stalking around the corner and she saw that he looked upset.

"What's wrong?"

"Wanda just called me. She always manages to get me going."

She had imagined that when people got divorced they would get out of each other's lives, but Dash always seemed to be having conversations with his first ex-wife. Of course, they had children together, and she supposed that made a difference, but since their son was twenty-four and their daughter twenty-two, she couldn't imagine what they had left to talk about. In general, she tried not to think about his kids, especially since both of them were older than she was.

"Didn't you tell me that Wanda had remarried?"

"A long time ago. A man named Edward Ridgeway. Not Ed, mind you. Edward."

"Why does she bother you so much?"

"Revenge, I guess. She still doesn't feel like she's settled old scores. She called to tell me that Josh is getting married the day after Christmas."

"That's only three weeks away."

"Nice of her to let me know my son's getting married, isn't it? Now I have to go to Tulsa for the wedding." He looked grim.

"You don't want him to get married?"

"He's twenty-four. I guess that's up to him, and anything that'll cut him loose from Wanda's apron strings is probably a good thing. I just hate the idea of letting her lead me around by the nose for two days. She was a sweet little thing when I married her, but over the years she's turned into a barracuda. Not that I should blame her. All that tomcattin' of mine hurt her pretty bad."

He began to walk away, and then slowly turned back. She could see that he had something on his mind, and she regarded him quizzically. He shoved his hand in his pocket.

"Honey, you wouldn't want to— Never mind. Bad idea."

"What?"

"Nothing, I was just—" He shifted his weight. "I was thinking about asking if you wanted to go to Tulsa with me for the wedding. Sort of act like a buffer. But I don't expect you'd want to leave your family so close to Christmas."

She thought of Chantal, who was growing plump and lazy on junk food and game shows right along with her idiotic stepfather, Buck. And of Gordon, who still hadn't picked up a paintbrush. She thought of Sophie, who spent more time in bed than out of it and refused to follow any of the doctor's orders. The idea of getting away from all that and being with Dash would be the best Christmas present she could have.

"I'd love to go with you, Dash. It'd do me good to get away for a while."

That evening she pulled down the sloping drive into the garage of their house in Pasadena. It was dark as she let herself in through the mudroom off the garage. She flicked the light switch, but the bulb seemed to be burned out, and she fumbled with the door leading into the kitchen. When she opened it, she was startled to see the glow of candlelight.

"Happy birthday!"

"Happy birthday, Honey!"

Flabbergasted, she saw all of her family standing in a half circle around the kitchen table. Sophie had dragged herself out of bed, Buck had thrown a sports shirt on over his undershirt, Chantal had poured the extra twenty pounds she'd gained into a pair of crimson slacks, and, reflected in the lenses of Gordon's new wire-rimmed spectacles, were the flames of twenty pastel candles sitting on top of a birthday cake.

They hadn't forgotten. They had finally remembered her birthday. Tears stung her eyes and she felt years of stored resentment melting inside her.

"Oh, my . . . It's—" Her words grew choked. "It's beautiful."

All of them laughed and even Sophie smiled, because the cake wasn't beautiful at all. Three layers tall, it was lopsided and unevenly coated with the ugliest shade of blue frosting Honey had ever seen. But the fact that they had done this for her, baked the cake themselves, made it the most precious gift she had ever received.

"I can't—I can't believe you did this." She struggled not to cry.

"Well, of course we did it," Chantal said. "It's your birthday, isn't it?"

They were off by one day, but that was meaningless. She was filled with love, joy, and an aching sense of gratitude.

Gordon gestured toward the cake. "I baked it, Honey. Me, myself, and I."

"I helped," Chantal threw in.

"We all helped," Buck said, scratching his belly like a beardless Santa Claus. "Except for Sophie."

"I picked out the icing color," Sophie said, looking hurt.

Their faces glimmered before her, soft, beautiful, and beloved in the golden light of the flickering candles. She forgave them all their foibles and knew that she was right to have stuck by them. They were her family. She was part of them and they were part of her, and every one of them was precious.

Gordon grinned like a schoolboy with a secret. Sophie's fat cheeks dented in a distracted smile, and Chantal's blue eyes glowed in the candlelight. Embarrassed by the depth of her emotions, Honey dabbed self-consciously at her cheeks.

"All of you— I—" She tried to tell them what was in her heart, but the feelings ran too strong and her throat constricted.

"Come on, Honey. Cut the cake!"

"Cut it, Honey. We're all hungry."

"It sure is going to taste good."

She laughed as Buck thrust a large knife into her hand and pushed her toward the cake. "Blow out the candles."

"Happy birthday to you, happy birthday to you . . ."

She blew out the candles, laughing through her tears. Once again, she tried to find the words that would express what this meant to her.

"I'm so happy . . . I—"

"Cut straight down through the middle," Gordon said, directing her hand. "I don't want you to ruin my artwork."

A tear dripped off her chin as she pointed the knife into the center. "This is wonderful. I'm so—"

The cake exploded.

Screams of laughter erupted as chunks of chocolate flew everywhere. Cake shot up into Honey's face, clots of blue icing stuck to her skin and clung to her clothes. Bits and pieces splattered against the wall and dropped to the floor.

They had all drawn back from the table in a single, unified motion just as she had cut into the center, and they were untouched. Only she had been hit.

Buck clutched his stomach. Their laughter grew louder. Even Sophie had joined in.

"Did you see her face?"

"We fooled you," Chantal cried. "It was all Gordon's idea. Gordon, you're so smart!"

"I told you it would work!" Gordon hooted. "I told you! Look at her hair!"

Chantal clapped her hands as she described her husband's cleverness. "Gordon cut a hole in the middle of the cake, and then he stuffed it with this big balloon blown up real full of air. We broke three of them trying to get it just right. Then we iced the whole thing so you couldn't tell, and when your knife poked through the balloon—"

Honey's chest heaved and she stumbled backward, staring at them. They were gathered around the ruined feast like a pack of jackals who had gorged on a banquet of malice. Their spitefulness choked her. She would leave them, pack her suitcase and never see them again.

"Uh-oh, she's mad," Gordon taunted. "She's going to be a bad sport, just like always."

"You're not going to be a bad sport, are you, Honey?" Chantal stuck out her lip. "We've had so much fun. You're not going to spoil it."

"Darn," Buck said. "We should of knowed."

"No," she said, her voice a tight, painful whisper. "I'm not going to be a bad sport. It—it was a great joke. Really. I'd—I'd better get cleaned up."

Turning her back on them, she fled through the hallway into the back wing of the house, clots of cake and icing dropping off her pretty silk blouse and linen slacks. The pain inside her made it hard to breath. She was going to move away. She would leave them and never come back. She would—

A choking sound slipped from her. And then what? Who would take their places? Not Dash. She had been building dream castles where he was concerned. He could have any woman he wanted, so why would he take her? This family was all she had.

The clattering began in her brain. The lonely clickety-clickety clattering of a ghost roller-coaster car creaking up a wooden incline. She squeezed her eyes shut trying to block out a painful, persistent voice that told her all of her success, all of her money, all the pretty clothes in the world wouldn't disguise the fundamental unlovableness that lived at her core.

Black Thunder's coaster car creaked up the lift hill. But no matter how hard she tried to imagine it, she couldn't make it shoot over the top.

15

Honey and Dash flew into Tulsa the day after Christmas for his son's wedding. They barely spoke to each other on the flight, and she suspected he regretted inviting her. She should have told him she couldn't come, but she had followed him just as she always did, ready to receive whatever crumbs of affection he tossed in her direction.

As she got off the plane, she told herself that anything was better than spending the rest of the holiday with her family. Even the birthday party the cast and crew had given her three weeks ago hadn't dulled the memory of what had happened. Since then, she had spent most of her time at home sequestered in her bedroom.

The Tulsa airport was crowded with holiday travelers. Inevitably, many of them recognized Dash, who was unmistakable with his tall stature, his Stetson, and an aged shearling jacket. She walked anonymously at his side. With her eyes shielded by large sunglasses and hair tumbling in sexy disarray, no one in the crowd recognized her as the tomboy Janie Jones.

She had chosen her clothes defiantly, not only because they were so unlike Janie's outfits but because she knew how much he would dislike them. A soft, golden-brown oversized sweater slipped off one shoulder. She wore it with a pair of slim-cut black leather pants, a belt of gold links, matching gold hoop earrings, and little black flats with a bronze diamond appliquéd over the vamp. A fur jacket was draped over her arm, completing an ensemble that looked both sexy and expensive.

Dash, predictably, had frowned when he met her at LAX. "I don't see why you had to wear something like that. Those pants are too damn tight."

"Sorry, Daddy," she had mocked him.

"I'm not your father!"

"Then stop acting like one."

He had given her an angry glare and looked away.

Now the holiday travelers gathered around him. "We love your show, Mr. Coogan."

"Could I have your autograph for my daughter? She wants to be an actress someday. Of course she's only eight, but—"

"We sure like that Janie. Is she a dickens in real life, too?"

Dash glanced over his shoulder at Honey, who had moved off to the side and was attracting her own share of attention from several of the men, although not because of her celebrity. "She's a dickens, all right."

Later, as they got into the rental car, he began to scold her again. "I don't know why you couldn't have worn something respectable. Everybody was looking at you like you were—I don't know."

"Like I was your Playmate of the Month?"

He threw the Lincoln into gear and refused to respond.

The wedding was scheduled for seven that evening. They checked in at the same hotel where the reception was being held. Honey discovered that Dash had booked them separate rooms on different floors, as if closer accommodations would contaminate him. After getting rid of their luggage, they headed for Wanda Ridgeway's house.

Thoroughbred Acres was one of Tulsa's newer upscale housing developments. As they drove through the entrance pillars, Honey noticed that all the streets were named after famous racehorses. The Ridgeway house, a large colonial, sat on Seattle Slew Way. Although it was only noon, the Christmas lights surrounding the porch were lit, and milk cans decorated with sprigs of greenery sat in a cluster beside the front door. As Honey followed Dash up the walk, she recalled what she knew about him and his first wife.

He and Wanda had met when the rodeo Dash was riding in had come to the small Oklahoma town where she lived. By the time he had left, she was pregnant, a fact he didn't find out about until three months later when she tracked him down in Tulsa. He was nineteen, she eighteen.

According to Dash, Wanda was the sort of woman who wanted to stay in one place all her life and organize charitable fund-raisers. From the beginning she had hated his nomadic life-style, and the marriage was over even before their second child was born. She had never forgiven Dash, not for his wandering eye or for throwing her life off track.

Her enmity was carefully concealed, however, as she admitted Dash and Honey into the two-story foyer and greeted her ex-husband with a hug. "Randy, darlin', I'm so glad to see you."

She was plump and pretty, a bit overdressed in ruffled silk. Her hair was arranged in the sprayed blond helmet so comfortable on the heads of well-to-do women in the Southwest, and her fingers flashed with diamonds. The Ridgeway Christmas tree stood directly behind her, decorated entirely with wooden hearts, burlap bows, and miniature flour sacks.

"Josh said you wouldn't show up, and you know how Meredith is with all that prayin', but I told him his daddy wouldn't miss his wedding, not for anything. And his bride, Cynthia, is just the sweetest thing. Josh! Meredith! Your daddy's here. Yoo-hoo! Oh, damn, Meredith's still at her Bible study and Josh had to make a last-minute trip to the travel agent."

She turned to Honey. "Now who's this? You didn't get married again, did you?"

But unlike the fans at the airport, Wanda had the eyes of a hawk, and even before Honey had slipped off her sunglasses, she recognized her ex-husband's traveling companion. Her lips thinned ever so slightly. "Well, if it isn't your sweet little costar. What a surprise. And aren't you the dearest little thang. Edward, you'll never guess who's here? Ed-*ward!*"

A middle-aged man with thinning hair, gentle eyes, and a slight paunch appeared in the foyer from the back of the house. "Well, hello there, Dash. I had the fan on in the bathroom and didn't hear you come in."

"Edward, look who Randy brought with him. Little Honey Jane Moon, one of your favorite TV people next to J.

R. Ewing and *Three's Company*. Isn't she just cute as a baby's *be*-hind?"

"Hello, Miss Moon, and welcome. Well, now, this is an honor. Yes it is. My, you sure do look grown-up in real life." His glance was admiring but not lecherous, and Honey decided she liked Edward, despite the fact that his red bow tie was embedded with blinking green lights.

After their coats and Dash's Stetson had been disposed of in a closet lined with peg hooks and organizer shelves, Wanda led them into a cavernous family room complete with every variety of painted wooden goose, straw wreath, and wicker basket. The room smelled of clove-scented potpourri bubbling away in ceramic pots printed with fat red hearts.

Wanda pointed toward a bar at one end decorated with pewter tankards and golf prints. "Get Randy a drink, Edward. And there's some soda pop in the refrig for Honey."

"If you don't mind, I'd rather have wine," Honey said, deciding she'd better assert herself before Wanda bulldozed her six feet under.

Dash frowned at her. "A Seven-Up'd be fine for me." He sank down onto a couch strewn with ruffled red-checked gingham pillows. Honey took the seat next to him and contemplated the character of a woman who would offer liquor to a recovered alcoholic.

The telephone rang. Wanda bustled off to answer it, and Edward was making enough noise with an ice-cube tray for Honey to whisper to Dash without being overheard.

"I don't know how you ever had the nerve to say that I talk more than any of your ex-wives. Wanda could set a land-speed record."

For the first time that day, he smiled at her. "Wanda settles down after a while. You never do."

Wanda had barely returned to the room before a young woman appeared in the doorway. She was thin and, at first glance, rather plain, with auburn hair and a wan complexion. Closer inspection, however, revealed fine, regular features that would have been attractive if they had been enhanced with a few basic cosmetics. When she saw Dash sitting on the couch, her pale lips drew up in a smile and she became almost pretty.

"Daddy?"

Dash had jumped up the moment he saw her, and he met her in the center of the room, where she disappeared into his arms like a rabbit diving into a hole. "Hi, there, pumpkin. How's my girl?"

As Honey watched them together, the ache of familiar pain spread through her. Despite separations and divorces, these people were still a family, and they had bonds that nothing could ever break.

"Praise the Lord," she said softly. "I knew He would bring you here today."

"A seven-forty-seven brought me here, Merry."

"No, Daddy. Our Lord did." An expression of intense certainty settled over her, and Honey watched curiously to see how Dash would respond.

He chose to retreat. "Meredith, I want you to meet somebody special. This is Honey Jane Moon, my costar on the show."

Meredith turned. As she spotted Honey, she looked as if her father had just kicked in her rabbit's hutch. Her pale lips narrowed until they almost disappeared, and her gray eyes grew opaque with hostility. Honey felt fried, as if Meredith had hit her with a lethal dose of electrical current.

"Miss Moon. The Lord be with you."

"Thank you," Honey replied. "You, too."

Wanda tossed down a Jack Daniels in one gulp. "No more Jesus stuff, Meredith. You could take the fun out of an orgy."

"Mother!"

Dash chuckled. Wanda looked over at him and smiled. For a few seconds the hostilities fell away and Honey had a brief glimpse of what it must have been like for them when they were young.

She was glad to see the moment fade as Wanda began outlining the afternoon's schedule. Relatives would be arriving any minute, she told them. The caterers had set up a buffet table in the dining room and she hoped no one was allergic to shellfish. Everybody needed to be at the church by six-thirty sharp. The dinner-reception at the hotel was dressy and she hoped dear little Honey had brought something special to wear.

Dear little Honey excused herself to use the powder room. A conch shell full of pastel soap conch shells sat on the basin along with another bubbling container of potpourri. The room smelled like pumpkin pie served with lilacs. When she emerged, Wanda had gone to the dining room to badger the caterer and the groom had returned.

Although Meredith Coogan bore little resemblance to her father, her twenty-four-year old brother Josh looked like a blurred and softened version of Dash, one in which all of the older man's angular lines and hard planes had been tamed and weakened. Josh acknowledged the introduction to Honey and was making a polite inquiry about their trip when Wanda returned to the room and interrupted.

"Did Josh tell you about his new job with Fagan Can?"

"No, I don't believe he did," Dash replied.

"He's going to be a supervisor in their accounting department. Tell your father all about it, Josh. Tell him what an important man you're going to be."

"I don't think I'll be all that important, sir. But it's steady work and Fagan is a well-established firm."

Wanda gestured toward him with a glass of bourbon. "Tell your father what a nice office they're giving you."

"It's very nice, sir."

"On the *corner* of the third floor," Wanda reported.

"The corner?" Dash tried to look suitably impressed. "Well, now."

"Two windows." She held up her fingers in case Dash couldn't count.

"Two. Isn't that something."

The doorbell rang, and Wanda once again excused herself. Dash and Josh regarded each other uncomfortably, each at a loss for anything more to say.

Honey stepped in to ease the tension. "Too bad you didn't have Josh working for you in your wild days, Dash. Maybe he would have kept the scum suckers away."

Dash smiled.

Josh looked puzzled. "Scum suckers?"

"She's referring to my well-known problems with the IRS," Dash offered.

Josh's forehead crumpled in an earnest furrow. "You shouldn't joke about the IRS, sir. Not with everything you've been through. Tax problems aren't a laughing matter."

Dash glanced longingly toward the bar.

Wanda and Edward's relatives began to arrive until the house was filled with a dozen more people. Honey's head had started to ache, and she tried to find sanctuary next to a silk ficus tree potted in a milk bucket. A brief lull fell over the room only to be broken by Meredith's small, sincere voice.

"I'm holding a prayer meeting in the living room at six o'clock. I'd like everyone to attend."

Wanda threw up her hands. "Don't be ridiculous, Meredith. I have a million things to do, and I certainly can't waste time praying."

One of the aunts giggled nervously. "I'm sorry, Meredith, but it's going to take me forever to do my hair."

Others chipped in with their excuses, obviously having already experienced one of Meredith's prayer sessions.

Dash took a few steps toward the door. "Honey and I have to go to the hotel to change, so it'll be easier if we just meet you all at the church."

Meredith looked crestfallen, and perhaps because Honey had been feeling so miserable herself, she experienced a moment's sympathy.

"The hotel's not that far away, Dash. We can stop here first."

Dash gave her his steeliest glare.

Meredith gazed at Honey, resentment oozing from every pore. "That's a wonderful idea," she said stiffly.

Dash, however, didn't think it was a wonderful idea at all, and as they drove to the hotel he told Honey he had no intention of going to Meredith's prayer meeting. "I love my daughter, but she's crazy when it comes to religion."

"Then I'll go by myself," she retorted stubbornly.

"Don't say I didn't warn you."

Honey dressed for the wedding in the gown that she had once considered wearing to the ranch, a delicately beaded silvery-blue sheath the exact color of her eyes. She fluffed her hair and clipped crystal clusters to her ears, but even though the mirror told her that she looked almost beautiful, she wasn't reassured. When Dash saw her, he would find something to criticize. The neck would be too low, the skirt too tight, her jewelry too flashy.

Dash had made arrangements to hitch a ride to the church with one of Josh's ushers, so she returned to the house by herself, hoping she wouldn't regret the impulse that had led her to accept Meredith's invitation. Meredith's face fell when she realized that Honey had come alone.

"Sorry," Honey said. "I guess your father isn't much for prayer meetings."

Honey could almost see Meredith's internal struggle as she tried to reconcile her obvious dislike of Honey with her need to evangelize. She wasn't too surprised when evangelism won.

Meredith led her into a living room that looked as it had just come out of plastic wrappers and gestured toward the velour sofa. As they took seats at opposite ends, Honey experienced an almost irresistible urge to delve into her handbag for lipstick and mascara. Meredith's lack of cosmetics combined with her dowdy polyester print dress made her much homelier than she needed to be. Honey began to understand what Liz Castleberry had gone through with her.

Meredith spoke stiffly. "Are you saved, Miss Moon?"

Honey had always rather enjoyed theological discussions and she gave the question serious consideration. "That's not an easy question to answer. And please call me Honey."

"Have you given yourself to the Lord?"

She remembered that long-ago spring when she had prayed to Walt Disney. "I suppose it depends. I consider myself a spiritual person, Meredith, but my theology isn't all that orthodox. I guess I'm a searcher."

"Doubts come from the devil," Meredith said harshly. "If you live in faith, there's no need to question."

"I have to question. It's my nature."

"Then you'll go to hell."

"I don't want to offend you, Meredith, but I don't think anyone has the right to pass judgment on somebody else's salvation."

But Meredith refused to back down, and Honey gave up all hope of a stimulating discussion. For the next half hour, Meredith quoted scripture and prayed over her. Honey's headache returned, but after a while, everything about Meredith softened. She prayed fervently, her face infused with joy, a young woman blissed out on Jesus.

"Smile, Randy. Everybody's watching us, dammit."

"They want to see if I'm gonna body-slam you to the dance floor."

The cloying scent of Wanda's hair spray was making Dash's stomach go crazy. He sidestepped to avoid another couple and told himself he didn't need a drink.

Wanda winced. "You stepped on my goddamn foot. Watch yourself, will you? God, you're a terrible dancer."

"You're the one who wanted to put on a show. You had to let all your friends see how well you've managed your ex-husband. Got him dancing with you, eating right out of your hand like a tame little puppy dog."

The stiff social smile never left her face. "I hate it when you're like this. At your own son's wedding. You are so mean, Randy Coogan. You've always been a mean, cold-hearted, lying, cheating bastard."

"You're never going to let it go, are you? We've been divorced for nearly twenty years, but you still want my last drop of blood."

"That's the only thing besides tits all your ex-wives have in common."

Honey swept past with Josh's best man, and the wedding photographer snapped her picture. Dash figured it would show up in one of the tabloids sooner or later. Several times during the fall photographers had caught her when she looked a lot older than seventeen. Instead of questioning her age, they ran the photos with captions like "Child star growing up too fast" or "Honey Jane Moon out past her bedtime."

Dash's jaw tightened. For somebody who didn't know how to dance, Honey had been doing a good job of it for almost four hours. And that wasn't all she was doing. More than a few times, he'd seen her reaching for a champagne glass.

All evening there had been something wild about her that he didn't like—the way she tossed her head, the throaty laughter that seemed to be coming from a woman instead of a kid. He tried to tell himself that he was just imagining the way all the men were looking at her. After all, she wasn't the most beautiful woman there, not even in that sparkly blue dress that fit too damn tight over her butt. She was cute, no doubt about it, but she was too little and baby-faced to be beautiful. He liked women who looked like women. Hell, there were lots of women who were prettier than Honey.

Still, he couldn't deny that there was something about her that might attract a certain type of man. The type who might like baby-faced little girls more than twenty years too young for them.

A voice that hadn't bothered him since the night of Liz's party when he'd caught Honey kissing that boy began to whisper to him. *A drink will make you forget about her. You don't need her when you can have me.* It was the siren's voice, the deceiving voice all drunks carry around inside them. *I can make you feel better. I can take away the pain.*

Wanda's words jabbed at him like her mascara-spiked eyelashes. "I don't know how you could bring her here and humiliate your own flesh and blood. Everybody's acting like Honey's your real daughter. Poor Meredith's been on the verge of tears all night."

Wanda called out a cheery greeting to one of the guests and then lowered her voice to a vindictive hiss. "I suppose I should be grateful that the people here don't know you as well as I do. I can see what's going on in your mind, and it makes me sick. How can you look at yourself in the mirror? She's younger than your own daughter."

He caught the enticing scent of the bourbon she had been drinking cutting through her hair spray, and his mouth went dry. "There's nothing going on in my mind—not like you mean—so just you get your own mind out of the gutter."

Her hand clamped his, trying to hurt. "Don't bullshit me, Randy. You might be able to fool everybody else here, but you can't fool me. I've seen the way you look at her when you think nobody's watching. And I'll tell you this, mister. It curdles my stomach. They're all cooing about how cute she is and how sweet it is that you act like father and daughter in real life. But that's not the way it is between you two at all."

"Now that's where you're wrong," he sneered. "It's just like that between us. Exactly. I've practically been raising that girl."

"Bullshit," she hissed through her frozen smile. "You make my skin crawl."

He'd had all he could take. He spotted Edward approaching with the bride in his arms and stepped in front of them. "The night's almost over, Edward, and I haven't had a chance to dance with my new daughter-in-law."

Wanda glared at him, but there were too many people around for her to dig in. The women changed places. Josh's new wife, Cynthia, was a pretty, vivacious blonde with blue eyes and big teeth. As he drew her close, he caught the scent of a new brand of hair spray.

"Did Josh tell you about his job, Father Coogan?" she asked as they took their first steps.

He winced at her form of address. "Why, yes. He did mention it." The netting on her headpiece poked dangerously near his eye, and he drew back his head. He felt as if he had been at the mercy of women with sharp points and razor edges all night. Honey whipped by in a soft cloud of champagne bubbles, laughing and dancing for all she was worth.

Forget about her, the siren whispered. *Let me soothe you. I'm smooth and soft, and I go down easy.*

". . . Fagan Can is an important company, but you know

Josh. Sometimes he needs a little push, so I told him when he was interviewing, I said, 'Now, Josh, you go in there and you look those men right in the eye and let them know you mean business.'" She winked. "The company's giving him a corner office."

"So I understand."

"An office with"—she lowered her voice to a stage whisper—"*two* windows."

The dance was endless. She chattered on about corner offices, china patterns, and tennis lessons. The ballad finally drew to a close, and she bustled off to claim her new husband. Josh sprang to her side, gazing at her earnestly to make certain he hadn't committed some unknown offense.

Congratulations, son, Dash thought sadly. *You managed to marry your mother, after all.*

He had to have a drink.

One of Cynthia's bridesmaids passed by and he grabbed her. She giggled at the honor of dancing with the legendary Dash Coogan, but he barely noticed because the siren's voice had grown more insistent, and he could feel all his years of sobriety slipping away.

Come to me, lover. I'm all the woman you need. I'll purr and I'll coo and I'll make you forget about Honey.

Honey swept by and shot him a hostile glare. Raucous, drunken laughter swirled around him, and the clatter of ice cubes was amplified in his head until it formed a crazed percussion to the music.

He hated to dance, but he moved from one bridesmaid to the next, afraid that if he stopped, the siren would claim him. The evening groaned on, and the bride and groom left. Before long, the guests began to depart. The seductive smell of liquor filled his lungs—wine, scotch, and whiskey overpowering the scents of food and flowers.

Just have one, the siren whispered. *One won't hurt.*

As the band finished its final set, the voice of the siren had grown so loud he wanted to clamp his hands over his ears. If he left the dance floor, he knew he would be lost.

"We haven't had a chance to talk, Daddy. Let's go talk."

He jumped as Meredith appeared from nowhere. His tongue felt cumbersome, and he was afraid she would notice he was sweating.

"We—we haven't danced, Merry. The evening's almost over and I haven't danced with my best girl."

She looked at him strangely. "The band's packing up. Besides, I told you earlier, Daddy. I don't believe in dancing."

"I forgot."

He had no choice but to follow her to one of the empty tables near the dance floor. Abandoned wineglasses and tumblers with amber residues floating in their bottoms sat on the linen tablecloths. They multiplied in front of his eyes until there seemed to be a battalion of them spread before him, like enemy soldiers on the march.

She pulled her skirt down over her knees as she took the seat next to him. "Stay at the house tonight, Daddy. You can have my room. Please. I hardly ever get to see you."

His fingertips brushed against a glass with an inch of precious watered-down liquor in the bottom. "I—I don't think that's a good idea. Your mama and I don't do too well when we're cooped up together."

"I'll keep her away from you. I promise."

"Not this time."

Pick me up, lover. Just one little sip and you'll forget all about her.

Her voice hardened. "It's Honey, isn't it? You've got plenty of time to spend with her, but not with me. You think she's perfect—a chip right off the old block. She talks like you. She even drinks like you. It's too bad she's not your daughter instead of me."

The glass burned his fingers. "Don't be childish. This doesn't have anything to do with Honey."

"Then spend some time with me tomorrow morning."

The world was reduced to the shimmering liquid in the glass before him and the agonizing need that pounded in his skull. "I'd love to spend time with you, Merry. I just don't want to do it praying."

Her voice broke. "You have to accept the Lord, Daddy, if you're going to have life eternal. I pray for you all the time. I tremble for you, Daddy. I don't want you to end up in hell."

"Hell's relative," he said harshly.

Gotcha!

His fingers clamped around the glass. It fit into his palm like a million old memories. Sweat broke out on his forehead as the siren gobbled him up. He couldn't stop himself, and he raised his head, ready to lift the tumbler to his lips, but before it got there, he spotted Honey on the other side of the nearly deserted room.

She was standing by the windows with a young stud smeared all over her like baby oil. His beautiful little Honey with the sassy mouth and big heart wasn't doing one thing to get away from him, just smearing herself closer and rubbing against him.

Meredith began to pray.

He shot up from the chair, knocking over the glass.

"Daddy!"

He barely heard her as he stalked across the room. The walls spun around him. His shirt clung to his chest beneath his jacket.

Come back! the siren wailed. *Don't go to her! I'm the one who'll never leave you! Only me!*

When he reached Honey's side, he didn't ask permission or beg anyone's pardon. With one hard yank, he pulled her away from the slimy bastard who was trying to dry-hump her right there in front of everybody and hauled her toward the door.

She made a small gasp, but he didn't give a shit if he hurt her. He didn't give a shit about anything except getting Honey away and putting an end to the jealousy that was eating him up.

"Dash, what's—"

"Shut up. You're acting like a goddamn whore."

She looked stunned, and then her eyes narrowed. "You bastard."

He wanted to whip the back of his hand right across her snotty little mouth. The silver chain on her evening purse

Seconds ticked by, and then an expression of disgust crossed his face. In two steps he reached the bottom of the bed and flung the bottle into the trash can that sat nearby with such force that the container fell to its side. A small amount of champagne frothed onto the carpet.

He turned back to her as she stood in the center of the mattress. His features were harsh, impossible to read. She began to walk awkwardly away from him until she reached the headboard. She leaned against the wall for balance, a position that thrust her breasts slightly forward.

He went very still. She watched as his eyes slid down over her. Seconds slipped by, one giving way to another. The rush of blood in her ears grew louder. Following his gaze, she saw that her dress had ridden far up on her thighs. A dangerous excitement, stronger than fear, took hold of her. Placing the palms of her hands flat on the wall behind her, she angled her hips forward more sharply so that her dress rode higher.

"Stop it," he said hoarsely.

The wildness that had been skimming around her all evening took possession. She parted her thighs. "What's the matter, cowboy?" she said huskily. "Can't you take a little heat?"

"You don't have any idea what you're doing."

"Poor Daddy," she said, her voice soft and mocking.

"Don't call me that," he said harshly.

She pushed her spine away from the wall and began walking down the length of the bed toward him, her stockinged feet sinking into the mattress. The champagne fired her, giving her courage and daring and igniting a primitive instinct. She began a mocking croon to him, taunting him with a relationship that didn't exist, prodding him so that he would be forced to acknowledge that he was hiding behind a lie.

"Oh, Daddy mine. Sweet Daddy . . ."

"I'm not your daddy!" he burst out.

"Are you sure?"

"Don't—"

"Are you sure you're not my daddy?"

"I won't—"

"Be sure, Dash. Please."

He stood frozen before her, his head below hers for once. Her body moved in awkward rhythm to the unsteady surface beneath her feet. He didn't move as she leaned forward to wrap her arms around his neck.

"I'm sure," she said.

When he didn't reply, she took his mouth, kissing him hungrily, using her tongue and her teeth to have all of him. She drew his lips between hers, invading him as if she were the woman of experience and he the novice.

He was like ice and steel. Frozen. Unyielding.

She didn't stop. If they had just this one moment of truth between them, she would wring it dry and make it last forever. The only barriers that separated them were the ones he had erected in his mind. She stroked deep into his mouth.

A groan erupted from the back of his throat and his hand tangled in her hair. He drew her down until she fell against him and he was taking all her weight. His mouth opened, and he overpowered her.

His kiss was rough and deep, full of dark need. She wanted to drown in it. She wanted all of her body to fit through his mouth so she could hide herself away inside him. At the same time she wanted to grow in size and strength until she could overpower him and force him to love her as she loved him.

And then she felt him shudder. With an awful hiss, he drew his head back. "What do you think you're doing?"

She collapsed to her knees on the bed. Reaching out, she wrapped her arms around his hips and crushed her cheek against the strong, flat muscles of his abdomen. "Exactly what I want to do."

He grabbed her shoulders, pushing her away. "That's enough! You've gone far enough, little girl."

She leaned back on her heels. Speaking softly, she said, "I'm not a little girl."

"You're twenty years old," he said harshly. "You're a kid."

"Liar," she whispered.

His eyes grew dark with pain, but she had no pity. This was her night. Probably the only night she would have. Without questioning what she was about to do, she slipped her hands to the back of her neck and reached beneath her hair for the tiny hook and eye at the top of her gown. When it was free, she tugged on the zipper. It made a small hiss in the quiet of the room, and the dress fell from her shoulders.

She dropped her feet over the side of the bed and stood. The dress slipped off her hips to the floor, leaving her in a lacy bra, shimmery silver stockings, and ice-blue tap pants.

His voice was hoarse. "You're drunk. You don't even know what you're asking for."

"Yes, I do."

"You're hot, and you want a man. It doesn't make any difference which one."

"That's not true. Kiss me again."

"No more kisses, Jane Marie."

"You're pathetic," she retorted, refusing to let him hide behind a make-believe relationship.

"I'm not—"

She caught his strong wrist and drew his hand to her breast, pressing it over the fullness. "Can you feel my heart pound, Dash?" She rubbed the palm back and forth so that her nipple hardened beneath the silky fabric. "Can you feel it?"

"Honey . . ."

She clasped his large hand beneath both of her smaller ones and slid it down between her breasts, over her ribs. "Can you feel me?"

"Don't . . ."

She paused for only a moment before she slipped it over the silky fabric of the tap pants and then between her legs.

"Christ." He touched her, closed around her, then pulled back as if she had burned him.

"We're going to stop this right now, you hear me?" he roared. "You're drunk, and you're acting like a whore, and that's the end of it."

"You're scared, aren't you?" She lowered her eyes to the

front of his trousers. "I can see how much you want me, but you're too afraid to admit it."

"That's smut talking. You don't have the slightest idea what you're saying any more than you have any idea what sex is all about. I'm a hundred years older than you. You're just a kid."

"You're forty-three. That's hardly ancient. And you didn't kiss me like I was a kid."

"Not one more word. I mean it, Honey."

But she was in too much pain to stop. Setting her jaw, she attacked him.

"You're such a coward."

"That's enough."

"You don't have the guts to admit the way you feel about me."

"Stop it!"

"If I were a coward like you, I couldn't look at myself in the mirror."

"I said to stop!"

"I'd kill myself. I really would. I'd take a knife and stick it—"

"I'm warning you for the last time!"

"Coward!"

He grabbed her arm, nearly hauling her off her feet as he drew her up against him. His face twisted, and as his mouth drew near hers, he hissed, "Is this what you want?"

The kiss was hard and consuming, and she should have been frightened, but the fire inside her burned too hot.

Her responsiveness fanned his anger instead of cooling it. Drawing back from her, he stripped off his jacket. "All right. I'm done playing games with you. If that's what you want, I'm going to give it to you."

He whipped off his tie and tugged at the front of his shirt, sending the onyx studs flying. He was breathing heavily, and there was an air of desperation about him. "Don't you think for one minute that you can come crying to me afterward."

She watched as he stripped off his cummerbund and shirt. "I won't cry."

"That's only because you don't know a damn thing about

what's going to happen to you." He pitched a shoe across the room. "You don't know anything, do you?"

"Not—not from practical experience."

He yanked off his other shoe, throwing it against the bed stand with a curse. "Practical experience is the only thing that counts. And don't think I'm going to make it easy on you. That's not the way I do it. You wanted yourself a lover, little girl. Now you got yourself one big time."

All her muscles went weak, and her wildness was replaced by fear. But even fear couldn't make her flee the room, because she needed his love too badly.

"Dash?"

"What do you want?"

"Do you—Should I take off the rest of my clothes now?"

His hands froze on the waistband of his trousers. He sank down into the chair behind him. For a moment he did nothing. She held her breath, praying that the man she loved would reappear instead of this dangerous stranger who was trying so hard to frighten her and succeeding all too well. But as his mouth thinned, she knew he wasn't going to relent.

"Now that's a real good idea." He stretched out his legs and crossed them at the ankles as he inspected her. "You just take everything off nice and slow while I watch."

"Why are you making this so terrible?"

"What did you expect, little girl? Did you think it was going to be poetry and kisses? If you wanted that, you should have picked yourself a schoolboy. Somebody as new to the game as you are. Somebody with nice manners who'd take time with you and wouldn't hurt you like I'm going to."

"You won't hurt me."

"Now that's where you're wrong. I'm gonna hurt you, all right. Look at how much bigger I am. Get that underwear off. Or are you ready to admit you've made a mistake?"

She wanted to run from him, but she couldn't. No one had ever found her worthy of love, and if this was the only kind he could give her, then she would take what he had to offer. Her hands trembled as she reached behind her to the clasp of her bra.

He shot up from the chair, his face contorted with fury. "This is your last chance. Once that bra comes off, I'm gonna be all over you."

She opened the clasp awkwardly and let the straps slip from her shoulders.

A muscle near his cheekbone ticked. "When that bra comes off, it'll be too late. I mean it. You're gonna wish you'd never been born." The lacy garment dropped to the floor. "When that bra comes off, you're gonna wish—"

"Dash?" Her voice trembled, barely a whisper. "You're really scaring me. Could you—Could you just hold me for a minute first?"

All his bluster disappeared. His shoulders dropped, and his mouth contorted with raw pain. Groaning, he reached out and wrapped her in his arms. Her breasts nestled into the warmth of his bare chest like small birds.

His voice blew across her ear, soft and sad. "I'm so afraid for you, Honey."

"Don't be afraid," she whispered. "I know you can't love me back."

"Sweetheart—"

"It's all right. I love you enough for both of us. I love you so much."

"You only think you do."

"I do," she said fiercely. "More than I've ever loved anyone in my life. You're the only person who's ever really cared about me. Don't be mad at me."

"Sweetheart, I'm not mad at you. Don't you understand? I'm mad at myself."

"Why?"

"Because I'm no good for you."

"That's not true."

He sighed, a ragged sound. "You deserve so much better. I won't mean to hurt you, but before we're done, I'll break your heart."

"I don't care. Please, Dash. Please love me, just for tonight."

He stroked her hair for a very long time. Then his hands slid down over her bare back to her hips. "All right, sweetheart. I'll love you. God forgive me, but I can't help myself."

He kissed her forehead and cheeks. He stroked her until his own breathing grew labored, then laid claim to her mouth. His kiss was demanding, and she lost herself in its wonderful strength. The power of his arousal pressed against her belly as his hands moved up along her sides. Dropping his head, he kissed her young breasts and suckled on them until she was weak with need.

"I never knew," she gasped.

"I'll show you, sweetheart," he replied.

Laying her on the bed, he drew off her panties and stockings. For a moment she was afraid she would do something wrong, and she tensed.

"You're so beautiful."

Relaxing, she let him separate her legs and stroke the soft, firm skin of her inner thighs. Before long, she felt herself surrendering, every part of her trusting him. When he parted her, she yielded up to him. She didn't fight his fingers as they made the passage easier. She welcomed him with hot, racing joy when he was naked and lying between her open thighs.

"Easy now, sweetheart," he said, his voice a rasp as he continued to stroke her. "Don't tense up on me."

She didn't. She let her arms fall wide and open on the bed, all of her open and trusting. He knew where to touch, where to stroke. He'd been making love to women for longer than she'd been alive, and he understood the mysteries of her body better than she did.

When he took slow possession, she received him with wonder and passion, barely feeling the pain because he had prepared her so well. He fondled her and caressed her, displaying infinite patience even though his own body was slick with sweat. Again and again he took her up to the peak, but he wouldn't let her fly.

She began to plead with him in short gasping breaths. "Please. I need . . ."

"Quiet now."

"But I have to . . ."

"No more. Hush."

He kissed her and stroked her and drew back his head to watch her as she begged for release.

"I'm going to . . . die."

"I know, sweetheart. I know."

His eyes filled with smoky tenderness, and she began to cry.

He smiled and let her soar.

17

Honey lay in his arms afterward, her head on his shoulder. He toyed idly with her hair, wrapping silky curls around his big brown fingers while she discovered the textures of his chest and explored old scars that she had seen but never touched.

He was quiet.

She wasn't.

"I never thought it would be so wonderful, Dash. It didn't hurt at all, and I wanted it to last forever. I was worried— You know, you read about it in books, and that sort of gives you high expectations. But then you've got to ask yourself, is that the way it really is?" She touched a scar near his nipple. "Where did this one come from?"

"I don't know. Montana, maybe. I worked on a ranch up there."

"Uhmm. I can't imagine anything more wonderful than sex. I was afraid that I'd be—You know, since I haven't had any practice, I thought I might be sort of a dud." She lifted her head, her forehead wrinkling. "I wasn't a dud, was I?"

He kissed the tip of her nose. "You weren't a dud."

Reassured, she lay back down and resumed her stroking. "But I still don't know a lot, and really, I don't see why we can't do it again. I'm not sore. Really, I'm not. And I want to make sure I satisfy you—I know that's important. And I haven't done any—you know—oral sex or anything."

"Jesus, Honey."

She propped herself up on her elbow to look at him. "Well, I haven't."

A faint, ruddy glow stained his cheekbones. "For pete's sake, where do you get your ideas?"

"I may not have had a lot of experience, but I'm a big reader."

"Well, that explains it."

"And another thing . . ."

He groaned.

"Everything happened so fast. Well, not fast. Really slow, which was wonderful. But I got a little crazy. Which wasn't my fault because everything you were doing to me was making me crazy. Not crazy, exactly, but—"

"Honey?"

"Uh-huh?"

"Do you think you could sort of wander toward the point you're trying to make before both of us die of old age?"

She toyed with the edge of the sheet where it lay over his waist. "My point—" She hesitated. "It's a little embarrassing."

"It's hard to imagine there's anything much left that *could* embarrass you."

She gave him a glare that was supposed to be withering, but she was so happy that it fell short of the mark. "What I'm trying to say is that—In the heat of passion, so to speak, I didn't get a chance to . . . I didn't actually . . . " She stroked the edge of the sheet. "The point is . . . " She took a deep breath. "I want to look."

His head shot up. "You what?"

Now she was the one with the ruddy cheekbones. "I want to . . . *look* at you."

"Sort of like a science experiment?"

"Do you mind?"

He chuckled and then dropped his head back to the pillow. "No, sweetheart, I don't mind. Look away."

She drew back the sheet, and within a very short time

Dash seemed to set aside all his reservations because they were making love again.

He was in the shower when room service banged on the door the next morning. He had ordered coffee and she had ordered waffles, sausage, toast, juice, and blueberry cheesecake. She wanted to eat everything, taste everything, do everything. She smiled and hugged herself. She was all woman. One hundred and two pounds of female dynamite. The meanest and toughest hombres in the West hadn't been able to whip Dash Coogan, but she had brought the king of the cowboys right to his knees.

Sashaying through the living room, all sexy and full of herself, she secured the belt of the robe she had thrown on after she had come out of the shower and opened the door. "Bring it right—"

Wanda Ridgeway pushed past her and stormed inside. "He's here, isn't he? He wasn't in his room. I know he's here."

"Mother, please." Meredith reluctantly followed.

Dash and Wanda had been divorced for years, but Honey was immediately guilt-stricken. "Who—who are you talking about?"

The sound of the shower could be heard clearly from the direction of the bedroom, and Wanda gave her the sort of look that grown women give children who are caught in a lie.

"Mother thinks my father is here," Meredith said stiffly.

"Dash?" Honey widened her eyes just as Janie did when she was trying to wiggle out of a tight spot. "You think Dash is here?" She gave a phony laugh and widened her eyes even more. "Why, that's ridiculous." Another phony laugh. "Why would Dash be using my shower?"

"Then who is it?" Wanda asked.

"A man—I—I met a man at the wedding. . . ."

Reddening, Meredith turned toward her mother. "I told you he wasn't here. You always think the worst of him. I told you—"

"She's lying, Meredith. Your whole life you've blamed me for the divorce. Despite all your hellfire talk, you still think your father walks on water. You think that he's all lit up with a great big halo just like Jesus. Well, your father couldn't walk on water if it was made out of concrete. His zipper broke up our marriage; not me."

The shower stopped.

Honey darted a nervous glance toward the doorway. "I don't mean to be rude, but if there's nothing else. . . ."

"Hey, Honey. Come in here and dry my back."

Meredith sucked in her breath at the sound of her father's voice. Wanda lifted her head in triumph.

"His shower was broken," Honey stammered. "I was with another man, but he left. And then Dash called and said his shower was broken, and he asked if he could use mine."

Dash came through the door, drying his hair with one towel, another wrapped around his hips. "Honey—"

He broke off.

Wanda crossed her arms over her chest, her expression smug. Meredith gave a hiss of outrage.

Dash went still for only a moment before he resumed drying his hair. "What are the two of you doing up so early?"

"How could you?" Meredith gasped.

"It's not what you think, Meredith." Honey rushed to his side. "Dash, I was just telling Wanda and Meredith about how the shower in your room wasn't working. And you called to ask if you could use mine. And since my—uh—companion for the night had left, I said that would be fine, and—"

Dash looked at her as if she'd lost her mind. "What the hell are you talking about?"

"Your broken shower?" Honey inquired weakly.

He slipped his towel down around his shoulders, grasping the ends with his hands as he turned to Meredith. "There wasn't any broken shower, Merry. Honey and I spent the night together, and since we're both consenting adults, it's nobody's business but ours."

Wanda's eyes glittered with malicious satisfaction. "Your daughter finally gets to see for herself exactly what kind of man her father is."

Meredith's lips trembled and then contracted bitterly. "I'm going to pray for you, Daddy. I'm going to spend the rest of this day on my knees praying for your everlasting soul."

Dash whipped the towel from his neck. "Don't goddamn bother! I don't need anybody praying for me."

"Yes, you do. You need all the prayers you can get." Meredith glared at Honey. "And you! You're an affront to every woman who values the sanctity of her own body. You tempted him just like the whores of Babylon."

Meredith had hit too close to the truth, and Honey winced. Dash, however, took a step forward.

"You stop right there," he said, his voice low with warning. "Don't you say another word."

"That's what she is. She—"

"Enough!" Dash roared. Before Honey knew what was happening, he had drawn her to his side. She went weak from the rush of feelings that his protectiveness evoked within her.

"If you want to stay part of my life, Meredith, you're going to have to accept Honey, because she's going to be part of it, too."

Honey's head lifted to look at him.

"I'll never accept her," Meredith said bitterly.

"Maybe you'd better think about what you're saying before you go slamming too many doors."

"I don't have to think about it," she replied. "If I accepted this sordid relationship, it would become my sin, too."

"You're going to have to work that out for yourself," he said.

Wanda stepped forward. "Go hold the elevator for us, Meredith. I'll be along in a second."

Meredith obviously had more on her mind that she wanted to say, but she didn't have the nerve to defy her mother. Refusing to look at her father, she darted Honey a hate-filled glance and did as she was told.

"You had to bring her here, didn't you?" Dash said after Meredith had left.

Wanda stiffened. "You haven't had to live with her.

You've been the good guy who breezes into town every few years with an armload of presents. I've been the nasty bitch who sent her daddy away. She's twenty-one years old, and I'm sick of living with her blame."

His mouth drew tight. "Just get out."

"I'm on my way." She slipped her purse strap higher on her shoulder, and then some of her malice seemed to fade. She looked from Dash to Honey and back to Dash. She shook her head.

"You're getting ready to screw everything up again, aren't you, Randy?"

"I don't know what you're talking about."

"Every time you start to get your feet back on solid ground, you do something to spoil it. As long as I've known you, that's been your way. Just when things are getting good for you, you always manage to ruin it."

"You're crazy."

"Don't do it, Randy," she said quietly. "This time, don't do it."

Silence fell between them. His face was rigid, hers pensive. She gave his arm an awkward pat and left them alone.

Honey's eyes raced from the closed door to Dash. "What did she mean? What was she talking about?"

"Never mind."

"Dash?"

He sighed and gazed out the window. "She knows I'm going to marry you, I guess."

Honey swallowed hard. "Marry me?"

"Go on and get dressed," he said harshly. "We've got a plane to catch."

He wouldn't talk about his startling announcement during the flight, or even after they reached Los Angeles. Finally, she gave up trying. On the freeway from the airport, he swore at other drivers and cut them off. But even his bad temper couldn't dampen the choir of angels singing inside her.

He had said he was going to marry her. Her world had split open like an egg, revealing a jeweled center.

He swore darkly and cut between two vans. She realized they were heading toward Pasadena instead of to the ranch, and her stomach began to cramp. He was taking her home. What if he hadn't meant what he'd said at all? What if they weren't getting married, and he was trying to find a way to tell her he'd changed his mind?

"I'll bet you didn't pack a single pair of jeans in that suitcase."

He sounded so accusing that she grew defensive. "We were going to a wedding."

"You always have a smart comeback, don't you?"

She opened her mouth to respond, but before she could speak, he went on. "Now here's the way we're going to do this. I figure the best thing is to go down to Baja. We'll get married there and then camp for a few days. We've got another week before we have to be back on the set, and we might as well make the most of it."

The choir of angels burst into a chorus of alleluias. "You mean it?" she breathed softly. "We're really getting married?"

"What do you suggest as an alternative? Did you want to have an *affair?*" He spit out the word as if it were a particularly loathsome obscenity. "Did you want to *live together?*"

"Everybody else does it," she said tentatively, trying to understand his mood.

He looked completely disgusted with her. "Is that all the value you put on yourself? I'll tell you one thing, little girl. I've been low in my life, but I've never been so low that I didn't marry a woman I loved."

He loved her! The knowledge radiated inside her like a sunburst. She no longer cared about his bad mood or anything else. He had said that he loved her, and she was going to be his wife. She wanted to throw herself into his arms, but there was something so forbidding about him that she didn't quite have the nerve.

He didn't speak again until they arrived at her house. "I'll give you ten minutes to get rid of all those fancy clothes and pack some jeans and boots. We'll spend the night at the ranch and then set out first thing tomorrow morning. It'll get cold at night, so bring a set of long underwear. And you're going to need your birth certificate."

Birth certificate! They really were going to do it. Giving a little whoop of happiness, she reached across the car to hug him, then raced into the house to do as he had directed.

None of her family seemed to have noticed that she'd been gone. She packed quickly and told Chantal she wouldn't be home for a few days. Chantal wasn't curious enough to ask for an explanation, and Honey didn't give one. Part of her still couldn't believe that Dash Coogan was really going to marry her, and until it had happened, she didn't want to jinx herself by telling anybody.

He was drumming his fingers impatiently on the steering wheel when she returned to the car. "You didn't have to wait out here," she said as she climbed in. "You could have come inside."

"Not with that bunch of cannibals."

She decided there would be time enough to sort out his opinion of her family after they were married, but she couldn't as easily dismiss something he had said earlier. As the car shot onto the Ventura, a small chill clouded her happiness.

"Dash? What you said earlier about always marrying the women you loved. I don't want to be loved the same way you loved your other wives. I want—I want it to be forever."

He glared at the freeway in front of him. "That just goes to show what you know."

18

They were married the next afternoon in Mexicali, just across the border. The ceremony took place in some sort of government office—Honey wasn't certain what kind since she couldn't read the Spanish signs and Dash still wasn't being communicative. Both of them were wearing jeans. She held a bouquet of flowers he had bought from a street vendor outside, and her ring was a plain gold band from a nearby jewelry shop.

The walls were thin and a radio blared Spanish rock songs from the next office. The official who married them had a gold tooth and smelled like cloves. As the ceremony ended, Dash grabbed the copy of their marriage certificate and dragged her outside, all without kissing her.

The warm afternoon air was fetid from the stench of the irrigation canals and fertilizer spray, but she breathed it in joyously. She was Mrs. Dash Coogan. Honey Jane Moon Coogan. She was finally part of someone else.

He pulled her toward his jeep, which was parked at the curb and filled with their camping gear. She knew from past discussions that the vehicle had been specially modified to handle the rough terrain of the wilderness camping he enjoyed. As he drove into one of the government-owned Pentex gas stations to fill the thirty-gallon tank, she remembered all the times he'd set out on one of these camping trips without her and how she had dreamed of going along. Now she was doing it in a way she had never imagined.

They headed west from Mexicali on Highway 2. Heat waves rose off the pavement, and litter blew across the highway. Abandoned tire treads lay at the side of the road like dead alligators, and tired old billboards scarred the bleak landscape. A truck filled with field workers blasted by, its horn squalling. Honey stuck her hand out the open window and waved at them gaily.

"Do you want to get your arm ripped off?" Dash snarled. "Just keep those hands inside."

Having the marriage ceremony behind them obviously hadn't improved his mood. She told herself that sooner or later he would let her know what was eating at him, but until then she was going to hold her tongue.

She had visited Tijuana several times with Gordon and Chantal, but this part of Baja was new to her. The land was parched and forbidding, a gnarled finger poking into the sea. Several miles west of Mexicali, the highway crossed the top of Laguna Salada, a wide, dry lake bed that extended as far as she could see. Its surface was marked with tire tracks from jeeps and ATVs.

As she stared at the dry moonscape of the lake bed, her eyes began to feel heavy. They had arrived at the ranch just after dark and eaten a silent meal. Afterward, he had brusquely directed her to one of the guest rooms, where she had tossed all night, unable to sleep because she was afraid he would change his mind by morning. She glanced down at the gold circlet on her finger and tried to absorb the fact that they were truly married.

Her shoulder banged against his as he abandoned the highway and began heading across the dry lake bed. "We're camping for the night in one of the palm canyons," he said brusquely. "It's not too accessible, so the developers haven't gotten hold of it yet."

"Not too accessible" proved to be an understatement. The gears of the jeep ground painfully when the small vehicle finally cleared the lake bed and assaulted the steep, rocky slopes that rose off its western edge. For an hour they followed a road that was little more than a rutted track, jolting and jarring her until she felt bruised. Finally, it passed through a narrow cleft in the rocks into a tiny palm-shaded canyon.

Granite walls, wild and rugged, rose high on the sides. She saw the twisted silvery limbs of elephant trees interspersed with palm and tamarisk. As Dash stopped the jeep, Honey heard the sound of running water. He climbed out and disappeared into the trees. She got out herself, stretched her limbs, and looked around for the source of the sound. Behind her, a small waterfall tumbled in a lacy silver mist from the harsh cliff face.

Dash came out of the trees, zipping his pants as he walked. Honey quickly looked away, both embarrassed and fascinated by this intimacy that was exactly the sort of thing she had always imagined a man would do in front of his wife.

He nodded toward the waterfall as he began unloading the jeep. "These canyons are one of the few places with fresh water in all of Baja. There's even a hot springs. Most of the peninsula is dry as dust, and water's a lot more precious than gold. Grab those tent poles."

She did as he told her, but as she was pulling the poles from the back, she caught the end of the longest one on the jeep's frame and they all clattered to the ground.

"Damn it, Honey, watch what you're doing."

"Sorry."

"I don't want to have to spend this entire trip cleaning up your messes."

She bent down to retrieve the poles.

"And do you mind telling me why you're wearing those sandals? I distinctly remember telling you to bring boots."

"I did," she said. "They're with my clothes."

"What good are they going to do with your clothes if we're in the middle of the desert and you run into a rattler?"

"We're not in the middle of the desert," she pointed out as she rose to her feet with the tent poles clutched in her arms.

"You've been spoiling for a fight ever since yesterday, haven't you?"

She stared at him, unable to believe his gall. He was the one who'd been acting as if he'd sat on a porcupine.

He poked the front brim of his Stetson back with his thumb, his expression belligerent. "We might as well set down a few rules right now. That is if you're not too busy dropping things to listen."

"I've never been camping before," she said stiffly. "I don't know anything about it."

"I'm not talking about camping. I'm talking about the two of us." He advanced on her until only a few feet separated them. "First off. I'm the boss. I'm set in my ways and I don't have any intention of changing a single one of them. You're going to have to do a lot more accommodating than me, and I don't want to hear any bitching about it. Understood?"

He didn't wait for her response, which was a good thing.

"I don't concern myself with housework. Expressions like 'splitting the work load' aren't even part of my vocabulary. I don't run a washing machine; I don't worry about whether there's coffee in the cupboard. We hire somebody to do that or you take care of it. Either way." His eyes narrowed. "And that parasite family of yours. If you want to keep supporting them that's your business, but I'm not giving them a penny, and they're not coming within ten miles of the ranch. Is that understood?"

He sounded as if he were giving her terms for parole.

"And another thing." His scowl grew blacker. "Those birth control pills I saw in your case. From now on they're one of your basic food groups, little girl. I already ruined one set of children, and I don't have any intention of ruining another."

"Dash?"

"What?"

She set the tent poles on the ground, then looked up at him, trying to keep her gaze steady. "I've been doing my best not to lose my temper with you, but you've pushed me right to the edge. You know that, don't you?"

"I've barely got started."

"Now that's where you're wrong. You're all done."

His jaw jutted forward. "Is that so?"

"It's so. I never used to be much of a crybaby, Dash Coogan, but since I fell in love with you, I've done more than my share. And I'm warning you right now that you're upsetting me, which means I'll probably start crying pretty soon. I'm not proud of it—as a matter of fact, I'm ashamed —but that won't change the outcome. So if you don't want to spend the rest of this sorry excuse for a honeymoon with a crying wife, I suggest you start acting like the gentleman I know you can be."

His head dipped. He kicked at the ground with the toe of his boot. When he spoke, his voice was soft, a bit hoarse. "Honey, I've never been faithful to a woman in my life."

A spike of pain drove right through her.

He gazed at her, his eyes unhappy. "When I think about my track record and all these years we've got stretching between us, not to mention the fact that we're going to put an end to two careers, I can't believe I'm doing this. It doesn't matter so much about me, but I can't stand the idea of hurting you. I know I must be crazy, Honey, but I don't seem to be able to help myself when it comes to you."

All of her resentment faded, and she was filled with tenderness. "I think I'm a little crazy, too. I love you so much I can hardly stand it."

He pulled her against his chest. "I know you do. And I love you even more. That's why there's no excuse for what I've done."

"Please, Dash, don't talk like that."

He stroked her hair. "You got under my skin when I wasn't even looking, just like a chigger. Everything would have been all right if you hadn't grown up on me, but all of a sudden you weren't a kid anymore, and no matter how hard I tried, I couldn't make you turn back into one."

For a long time the only sound was the rush of the waterfall behind them.

By the time they had set up camp, the sky had clouded over and a chilly drizzle had plunged the temperature down into the forties. Honey was cold, wet, and happier than she could ever remember.

"Do you mind getting the last of the food?" He zipped the front of the small tent he had set up.

She reached inside the jeep, but before she could pull out the large food tin he had sprung to her side and taken it from her.

"It's not heavy," she protested. "I can do that."

"I expect you can." Leaning down, he brushed his lips over hers.

She smiled to herself as she remembered all the chest-pounding he'd been doing. Dash Coogan had more bluster than any man she'd ever known.

An icy gust of wind blew through the camp site, rattling the wet palm fronds, and she shivered. "I thought this was supposed to be a tropical climate."

"You cold?"

She nodded.

"That's good."

She looked at him quizzically.

"The weather can change fast around here, especially in the winter." He sounded pleased. "This is about the only time of year you need a tent. Normally, I'd have just brought a sun fly to give us shade, keep out the bugs, and let the breeze through. Grab some dry clothes for both of us and that long underwear of yours while I put this away."

She did as he asked, but as she began to head toward the tent to change, he stepped in front of her. "Not that way." Taking her hand, he wrapped a poncho around their dry clothing and began to lead her into the palms.

The temperature was dropping by the minute, and her teeth had started to rattle. "I'm afraid I'm too cold for a hike, Dash."

"Come on now. You're tougher than that. A little nip in the air never hurt anybody."

"It's a lot more than a nip. I can see my breath."

He grinned. "Is it my imagination or are you starting to whine?"

She thought of the tent and those fluffy down sleeping bags where they could be curled up right now and where she could be getting more lessons in lovemaking. "It's definitely not your imagination."

"I can see I'm going to have to get you toughened up."

He led her through a breach in the trees and she caught her breath. Before them in a nest of ferns and mossy rocks lay a small pool with steam curling from its surface into the chilly air.

"I told you there was a hot springs here," he said. "Now what do you say the two of us strip off these clothes and get down to some serious hanky-panky?"

She was already unbuttoning her blouse, but her fingers were clumsy with the cold and he finished undressing first. When he was naked, he helped her peel the wet denim from her legs and then drew her into the pool until he was standing waist deep, but only her breasts and shoulders were exposed. The water felt hot and wonderful against her cold skin. Above the surface her breasts were covered with gooseflesh, her nipples puckered into hard little pebbles. He dipped his head and caught one in the warmth of his mouth. She arched her neck at the gentle suction. His mouth moved to the other nipple.

After a while he released her and began sluicing warm water over her chilled shoulders, not letting her dip beneath the surface, but warming her with the water and the palms of his big brown hands.

She began to stroke his hips and the fronts of his thighs beneath the water. Her nipples softened and spread like summer buds beneath his warm fingers. Her hands grew more adventuresome. She stroked him until he groaned.

They were near the center of the pond now, and the water had grown deeper until the tops of her shoulders were covered. "Wrap your legs around my waist," he said huskily.

She licked at the beads of moisture that had formed on his cheekbones and did as he asked.

He played with her beneath the water, his fingers on a rampage, making her gasp as they explored every part of her.

"Dash . . ." She tightened her strong young thighs around him.

He groaned out her name and drove home.

They stayed in the palm canyon for two days, and during that time Dash seemed to grow younger before her eyes. The harsh lines at the corners of his mouth faded and the bleakness in his green eyes disappeared. They laughed and wrestled and made love until sometimes she wondered which of them was the twenty-year-old. She cooked bacon and eggs on the Coleman stove, and had tears in her eyes the morning of the third day when they left their canyon behind. Dash wanted her to see everything, and since the weather had once again grown hot, they were to spend the next few nights camping along the Gulf of California, or the Sea of Cortés, as it was also called.

"That was the best time I ever had in my life," she sighed when they were back on the highway heading south.

"We'll come here again." His voice grew surprisingly

grim. "I imagine we'll have time for a lot of camping in the future."

"What's wrong with that? You love to camp."

"I like to camp when I'm on vacation. Not because both of us are going to be unemployed."

She set her jaw. "I don't want to talk about it."

"Honey—"

"I mean it, Dash. Not now."

He let her have her way and began identifying some of the vegetation and pointing out the volcanic rock formations. As they drove farther south with the hot breeze blowing through the open windows of the jeep, she saw abandoned automobile bodies everywhere, and she began to feel uneasy. There was something almost apocalyptic about the landscape: bleak, parched vistas scabbed with rusted automobile hulks lying on their backs like dead beetles, skeletal vegetation sucked dry of moisture, crumbling roads spotted with animal carcasses. Even the most dangerous switchbacks had no guardrails, just clusters of memorial crosses marking the spot where loved ones had been lost.

An irrational fear came over her, not for herself but for Dash. "Let me drive," she said abruptly.

He looked over at her quizzically. She knew he was a good driver, but she wanted to be behind the wheel. Only if she were in control of every motion of the automobile, every nuance of the road, could she protect him from harm.

"There's a beach-shack restaurant not far from here where we can eat lunch," he said. "The food's real good. You can take over from there."

She forced herself to draw a series of deep breaths and, gradually, she began to relax.

"Shack" was a generous description for the restaurant. It was made of adobe that had once been painted a bilious shade of green, and the mismatched tables were set outside on a crumbling patio overlooking the sea. The patio was shaded by a dilapidated roof covered with flapping tar paper and supported by splintered wooden posts.

"I know the IRS still takes most of your paycheck, Dash, but I thought you could afford better than this."

"You just wait," he said with a grin as he led her to a wooden table with a square of well-scrubbed linoleum nailed over the top.

"Señor Coogan!"

"Hola! Cómo estás, Emilio?"

Dash rose as an elderly man came toward them. They exchanged greetings in rapid-fire Spanish and then Dash introduced her, but since she didn't speak the language, she wasn't certain exactly how he identified her. Eventually Emilio bustled off through a banging screen door into the kitchen.

"I hope you're hungry." Dash took off his hat and set it on an empty chair.

For the next half hour, they feasted on one of the best meals Honey had ever eaten: quesadillas made of tender flour tortillas with goat cheese bubbling from the sides, succulent lime-seasoned chunks of abalone, avocados stuffed with plump shrimp that hinted of saltwater and cilantro. Occasionally one of them would spear an especially tender morsel and feed it to the other. Sometimes they kissed between bites. Honey felt as if she'd known how to be a lover all her life.

She was too full to eat more than a few bites of the fat fig tart that was their dessert. Dash had put down his fork, too, and was gazing out at the sea. She saw a ridge in his hair where he had taken off his hat, and she reached out to smooth it, barely able to believe that she now had the right to do this sort of thing.

He caught her hand and drew it to his lips. When he let her go, his expression was solemn. "As soon as we get back—"

She tugged her hand away. "I don't want to talk about it."

"We have to talk. This is serious, Honey. The first thing I want you to do is see a good lawyer."

"A lawyer? Are you trying to divorce me already?"

He didn't smile. "This isn't about divorce. Every penny of your money has to be locked up tight so the IRS can't take it away from you because of me. I won't have you paying for my financial mistakes. It was stupid of me not to have thought of it right away so we could have taken care of it before we ran off to get married. I don't know—I'm not good about money."

She saw how distressed he was, and she smiled at him. "I'll take care of it, okay? Don't worry."

Her reassurance seemed to satisfy him, and he leaned back in his chair. But now that he had raised the specter of their future, it hung between them. She knew she had to stop being such a coward and face the topic she wanted to avoid. She toyed with the label on the bottle of mineral water she had been drinking.

"Maybe it'll be all right, Dash. Nobody has to know. We can keep our marriage a secret."

"Not a chance. The tabloids have probably already found out. You think that guy who married us is going to keep his mouth shut?"

"He might."

"And what about the clerk who did the paperwork? Or the jeweler who sold us your wedding ring?"

She sank back in her chair. "So what do you think will happen?"

"Our P.R. people will fall all over each other trying to do damage control. It won't do a damned bit of good, but they'll go through the motions anyway so they look like they're earning their paychecks. The tabloids will have helicopters flying over the ranch trying to get photos of the two of us naked. Columnists will write about us in the newspapers. The comics are going to have a field day. We'll be fair game for every monologue on the Carson show. We won't be able to turn on the set without hearing some smartass take a poke at us."

"It won't be—"

"The production company and bullshit artists at the network will convince each other they can make script adjustments and revise the concept. But no matter what they try to do, audiences are going to puke, and *The Dash Coogan Show* will be history."

She was furious with him. "You're wrong! You're always looking at the bad side. That's one thing I can't stand about you. When the slightest little thing happens, you have to act like it's the end of the world. Audiences aren't stupid. They know the difference between real life and a television program. The network wouldn't drop the show for anything. They've made millions. It's one of the most successful shows in history. Everybody loves us."

"Who are you trying to convince? Me or yourself?"

His gentleness was her undoing. She looked out at the ocean where the waves were sparkling in the afternoon sun, and her shoulders sagged. "We haven't done anything wrong. We love each other. I'm not going to be able to stand it if people try to make something obscene out of the two of us. This is real life. Not a television show."

"But our audience doesn't know us, Honey; they only know the characters we play. And the idea of Janie Jones and her pop running off to get married is just about as repulsive as you can get."

"It's so unfair," she said softly. "We haven't done anything wrong."

His eyes were steady and searching. "Are you sorry?"

"Of course not. But you seem to be."

"I'm not sorry. Maybe I should be, but I'm not."

Their tension eased as each looked into the other's eyes and saw only love.

That afternoon they set up camp on a crescent-shaped white-sand beach tucked into a secluded cove. Dash showed her how to chip fist-sized oysters from the rocks with a hammer and chisel. They squeezed fresh lime juice over them and ate them raw.

It was too chilly for swimming, but Honey insisted on wading, and afterward Dash warmed her feet between his thighs. They made love to the sound of the surf.

The following night they took a room in a small hotel so they could bathe in warm water. After Honey discovered the pleasures of showering together, she went on tiptoe to whisper what she wanted to do to him.

"Are you sure?" he asked, his voice husky.

"Oh, yes. I'm sure, all right."

This time, she was the one who led him to the bed.

The next day they drove deep into the desert and pitched camp. She saw the contorted trunks of elephant trees and granite boulders sculpted by the wind into fearful shapes. Stretches of cardon cactus with vultures perched in their upthrust arms were etched in stark relief against the sky. That evening as they sat around the small fire Dash had made, she watched with apprehension while the sun faded.

"I don't know if I'm going to like this."

"You haven't seen the stars until you've seen them from the desert."

The sun dipped beneath the horizon and a great swarm of birds flew up. She caught her breath. "How beautiful. I've never seen so many birds."

He chuckled. "Those are bats, sweetheart."

She shuddered and he drew her down beside him on the sleeping bag he had unfolded. "Nature isn't prettied up here. That's why I like it. This is life stripped down to its bare bones. Don't ever be afraid of it."

Gradually, she relaxed as she lay on his shoulder and he covered her breast with his palm. The desert was alive with night sounds. Time slipped by as one star after another poked through the sky. Without any city lights to blur their brilliance, she felt as if she were seeing stars for the first time.

Slowly she came to understand what he meant. Everything was so elemental that the two of them seemed to have been peeled bare until nothing was left separating them. No subterfuge, no secrets.

"When we get back, Honey, it's not going to be easy. I just hope you're tough enough to take it."

She propped herself up on one elbow and gazed down at his familiar, beloved face. "Both of us know I'm tough enough," she said softly. "But are you?"

She could almost see him withdrawing from her, and the closeness between them dissolved.

"That's ridiculous." He angled up until he was sitting on the sleeping bag, his back toward her.

Perhaps it was the spell cast by the desert, but she felt as if a blindfold had been pulled away from her eyes. She could finally see him clearly—not just what he wanted her to see, but everything there was. The vision scared her, but his love had given her courage so she sat up and gently touched his back. "Dash, it's way past time for you to finish growing up."

His muscles stiffened beneath her hand. "What are you talking about?"

Now that she had begun this, she didn't want to finish it. What if she was wrong? Why did she think she knew things about him that the grown women he'd married didn't? And then she reminded herself that those grown women had all lost him.

Getting on her knees, she moved around so that she could see his face. "You have to accept the fact that this marriage is the end of the line for you. And you're not going to get out of it by conveniently tumbling into another woman's bed just so I'll divorce you."

His eyes narrowed, and he shot up from the sleeping bag. "You're not making one bit of sense."

"Bull. You've been using your zipper as an escape hatch since the first time you got married. Your other wives let you get away with it, but I won't." Her heart began to thud, but she'd gone too far to back down, and she rose to stand beside him. "I'm telling you right now that if I find you in bed with another woman, I might take a gun to you, I might take a gun to her, but I'm not divorcing you."

"That's the stupidest thing I ever heard you say! You're practically giving me permission to be unfaithful to you."

"I'm just telling you how it is."

"See, this is exactly what I was afraid of." His speech grew choppy, a clear sign that he was agitated. "You're too young. You don't know the first thing about being married. No woman with half a brain in her head tells her husband something like this."

"I just did." She bit down on her bottom lip to keep it from trembling. "I'm not divorcing you, Dash. No matter how many women you sleep with."

Even in the firelight she could see that his face had grown

ruddy with anger. "You're just plain stupid, you know that?"

Some of her fear began to slip away, and she gazed at him with wonder. "I'm really scaring you, aren't I?"

He scoffed at her. "I'm not scared. Hell, no. It's just hard to believe how stupid you are."

She pushed some more. "I can't do anything about the way you grew up. Those welfare people shifted you from one family to another, not me."

"That doesn't have anything to do with it."

"I'm not going to disappear on you like those families did. You can love me as much as you want, and nothing bad's going to happen. I'm your wife for the rest of your life, and no matter how hard you try, there isn't anything you can do to drive me away."

She could see him trying to find a way out. He even opened his mouth to retort, but then a great stillness came over him. Reaching out, she closed her hand over his.

The cactus creaked in the night wind. He spoke softly, still not looking at her. "You really mean it, don't you?"

"I really mean it."

He gazed at her, and even though he cleared his throat, his voice was husky with emotion. "You're the damnedest, most aggravating female I've ever met."

At first she thought it was a trick of the firelight, but then she knew it was no trick at all. Dash Coogan had tears in his eyes.

The
Drop
1989-1990

19

"Do you still feel bitter toward Dash and Honey?"

The *Beau Monde* reporter crossed her legs as she asked the question and regarded Eric through the red metal frames of her glasses. Laurel Kreuger reminded him of a Gap ad. She had a New York intellectual look—slim and attractive with short no-fuss hair and minimal makeup. Her clothes were casual and oversized: turtleneck, baggy khaki trousers, boots, a Soviet army watch.

A *Beau Monde* cover story was worth some inconvenience, but she had been interviewing Eric on and off for several days; it was Sunday, his only day off, and he was getting tired of it. Trying to channel his restlessness, he rose from one of the hotel penthouse's two facing couches and wandered over to the window, where he lit a cigarette and gazed down at Central Park. The trees were still bare of leaves, and their branches whipped in the March wind. He felt a momentary nostalgia for California, even though he'd only been away for a month.

He finally replied to her question. "Dash and Honey got married at the end of eighty-three, more than five years ago. I've been too busy since then to give it much thought. Besides, I was basically already off the show when it happened."

As he exhaled, the smoke spread skeletal fingers against the glass, blurring but not quite obscuring his reflection. His face seemed both sparer and harder than it had been during his years on the Coogan show, although it had lost none of its male beauty. If anything, the sullen, brooding quality he had exhibited in his twenties had, in his thirties, matured

251

into a dark sexuality that made the alienated antiheroes he frequently played on-screen so dangerously compelling.

The Manhattan Sunday traffic crept by far below as the reporter continued her probing. "Regardless of the fact that you were no longer a regular on the Coogan show, you were certainly outspoken at the time."

He drifted back over to the couch where he had been sitting facing her. "A lot of us were. If you'll remember, we had four seasons of that show in the can, and the producers were just getting ready to put it up for syndication. We were all expecting to make a lot of money on that deal. When news of Dash and Honey's marriage broke, it went right down the toilet. Ross Bachardy had to give the show away."

"That sounds bitter to me."

"Money's money." He sank back onto the striped cushions. "If I'd known what was going to happen with my career, I wouldn't have worried."

"Apparently being nominated for this year's Best Actor Oscar changes one's perspective."

"Not to mention one's bank account."

"So you decided to forgive the lovebirds their transgressions?"

"Something like that."

"Do you still talk to either one of them?"

"I was never close to either Dash or Honey. I speak to Liz Castleberry every few months."

"Coogan still shows up once in a while in commercials and doing guest shots, but Honey's pretty much a mystery lady," Laurel said. "Occasionally somebody will spot her on the Pepperdine campus taking a class, but other than that, she doesn't seem to leave their ranch very much."

"A major waste of talent. She never had any idea how good she was. Still, I'm not surprised she's made herself scarce. The press beat up on her pretty badly."

"She lied about her age for so long that no one believed her when she finally told the truth. The fact that people thought she was seventeen instead of twenty when she and Coogan ran off made it even worse."

He stabbed his cigarette into the ashtray next to him.

"Ross Bachardy was the one who concealed her age, not Honey."

"You sound like you're defending her."

"In some ways, she got a bum rap. In other ways, she and Dash screwed over a lot of people's futures."

"But not yours."

"Not mine."

She glanced at the notebook in her lap. "You've been getting some heady press lately. Gene Siskel said he expects you to be the premier actor of the nineties."

"I appreciate the vote of confidence, but predictions like that are a bit premature."

"You're only thirty-one years old. You've got a lot of time to prove the critics right."

"Or wrong."

"You don't believe that, do you?"

"No, I don't believe that."

"You certainly are self-confident. Is that why you decided to come to New York to do *Macbeth?*" She glanced down at her tape recorder to make certain the cassette wasn't running out.

He put his finger to his lips. "The Scottish play."

She regarded him quizzically.

"Actors consider it bad luck to refer to this play by its title. It's an old theatrical superstition."

Her mouth gave a wry twist. "Somehow I don't think you're the superstitious type."

"We have another two weeks before we finish our run, and I'm not taking any unnecessary chances, especially in a production this risky."

"I'll say it's risky. Casting you and Nadia Evans, two of the screen's reigning sex symbols, as Lord and Lady Macbeth was hardly conventional. The critics walked into the theater with their fangs bared. Both of you could have fallen on your faces."

"But we didn't."

"It's the sexiest production of *Mac*—er the Scottish play I've ever seen."

"Sexy's easy. It's all that blood and guts stuff that's hard."

She laughed, and a current of sexual chemistry sparked between them. It wasn't the first time it had happened, but once again he dismissed the idea of taking her to bed. It was more than the AIDS crisis that had made him selective about his bed partners. His first year with Lilly, when he had tried so hard to establish real sexual intimacy with her, had stripped him of his ability to enjoy sex for its own sake. He no longer went to bed with women he didn't like, and he definitely didn't go to bed with members of the press.

"You don't give a lot away, do you, Eric?"

He reached for his cigarettes, stalling for time. "What do you mean?"

"I've been interviewing you for several days, and I still don't have the foggiest notion what makes you tick. You're probably the most closed person I've ever met. And I don't just mean the way you dodge personal questions about your divorce or your past. You don't ever let anything slip, do you?"

"If I could be any tree in the world, I'd be an oak."

She laughed. "I must admit you've surprised me. Tell me why—"

But before she could begin another line of questioning, the door of the penthouse burst open and Rachel Dillon charged in. Her dark, tangled hair flew back from a small, delicate face whose soft features were marred only by a smear of chocolate near her mouth and a round Band-Aid plunked at the center of her forehead. Along with purple jeans and pink high-top sneakers, she wore a Roger Rabbit sweatshirt accessorized with a cast-off rhinestone necklace that had belonged to her mother. She was six weeks shy of her fifth birthday.

"Daddy!" She squealed with delight as if she hadn't seen him in weeks when, in fact, they had only been separated for a few hours. Throwing out her arms and nearly sending a vase of silk flowers toppling in the process, she raced toward him.

"Daddy, guess what we saw?"

She didn't notice the copy of the Sunday *Times* that lay on the floor directly in her path. Rachel never noticed any obstacles between herself and what she wanted.

"What did you see?" With a well-practiced motion, he swept her up just as she slid on the papers, catching her before she could bang her head on the nearby coffee table. She threw her arms around his neck, not out of gratitude for being rescued from potential disaster but because she always gave him crushing bear hugs after even the shortest separations.

"You guess, Daddy."

He drew her wiggling, energy-charged form into his lap and breathed in her particular strawberry scent of little-girl's hair faintly overlaid with sweat, since Rachel never walked when she could run. A panda-shaped barrette dangled from the very end of a dark brown lock. While he gave her question serious consideration, he slipped it off and set it on the end table. Rachel's barrettes were everywhere. He'd even pulled one out of his pocket in the middle of a press conference thinking it was his cigarette lighter.

"You saw a giraffe or Madonna."

She giggled. "No, silly. Daddy, we saw a man do peepee on the sidewalk."

"And that's what we love about the Big Apple," he replied dryly.

Rachel nodded her head vigorously. "Daddy, he did. Right on the sidewalk."

"Your lucky day." He gently touched the Band-Aid on her forehead. "How's your owie?"

But Rachel refused to be distracted. "Daddy, even Becca the goody-goody looked."

"Did she now." Eric's eyes grew soft, and he gazed across the room toward Rachel's twin sister Rebecca, who had just come through the door and was holding hands with Carmen, the girls' nanny. She gave him her sweet smile. He winked at her over the top of her sister's head in the secret signal they had developed. *Rachel got here first as usual, but she'll soon be bored, and then you and I can settle in for a nice long cuddle.*

"Daddy, did Mommy call on the telephone?" Rachel bumped his chin with the top of her head as she spun around. "Daddy, she said she'd call me today."

"Tonight, honey. You know she always calls at bedtime on Fridays."

Growing bored right on schedule, Rachel bounced off his lap and raced over to her nanny to grab her hand away from Becca. "Come on, Carmen. You said we could do finger paints." Before she left for the bedroom, she turned back to her sister. "Becca, don't be mushing with Daddy all day, you pokey. After me and Carmen finish, I'm gonna show you how to tie your shoe." Her face grew stern. "And this time you better do it right."

Eric resisted the urge to leap in and protect his fragile, damaged daughter from her domineering sister. Rachel was impatient with Becca's slowness, but she was also big-hearted and fiercely protective of her. Although he had discussed her sister's Down syndrome with her as soon as she was old enough to understand, she refused to accept Becca's slowness and was merciless in her insistence that she keep up. Maybe in part because of her unrelenting demands, Becca was progressing more rapidly than the doctors had expected.

Eric knew that, despite public perception, children born with Down syndrome were not all the same. They ranged from being mildly to moderately retarded, with a wide variation in mental and physical abilities. The extra forty-seventh chromosome that caused Rebecca's Down syndrome had left her mildly retarded, but there was no reason to believe she couldn't live a full and useful life.

As Rachel disappeared, Becca came toward him, her thumb in her mouth. The girls were fraternal twins instead of identical ones, but despite Becca's slightly slanted eyelids and the gently depressed bridge of her nose, they still bore a strong resemblance to each other and to him. Smoothly extracting her thumb, he gathered her into his arms and kissed her forehead. "Hi, sweetheart. How's Daddy's girl?"

"Becca is boo-tee-full."

He smiled and hugged her. "You certainly are."

"Daddy boo-tee-full, too." Becca's speech was slower than Rachel's, full of word omissions and sound substitutions. Although it was difficult for strangers to understand her, Eric had no trouble.

"Thanks, champ."

As she settled back against his chest, a deep sensation of peace came over him, just as it always did when he held her. Although he could never have explained it to anyone, he felt as if Becca were the universe's special gift to him, the only absolutely perfect thing in his life. He had always feared himself around the defenseless, but protecting this fragile child had begun to remove that haunting burden. In a way that he didn't entirely understand, the gift of Rebecca had let him atone for what he had done to Jason.

He had gotten so wrapped up in his daughters that he had nearly forgotten Laurel Kreuger, who was avidly taking in this scene of domesticity. Although he had never made any attempt to hide Becca's condition, he hated exposing his children to the press, and he absolutely forbade having them photographed. Even though it wasn't Laurel's fault the children had come back early from their outing, he resented this intrusion into his privacy.

"That's it for today, Laurel," he said abruptly. "I have some business to attend to this afternoon."

"We were scheduled for another half hour," Laurel protested.

"I didn't know that the girls would be back so soon."

"Do you always drop everything for them?" Her question held the faintly judgmental undertone of someone who has never been a parent.

"Always. Nothing in my life—not *Beau Monde,* not even my career, is as important as my daughters." It was the most revealing statement he had made to her since their interviews began, but he could see that she didn't believe him. Despite the fact that she had been dismissed, she made no move to gather up her tape recorder or notebook.

"You and your ex-wife have joint custody, don't you? I'm surprised you didn't leave the girls with her for the past few months instead of uprooting them by bringing them all the way across the country."

"Are you?"

She waited for him to explain, but he remained silent. He had no intention of letting her know that Lilly was incapable of dealing with the girls for very long. In theory, the girls were supposed to divide their time equally between their parents, but in practice they were with him ninety per cent of the time.

Lilly loved both her daughters, but for some reason that he couldn't fathom, she blamed herself for Becca's condition and her guilt made her ineffectual at meeting her daughter's special needs. In some ways the situation was even worse with Rachel. For all Lilly's intelligence, she seemed to lack the resources to deal with her strong-willed daughter, and Rachel rode roughshod over her.

Laurel continued to watch him cuddle Becca. "You're going to spoil your reputation as the last of the tough guys. Although that might not be a bad idea. Some critics call it your fatal flaw. They say that no matter what role you play, you always seem alienated."

"That's crap."

"Not according to a recent critical analysis of your work." She flipped over some pages in her notebook. "I quote, 'Eric Dillon's solitary performances mark him as one of society's loners. He is an actor who lives on the edge: sexually dangerous, permanently alienated, a voluntary discard. We feel his pain, but only as much as he allows. He gives us a twisted sort of brilliance, hard and difficult to crack. Ultimately, Dillon is gorgeous, hostile, and ruined.'"

He shot up from the couch, his daughter caught firmly in his arms. "I said that's enough for today."

Becca looked up at him, her eyes widening with alarm. He forced his muscles to relax and rubbed her arm. Then he glared at the reporter.

Apparently Laurel decided she'd pushed him far enough because she immediately gathered up her things and stuffed them into her tote bag. When she was on her way to the door, however, she hesitated.

"I have a job to do, Eric. Maybe after all this is over, we could—You know. Have a drink or something."

"Or something," he said coldly.

After Laurel had left, he soothed Becca, then sent her off to play with her sister while he made some phone calls. When he was done, he went into the spacious room the girls shared and nodded at Carmen so she could slip away to take a much-needed break. Crossing to the end of the room, he observed Becca sitting at the low table patiently finger-painting red circles on white butcher paper.

Transporting the girls across the country for three months hadn't been easy. The hotel room was set up with their play equipment, along with multicolored plastic milk crates filled with toys and books. He'd arranged for a special school and a speech therapist for Rebecca and put Rachel into a private nursery school. Still, he believed the advantages of keeping the girls with him outweighed the disadvantages of uprooting them.

Rachel, growing bored with finger-painting, began to practice her cartwheels. There was too much furniture in the room for gymnastics, and he waited for the inevitable, which wasn't long in coming. As she threw herself over, she caught her heel on the corner of one of the milk crates and gave a howl of outrage.

He squatted down. "Here, let me rub it."

She glared at him, transferring the sole responsibility for her gymnastic failure onto him.

"Daddy, you ruined it! I was doing it right till you came in! It's all your fault."

He lifted one eyebrow, letting her know that he had her number.

She was one of the few people in the world who didn't have any qualms about facing him down and she returned him raised eyebrow for raised eyebrow. "Cartwheels are stupid."

"Uh-huh," he replied noncommittally. "Doing them in here isn't too smart, either."

He straightened and walked over to stand behind Becca, brushing his hand along the side of her neck. "Good work, champ. Give it to me when it's dry, and I'll hang it in my dressing room at the theater." He turned back to Rachel. "Let me see your painting."

She regarded him sullenly. "It's stupid. I ripped it up."

"I think somebody needs a nap."

"Daddy, I'm not cranky. You always say I need a nap when you think I'm being cranky."

"My mistake."

"Daddy, only babies take naps."

"And you certainly aren't a baby."

Becca piped up from the table. "Me want to show Patches Becca's painting, Daddy. Me want to show Patches."

Rachel's crankiness instantly vanished. She jumped up and raced over to grab Eric's leg. "Yeah, Daddy! Let Patches play with us. Please."

Both girls regarded him with eyes so full of entreaty that he laughed. "Couple of con artists. All right. But Patches can't stay too long. He told me he has to perform some major carnage this afternoon. Not only that, he has a meeting with his agent."

Rachel giggled and ran for her bureau, where she quickly pulled open a drawer and extracted a pair of her navy blue tights. She raced back to him, the tights extended, and then rushed for the Band-Aid box.

"Not a Band-Aid again," he protested as he sat down in one of the small chairs, wrapped the navy tights around his head, and then knotted the legs to the side in the manner of a pirate's scarf. "You're going to end up with a father who's lost half of his right eyebrow. Let's just pretend."

"Daddy, you got to do the Band-Aid," Rachel insisted, just as she always did when he protested. "You can't be Patches without a patch, can he, Becca?"

"Becca want to see Patches."

He grumbled as he peeled the wrapper from the adhesive strip and secured it at a diagonal across his right eye, from the inside corner of his eyebrow to the outer edge of his cheekbone. Becca's thumb crept toward her mouth. Rachel leaned forward in anticipation. They watched in silent fascination, waiting for that magical transformation when their daddy changed into Patches the Pirate. He took his time. No matter how humble his audience, that special moment of transformation was sacred to him, the time when the boundary between illusion and reality grew indistinct.

He breathed once. Twice.

Rachel squealed with delight as he squinted his eye beneath the Band-Aid, crooked one edge of his mouth, and completed the transfiguration.

"Well, now, and what do we 'ave 'ere? Two bloodthirsty wenches, if me eyes ain't deceivin' me." He gave them his fiercest glower, and was rewarded with piercing squeals. Rachel began to run away from him, as she always did. He jumped up from the small chair and quickly scooped her off her feet.

"Not so fast, me pretty. I've been lookin' for some 'earty mates to carry off on me pirate ship." His eyes traveled from Rachel, squealing with delight and squirming beneath his arm, to Becca, watching gleefully from her seat at the table. He shook his head. "Nah. On second thought, I'll be throwin' you back. The two of you look puny." He set Rachel down and, arms akimbo, regarded her ferociously.

Rachel immediately grew indignant. "We're not puny, Patches. Feel this." She raised her arm and made a muscle. "Becca, show Patches your muscle."

Becca did as she was told. Eric dutifully leaned down and examined both sets of thin little arms. As always, the fragile delicacy of their bones struck fear into his heart, but he hid it and whistled with admiration. "Stronger than you look, the both of you. Still . . ." He fixed Becca with a dark scowl. "Are you good with a rapier, lass?"

"He means a sword," Rachel whispered loudly to her sister.

Becca nodded. "Vewwy, vewwy good."

"Patches, me too," Rachel squealed, "I'm great with a

rapier." She launched them into the part of the game she liked the best. "And I can cut off a bad guy's head in a single swoop."

"Can you now?"

"I can even open his stomach and let his blood and guts and brains spill out without blinkin' me eye."

Eric was noted for his faultless concentration, but he nearly lost it as Rachel tried, for the first time, to copy his accent. He had invented the rules of this particular game, however, and he checked any display of amusement. Instead, he regarded them doubtfully.

"I don't know. Raidin' and plunderin' is serious work. I need somebody with a strong 'eart fightin' at me side. The truth of it is . . ." He sank down into the chair next to Becca and whispered conspiratorially. "I'm not too fond of the sight of blood."

Becca reached out and patted his shoulder. "Poor Patches."

Impish lights sparked Rachel's eyes. "Patches, what kind of pirate can't stand blood?"

"Lots of 'em. It's a 'azard of the occupation."

"Patches, me and Becca love blood, don't we, Becca? If you let us come with you, we'll protect you."

"Me protect Patches," Becca offered, winding her arms around his neck.

He shook his head doubtfully. "Mighty dangerous, it is. We'll be raidin' ships full of lions with jaws powerful enough to eat up little girls." They listened wide-eyed as he described the perils of their raid. He'd learned from experience that they were especially taken with cargoes of exotic animals, but any reference to either robbers or big dogs frightened them.

Eventually Rachel spoke the words she said each time. "Patches, can my mommy come with us?"

He paused for only a moment. "Is she strong?"

"Oh, yes. Very strong."

"She's not afraid of blood, is she?"

Rachel shook her head. "She loves blood."

"Then we'll take her right along with us."

The girls giggled their pleasure and his heart swelled. In fantasy at least, he could give them the mother who was so frequently absent from their daily lives and so very ineffectual when she was present.

Then Patches the Pirate settled down to spin magic yarns of sea voyages, tales complete with valiant little girls sailing the seven seas and vanquishing all their enemies. They were tales of bravery and determination, tales where little girls were expected to stand their ground right along with the men and fight to the end.

Spellbound, the children clung to every word. As they listened, they heard only the rich bounty of their father's imagination. They were too young to understand that they were watching the man who was perhaps the best actor of his generation play the only role of his career in which he was alienated from absolutely no one.

20

"Did Daddy win?" Rachel raced into the living room, her red nightgown flying behind her, bare feet slapping the black and white marble floor.

Lilly reluctantly drew her attention from the television entombed in a pebbled gray cabinet. She had just finished redecorating the Coldwater Canyon home she and Eric had once shared. The doorways were now framed by Ionic columns topped with broken pediments, and the neo-Roman furniture was upholstered in white canvas. The light gray walls served as a background for first-century marble sculptures, French torchère lamps, and a wall-sized surrealistic canvas of a supersonic jet flying through the center of an enormous red apple. At first she had adored the new decor, but now she had begun to think so much neoclassicism was too cold.

"Don't run, Rachel," she admonished her daughter. "Why aren't you asleep? It's after nine. I hope you didn't wake Becca."

"I want to see if Daddy winned his Oscar. And I'm scared of a thunderstorm."

Lilly looked through the windows and noticed the trees were whipping in the wind. Southern California was having a terrible drought, and she suspected this storm would pass over without a drop falling as the others had, but she knew she would have trouble convincing her strong-willed daughter of that. "It's not going to rain, Rachel. It's just some wind."

Rachel gave her the mutinous look that seemed to be permanently stamped on her face. "I don' like thunderstorms."

In the background the Academy Award broadcast faded into a commercial. "There's not going to be a thunderstorm."

"Yes there is."

"No, there isn't. We're having a drought, for God's sake."

"Yes there is."

"Dammit, Rachel, that's enough!"

Rachel glared at her and stomped her foot. "I hate you!"

Lilly squeezed her eyes shut and wished Rachel would disappear. She couldn't handle her as Eric did. Yesterday when she'd picked the girls up at their father's, Rachel had started to go outside in her socks. When Eric had ordered her to put shoes on, she'd screamed that she hated him, but it hadn't seemed to bother him. He'd glared right back at her and said, "Tough luck, kiddo. You're still going to wear your shoes."

Lilly knew that she would have given in. It wasn't that she didn't love her daughter. At night when Rachel was asleep, Lilly could stand forever by her bed and simply gaze at her. But during the daytime, she felt so incompetent. She was like her own mother, a woman who simply wasn't maternal. Her mother had left Lilly to be raised by her father, and Lilly was doing the same with her daughters. Sometimes it was better that way.

Even so, she found herself resenting Eric's relationship with the girls. She knew they loved him more than they loved her, but being a parent was easier for him. He never lost his temper with Rachel, and Becca's condition didn't terrify him the way it terrified her.

"Look, there's Daddy!" Rachel squealed, her quarrel with her mother temporarily forgotten. "And Nadia. She's real nice, Mommy. Not like when her and Daddy was in *Macbeth* and she screamed all the time. She gave me and Becca Gummi Bears."

The camera was panning the front rows of the star-studded audience that was packed into the auditorium of the Dorothy Chandler Pavilion. Eric's date for the Academy Awards was Nadia Evans, his *Macbeth* costar. Lilly was jealous, although she knew she had no right to be. Eric had been a faithful husband; it was her infidelities that had ended their marriage.

Even after Eric had discovered she was having an affair with Aaron Blake, one of Hollywood's more exciting young actors, he hadn't insisted on a divorce. But Lilly hated the frustrations of trying to be a wife and mother, she hated the relentless intimacy of the marriage bed, and she hadn't seen any point in postponing the inevitable. Eric had never loved her—she knew he wouldn't have married her if she hadn't been pregnant—but he had treated her well, and having been the child of a hostile divorce, she wanted to retain at least the semblance of an amicable relationship with him.

Lilly studied Nadia Evans as the camera lingered on her and tried to take some satisfaction from the fact that she was just as beautiful as the actress. She was even slimmer now than she had been before her pregnancy, and she loved the deeper hollows in her cheeks. Recently she had been wearing her silver-blond hair in a ballerina's knot low on her neck to further emphasize her facial bones.

The Best Actor nominees were read off, and Lilly's resentment settled in deeper. She was a child of Hollywood, and every part of her yearned to be at his side now, sharing this moment.

"Mommy, do you think Daddy will win?"

"We'll see."

Rachel, for once motionless, stood in the center of the black and white marble floor and gazed at the television.

"And the Oscar goes to . . ."

Lilly snatched the remote control and punched up the volume.

"Eric Dillon for *Small Cruelties!*"

Rachel giggled and clapped her hands. "Mommy, he winned! Daddy winned!"

Lilly sagged back into the couch. This was what she got for divorcing him. She should have been the one sitting with him when he won, not Nadia Evans. If only they were still married, this would have been her night of triumph, too.

But it was too late for regrets. She remembered his icy fury when he had discovered she was having an affair and wondered what he would have done if he had known that Aaron Blake wasn't the only lover she had taken while they were married. Her stomach coiled in self-disgust. Every time she took a lover, she thought he would be the one who could fill up the empty spaces in her life. But it never happened. The only man who had given her lasting happiness was her father.

Nadia kissed Eric. He got up from his seat and took a hop step down the aisle, stopping as people rose to thump him on the back. When he got to the stage and received the Oscar, he turned to the audience and grinned, holding the gold statue high over his head.

The audience finally quieted, and he began to speak. "This shouldn't mean so much, but it does . . ."

She couldn't watch any more, and she snatched the remote control and punched the power button.

"I want to see Daddy!" Rachel protested.

"You'll see him tomorrow. It's bedtime."

"But I want to watch. Why did you turn off the TV?"

"I've got a headache."

A clap of thunder boomed outside the window, bringing noise but no rain. Rachel's finger plopped into her mouth, a clear sign that she was upset.

"Tuck me in, Mommy."

As Lilly gazed down at Rachel, her heart filled with love for this child who so seldom asked for any affection from her. They walked down the hallway together, temporarily at peace. She paused for a moment outside the door of Becca's room and gazed inside at the still little bundle lying under the covers.

What if that damaged child were punishment for her own sins? She tried to redirect the agonizing path her thoughts always took when she looked at Becca and found herself wondering what her life would be like if she hadn't let Eric talk her out of the abortion. But as she turned away from the room, she knew that no matter how ineffectual and resentful these children made her feel, she didn't regret having given birth to them.

They passed the group of enlarged photographs she had taken before she'd married Eric and abandoned her cameras. She had always meant to do portraits of the girls, but somehow she'd never gotten around to it. They entered Rachel's bedroom, which was decorated in pink and lavender hearts, although the feminine ambience was spoiled somewhat by Rachel's Hulk Hogan posters.

Rachel climbed on the bed, her small round bottom sticking up in the air for a moment before she slipped beneath the covers. Lilly was arranging them over her when another clap of thunder rattled the windows.

"Mommy!"

"It's all right. It's just thunder."

"Mommy, would you sleep with me?"

"I'm not ready to go to bed yet."

Rachel looked mulish. "Daddy lets me sleep with him. Daddy sleeps with me and cuddles me all night long."

Lilly froze. A painful, high-pitched noise began to whine in her head, gradually growing more shrill. She could barely summon the breath to speak. "What—What did you say?"

"Daddy . . . He sleeps with me if I'm scared. Mommy, what's wrong?"

The noise in Lilly's head became a great whirlpool sucking her into its center. The whirlpool spun her faster, and the noise shrieked in her brain until she felt as if she were coming apart. She collapsed on the side of the bed and tried to keep from fainting.

Rachel's voice called to her from far away. "Mommy? Mommy?"

The room began to settle around her, and she tried to tell herself there was nothing in Rachel's innocently spoken words to have inspired such a deep, unreasonable fear, but she felt as if she had been threatened at the most fundamental level of her existence.

Her fingers clasped the edge of the cover as she slowly pushed out the words. "Does Daddy sleep with you very often?"

Another clap of thunder rattled the windows. Rachel gazed out with trepidation. "Mommy, I want you to sleep with me."

Lilly tried to keep her voice from trembling, but the coldness in her limbs made that impossible. "Tell me about Daddy."

Rachel's eyes didn't move from the window. "Thunder's scary. Daddy says I don't have to be scared. His hair tickles."

Lilly's heart began to race so fast that she could barely breathe. "What—what do you mean his hair tickles?"

"It tickles my nose, Mommy."

"The hair on his—on his head?"

"No, silly. His tummy." She pressed her hand to the center of her chest. "Here."

Lilly's knuckles had turned white from gripping the edge of the cover. "Doesn't Daddy—Well, of course he does." She tried to force a laugh through her stiff lips, but it emerged as a sob. "Of course Daddy has his—his pajamas on when you get in bed with him, doesn't he?"

Rachel once again looked toward the window. "I'm scared of boomers, Mommy."

"Listen to me, Rachel!" Her voice rose to a shriek. "Does Daddy wear his pajamas when you get in bed with him?"

Rachel's forehead puckered. "Daddy doesn't wear jammies, Mommy."

Oh, God. Dear God. She wanted to run from the room, run from the awful black whirlpool sucking her toward the unspeakable. Her teeth began to chatter. "Does Daddy— Has he ever . . . touched you, Rachel?"

Rachel's thumb crept into her mouth and she nodded.

Blood no longer flowed through her veins, but knife-sharp slivers of ice. She gripped her daughter's shoulders. "Where does he touch you?"

"Becca's asleep."

She wanted to disappear, to jump from her own skin and from the monstrous whirlpool that seemed about to carry her away, but she couldn't abandon her daughter. "Think very carefully, Rachel. Has Daddy ever touched you—" *No! Don't say it. You're not allowed to tell.* "Has Daddy—" Her voice broke on a sob.

Rachel's eyes were wide with alarm. "Mommy, what's wrong?"

The words spilled out in a rush. "Has he ever . . . touched you . . . between your . . . legs?"

Rachel nodded again and rolled over, facing the window. "Go away, Mommy."

Lilly began to sob. "Oh, baby." She pulled her small daughter into her arms, covers and all. "Oh, my sweet poor baby."

"Mommy, stop! You're scaring me!"

Lilly had to ask the final question, the unspeakable one. *Don't let it be true. Please don't let it be true.* She drew back enough to see her daughter's face, no longer rebellious but pale with apprehension. Lilly's tears dropped onto the satin binding of the cover.

"Did Daddy—Oh, Rachel, sweetheart. . . . Did Daddy ever show you—show you his penis?"

Wide-eyed and frightened, Rachel nodded. "Mommy, I'm scared."

"Of course you are. Oh, my poor, poor baby. I won't let him hurt you. I won't ever let him hurt you again."

Lilly rocked her and crooned, and as she clasped her daughter's small body to her breast, she made a vow to protect her. She might have failed Rachel in some ways, but she wouldn't fail her in this.

"Mommy, you're scaring me. Mommy, why are you calling me Lilly?"

"What, sweetheart?"

"You said Lilly. That's your name. That's not my name. You said 'poor Lilly.' "

"Oh, I don't think so."

"You did, Mommy. 'Poor Lilly.' "

"Go to sleep, sweetheart. Shh. . . . Mommy's here."

"I want my daddy."

"It's all right, sweetheart. I won't ever let him hurt you again."

Eric didn't return home until seven that morning. There had been interviews, photographers, three different parties ending with a buffet breakfast. Nadia had finally given out at four, but it was the biggest night of his life, and he hadn't been ready for it to end.

He stepped out of the limo onto the cobbled entryway that led to his house. His collar was open, his bow tie undone, and the jacket of his tuxedo was draped over his arm. In his hand the gold statue of Oscar glimmered in the early morning sun. He had the feeling that everything in his life had come together. He had his work and his daughters, and for the first time since he was fifteen, he didn't hate himself.

The limo pulled away, and he saw Lilly standing by her car waiting for him. His euphoria faded. Why couldn't she have let him have one day to enjoy his success? But as she came toward him, his annoyance was replaced with alarm. Lilly was always meticulous about her appearance, but her clothes were wrinkled and her hair had come undone from its careful ballerina's knot.

He hurried over to her, noticing that she had eaten off her lipstick and old mascara had smudged under her eyes. "What's wrong? Is something wrong with the girls?"

Her face tightened, looking pinched and ugly. "Something's wrong, all right, you perverted bastard."

"Lilly . . ."

As he reached out to take her arm, she jerked away, snarling at him like a cornered animal. "Don't touch me! Don't ever touch me!"

"Maybe you'd better come inside," he said, forcing his voice to sound calm.

Without giving her a chance to refuse, he went to the front door and unlocked it. She followed him into the house, moving through the foyer and off to the living room on the left. Her breathing was heavy and agitated.

The room was sparsely furnished, with white walls, pale wood, and some comfortable sofas upholstered in light, nubby fabric. He laid his coat and the Oscar on a chair that sat near a rough-hewn cupboard displaying baskets, Mexican tinware, and figures of saints. The early morning sun streamed through the windows, casting rectangles of light on the floor. He walked into one of them.

"Let's get this over with so I can go to bed. What is it this time? Do you need more money?"

She spun toward him, her face pale with distress, her lips quivering. Guilt replaced his annoyance, the guilt he always felt when he was with her because she wasn't a bad person, yet he hadn't been able to love her the way she needed.

He softened. "Lilly, what's wrong?"

Her voice broke. "Rachel told me. Last night."

"Told you what?" His forehead puckered in alarm. "Is something wrong with Rachel?"

"You should know that better than anyone. Did you do it to Becca, too?" Her eyes filled with tears. She sagged down onto the couch, her hands crumpling into fists in her lap. "My God, I can't bear to think that you might have touched Becca, too. How could you, Eric? How could you be so sick?"

Genuine fear had begun to grip him. "What's happened? Jesus, tell me!"

"Your dirty little secret is out," she said bitterly. "Rachel told me all about it. Did you threaten her, Eric? Did you threaten to do something terrible to her if she told?"

"Told what? For God's sake, what are you talking about?"

"What you've been doing to her. She told me—She told me that you've been sexually molesting her."

"What?"

"She told me everything."

A deathlike stillness came over him. His voice was a soft rasp. "You'd better explain what you're talking about. Start at the beginning. I want to hear everything."

Lilly's eyes narrowed with hatred. Her speech was rushed and shrill. "Last night I was tucking Rachel into bed. There was some thunder, and she asked me to get in bed with her. When I said no, she told me that you let her sleep with you."

"Sure I let her sleep with me when she's scared. What's wrong with that?"

"She said you don't wear pajamas."

"I never have. You know that. When the girls are around, I sleep in a pair of briefs."

"That's sick, Eric. Letting her in bed with you."

His alarm was changing into anger. "There's nothing sick about it. What the hell's wrong with you?"

"So much righteous indignation," she scoffed. "Well, don't bother, because she told me all of it, you bastard." Lilly's face twisted until it was ugly with hatred. "She said she's seen your cock."

"She probably has. Christ, Lilly. Sometimes they walk in on me when I'm getting dressed. I don't go out of my way to flaunt myself in front of them, but I've never made a big deal out of it."

"You bastard. You think you've got an answer for everything. Well, that's not all she said. She told me you touch her between her legs."

"You're a liar! She wouldn't say that. I've never touched her—" But he had. Of course he had. Carmen usually bathed the girls, but sometimes he did.

"Listen to me, Lilly. You're putting some kind of sick interpretation on something that's perfectly normal. I've bathed those girls on and off since they were babies. That's what Rachel was talking about. Ask her. No, we'll ask her together."

He moved toward her, ready to drag her back to her house and his daughters if necessary, but she jumped up from the couch and the fear on her face stopped him.

Her teeth were bared, her too-thin face fierce. "You're not going to get within a mile of her. I'm warning you right now, Eric. Stay away from those girls or I'll have you thrown in jail so fast your head will spin. I may not be much of a mother, but I'll do whatever I have to do to keep them safe. If I think you're posing the slightest threat to them, I'll go to the authorities. I will. I mean it. I'll keep quiet as long as you stay away, but the moment you come near those girls, you'll find this filthy perversion of yours smeared over every paper in the country."

She fled from the room.

"Lilly!" He started to go after her, but then he made himself stop. He had to pull himself together and think.

His cigarette pack was empty. Crushing it in his fist, he threw it across the room toward the fireplace. The conviction he had seen in Lilly's eyes chilled him. She truly believed what she was saying. But how could she believe he was capable of something so obscene when she knew how much he loved those girls? He began pacing the floor, trying to remember everything he had ever done with his daughters, but it was so impossible, so ridiculous.

Gradually, he grew calmer. He had to stop reacting emotionally and think logically. This was another one of Lilly's trips off the deep end, and he should be able to prove that without any difficulty. The whole thing was so patently absurd. Fathers all over the country bathed their children and took them into bed when they were frightened. His lawyer would straighten it out in no time.

"I've been taking a crash course in child sexual abuse since your phone call, Eric, and I'm afraid this may not be quite as easy as you think."

Mike Longacre leaned forward over his desk. He was in his late thirties, but thinning hair and a tendency toward pudginess made him look older. He had been Eric's lawyer through the divorce, and the men had developed a distant sort of friendship. They'd done some deep-sea fishing together, played racquetball, but they had little else in common.

Eric shot up from his chair and thrust one hand back through his hair. He hadn't had any sleep; he was running on cigarettes and adrenaline. "What do you mean it's not easy? The whole thing is incredible. I would no more harm my daughters than I'd cut off my arm. Lilly's paranoia is the danger to them, not me."

"Sexual abuse of children is a tricky area."

"Are you telling me you actually think Lilly can make this stick? I told you what she said. She obviously twisted some innocent remarks Rachel made. There's nothing more to it."

"I understand. I'm simply advising you that we have to tread carefully here. Sexual abuse of children is the one area of the law where the accused has no rights. You're guilty until proven innocent. Remember that a sickening number of these charges are true, and the court's primary concern is protecting the children. Countless fathers are molesting their daughters every day."

"But I'm not one of them! My God, my children don't need protection from me. Goddamnit, Mike, I want this thing stopped before it goes any farther."

The lawyer toyed with his gold pen. "Let me tell you a little about what can happen here. Everyone used to believe that children never lied about sexual abuse, but we've discovered that they can be coached. Let's say the mother has gotten a lousy divorce settlement. Her husband is driving a BMW and she can't pay her grocery bill. Maybe he wants to challenge the custody arrangement, or he isn't making his child support payments."

"None of this applies to Lilly. I've given her everything she's wanted."

Mike held up his hand. "For whatever reason, women frequently feel powerless in divorce cases. Maybe the kid says something that starts her thinking. She begins asking questions. 'Daddy touched you here, didn't he?' She pops a piece of candy in the kid's mouth, and when the kid says no, she hands out another piece of candy. 'Are you sure? Now think hard.' The kid is getting all this extra attention and begins to fabricate to keep Mom happy. There have even been cases where mothers have threatened to kill themselves if the children don't say what she tells them."

"Lilly wouldn't do that. She's not a monster. Jesus, she loves the girls."

There was a moment of silence in the office. "Then what's going on here, Eric?"

Eric swallowed hard and looked up at the ceiling. "I don't know. God help me, I don't know."

He turned back to the attorney, struck by a new thought. "Rachel's a hardheaded little girl. Even though she's just turned five, I don't know how much she could be influenced. We'll hire the best psychiatrists in the field. Let them talk to her."

"In theory, that's a good idea, but in practice it backfires all the time."

"I don't see how. Rachel's well adjusted. She's articulate. She's—"

"She's also a child. Listen to me, Eric. We're not dealing with an exact science. Most of the professionals who specialize in child abuse cases are well trained and competent, but it's still a relatively new discipline. Even the most capable make mistakes in judgment. There have been a lot of scary cases. For example, a little girl is given an anatomically correct male doll. She's never seen anything like this before, and she pulls on its penis. Bingo. The overzealous expert takes this as a sign of abuse. I'm not exaggerating. These things happen all the time, and there aren't any guarantees. I'm sorry. I'd like to be able to reassure you that a psychiatric exam of Rachel would exonerate you, but I simply can't. The truth is, you'll be playing Russian roulette if you press the issue."

Mike gave him a slow, steady gaze. "You also have to remember that Rebecca would be questioned. I imagine she could be influenced quite easily."

Eric squeezed his eyes shut, his flicker of hope dying. His sweet little Becca would do anything or say anything if she thought it would please.

Mike's chair squeaked as he shifted his weight. "Before you even think about challenging Lilly, you need to understand the consequences. Once she goes public with her accusations, everything happens quickly and none of it is good. The girls will be taken away from you while the investigation goes on."

"How can that happen? This is America. Don't I have any rights?"

"It's as I said. In child abuse cases you're guilty until proven innocent. The system has to work that way for protection, and the best you can hope for while the investigation goes on is supervised visitation. The investigations themselves are supposed to be kept confidential, but the girls' teachers will be questioned, friends and neighbors, all the hired help. Anyone with half a brain will be able to figure out what's going on, and since you're involved, I can guarantee it'll hit the papers long before the courts get hold of it. I don't think I need to elaborate on what being accused of child molestation will do to your career as a leading man. The public will put up with a lot, but—"

"I don't give a shit about my career!"

"You don't mean that." He held up his hand and went on. "The girls will be forced to undergo medical examinations. A series of them if this drags on."

Eric felt sick. How could he put his babies through something like that? How could he hurt them that way? They were innocents. When they were born, he had thought he had broken the cycle, but once again it had caught him up. Why did he always have to hurt the innocents?

"The examinations will prove they haven't been abused," he said.

"Maybe in an ideal world. The truth of the matter is that in the majority of cases, there isn't any physical evidence. Most sexual abuse involves fondling or oral copulation. An intact hymen is no proof that a child hasn't been molested."

Eric felt as if the walls of the office were closing in on him. He hadn't believed—He hadn't even let himself consider the possibility that he might lose his daughters. Any minute now he'd wake up, and this would only be a nightmare.

The lawyer shook his head. "The minute these charges become public, a man has a loaded gun pointed at his head. For someone who's a celebrity, it's even worse. On the positive side, I've seen some fathers go bankrupt defending themselves in these cases, and you don't have to worry about that."

Pain and frustration made Eric's voice sharp. "Is that the best you can do for hope? That I can afford to defend myself? What the fuck kind of comfort is that?"

Longacre stiffened. "It probably wasn't wise for you to have taken your daughters into bed in the first place."

Eric's rage exploded. He vaulted across the desk and grabbed the attorney by the collar of his shirt. "You son of a—"

"Eric!"

As he drew back his fist, the alarm in Longacre's eyes stopped him, and he forced himself to let go.

Mike gasped for breath. "You fool."

Eric was trembling as he pulled away. "I'm sorry. I—"

Unable to say more, he fled from the office and drove frantically to Lilly's house. He had to get to his children. But when he arrived at the house, everything was locked and the curtains were drawn.

He found the gardener working by the pool in the back. The man said Lilly had left the country. And she had taken the girls with her.

Three weeks later Eric flew to Paris, where his team of private investigators had located Lilly and the girls. As he stared blindly out the window of the taxi that was moving through the traffic on the quai de la Tournelle, he knew that the last weeks had been the longest in his life. He had smoked too much, drunk too much, and, in the wake of his Oscar triumph, been unable to concentrate on his work.

As the taxi crossed the pont de la Tournelle to the tiny Ile Saint-Louis that sat in the center of the Seine, the driver kept grinning at Eric in his rearview mirror. Eric had long ago accepted the fact that there were few places left in the world where his face wasn't recognized. He looked off to his left toward the neighboring Ile de la Cité's famous landmark, but Notre-Dame's slender spire and flying buttresses barely registered in his mind.

The Ile Saint-Louis sat between Paris's Right and Left banks where it formed the period to the Ile de la Cité's exclamation mark. The island was one of Paris's most exclusive and expensive neighborhoods and had housed a number of luminaries over the years, including Chagall and James Jones as well as current residents such as Baron Guy de Rothschild and Madame Georges Pompidou.

The taxi let Eric out in front of the address the investigators had given him, a seventeenth-century town house located on the fashionable quai d'Orléans. Across the Seine the Left Bank glimmered in the late morning light. As Eric paid the fare, he looked up toward the second floor windows and saw the draperies move. Lilly had been watching for him.

As desperately as he yearned to see his daughters, he knew the situation was too explosive for him to give in to the urge to arrive unexpectedly, and so he had called Lilly early that morning. At first she had refused to see him, but when she realized he was going to come whether she wanted him to or not, she had agreed to meet him at eleven when both girls would be gone.

The town house was built of limestone, and the intricately carved wooden front door was enameled a rich shade of blue. White shutters, their top halves open to reveal pots of trailing pink ivy geraniums, graced the long, narrow windows. He was about to lift the knocker when the door swung open and Lilly stepped out.

She looked tired and drawn, even thinner than he remembered, with faint purple smudges lodging in the hollows beneath her eyes. "I warned you to stay away," she said, hugging her arms beneath her silk blouse, although the morning was warm.

"We have to talk."

He saw a group of tourists coming toward them and turned his head away. The last thing he needed to do while he was trying to reclaim his life was sign autographs. He snatched a pair of sunglasses from the pocket of his white cotton dress shirt and shoved them on. "It's too public here. Can't we go inside?"

"I don't want you near their things."

The cruelty of her comment filled him with rage, and he wanted to strike her. Instead, he grasped her upper arm so hard that she winced and pulled her along the tree-lined quay toward a bench that faced the river.

The setting was idyllic. Tall poplars cast dappled shadows over the walk. A fisherman stood on the banks near a graceful iron light pole. A pair of lovers walked by, their bodies so intertwined it was difficult to tell where one began and the other ended.

She sat down on the iron bench and began clenching and unclenching her hands. He remained standing and stared blindly out toward the water. For the rest of his life, he would hate this beautiful city.

"I'm not giving in to your threats any longer, Lilly. I'm going public. I've decided to take my chances in court."

"You can't do that!" she cried.

"Just watch me."

He looked down at her. Her fingernails had been bitten so far down that the cuticles were bloody.

She gasped for breath as if she had been running. "The publicity will ruin your career."

"I don't care anymore!" he exclaimed. "My career doesn't mean anything without my children."

"What's the matter?" she sneered. "Can't you find anybody else who'll give you your sexual thrills?"

He grabbed her. She gasped, trying to pull away from him by cowering into the bench. His rage was a blinding white light, and he knew that if he didn't let her go, he would hurt her.

With a dark oath, he dropped her arm and whipped off his sunglasses. They snapped in his hands, and he hurled them into the Seine. "God damn you!"

"I won't let you near them!" she cried, jumping up from the bench. "I'll do whatever I have to. If you go to court or do anything to try to get them back, I'll send them underground."

He stared at her. "You'll do what?"

A pulse beat frantically in a thin blue vein near her temple. "There's an underground system that protects children when the law won't. It's illegal, but effective." Her gray eyes darkened with bitterness. "I knew you'd try to get to them, so I've learned a lot about it in the past few weeks. All I have to do is say the word, Eric, and the girls will disappear. Neither of us will have them then."

"You can't mean that. You wouldn't send them into hiding with strangers."

"The strangers won't molest them, and I'll do whatever I have to do to keep them safe." Her face sagged. He saw how tired she looked, but he felt no pity for her.

"Please," she whispered. "Don't make me send them away. They've already lost their father. Don't make them lose their mother, too."

Beneath her exhaustion he saw determination, and he knew with sickening certainty that she wasn't making an idle threat. Her conviction in his guilt was absolute.

The ball of pain spun inside him, growing larger with each revolution. "How can you believe I'd hurt my daughters?" he asked hoarsely. "What did I ever do to make you think I'm capable of something like this? Jesus, Lilly, you know how much I love them."

Tears rolled down her cheeks. "I don't know anything anymore except that I have to protect them. I'll do that, even if it means giving them up to strangers. No little girls should have to suffer what they've suffered."

She turned to leave.

He took a quick step after them, his voice raw with

desperation. "Just tell me how they're doing. Please, Lilly. At least do that for me."

She shook her head and walked away, leaving him more alone than he'd ever been in his life.

21

EXTERIOR.
PASTURE FENCE NEAR THE RANCH HOUSE—DAY

Dash and Janie are standing by the fence. Dash holds a crumpled letter in his fist.

JANIE
Did Blake write you? When's he coming home on leave?

DASH
This letter isn't from Blake. It's from your grandmother.

JANIE
(excited)
My grandmother? I didn't even know I had one of those!

DASH
Do you remember all the stuff I told you about your ma?

JANIE
(cheerfully)
I remember. You said she was the sweetest thing you'd ever met and you couldn't figure out how she gave birth to a spawn of Satan like myself.

DASH

She was sweet, Janie. But I also told you she was
an orphan, and that was a lie.

JANIE

A lie? Why'd you lie, Pop?

DASH

Your mama's parents kicked her out of the house
when she was only seventeen years old. They
were pretty strict people. She wasn't married.
And she was pregnant with you.

JANIE
(puzzled)
You mean you and Ma had to get married?

DASH

I married your ma because I wanted to. There
wasn't any *have to* about it.

He gazes down at the letter.

DASH

Apparently your grandfather died last year,
and your grandmother's getting old. She wants
to see you, so she hired some private detectives
to track us down. According to this letter, she'll
be here day after tomorrow.

JANIE

Wow! I can't believe this. Do you think she'll
have one of those buns on top of her head and
bake pies?

DASH

Janie, there's somethin' I got to tell you. Maybe I
should have told you a long time ago, but—I
don't know—I couldn't seem to bring myself to
do it. Now I guess I don't have any choice. Your
grandmother knows the truth, and if I don't tell
you, she will.

JANIE
You're starting to make me nervous, Pop.

DASH
I'm sorry, Janie. I don't know how else to say this but straight out. Your Ma was already pregnant with you when I met her for the first time.

JANIE
But that doesn't make sense. How could—Are you trying to tell me—Do you mean that you're not really my father?

DASH
I'm afraid that's about the size of it.

"Stupid, stupid, stupid." Honey slammed the covers holding the final script of *The Dash Coogan Show*.

"I hope you're not talking about me." Dash came through the door of the motor home where Honey was curled up on the couch. He wore jeans and cowboy boots with a tweed sports coat. A silver and turquoise thunderhead bolo glimmered at the collar of his denim shirt.

Although they'd been married for five years, her heart gave the funny jump-skip that still happened when he came up on her unexpectedly. She didn't think she'd ever get enough of looking at that legendary face—those rough-hewn features so elemental that they seemed to have been carved by the wind and then baked by the desert sun.

He pocketed the key he'd used to open the door, leaned down, and kissed her. "I know I haven't taken all those fancy college classes like somebody I could mention, but I don't consider myself stupid."

She laughed and wrapped her arms around his neck to pull him closer. "You're sly as a fox, you old cowboy."

He kissed her again, sliding his hands beneath the baggy powder-blue knit sweater she was wearing with a short white denim skirt. "I thought you were going to work on that paper you got due."

"I am. I just—" She released him. "Yesterday I was straightening up that mess you call a den, and I found the scripts from our final season. I decided to bring the last one along to reread. See if the Fatal Episode was as bad as I remembered."

He took off his sports coat and tossed it over a chair. "You could have asked me. I'd have told you it was even worse than you remembered."

She rose from the couch and walked a few steps to the coffeepot she kept going whenever she went on location with Dash. They were in a rough East Los Angeles neighborhood where he was shooting a low-budget television movie about a Texas cop on assignment with the LAPD. She handed him a mug and then poured another for herself. Leaning back against the small counter, she crossed her ankles, which were encased in the powder-blue socks she was wearing with her white Keds. When she had gotten dressed that morning, Dash had told her she looked all of thirteen and he would appreciate it very much if she didn't get him arrested for something unsavory like statutory rape.

She took a sip of coffee. "I don't know why the writers thought that kind of stupid explanation about Dash not really being Janie's father would make audiences forget they were watching a married couple pretend to be father and daughter."

He sat down on the couch and leaned back. When he stretched out his legs, his cowboy boots reached halfway down the center of the motor home. "By the time the Fatal Episode aired, we didn't have any viewers left anyway, so I guess it didn't matter."

"It mattered to me. I hated the idea that they tried to save the show by deciding that Dash and Janie weren't really father and daughter. That was even stupider than Bobby's dream on *Dallas*."

"It was Pam's dream, not Bobby's. And nothing could be that stupid."

A police siren from the street outside penetrated the thin shell of the motor home. Dash scowled. "Damn. I don't know why I let you talk me into bringing you along today. This neighborhood's too dangerous."

Honey rolled her eyes. "Here we go again. Papa Dash being overprotective."

"Overprotective! Do you have any idea how many drug murders and gang shootings have happened around here just in the last few months? And this two-bit production company didn't hire any security people. They probably don't even have a city permit to film."

"Dash, I've kept the door locked, and I'm not going out. You know I have to write my English lit paper, and this is a perfect place to do it because there aren't any distractions. If I were home, I'd be out riding, or digging in the flower bed, or baking you a chocolate cake."

He sputtered some more, and she gave him a sympathetic smile. She tried not to tease him too much about his overprotectiveness because she understood that he couldn't help himself. No matter how certain he was of her love, he could never completely set aside the little boy buried inside him who was afraid the person he loved most was going to be snatched away.

"It's my fault," he grumbled. "I like having you around so much I lose my common sense. Rub my neck, will you? That fight scene yesterday got me all stiff."

He turned sideways, and she went over to the couch, where she knelt in back of him. She pushed her hair behind one ear. As she cocked her head, it tumbled forward on the opposite side and fell in a honey-colored waterfall over his shoulder. He leaned against her and she began massaging the muscles of his shoulders, closing her eyes for a moment to absorb the solid, familiar feel of him. Their marriage had brought her more happiness than she had ever believed possible, and even all the professional and financial difficulties that had followed had never made her regret what they had done.

"I'm too old for these cops and robbers pictures," he grumbled.

"You won't be fifty till summer. That's hardly ancient."

"Right now I feel like it is. Maybe trying to keep up with the sexual excesses of my twenty-five-year-old child bride has something to do with it."

She buried her lips in the side of his neck while her hands trailed down along the front of his shirt to the waistband of his jeans. "Want to knock off a quickie?"

"Didn't we do that early this morning?"

"Anything that happens before six o'clock counts for the day before."

"Now why's that?"

"It's all a matter of relativity. I learned about it in that philosophy class I took last year." She slipped her fingertips inside his waistband. "It's far too complex for me to explain to an ignorant cowpoke, so I'm afraid you'll have to take my word for it."

"Is that so?" He leaned forward so abruptly that she upended over his shoulder.

"Hey!"

He caught her in his lap before she could sprawl to the floor. "It seems to me somebody's getting a little too smarty-pants to fit into her britches."

She squirmed into a more comfortable position in his arms and gazed up into that wonderful face. "Are you ever sorry you married me?"

He cupped her breast and gently kneaded it. "About a hundred times a day." And then the teasing light faded from his green eyes and he drew her against him with a muffled groan. "My sweet little girl. Sometimes I think my life didn't start until the day I married you."

She lay contented against him. Maybe their marriage was even more precious to her because it wasn't perfect. They'd had so many problems right from the beginning: their guilt over the demise of the TV series, the humiliation they had suffered from the press, the fact that his daughter hated her guts.

Most of their problems hadn't gone away. They'd only recently emerged from their financial troubles. Instead of sheltering the money she'd brought into their marriage, she'd used most of it to put a big dent in his IRS debt. He'd been furious when he'd found out, but she didn't regret a single penny. The debt was finally paid off, and they had begun to set aside money for the future.

A worse problem was the beating his professional career had taken as a result of their marriage. It saddened her to see him forced to accept roles in second-rate television movies such as the one he was shooting now. He shrugged off her concern by saying he'd never been much of an actor anyway, and any work was good work.

Maybe he wasn't a versatile actor, but to her mind, he was something even better. He was a legend, the last of the solitary individualists who wore a white hat and stood for decency. No matter how much they had needed the money, she wouldn't let him accept any parts that tarnished that image.

As her nose brushed against his shirt collar, she knew that the biggest conflict between them—the one that never went away—was Dash's refusal to let her have a child. The issue lurked like an unwelcome visitor in all the invisible corners of their existence together. She yearned for his baby, dreamed of bassinets and snap-legged sleepers and a sweet little down-covered head. But he said he was too old for a baby and that he'd already proven he didn't know how to be a father.

She no longer believed his excuses. She knew he was afraid something would happen to her in childbirth, and he needed her too much to take the risk. What she didn't know was how she could fight a fear that was rooted in love.

He poked his finger through one of her curls. "I almost forgot to tell you. Apparently there was a news report about Eric Dillon on television a couple of hours ago."

"That arrogant little bastard."

"Dillon's at least six feet tall. I don't know why you call him little."

"Six feet is still four inches shorter than you. That makes him little in my book."

"That's a pretty narrow definition of short, especially

coming from somebody who can't even reach the top shelf of her kitchen cupboards."

"I notice that you're not debating the fact that I called him a bastard. Since he won his Oscar last month, he's probably even more insufferable than I remember."

"He wasn't that bad, Honey. You shouldn't blame him for the fact that you fell in love with him and he had to spend all his spare time hiding out from you."

"I did not fall in love with him, Dash Coogan. I just had a crush. You were the one I fell in love with."

He grinned. "I've been thinking. How do you feel about going up to Alaska this summer and doing some backpacking along the Chilkoot Trail?"

"That's a wonderful idea. I've always wanted to go to Alaska."

"We don't have to. I may not be a multimillionaire, but I can afford something better for you than a tent. If you want to go to Paris or something—"

"I do. But not with you. I can just hear you complaining about the traffic and the fact that everybody's speaking French. Maybe the next time Liz goes to Europe, I'll go with her."

"That sounds like a good idea."

They smiled at each other, both of them knowing she wouldn't go anywhere without him. She'd lived through an entire childhood without anyone to love her, and now that she had Dash, she didn't want to be with anyone else. She was dependent on him in a way that she had never permitted herself to be dependent on anyone, even when she was a child. He was both her greatest strength and her greatest weakness.

She shifted her weight to avoid the corner of his belt buckle where it was digging into her waist and remembered that she had interrupted him. "So what did you hear about Eric?"

"Oh, yeah. Apparently he tried to straighten out a curve on Mulholland last night. He was driving drunk, the stupid son of a bitch."

"I hope he's all right."

"I guess it was pretty serious. Some broken bones; I don't know what all. Luckily, no one else was involved."

"It's hard to feel a lot of sympathy for him, isn't it? He just won an Oscar. He's rich and successful, at the top of his career. And he's got two little girls. How could he be so self-indulgent?"

"Remember that he grew up with lots of money. I doubt he ever had to work too hard for anything. People like that don't have a lot of depth to them."

"It's funny, though, how somebody who's so obviously shallow can turn in the performances he does. Sometimes when I watch one of his films, he makes me shiver."

"That doesn't have anything to do with his performance. It's your leftover sexual attraction to him."

She laughed and threw herself against him, toppling him back against the couch so that he bumped his head on the wall.

"Damn little hellcat," he murmured against her mouth.

She pulled his shirttail from his jeans. "How much time do we have before you need to be back on the set?"

"Not much."

"Doesn't matter." The snap on his jeans gave way beneath her fingers. "You've been so quick on the trigger lately that I'm sure we can manage."

He reached back to close the open set of blinds on the motor home window. "Are you casting aspersions on my staying power?"

"I absolutely am."

His hands slid beneath her sweater and unfastened her bra. He brushed his thumbs over her nipples. "If you wouldn't wiggle around so much and make all those moaning sounds in my ear, I might last longer."

"I do not moan. I—" She moaned. "Oh, that's not fair. You know I'm sensitive there."

"And about a hundred other places."

Within minutes, he had located half a dozen of them.

Their lovemaking was filled with laughter and passion. As

sometimes happened when they were finished and Honey lay against his chest, she could feel tears welling in her eyes.

Thank you for giving him to me, God. Thank you so much.

Dash locked the door of the motor home behind him when he left. She opened the blinds so she could watch him walk away with that rolling, bowlegged gait she loved. Her very own cowboy husband. If she could only convince him to let her have a baby, she'd never ask for anything else again.

The view from the window was grim and depressing. The production vehicles and motor homes were grouped together in what had once been the parking lot for the abandoned light-bulb factory across the street, where the crew was gathered to film today's scenes. The factory's brick walls held spray-painted obscenities and gang messages. As always happened on location, a small crowd had formed to watch the actors: kids truant from school, people who had wandered out from the local shops, an assortment of vagrants. A street vendor was even selling ice cream bars.

Still, she didn't let the festive atmosphere delude her. For once, Dash was right to be cautious; this was a dangerous neighborhood. When they'd gotten out of their car that morning, she'd seen a broken hypodermic needle lying in a weedy hole in the asphalt.

She turned away from the window and walked over to the table where she was working on the paper for her lit class. She regarded the notes she had made without enthusiasm. She was twenty-five years old, too old to be going to school. Maybe that was why she was having so much difficulty getting started on this paper. Since she had no specific career goal in mind, she took classes more to fill time than for any other reason. All she wanted from life was to be Dash Coogan's wife, the mother of his child, and to play Janie Jones for the rest of her life. But if she told Dash school had begun to seem pointless, she knew exactly what he would say.

"Damn right it is. Give that underworked agent of yours a

phone call and get your cute little butt back to work in front of the cameras where you belong."

Dash persisted in believing that she was a great actress despite the fact that she'd only played one part. She wished he were right and her talent was genuine instead of a gimmick. Not even to him would she confess how much she missed acting.

Occasionally when he was away from the ranch, she read scenes from plays aloud: everything from Shakespeare to Neil Simon and Beth Henley. But it was always a disaster. She sounded phony and stilted, like an actor in a junior high play, and any fantasies she had about going back in front of the cameras quickly dissolved. In the past five years she'd lived through a humiliating amount of abuse from the press and the public. The only thing they hadn't been able to take away from her were her performances as Janie Jones, and she wouldn't let anything tarnish that.

She settled at the table to work, but she couldn't seem to concentrate. Instead, she found herself thinking about her last phone conversation with Chantal. As usual, Chantal had wanted money, this time so she and Gordon could take a cruise.

"You know I can't afford that," Honey had said. "I don't have a source of income now, and I've been telling you for the past year that I can't keep up the payments on your house much longer. Instead of cruises, you need to start thinking about finding some place less expensive to live."

"Don't start nagging me, Honey," Chantal had replied. "I can't take any more pressure now. Me and Gordon have both been under a lot of stress these last six months, ever since those doctors told me about my fallopian tubes and all. It's hard facing the fact that I can't ever have a baby."

Chantal had said the one thing guaranteed to win Honey's sympathy, and she had immediately softened. "Chantal, I'm sorry about that. You know I am. Maybe I should send you to another doctor. Maybe—"

"No more doctors." Chantal had said. "They've all told me the same thing, and I can't stand any more of those examinations. Besides, Honey, if you can find the money to pay all those doctor bills, I don't see why you can't come up with enough for a cruise."

Last night when Honey had mentioned the conversation to Dash as the two of them were getting ready for bed, he'd started badgering her again.

"Chantal's just using you. To tell the truth, I think she's more relieved than sorry that she can't get pregnant. She's too lazy to have a baby. Don't you realize that by making Gordon and Chantal so dependent on you, you've robbed them of the chance to become productive people? I know you always think you know what's best for everybody else in the world, but that's not necessarily true."

She'd slapped down her hairbrush and glared at him. "You don't understand, Dash. It's not in Chantal's nature to be productive."

"It's in anybody's nature if they're hungry enough. And what about Gordon? He's got two arms and two legs. He's perfectly capable of carrying his own weight."

"But you don't understand how it was when I first came to L.A. Gordon threatened to take Chantal away from me. She was all I had, and I couldn't let that happen."

"He was manipulating you, is what he was doing."

"That may be, but I can hardly turn my back on Chantal now that Sophie's gone. It's been three years since Sophie died, and she still hasn't gotten over it."

"If you ask me, you've mourned your Aunt Sophie a lot longer than Chantal ever did."

"That's a dirt-rotten thing to say."

He'd begun noisily brushing his teeth, effectively shutting off further conversation. She'd stomped into the bathroom and closed the door, not wanting to admit even to herself that he was at least partially right. Sophie's death seemed to have hit her harder than Chantal. But it had been so unnecessary, so lacking in dignity. Her aunt had choked on the wing bone in some store-bought fried chicken Gordon had heated up in the microwave.

At least Buck Ochs was gone. Sophie hadn't even been cold in her grave before he'd brought home a hooker. To

Gordon's credit, he'd thrown Buck out, and the last Honey had heard, Sophie's former husband had gone to work in a park near Fresno.

She pushed away thoughts of her family and forced herself to get to work on her paper. Two hours later, with her notes organized and the first few pages written, she rose to pour herself a fresh mug of coffee. As she glanced through the back window, she saw Dash walking across the narrow, dirty street toward the motor home.

Once again, her heart gave that silly hop-skip. She looked at her watch and saw that it was nearly four o'clock. Maybe he was done for the day and they could go home early. With a smile, she set down her coffee, unlocked the door, and stepped outside.

The late afternoon was hot and humid, more like July in South Carolina than May in southern California. The vans and trucks surrounding her were jammed so close together that the air couldn't circulate, and everything smelled of gasoline and exhaust fumes. As Dash crossed from the street into the parking lot, she waved at him.

He lifted his arm to wave back, but halfway up, his hand stalled. He was close enough that she could see him frown. Just then, she heard the muffled sound of a woman's cry. She turned sharply.

Off to her right, two of the larger motor homes were parked parallel to each other, forming a narrow, dark tunnel less than five feet across. She saw a flash of movement toward the rear of the vehicles and took a quick step forward.

A thin, swarthy-faced man wearing a ripped red T-shirt and shiny black pants was dragging a young Hispanic woman into the confined space. Horrified, Honey watched as the man rammed the woman against the side of the larger vehicle and made a grab for the purse she held clamped in her arms. The woman screamed, hunching her shoulders to protect the purse at the same time she struggled to free herself from him.

The woman and her assailant were less than thirty feet away, and, instinctively, Honey began to rush forward, but before she could go far, she heard the thud of running feet behind her. Dash shot past, giving her a hard shove in the center of her back that sent her sprawling.

She gasped as her bare knees scraped on the asphalt and the heels of her hands slid over the rough surface. The pain was sharp, but not as sharp as the sense of dread that swept through her. She jerked her head back up.

From the ground she could see it all. She could see the pattern of bright yellow flowers on the skirt of the woman's dress, hear her cries for help as she foolishly clung to her purse.

Dash stood not far from the point where Honey lay, his back to her, legs braced. Her heart pounding, she opened her mouth to yell at him to be careful, not to play the hero, not to—

"Let her go!" Dash called out.

Time hung suspended, so that the most insignificant details would be forever etched in her mind with grotesque clarity. The veins of cracked asphalt that led to her husband's boots, the raveling hanging from the hem of his jeans. She felt the hot sun beating down on her back, smelled the asphalt, saw the long shadow cast by his tall frame. Dominating it all was the wild, drug-crazed expression in the eyes of the woman's assailant as he stood at the end of that dark tunnel formed by the production vehicles and spun to face Dash.

In one grotesque motion, the man snatched a snub-nosed pistol from the waistband of his shiny black pants and raised it. A horrible scream spilled from her throat as she watched the wild-eyed addict fire two shots.

Dash twisted and crumpled to the ground in a slow, awkward movement. A cloying gray fog enveloped her, making everything seem unreal. In the narrow tunnel the woman fell, too, a bright yellow blur, as the addict shoved her down and ran away, the purse lying forgotten at her side.

Dash's arm lay over the cracked pavement. Honey saw his bare wrist, the broad back of his hand. Sobbing like a wounded animal, she began to crawl toward him on her hands and her bloody, scraped knees. Through the gray fog, she told herself that everything would be all right. Just seconds ago she had waved at him. None of this was real because nothing this ghastly could happen without warning. Not so quickly, not without an omen.

She was barely aware of the shouts of the crew members as they came running from the other side of the street. She saw only her husband's fingers clawing at the asphalt.

She struggled to her knees beside him, her body shaking with wrenching sobs. "Dash!"

"Honey . . . I'm . . ."

Gripping his arms, she turned him so that his head and one shoulder were resting in her lap. A big stain was spreading over his chest like a sunburst. She remembered that he'd had a wound like this in one of his films, but she couldn't think which one it was.

She cupped his cheeks and whispered on a sob, "You can get up now. Please, Dash . . . Please, get up . . ."

His eyelids flickered, and his mouth began to work. "Honey . . ." He whispered her name on a horrible wheeze.

"Don't talk. Please, God, don't talk . . ."

His eyes locked with hers. They were full of love and bleak with pain. "I knew . . . I'd . . . break . . . your . . . heart," he gasped.

And then his outspread hand went limp.

Inhuman, wrenching sounds slipped from her throat. The asphalt was so black, his blood so red. His eyes stared up at her, open but unseeing.

One of the crew members touched her, but she shook him off.

She cradled her husband's head in her lap, stroked his cheek while she rocked and whispered to him. "You're going . . . to be fine. You're all right . . . My darling . . . My own . . . cowboy."

His warm blood seeped through her skirt, making her thighs sticky. She continued to rock him. "I love you, my darling. I'll . . . love you . . . forever." Her teeth were chattering and her body convulsing with shivers. "Nothing bad can happen. Not a thing. You're the hero. The hero never . . ."

She pressed kisses to his forehead, the ends of her hair dipping in his blood, tasting the blood in her mouth, muttering that he wouldn't die. She would die instead of him. She would take his place. God would understand. The writers would fix everything. She stroked his hair. Kissed his lips.

"Honey." One of the men touched her.

She lifted her head and her face contorted with fury. "Go away! Everybody go away! He's all right."

The man shook his head, his cheeks wet with tears. "Honey, I'm afraid Dash is dead."

She pulled her husband's beloved head closer against her breasts and rested her cheek against his hair. She spoke fiercely in a flood of words. "You're wrong. Don't you understand? The hero can't die! He can't, you stupid God! You can't break the rules. Don't you know? The hero never dies!"

It took three medics to pull her away from Dash Coogan's lifeless body.

22

The room was stifling, but she lay on the bed wrapped in Dash's old sheepskin coat. Beneath it her nylons stuck to her legs and the black dress she had worn to the funeral was soaked with perspiration. She kept her face buried in the collar of the coat. It held his scent.

Sweaty tendrils of hair clung to the back of her neck, but she didn't notice. Liz had come and gone, bringing a plate of food that Honey couldn't eat and trying to talk her into staying at the beach house for a few weeks so she wouldn't be alone. But Honey wanted to be alone so she could find Dash.

She curled tighter into the coat, her eyes pressed closed. *Talk to me, Dash. Let me feel you. Please, please let me feel you so I know you're not gone.* She tried to make her mind go blank so Dash could reach her, but a terror so black she wanted to scream swept through her. Her mouth opened against the soft collar.

She wasn't aware that someone had come into the bedroom until she felt the mattress sag next to her. She wanted to strike out at all of them and make them leave her alone. They had no right to intrude on her privacy like this.

"Honey?" Meredith spoke her name and then began to cry. "I—I want to ask you to forgive me. I've been hateful and jealous and vindictive. I knew it was wrong, but I couldn't stop myself. All I—All I ever wanted was for Daddy to love me, but he loved you instead."

Honey didn't want Meredith's confidences, and she had no comfort to give. She pushed herself up on the bed and sat on the edge with her back to Meredith. She clutched the lapels of Dash's sheepskin jacket around her. "He loved you, too." She spoke woodenly, knowing she had to say the words. "You were his daughter, and he never forgot that."

"I—I was so hateful to you. So jealous."

"It doesn't matter. Nothing matters."

"I know Daddy is at peace and we should be giving praise instead of grieving, but I can't help it."

Honey said nothing. What did Meredith know of a love so strong that it was as fundamental as oxygen? All of Meredith's emotions were directed safely toward heaven. Honey willed herself to disappear inside Dash's jacket until Meredith left.

"Could you—Could you forgive me, Honey?"

"Yes," Honey replied automatically. "I forgive you."

The door opened and she heard Wanda's voice. "Meredith, your brother's leaving. You need to come and say good-bye."

The mattress moved as Meredith rose. "Good-bye, Honey. I'm—I'm sorry."

"Good-bye, Meredith."

The door shut. Honey rose from the side of the bed, but as she turned toward the window, she saw that she still wasn't alone. Wanda stood watching her. Her eyes were red with weeping, her sprayed blond bubble flattened on one side. At the funeral she had carried on as if she were the widow instead of Honey.

She dabbed at her eyes and sniffed. "Meredith's been jealous of you from the first time she saw you and Randy on TV. He wasn't much of a father to her—I guess you know about that—and watching the two of you being so close was like an open wound to her."

"It doesn't matter now."

Wanda's perfume bore the heavy scent of carnations. Or maybe it wasn't her perfume. Maybe Honey was smelling the overpowering scent of all the funeral floral arrangements.

"Is there anything I can do for you?" Wanda asked.

"Make everybody go away," Honey replied dully. "That's all I want."

Wanda nodded and moved to the door where she blew her nose, then spoke briskly. "I wish you well, Honey. I admit I didn't think Randy should have married you. But all of his ex-wives were at that funeral today, and the three of us together never gave him as much happiness as you did in a single day."

Dimly, Honey realized that it had taken a generosity of spirit for Wanda to make that statement, but she only wanted to be rid of her so she could lie down on the bed again and close her eyes and try to reach Dash. She had to find him. If she couldn't find him, she would die herself.

Wanda left, and within an hour, the rest of the guests were gone, too. As night fell, Honey walked aimlessly through the house in her stockinged feet. His coat hung so long on her that when she slipped her hands into the pockets, her fingers couldn't touch bottom. Eventually, she curled up in the big green leather chair where he used to sit watching television.

The man who had murdered Dash was an addict out on parole. He'd been killed in a gun battle with the police several hours after Dash had died. Everybody seemed to think she should feel better because Dash's murderer was dead, but revenge meant nothing to her. It couldn't bring Dash back.

She must have dozed because when she awakened it was past two in the morning. She went into the kitchen and began aimlessly opening cupboard doors. His favorite coffee mug sat on the shelf; an open pack of his spearmint LifeSavers lay by the sugar bowl waiting for him. She walked into their bathroom and saw his toothbrush in a blue china holder on the counter. She rubbed her thumb over the bone-dry bristles and then slipped it into her pocket. On her way out of the bedroom, she extracted a pair of his socks from the laundry hamper and put them in the other pocket.

There was no moon overhead when she went outside, only the faint glow from the light bulb above the door of the stables. As she crossed the yard toward the paddock, the stones tore holes in the feet of her nylons, but she paid no attention. She made her way to the fence where they had stood together so many times.

She waited and waited.

Finally, her legs gave out and she sank down into the dirt. She pulled his toothbrush from one pocket and his socks from the other. They formed a warm damp ball in her hand. Tears wet her cheeks as the silence suffocated her.

She slipped his toothbrush into her mouth and sucked on it.

As the weeks passed she grew thin and frail. Occasionally she remembered to eat, more frequently she didn't. She slept at odd times and in short snatches, sometimes in his chair, sometimes in their bed with an article of his clothing pressed to her cheek. She felt as if she had been tipped over and emptied of every emotion except despair.

The newspapers had relentlessly chronicled Dash's death, and helicopters hired by the paparazzi buzzed the ranch for a photograph of the grieving widow, so she spent most of her time inside the house. Ironically, Dash's death had given their marriage a posthumous respectability, and instead of being the butt of everyone's jokes Dash was a martyred hero, while her name was spoken with respect.

Newspaper articles described her as brave and courageous. Arthur Lockwood drove to the ranch to tell her he was being plagued with requests to interview her and that several important producers wanted to cast her in their next pictures. She stared at him blankly, unable to understand.

Liz began tormenting her with healthy casseroles, vitamins, and unwanted advice. Chantal and Gordon appeared to plea for money. Her hair began to fall out, but she barely noticed.

One afternoon early in August, three months after Dash's death, she was maneuvering the narrow canyon road coming back from a visit with Dash's attorney when she realized how easy it would be to take one of the bends too wide. With a quick press on the accelerator, she could fly through the guardrail and crash into the canyon. The car would roll, then become a blazing fireball incinerating all her pain.

Her hands trembled as they clutched the steering wheel. The burden of pain had grown too crushing, and she simply couldn't bear it any longer. No one would care very much if she died. Liz would be upset, but she had a full, busy life and she would soon forget. Chantal would cry at her funeral, but Chantal's tears were cheap; she wouldn't cry much harder than she did when one of her soap opera characters died. When people didn't have a real family, they could pretty much die unmourned.

Family.

It was all she had ever wanted. A person who would love her without condition. A person she could love back with all her heart.

A sob racked her body. She missed him so much. He had been her lover, her father, her child, the center of everything good in her life. She missed his touch and scent. She missed the way he swore, the sound of his footsteps crossing the floor, the scrape of his whiskers against her cheek. She missed the way he turned the newspaper inside out so that she could never find the front page, the sounds of Sooners games blaring from the television. She missed his daily rituals of shaving and showering, the abandoned towels and underwear that never quite hit the hamper. She missed all the flotsam and jetsam that had been part of Dash Coogan.

Through the blur of tears, she watched as the needle on

the speedometer edged upward. The tires squealed as she careened around a curve. A push on the accelerator, a twist of her hands, and all the pain would be gone.

Unbidden, the memory of a young girl with chewed hair and worn-down flip-flops came back to her from another lifetime. As the speedometer inched higher, she wondered what had happened to that fierce little sixteen-year-old who had believed anything was possible. Where was the child who had taken off across America in a battered pickup truck with only guts to keep her going? She could no longer remember what that kind of courage felt like. She could no longer remember the child she had been.

Find her, a voice inside her head whispered. *Find that little girl.*

Gradually, her foot eased on the accelerator, not from any renewed desire to live, but simply because she was too tired to maintain the pressure.

Find her, the voice repeated.

Why not? she thought dully. The only thing she had better to do was die.

Ten days later the humid South Carolina heat consumed her as she stepped out of her air-conditioned Blazer onto the crumbling asphalt parking lot of the Silver Lake Amusement Park. Knee-high weeds grew through the gaping holes in the pavement and rust-streaked concrete obelisks showed where light posts had once been mounted. Her legs were rubbery. She had been on the road for several days, stopping at odd times to check into a motel and sleep for a few hours before she drove on. Now she was exhausted to the very marrow of her bones.

She squinted dispiritedly into the blazing sun and gazed at the boarded-up park entrance. She had owned the park for years, but she had never done anything with it. At first she simply hadn't had enough time to manage both her career and the park. After she'd married Dash, she'd had time, but not the money.

The roof on the ticket booth had collapsed and the flamingo-pink paint on the six stucco gate pillars was peeled

and dirty. Over the entrance the letters on the sign that
dangled crookedly were barely visible.

S lver Lak Amusem   Par
Home of th Legendar Bl ck Thu der
Roll r Coast
Thrillz 'n' Ch llz fo th Entir Fam ly

She lifted her head and took in the view she had crossed a
continent to see—the ruins of Black Thunder. Above the
decay of the park, the mighty wooden hills still soared into
the scorched Carolina sky. Neither time nor abandonment
had been able to destroy it. It was indomitable, the greatest
wooden roller coaster in the South, and nothing could spoil
its majesty—not the dilapidated buildings, the sagging
signs, the tangled undergrowth. It hadn't been operable for
eleven years, but it still waited patiently.

She lowered her eyes to escape the flood of painful
emotion. In the old days she would have been able to see the
top half of the Ferris wheel and the curving arms of the
Octopus rising above the ticket booth, but the rides were
gone and the parched sky held only a fireball sun and Black
Thunder.

The humidity enshrouded her, thick and suffocating,
making her perspire through the waistband of her khaki
shorts. The sun beat down on her thin shoulders and bare
legs as she began walking along the perimeter of the fence,
but the pines and undergrowth prevented anything more
than an occasional glimpse inside the park. Eventually she
came to the old delivery entrance. It was fastened with a
length of chain and a rusted padlock, both without purpose
since the fence nearby had been slit long ago. The park must
have been a popular place for scavengers when it still held
the possibility of salvage. Now, even the vandals seemed to
have abandoned it.

The chain-link prongs scratched her legs as she climbed
over the fence. She made her way through the scrub and
then slipped between two disintegrating wooden buildings
that had once held heavy equipment. She walked on, passing

beneath Black Thunder's colonnade of weathered southern-pine support columns but unwilling to look upward into the massive curving track for fear of the damage she would see. She moved out into the center of the park.

A chill gripped her as she saw the disintegration. The Dodgem Hall had collapsed and, farther on, the picnic pavilion was overgrown with scrub. Broken sidewalks led nowhere; circles of barren earth marked the spots where the Scrambler and Tilt-a-Whirl had once stood. Through the trees she could glimpse the murky surface of Silver Lake, but the *Bobby Lee* had long ago sunk to the bottom.

Dirt sifted through the open weave of her sandals as she made her way to the abandoned midway. Her footsteps padded the ground in the silence. A pile of rotted timbers lay in the weeds, and a tattered blue plastic pennant, dull with dirt, was snared on a nail head. The hanky-panks were gone, the scent of popcorn and candy apples replaced by the smell of decay.

She was the only person left on earth.

As she stood in the park's vacant heart, she finally lifted her eyes back to the sky so she could take in the entire skeleton of Black Thunder as it encompassed her abandoned universe. Her eyes stung as she followed the invincible lines of the mythic coaster: the great lift hill followed by the plunge toward the earth at an angle sharp enough to penetrate the very bowels of hell, all three hills with their glorious, thrice-delivered promises of death and resurrection, the heart-stopping spiral down to the water and the smooth, fast delivery into the station. Somewhere on that wild, racing ride she had once been able to touch eternity.

Or had she? She began to tremble. Was the certainty that she had been able to find her mother when she had ridden that coaster nothing more than the fancy of a child? Had the coaster really delivered her into the presence of God? She knew that her belief in God had been born on that coaster as surely as that same belief had been washed away by Dash Coogan's blood.

As she stared at the great ribs of Black Thunder etched against the parched sky, she cursed and begged God, both at the same time. *I want him back! You can't have him. He's mine, not yours! Give him back to me. Give him back!*

The ferocious sun burned through her hair into her scalp. She started to sob and sank to her knees, not to pray but to curse. *You fucker. You awful fucker.*

But even as she squeezed her eyes shut the silhouette of Black Thunder's three mighty hills stayed etched on her lids. The horrible obscenities continued to spill from her until they gradually assumed the cadence of ritual.

Exhausted, a stillness came over her. She opened her eyes and lifted them to the mountaintops as those in despair had done for centuries. Hope. Black Thunder had always given it to her. And as she stared at those three wooden peaks, she was filled with the absolute certainty that the coaster could transport her to some eternal place where she could find her husband, a place that existed beyond the temporal, a place where love could live forever.

But Black Thunder had no more life left in it than Dash Coogan's body, and it was incapable of transporting her anywhere. The massive skeleton stood crippled and impotent against the August sky, no longer bearing promises of hope and resurrection, no longer promising anything except dry rot and decay.

She stumbled back to her car, the weight of her weariness overwhelming. If only she could make Black Thunder run again. If only . . .

Climbing inside the suffocating interior of the car, she leaned back against the seat and fell into an exhausted sleep.

23

Sheri Poltrain had been working behind the register at the Gas 'n' Carry in Cumberland County, North Carolina, for three years. She'd been robbed twice and threatened with bodily harm half a dozen times. Now as the stranger approached the register of the convenience store, she tensed. She was better acquainted with trouble than most women, and she knew when it was walking toward her.

He looked like a biker, except the wrists and hands exposed beneath the sleeves of his unzipped brown leather jacket were clean and free of tattoos. And he didn't have a beer gut. Not even close. Through the open front of his jacket, she saw a belly as flat as the stretch of rainy county highway that ran past the gas pumps outside. He was at least six feet tall, with good shoulders, a muscular chest, and faded jeans that clung to one of those narrow, tight butts men never had the good sense to appreciate. No. There was definitely nothing wrong with his body. In fact, it was pretty incredible. What was wrong with him was his face.

He was just about the meanest-looking son of a bitch she'd ever seen. Not ugly mean. Just cruel mean. Like he might put out cigarettes on sensitive parts of a woman's body without ever changing his expression.

His hair, damp with the chilly late November drizzle that fell outside, was dark brown, almost black, and it hung nearly to his shoulders. It was clean but shaggy. He had a strong, perfectly shaped nose and the kinds of bones she'd once heard somebody describe as chiseled. But great bones couldn't make up for those thin lips and that hard mouth that didn't seem to have learned how to smile. And great bones couldn't make up for the coldest, single blue eye she had ever seen in her life.

She told herself not to stare at the black patch that covered his other eye, but it was hard to ignore. With that black patch and emotionless expression, he looked like some kind of modern-day pirate. Not the blow-dryer kind on the cover of one of the romance novels that sat on the rack next to her register, but the nasty kind who might pull a Saturday night special out of his back pocket and empty it into her belly.

She looked uneasily down at the digital display on her register that told her how much gas he had pumped into the mud-splattered gray GMC van that sat outside. "That'll be twenty-two even." She wasn't the type to let any man see that she was afraid, but this one gave her the heebie-jeebies, and her voice wasn't as firm as usual.

"Also a bottle of aspirin," he said.

Her eyes flickered with surprise at his faintly accented speech. He wasn't an American, but a foreigner. He sounded like he was from the Middle East or somewhere. The notion sprang into her mind that he might be some kind of Arab terrorist, but she didn't know if Arab terrorists could have blue eyes.

She removed an aspirin bottle from the cardboard display behind her and slid it across the counter. There was something dead in that single visible eye, an absence of any sort of life force that gave her the creeps, but when he withdrew nothing more threatening than a wallet from his back pocket, her curiosity poked through one small corner of her fear.

"You stayin' around here?"

The look he gave her was so threatening she quickly returned her attention to the register. He laid thirty dollars on the counter, picked up the aspirin bottle, and walked out of the store.

"You forgot your change," she called after him.

He didn't bother to look back.

Eric removed the seal from the aspirin bottle. As he rounded the back of the van, he pulled off the lid and took out the cotton wad. It was a chilly, drizzly Saturday afternoon in late November, and the dampness was bothering the leg he had injured in his auto accident. When he was behind the wheel, he swallowed three pills with the cold coffee dregs in his Styrofoam cup.

After his car had crashed through the guardrail last May, he'd spent a month in the hospital and another two months in physical therapy as an outpatient. Then in September, he'd started work on a new film. They'd considered delaying shooting because of his injuries, but he'd made good progress, and they had eventually decided to work around them instead, giving him a stunt double for a number of scenes he would normally have done himself.

The picture had been finished ten days ago. Afterward, he was scheduled to fly to New York to discuss a play, but at the last minute he'd decided to drive instead, hoping the solitude would help him pull himself together. After a few days, the solitude had become more important than his destination, and the closest he'd gotten to Manhattan was the Jersey Turnpike.

He was heading south on the back roads, traveling in a GMC van because it was less conspicuous than his Jag. At first he'd had vague ideas of visiting his father and step-mother on Hilton Head, where they'd retired a few years ago. But it hadn't taken him long to figure out that they were the last people he wanted to see, even though they'd been urging him to visit for years, ever since he'd grown famous. Still, he had six more weeks to kill before he had to start work on another film, and he had to do something to fill the time, so he kept on driving.

As he pulled away from the pumps, he caught sight of the female attendant watching him through the plate-glass window. She hadn't recognized him. No one had recognized him since he'd left L.A. He doubted that even his friends would have known him unless they looked closely. The phony accent he'd used in his last film, along with the longer hair he'd grown, had successfully concealed his identity for three thousand miles. Even more important than anonymity, the disguise afforded him at least temporary escape from being himself.

He turned out onto the wet county road and automatically patted his jacket pocket for his cigarettes only to remember he no longer smoked. They wouldn't let him smoke in the hospital, and by the time he was dismissed, he'd fallen out of the habit. He'd fallen out of the habit of enjoying all of life's sensory pleasures. Food no longer held any appeal, and neither did liquor or sex. He could no longer even remember why they had once been so important. Ever since he'd lost his children he felt as if he belonged more to the world of the dead than the living.

In the seven months since Lilly had taken the girls, he'd learned more than most lawyers knew about the sexual abuse of children. While he had lain in his hospital bed, he'd read stories of fathers violating tiny babies in unspeakable ways, of perverted, twisted men who preyed upon one daughter after another, betraying the most sacred trust that could exist between two human beings.

But he wasn't one of those monsters. He was also no longer the naive hothead who had stormed Mike Longacre's office demanding that his attorney put an end to Lilly's false accusations. Now he knew that the law was also full of injustice.

No matter what personal sacrifices he had to make, he wouldn't let his children end up in the underground, where they would be deprived not only of their father but of their mother as well. So he stayed away from them, relying on the international fleet of detectives he had hired to keep them under watch. With an increasing sense of dull resignation, he followed Lilly's wanderings with the girls, first to Paris and then to Italy. They'd spent August in Vienna, September in London. Now they were in Switzerland.

Everyplace she went, she engaged new governesses, new tutors, new specialists, all of whose bills he paid. From the interviews the detectives held with those she had hired, he knew that Becca was regressing and that Rachel had become increasing difficult to control. Lilly herself was the only stability the girls had, and forcing them into the underground would end even that.

Even so, he ached for his daughters so badly that he was sometimes tempted. Over the past seven months his pain had gone beyond the torture of a raw, gaping wound into something more primal, a desolate emptiness of the soul that was worse than any physical anguish because it was a living death. For a while he had been able to direct his despair into the role he was playing, but when the filming was done, he had lost his place to hide.

He had also gradually lost the ability to see any of the world's beauty, and now he only registered its horror. He could no longer read newspapers or watch television because he couldn't endure another account of a newborn baby abandoned in a trash can, umbilical cord still attached to its small, blue body. He couldn't read about another severed head found in a cardboard carton, or a young woman gang raped. Murders, mutilations, evil. He had lost his ability to separate his own pain from the suffering of others. All the world's pain belonged to him now, one atrocity after another, until his shoulders were bowed with the weight and he knew he would break if he didn't find a way to protect himself.

And so he was running, hiding away inside the skin of someone he'd invented, a persona so menacing that ordinary people drew away from him. He played jazz tapes instead of listening to the radio, slept in his van rather than a motel room with its beckoning television, avoided big towns and newspaper stands. He sheltered himself in the only way he knew how because he had grown so fragile he was afraid he would shatter.

A tractor-trailer rig kicked water at his van as he turned from the county access road out onto a state highway. The wipers made several half-moon passes over the windshield before he could see. Through the blur he spotted a blue road sign imprinted with the white H that indicated a nearby hospital. It was what he'd been looking for, the fragile thread that allowed him both to protect himself and try to save his soul at the same time.

He followed the blue and white hospital signs through a two-stoplight town until he came to a small, unassuming brick structure. He parked in the farthest corner of the lot away from the hospital building and climbed into the back of the van. The seats had been removed so there was an area big enough to stretch out his bedroll, which was now neatly folded away next to an expensive leather suitcase that held his clothes. He pushed it aside and drew forward a cheap vinyl suitcase.

For several moments he did nothing. And then, with something that might have been either a curse or a prayer, he opened the lid.

"'Ow does a bloke get some service around 'ere?"

Nurse Grayson's head shot up from the chart she had

been studying. She was generally unshockable, but her mouth dropped open at the improbable figure who stood on the other side of the nurse's station desk, grinning devilishly at her.

He wore a frizzy red wig topped with a black pirate's scarf knotted at the side. A purple satin shirt was tucked into voluminous black trousers that were spangled with saucer-sized red and purple polka dots. A single exaggerated eyebrow arched into the clown white that covered his face. He had a bright red mouth, another dot of red on the end of his nose, and a purple patch shaped like a star covering his left eye.

Nurse Grayson quickly recovered. "Who are you?"

He gave her a naughty grin that made her forget she was fifty-five years old and long past the age where she could be taken in by a charming scoundrel.

He sketched an overly dramatic bow before her, tapping his forehead, chest, and waist. "Patches the Pirate is me name, me pretty, and a more pitiful excuse for a sea dog, you'll never set eyes on."

Despite herself, his mischievous manner drew her in. "Now why is that?"

"Can't stand the sight of blood." He gave a comical shudder. "Miserable stuff. Don't know 'ow you tolerate it."

She giggled, and then belatedly remembered her professional responsibilities. Casually lifting her hand to tidy any errant salt-and-pepper curls that might have escaped her cap, she inquired, "Can I help you with something?"

"It's the other way around, now isn't it? I'm 'ere to entertain the kiddies. The bloke from the Rotary Club told me to show up at three. Did I get the time wrong again?" His look was devilish and unrepentant. "In addition to bein' afraid of blood, I'm also unreliable."

The single eye not covered by the patch was the brightest turquoise she had ever seen—as crystal clear as a candy mint. "No one told me that the Rotary had arranged for a clown to visit the children."

"Didn't they now? And I 'ave to be in Fayetteville by six

to entertain at the Altar Guild bazaar. It's lucky for me that you've got an understanding 'eart, in addition to a beautiful face. Otherwise, I wouldn't be able to earn the fifty bucks the Rotary's payin' me."

He was full of the devil, but so charming she couldn't resist. Besides, the rain had kept visitors down this afternoon, and the children could use a little entertainment. "I suppose there's no harm."

"Not a bit."

She came out from behind the desk and began to lead him down the hall. "As you can see, we're a small hospital. We only have twelve beds in Pediatrics. Nine of them are filled."

"Anyone I should know about?" the clown asked softly, all traces of mischievousness fading.

If she'd had any doubts about letting him onto the floor without official authorization, they vanished instantly. "A six-year-old named Paul. He's in one-oh-seven." She pointed toward the end of the hall. "He's had a rough time with pneumonia, and his mother's been too busy with her boyfriend to visit very often."

The clown nodded and made his way to the room she had pointed out. Moments later, Nurse Grayson heard the cheerful gravel of his voice.

"Ahoy, there, mate! Me name's Patches the Pirate, and I'm the mangiest dog that ever sailed the seven seas. . . ."

Nurse Grayson smiled as she made her way back to the nurses' station and congratulated herself on her good judgment. There were times in life when it paid to bend the rules.

Eric spent that night parked off the side of a dirt road in a small clearing just over the South Carolina border. When he emerged from the van the next morning, still dressed in his jeans and T-shirt from the day before, his mouth felt like dull metal from bad food and too many nightmares.

He'd bought the clown costume a week ago in a shop near Philadelphia, and since then he'd stopped at a small-town hospital nearly every day. Occasionally he called ahead, posing as a civic leader. Most of the time, however, he just followed the blue and white signs as he'd done yesterday and talked his way in.

Now he couldn't shake off the suffering of the little boy at the hospital yesterday. The child was thin and frail, and his lips bore a faint bluish rim. But it was the boy's pathetic delight at receiving Eric's undivided attention that had been wrenching. Eric had stayed with him for the rest of the afternoon and then gone back that evening and done magic tricks until the child had fallen asleep. But instead of feeling good about what he'd done, he could only think about all the children he hadn't been able to comfort, all the pain he couldn't stop.

The chilly dampness seeped through his T-shirt. As he worked the kinks out of his muscles, he gazed up into the gunmetal-gray sky. So much for sunny South Carolina. Maybe he should get back on I-95 and head directly for Florida. For a while now, he'd had vague ideas of hanging around the clowns at Ringling Brothers winter quarters in Venice for a few weeks. Maybe he'd get a chance to perform for well children, for a change, instead of sick ones. The idea of being with children who weren't suffering tantalized him.

He climbed back into the van. He hadn't showered in two days, and he needed to check into a motel so he could clean up. In the past he'd always been impeccable about personal cleanliness, but since he'd lost his children he'd grown lax. But then he'd grown lax about a lot of things, like eating and sleeping.

Half an hour later, he felt a tug on the steering wheel and knew he had a flat. He pulled over to the shoulder of the two lane highway, climbed out of the van, and went around to the back to get the jack. It had started to drizzle again, and at first he didn't see the splintered wooden sign that leaned in the palmettos at the side of the road. But the bad tire was mud slicked, and when he pulled it off, it got away from him and rolled into the ditch.

He spotted the sign as he bent over to reclaim the tire. The letters were faded, but he could still make them out:

SILVER LAKE AMUSEMENT PARK
Home of the Legendary Black Thunder
Roller Coaster
Thrillz 'n' Chillz for the Entire Family
Twenty Miles Straight Ahead,
Left 3 Miles on Rt. 62

Silver Lake Amusement Park. He felt the tug of familiarity, but he couldn't remember why. It wasn't until he secured the last lug nut on the spare that he recalled the name. Wasn't that the place Honey had talked so much about? He remembered the way she had entertained the crew with stories about growing up in an amusement park in South Carolina. She had spoken of a boat that had sunk to the bottom of the lake and a roller coaster that was supposed to be famous. He was almost certain it had been the Silver Lake Amusement Park.

He secured the hubcap with the heels of his hands and then looked thoughtfully back at the sign. His jeans were wet and muddy, his hair dripping down the back of his neck. He needed a shower, clean clothes, and a hot meal. But so did the majority of the world's population, and as he stood where he was, he wondered if the park was still in existence. The condition of the sign made it doubtful. On the other hand, anything was possible.

Maybe the Silver Lake Amusement Park was still open. And maybe they needed a clown.

24

"Honey, it's raining!" Chantal shouted. "You stop working right now."

From Honey's perch high atop Black Thunder's lift hill, she looked down at the miniature figure of her cousin gazing up at her from beneath the small red dot of an umbrella.

"I'll be down in a few minutes," she shouted back. "Where's Gordon? I told him to come right back."

"He's not feelin' good," Chantal yelled. "He's taking a little rest."

"I don't care if he's dying. You tell him to get back up here."

"It's the Lord's day! You shouldn't be workin' on the Lord's day."

"Since when did either of you ever care about the Lord's day? Neither of you likes to work on any day."

Chantal walked away in a huff, but Honey didn't care. Gordon and Chantal's free ride was over. She drove another nail into the catwalk she was building at the top of the lift hill. She hated rain and she hated Sundays because the restoration work on the coaster ground to a halt. If she had her way, the construction crew would be on the job seven days a week. They weren't union members, so they could work longer hours.

Ignoring the rain, she continued to nail together pieces of the catwalk. It frustrated her that she wasn't strong enough to do the harder jobs, such as repairing the track. The crew, under the supervision of the roller-coaster restoration expert she had hired to oversee the job, had spent the first two months removing the old track and repairing the frame wherever it was damaged. Luckily, much of it was still sound. The concrete footings had been installed in the sixties, so they didn't have to be replaced. All of them had been worried about cracks in the ledgers, the giant boards the track rested on, but there hadn't been as many as they'd feared.

Still, rebuilding the entire track was a massive and expensive project, and Honey was rapidly running out of money. She had no idea how she would finish financing the new lift chain and engine that still had to be installed, not to mention the electrical system, as well as air-compressor brakes to replace the old hand-operated ones.

The rain was falling more steadily and her footing had

grown precarious. Reluctantly, she lowered herself over the side and began the long climb down the frame that they were using like a ladder until the catwalk was complete. Her body no longer screamed in protest as she made the arduous descent. She was thin, hard-muscled, and weary from two months of backbreaking work, seven days a week, as many as fourteen hours a day. Her hands bore a ridge of calluses across the palms as well as a network of small wounds and scars from mishaps with the tools she had gradually learned to use with some degree of competence.

When she reached the ground, she pulled off her yellow hard hat. Instead of heading to her makeshift home, she walked through the dripping trees toward the other end of the park. Any fleeting thoughts she'd had about living in Sophie's trailer had vanished upon her first inspection. The roof had collapsed, the robin's-egg-blue shell had caved in on one side, and vagrants had long ago stripped it of everything useful. After having the wreckage removed, she'd installed a small silver trailer on the same site.

Now, however, her destination wasn't her own temporary home but the Bullpen, the ramshackle building that had once housed the unmarried men who worked in the park. Currently Gordon and Chantal lived there. She was glad the Bullpen sat at the opposite end of the park from her trailer. It was bad enough being around people all day. At night, she needed to be alone. Only when she was alone could she feel the possibility of some connection with Dash. Not that she really thought it would happen. Not until she could ride Black Thunder.

She'd snared her hair in a rubber band at the back of her neck, but wet strands stuck to her cheeks and her sweatshirt was soaked through to her skin. If Liz could see her now, she'd be wringing her hands. But Liz and California were part of another universe.

"Who is it?" Chantal said in response to Honey's knock.

Honey set her teeth in frustration and jerked open the door. "Who do you think it is? We're the only people here."

Chantal jumped up nervously from an old orange Naugahyde couch where she'd been reading a magazine and sprang to attention like an employee whose boss had caught her loafing. The interior of the Bullpen was made up of four rooms: a crude living area that Gordon and Chantal had furnished with odds and ends bought from Good Will; the sleeping area that used to hold wooden bunk beds but now contained an old iron-framed double bed; a kitchen; and a bathroom. Although the interior of the house was shabby, Chantal was keeping it neater than she'd kept any of their houses.

"Where's Gordon? You told me he was sick."

Chantal tried to slide the magazine under an ugly brown velour pillow. "He is. But he still went out back to change the oil on the truck."

"I'll bet he didn't go out until after you told him I was looking for him."

Chantal quickly changed the subject. "You want some soup? I made some nice soup a little while ago."

Honey threw off her wet sweatshirt and followed Chantal into the kitchen. Old metal cupboards covered with bile-green paint lined two of the walls, one of which held the park's only working telephone. The gold Formica counter-tops were dull and stained with use, and the linoleum floor had cracked like drought-stricken earth.

Because Honey and Gordon were working on the coaster all the time, Chantal was the only one free to take care of their meals, and she had learned that if she didn't cook, none of them ate. Surprisingly, the work seemed to have been good for Chantal. She'd lost a lot of the weight she had gained over the years and had begun to look like a more mature version of the eighteen-year-old who had won the Miss Paxawatchie County beauty contest.

"Opening a can and heating up the contents doesn't constitute *making* soup," Honey snapped as she took a seat at one end of an old picnic table they had moved inside. She knew she should encourage her cousin instead of criticizing her, but she told herself she simply didn't care about Chantal's feelings anymore.

Chantal's mouth tightened with resentment. "I'm not as good a cook as you, Honey. I'm still learning."

"You're twenty-eight years old. You should have learned a long time ago instead of spending the past nine years heating up frozen dinners in the microwave."

Chantal reached into the cupboard for a bowl, then took it over to the old gas stove and began filling it with chicken noodle soup. "I'm doing my best. It hurts my feelings when you're so critical."

"That's too bad. If you don't like the way I'm running things around here, you can leave any time." She hated her surliness and bad temper, but she couldn't seem to stop. It was like those early days on the Coogan show when any sign of weakness would have broken her.

Chantal's hand tightened around the ladle. "Me and Gordon don't have any place to go."

Honey set her mouth in an unforgiving line. "Then I guess you're stuck with me."

Chantal regarded her sadly, her voice quiet. "You've changed, Honey. You've gotten so hard. Sometimes I barely recognize you."

Honey took a spoonful of soup, refusing to let Chantal see that her words hurt. She knew that she was hostile. The men on the crew never joked around with her like they joked with each other, but she told herself she wasn't trying to win any popularity contest. All she cared about was finishing Black Thunder so that she could ride it again and maybe find her husband.

"You used to be so sweet." Chantal stood by the sink with her arms hanging at her side, her face full of regret. "And then after Dash died, I think something twisted inside you."

"I just decided to stop letting you and Gordon freeload off me, that's all."

Chantal bit down on her bottom lip. "You sold our house right out from under us, Honey. We loved that house."

"I needed the money. And I sold the ranch, too, so it wasn't like I was singling you out for persecution." Selling the ranch was the most difficult decision she'd ever had to make, but she'd ended up liquidating almost everything to finance the restoration of the coaster. All she had left was her car, some clothes, and this park. Even so, she still didn't have enough money, and she would be lucky to make it to January before what she had left ran out.

She refused to think about it. She wouldn't let anything sway her from the determination that had been born in her the day she had returned to the park and had seen Black Thunder again. Sometimes she thought her decision to rebuild the coaster was all that was keeping her alive, and she couldn't let sentiment weaken her.

"This whole thing's crazy," Chantal cried. "Sooner or later, you're going to run out of money. And then what'll you have? A half-finished roller coaster that no one will be able to ride sitting in the middle of a place where nobody ever comes."

"I'm going to find a way to raise more money. There are some historical groups interested in restoring wooden coasters." Honey avoided meeting Chantal's eyes. None of those groups had the resources to come up with the large amount of money she needed, but she wasn't going to admit as much to Chantal. Her cousin already thought she was crazy. And maybe she was.

"Just suppose a miracle happens and you finish Black Thunder," Chantal said. "What good will it do you? Nobody's going to come to ride it because there isn't a park here anymore." Her eyes grew dark with urgency. "Let's go back to California. All you'd have to do is pick up the phone and somebody'd hire you to be in a TV show. You could make lots of money."

Honey wanted to put her hands over her ears. Chantal was right, but she couldn't do it. As soon as audiences saw her trying to play a part other than Janie Jones, they'd realize what a fraud she had been as an actress. The record of those performances was the only thing that she had left in which she could take pride, the only thing she couldn't sacrifice.

"This is crazy, Honey!" Chantal exclaimed. "You're throwing away everything. Are you trying to put all three of us in a grave right along with Dash Coogan?"

Honey slammed down her spoon, splashing soup every-where, and jumped up from the table. "Don't you talk about him! I don't even want to hear you mention his name. I don't care about houses or California or anybody coming to the park. I don't care about you and Gordon. I'm restoring this coaster for *me* and not for anybody else."

The back door had opened, but she didn't notice until Gordon spoke. "You shouldn't yell at Chantal like that," he said quietly.

She spun around, her teeth barred. "I'll yell at her any way I want. You're both worthless. The two most worthless people I've ever met in my life."

Gordon studied a point just above her right eyebrow. "I've been working right by your side, Honey, ever since we came out here. Ten, twelve hours a day. Just like you."

It was the truth. Today's absence was rare. Gordon worked with her on Sundays and in the evenings after the men had left. She had been surprised to see that hard work even seemed to agree with him. Now as she noticed how pale he was, she realized he had probably been telling the truth when he had said he wasn't feeling well, but she didn't have any sympathy left to waste on anyone, not even herself.

"The two of you had better not push me. I'm in charge, and you need to decide right now how it's going to be." Her mouth twisted bitterly. "The old days are gone when you could get anything out of me you wanted just by threatening to leave. I don't care anymore if you go. If you don't think you can live with my decisions, then pack your bags and be out of here by tomorrow."

Brushing past him, she stalked out the back door and down the crumbling concrete steps. Why did she let them stay? They cared about her money, but not about her. And she didn't care about them anymore. She didn't care about anyone.

A chilly, wet blast of wind hit her, and she remembered that she'd left her sweatshirt behind. Off to her left she could see Silver Lake, its rain-cratered surface slate gray and fetid under the December sky. A vulture swooped over the ruins of the Dodgem Hall. The land of the dead. The park was a perfect place for her.

She slowed her steps as she entered the trees and the

emptiness enveloped her. Wet brown needles stuck to her work boots and the bottoms of her jeans. She wished she could rebuild the coaster by herself so she could get rid of everyone else. Maybe in the solitude Dash would talk to her. She sagged against the scaly bark of a longleaf pine, her breath forming a frosty cloud in the air, grief and loneliness overwhelming her. *Why didn't you take me with you? Why did you die without me?*

Only gradually did she grow aware of the fact that a man was standing in the far end of the clearing near her trailer. Chantal had said it wasn't safe for her to live so far away from them, but she had paid no attention. Now the hair at the back of her neck prickled.

He lifted his head and spotted her. There was something ominous about the still way he held himself. She'd encountered several vagrants since she'd returned to the park, but they'd run away when they saw her. This man didn't look as if he intended to run anywhere.

Until that moment she hadn't thought she cared enough about her personal safety to experience fear again, but even from sixty feet away, she could feel the man's menace. He was much larger than she, broad-shouldered and strong, with long, wild hair and a frightening black eye patch. Rain glistened on his leather jacket, and his jeans were muddy and soiled.

When he didn't come any nearer, she experienced a flicker of hope that he would turn away. But he began to move toward her instead, taking slow, threatening steps.

"You're trespassing." She barked out the words, hoping to intimidate him in the same way she'd intimidated so many others.

He said nothing as he came closer, then stopped in the shadows less than twelve feet away.

"What do you want?" she demanded.

"I'm not certain." His words were colored by a faint foreign accent she couldn't quite identify.

An icy finger of dread trickled down her spine. She was alarmingly aware of the emptiness of the clearing, the fact that even if she screamed, Gordon and Chantal wouldn't hear her.

"This is private property."

"I am not hurting anything." There was no intonation to his speech, just that soft, alien accent.

"You go on and get out of here," she ordered. "Don't make me call my watchman."

She wondered if he suspected there wasn't a watchman, because her empty threat didn't intimidate him.

"Why would you do that?" he asked.

She wanted to run, but she knew he would overtake her long before she could reach Chantal's trailer. As he stood staring at her, she had the frightening sense that he was trying to make up his mind about something. Her own brain quickly supplied a possibility. He was trying to decide whether he should kill her or just rape her. For a moment something about him seemed familiar. She thought of all those true-crime television shows Gordon and Chantal watched and wondered if she could have seen him on one of them. What if he was a fugitive?

"You don't know me, do you?" he finally said.

"Should I?" Her nerves were stretched so tautly she wanted to scream. One wrong word and he would be on her. She stood frozen until he took another step forward.

She instinctively moved back, holding out her arm as if that frail barrier could keep him away. "Don't come any closer!"

"Honey, it's me. Eric."

Only gradually did his words penetrate her fear, but even then it took a few moments before she realized who it was.

"I didn't mean to scare you," he said, in a flat, dead voice that no longer held any trace of accent.

"Eric?"

It had been years since she had seen him in person, and the many newspaper and magazine photographs of him bore no resemblance to this menacing-looking one-eyed stranger. Where was the sulky young heartthrob she had known so long ago?

"What are you doing here?" Her voice was harsh. He had no right to frighten her like that. And he had no right to intrude on her privacy. She didn't care if he was Mr. Big Shot in Hollywood. She was long past the point when she was impressed by movie stars.

"I noticed a sign about twenty miles from here and remembered how you used to talk about this place. I was just curious."

She took in the eye patch and his unkempt appearance. His clothes were muddy and wrinkled, his hands dirty, his jaw dark with stubble. It was no wonder she hadn't recognized him. She remembered his automobile accident, but she no longer felt pity for people who were lucky enough to emerge from accidents with their lives intact.

She didn't like the fact that she had to tilt her head to look him in the eye. "Why didn't you tell me who you were right away?"

He shrugged, his face blank of any expression. "Habit."

Uneasiness crept through her. He stood silently, making no attempt to explain either his presence in the park or his menacing appearance. He simply returned her gaze with one clear blue, unflinching eye. And the longer he looked at her, the more she had the disturbing sense that she was staring into a mirror image of her own face. Not that she saw a physical resemblance there. It was something more fundamental. She saw a bleakness of the soul she knew all too well.

"You're hiding out, aren't you?" she said. "The long hair. The phony accent. The eye patch." She shivered against the cold.

"The eye patch is for real. They wrote it into the script for my last film. As for the rest, I wasn't trying to scare you. The accent's automatic. I use it to keep the fans away. I don't even think about it anymore."

But he seemed to be trapped in something more fundamental than a ruse to avoid being recognized by his fans. As a runaway herself, it wasn't difficult to recognize another, although what he had to run from she couldn't imagine.

He stared off into the distance. "No neighbors. No satellite dish. You're lucky to have this place."

He hunched his shoulders against the damp wind, still not bothering to look at her. "I'm sorry about Dash. He never liked me much, but I genuinely admired him."

His condolences sounded begrudging, and she bristled. "Not as an actor, I bet."

"No. Not as an actor. He was more a personality than anything else."

"He always said he played Dash Coogan better than anybody." She clamped her teeth together so they wouldn't chatter. She didn't show her weaknesses to anybody.

"He was his own man. Not many people can say that." Turning his head, he looked past her toward the sliver of lake visible through the trees.

She remembered a newspaper photograph she'd seen of him the day before the Academy Awards: mousse-slicked hair, RayBan sunglasses, unstructured Armani suit. The photograph hadn't shown his feet, but they had probably been sockless and stuffed into a pair of Gucci loafers. It struck her that he was a man of a thousand faces, and his vagabond's guise was merely one of them.

"You've got a lot of space here," he said.

"And not very many people," she replied. "Which is the way I want to keep it."

He didn't take the hint. Instead, he glanced toward the trailer. "You wouldn't happen to have a shower rigged up in there with some hot water?"

"I'm afraid I'm not in the mood for company."

"Neither am I. I'll be back as soon as I get some clean clothes from my van."

By the time she opened her mouth to tell him to go to hell, he had disappeared into the trees. She stalked into the trailer and momentarily considered locking the door. But an enormous weariness had settled over her, and she realized she simply didn't care. Let him take his shower. Then he would go away and she could be alone again.

She was shivering, and she wasn't about to wait around in wet clothes while Mr. Movie Star used up all her hot water. Let him take the leftovers. As she peeled out of her work clothes and stepped into the shower, she wondered what had happened to him. Other than his divorce and the automobile accident he had obviously survived, she had never heard of a single traumatic event in his life. He was one of God's chosen, given fame and fortune as if he'd been sprinkled with fairy dust at birth. What right did he have to act as if he were living out a Greek tragedy?

After she had dried off, she slipped into a pair of worn gray sweats she kept on the back of the door, then left the bathroom for the tiny, utilitarian bedroom that occupied the back. She didn't bother to look toward the trailer's living area to see if he had returned, but a few moments later she heard the bathroom door click shut and then the sound of the shower running.

When she had finished combing the snags out of her wet hair, she went to the small kitchen that ran along one side of the living area. She thought about making a pot of coffee, but she didn't want Eric to stay that long, so she filled the sink with water and began washing the dirty cups and glasses that had accumulated over the last few days.

When he emerged from the bathroom, he was wearing clean jeans and a flannel shirt. His long hair was slicked back from his face, and he had shaved. She hadn't intended to ask any questions that would prolong his visit, but once again the eye patch caught her attention.

"Is your eye injury permanent or temporary?"

"Permanent. At least until I have surgery. Even then, who knows? It's not a sight for weak stomachs."

This time a stirring of pity disturbed the shell she had erected around herself. The loss of an eye would be difficult for anyone, but it must be especially devastating for an actor who was being deprived of one of the most fundamental tools of his trade.

"I'm sorry," she said. The apology sounded resentful, and she thought how much she disliked this tough, hard person she had become.

He shrugged. "Shit happens."

Doesn't it just, she thought. So that was the reason he was running away. He had injured his eye in an accident, and he couldn't face up to it.

He wandered across the short-pile gray carpet to the back window and gazed through it. She began retrieving cups from the soapy dishwater.

"You don't have any TV here. That's good."

"Most of the time I don't even see a newspaper."

He nodded brusquely. And then, "What are you doing here?"

She'd been waiting for the question. Everyone was full of questions. The townspeople, the workmen, Liz. Everybody wanted to know why she had left L.A., and why she was spending a fortune trying to rebuild a roller coaster that sat in the middle of a dead amusement park. Since she could hardly tell people she was rebuilding it so she could find her husband, she generally explained that the country's great wooden coasters were endangered historical landmarks, and she was trying to save this one. But she didn't owe Eric any explanations, and so she said brusquely, "I needed to get out of L.A., so I'm restoring Black Thunder. The roller coaster."

She waited for him to prod her with more questions, but instead he turned to face her. "Look, it's obvious that you don't want company, but I'd like to hang around for a couple of days. I'll stay out of your way."

"You're right. I don't want company."

"That's fine. Neither do I. That's why this is a good place for me."

She pulled a mug out of the water and rinsed it. "There's nowhere for you to stay."

"I've been sleeping in my van."

She grabbed a dish towel and dried her hands. "I don't think so."

"Afraid?"

"Of you? Hardly."

"Rebuilding that coaster must be a lot of work. Maybe you could use another set of hands."

She gave a short laugh. "Construction work isn't for movie stars. It plays hell with those hundred-dollar manicures."

He didn't rise to her taunt; he barely seemed to have heard her. "Just do me a favor. Don't tell anybody who I am."

"I didn't say you could stay."

"You won't even know I'm here. And one more thing. Every couple of days I'll be taking some time off. Since I won't be on the payroll, it shouldn't be a problem."

"Need to get your hair done?"

"Something like that."

She didn't want him around, but she could use another set of hands—especially since she didn't have to pay him wages.

"Fine," she snapped, "but if you get on my nerves, you have to go."

"I won't be around long enough to get on your nerves."

"You're already just about there, so don't push it."

He shoved one hand in the back pocket of his jeans and studied her openly, taking in her damp hair, the worn gray sweats, her feet stuck in a pair of Dash's old wool socks. The only jewelry she wore was her wedding band, but in the past few months tools had deeply notched the gold in several places. She couldn't remember the last time she'd used makeup. Her twenty-sixth birthday wasn't for another few weeks, but her face was lined and tired, her eyes haunted. She knew from her infrequent glances in the mirror that nothing of the girl she had been remained.

He stared at her without apology and she began to experience a strange sense of commonality. For some reason that she didn't understand, nothing mattered to him. She could tell him everything or withhold it all. He was encapsulated in his indifference, and no matter what she revealed, he wouldn't offer either sympathy or condemnation. He simply didn't care.

The irony wasn't lost on her. For years she had regarded Eric Dillon with antipathy. Now, he was the first person she'd met since Dash's death whose presence she could tolerate.

The next morning Chantal came running to her as soon as she met Eric to launch a vehement protest against Honey hiring such a dangerous-looking stranger.

"That Dev is going to murder us in our beds, Honey! Just look at him."

Honey glanced over at Eric, who was stacking a pile of two-by-sixes in the frosty morning air. Dev? So that was the name he was using. Short for devil?

He was wearing a hard hat like everyone else, but he had snagged his hair into a ponytail that formed a blunt comma at the back of his neck. His flannel shirt was open at the throat, and she could see a T-shirt beneath. He had on a pair of scuffed work boots and jeans with a hole at the knee. His current outfit seemed just as much a part of him as the Armani suits. The curious thought flashed through her mind that everything he wore was costume instead of clothing.

"He's all right, Chantal. Don't worry about it. He used to be a priest."

"He did?"

"That's what he said." Honey swallowed the last of her coffee and tossed aside her paper cup. She smiled cynically as she mounted the frame and began to climb the lift hill. The idea of Eric Dillon as a priest was the first thing that had struck her funny in a long time.

When she arrived at the top, she attached her safety line and gazed back down to the ground. Eric was reaching up to fasten a two-by-six to the rope that hauled up the lumber. Ponytails weren't normally a hairstyle she liked on men, but with his thin nose, sharp-bladed cheekbones, and dramatic eye patch, he definitely pulled it off. She could just imagine what Dash would have said about it, and she smiled to herself as she created a little dialogue between them, something she liked to do to give herself a sort of bittersweet comfort.

"Now why would anybody who calls himself a man want to wear something like that?" he would say.

She'd look dreamy-eyed in a way that would be guaranteed to aggravate him. "Because it's incredibly attractive."

"Makes him look like a pansy."

"You're wrong, cowboy. He looks all man to me."

"Well, then, if you think he's so damn good-looking, why

don't you use him to satisfy that itch that's starting to wake you up at nights."

She nearly hit her thumb with her hammer, something she hadn't done in a month. Where had that thought come from? There wasn't any itch. None at all.

She took a vicious swing, but her imagination refused to be stifled, and she could hear Dash say, *"I don't see what's so wrong with having an itch. It's long past time. I didn't raise you to be a nun, little girl."*

"Stop talking to me like a father, dammit!"

"Part of me is your father, Honey. You know that."

She began frantically running numbers from her dwindling bank account in her head to block out any more imaginary conversations.

25

True to his word, Eric stayed out of her way, and she had little conversation with him after that first day. His van was parked between two of the old storage buildings not far from the delivery entrance. In the evening, while she was eating dinner with Chantal and Gordon, he used her shower.

From the beginning he managed to blend in with the workmen, and what he lacked in skill he made up for in muscle and tenacity. After two weeks she had to remind herself that he truly was Eric Dillon and not the man he had created; a long-haired, one-eyed foreigner who had introduced himself to everyone as Dev.

Several times each week he disappeared for part of the afternoon. Despite herself, she began to wonder where he went for those four- or five-hour stretches. The third time he disappeared it finally occurred to her that he must have a woman somewhere. A man like Eric Dillon was hardly going to give up sex just because he'd lost an eye.

She slammed her hammer down on a nail she was driving into the catwalk. Lately, when she should have been thinking about coming up with the money she needed to finish the coaster, she had been thinking about sex, and last night she'd had another disturbing dream, one in which a faceless man approached her, obviously with the intention of making love. She wanted that part of her buried with Dash, but her body seemed to have other ideas.

She shoved the hammer back into her tool belt, determined not to think about it. Even thinking about sex was a betrayal of what she and Dash had meant to each other.

That evening during dinner, Chantal and Gordon were abnormally quiet. Chantal picked at the too-salty tuna casserole she had prepared, then finally pushed it away and went to the refrigerator for a Pyrex casserole full of red Jello.

Gordon cleared his throat. "Honey, I've got something to tell you."

Chantal fumbled the casserole as she set it on the table. "No, Gordon. Don't say anything. Please . . ."

"I'm just about broke, so if you're after money, forget it." Honey pushed aside the soggy potato-chip crust with the vague hope of finding a small chunk of tuna.

Gordon banged down his fork. "It's not money, dammit! I'm going away. Tomorrow. They're hiring construction workers up near Winston-Salem, and I'm going to get a job."

"Sure you are," Honey scoffed.

"I mean it. I'm not going to work for you anymore. I'm tired of taking your money."

"Why do I find that hard to believe?" She shoved back her plate and said sarcastically, "What about your great career as an artist? I thought you weren't ever going to compromise yourself."

"I guess I've been doing that since you picked me up on that Oklahoma highway," he said quietly.

Honey felt the first prickle of uneasiness as she realized that he was serious. "What brought about this sudden change of heart?"

"These past few months have reminded me that I like hard work."

Chantal was staring down at the table. She sniffed. Gordon regarded her miserably. "Chantal doesn't want to go. She—uh—she may not be coming with me."

"I haven't made up my mind yet."

"He's bluffing," Honey said sharply. "He won't leave you behind."

Gordon gazed at Chantal, and his eyes were tender. "I'm not bluffing, Chantal. Tomorrow morning I'm driving out of this place with or without you. You have to make up your mind whether you're going to stand by me or not."

Chantal started to cry.

Gordon rose from the table and turned his back on them. His shoulders heaved, and Honey realized he was near tears, too. She hid her own growing panic beneath anger.

"Why are the two of you doing this? Just go! Both of you." She sprang to her feet and spun on her cousin. "I can't support you any longer. I've been trying to find a way to tell you, and it looks like this is it. I want you out of here tomorrow morning."

Chantal jumped up from her chair and confronted her husband. "See what I mean, Gordon? How can I leave her like this? What's going to happen to her?"

Honey stared at her. "Me? You're worried about leaving me? Well, don't be. I'm tough. I've always been tough."

"You need me." Chantal sniffed. "For the first time in as long as I can remember, you need me. And I don't have any idea how to help you."

"Help me? That's a laugh. You can't even help yourself. You're pitiful, Chantal Delaweese. If you wanted to help me, why didn't you take some of the responsibility off my shoulders when I was busting my rear on the Coogan show? Why didn't you do something to help out then instead of lying around on the couch all day? If you wanted to help me, why didn't you act like you cared about somebody other than Gordon? If you wanted to help me, why didn't you bake me a birthday cake that didn't *blow up?*"

To Honey's dismay, her eyes stung with tears. There was a long silence broken only by the harsh sound of her breathing as she struggled for control

330

Finally, Chantal spoke. "I didn't do any of that because I sort of hated you then, Honey. All of us did."

"How could you hate me?" Honey cried. "I gave you everything you wanted!"

"Remember when you made me enter the Miss Paxawatchie County contest because you were trying so hard to keep us off welfare? Well, it's like me and Gordon have been on welfare all these years. Not because we needed help like somebody with lots of kids and no way to feed them. But because it was easier to take a free handout than work. We lost our dignity, Honey, and that's why we hated you."

"It wasn't my fault!"

"No. It was ours. But you made it so easy."

Gordon turned back to Chantal, his expression miserable. "I need you, too, Chantal. You're my wife. I love you."

"Oh, Gordon." Chantal's lips trembled. "I love you, too. But you can take care of yourself. Right now, I don't think Honey can."

Honey's throat closed tight with a nearly uncontrollable rush of emotion. She fought against it, struggling to keep her dignity. "That's the stupidest thing I ever heard you say, Chantal Booker Delaweese. A woman belongs with her husband, and I don't want to hear another word about you staying here with me. As a matter of fact, I'll be glad to have you gone."

"Honey . . ."

"Not one more word," she said fiercely. "I'm saying my good-byes right now, and both of you had better be out of here first thing tomorrow." She grabbed her cousin and drew her into her arms for a crushing hug.

"Oh, Honey . . ."

She pulled away and extended her hand toward Gordon. "Good luck, Gordon."

"Thanks, Honey." He took her hand, and then he hugged her, too. "You take care, you hear?"

"Sure." Moving away, she headed toward the back door, where she forced a smile that made her jaw muscles ache, then rushed outside.

She ran across the park. Her hair came free and flew about her head, lashing her cheeks. Her feet thudded on the hard ground. As the trailer came into sight, she gasped for air, but she didn't stop running.

She stumbled on the step and caught herself just before she fell. When she got inside, she pushed the door shut and leaned back against it, using her body to stave off the monsters. Her chest heaved, and she tried to calm herself, but she had passed the point of reason, and her fear consumed her.

For months she had been telling herself she wanted to be left alone, but now that it had happened, she felt as if she had been cast loose in space, aimlessly whirling, disconnected from all human life. She was no longer part of anyone. She had no family left. She lived alone in the land of the dead, only her obsession with Black Thunder keeping her alive. But Black Thunder had no plasma, no skin, no heartbeat.

Gradually, she became aware of the noise of water running. At first she couldn't think what it was, and then she realized that Eric was using her shower. Normally he was gone by the time she returned from her dinner, but she had come back earlier than usual.

She pressed her hands to her temples. She didn't want to be alone. She couldn't be alone. *I can't bear it anymore, Dash. I'm so afraid. I'm afraid of living. And I'm afraid to die.*

Her teeth began to chatter. She stepped away from the door, holding onto the counter for support. The fear was sucking at her bones, gobbling up little bits of her. She had to make it go away. She needed a connection with someone. Anyone.

Numbly, she turned toward the short, narrow hallway and stumbled the few short yards that took her to the bathroom door. She told herself not to think. Just to keep herself alive.

Forgive me. Oh, please, forgive me.

The knob turned in her hand.

Steam enveloped her as she entered. She pressed the door shut behind her and stood against it, struggling to breathe.

He had his face turned to the nozzle, his back toward her. His body was too large for the rectangular shower stall, and when he moved, his shoulders bumped into the sheets of cheap plastic that formed the walls, making them rattle. She could discern the outline of his back and buttocks through the steam-clouded walls, but none of the details. His body could have belonged to any man.

Squeezing her eyes shut, she kicked off her shoes. Then she crossed her arms over her chest and peeled both her sweatshirt and T-shirt over her head. Her bra was lacy and delicate, pale shells of mint green, the remaining token of femininity she hadn't been willing to abandon to the world of hard hats, work boots, and Skil saws. With a dull sense of inevitability, she unsnapped her jeans and pulled them slowly down over her legs, revealing the fragile pair of panties that matched her bra.

Her legs had begun to shake and she steadied herself with a hand on the rim of the sink. If she didn't find a human connection, she would break apart. A connection with anyone.

Her reflection floated before her in the steam-fogged mirror above the sink. She could make out tangled hair, the indistinct outlines of her features.

The water stopped running. She whirled around. Eric turned in the shower stall and went absolutely still as he saw her standing there.

She said nothing. The steamy plastic panels continued to blur the distinguishing lines of his features in a way that comforted her. He could be any man, one of the faceless men in her dreams, an anonymous man whose only purpose was to take away her fear of being alone and unloved.

Slowly he turned his back to her, and the shower door made a hollow *ping* as he opened it. Reaching through with one dripping arm, he retrieved his towel from the wire hook outside. His eye patch dangled from a black cord beneath. Still standing in the shower, he passed the towel through his wet hair, pushing it away from his face, then reached for the black patch and secured it over his head to spare her the sight of his mutilated eye.

Her heart thudded relentlessly in her chest. The steam was beginning to make her skin glisten. Naked except for the fragile pieces of mint-green lace, she waited for him to emerge.

He stepped through the shower door, watching her as he rubbed the towel in slow circles over the dark, matted hair on his chest. The bathroom was small, and he was so close she could have touched him. But she wasn't ready to touch, and her gaze dropped to his sex. It lay heavy against his thigh, the heat distending him. This was what she wanted from him. Only this. The connection.

She kept her eyes averted from his face so that she would know him only as a body. His torso was perfectly sculpted, the musculature deliberately defined. She saw an angry red scar near his knee and looked away, not because she was repulsed, but because the scar personalized him.

He passed the towel over his buttocks and thighs. She could feel her hair curling in the steam, forming baby corkscrews around her face. Beads of moisture had gathered between her breasts. They dampened her thumb as she unfastened the front clasp on her bra and let the pale green lace drop away like fragile teacups.

She sensed his eyes upon her breasts, but she would not look at his face. Instead, she studied the indentation at the base of his throat where a trickle of water had collected. His arm moved toward her, the tendons strong and clearly defined. She caught her breath as he passed his hand over her breast.

The dark tan of his arm looked foreign and forbidden against the paleness of her skin. He flattened his palm against her rib cage, slid it down over her stomach and inside the waistband of her panties. Tendrils of fire licked at her nerve endings. Her body felt hot and swollen. He slipped down her panties.

As soon as she stepped out of them, she knew she had to touch him. Leaning forward, she dipped her mouth to the moisture that had cupped at the base of his throat. Her nostrils quivered as she caught the clean scent of his skin.

She pressed her nose to his chest, a nipple, turned her head toward his underarm, softly breathing him in.

Ribbons of her pale hair streamed over his damp chest, adorning his darker skin with gentle ornamentation. He flattened his hands over her back. She trembled at the sensation of once again being enclosed in a man's arms. He slid his hands down along her back to her buttocks, cupping them to draw her against him. She felt him hard and moist against her belly.

She waited for him to speak, to ask all the "why's" and "what's" that would send her flying away from him. But instead of speaking, his head dipped to the curve of her neck. She caught the backs of his thighs and squeezed them. Then she arched her neck and offered him her breasts.

He lowered his lips to her collarbone before claiming the swell of flesh below. Her skin was alive to sensation: the dampness of their flesh, the pleasuring pain of his whiskers, the soft whip of his wet, dark hair. And then she felt the demands of his mouth as he encompassed her nipple and drew it deeply inside. His eye patch brushed over her skin.

He reached between her legs from behind and opened her. She moaned and encircled his calf with her leg, trying to climb his body so that she could take him in. But he held her off, stroking her and touching her in ways that made her gasp with need.

Only once did she turn cold. When he put her away from him and reached for his pile of clothing on the floor.

Keeping her eyes averted from his face, she watched his hands, too befuddled by the urgency of her need to understand why he should be taking a wallet from his jeans. What he wanted there. And then as he slid out the small foil packet she understood and hated the necessity because faceless men should have no need for small foil packets. Faceless men should have bodies that blindly served, without the power to reproduce, without the dangers of disease.

She turned her back while he readied himself.

And then his hands came around her to toy again with her breasts until she sobbed. He turned her. She propped her arms over his shoulders as he lifted her, wrapped her legs around his waist. He pressed her to the thin bathroom wall so that her spine was flat against it.

"Are you ready?" he whispered, his voice smoky.

She nodded her head against his cheek and pressed her eyes shut as he pushed himself inside her.

Her hair tumbled down over his back, and her thighs clasped him with their work-strengthened muscles. She clung to him, whispering *yes* and *yes*. Her body was so starved, so desperate.

Gently, he used her.

Tears seeped from her eyes and trickled along his damp spine. He held her in his strong arms, stroked her so deeply, caressed her so tenderly. She cried out with her climax, and then gripped his shoulders tighter while he drove to find his own release. She stoically bore his weight as he leaned shuddering against her.

Gradually he withdrew and lowered her to the floor. His breathing was harsh and uneven. She saw his arm move and knew he was about to draw her close. Quickly, she backed away, not looking at him, not letting him touch her. Within seconds, she had left him alone while she closed herself in the small bedroom across the hallway.

Much later, when she emerged, he had disappeared. She could find no sign that he had even been there except for the droplets of water still clinging to the walls of the shower. She dried them off before she stepped inside herself.

He couldn't take any more hurt!

Eric's knuckles were white as he gripped the van's steering wheel. Why had he let another wounded person into his life? He had been trying to get away from suffering, not plunge in deeper. He wanted to drive away, but he had not even been able to put the key in the ignition.

Her face was imprinted on the windshield in front of him: those luminous, haunted eyes, that full mouth trembling with need. God, he'd been dreaming about that mouth from the moment he had seen her again. It was soft and sensual, and it drew him as if it had magic powers. But he hadn't even kissed her, and he doubted she would have let him if he'd tried.

Instead of finding sanctuary in this dead amusement park, he had plunged himself deeper into hell. Why was he so drawn to her? She was cold and tough, with a grim, single-minded determination that was at odds with her small stature. Even the men on the construction crew shied away from her. They had been stung too often by her razor-sharp tongue. She was the same little monster she'd been that second season of the Coogan show, a hundred years ago.

Over the trees he could see the top of the lift hill. He didn't understand what there was about the coaster that obsessed her, but he had begun to hate those moments when he looked up from the ground and saw her small body entwined with the frame of the great wooden beast until she and the coaster almost seemed to be one. Her obsession frightened him.

Who was she? Not the needy, love-struck girl who had once reminded him of his little brother. Not the tough, sharp-tongued boss lady in the yellow hard hat, either. Sometimes when he looked at her, he thought he saw another woman standing slightly apart from her—a saucy, laughing woman with a loving heart and wide-open arms. He told himself the image was an illusion, a mental hologram he had created out of his own despair, but then he wondered if he might not be seeing the woman she had been when she was married to Dash Coogan.

Tonight, her beauty had clawed at his guts. The strength, the tragedy, the awful vulnerability. But they had come together like animals instead of human beings. Even when their bodies were locked together, they had given nothing of themselves to each other, so that in the end he could use her as she was using him, impersonally, as a safe receptacle.

But it hadn't worked that way. The thing that terrified him—the thing that made sweat break out on his body and his stomach clench—was the way she had made him feel.

For the space of time while he had held that fragile female body—a body that demanded nothing more from him than sexual release—he had felt all the fiercely protective layers he'd erected around himself slip away, leaving him ready to go to the ends of the earth to console her.

As he sat staring blindly through the window of the van, he knew that he should leave just as surely as he knew he was going to stay. But he would never let himself be so vulnerable to her again because he had no place left inside him to hold anyone else's pain. They said he was the best actor of his generation, and he was going to use his talent. From this moment on, he would wrap himself so tightly inside his identities that she would never again be able to touch him.

The next day Honey drove herself relentlessly, trying to shut out the events of the night, but as she inspected a section of track with the project foreman, the images washed over her. How could she have done it? How could she have betrayed her marriage vows like that? Self-hatred gnawed away at her, a bleak antipathy toward the person she had become.

For the rest of the day she threw herself into her work with a ferocity that, by evening, left her drained and weak. As she dropped to the ground and unfastened her tool belt, she heard someone approaching her from behind. Even before she turned, she could feel who it was and she tensed.

Eric regarded her with a face empty of any expression. Instead of feeling relieved that he wasn't forcing her to acknowledge what had happened, she felt chilled. If it weren't for the small aches in her body, she would think that she had imagined the whole thing.

"I understand that your cousin and her husband have left," he said in his carefully accented English. "Would you mind if I move my belongings into the Bullpen? It's more comfortable than my van."

She had tried to forget about the empty Bullpen. All day she had looked down at the vacated building expecting to see Gordon's truck parked there, but he and Chantal were gone.

"Suit yourself," she said stiffly.

He nodded and walked away.

When she returned to her trailer, she heated a can of beef stew for her own dinner and tried to block out her loneliness by running numbers on her calculator. The figures hadn't changed. She could meet her payroll through the first week of January, and then she would have to shut down.

Grabbing a soft blue cable-knit cardigan, she let herself outside. The night was clear, the sky dotted with silver stars. She hoped Chantal and Gordon were all right. It would be Christmas in less than two weeks. Last Christmas, she and Dash had camped in the desert and he'd given her handmade gold earrings shaped like crescent moons. She'd put them away in her jewelry box after he died because she couldn't bear looking at them.

She picked her way along the overgrown path that led to the lake and stood on the bank to gaze out over the water. The government had finally forced the Purlex Paint Company to stop its pollution, but it would be several years before the lake began to come to life again. Now, however, the darkness concealed its polluted condition, and moonlight formed silver streamers on its still surface.

She turned her back on the lake and let her eyes rise above the trees to the hills of Black Thunder, dimly visible in the moonlight. Everybody thought she was crazy to be rebuilding the coaster. How could she explain this unrelenting drive to find some sign that Dash was not lost to her? In saner moments she told herself that Black Thunder was only an amusement-park ride and that it held no mystical powers. But her rational mind was silenced by the driving urgency that insisted she could only restore her soul by taking a ride through her nightmares on Black Thunder.

Her shoulders sagged. Maybe everybody was right. Maybe she was crazy. She could feel her eyes fill and the wooden hills wavered before her. *You damned old cowboy. You broke my heart, just like you said you would.*

A movement in the pines distracted her. Alarmed, she saw the dark figure of a man standing there. He stepped out of the shadows, and she realized that it was Eric. She felt a jolt of panic at the idea of being alone with him.

As had become her practice when she wanted to hide her fear, she grew angry. "I don't like being spied on. You just wore out your welcome."

His single blue eye regarded her dispassionately as he came toward her. "Why would I be spying on you? Actually, I was here first."

"It's my lake," she retorted, dismayed at her own childishness.

"And you're welcome to it. From what I can see, nobody else would want it."

Even though they were alone, she realized that he was speaking to her with the faint tinges of a Middle Eastern accent. She also realized that if she continued to snap at him, he might think last night had some real meaning to her. She took a shaky breath and attempted to regain her dignity.

"The lake's starting to come back," she said. "A paint company used it as a dumping ground for years."

"This place is too isolated for you to be living alone. I found a vagrant hanging around the Bullpen this evening. Now that your relatives are gone, maybe you should consider renting a room in town instead of staying out here by yourself."

He didn't realize that he was more dangerous to her than any vagrant, and her slim hold on composure snapped. "I don't remember asking for your opinion."

The face that was so expressive on the screen slammed shut like a screen door with a too-tight spring. "You're correct. It's not my business."

Despite the accent he had thrown up like a barrier, memories of the night before rushed over her and she struggled against her panic in the only way she knew. "You hide behind that accent, don't you?" she said contemptuously. "And you're hiding more than your famous face. Well, you may forget who you are, but I don't, and I'm sick of you acting like some kind of nut case."

His jaw tightened. "The accent's automatic, and I'm

hardly the nut case." She sucked in her breath, waiting for him to confront her with having come to him. But instead, he said, "I'm not the one who's building a roller coaster in the middle of nowhere. I'm not the one running around like some pint-sized version of Captain Ahab obsessed with her own goddamned Moby Dick."

"Better than Moby Dickless!" She wasn't obsessed. *She wasn't!* This was simply something she had to do so she could live again.

"What does that mean?" His accent was gone, his face shadowed.

She went on the attack, trying to sink her teeth into the softest part of his flesh, trying to make the kill first. "What kind of coward are you, running away just because you lost your stupid eye? *At least you're alive, you bastard!"*

"You little shit. You don't know what it looks like under here." He jabbed his fingers in the direction of the black patch. "There isn't an eye there. Just a mass of ugly red scar tissue."

"So what? You've got a spare."

For a moment he didn't say anything. Her stomach felt sick at what she was doing, but she didn't know how to take back the words.

His lips curled in mockery, and he spoke softly. "I always wondered what happened to Janie Jones, and now I know. Life threw her one too many hard knocks and now she's right back where she started—a bossy little bitch hiding behind a big mouth."

"That's not true!"

"Jesus. It's too bad Dash isn't still alive. I'd lay money he'd throw you over his knee and beat some sense into you just like he did when you were a kid."

"Don't you talk about him," she said fiercely. "Don't you even speak his name." Tears were glistening in her eyes, but he appeared unmoved.

"What in the hell are you doing here, Honey? Why is rebuilding that coaster so important to you?"

"It just is, that's all."

"Tell me, damnit!"

"You wouldn't understand."

"You'd be surprised at how much I can understand."

"I have to do it." She looked down at the hands she was twisting in front of her and her anger faded. "When I was a child that coaster meant a lot to me."

"So did my Swiss army knife, but I wouldn't give up everything to get it back."

"It's not like that! It's about—it's about *hope.*" She winced, appalled by what she had revealed.

"You can't make Dash come back," he said cruelly.

"I knew you wouldn't understand!" she exclaimed. "And when I need lectures from you, I'll let you know! You're running away just as much as I am and for a lot less reason. I read the papers. I know you have children. Two little girls, right? What kind of father are you to disappear on them like this?"

He gave her a look so taut with restrained rage that she wished she'd kept her mouth shut.

"Don't make judgments about things you don't know anything about." Without another word, he stalked away from her.

For the next few days Eric only spoke to her when the men were around, and he always used the voice of Dev, the construction worker. The voice began to haunt her dreams and make her body ache with sensations she didn't want to acknowledge. She kept reminding herself that Eric was a gifted and disciplined actor with complete control over any character he created, but the menacing-looking construction worker was assuming an identity separate from Eric in her mind. She did everything she could to stay away from him, but in the end her escalating money problems made that impossible.

On a Tuesday afternoon, four days after their confrontation by the lake, she made up her mind to approach him. She waited until the men stopped for lunch. Eric had been loading old sections of track into the back of a flatbed, and he pulled off his gloves as she came near.

She held out a brown paper bag. "I noticed you haven't been eating lunch, so I fixed this for you."

He hesitated for a moment, then took it from her. He was clearly wary, and it occurred to her that he had been avoiding her as much as she was avoiding him.

"I only brought along one thermos, though, so we'll have to share." She began to walk, hoping he'd follow. After a few seconds, she heard his footsteps.

She moved away from the men to the spot where the carousel had once stood. Not far away an old sycamore had fallen in a storm. She sat down on it, put the thermos on the ground, and opened her lunch sack. A moment later he straddled the trunk and pulled out the peanut butter sandwich she'd made that morning. She noticed that he bunched the plastic wrap around the bottom part to protect it from his grimy hands, and she remembered that he had grown up in a wealthy family where clean hands would have been required at the dinner table.

"I cut it into triangles instead of rectangles," she said. "It's the closest I come to gourmet cooking these days."

The corner of his mouth ticked in something that might have been his version of a smile. She felt a sharp pang as she remembered how much she and Dash used to laugh.

He gestured toward the barren circle of earth in front of them. "One of the rides must have been here."

"The carousel." The first time she had seen Eric, his eyes had reminded her of the bright blue saddles on the horses. She opened her own lunch bag, trying to overcome her uneasiness as she pulled out her sandwich. She knew this was a bad idea, but she hadn't been able to come up with a better one.

Slipping a corner of the peanut butter sandwich in her mouth, she chewed it without tasting, swallowed, then set it in her lap. "I have something I want to talk to you about."

He waited.

"I'm going to have to call off the restoration work if I can't come up with some cash in the next few weeks."

"I'm not surprised. It's an expensive project."

"The truth of the matter is, I'm broke. What I wanted to

ask you—" The chunk of sandwich seemed to be stuck in her throat. She swallowed again. "I was thinking that you . . . That is, I was hoping you might—"

"You're not going to hit me for a loan, are you?"

Her carefully planned speech vanished from her mind. "What's so horrible about that? You must have a few million stashed away, and I only need around two hundred thousand."

"That's all? Why don't I just whip out my checkbook right now?"

"I'll pay you back."

"Sure you will. That coaster's going to be earning you a fortune. What do you figure? Maybe five bucks a week?"

"I'm not planning on paying you back from the coaster. I know it won't make a profit. But as soon as I finish Black Thunder and it's running again, I'm—" She stumbled on her words. This was going to be even harder than she had thought. As she spoke, she knew she was giving up the only thing she had left that was of any value to her. "I'm calling my agent this evening. I'm going back to work."

"I don't believe you."

She felt sick. "I have to. If acting is the only way I can get Black Thunder running, then I'll do it."

"Something good might come out of this after all."

"What do you mean?"

"You should never have stopped performing, Honey. You didn't even give yourself a chance to find out what you could do."

"I can do Janie Jones," she said fiercely. "That's it. I'm a personality, just like Dash. I'm not an actress."

"How do you know that?"

"I just do. I used to listen to all that talk of yours about internal technique, affective memory, the Bucharest school. I don't know anything about those things."

"That's just vocabulary. It doesn't have anything to do with talent."

"I'm not going to debate this with you, Eric. All I'm saying is that I can pay you back. I'll have my agent put together some ironclad contracts—film roles, TV movies, commercials—anything that pays. By the time people figure out I'm not Meryl Streep and the job offers stop, you'll have your money back with interest."

He stared at her. "You'd sell your talent that cheap?"

"It's not exactly talent I'm selling, is it? Notoriety might be a better word."

His lips thinned. "Why don't you just pick up the phone and call one of the big men's magazines? They'd give you a fortune for a nude layout. Think about it. You'd have the money you need to finish rebuilding your roller coaster, and guys all over America could jerk off to naked pictures of Janie Jones."

He had made a direct hit, but she wasn't going to let him see it. "How much do you think they'd give me?"

He balled the paper sack and, with an exclamation of disgust, threw it on the ground.

"I'm kidding," she said tightly. "You were getting so sanctimonious."

"I wonder. If nude photos were the only way you could get the money, would you do it?"

"I guess I'd have to think about it."

"I'll bet you would." He shook his head in wonder. "Damn it, I think you'd actually do it."

"So what? My body doesn't mean anything to me anymore."

A subtle tension came over him, and she suspected he was remembering the way she had offered herself to him. She seized the chance to tell him indirectly that their lovemaking had no significance to her.

"My body isn't important, Eric. It doesn't mean anything! Now that Dash is dead, I just don't care anymore."

"I sure as hell think he'd care."

She looked away.

"He would, wouldn't he?"

"Yes. Yes, I guess he would." She drew a shaky breath. "But he's dead, Eric, and I have to rebuild this coaster."

"Why? Why is it so important to you?"

"It's—" She remembered the night by the lake. "I tried to tell you before, and you wouldn't understand. It's just something I have to do, that's all." A long silence fell as she attempted to get herself back under control.

He studied the scuffed toe of his work boot. "Exactly how much do you need?"

She told him.

He gazed out toward the clearing that had once marked the site of Kiddieland. "All right, Honey. I'll make a deal with you. I'll loan you your money, but on one condition."

"What's that?"

He turned to her, his single blue eye regarding her so intently she felt burned. "You'll have to sign yourself over to me."

"What are you talking about?"

"I mean that I'll own your talent, Honey. Every bit of it until the loan's paid off."

"What?"

"I choose your projects. Not you and not your agent. Only me. I decide what you can and can't do."

"That's ridiculous."

"Take it or leave it."

"Why should I? You'd never hand your career over to someone else."

"Not in a million years."

"But you expect me to."

"I don't expect anything. You're the one who wants the money, not me."

"What you're talking about is slavery. You could put me in hemorrhoid commercials or make me do auto shows at a hundred dollars a pop."

"Theoretically."

"I don't have any reason to trust you. I don't even like you."

"No, I don't expect you do."

He said the words so matter-of-factly that she was ashamed. Obviously, he didn't expect anything more from her.

Snatching up her uneaten lunch, she rose from the log and gave him a hostile glare. "All right. You've got a deal. But you'd better not cross me, or you'll regret it."

He watched her as she stalked away. *Big talker,* he thought to himself. She was still swinging those fists just as she had when she was a kid. Still daring the world to cross her. And had it ever.

He couldn't tolerate watching her shadowbox with ghosts much longer. And the worst ghost of all was that damned roller coaster. She had said the coaster was about hope, but he had the uneasy sense that she somehow thought Black Thunder could bring her husband back. He stood and picked up the remnants of his lunch. He couldn't imagine what it would be like to be loved as Honey loved Dash.

Even though he didn't have to be back in L.A. for two weeks his mind screamed at him to leave now. Take himself as far from the grieving Widow Coogan as he could get. That's what he should do. But instead of disengaging himself from her, he had just become even more entangled, and when he asked himself why, he could only come up with one answer.

In some strange way, he felt as if he had just taken a giant step toward finally earning Dash Coogan's respect.

26

Not a single red bow or a sprig of holly decorated the interior of her trailer on Christmas morning. Honey had planned to endure the holiday rather than celebrate it, but when she got out of bed, she couldn't make herself climb into her work clothes for another day of solitary labor.

As she stared at herself in the bathroom mirror, some small shred of vanity poked at her. Dash used to tell her how pretty she was, but the small face that looked back at her was gaunt and haunted, a street urchin grown old too quickly. She turned away in disgust, but instead of walking out of the bathroom, she found herself kneeling down to search the tiny storage space below the sink for the hot rollers she had stuck there when she had moved in, along with her makeup.

An hour later, dressed in a silky turtleneck and pleated trousers of antique rose wool, she finished brushing out her hair. It fell in loose waves to her shoulders and shone like warm honey from the conditioner she had used. Makeup camouflaged the circles under her eyes while mascara thickened her lashes and emphasized her light blue irises. She dusted her cheekbones with blush, slicked on a soft pink lipstick, and fastened the gold crescent moons Dash had given her into her lobes. Her eyes began to sting as she watched one of the moons tangle with a tendril of hair, and she quickly turned away from her reflection in the mirror.

When she reached the trailer's living area, she poured herself a cup of coffee and went to the table next to the couch for the brown envelope she had put there several days earlier. It had a message scrawled across the front in Chantal's childish handwriting. "Do Not Open Until December 25. This Means You!" She tore apart the envelope flap and pulled out a lumpy package wrapped in white tissue paper with a note affixed to the top.

Dear Honey,

Hope you have a Merry Xmas. Me and Gordon like Winston-Salem. We found a place to stay in a real nice trailer park. Gordon likes his job. He said to tell you he's got a present for you, but you won't get it for a while. I made a friend. Her name is Gloria and she taught me how to croshay.

I'm still thinking you should go back to L.A. I don't think Dash would like what your doing to yourself. I miss you. I hope you like your present.

Love,
Chantal (and Gordon)

P.S. Don't worry. If you go back to L.A., me and Gordon won't come with you.

Honey blinked her eyes and unwrapped the tissue paper. With a shaky smile she drew out the first real present she had received from Chantal since they were children, a hand-crocheted cover for a roll of toilet paper. It was made of neon-blue yarn and ornamented with misshapen yellow loops to represent flowers. She carried it to the bathroom, where she stuffed it with a spare roll and set it in a place of honor on the back of her toilet.

That done, she tried to think of something else to occupy her time. Impulsively, she snatched up a gray wool jacket, grabbed her purse, and headed for her Blazer. She would turn the radio up and take a long drive.

Only Christmas carols were playing on the local stations, so she snapped the radio off before she reached the town limits. The weather was in the high fifties and clear, and she had just decided to drive over to Myrtle Beach to watch the ocean when she spotted Eric's van stopped at a traffic light several blocks ahead of her. She remembered his mysterious disappearances and wondered if he were on his way to meet a woman. The idea made her feel sick.

She wasn't planning to follow him, but when he turned off Palmetto Street, she found herself turning, too. A number of holiday travelers were on the road, and she didn't have any trouble keeping several car lengths between them. To her surprise, he pulled into the parking lot of Paxawatchie County's major hospital.

She parked her car a few rows over from the van and waited. Several minutes ticked by. Her mind drifted to Dash, and because that was too painful, she thought about the work that lay ahead before Black Thunder could once again fly over the tracks.

She returned her attention to the van as the back doors swung open. And a clown stepped out.

He was dressed in a purple shirt tucked into baggy polka-dotted trousers, and his hair was covered by a frizzy red wig tied with a pirate's scarf. In one hand he held a bundle of multicolored helium balloons, in the other a plastic trash bag that looked as if it might be stuffed with presents. Just as she decided she had followed the wrong van, the clown tilted his head and she caught a glimpse of a purple star-shaped eye patch. For a moment she felt disoriented.

Eric Dillon had still another face.

Who was he? How many identities did he have? First Dev. Now this. She wanted to drive away, but she couldn't. Without stopping to think about what she was doing, she followed him inside.

He had disappeared by the time she got to the lobby, but it wasn't difficult to find his trail. An elderly woman sat in a wheelchair holding a red balloon. A child with an arm cast held a green one. Further on, she came upon a patient lying on a gurney with an orange balloon floating overhead. But the trail ran out in a back hallway.

She tried to talk herself into leaving, but instead she approached a nurses' station. "Excuse me. Did you happen to see a clown go by earlier?" The question sounded ridiculous.

The young nurse behind the desk had a sprig of artificial holly stuck in her plastic name tag. "You mean Patches?"

Honey nodded uncertainly. This must not be Eric's first visit to the hospital. Was this where he came when he disappeared?

"He's probably doing a show for the kids today. Hold on." She picked up her phone, asked a few questions of the person on the other end, then hung up. "Pediatrics on three. They're starting now."

Honey thanked her and headed for the elevators. As soon as she stepped out onto the third floor, she heard squeals of laughter. She followed the sounds to a lounge at the end of the corridor and stopped. It took all of her courage to look inside.

A dozen very young children, probably between four and eight years old, were gathered in the cheerfully decorated room. Some wore hospital gowns, others robes. They were black, Asian and white. Several sat in wheelchairs and a few were hooked up to IVs.

Beneath his curly red wig, Eric's face was disguised in clown white. He had one large eyebrow drawn on his forehead, a scarlet mouth, a red circle at the end of his nose, and the purple star-shaped eye patch. He was concentrating on the children and didn't see her. Fascinated, she watched.

"You are not Santa Claus!" one of the children called out, a small boy in a blue robe.

"Now that's where yer wrong," Eric retorted belligerently. "I got a beard, don't I?" He stroked his smoothly shaven chin.

The children greeted this observation with vigorous shakes of their head and shouts of denial.

He patted his flat waist. "And I got a big fat stomach?"

"No, you don't!"

"And I got a red Santy Claus suit." He plucked at his purple shirt.

"No!"

A long pause fell. Eric looked bewildered. His face puckered as if he were about to cry, and the children laughed harder.

"Then who am I?" he wailed.

"You're Patches!" several of them squealed. "Patches the Pirate!"

His face cracked open in a smile. "That I am!" He pulled at the waistband of his baggy red and purple polka-dot trousers and half a dozen small balloons floated up and out. Then he broke into "Popeye the Sailor Man," substituting the name Patches and performing something close to an Irish jig.

Honey watched in bewilderment. How could a person who was driven by so many private devils set them aside to perform like this? His accent was a comic mixture of Cockney, Long John Silver, and Popeye's nemesis Bluto. The children were clapping with delight, completely caught up in the enchanted spell he was so effortlessly weaving about them.

As he wound up for his finish, he pulled three rubber balls

from his pants pocket and began juggling them. He was a clumsy juggler, but he was so enthusiastic that the children loved it. And then he saw her.

She froze.

One of the balls slipped from his grasp and bounced across the lounge. Several seconds ticked by as he stared at her, and then he immediately returned his attention to the children.

"I missed it on purpose," he growled, planting his hands on his hips, glaring at them, daring them to contradict him.

"You did not!" a few of them countered. "You dropped it!"

"You all think yer so smart," he glowered. "I'll 'ave you know I was trained in the arts of juggling by Corny the Magnificent 'imself!"

"Who's that?" one of the children asked.

"You never 'eard of Corny the Magnificent?"

They shook their heads.

"Well, then. . . ." He began spinning a magical yarn of jugglers and dragons and a beautiful princess with a wicked spell cast upon her that had made her forget her name and left her cursed to wander the globe trying to find her home. With facial expression and gesture, he created imaginary pictures so vivid they could have been real.

She had seen what she'd come for, but she couldn't make herself leave. Strands of the snare he had woven about the children entrapped her, and as she listened, it became impossible to remember who existed behind that clown's face. Eric Dillon was dark and damned; this pirate clown exuded a joyous, enchanting charm.

Patches shook his head dolefully. "So beautiful the princess is, and so sad. 'Ow would you like it if you couldn't remember yer name or where you lived?"

"I know my name," one of the bolder little boys called out. "Jeremy Frederick Cooper the third. And I live in Lamar."

Other children called out their names, and Patches congratulated them on their excellent memories. Then his shoulders hunched forward and he looked doleful. "Poor princess. If only we could 'elp her." He snapped his fingers. "I got me an idea. Maybe all together we can break that wicked spell."

There was a chorus of agreement from the children, and one little girl wearing eyeglasses with clear plastic frames lifted her hand.

"Patches? How can we help the princess if she's not here?"

"Did I say she wasn't 'ere?" Patches looked befuddled. "Naw, I didn't say that, mate. She's 'ere, all right."

The children began to look around, and Honey felt the first twinge of alarm.

"'Course she's not wearin' 'er princess clothes," Patches said.

Her palms began to sweat. Surely he wouldn't . . .

"On accounta the fact that she doesn't remember who she is. But she's beautiful just like a princess should be, so it's not 'ard to pick 'er out, now is it?"

A dozen sets of eyes landed on her. She felt as if she had been pinned to the wall like a dead butterfly. She spun toward the door.

"She's leaving!" one of the children called out.

Before she could clear the doorway, a rope dropped over her head and tightened around her waist, pinioning her arms to her side. Stunned, she stared down.

She'd been lassoed.

The children shrieked with laughter while she stared at the lariat, unable to believe what she was seeing. He began to reel her in. The children cheered. She stumbled backward, embarrassment making her even more awkward. How could he do this to her? He knew that she wasn't ready for anything like this. Her body bumped against his.

"She's shy around strangers," Patches said, beginning to untangle her from his lariat. As soon as he freed her, he threw his arm around her shoulder, ostensibly to give her a hug but, in reality, to pin her to his side. "Don't worry, Princess. None of these blokes'll 'urt you."

She looked out at the children and then back at him, her expression beseeching.

"Poor princess. Looks like she's lost 'er voice, too." He actually seemed to be teasing her. She wanted to push herself away in outrage, but she couldn't do it with the children watching.

"Where's your crown?" one skeptical little boy with an IV in his arm asked.

She waited for Eric to respond, but he kept silent.

The seconds ticked by.

He looked down at the fingernails on his free hand, then began an elaborate show of inspecting and buffing them while he waited for her to speak.

"Tell us, Princess," the little girl with the eyeglasses said softly.

"I—uh—I don't remember," she finally managed.

"See wot I told you?" Patches snapped one suspender with the hand he'd been buffing. "Memory like a piece a Swiss cheese. Full of 'oles." He sounded smug, and it irritated her.

"Did you leave it under your bed?" the little girl asked. "I left my Lite Brite under my bed."

"Uh—no, I don't think so."

"In the closet?" another child offered.

She shook her head, conscious of the clown's arm clamped around her shoulders.

"In the bathroom?" said a little boy with a lisp.

She realized they weren't going to let up on her, and she blurted out, "I—uh—I think I left it at the Dairy Queen." Now where had that ridiculous notion come from?

Patches's arm dropped from her shoulders, but instead of helping her out, he sounded distinctly skeptical. "You left yer princess crown at the Dairy Queen?"

He clearly wasn't going to make this easy. "It—It was giving me a headache," she said. And then, a bit more firmly as her sense of pride poked through, "Crowns do that."

"I wouldn't know. I only wear me pirate's scarf." She waited for him to give her a way out, but instead he said, "I 'eard a rumor about princesses and wicked spells."

"You did?"

"It came to me on good authority."

"Is that so?" She had begun to relax a little.

"I 'eard that a wicked spell on a princess can be broken if the princess in question . . ." He winked at the children. ". . . kisses a 'andsome man."

The boys groaned and the girls giggled.

"Kisses a handsome man?"

"Works every time." He began to preen for the children, tidying his wig and smoothing his painted eyebrow with his little finger. The children, anticipating what was coming, laughed harder.

His mischief was contagious, and she concealed a smile. "Is that so?"

"Bein' a charitable person and all . . ." He dusted the seat of his pants. ". . . I've decided to offer meself fer the job."

With comic lechery, he leaned toward her, his mouth outrageously puckered.

She almost laughed. Instead, she studied his pursed lips for several beats. Then she looked at the children and rolled her eyes. They giggled, and the sound filled her with a glow of pleasure.

She turned back to the clown. "A kiss?" She said the word as if he'd suggested cod liver oil.

Patches nodded. And with his mouth still puckered said, "A big smacker, Princess. Right 'ere." He pointed toward his painted lips.

"From a handsome man?" she inquired.

Still puckered, he flexed his muscles and preened.

She looked back at the children, and they laughed harder. "A kiss from a handsome man, huh? Well, all right, then."

Stepping past him, she approached a little boy with chocolate-brown skin and a leg cast. Bending down, she offered him her cheek. He blushed, but dutifully planted a quick kiss there. The children hooted at his embarrassment.

She straightened. Patches's painted smile had stretched like elastic over his face. And then the noise died down as all of them waited to see if the kiss would work.

She went very still in the time-honored manner of a princess shaking off a wicked spell. Gradually, she widened her eyes until they were huge with wonder.

"I remember! I'm from . . ." *Where?* Her muse deserted her. "I'm from Paxawatchie County, South Carolina!" she exclaimed.

"That's right here, Princess," a child with a lisp said.

"Is it? Do you mean I'm home?"

The children nodded.

"Do you 'member your name?" one of them asked.

"Why, I do. My name is—Popcorn." It was the first word that came into her head, inspired, no doubt, by the smell drifting into the lounge from the small kitchenette next door.

"That's a dumb name," one of the older boys observed.

She stood her ground. "Princess Popcorn Amaryllis Brown from Paxawatchie County, South Carolina."

The clown's blue eye twinkled in the white face paint. "Well now, Princess Popcorn. Since you've remembered yer name, maybe you'd 'elp me give out some Christmas presents 'ere."

And so she helped him distribute the presents he had brought, which turned out to be expensive hand-held video games. The young patients were delighted, and as she laughed with them, she felt lighthearted for the first time in months.

Finally the nurses appeared to lead the children back to their beds. Patches promised to stop by their rooms to see each one of them before he left.

When they were alone in the lounge, he turned away from her to pack up his tricks. While he gathered up his lasso and stowed it in the bag he had brought, she waited for him to speak, but he said nothing. She bent down to pick up one of the balls he had dropped. When he turned back toward her, she held it out.

"How long have you been doing this?" she asked quietly.

She had expected him to sidestep her question, but, instead, he looked thoughtful. As soon as he began to speak, she realized why.

"Well, now, Princess. Corky musta taught me to juggle not long after we sunk the *Jolly Roger*."

Not only had he deliberately misinterpreted her question, but he had retained his identity as Patches. She shouldn't have been surprised. When Eric was in character, he stayed that way. She didn't stop to examine her sense of relief. She only knew that she felt safe talking with this pirate clown, and she didn't feel at all safe with Eric Dillon.

"You said his name was Corny," she corrected.

"There were two of 'em. Twins."

She smiled. "All right, Patches. Have it your way."

He had packed up his props and now he turned toward the door. "I'm gonna visit some of the older kids now, Princess. You want to come with me?"

She hesitated, and then she nodded.

And so Patches the Pirate and Princess Popcorn Amaryllis Brown spent Christmas afternoon visiting the children on the third floor of the Paxawatchie County Hospital, dispensing comfort, magic tricks, and video games. Patches told all the older boys that she was his girlfriend, and Princess Popcorn Amaryllis said that she most certainly was not. She said that princesses didn't have boyfriends; they had suitors instead. And that none of those suitors were clowns.

Patches said the only suit he owned was the one he was wearing, but he'd buy a new one if she'd give him a kiss. And so it went.

That afternoon, she heard something she had not heard in months. She heard the sound of her own laughter. There was something magical about him, a gentleness that drew in the children and made them feel free to clamber on his lap, to tug at his legs, a mischievous charm that let her set aside her grief if only for a few hours and wish that she could crawl into his lap, too. The thought brought her no pangs of guilt, no sense of disloyalty to Dash's memory. After all, there was nothing at all wrong with wanting to embrace a clown.

It was nearly dark when they left the hospital. Even then, he did not set aside the character of Patches. As they walked across the parking lot, he continued to flirt outrageously with her. And then he said, "Visit the kiddies with me later this week, Princess. We can try out this trick with daggers I been thinkin' about."

"Would it happen to involve using me as a target?"

"'Ow'd you know?"

"Intuition."

"It's perfectly safe. I 'ardly ever miss anymore."

She burst into laughter. "No, thank you, you rascal."

But as they reached his van, her laughter faded. When he climbed inside, this pirate clown would disappear, and he would take the princess with him. She felt just like all the sick children who had called out to him not to go. She thought of her empty trailer and the harsh, grim-faced man who shared the park with her. The soft, wistful words slipped out before she could stop them.

"I wish I could take *you* home with me."

She heard the briefest hesitation before he set down his bag and said, "Sorry, Princess. I promised me mates I'd go on a raid with 'em."

She felt incredibly foolish. In an attempt to recover, she clucked her tongue. "Carousing on Christmas night, Patches? You don't have any shame. And I was going to fix a real dinner, for a change."

There was a short silence. For the first time that afternoon, the clown seemed to lose some of his cockiness. "Maybe I'll—I could send one of me mates over instead. To keep you company."

His reply was a dash of cold water. It also made her feel vulnerable. She looked quickly down at the toes of her shoes. "If his name is Eric, I don't want to see him."

"Don't blame you," he replied without a lost beat. "Bad piece a work, that one."

Silence fell between them. The parking lot was quiet and the night clear. As if compelled, she lifted her chin and gazed into the clown's white face. Her brain knew who resided behind the makeup, but it was Christmas, the night ahead was long, and her heart stepped across the boundary of logic.

"Tell me about him," she said softly.

He shoved his hands in his pockets and said dismissively, "'E's not a subject fit fer the tender ears of a princess."

"My ears aren't all that tender."

"Just watch out for 'im, that's all."

"Why's that?"

"Yer too pretty, doncha see? Threatens 'im if 'e thinks a woman might be as good-lookin' as 'e is. Vainest man I ever knew. Doesn't like anybody sharin' 'is mirror space. First thing you know, 'e'll be stealin' yer 'air rollers, and walkin' off with yer makeup mirror."

She smiled, suddenly glad that he wasn't being serious. But then his brow puckered beneath the red eyebrow, and she could feel him growing tense.

"The truth is, Princess . . ." He pulled a key from his pocket and fit it in the rear door lock. "I think yer need to stay as far away from 'im as yer can. Seems like you've 'ad enough trouble in yer life—wot with that wicked curse and everything—without addin' to it. 'E's got a ice cube for a 'eart, that one."

She thought of the children clamoring for his attention, the hugs he had given, the comfort he had offered. Some ice cube.

"I used to think that was true," she said stiffly, "but I don't believe it anymore."

"Now don't you turn soft on me, Princess, or I'll 'ave to go against me better judgment and give you some advice."

"Go ahead."

He leaned against the back of the van and met her eyes unflinchingly. "All right. You were smart to take 'is money for one. The bloke's so rich 'e won't miss a penny. And you need to do wot 'e says about yer career. 'E won't steer you wrong there, and you can trust 'im." He pushed one hand into the pockets of his baggy trousers. "But that's all yer gonna get from 'im. 'E's not good with fragile people, Princess. 'E doesn't mean to 'urt 'em, but it always 'appens."

She was the one who looked away. "I shouldn't have— That night in the bathroom—I was tired, that's all."

"It wasn't a smart thing to do, Princess." His voice grew

husky. "Yer not the kind of woman can take somethin' like that lightly."

"Yes I am!" she exclaimed. "That's exactly how I took it. It didn't mean anything because I'm still in love with my husband. And he would have understood!"

"Would 'e?"

"Of course. He understood about sex. And that's all it was. Just sex. There was nothing wrong."

"That's good, Princess. Then you don't 'ave anything to regret."

It should have been true, but it wasn't, and she didn't understand why.

He gave her a gentle smile and climbed into the van. "So long, Princess."

"So long, Patches."

The engine started immediately, and he pulled out of the parking lot. She watched as the van turned the corner and disappeared. In the distance church bells softly chimed. Above her head the stars popped out one by one.

Grief settled over her in a great heavy cloud.

27

Eric appeared at the door of her trailer that night. He wore black jeans and a dark jacket over a charcoal-gray sweater. His long hair was windblown, his single eye just as mysterious and unrevealing as the black patch that covered its mate. A creature of the night.

He hadn't visited her trailer since he'd moved into the Bullpen, and the belligerent set to his mouth indicated that he wasn't going to ask her if he could enter. Instead, he stood outside glaring at her as if she were the interloper.

She was ready to make a nasty comment when she was

struck with the irrational sense that the pirate clown would be disappointed in her if she didn't offer hospitality to his friend. The idea was crazy, but as she stepped back from the door to let him in, she reminded herself that everything had been crazy that fall. She was living in a dead amusement park, building a roller coaster that led to nowhere, and the only person she had been happy with was a one-eyed pirate clown who wove magic spells around sick children.

"Come in," she said begrudgingly. "I was just getting ready to eat."

"I don't want anything." His tone was equally hostile, but he stepped inside.

"Eat anyway." She pulled a second plate from the cabinet and ladled out a chicken breast for him along with a generous serving of rice and one of the rolls she had defrosted from the freezer. She set a place for him opposite hers at the small table and sat down to eat.

Silence fell between them. The chicken tasted dry in her mouth, and she picked at her food. He ate mechanically, but rapidly enough that she knew he was hungry. She found herself searching for some microscopic dab of clown white that he had missed when he showered, or a tiny speck of rouge at his hairline, anything to link him with the gentle, playful clown, but she saw nothing except that hard mouth and those darkly forbidding features. His transformation was complete.

He pushed back his plate. "I've been in touch with your agent, and I've had some scripts sent to me. I'm going to make a decision about your first project soon." His voice was brusque and businesslike, without even the slightest trace of the clown's humor.

She gave up any further attempt at eating. "I'd like a little say in this."

"I'm sure you would, but that wasn't our agreement."

"You didn't waste any time."

"You owe me a lot of money. I want you to know up front that I'm not going to chose a comedy, and that the part won't bear any resemblance to Janie Jones."

She stood and snatched up her plate. "That's all I can do, and you know it."

"You did a pretty good job of playing a princess."

She walked over to the sink and wrenched on the faucet. She didn't want to talk to him about the princess or what had happened between them today. The afternoon had been too wonderful, and she couldn't bear to have it corrupted.

"It's the same thing," she said, hoping to put an end to the discussion.

"It's not even close." He brought his own plate over and set it in the sink.

She shoved it under the faucet. "Of course it is. Janie was me and so is the—princess."

"That's the mark of a good actor. Instead of trying to create a character from whole cloth, the best actors create characters from aspects of themselves. That's all you did with Janie, and it was the same thing today."

"You're wrong. Janie wasn't just part of me; Janie was me."

"If that were true, you'd never have married Dash."

She clenched her teeth, refusing to let him force her into an argument.

He walked across the trailer toward the table. "Think about all the battles you fought over the years with directors. I can remember dozens of times when you'd complain about a line of dialogue or a particular action by saying that Janie wouldn't do something like that."

"I hardly ever won those battles, either."

"Exactly my point. You were forced to say the line the way it was written. You did whatever the script required. And it wasn't you."

"You don't understand." She spun around to confront him. "I've tried. I've read aloud all sorts of different parts, and I'm terrible."

"That doesn't surprise me. You were probably *acting* instead of just *being*. Open up some of those plays again, but this time don't try so hard. Don't act. Just be." He sat down on the straight-back chair near the table and stretched out his legs, not quite looking at her. "I've just about decided on a television miniseries that you've been offered. It's set during World War Two."

"Unless I get to play a feisty woman from the South who was raised by a broken-down rodeo rider, I'm not interested."

"You'd be playing a North Dakota farm woman who becomes involved with one of the detainees at a Japanese internment camp that adjoins her property. The hero is a young Japanese-American doctor who's imprisoned there. The farm woman's husband is fighting in the South Pacific; her only child has a life-threatening disease. It's good melodrama."

She stared at him, aghast. "I can't do something like that! A farm woman from North Dakota. You have to be joking!"

"From what I've seen, you can do anything you set your mind to." He gazed toward the front window of the trailer, which was pointed in the direction of Black Thunder.

"You're going to be a real bastard about this, aren't you?"

"Haven't you figured it out yet? I'm a real bastard about everything."

"You weren't this afternoon." The words slipped out before she could stop them.

His face stiffened as if she had committed some breach of protocol, and when he spoke, his voice was full of cynicism. "You really fell for that clown routine, didn't you?"

Every part of her turned to ice. "I don't know what you mean."

"My favorite part was the way you stood out there in that hospital parking lot and pretended it was all real." He leaned back in the chair and scoffed at her. "God, Honey, you really made an ass of yourself."

Pain swelled inside her. He was taking something beautiful and making it ugly. "Don't do this, Eric."

But he was on the attack, and he didn't waver. This time he would make certain he drew first blood. "You're—what? Twenty-five, twenty-six years old. I'm an actor, sweetheart. One of the best. I get bored sometimes and practice on the little kids. But it's all bullshit, and I sure as hell didn't expect you to get sucked in."

Her head had begun to pound and she felt ill. How could someone so physically perfect be so very ugly? "You're lying. It wasn't like that at all."

"I've got news for you, sweetheart. There's no Santa Claus, no Easter Bunny, and there aren't any magical clowns." He banged the front legs of the chair to the floor and swooped in for the kill. "About the best you can hope for in life is a full belly and a good fuck."

She drew in her breath. His upper lip had curled in a sneer and he was looking her over from head to toe as if she were a whore he might buy for the night. All the screen's bad boys flashed before her eyes. Every one of them was sitting before her right now, sullen, insolent, cruel—arms crossed, legs stretched out to kingdom come.

All the screen's bad boys.

And at that moment she saw through the smoke screen he had thrown up with his actor's bag of tricks. He was playing another part. With perfect clarity, her vision penetrated the insolence to find the pain, and it so perfectly matched her own that all her anger dropped away.

"Somebody ought to wash your mouth out with soap," she said softly.

"I'm just getting started," he sneered.

Her voice was a whisper. "Let it go, Eric."

He saw the compassion in her face and shot up from the chair, a world of pain coloring his words as he shouted at her. "What do you want from me?"

Before she could respond, he grabbed her shoulder and turned her toward the back of the trailer where the bedroom lay. "Never mind. I already know." He gave her a nudge forward. "Let's go."

"Eric . . ." She understood right then exactly what he was trying to do. Turning back to him, she gazed up into a face that was contorted with cynicism, and she felt no anger at all because she understood it was an illusion.

He wanted her to tell him to go to hell, to kick him out of the trailer, out of her life, to call him every despicable name she could think of. He wanted her to control something he couldn't control himself—the mysterious force that was drawing them together. But the December night on the other side of the trailer's silver shell loomed huge and empty, and she could not send him out into it.

He cursed softly. "You're going to let me do it, aren't you? You'll let me take you in there and fuck you."

She squeezed her eyes shut to hold back the tears. "Shut up," she whispered. "Just, please . . . shut up."

The armor of his defenses crumbled. With a groan, he pulled her into his arms. "I'm sorry. God . . . I'm sorry."

She felt his lips in her hair, on her forehead. His sweater was soft under her palms, the muscles beneath it taut and hard. He caressed her through her clothing—breasts, belly, hips, claiming everything, his touch sending fire licking through her veins.

She grew drunk with his scent: the wool of his sweater, piney soap and clean skin, the citrus tang of the shampoo he had used in his hair. He tilted up her chin to kiss her. Her mind screamed an alarm. Kissing was taboo. Only that.

Ducking her head, she worked the snap on his jeans, and they were naked by the time they reached her bed. It was narrow, designed for one instead of two, but their bodies were so intertwined it didn't matter.

Their passion was a hot, slick monster. She gave him all her secret parts to do with as he wished and took the same from him in return. Primordial serpent, soft devouring beast. They used their hands and mouths; probing, demanding, starved with need.

She did not know the man she accepted between her thighs. He was not a movie star, not a construction worker or pirate clown. His language was rough, his face grim, but through it all, his hands were as giving and gentle as the tenderest of lovers.

In the brief seconds afterward when her body hadn't yet settled back to earth but while he still lay atop her, she stroked his cheekbones with the pads of her thumbs. Inadvertently, her thumb slipped beneath the black eye patch. Without conscious thought, she felt for the disfiguring ridge of scar tissue he kept hidden away.

And encountered only the thick fringe of his eyelashes.

She sucked in her breath. Her thumb brushed over the configurations of a normal eye.

There isn't an eye there, he had said, *just a mass of ugly scar tissue.*

He drew away from her. Sat up on the edge of the narrow bed. "I wish I still smoked," he murmured.

She pulled the sheet over her naked body and stared at the strong muscles of his back. "There's nothing wrong with your eye."

His head shot up, and then he gathered his clothes and went into the bathroom.

She tucked the sheet high under her arms, drew up her knees. She began to shiver as all her misery washed back over her.

He came out of the bathroom wearing his jeans and drawing the sweater over his head, his black eye patch anchored firmly in place. He stopped in the doorway, looming there in the shadows, mysterious and dangerous.

"Are you all right?" he asked.

Her teeth were chattering. "Why did you lie to me about your eye?"

"I didn't want anyone to recognize me."

"I already knew who you were." Her voice broke on a quiver. "Don't lie, Eric. Tell me why."

He braced his arm on the door frame, and his voice was so low she barely heard the words.

"I did it because I couldn't live in my own skin any longer."

Turning on his heel, he left her alone in the small silver trailer.

Eric pulled off the interstate at a rest area in northern Georgia, one of the state-operated facilities with toilets, water fountains, and vending machines. It was three in the morning, and he had been keeping awake on coffee and the sugar hit from a stale Reese's Cup he'd found in his glove compartment. He hadn't made up his mind whether he would ditch the van in Atlanta and fly back to L.A. or whether he would keep driving.

The rest stop was nearly empty on this Christmas night. Not empty enough, however, for him to abandon his eye patch. He slipped it back over his head, then got out of the van and walked past the glass case that held a map of the Georgia highway system. Inside the low brick building a poorly dressed teenage girl sat on one of the benches holding a sleeping baby. She looked hungry, exhausted, and desperate.

Pity stirred the numbness inside him. She was too young to be alone in the world. He dug into his pockets trying to see how much change he had left and hoping it was enough to leave her with some food, but at that moment she looked up at him, and fear joined the other tragedies in her eyes.

She clutched her baby more tightly to her chest and sank back into the bench as if the wood could protect her from his menace. He could hear the quickened sound of her breathing and was sickened by the fear he was causing her. Quickly, he turned away to the vending machines. She was little more than a baby herself, another one of the innocents. He wanted to buy her a house, send her to college, give her a teddy bear. He wanted to buy a future for her baby, warm clothes, turkey dinners, teachers who cared.

The injustices of the world again overwhelmed him, and his head bowed under the crushing burden. He had money and power, and he should be able to fix it all. But he couldn't. He couldn't even protect the people he loved the most.

He shot the vending machines full of change. Instead of houses and college educations, packets of junk food clanked out, potato chips and candy bars, cookies shaped like elves and cupcakes shot full of chemicals—the bounty of America. He gathered it up and snatched the remaining bills from his wallet without counting them. Then he placed it all in a mute offering on the empty bench across from where she sat and left her alone.

By the time he reached the van, he knew he had to turn back. He had tried to run from all the evils that he wasn't able to correct, but even at the Silver Lake Amusement Park he hadn't been able to find sanctuary. It was a kingdom of the dead, ruled by a princess who was dying from grief. And she was the one innocent left that he might be able to save.

In less than a week, he needed to be back in L.A., but before he left he had to try to help her. Except how could he do it? When he was with her, he only hurt her. He remembered the way she had been at the hospital with the children, full of laughter and love, free of ghosts. And the person who had brought her back to life was a pirate clown, a jokester with an endless capacity for giving and a fearlessness about offering himself.

He knew he couldn't help her, but maybe the clown could.

When Honey returned to her trailer after work on Wednesday, two days after Christmas, she found a dress box sitting inside the door. Taking it over to the table, she opened it. Inside lay a white tulle princess dress spangled with silver moons and stars the size of half dollars. She lifted it out and saw what was beneath. A rhinestone tiara and a pair of purple canvas basketball sneakers.

With it was a note that said simply, "Thursday, 2:00 P.M." Instead of a signature, at the bottom of the card was a drawing of a small, star-shaped eye patch.

She pulled it all to her chest: the dress, the purple sneakers, the tiara. Blinking hard, she bit down on her lip and tried to think only of the clown and not what had transpired between herself and Eric on Christmas night. He had showed up for work today, but the only time he had looked in her direction had been with Dev's cynical eye.

The following afternoon when she entered the hospital, she was both nervous and excited. She didn't know whether it was because she'd see the clown again, or simply because, wearing the white tulle princess gown, she no longer felt like herself. Still, she knew she had to be cautious. After Eric's taunting, there was no way she would again fall under the spell of the pirate clown. The kinship she had imagined with him didn't exist. This time she wouldn't forget who lay beneath the white face and silly wig.

When she reached Pediatrics, the nurse directed her to one of the rooms at the end of the corridor. There she found two empty beds. Their occupants were sitting on the clown's lap, and they were wide-eyed as they listened to him read *Where the Wild Things Are.*

He must have read the book many times because she noticed that he seldom looked down at the words. Instead, he maintained eye contact with his small audience as he alternated between playing the parts of Max and the fearsome Wild Things.

He turned the last page. ". . . and it was still 'ot."

The girls giggled.

"I was pretty scary when I read that story, wasn't I?" he boasted. "I scared all of you, didn't I?"

They nodded their heads so agreeably that he laughed.

She stepped hesitantly into the room. The girls had been so absorbed in the story that they hadn't noticed her until then. Their eyes widened and their mouths formed small round ovals at the sight of her costume.

The clown's eyes swept over her, and he made no effort to hide his appreciation of her appearance. "Well now, look who's 'ere. It's Princess Popcorn 'erself."

One of the children on his lap, an earnest brown-skinned moppet with a bandage covering the left side of her face, leaned toward him and whispered, "Is she really a princess?"

"I absolutely am," Princess Popcorn said, stepping forward.

They continued to regard her in wide-eyed amazement. "She's beautiful," the other offered.

Awe-struck, they took in the tiara that nestled atop her tumble of honey curls, the white tulle princess gown with its glimmering moons and stars, the purple canvas basketball sneakers. Their small mouths gaped. She was glad she'd taken extra care with her hair and makeup.

"I couldn't agree more," Patches said softly. "Definitely the most beautiful princess in America."

Just like that, she could feel herself slipping under his spell, but this time she fought against it by primly pursing her soft rose lips. "Pretty is as pretty does. What's inside a person is a lot more important than what's outside."

Patches rolled his single turquoise eye. "'Ew writes yer material, Princess? Mary Poppins?"

She threw him a haughty look.

"What's that under your eye?" one of the girls asked, sliding down off his lap.

She had momentarily forgotten about the small purple star she had drawn high on her left cheekbone. Avoiding the clown's gaze, she reached inside her tote bag for her sable makeup brush and a pot of orchid eye shadow.

"It's a star, just like Patches's. Would you like one, too?"

"Could we?" they inquired breathlessly.

"You certainly could."

The visit flew by. Patches told jokes and performed his magic tricks while she painted stars on the children's faces. Some of the children had been there on Christmas Day, but a number of them were new patients. While the boys were more interested in Patches's magic tricks, the girls stared at her as if she had just stepped out of the pages of their favorite fairy tale. She combed their hair, let them try on her tiara, and reminded herself to buy another pot of orchid eye shadow.

Patches, in the meantime, flirted with all the little girls, the nurses, and most of all with her. She couldn't resist him any more than the children could, and even though she had promised herself she wouldn't again fall under his spell, there was something so irresistible about him that she let all of her sensible resolutions dissolve.

When it was finally time to leave and they were riding the elevator downstairs, she warned herself to be wary. But he would disappear in a few more minutes, and what real harm was there in holding on to the illusion just a little longer?

"Next time you're not lassoing me," she said.

"You don't know 'ow to 'ave a good time, Princess."

"We'll do knives instead."

His face brightened as the doors slid open. "Really?"

"Yes. I'll throw."

He laughed. They walked through the lobby and out into the parking lot. The days were short and dusk had settled.

He led her toward her car, but when they got there he hesitated, as if he, too, weren't ready for them to part.

"Will you come back with me on New Year's Day?" he asked. "It'll be me last visit before I take off to sail the seven seas."

New Year's was just four days off. If only Eric would go away and leave Patches behind. "Sure." She pulled her keys from inside her tote, knowing she had to separate herself from him but not willing to climb into her car.

He took her keys. She looked up at him and saw that he seemed troubled.

"I've been thinking about that coaster of yers," he said. "I'm worried about you."

"Don't be."

He unlocked the door and handed over her keys. "It won't bring back yer 'usband, Princess."

She stiffened. The headlights of a car pulling out of the parking lot turned the moons and stars on her dress into shimmering sparks. Her brain warned her that if she tried to explain, he would mock her later, but her heart couldn't believe this pirate clown could ever harm her. And maybe he would understand what Eric couldn't.

"I have to." She bit her lip. "The world isn't much good without hope."

"What kind of 'ope are you talkin' about?"

"Hope that there's something eternal about us. That it wasn't just some random cosmic accident that put us here."

"If yer tryin' to find God on that coaster of yers, Princess, I think you'd better look somewhere else."

"You don't believe in God, do you?"

"I can't believe in somebody that lets so much evil 'appen in this world. Little children suffering, murder, starvation. Who could love a God who 'as the power to stop all that, but doesn't use it?"

"What if God doesn't have the power?"

"Then 'e's not God."

"I'm not sure about that. I can't love the kind of God you're talking about, either—a God who would decide it was time for my husband to die and then send a dope addict to murder him." She took a quick breath, swallowed. "But maybe God isn't as powerful as people think. Maybe I could love a God who didn't have any more control over the random forces of nature than we have. Not a Santa Claus God of reward and punishment . . ." Her voice became a whisper. ". . . but a God of love who suffers with us."

"I don't think a roller coaster can teach you that."

"It did once. When I was a child. I'd lost everything, and Black Thunder gave me back hope."

"I don't think it's 'ope you want. And I don't even think it's God. It's yer 'usband." He pulled her into his arms. "Dash isn't comin' back, Princess. And it would tear 'im apart to see you sufferin' like this. Why don't you let 'im go?"

She felt the gentle pressure of his jaw on the top of her head and the warmth of his arms seemed like the safest place she had been in longer than she could remember. But because this silly clown had begun to mean too much to a woman who was still grieving over her husband's death, she pulled away from him and spoke fiercely.

"I can't let him go! He's the only thing I've ever had that was all mine."

She threw herself inside her car, but not until she had cleared the parking lot did she look back in her rearview mirror. The clown had disappeared.

28

Honey stood in the fading afternoon light on the porch of the Bullpen and asked herself what she was doing there. It was New Year's Day, and she had spent her entire hospital visit avoiding the clown. She had even slipped out early so she wouldn't have any more private parking-lot conversations with him. Tomorrow he was leaving, and it would all be over.

As she turned the knob and walked inside, the tulle skirt of her princess gown rustled in the stillness. She knew she had to hurry. Although he had been occupied with the children when she had left, she didn't know how much longer he planned to stay, and she would be mortified if he caught her going through his things.

She bit her lip as she stepped inside the musty room, ashamed of herself and yet unable to leave. His identities swirled in her head, separating, melding, and separating again: the menacing Dev, the warm, loving clown, and Eric himself, a dark enigma. Surely there would be something in his belongings that would tell her who he was. She had to put an end to this sick fascination. Otherwise, she would be left with another ghost.

His windbreaker was thrown over the orange vinyl couch, and through the doorway she could see a pair of jeans tossed on top of the old iron-framed double bed. Eric's clothes. An old flannel work shirt that belonged to Dev hung over the back of a chair. As she looked at these bits and pieces of his identity, she felt a despondency that was different from the ever-present pain of Dash's death.

Once he left tomorrow, she probably wouldn't ever see him again, not even when she went back to L.A. Eric lived in the insulated world of the superstars, so their paths weren't likely to cross by accident, and the decisions he made about her career would be handled through her agent. She had only now to solve the mystery, and to convince her heart that Eric and the clown were really one.

She smelled the particular odor of greasepaint even before she walked into the bathroom. Like many actors, he stored his makeup in a fishing-tackle box, which lay open on the lid of the toilet. A tube of clown white and small round tins of red and black rested on the back of the sink, along with a dark pencil and several sable brushes. She slumped against the door frame and stared blindly at the makeup. It was true then.

She gave a small, shaky laugh at her own silliness. Of

course it was true. She knew they were the same person. Her mind did, anyway. But somehow her heart kept refusing to make the final connection. Again, she wished Eric would go and leave the clown behind. Everyone loved clowns. Caring about a clown wasn't a betrayal.

"Well, now, look who came callin'. Princess Popcorn 'erself."

She spun around.

He stood a few feet away, the painted smile on his face curling around a genuine one beneath. She began to stammer an explanation for her presence, but then realized he didn't seem to care. It was almost as if he had been expecting to find her waiting for him.

"Yer crown's crooked," he said with a grin.

"It's not a crown. It's a tiara." She was nervous, and when she reached up to take it off, her hair became tangled in the combs that secured it.

"'Old on there, Princess. Let me 'elp you."

He stepped forward and extracted the tiara from her hair. The touch of his hands was so gentle she had to fight against the soft sensations spreading through her. "You do that like you've had lots of practice."

"I'm good friends with a couple of little girls who've got long 'air, too."

His easy manner disappeared. He turned his back on her and walked out into the living area. She followed him.

"Tell me about them," she said.

He stood by the window with its shabby, water-spotted curtain and toyed with her tiara. His strong, thin fingers, tan from the sun, looked out of place against the delicate filigree of metal and rhinestones. They were indisputably Eric's hands—hands that knew her intimately—and she looked away from them.

"Their names are Rachel and Rebecca. Rachel's a lot like you, Princess. She's tough and stubborn, and she likes gettin' 'er own way. Becca is—Becca is sweet and soft. 'Er smile could stretch yer 'eart wide open."

He fell silent, but even from the other side of the room, she could feel the strength of his love for his daughters.

"How old are they?"

"They're five. Six in April."

"Are they ugly like you?"

He chuckled. "They're the prettiest little girls you ever saw. Rachel's 'air is dark like mine. Becca's is lighter. They're both tall for their age. Becca was born with Down syndrome, but that 'asn't stopped 'er one bit." He turned the tiara in his hands and ran his thumbnail over the small combs, making a soft, pinging sound. "Becca's got lots of determination—always 'ad, right from the beginning—and her sister Rachel makes 'er keep up." Again, his thumbnail scraped over the prongs. "At least she used to. . . ."

He gazed at her, cleared his throat. "They would 'ave loved you in that outfit, Princess. Both of 'em are suckers for royalty."

He looked as if he wished he hadn't said so much, but there was even more he hadn't told her. Why was he separated from these daughters he obviously loved so much?

He walked over to her and handed back the tiara. "I'm leavin' tomorrow, you know."

"Yes, I know."

"I'm gonna miss you. Princesses like you don't grow on trees, now do they?"

She prepared herself for the joke that would come, but the mouth beneath his clown's painted grin was unsmiling. "You don't know 'ow beautiful you are, do you, Princess? You don't know 'ow just lookin' at you makes me old 'eart thump."

She didn't want to hear this. Not from the clown. She was too vulnerable with him. But if not from the clown, then who? She tried to smile. "I'll bet you say that to all the princesses."

He reached out and touched her hair. "I never said it to a one. Only you."

A traitorous weakness spread through her. She looked up at him with pleading eyes. "Don't . . ."

"Yer the sweetest princess I ever met," he said huskily.

She no longer knew who she was talking to, and tiny wings of panic began to beat at her insides. "I have to go now."

She turned her back on him and walked to the door. But when she got there, she stopped. Keeping her eyes straight ahead so that she didn't have to look at him, she whispered, "I think you're wonderful."

She groped for the door knob. Twisted it in her hand.

"Honey!"

It was Eric's voice, not the clown's. She spun around.

"I'm tired," he said, "of being a prisoner."

And then, as if it were happening in slow motion, he pulled off his wig and eye patch with a single movement of his arm.

His silky hair looked as black as the midnight sky next to his stark white face. His turquoise eyes were full of agony. *Run away!* her mind screamed. But she stood paralyzed as he withdrew the oversized white handkerchief that protruded from his pocket and lifted it to his face.

"Eric, no . . ." She took an involuntary step forward.

The lip rouge smudged into the white, the large eyebrow blurred. Helplessly she watched as he removed the layers of makeup.

It was a little murder.

Her eyes began to sting but she blinked the tears away. Bit by bit, the clown disappeared. She told herself she wouldn't give in to grief. She was already mourning the passing of one good man, and she would not mourn another. But the tears continued to form.

He was the instrument of his own destruction. When he was done, he dropped the soiled handkerchief and met her gaze full on.

Residues of his clown's makeup still clung to his skin and eyelashes, but there was nothing comical about his appearance. The face that had been revealed was one she knew— strong, handsome, unbearably tragic. She understood that he had made himself vulnerable to her in a way he had never done with anyone else, and it filled her with fear.

"Why are you doing this?" she whispered.

"I wanted you to see me."

There was a naked, hungry expression in his eyes that she

had never witnessed before, and in that moment she knew he was going to tear her apart just as Dash had done. Even so, she couldn't turn away. All of her old assumptions about him no longer worked, and she realized she would never be free of him if she couldn't unlock his mysteries. "What are you running from?"

He gazed at her with haunted eyes. "From myself."

"I don't understand."

"I destroy people." He spoke so quietly she barely heard him. "People who don't deserve it. The innocents."

"I don't believe you. You're the gentlest man I've ever seen with children. It's as if you can read their minds when you talk to them."

"They need to be safe!" he exclaimed, the statement exploding into the quiet of the room.

"What do you mean?"

"Children are real and precious, and they need to be safe!" He began to pace, and she felt as if the room had grown too small to contain him. When he spoke, the words tumbled from his lips as if they had been dammed up for too long.

"I wish there was a place where I could keep them all safe from harm. Where there weren't any car accidents or diseases or anyone who could hurt them. A place where there were no sharp corners or even any Band-Aids, because no one would ever need them. I wish I could make a place where all the kids that nobody wanted would come to stay."

He stopped walking and gazed into space. "And I could spend my time in this clown's costume making them laugh. And the sun would shine, and the grass would be green." His voice faded to a whisper. "The only rain that fell would be gentle, with never any thunder. And my arms would be as wide as the world so that I could stretch them out and protect everything that was too small and too tender to protect itself."

Tears glistened in her eyes. "Eric . . ."

"And my daughters would be there. Right in the middle where nothing bad could ever get to them."

It was his children. He had stripped himself bare, and she understood that whatever haunted him, whatever was driving him to the edge, was connected with his children.

"Why aren't you with them?"

"Their mother won't let me see them."

"But how could she be so cruel?"

"Because she believes—" His mouth twisted. "She won't let me near them because she believes I molested them."

The word, coming from his lips, wouldn't register in her mind. "Molested them?"

He spoke through clenched teeth, every syllable tortured. "She believes that I sexually abused my daughters." His face was ageless and emptied of all hope.

Stunned, she watched as he twisted away from her and fled from the Bullpen. His feet pounded on the wooden steps, and then all was quiet.

She stared at the empty doorway. Seconds ticked by as she tried to take in what he had said. Her brain dredged up old newspaper stories about scoutmasters, teachers, priests—men who ostensibly loved children but were found to have been molesting them. But her heart dismissed the possibility that he could be one of these men. There were many things in life of which she was uncertain, but nothing on earth could ever convince her that Eric Dillon, in any of his guises, could willfully hurt a child.

She ran outside after him. It was dusk and the sky was streaked with garish ribbons of scarlet, lavender and gold. He had disappeared. She ran through the trees toward the lake, but both the eroding shoreline and the crumbling pier were vacant. For a moment she didn't know what to do, and then a stillness inside her told her where he must be.

As soon as she cleared the trees, she saw him climbing Black Thunder to the top of the lift hill. Despite his hostility toward the coaster, he had instinctively chosen the same destination that so relentlessly drew her. Human beings had always gone to the mountaintop whenever they needed to find the eternal.

His purple shirt and polka-dot trousers blended in with the blazing Technicolor sunset behind him as he made his purposeful climb to the top. She understood the necessity of his journey because she had made it so many times herself, but something inside her couldn't let him make it alone.

Drawing the billowy tulle of her skirt through her legs from the back, she tucked as much of the excess material into the gown's sash as she could manage and began her ascent. She had made the climb a hundred times before, but never with the encumbrance of five yards of white tulle, and she moved awkwardly. Halfway up she tripped. She caught herself just before she lost her footing and swore softly.

The sound was enough to draw Eric's attention and he called down to her in alarm. "What do you think you're doing? Get down. You're going to fall."

Ignoring him, she stuffed the gown back into her sash with one hand while she held on with the other.

He was over the rail in a second, on his way down the side of the frame to meet her. "Don't come any farther. You're going to trip."

"I've got the instincts of a cat," she said, as she resumed her climb.

"Honey!"

"Quit distracting me."

"Jesus . . ."

His shiny black pirate's boots and then the legs of his purple trousers came into view. "I'm under you," she warned. "Don't come any farther."

"Hold still. I'm going to move alongside you and help you back down."

"Forget it," she said breathlessly. "We're a lot nearer the top than the bottom, and I don't have the energy to climb back down right now."

He must have decided it was more dangerous to argue with her than to let her do as she wanted because he stayed at her side until they reached the top. Then he slid under the rail and, grasping her arms, drew her up beside him.

They collapsed next to each other, sitting on the track, their legs hanging through the spaces between the ties. "You're crazy," he said.

"I know." Her skirt billowed over both of them and down

through the open framework. Pieces of tulle snagged on rough surfaces in the wood, and the moons and stars in her lap caught fire from the sunset.

They were silhouetted against the color-streaked sky with the world in miniature below them—treetops like small green sponges, the lake a mirrored sliver, the tiny finger of a faraway church steeple. From their perch in the sky, they were forced to remember that another more dangerous world existed beyond the safe parameters of this dead amusement park.

She gazed down the legendary first drop. "Do you know what happens when you hit the bottom?"

"What?"

"You go back up again," she said softly. "Always back up. With a roller coaster, hell is only temporary." *Please, God, let it be true.*

"When you've been accused of molesting the two people you love the most, hell is a way of life," he said harshly. "Fathers do it all the time, you know. Inhuman, perverted bastards, desecrating the most sacred responsibility a man can have."

"But not you," she said. She spoke the words with certainty, not questioning.

"No, not me. I'd kill myself before I'd hurt my daughters. I don't mean that as a figure of speech, Honey. I mean it literally. I love them more than my own life."

"Why did their mother accuse you?"

"I don't know!" he exclaimed. "I don't know why. I only know that she believes it's true. She truly believes I've done these—these unspeakable things to them." He ran his fingers through his hair, his speech growing agitated. The words had been held back for too long, and now they came in torrents. As they sat in the fading light of a new year at the top of the lift hill, he told her of the death of his stepbrother Jason and how his guilt had haunted him for years. He spoke of his marriage to Lilly and the birth of his twin daughters, of the joy the girls had brought him and the horror of their mother's accusations.

As she listened to him, she didn't once doubt that he was telling the truth. She remembered the games he had played with her: the harsh words, the air of menace he could assume at will. All of it was illusion. Only the clown's gentleness had spoken the truth about who he was.

She heard what he wasn't saying, too, and glimpsed the awful sense of responsibility he seemed to bear for all of the evil in the world. Finally, she understood his curse. He thought he should fix everything.

She couldn't address that pain, but she could address the other. "You may be hurting your daughters even more by not fighting for them," she said gently. "Losing a parent when you're so young is a terrible thing. It changes you forever. My mother's death shaped everything I've ever done, even the way I fell in love. Because of her death, I've spent my whole life trying to make a family for myself. Dash had to be my father before he could be my husband. You don't want that for them, Eric. You don't want them to spend their adult lives looking for you in every man they meet."

His face was haunted, his despair so absolute that she yearned to give him physical comfort, but she was afraid to reach out to him. Afraid he would misunderstand. She had allowed him to make love to her, but now a simple touch on the knee was too intimate.

"I can't do anything," he said. "Lilly's going to put them into the underground if I make a move to get them back. Then they won't have anyone."

Honey felt sick. She couldn't imagine any woman being so vindictive. Why did Lilly hate Eric so much? For the first time, she truly grasped the complexity of his dilemma.

"I'm sorry," she said.

He stood up, rejecting her pity. "Let's climb back down. Stay with me."

The descent was easier than the ascent. Even so, Eric stayed beside her, his hand catching her arm whenever he thought she looked unsteady. By the time they reached the ground, the sunset had faded and it was nearly dark.

They stood quietly for a moment. His face was in deep shadow. Beneath all the masks he had thrown up, all his identities, she felt the goodness that ran like a core of gold straight through him. "I can't imagine what your daughters must be feeling to have lost you."

To her surprise he lifted his arm and buried his hand in her hair. At first he said nothing, simply wove a strand through his fingers. When he spoke, his voice was husky and vulnerable. "And what are you going to feel when you lose me?"

The flutters of panic returned. He mustn't touch her. Not like this. She wasn't his to touch. "I don't know what you mean."

"Yes, you do. Tomorrow when I leave. Will it make any difference to you?"

"Of course it'll make a difference." She pulled away from him and walked toward a pile of scrap lumber.

"One fewer pair of hands to work on your coaster?"

"That's not what I mean."

"Then what?"

"I'll—" She turned back to him. "Don't ask me questions like that."

"Come back with me, Honey," he said quietly. "Leave the coaster and come back to L.A. with me. Now. Not three months from now when it's done."

"I can't."

"Why not?"

"I have to finish building it."

All his softness disappeared, and his mouth set in a grim, harsh line. "How could I forget? You have to build your great monument to Dash Coogan. Why did I think I could compete with that?"

"It's not a monument! I'm trying to—"

"To find God? I think you've got God and Dash tangled up in your mind. It's Dash you want to find on that coaster."

"I love him!" she cried.

"He's dead and no roller coaster in the world has the power to bring him back."

"He's not dead to me! Not ever to me. I'll always love him."

The light was too dim to see clearly, and so she wasn't certain that she saw him wince. But the sorrow in his voice was unmistakable. "Your body wasn't as faithful as your heart, was it?"

"That was just sex!" she cried, as much to herself as to him. "Dash wouldn't have cared about that. He understood about sex."

His voice was low and flat. "What did he understand?"

"That sometimes it's—Sometimes it's meaningless."

"I see."

"We've both been lonely, and—Don't try to make me feel guilty. We didn't even kiss, Eric."

"No, we didn't, did we? You did other things with that beautiful mouth of yours, but you wouldn't kiss me."

He took a step toward her, and she knew he was about to change that. She told herself to move away, but her feet remained rooted to the ground. At that moment she would have given all she had for him to slip one of his masks back on—any of them. She finally realized how much his protective identities had also protected her. Stripped bare as he was now, no barriers separated them. Not skin or bone. She could feel the pain of his yearning as if it were coming from her own heart.

"Do you know that I've been dreaming about your mouth?" His eyes were dark, his voice husky.

"I'm cold," she said. "I'm going back to the trailer."

"How it would feel. What it would taste like." He cupped her arms in his palms. His breath was soft. She couldn't move as he lifted his hand and gently brushed his thumb over her lips.

They parted automatically. It had been so long since she had been kissed, and he was so very beautiful, right to the center of his soul. His thumb outlined her bottom lip, touched the bow at the top. He dipped his head, and his thick, dark lashes fanned his cheekbones.

She felt the warmth of his mouth draw nearer and was

pierced with a longing so fierce that she knew if she gave into it, she would have committed such an unforgivable act of betrayal that she could never again live with herself.

Just as his lips were about to settle over hers, she jerked away. "No! No, I won't do this! I won't betray my husband."

She had never seen anything as sad as the expression on his face. His eyes shimmered with pain that pierced her to the very core, and he seemed to collapse into himself.

"I'll bet you would have kissed the clown," he whispered.

She ran from him then, fleeing his presence and the sweet, sad seduction she had almost not been strong enough to resist.

Eric stood next to the coaster long after she had disappeared into the trees. His eyes were dry and scratchy. He told himself he had been living with pain for so long that a little more wouldn't make any difference, but logic couldn't ease the anguish. As the night wind whipped the trees, he found himself remembering the child she had been, the way she had followed him with those puppy-dog eyes, begging him to pay attention to her. Even then, something about her had drawn him in.

Now she was a woman, and he loved her. Despite her hostility and her rejection, he knew that she understood him in a way no one else ever had. Although she had never had a child herself, she understood the depth of his love for his children. And her fierce, disciplined drive to finish her coaster—no matter how much it might alarm him—mirrored his own obsession with his work. She even seemed to know why he had to live in other people's skins. Despite the differences in their backgrounds, despite the lies and deceptions, she felt like the other half of himself.

And she didn't want him. Instead she wanted a dead man.

A fresh attack of pain began to rush at him, howling and yipping, ready to sink its teeth in. Before that could happen, his mouth gave a savage twist, and he flung up his shield of cynicism.

He was the Prince of Studs. Women came after him, not the other way around. All he had to do was snap his fingers and they lined up for his pleasure. He could have them any way he wanted: blond, brunette, old, young, big tits, long legs, step right up and let the big star take his pick. The women of the world were his to command.

Upside down? *Certainly, sir.*

Two for one? *We aim to please.*

But this woman didn't understand the rules.

She didn't understand the most basic fucking rule of the universe! She didn't understand that big movie stars were *entitled to any woman they wanted!*

This woman didn't care that he might be the best goddamn actor of his generation. He could be a bricklayer for all the difference it would make to her. She didn't care that he was a millionaire twenty times over, or that she was the only person in the world he had ever spilled his guts to. And she didn't even read goddamn *People* magazine, so how could she know that he was Sexiest goddamn Man Alive?

Eric turned away and headed back to the Bullpen to pack his things. As he left Black Thunder behind, he knew that he had done a lot of stupid things in his life, but the stupidest thing he'd ever done was to fall in love with the grieving Widow Coogan.

Into the Station

Station

1990

29

"Daddy!" Lilly jumped up from her living room couch where she had been resting from her unpacking chores and raced across the black and white marble floor to her father.

"Hello, darling." In the seconds before Lilly was encompassed in Guy Isabella's arms, she noted with relief that he looked as handsome as ever. His thick, silvered-blond hair gleamed in the late January sunlight that streamed through the windows. A cantaloupe-colored sweater lay knotted over the shoulders of his Egyptian-cotton shirt. His pleated linen trousers were baggy and stylishly wrinkled. When he'd visited her in London four months earlier, she'd suspected he'd had a face-lift, but he was secretive about the exotic cosmetic treatments that kept him looking closer to forty than fifty-two, and she hadn't asked.

"I'm so glad to see you," she said. "You don't know how horrible everything's been." Drawing back, she gazed up at him. "You have an earring." She stared at the small gold hoop in his earlobe.

His eyes crinkled at the corners of his tightly stretched skin as he smiled. "You noticed. One of my lady friends talked me into it not long after our visit in London. What do you think?"

She hated it. There had been enough changes in her life recently, and she wanted her father to stay the same. Still, she wasn't going to ruin their reunion with criticism. "Quite dashing."

His tawny eyebrow arched as he regarded her critically, taking in the long red knit sweater that hung too loosely from her shoulders over a pair of silky black leggings. "You look terrible. Didn't you say you were going to spend New Year's in St. Moritz with André and Mimi? I thought you'd be rested."

"Hardly," Lilly replied bitterly. "The new nanny quit so I had to take the girls with me. Becca wasn't a problem. She doesn't talk very much anymore, but Rachel was uncontrollable. After the first day, André and Mimi were aching to ask me to leave, but they're much too polite, so Mimi contented herself with helpful comments about my shortcomings as a disciplinarian. Then Rachel deliberately knocked a glass of grape juice on Mimi's Daghestan rug, and Mimi reverted to her fishwife roots. It was dreadful. We left for Washington two days later."

"Did your visit with your mother go well?"

"What do you think? Rachel has always exhausted her, and Becca—You know mother. She's not good with any sort of imperfection."

"I can imagine." He began to look around him, rubbing his hands together. "Where are my granddaughters? I can't wait to see Rachel again. And Becca, too, of course. I'll bet they've grown like weeds."

"Like nasty little weeds," Lilly murmured under her breath. Guy looked at her quizzically. "I called a service to get a sitter for the afternoon. She's taken them out for pizza and then to the park. I told her to keep them there for a couple of hours, but I doubt that they'll last that long. Rachel will attack another child or Becca will wet her pants or there'll be some other disaster and they'll be back."

"You need to discipline Rachel, Lilly."

"Don't you lecture me, too." She turned away from him and walked toward the windows. "How am I supposed to discipline her? She's hostile and difficult, and if I try to punish her, she runs away. I lost her for three hours last fall. After we found her, she went into my closet with a pair of scissors and deliberately cut up my new evening gown."

"I was hoping things would get better."

"How can they get better? She hates me, Daddy." Lilly crossed her arms over her chest and, biting her bottom lip, murmured, "And sometimes I hate her."

"You don't mean that?"

"No, of course I don't," she said wearily. "Except sometimes I do mean it. She makes me feel like such a failure." She reached down for the cigarette pack she'd left on the table that sat between the windows.

"You're smoking!"

Her hands faltered as she opened the pack. She hadn't intended to smoke in front of her father. He might sometimes be a bit too liberal in his use of alcohol, but he was a fanatic when it came to tobacco. "You have no idea of the strain I've been under."

He eyed her with such disapproval that she set down the pack. He walked over to the couch and carefully tugged on his trouser legs as he took a seat. "I can't understand why you're putting such pressure on yourself. I know you love to travel, but you've had so many addresses in the past nine months even I can't keep up with you. You're obviously exhausted. But I won't lecture you anymore, darling. At least you've had enough sense to come home so I can look after you."

"I'm only here for a few days. Just long enough to clear up some business affairs, and then we're going back to Paris."

"That's ridiculous, Lilly. You can't keep on moving around like this. Why do you have to leave so soon?"

"Eric's in town."

"All the more reason to stay. The way you've let him abdicate responsibility for the girls baffles me. You know I never liked him, Lilly, but I still can't believe how he's turned his back on his daughters."

Lilly looked away so she didn't have to meet his eyes. She had never told him about Eric. She was too ashamed. "Fatherhood was just another acting role for him. Once he mastered the part, he got tired of it."

"It's still hard for me to understand. He seemed to care about the girls so much."

"He's an actor, Daddy."

"Even so—"

"I don't want to talk about it."

He stood and came over to her. "But Lilly, you can't keep

391

running. It's not good for the girls, and it's not good for you. You've always been high-strung, and it's obvious that raising Rachel and Rebecca by yourself is too much for you. You're as thin as a rail and you look exhausted. You need some pampering, darling." He gave her a smile that gently crinkled the creases at the corners of his eyes. "How about a few weeks at a spa? There's a new place near Mendocino that's wonderful. I'm going to send you there as soon as possible. It'll be my Christmas present."

"You've already given me a dozen presents."

"Nothing's too good for my baby." He drew her into his arms, and she pressed her cheek against his smoothly shaven jaw. As he held her there, she began to feel nauseated. She took a deep breath, waiting for the comfort his presence always gave her, but the musky smell of his cologne seemed to make her even queasier. Disturbed, she pulled away from him.

"Is something wrong?"

"Jet lag, I guess. I feel—It's all right. My stomach is just a little upset."

"That settles it. I'm taking the girls home with me tonight."

"No, really—"

"Not another word. Every time I offer to take them, you put me off. Do you realize that you've never once let me have my granddaughters? Not once since they were born. And I can't count the number of times in the past nine months that I've asked you to fly them to California to stay with me for a few weeks, but you always have excuses. No more, darling. You're under enormous strain, and if you don't get some rest soon, you'll be ill."

A headache had begun to throb at her temples. "They're too big a handful, Daddy."

"That's what you always say."

"Becca's been wetting the bed, and she's having so many problems with her speech that it's hard to understand her. Rachel gets more rebellious all the time; she won't do anything she's supposed to. I'd put her in a school somewhere, but I don't want Eric—" She broke off. "Anyway, you're not used to young children. They'd be too much for you."

"Not for a few nights. That won't be a problem at all. And don't forget that I raised you, Princess."

Lilly's stomach began to roll again, but before she could say anything, she heard the sound of the front door crashing open.

"I'm not one bit sorry!" Rachel shrieked in that loud, determined voice that made Lilly want to cover her ears. "It was my swing, and that boy tried to take it!"

Lilly pressed her thin fingers to her temples to try to keep her head from blowing apart. The argument between her daughter and the sitter who was supposed to have kept the girls occupied accelerated.

Rachel stormed into the living room, her dark hair flying wildly around her face. "You're a stupid baby-sitter! And I'm not doing anything you say!"

The sitter appeared with Becca in tow. She was an elderly woman, and she looked frazzled and angry. "Your daughter deliberately attacked a little boy," she announced. "And when I reprimanded her, she cursed me."

Rachel's light blue eyes were hostile, her mouth set in a mulish line. "I only said the S word, and he took my swing."

Guy stepped forward. "Hey, sweetheart. How about a kiss for your grandfather?"

"Grandpa Guy!" Rachel's hostility evaporated as she raced toward him. He hoisted her into his arms. Her legs were long, and her sneakers banged against the knees of his linen trousers. Lilly felt something horrible uncoiling inside her chest at the sight of her daughter in her father's arms. She suspected it was jealousy and she was ashamed.

While her father talked to Rachel, she got rid of the sitter and pulled Becca out from behind one of the neo-Roman chairs where she had gone to hide. To her disgust, she saw that Becca's pink corduroy slacks were wet.

"Becca, you wet yourself again."

Becca sucked on her thumb and watched her sister and grandfather with dull, disinterested eyes.

"Daddy," Lilly said nervously. "Don't you want to say

hello to Becca?" Guy reluctantly set Rachel down and turned toward her.

"She's W-E-T," Lilly warned.

"Mommy just told Grandpa you wet your pants again," Rachel announced to her sister. "I told you not to be a baby anymore."

"Well, now, accidents happen, don't they, Rebecca?" Guy patted Becca on the head but didn't pick her up. Lilly's father was no more comfortable with Rebecca than her mother, Helen, but at least he was more discreet about it. He pulled some cinnamon candies from the pockets of his linen slacks and handed them to the girls, just as he had done with her when she was a little girl. The familiar sight of those candies made her feel queasy again. She wondered if she were coming down with the flu.

"Unwrap it like this, Becca." Rachel extended her own candy toward her sister and showed her how to pull on the ends.

"Here, let me help," Guy said.

"No, Grandpa. Becca has to do things for herself or she won't learn. That's what Daddy says. Everybody keeps doing things for her, and it's made her lazy." She splayed her small hand on her hip and glared at her sister. "Unwrap it yourself, Becca, or you can't have it."

Guy plucked the candy from Becca's fingers. "Now, Rachel, there's no need for that." He unwrapped the candy and gave it to Becca. "Here, sweetheart."

Rachel gazed at him with disgust. "Daddy says—"

"What your father says isn't important anymore," Lilly snapped. "He's not here, and I am."

Guy saw that Lilly was upset and he came over to comfort her. Becca began to cry. Red syrup from the candy leaked from the corner of her mouth. Rachel glared at her mother and then turned to her sister.

"Crying's for babies, Becca. Daddy'll stop being so busy soon and have time for us. He will! How many times do I have to tell you?"

"That son of a bitch," Guy muttered, his voice so low that

only Lilly could hear. "How could he do this to them? Still, I suppose it's all for the best. They're young enough now to adjust. If he had abandoned them when they were older, it would have been doubly traumatic."

Lilly couldn't imagine how anything could be more traumatic than what had already happened. She was ruining her own life trying to protect children who weren't the slightest bit grateful, but she couldn't weaken. Even if her daughters hated her for it, she would protect them from their father's perversion.

Guy had gone back over to the girls, and Rachel gave a squeal of delight at something he had said. "Really? Can me and Becca get pizza, too? And can I watch television before I go to bed?"

"Absolutely." Guy tousled her hair.

Lilly's heart slammed against her rib cage. "Daddy—"

"Not another word, Lilly." He regarded her sternly. "You need a rest, and the girls are going to stay with me for a few days so you get it."

"No, Daddy, I don't—"

"Help your sister change into some dry clothes, Rachel, and then we'll go."

Lilly tried to protest, but her father paid no attention. Her head was pounding, her stomach rolling. She hated the idea of her daughters going off with her father, and she hated herself even more for being so jealous. What kind of mother was she to resent a loving grandfather's relationship with his own grandchildren?

She forced herself to return several changes of their clothing to the suitcase she had just unpacked. The upheaval in her stomach grew worse. While her father was occupied with the girls, she slipped into her bathroom and vomited.

She felt better with her stomach empty, but her head was still pounding. She quickly swallowed three aspirin and went back into the bedroom.

The excitement of staying with her grandfather had overstimulated Rachel. She was running up and down the back hallway and screeching at the top of her lungs. Guy, however, seemed to have the magic touch with her and when he told her to settle down, she obeyed.

They were ready to leave when they discovered that Becca had disappeared. Rachel found her hiding in the back of Lilly's closet. Her pants were wet again, and Lilly had to change her.

"Don't forget, Mommy," Rachel said as she stood at the front door holding her grandfather's hand. "If Daddy calls while we're gone, tell him to come get us."

For nine long months, every time she left the house, Rachel had said the same thing. Lilly clenched her teeth, an action that intensified the throbbing in her head, but painful experience had taught her that Rachel would refuse to leave if her request was ignored. "I won't forget," she said stiffly.

"Kiss your mother good-bye, girls," Guy said.

Rachel obediently gave Lilly a loud smack. Becca was unresponsive.

Guy pecked Lilly's cheek. "Don't worry about a thing, darling. Call some friends and enjoy yourself for a few days. The girls and I will be fine."

Lilly felt as if someone had taken a hammer and chisel to her head. "I don't know. The girls are so . . ."

"Don't fret, darling. Come along, girls. How about a stop for ice cream on the way?"

Rachel gave an earsplitting shriek and tugged on her grandfather's hand. Becca followed obediently. Guy held the door of his Jaguar sedan open and they clambered inside. His hair glinted in the California sunshine, and his straight white teeth flashed as he smiled. He was so handsome. So horribly, obscenely handsome.

"Their seat belts!" Lilly called out. "Don't forget their . . ."

Guy had already fastened the belts, and he waved his hand to indicate that he had heard. Moments later, he was backing down the drive.

Lilly rushed forward. "Be good!" she called out. "Don't do what Grandpa tells you." She caught her breath. What was wrong with her? "I mean—"

She felt cold and feverish at the same time, and she stumbled slightly as she made her way back inside the house and to her bathroom. Even though it was still light outside, she swallowed two sleeping pills. Her father was right. She was falling apart, and she had to get some rest. She climbed into bed without removing her clothes.

Afternoon slipped into evening, and the nightmares engulfed her. In her dreams she was running. A faceless woman raced after her, hands with blood-red fingernails extended and splayed. One by one those long blood-red nails shot off the ends of her fingers, turned into daggers, and stabbed her in the back. Lilly turned to her father for help, only to realize that he held the biggest dagger of all and it was pointed at Rachel. The horror enveloped her. And then it wasn't her father coming after her, but Eric, and he wanted Rachel. Mustering all of her strength, she cried out.

The strangled sound of her own scream awakened her. The room was dark, and for a moment she didn't know where she was. She gripped the cover, afraid to sit up, afraid to move for fear some indefinable horror would claim her. Her hair was stuck to her cheeks like a web, and she could hear a horrible pounding in her ears.

Eric's face swam before her eyes, a vision of filth and decay all the more obscene because of his physical perfection. As she struggled to clear her mind from the aftereffects of the sleeping pills she had taken, she was flooded by a paralyzing realization that she had made a horrible mistake by not telling her father about Eric. What if Eric went to Guy's house and took Rachel? Her father didn't know about Eric's perversion. He wouldn't know that he shouldn't hand her over. What if Guy let Eric have her?

Through the fog of her sleeping pills and the lingering horror of her nightmare, she was gripped by the awful certainty that Eric had done just that. He had taken Rachel, and her daughter was in desperate trouble.

Her body was leaden, and the bile rose in her throat as she remembered that Becca was with her father, too. But then she knew that Eric would never molest Becca. Her condition would repulse him. Rachel was his target. The stronger daughter.

Whimpering, she climbed from the bed and groped for her shoes. Then she staggered from the room, still trying to escape from her narcotic-induced fog. Her purse lay on the glass-topped credenza in the hallway, and she dug through the rubble of crumpled tissues, animal crackers, and boarding passes until she found her car keys. Gripping them in her fist, she picked up her purse and stumbled through the kitchen on her way to the garage. She had to get to Eric before he could hurt Rachel.

A set of Danish cutlery mounted in a polished block of teak caught her eye. After only a moment's hesitation, she pulled a heavy knife from its slot and placed it in her purse. She squeezed her eyes shut, the lids trembling. She knew she wasn't a good mother. She was self-centered, impatient, and she never seemed to do the right thing. But she loved her daughter, and she would do whatever was necessary to protect her.

Eight miles away in the hills of Bel Air, Guy Isabella tucked the covers around his granddaughter's small body with one hand while he clasped a tumbler of whiskey with the other.

"Why can't I sleep with Becca, Grandpa Guy?" Rachel gazed apprehensively up at the room's high ceiling and then over at the tall windows with their diamond-shaped leaded-glass panes. Grandpa Guy had told her this used to be her mother's room, but Rachel didn't like it. It was dark and spooky.

"Rebecca has been asleep for almost an hour," her grandfather said. The ice cubes clinked in his glass. "I didn't want you to wake her."

"I'd be real quiet. I might get scared if I have to sleep by myself."

"Nonsense. You won't be scared." He ran the tips of his fingers over Rachel's lips. "Grandpa Guy will check on you before he comes to bed."

"I want to sleep with Becca."

"Don't be afraid, sweetheart. Grandpa Guy will be near."
Bending down, he pressed his lips lightly over Rachel's.

Eric rubbed his eyes and stared at the telephone next to
his bed as he unbuttoned his shirt. How many times in the
three weeks since he'd returned had he wanted to call
Honey? A hundred? A thousand? He told himself that it was
a good thing the park's only telephone was in the Bullpen
where she wouldn't hear it if he finally gave into temptation.
She had already let him know in every way possible that he
couldn't compete with a ghost, and he had no intention of
groveling.

It was nearly midnight, and he had been up since five, but
even though he was exhausted, he knew he wouldn't be able
to sleep for more than a few hours. His new role was both
physically and emotionally demanding, and he wasn't giving it his best, but he couldn't seem to manage all the peeling
away of layers that he had to go through to get to the heart of
a character. Maybe because he still hadn't managed to put
himself back together since the night he had peeled himself
away for Honey. How could he do his actor's job of entering
another person's soul when he felt so personally exposed? It
was as if he had left part of himself behind with her, and
until he was complete again, he would drift.

The idea made him angry. He had to scrub her memory
from his mind, erase the sound of her laughter as she had
played with the children at the hospital, drive out the images
of the two of them making love. Most of all, he had to forget
her soft, sweet compassion the night he had taken off his
clown's mask and laid himself bare to her.

The ringing of the doorbell interrupted his disturbing
thoughts. He frowned. His Nichols Canyon house was
tucked away on a nearly inaccessible road, hardly a convenient spot for drop-in company. He didn't bother to rebut-
ton his shirt as he made his way from his bedroom to the
front entry. When he reached the door, he peered through
the peephole and then quickly turned the knob.

"Lilly?"

Her teeth were chattering, and her skin looked pale and

pinched. She had cut her hair since he had seen her and it hung about her face in silvery-blond wisps that made her eyes look huge and haunted.

She stared at him as if she were looking at something profane. Her eyes took in his unbuttoned shirt and then dropped to the open snap on his jeans. Her mouth began to quiver. "Where is she?"

He shoved one hand wearily back through his hair. "What do you want, Lilly?"

"What have you done with her?"

She grabbed the door frame for support and he reached for her arm, beginning to grow alarmed. "What's wrong?"

She tried to pull away from him, but he drew her inside. He led her into the living room and pushed her down on the sofa. Her breathing was quick and shallow, and she was clutching her purse to her chest. He grabbed a bottle of brandy from the bar and splashed some into a glass.

"Drink this."

The rim of the glass clinked against her teeth. She swallowed and then coughed.

"Tell me what's happened?" he demanded. "Is something wrong with the girls?"

She passed a trembling hand over her mouth and rose unsteadily to her feet. Instinctively, he reached out to catch her, but she drew back. "Where is she?"

"Who?"

"Rachel! I know you have her."

His heart missed a beat. "I don't have her. For God's sake, what's going on?"

"I don't believe you. You took her from my father. Where have you put her? Where is she?"

"I didn't even know you were back in town. How could I have taken her? Are you telling me you don't know where she is?"

"Liar!" she shrieked. Bolting past him, she ran toward the back of the house.

He rushed after her and then watched as she threw open the door of the guest room. When she saw that it was empty, she moved onto the next room and the next until she reached his bedroom. His gut churned as he stopped inside the doorway. She stood in the center of the room clutching her purse to her chest, her eyes opalescent with terror.

"What have you done with Rachel?" she whispered hoarsely.

He forced himself to stay calm. She was barely holding onto the threads of reason, and if he said the wrong thing, he could push her over the edge. Sounding as composed as he could manage, he stepped cautiously into the room.

"When did you last see her?"

"Daddy took her for the night." Her speech was choppy, and she was twisting her purse strap around her fingers. "Becca, too. He took Becca, too. I knew I shouldn't let them go, but I was so tired."

"It's all right, Lilly," he said soothingly, moving a little closer. "You didn't do anything wrong."

"Yes, I did!" She began to whimper. "You don't understand. I never told him about you. He didn't know that you could hurt Rachel."

"I haven't hurt Rachel," he said quietly. "You can see she's not here. I love her. I'd never hurt her."

"Liar!" she shrieked. "Daddy loved me! He loved me, and he hurt me."

He could feel the hair begin to stand up on the back of his neck. "Lilly, what are you talking about?" He moved too quickly and she shrank back.

"Don't touch me!" Her eyes were wild, the pupils dilated. "You'll hurt me. You'll hurt me like you hurt Rachel."

He froze in his tracks.

She began to cry. "She doesn't like it when you hurt her . . . but she can't make you stop." Her voice grew higher in pitch, more childlike. "You tell her not to . . . make any noise . . . when you touch her. Don't make any noise, sweetheart. I won't hurt you. Just shut your eyes. But she can't . . . shut her eyes. And you . . . smell like whiskey."

"Lilly, I don't even drink whiskey."

"She doesn't like . . . that whiskey smell," Lilly sobbed.

"And she doesn't like it when—when you turn on the radio." She gulped for air. "And you say, 'Just shut your eyes and—and listen to the music, Lilly.'"

The horror of complete comprehension washed over him. "Christ."

"And then sometimes—" Her voice broke, became a whisper. "Sometimes the music's playing . . . and the whiskey smell . . . and those hands."

"Oh, baby . . ."

"It's like a terrible dream, except sometimes when those hands feel good." She shattered before him, her voice almost inaudible. "And that's the worst thing of all." With a cry, she slid down the wall and crumpled like a broken toy on the floor.

He rushed toward her, wanting to hold her, to help her. She screamed and grabbed for her purse.

"No!" she shrieked. *"No more!"*

He gasped as a sharp pain pierced his side. Jerking back, he saw the blade in her hand and realized she had stabbed him. She moaned in horror and dropped the knife, staring at the blood welling from his side. Through his pain he saw her face grow ashen and knew the exact moment when the past and present clicked together in her mind.

"Dear God," she whispered. "Oh, God, no . . . What have I done?"

Eric pressed one hand to his side against the welling blood. He thought it was only a flesh wound, but there was no time to make certain. For now he could think only of his daughter.

"Is Rachel with your father now?" he demanded. "Is that where she is?"

Lilly's eyes were terror-stricken but lucid. "Oh, God, Eric," she whispered. "It was never you. It was him all along. He did those things to me, but I blocked them out. And now I've let him take the girls."

He pulled her to her feet. "Let's go."

Her eyes were dark with horror. "You're bleeding. I cut you."

"I'll worry about it later." He snatched up the T-shirt he'd thrown over the bottom of his bed earlier and wadded it against his side.

"Oh, Eric. I'm sorry. What have I done? Oh, God, I'm sorry."

"We don't have time. We have to get to them right away." But as he pulled her from the bedroom, he wondered if it was already too late.

The keys were still in the ignition of her car. He pushed her into the passenger seat and jumped behind the wheel. The tires squealed as he backed down the narrow drive. The digital clock on the dashboard read 11:48. Almost midnight. The perfect time for a monster to molest a little girl.

Lilly sobbed next to him, her arms wrapped around her chest as she rocked back and forward. "Not Becca . . . He won't hurt Becca. It's Rachel." Her sobs intensified. "How could he do it? I loved him so much. Please, Eric. Don't let him hurt her. You don't know what it's like. Please."

He gritted his teeth and shut out the heart-wrenching sounds of her pleas. Over the years he'd driven in a dozen movie car chases, but now it was for real, and as he floored the accelerator, he blotted everything from his mind except the dangerous, twisting canyon road and the little girls whose life would never be the same if their father didn't reach them in time.

30

A funny, bad smell woke Rachel. She couldn't remember what it was and then she knew it was booze like Mommy's parties. She huddled more deeply into the covers and rolled over onto her side. Her long nightgown was twisted around her waist.

The mattress moved and she started to poke Becca and tell her not to be such a wiggly worm, but then she remembered that she was at her Grandpa Guy's house and Becca wasn't in bed with her. She heard music playing and forced her eyes open. A red light glowed from the radio on her bedside table.

The mattress moved again. There was someone sitting on the other side of the bed. She felt scared. Maybe a wild thing had slithered out of the closet and was coming to get her. She wanted to call for her daddy, but she was too scared to make a sound, and then the bed moved again and she twisted around and saw that it was only her Grandpa Guy sitting on the other side.

"I was scared," she said.

He didn't speak. He just looked at her.

She rubbed her eyes. "Did my daddy call on the phone?"

"No."

"You smell bad, Grandpa. Like booze."

"A little good whiskey. It's just a little good whiskey, that's all." His words sounded funny, not like the way he usually talked, but slower, and he was saying each word carefully, like Becca's speech therapist. His hair was messed up, too. Grandpa Guy was always neat, and she was surprised to see him with messy hair.

"I'm thirsty. I want a drink of water."

"Let me . . . Let me rub your back."

"Now!" she insisted. "I'm very thirsty."

He swallowed the rest of the whiskey in his glass, then rose slowly from the side of the bed and left the room.

Wide awake now, Rachel waited until he had disappeared before she pushed back the covers and climbed out. Her bare feet padded across the carpet as she made her way into the hallway. It was long and as dark as a castle's, with a heavy wooden chest, big, ugly vases, and a wooden chair like a throne. Some swords that Grandpa Guy had used in one of his movies hung on the wall, and yellow lights that looked like candles were set into the dark red wallpaper. They glowed dimly, making her shadow huge.

Her tummy felt scared—Grandpa Guy's house was so big and dark—but she moved cautiously down the hallway until she got to her sister's room. She turned the knob carefully and pushed with both hands on the heavy door until it opened far enough for her to slip inside.

Becca was curled up in the middle of the bed making a funny *ptt-ptt-ptt* sound with her mouth like she did when she was sleeping. Sometimes the sound woke Rachel up and she'd give her sister a little kick, but now the familiar *ptt-ptt-ptt* made Rachel feel better. Rachel liked knowing that her sister wasn't scared or crying or something. Being Becca's sister was a big responsibility. Daddy used to tell her that she was sometimes too much of a fussbudget with Becca, but Daddy wasn't around now and Mommy was sort of scared of Becca, so Rachel felt responsible.

Her brow furrowed as she gazed at the bed. Becca was starting to forget Daddy, but Rachel couldn't forget. Mommy said Daddy was too busy to see them, but Rachel thought maybe he didn't want to see them anymore because she did so many bad things. Maybe if she was a goody-goody like Becca he would come get them. Her lips set stubbornly. And when he did come, she was going to hit him hard right in the middle of his heart because he shouldn't have made them stay with Mommy so long.

Becca moaned in her sleep and her mouth moved like she was getting ready to cry. Rachel crept over to the side of the bed and patted her. "Don't be scared, Becca," she whispered. "I'll take care of you."

Her sister quieted. Rachel was turning to leave when she saw a dark figure standing in the doorway. Her legs went all Jell-O, and then she knew she was just being a big scaredy cat because it was only Grandpa Guy.

She crept quietly over to meet him. He stepped back from the doorway to let her out of the room and closed the door. She looked up at him. He held her glass of water in his hand and another glass of booze in the other.

"Go back into your bedroom," he said, still talking in that funny, slow way.

She was getting sleepy again and she followed him. He was walking a little crooked, and he spilled some of her water on the carpet near her bed. When she spilled, she was supposed to clean up her mess, but Grandpa Guy didn't seem to notice.

He pulled back the covers on her bed. She got under them and took the glass from him. Holding it with both hands, she took a sip before she handed it back.

"Is that all you wanted?" He sounded like he might be mad at her.

She nodded.

"All right, then. Lie down and go to sleep." He had started to whisper, and she wondered if he was afraid he might wake Becca, but Becca was far away.

"I'll just rub your back," he said. "I'll rub your back for a little bit."

She didn't like the funny way he was talking, and she didn't like the way he smelled, but she liked getting her back rubbed, and she rolled obediently over onto her stomach and shut her eyes.

Grandpa Guy's hands reached under her nightgown. She lifted her hips so he could push it up far enough to reach her back. He began to rub. His hands felt nice, and she yawned. The music on the radio was soft and pretty. Her eyelids drifted shut. She thought about Max and the wild things in her favorite book. Maybe tomorrow Grandpa would read it to her. Maybe tomorrow . . .

She drifted on her bed like Max in his private boat.

And then something terrible jerked her awake.

The gold and black wrought-iron gates, some of the most elaborate in Bel Air, came into view. Eric jammed on the brakes, and the car fishtailed as it skidded to a stop. The clock on the dashboard read 12:07. It had taken him nineteen minutes to get here. What if he was too late?

He knew Guy didn't have live-in help. Everyone arrived in the morning and left after dinner. At night, Guy slept in the big mausoleum of a house alone. Alone except for two little girls.

Lilly's eyes were glued to the gates. "I forgot about the gates. Oh, God, Eric, they're locked. We can't get inside."

"I'll get in." He jumped from the car, ignoring the pain in his side where Lilly had stabbed him. He could do it all, he told himself. Drive fast cars at supersonic speeds, climb impenetrable barriers, break into locked houses, save the innocents. He'd done it a dozen times. He'd done it with his bare fists and with an Uzi in his arms. He'd done it bleeding from his gut and blind in one eye. But when he'd done it before, it had been make-believe, and this time it was all too real.

He found a toehold in the ironwork. The fence wasn't difficult to climb, but the pain in his side encumbered him. His shirt was blood soaked, and he hoped Lilly hadn't hit anything important when she'd cut him.

The house and grounds were protected with a series of photoelectric eyes. As he reached the top of the gate and threw his leg over the curling grillwork, he hoped he was setting off alarms everywhere—inside the house, at the security agency, right in God's ears. He dropped to the ground and sucked in his breath at the bolt of pain that shot through him. As he ran toward the house, he kept his hand shoved against his side where the blood was wet and slick. He sprinted to the front door and leaned on the bell with one hand while he pounded with the other on the carved panels.

"Open up! Open up, you son of a bitch!" As he slammed his fist against the door, he prayed that his daughters were safely tucked in bed, alone and untouched, but he wasn't enough of an optimist to believe it.

Seconds ticked by, each one lasting forever. Guy didn't appear, and Eric knew he couldn't wait any longer. He ran toward the thick growth of trees at the side of the house then along the east wing. As he reached the gardens at the back, the memory of the first time he had been here passed through his mind, the night Lilly had taken him to the playhouse and the twins had been conceived. The attraction he had once felt for her was so different from the meeting of the souls he experienced with Honey that it seemed to have happened to another person. He pushed away thoughts of Honey. They were an indulgence he couldn't afford.

Over the sound of his breathing, he heard water running in the hexagonal Mediterranean fountain. He ran toward the door that led into the kitchen. With one hand clasped to his side, he lifted his foot and smashed the lock.

The door splintered as he crashed through. For the space of a few seconds the pain in his side numbed him. He steadied himself as he became aware of the persistent beep of the security alarm. And above that beep, he heard a sound that froze his blood. Rachel's shrieks for help.

Rachel had wedged herself into the corner of her mommy's old bedroom. She was wearing only her underpants and she was screaming because the wild thing wasn't a friendly monster anymore but her own Grandpa Guy.

"Stop that screaming!" he yelled as he came toward her. "Stop it!"

The whole house was beeping, but Grandpa Guy didn't seem to hear it. He shoved a chair out of the way as he came nearer. He wasn't talking in that careful way anymore. His words were running together like too much food in his mouth, and he kept bumping into things, and his pants were open. She'd seen what was in there, and it was ugly.

"No!" she screamed. "No! I'm scared!"

She was crying and her nose was running. Everything had been nice at first when he was rubbing her back, but then he'd put his hand in her underpants. She knew about good touches and bad touches, and it woke her up. She had started yelling, but he had done another bad touch, so she had kicked him and jumped out of bed. But now he was coming after her.

"Come here, Rachel!" Grandpa Guy commanded. His teeth showed, and they were big and fierce. "Stop screaming and come here! I'm going to punish you if you don't come here."

He lurched forward and she screamed again. She ducked to run past him, but he caught her.

"No!" she screamed as his fingers dug into her arms. "No! I'm scared!"

"Be quiet!" His breath was stinky as he picked her up,

squeezing her so tightly that he hurt her. "Be quiet! I won't hurt you. Shh. I'm just going to rub you."

"I'll tell!" she screamed, trying to kick him. "I'll tell my daddy you touched me bad!"

"You won't tell." He carried her toward the bed and dropped her there. "If you tell, you won't see your mother again."

She started to sob.

He pulled away the covers that she had grabbed and reached for her underpants.

"No! No, don't do that!" Rachel kicked as hard as she could.

Grandpa Guy gave a grunt as one of her kicks landed. But then he pressed down on her and reached for her underpants again. Her arms and legs were so tired and shaky that she couldn't fight hard, but she didn't stop. She remembered her daddy and Patches and the pirate raids where girls could fight just as good as anybody else. She kicked again and screamed again and said the same words over and over.

"Daddy! Daddy!"

Eric took the front stairs two at a time, hauling himself up by the banister so he could move even faster until his feet barely seemed to be hitting the carpeted treads. His blood was pounding, his heart racing. Rachel's screams were coming from behind a closed door at the end of the hallway, and from the opposite direction he could hear the softer, more muted sound of Becca crying. He threw himself down the hallway and exploded into the room.

Guy was on the bed pressed over his daughter. He lifted his head and looked at Eric through alcohol-deadened eyes. There was nothing handsome about him now. His hair was disheveled, his face slack, every wrinkle visible. The room reeked of liquor.

Eric hurled himself across the room and hauled Guy from his daughter's small body.

"You bastard!"

"No . . ." Guy whimpered.

"I'm going to *kill* you, you son of a bitch!" Eric threw him against the wall, then went after him. Grabbing his shirtfront, he wrenched him up from the floor where he'd fallen and began to punch him. Blood lust roared in his ears and only the crunch of bone could make it stop. He struck again and again, shattering his face. Guy slumped into unconsciousness, but Eric didn't stop. Two innocent children had to be avenged, Rachel and her mother. Guy's head snapped back under the force of Eric's next blow.

"Daddy!"

Gradually the roaring in his ears subsided, and the world around him began to steady. As he came back into himself, he saw the ruin of the man before him. His cheekbone was shattered, and blood streamed from the mouth and nose of a face that would never again be called handsome. He released Guy's shirtfront, and Lilly's father crumpled to the floor.

Eric heard a sob and saw that Rachel was running toward him. With one long stride, he caught her to him and swung her up into his arms.

"Daddy! Daddy!"

She cried out his name and buried her face in his neck. The tiny bumps of her spine pressed against his fingers. His eyes squeezed shut from the strength of the love he felt for her while his heart slammed against his ribs. One of her knees dug into his wounded side, but he barely noticed the pain. He felt the soft fabric of her underpants against his arms and allowed himself to hope that he had arrived in time.

"It's all right, sweetheart," he crooned, gasping for breath. "Everything's all right. Daddy's here. Daddy's right here."

"Grandpa Guy . . . He tried to . . . He wanted to . . . hurt me."

"I know, sweetheart. I know." He kissed her cheeks and tasted the salt of her tears. In the distance he heard the sound of a police siren, but his only concern was the child in his arms.

"He wanted to hurt me," she sobbed.

"Daddy won't ever let him hurt you again."

Becca's crying had grown louder in the other room, and with Rachel still in his arms, he turned to go to her.

"I don't—I don't want . . . " Rachel's words got lost in a sob and her stranglehold on his neck tightened.

He stopped walking and stroked her back. "What, sweetheart? What don't you want?"

Her small ribcage heaved.

"Tell me," he whispered, his lips pressed to her cheek, his eyes full of tears.

"I don't want you . . ."

"What, baby?"

"I don't want you to—" She hiccupped. ". . . to see my underpants."

His heart melted in his chest and he slowly lowered her to the floor. "Of course you don't, sweetheart," he whispered. "Of course you don't."

Still holding her close, he reached for the soft yellow cotton robe with the border of dancing bears that had fallen to the carpet. Gently, he wrapped it around her and gave her back the privacy that was hers by right.

With Rachel clasped tightly in his arms, he carried her from the room and made his way down the hallway to reclaim his other daughter.

31

Honey had just finished making a phone call to one of the food vendors when she heard a banging on the back door of the Bullpen. "Come on in."

The door swung open and Arthur Lockwood entered. Even in the middle of a South Carolina amusement park, he managed to look like a Hollywood agent. Maybe because he always seemed to be waving papers.

"The people who are renting the rides are here," he said, "and you have to sign off on the carousel."

"The carousel wasn't supposed to be delivered until

tomorrow." She took the papers and scrawled her name across the bottom of them.

Arthur shrugged as she handed them back. "I don't work here. I'm just the messenger boy. When you get back to L.A., promise me that you won't tell anybody that I've been running around negotiating with hot dog vendors and Good Humor men. It spoils my image as a shark."

"I promise. And thanks, Arthur."

Arthur had shown up at the park two days ago to go over her contract for the television movie Eric had chosen as her comeback vehicle, the project he had discussed with her last Christmas about the Japanese internment camp. Filming would begin in a month. It was a wonderful script, but the part of the North Dakota farm wife seemed so far beyond her abilities she was glad that she was too exhausted to worry about it.

Arthur could have discussed the details of the contract with her by phone, and the fact that he had decided to put in a personal appearance told her that he hadn't been certain she would sign the contract in the end. But a deal was a deal, and no matter how painful the consequences, she wouldn't welsh.

Incredibly, Arthur hadn't uttered a single word of rebuke about the agreement she had made with Eric. He'd even approved the paperwork that made it official. Apparently the men talked frequently, but Arthur hadn't discussed the details of their conversations with her, and she hadn't asked. She tried to feel relieved that Arthur would be dealing with Eric instead of herself.

She wished she could ask him about Eric directly, but she couldn't seem to find the right words. Three months ago, at the end of January, Lilly had held a widely publicized press conference in which she had revealed the sexual abuse she had suffered as a child. According to reports, both Eric and her mother had been at her side during the press conference. There was no mention of the accusations Lilly had made against Eric, so Honey could only assume that those accusations had been the result of Lilly's own childhood trauma and that Eric had his children back.

She felt the sting of tears and busied herself with the clipboard that held a stack of grimy papers. "I hope Eric doesn't have any more projects lined up for me."

"Uh—we're talking." Arthur grew extremely interested in his Rolex. "It's getting late, and I have a plane to catch."

"Is he— You said he'd been injured."

"I told you, Honey. He's fine. It wasn't serious." He waved the carousel papers and kissed her cheek. "I'll hand these over on my way out. You take care now. Don't wear yourself out with the festivities this weekend."

He frowned at her, and she knew he was unhappy with the way she looked. Once again, she was finding herself unable to sleep. She was always on edge, and only the trips she continued to make to the hospital offered her any pleasure. She alternated between exhaustion and an almost manic aggressiveness that left her feeling as if she were about to jump out of her skin. But only by working hard could she drive away thoughts of Eric.

"I'll be fine." She saw Arthur off and then, after making another phone call, left the Bullpen herself.

She had decided to make an event of the reopening of Black Thunder on Saturday, three days from now. Since she was already deeply in debt, a few thousand more wouldn't make any difference. The county office of family services had given her a list of seventy-five needy families, and she had invited them all to enjoy an afternoon at the park. The event wouldn't be elaborate, but everything would be free: the food, a few rented rides for the younger children, some game booths, and, of course, Black Thunder.

As she walked back to the coaster, every part of her ached with a weariness brought about as much by tension as physical labor. Today was Wednesday. If all went well, Black Thunder would have its first test run that afternoon. That would give them another few days to work out any problems before the families arrived on Saturday for the coaster's official reopening. Two weeks later she would leave for California.

A crew was putting the final touches of paint on the shiny black station house as she approached. Inside under protective plastic sheeting sat the refurbished train with its seven purple and black cars. The electricians had been wiring up the control board, while the engineers and project foreman were engaged in a series of checks and cross-checks. Today the new lift chain would be rotated for the first time by Black Thunder's original flywheel, using power fed through the hundred-horsepower motor. The brake inspection was in progress, and by late afternoon they hoped to send the train out, its cars loaded with sandbags for its first run.

Only a fraction of the work crew remained, and without the shrill whine of power saws and the pounding of hammers, the construction site was abnormally quiet. She stopped next to a pile of scrap waiting to be hauled away and gazed at the enormous piece of artwork that hung over the entrance to the station house.

It was wonderful, even better than the artwork over the old House of Horror. The coaster stretched the length of the painting, rearing and bucking like a wild mustang against a terrifying sky of boiling clouds and runaway lightning bolts. Executed in violent purples, blacks, and stormy grays, the painting had the same uncontrollable energy as the ride. It had arrived from Winston-Salem, North Carolina, in the back of a construction truck. The bottom right hand corner held the signature of the artist—Gordon T. Delaweese. Gordon's talents were just one more thing she had been wrong about.

She remembered her last conversation with Chantal, a nonstop monologue in which her cousin had described all the wonders of the beauty school she was attending to learn how to do hair. Honey wearily rubbed her eyes. How many times had Dash told her that she should stop trying to run other people's lives?

Sandy Compton, the project foreman, came toward her. "Honey, we're about ready to load the cars with sandbags and send out the train."

She felt a combination of anticipation and anxiousness. It was finally going to happen.

"Don't be surprised if the train can't make the entire run

the first time," Sandy said. "Remember that the track's stiff, and we have to make adjustments. We're expecting trouble on the lift hill, and the spiral may give us problems."

She nodded. "I understand."

For the next three hours she watched as Black Thunder slowly came to life. The sandbag-laden train struggled to climb the lift hill. It stopped, then moved, then stopped again until a problem in the motor was corrected. When the train finally cleared the crest and plunged into the first drop, she felt as if she had been lifted off the ground herself. It managed the rest of the course, including the spiral, and by the time it had coasted into the station, everyone was cheering.

Black Thunder was rolling again.

The rest of the week flew by for Honey. The coaster was ready for human occupants by Thursday and the engineers were euphoric after their first test run. Although sections of the track still needed to be smoothed to take out some of the brutality, it was exactly what they wanted—a fast, dangerous ride, barely in control.

Late Thursday afternoon, the foreman approached Honey to tell her they had passed the safety inspection. And then he asked her if she wanted to go out on the next test ride.

She shook her head. "Not quite yet."

She didn't ride it on Friday either. Although she spent the day rushing to get ready for Saturday afternoon's celebration, it wasn't her work load that made her refuse, but the fact that there were too many people around. The board operator who would be running the ride had agreed to come to the park early Saturday morning before anyone else arrived. Only then, when she could be alone, would she take her ride.

She gazed around her. More than half the park was fenced off for safety reasons, but this section had sprung to life before her eyes. The equipment for the food vendors sat in place not far from Black Thunder's station house, and a rented carousel stood where the old one had once run. They had installed an inflated Moonwalk for the smaller children, and a variety of game booths, which were going to be run by members of a local church. But the real attraction was Black Thunder.

The coaster had cost her a million dollars to rebuild. She was broke and in debt, but she didn't regret anything. At dawn tomorrow she would climb into that first car and see if she could touch the eternal that would finally let her make peace with Dash's death.

She saw a little girl, one of the workmen's children, gazing up at the coaster. The child had craned her neck at such a sharp angle that the ends of her straight dark hair brushed the waistband of her jeans. Her expression was so intense with concentration that Honey smiled as she approached her.

"Hi. Are you looking for someone?"

"I'm waiting for my daddy."

The child's hair was held back from her face with a set of barrettes that didn't match. Along with her jeans, she wore a T-shirt appliquéd with a red and yellow satin tugboat, a pair of battered Nikes, and a neon-pink plastic bracelet flecked with silver glitter.

"This roller coaster's really big," she said.

"Yes, it is."

She turned to study Honey. "Is it scary?"

"It's pretty fierce."

"I wouldn't be scared," the child scoffed. "I'm not scared of anything." And then her face fell. "Except that I have nightmares."

"Did you ever ride a roller coaster?" Honey inquired.

"Only baby ones."

"That's too bad."

The child gave an indignant snort. "I was going to ride Space Mountain when we went to Disneyland, but my daddy wouldn't let me 'cause of the nightmares. He was *so* mean. And then he made us leave early just 'cause he said I was crabby."

Honey concealed her amusement. "Were you?"

"I sort of threw my ice cream cone, but I didn't mean to hit his shirt, and he shouldn't of made us leave."

Honey couldn't help but smile, especially since she wasn't the one responsible for raising this cute little hellion. Something about her made Honey remember another little girl who had also plunged dauntlessly into life.

The child regarded her reproachfully. "It wasn't one bit funny."

Honey immediately sobered. "I'm sorry. You're right. It definitely wasn't funny to leave Disneyland early."

"Daddy already said I can't ride Black Thunder. I even cried, but he wouldn't change his mind. He's *really* mean."

No sooner were the words out of her mouth than her face splintered into a wide grin as she caught sight of someone behind Honey's back.

"Daddy!" she shrieked. Arms and legs pumping, she took off.

Honey smiled as she heard an oof of expelled breath. Which one of her workmen had fathered this little stinker? Just as she was about to turn and see, she heard that unforgettable voice.

"Jeeze, it's only been five minutes, Rach. Watch that elbow. And I asked you to wait while I took Becca to the bathroom."

Honey's entire world tilted. Her emotions leaped between a piercing sense of joy and a suffocating fear. She was abruptly conscious of her dirty jeans and untidy hair. What was he doing here? Why hadn't he stayed away so she would be safe from him? Slowly, she turned to confront him.

"Hello, Honey."

The man who stood before her was no one she knew. He was an expensive stranger, an icon with a gilded Oscar on his mantel and the world's power brokers at his feet. The eye patch was gone. The long hair that she remembered so well had been civilized in a two-hundred-dollar haircut that didn't quite reach his collar. His clothes screamed money and European style: a designer shirt instead of soft flannel, loosely fitting slacks in a subtle gray-on-gray windowpane rather than faded jeans. He pulled off his costly sunglasses and slipped them into his shirt pocket. His turquoise movie-star eyes revealed nothing of what he was feeling.

She tried to get the pieces to click together so that she could connect the movie star with the clown, the construction worker, and, most of all, with the man who had let her see his private demons, but she couldn't make the link.

Not until he gazed down at his daughters. At that moment, his false identities faded away and she knew that the man who stood before her was the same one who had laid bare his soul that night four months ago while they sat on top of Black Thunder.

"It looks like you've already met Rachel," he said. "And this is her sister, Becca."

She dropped her eyes to the child whose hand was completely enveloped in his, but before she could say anything, Rachel broke away from his side and ran to her.

"Becca's got Down syndrome," she said in a fierce whisper that was loud enough to be heard by the world. "Don't say anything mean to her. Just 'cause she doesn't look like everybody else doesn't mean she isn't smart."

Honey found her tongue with difficulty. There was no use trying to explain to Rachel that her silence hadn't been caused by her sister's handicap, but by her father.

"Hello, Becca," she managed, her voice shaky. "I'm glad to meet you."

"Hi," Becca said shyly.

Apparently Honey had met Rachel's standard for behavior because she nodded her approval and returned to her father's side.

Honey slipped her fingertips into the pockets of her jeans and addressed Eric for the first time. "I—I thought you were working on a film."

"Just finished up. I decided I couldn't miss the great event." His eyes were expressionless as he looked up at Black Thunder.

"I didn't expect you," she said inanely.

"No, I don't imagine you did." His bad boy's mouth gave that cynical twist he hid behind when he was hurting. "How was your magical mystery ride?"

"I—I haven't taken it yet."

He lifted his eyebrow. "Waiting for a full moon?"

"Don't, Eric."

Rachel's voice interrupted, and her tone was decidedly condemning. "I thought you said Honey was a grown-up. She's *little.*"

"That's enough, Rach."

"I bet I'll be taller than her by the time I'm in third grade. She's a shrimp for a grown-up."

"Rachel . . ." Eric's voice held a note of warning.

"It's all right, Eric." There was something decidedly calculating about Rachel's comments, and through her own distress Honey felt a spark of admiration, not to mention a strange kinship. She knew all about this sort of challenge.

"I may be short, kiddo," she said. "But I'm tough."

"I'm tough, too," Rachel retorted.

"I can see that, but you have a way to go before you'll be as tough as I am." Honey stuck the tips of her fingers in the back pockets of her jeans. "I was running this place when I wasn't much older than you. It's what's inside a person that counts, not what's outside. Nobody who's got any sense *ever* messes with me."

"Oh, Lord," Eric muttered. "I knew this would happen."

Rachel regarded her with the first hint of respect. "Are you strong enough to fight a man?"

"A dozen of them," Honey replied without hesitation.

"I had to fight my Grandpa Guy. He was giving me bad touches."

Honey felt a jolt of outrage as she realized there was more to Lilly's story than had been made public. She concealed her dismay, and the only emotion she permitted herself to display was respect. "I'll bet he was sorry he tangled with you."

Rachel nodded vigorously. "I screamed and yelled real loud, and then Daddy beat him up. Grandpa Guy had to go to a special hospital for—" She looked uncertainly at her father.

"Alcoholics," he said, supplying the word.

"A hospital for alcoholics," Rachel continued. "And me

and Becca don't ever have to be alone with him again. And Daddy said I don't ever have to let anybody see my underpants."

"That's good," Honey replied. "Some things are private, aren't they?"

But Rachel was no longer interested in talking about the past. Her eyes returned to Black Thunder. "I'm not a baby. I don't see why I can't ride the roller coaster, Daddy."

"It's not negotiable," Eric said flatly.

Honey interrupted the argument she could see brewing. "Where are you staying?"

"The hotel in town."

"I don't see why we can't stay here like you did, Daddy." Rachel turned to Honey. "Daddy told us how he helped build Black Thunder, didn't you, Daddy? And he lived right here in the middle of the 'musement park."

"It's not much of a park, Rachel," Honey warned. "If you're expecting Disneyland, you're going to be disappointed. There's just what you see. Black Thunder and a few rented attractions that get sent back on Monday morning."

"I don't care. Why can't we stay in the park where you stayed, Daddy? Becca wants to, don't you, Becca?"

Becca nodded obediently. "Becca wants to stay here."

"Sorry, girls."

Rachel tugged on her father's arm. "If we stay at the hotel everybody'll bother you for autographs just like they did on the airplane. I want to stay here. And so does Becca. And she doesn't wet the bed anymore, Honey, so you don't have to worry."

Becca regarded Honey so sheepishly that she couldn't help but smile. "I wasn't worried at all."

Eric didn't look at Honey. Instead, he kept his eyes on his daughter. "I'm sorry, Rachel, but I don't think it's a good idea."

"Remember last time we stayed at the hotel, and I had a nightmare, and I couldn't stop screaming. That man came and pounded on the door and said he was calling the police."

Honey saw Eric's hesitation, and although she wasn't

privy to the details, she could guess his dilemma. "I don't mind, Eric," she said stiffly. "It's up to you."

"Please, Daddy! Pretty please!"

Eric shrugged. "I guess I don't have much choice, do I?"

Rachel squealed and began to hop up and down. Becca squealed, too, and also started jumping.

"Let's go look around." Rachel snatched Becca's hand and began running toward the rented carousel, which was just visible through the trees.

"Stay in sight," Eric called after them.

"We will," Rachel shouted back.

"They won't," Eric sighed.

He turned back to Honey. "You could have said no."

"And be forced into another shoot-out with your daughter? No, thank you."

He smiled. "She's pretty awful, isn't she?"

"She's wonderful, and you know it."

An awkward silence fell between them. He stuffed his hands into the pockets of his slacks. "I planned to come here alone, but Rachel went into a tailspin when I talked to her about it."

"I imagine she was afraid you wouldn't come back."

His face darkened. "As you may have gathered, Lilly's father attacked her, and she's had terrible nightmares almost every night since."

Honey felt sickened as he filled her in on the details.

"Just getting her to separate from me during the day has been difficult enough. The child psychologist who's working with us doesn't think I should push it, and I agree. Rachel needs to feel safe again."

"Of course she does."

"No child should have to endure what she has," he said bitterly.

Honey wanted to reach out to him, but instead she looked toward the roller coaster. "She's going to give you a hard time tomorrow about riding Black Thunder."

"I know. It's one of the reasons I shouldn't have brought her here, but I was too self-absorbed to think it through."

Why had he come? She was afraid to ask, and he didn't seem ready to volunteer the information.

"I think I need to go on a scouting mission," he said.

She glanced over toward the carousel. Just as he had predicted, the girls had disappeared. "Why are you here, Eric?"

His movie-star eyes caught her up. "I need to get on with my life, Honey. I want to find out if there's any future for the two of us, or if I'm just kidding myself."

His frankness both surprised and dismayed her. She realized the real Eric was something of a stranger to her, and she wasn't certain how to protect herself against him.

"Eric, I—"

Rachel's voice interrupted, calling from the other side of the trees. "Daddy! Come see what we found."

"I have to go. We'll pick you up for dinner at six."

"I don't think that's—"

"Wear something pretty."

She opened her mouth to argue, but he was already walking away.

Honey wore the only dress she had brought with her, a simple jade-green sheath that stopped well short of her knees. She accessorized it with matching opaque stockings and jade-green pumps. A heavy gold Egyptian necklace complemented the plain round neckline. Her only other piece of jewelry was her wedding ring.

"Neat!" Rachel spun in a circle in the middle of the living area of Honey's trailer. "This is so neat, Daddy! Why can't we live in a trailer like this?"

"I'll sell the house tomorrow."

"He's being sar-cat-sick, Becca."

"Sarcastic." He corrected her automatically while his eyes drank in the sight of Honey Jane Moon Coogan. She had bent forward so Becca could touch her necklace, and as he watched his daughter slip her hand into Honey's long hair, he tried not to think about how much he wanted to do the same thing.

"I get to sit next to Honey," Rachel announced as they left the trailer and walked toward the lot where his rental car was parked. "You sit in the front seat with Daddy, Becca."

To his surprise, Becca stamped her foot. "Me want to sit with Honey."

"No, dummy. I saw Honey first."

Honey stepped between the girls and took their hands. "All three of us will sit in the back. We'll let your daddy chauffeur us."

"Great," he muttered, beginning to wish that he'd brought the girls' nanny with him so he could have Honey to himself for a little while.

By the time dessert arrived, he was definitely wishing he'd brought the nanny along. His daughters had completely monopolized Honey's attention. Not that he could have had a lengthy conversation with her anyway. Every time he lifted his fork, someone else appeared at the table asking for his autograph.

Across from him Honey gave a soft whistle of admiration as Becca counted out their four water glasses. "That's terrific, Becca. You sure are a good counter."

Becca had blossomed since Eric had gotten her back. The bed-wetting had stopped, and her language skills had taken a giant leap forward. Normally shy around strangers, she was chattering like a magpie to Honey.

His gaze moved to her sister. Honey and Rachel had had several clashes of will during dinner, but Honey had won every one. He kept expecting Rachel to throw a tantrum in retaliation, but there seemed to be some kind of unspoken understanding between them. Not that he was entirely surprised. In every way except physical appearance, Rachel could have been Honey's child instead of Lilly's. Both these females he loved had crusty, aggressive exteriors and marshmallow interiors. They were affectionate, loyal, and fiercely protective. They also shared an entire truckload of negative traits that he didn't want to think about with pigheaded stubbornness leading the pack.

Across the table, Rachel was unhappy with the fact that

her sister had claimed Honey's attention, so she licked her spoon and stuck it on her nose. Honey ignored her until the spoon dropped off, then she complimented her on her dress.

He shifted his thoughts to Lilly. Just last week, they had talked. She was working with an excellent therapist—the same one who was helping him deal with Rachel's trauma— and she was more at peace than he could remember. To ease the guilt she felt over what she had put them all through, she had given him full custody of their daughters, believing he could help them heal in a way that she couldn't.

After one of her early sessions with the therapist, the two of them had talked.

"I love the girls so much," she had confessed, "but I've realized that the only times I'm really comfortable with them is when you're around to supervise. I wish I could be Auntie Mame."

"What do you mean by that?"

"You know. Fly into town. Shower them with presents. Kiss them like crazy. And then disappear, leaving you with the business of raising them. Do you think I'm horrible?"

He had shaken his head. "I don't think you're horrible at all."

He knew Lilly was coping with the events in her past in the best way she could, and so far the girls had been accepting of their mother's appearances and disappearances in their lives. His disappearances were another matter, however, which was why he'd been forced to bring them to South Carolina.

"Do you ever have nightmares?" Rachel asked Honey.

"Sometimes," Honey replied.

"Scary ones?"

Honey's eyes flickered toward Eric. She quickly looked away. "Pretty scary."

Rachel regarded her thoughtfully. "Are you going to marry my daddy?"

"Enough questions, Rach." Eric signaled for the bill.

As the waiter walked toward them, the knot in his gut confirmed that he didn't want to hear Honey's answer.

32

Honey kissed first Rachel and then Becca on their foreheads. "Night, girls."

"Sleep tight," Becca murmured, before snuggling down into the covers.

"Night, Honey." Rachel blew three loud kisses.

Honey slipped out of the bedroom while Eric said his good nights. She had been flattered when the girls had insisted she participate in their bedtime ritual, but now that it was over, she felt empty and alone. Dash had been wrong not to let her have a child.

Eric addressed his daughters from the doorway behind her. "Honey and I are going to take a little walk outside. We won't go far. The window's open, so I can hear if you call."

"Make sure you come back, Daddy," Rachel said.

"I will, Rach. I promise. I'll always come back." The emphatic quality of Eric's response indicated that this was a frequently repeated ritual between the two of them.

Honey didn't want to take a walk with him, but he was already at her side lightly clasping her elbow and leading her to the door. It was the first time that he had touched her.

The night was warm and the moon hung so low in the sky it looked as if it had been stolen from the backdrop of a high school prom. Eric had left his jacket and tie inside, and his shirt gleamed blue-white in the light.

"You were great with the girls. Rachel's so demanding that most adults tend to overlook Becca."

"It was my pleasure. You've done a good job with them, Eric."

"These past few months have been tough, but I think we're on more solid ground now. Lilly's given me full custody."

"That's wonderful, although a lot of men would regard that as more of a burden than a pleasure."

"I love being a father."

"I know you do." Once again she thought of how much she had always wanted to have a family of her own and to create for someone else the childhood she wished she'd had. The desire to be part of a group of people who loved each other had been the driving force behind her life for as long as she could remember, and she was no closer to obtaining it than she had ever been. Only during her marriage to Dash had she known what it was to be part of someone else, and the gift of love he had given her had been so precious that her life had ended when she lost it.

They walked for a few moments in silence until they reached the clearing that bordered the lake. Eric glanced back at the Bullpen. His actor's voice, usually so much under his command, sounded ragged. "Don't take that coaster ride tomorrow, Honey."

The prom-night moon hung behind him, outlining his head and shoulders in silver and making him look larger than life, just as he did on the screen. But this was no movie star who stood before her, only a man. An awful war began inside her—the irresistible urge to slide into his arms battling against the despair that even considering such an act of betrayal produced.

"Eric, I've given up everything to do this. I don't have anything left."

"You have a career waiting for you."

"You know more than anyone how much that frightens me."

"But you made your deal with me anyway," he said bitterly. "You sold your soul to the devil so you could take your magical mystery ride."

I sold my soul to an angel, she thought, but she couldn't risk saying any soft words to him, so she kept silent.

He gave a snort of disgust. "I can't even come close to filling Dash's shadow, can I?"

"It's not a competition. I don't make comparisons like that."

"Lucky for me, because it's not hard to figure out who'd be the loser." He spoke in a voice that held no trace of self-pity; he was merely reciting facts. "Dash will always wear the white hat, with a shiny tin star pinned to his vest. He stands for everything good, everything noble and heroic. But I've always walked too close to the dark side."

"Those are movie parts. They don't have anything to do with real life."

"Who are you trying to convince, Mrs. Coogan? Me or yourself? It comes down to one simple, inescapable fact. You've already had the best man, and you're not going to settle for second best."

"Don't even think that about yourself," she said miserably. "You don't have to take second place to anyone."

"If that's true, why is it so important for you to ride that coaster tomorrow morning?"

She had lost the vocabulary to explain. In the light of his relentless hostility, her belief in the power of a roller coaster ride seemed ridiculous. She had tried and failed to make him understand that she wanted back the faith in God she had lost, the belief that love was a more powerful force in the universe than evil. She could never make him understand her certainty that she could once again find hope in the eternal on that ride, and, in the process, say her good-byes to Dash. In frustration, she spoke words that were damaging instead of healing.

"I have to find him! Just one more time."

His eyes darkened with pain, and his voice was a hoarse murmur. "I can't compete with that."

"You don't understand."

"I understand that I love you and I want to marry you. And I understand that you don't feel the same way about me."

A rush of emotion so intense that it left her weak coursed through her. Eric was a man who had erected a million defenses against the hurts of the world, and all of them had come tumbling down. It made her love him more—this beautiful, tortured man who had been born with too much sensitivity to walk unscathed through the evils he saw around him. Except she wasn't free to love him. Her heart was still shackled by another love, one that she couldn't let go.

She turned her face up to his. "Eric, I'm sorry. Maybe after tomorrow morning I can think about the future, but—"

"No!" he exclaimed. "I'm not going to compete with a ghost any longer. I want something better than that."

"Please, Eric. This doesn't have anything to do with you."

"It has everything to do with me," he said fiercely. "I can't build my life with someone who's looking backwards." He shoved his fists into his pockets. "Bringing the girls here was a terrible mistake. They've had enough instability in their lives. I knew how much they'd like you, and I shouldn't have taken this risk with them. If it were just me, maybe I'd stand around and hold your hand for the next ten or twenty years while you decide whether or not you're going to climb out of the grave. But they've been cheated too many times, and I can't let anyone in their lives who doesn't have something better to give all of us than leftover love."

She wanted to shut out his pain. If only she didn't understand so well what he was feeling. "Don't you realize I want to give you something better than that?" she cried. "Don't you realize how much I want to love you back!"

Again, the bitter twist to his mouth. "Tough job, isn't it?"

"Eric—"

"Don't take that ride tomorrow morning," he said quietly. "Choose me, Honey. This time choose me instead of him."

She saw what it had cost him in pride to ask, and she hated herself for the pain she was giving him. "I'll do anything else you ask me," she said desperately. "Anything but that. It's the one thing I can't give up."

"And it's the only thing I want."

"I need that ride to set me free."

"I don't think you want to be set free. I think you want to hold on to Dash forever."

"He was the center of my life."

The beautiful planes of his face were bleak, bereft of hope.

"When you take your ride tomorrow morning, I hope you have your epiphany—or whatever it is you're expecting to happen—because otherwise you'll have paid an expensive price for nothing."

"Eric, please—"

"I don't want your pity. And I don't want your leftovers. Love has to be freely given, and if I can't have that, I don't want anything." His eyes held a sad dignity. "I'm tired of walking on the dark side, Honey. I want to walk in the light for a while."

He turned away from her. Her skin felt as cold as the grave as he walked back to his children and left her standing alone in the still, silent heart of her dead amusement park.

That night when she couldn't sleep, she pulled on her work clothes and made her way to Black Thunder. Fog had rolled in during the night, and the coaster was an eerie sight. The geometric lacework of the bottom half had an unearthly sulfurous glow from the yellow security lights that hung inside the frame. But the upper half had disappeared into the swirling fog, so that the tops of the great hills looked as if they had been snapped off.

She hesitated for only a moment before she began to climb to the top. Streamers of fog enclosed her, and before long, she could no longer see the ground. She was alone in the universe with the coaster she had given up everything to build.

When she reached the top, she sat on the track and drew up her knees. The night was as silent as death. She let herself drift far above the earth in a world of wood and fog. She found herself remembering the little girl she had been, the child who had once ridden the great wooden roller coaster straight through the valley of death. But she was no longer a child. Now she was a woman, and she couldn't hide the fact that she loved him.

Just Eric. Not the dangerous stranger with the black eye patch, not the pirate clown she had convinced herself it was safe to love, and not the millionaire movie star. His identities had been stripped away. There were none left for him to hide behind. Nothing left behind which she could hide her own feelings about him.

She pressed her cheek against her bent knee, huddling miserably into herself as tears leaked from the corners of her eyelids. He was right. Her love for him wasn't a free and joyous offering, as love should be. Instead, it was shadowed by the past, by the love she couldn't forget, the man she couldn't give up. Eric deserved something better than the leftover love she was offering. But the only way she could hope to free herself from the past was to ride the coaster, and if she did that, she would lose him forever.

Dash, I need your wisdom. I can't go on if I can't put you to rest. Tell me how I do that without betraying everything we meant to each other.

But the barrier of death remained impenetrable, and once again, he refused to speak to her.

She stayed at the top of the lift hill throughout the night. In the inky blackness before dawn, the silence was broken by the shrill screams of a child. The sound was distant—it came from the other side of the park—but that didn't make it any less chilling as over and over again Rachel Dillon screamed out the terror of lost innocence.

The sky was pearly gray, poised at that precise moment just before the full break of morning. Tony Wyatt, the board operator who would be running Black Thunder that day, walked toward Honey through the wet grass. The fog from the night before had lifted, and steam rose from the Styrofoam coffee cup he held. As he nodded, he looked as if he were barely awake.

"Mornin', Miz Coogan."

She stepped down off the bottom rungs of the ladder and greeted him. Her body ached from weariness. She was chilled, and her eyes were scratchy from lack of sleep. "I already walked the track," she said. "Everything looks fine."

"That's good. Heard a weather report driving over. It's going to be a nice day." He headed off to the station house.

Honey stared up at the coaster. If she took her ride, she would lose Eric, but if she didn't take it, she would never be able to come to terms with her past.

"Honey!"

Startled, she spun around and saw Rachel flying through the trees toward her. She was dressed in jeans and a pink sweatshirt that was turned wrong side out. Her hair hadn't been brushed and her expression was fierce with anger.

"I hate him!" she cried, coming to a stop in front of Honey. Her eyes were bright with unshed tears, her mouth trembling, but mulish. "I'm not going home! I'm going to run away! Maybe I'll die and then he'll be sorry."

"Don't say that, Rachel."

"We were supposed to stay for the celebration, but Daddy woke us up this morning and said we're going to the airport. We just got here yesterday! That means I won't get to ride Black Thunder."

Honey tried to blunt her pain at the news that Eric truly was leaving by concentrating on Rachel. "He wasn't going to let you ride it anyway," she reminded her gently.

"I would have made him let me!" Rachel exclaimed. Her eyes slid along the length of the coaster. "I have to ride it, Honey. I just have to."

Honey felt as if Rachel's need were her own. She didn't try to understand the kinship she experienced with this child; she simply accepted it. As she stroked her between her shoulder blades, she felt like crying herself. "I'm sorry, sweetheart. I really am."

Rachel shook off her sympathy. "It's because of you, isn't it? The two of you had a fight."

"Not a fight. It's hard to explain."

"I'm not going! He said he'd give us a special treat to make up for leaving, but I don't want a special treat. I want to ride Black Thunder."

"Rachel, he's your father, and you have to do what he tells you."

"You're damn right she does!" Eric's voice rang out from behind them. "Get over here right now, young lady."

He strode angrily through the trees with Becca in his arms. When he reached the clearing, he set her on the ground and then straightened to glare at his other daughter.

Rachel glared right back, her small body unconsciously

431

arranging itself in imitation of his, legs splayed, arms tense at her sides.

"No!" she shouted. "I'm not going to the airport with you! I don't like you!"

"That's tough. Get over here."

Honey's heart constricted in her chest. She saw by the exhaustion in his face that he had reached his limit. She wanted to plead with him not to leave, but she had no right. Why did he have to be so stubborn? Why did he insist on putting her to the test? But even as she asked herself the questions, she knew he had every right to expect all those things that she wasn't yet able to give.

"Now!" Eric bellowed.

Rachel began to cry, but she didn't move.

Honey took a half step forward, gripped by a sudden and unshakable certainty that Eric was wrong not to let Rachel ride Black Thunder. She forgot that she had no real connection to this child. She felt as if Rachel had come from her own body.

And at that moment, she knew what she had to do.

She grasped Rachel's hand and gazed over at Eric. "She has to ride Black Thunder first."

"The hell she does!"

"Don't stop her, Eric." Her voice dropped to a whisper, pleading. "Let her ride it for me. For herself."

All the angry tension seeped from his body, leaving him looking old and exhausted, a man who had fought one too many battles. "She's too young, Honey. She's only a baby."

Rachel's mouth snapped open to voice an indignant protest, but Honey squeezed her hand in a warning to be silent.

"She has to do this, Eric."

"I don't want her frightened."

"She's already been frightened. Her grandfather took care of that."

Turning her back to him, she knelt in front of Rachel. "I was just your age when I rode Black Thunder for the first time, and I was more frightened than I've ever been in my life. This ride is fierce. It wasn't designed for young children, sweetheart. The first drop is worse than any horror movie. You're so small that you'll come right off the seat, and the tops of your legs will slam against the lap bar. When you hit the spiral, you'll feel as if you're going to be sucked straight down to the bottom of the lake. It's going to scare you to death."

"Not me," Rachel scoffed. "I wouldn't be scared."

Honey gently cupped her cheek. "Yes, you will."

"You rode it."

"My uncle made me."

"Was he bad like my Grandpa Guy?"

"No, not like that. He just didn't like little kids very much."

"Did you cry?"

"I was too scared to cry. The train took me to the top of the lift hill, and when I saw how far it was down, I thought I was going to die."

"Like when Grandpa Guy squished on top of me."

Honey nodded. "Just like that."

"I want to ride," Rachel said stubbornly.

"Are you absolutely sure?"

Rachel nodded, and then her eyes began devouring the coaster with an intensity that Honey understood all too well. Both she and Rachel knew what it was to feel defenseless in the world. They knew that women had to find courage in different places from men. Without looking at Honey or her father, Rachel broke away and ran to the station house.

"Rachel!" Eric rushed forward, but Honey threw herself at him.

"Please, Eric! This is something she has to do."

He looked at her, his eyes defeated, full of pain. "I don't understand any of this."

"I know you don't," she whispered, finally allowing the full force of her love for him to rush over her. "You're big and you're strong, and you see life differently."

"I'm going with her."

"No, Eric. You can't. She has to do this alone." She looked up into his eyes, straight through into his soul, begging him to trust her. "Please."

Finally he nodded, the movement so full of reluctance that she knew what it had cost him and loved him all the more for it. "All right," he said. "All right."

She drew him toward the station house, and they passed beneath Gordon Delaweese's painting. Rachel had climbed into the first car, and her face was animated with a combination of excitement and apprehension. At the same time, she looked incredibly small and defenseless in the empty train.

Honey's hand trembled as she checked to make certain Rachel was secure under the lap bar. "It's not too late to get out."

Rachel shook her head.

Leaning down, Honey kissed her forehead. "When you're done," she whispered, "the nightmares will be gone forever."

Honey wasn't even certain if Rachel had heard. Her small fingers were white as they gripped the bar, and Honey saw that her excitement had been replaced with fear. Which was exactly as it should be.

She stepped back from the train to stand at Eric's side. Tension radiated from him, and she could sense the force of will he was exerting to hold himself back. Rachel was his most precious possession. She knew he didn't understand, and she was humbled at his trust in her.

She turned toward Tony, who was waiting at the control board, oblivious to the drama that was being played out before him. Then she nodded.

She and Eric rushed out from under the roof of the station house in time to watch the train begin its climb up the great lift hill. Behind them, Becca sat cross-legged in the grass watching her sister. Rachel's bright pink sweatshirt made her highly visible at the front of the long train of empty cars.

Ride it for me, sweetheart, she thought. *Set me free, too.*

Eric slipped his hand into hers. His fingers were cold, and she gripped them tightly. She could feel Rachel's terror in her own body as the car ground relentlessly toward the top of the hill. Her heart began to race, and she was perspiring. When Rachel reached the top and saw the drop, she would once again be forced to face her grandfather.

The car hung suspended at the apex of the hill, and Honey went rigid with fear, a fear that she knew was her own as much as Rachel's. And then as the train plunged down the drop and swooped into the second hill, she understood it all. She saw that she was Rachel and that Dash was her. That people who loved were always part of each other. She saw that her love for Dash didn't prevent her from loving Eric. Instead, it made it possible.

A joyous sunburst opened inside her. She turned to Eric. His face was tense with concern as his eyes followed the racing pink blur that was his daughter, fearing that she would try to stand, that she would fall out, that the coaster he had helped build would not carry her safely back to him. But Black Thunder did not desert those it sheltered anymore than God did, not even in the darkest of hours.

Honey's own fear had left her, and she understood how simple her love for Eric was. It held no dark corners, no psychological complexities. He was not a father to her. He wasn't her superior or her teacher. He didn't possess a lifetime of experiences of which she knew nothing. Eric was simply Eric. A man who had come into the world with too much feeling. A man who was as vulnerable as she, as needful of love.

She wanted to laugh and sing and enfold him in the universe of her love. He began to run, and she realized the train had cleared the spiral over the lake and was speeding back to the station. She followed him beneath the roof, her heart dancing.

The train screeched into the station. Rachel's face was stark white, her hands frozen around the bar, all her defiance gone.

Eric ran to her, and as the train braked to a stop, he reached out. "Baby . . ."

"Again," Rachel whispered.

"Yes!" Honey shouted out the word. Laughing, she threw herself at Eric. "Oh, yes, my love. Yes!"

The train left the station with Rachel Dillon in its front seat while Eric held Honey in his arms and felt those soft, full lips claiming his own.

At that moment he gave up trying to understand the drama these females he loved were playing out. Maybe women were even more different from men than he had assumed. Maybe they had to find the courage to face life in a different way.

Honey had smeared herself against him almost as if she were trying to inject herself into his body. Her mouth opened under his, and he knew that she was offering him all of her love, her loyalty, all the passion with which she attacked life. This woman who occupied his soul was giving him everything. And at that moment the jealousy he felt toward Dash Coogan slipped away forever.

"I love you!" Honey said against his lips. "Oh, Eric, I love you so much."

He groaned her name and lost himself in her mouth. They kissed while Rachel left her nightmares behind on the hills of Black Thunder.

"I think I've been waiting for you forever," he murmured.

"Do you still want to marry me?" she asked.

"Oh, yes."

"I want a baby."

"Do you? I'm glad."

"Oh, Eric . . . This is right. I finally know this is right."

He couldn't get enough of her mouth. It was sweet and rich, promising him love and abundance. It carried him through space, through time, into a place where only good existed. And as he settled into that miraculous place he heard a rough, weary voice, so deep it could have come from God's belly.

It's about time you took what was yours, pretty boy. I was just about ready to lose patience with you.

Startled, he drew back from her. Her eyes, still drugged from their kiss, opened and she looked at him quizzically. Feeling foolish, he reclaimed that sweet, soft mouth.

The train raced by and, for a few moments, all of them touched eternity.

Epilogue
1993

Honey located Eric and the girls through the glare of lights and the flash of strobes. As the applause finally quieted, she stepped to the Plexiglass podium and gazed down at the gold Emmy that had been placed in her hands.

"Thank you so much." Her voice cracked and the audience laughed. She laughed with them and leaned closer to the microphone.

"If anybody had ever told me that a puny little redneck girl from South Carolina could end up with one of these, I would have told them they'd been out in the sun too long."

More laughter.

"I've got a lot of people to thank, so I hope all of you will be patient with me for a minute." She began her list with Arthur Lockwood and then went on to name the people associated with *Emily,* the Hallmark Hall of Fame presentation on the life of Emily Dickinson that had earned her the award.

The gold lace skirt of her evening gown rustled as it brushed against the podium. "But most of all I have to thank my family. Families are funny things. People who have them don't always appreciate them. But if you've grown up without one, it's sometimes hard to find your place in the world.

"Tonight I want to acknowledge my family. It took me a long time to find them, but now that I have, I'm not letting a single one of them go. My stepdaughters Rachel and Rebecca Dillon, and their beautiful mother Lilly who shares them with me. Zachary Jason Dashwell Dillon who'll be two years old tomorrow and is the cutest toddler in the world. His baby brother Andrew, who's waiting in the greenroom right now for me to stop talking and bring him his next meal."

Everyone laughed.

"Two people I love in Winston-Salem, North Carolina, Chantal and Gordon Delaweese. A person I'm proud to call my friend, although it took us a while to get there— Meredith Coogan Blackman. And Liz Castleberry, the stubbornest lady I ever met in my life."

Liz smiled from her seat directly behind Eric.

"One person I love isn't here tonight, at least not physically." She paused, and a stillness fell over the crowd. "Dash Coogan was the last of America's cowboy heroes, and he was my hero, too. He taught me a lot of things. Sometimes I listened to him, sometimes I didn't. When I didn't, I was usually sorry."

She saw several people in the audience dab at their eyes, but she had made peace with Dash's death that day three years ago when Rachel had ridden Black Thunder, and she didn't feel like crying. Instead, she smiled. "I loved that cowboy, and I'll be grateful to him for the rest of my life."

She cleared her throat. "This last one's hard. Marriage is always a balancing act, and it's never a good idea for one partner to get too big a head, but I'm afraid that's what's going to happen here. People write a lot of things about Eric Dillon's talent, and most of it's true. But nobody writes about the important things. The fact that he's a wonderful father and the best husband a woman could have. The fact that he cares about other people so much that he sometimes scares me. That doesn't mean he's perfect, of course. It's hard living with a man who's prettier than all of your girlfriends put together."

Eric groaned good-naturedly as everyone laughed.

Honey gazed through the lights straight into his heart. "But if it weren't for Eric Dillon, I wouldn't be here tonight. He loved me when I wasn't lovable, and I guess when it comes right down to it, that's pretty much what family is all about. Thank you, sweetheart."

Eric watched from the second row, his chest so filled with love and pride he felt as if he would burst. It amazed him that Honey could thank him when she was the one who had given him everything.

She finished to wild applause and was escorted off into the wings. He knew that she would head first for the greenroom and their two-month-old son. Only after she had gathered up Andrew would she go to the reporters waiting to interview her.

In addition to questioning her about her career, he suspected the press would also ask her about the special camp for abused children the two of them had built on the site of the former Silver Lake Amusement Park. Honey had a theory that Black Thunder might help just a few of the children heal. Although he'd ridden Black Thunder dozens of times over the past three years, he had never found it to be anything more than a thrilling ride. However, when he'd been foolish enough to offer this opinion to Honey and Rachel, they had both been so outraged that he'd vowed to keep his mouth shut in the future.

The ceremony was drawing to a close when an all-too-familiar voice echoed in his head. *You've done all right by her, son. I'm proud of you.*

Eric suppressed a groan. Not now. Ever since Rachel had taken that damned roller-coaster ride . . .

His rational mind knew that he wasn't really hearing Dash Coogan's voice. After all, Honey never heard him, so why should he? But his irrational mind—That was another story entirely.

Rachel leaned across her sister and whispered, "Honey did good, didn't she, Daddy?"

He swallowed a lump in his throat and gazed at both of his daughters. "She did real good, sweetheart. Real good."

Damned right she did, the voice said.

He shifted in his seat, not altogether displeased with the idea that his family just might have a cowboy guardian angel looking out for them.

* * *

Susan Elizabeth Phillips

Three hours later, after the celebrations and congratulations were behind them, Eric and Honey moved through the bedrooms of their quiet house hand in hand, Honey in her golden gown, shoes kicked off, hair tousled; Eric with his bow tie undone and collar open. They went from one child to the next, straightening the covers, rescuing a teddy bear, removing a thumb from a small mouth. They stepped over toys and books, adjusted night-lights, and removed a leaking squirt gun from beneath a pink-and-lavender pillow.

Only when they were reassured that each child was safe for the night did they go to their own room and turn to each other.

They were finally home.

Author's Note

I am deeply indebted to the following people and organizations:

Tim Cole, who designed Black Thunder and served as my patient and enthusiastic technical adviser.

Randy Geisler and The American Coaster Enthusiasts.

The National Down Syndrome Congress.

My friends and fellow authors, who answered all the questions I couldn't: Joan Johnston, Jayne Ann Krentz, Kathleen Gilles Seidel. And Meryl Sawyer, for help above and beyond the call of duty.

Linda Barlow for her thoughtful critique and unflagging friendship.

Steve Axelrod for his continued wise counsel, and Claire Zion for her insights and support.

The members of my family who give me so much.

And my readers, who continue to enrich my life with their warmth and enthusiasm.

Susan Elizabeth Phillips
c/o Pocket Books
1230 Avenue of the Americas
New York, NY 10020

Hot Shot

Susan Elizabeth Phillips

To Bill Phillips, B.E.E., M.S.E.E., who, in 1971, told me of a time when ordinary people would have computers in their homes. He told me other dreams, too.

PROLOGUE

• •

For three terrifying days in 1958, the bride was the most famous child in America.

Eighteen years later, Susannah Faulconer once again felt like that panic-stricken seven-year-old. As she began walking at her father's side down the white runner that had been laid in a rigid path through the exact center of the Faulconer gardens, the heirloom pearl choker that encircled her throat seemed to be cutting off her breath. She knew the sensation was irrational since the choker wasn't the least bit tight and she had worn it many times, beginning with her debutante ball when she was eighteen. There was no reason for her to feel as if she couldn't breathe. No reason for her to experience such an overpowering urge to rip it from her throat and fling it into the crowd of well-dressed guests.

Not that she would actually do such a thing. Not proper Susannah Faulconer.

Although she was a redhead, people didn't tend to think of her that way, since her hair wasn't the fiery red of a slick Clairol ad, but a patrician auburn that conjured up images of a gentler time—a time of early morning fox hunts, tinkling teacups, and women who sat for Gainsborough. Beneath a Juliet cap, she wore her hair swept neatly away

1

from her face and simply arranged at the nape of her neck. The style was a bit severe for a bride, but it somehow suited her. Instead of an elaborate wedding gown, she wore a tea-length dress of antique lace. The open mandarin collar revealed a slim, aristocratic neck encircled by the lustrous five-strand heirloom pearl choker that was giving her so much difficulty. Everything about her bespoke wealth, breeding, and an old-fashioned sense of constraint out of place in a modern twenty-five-year-old woman.

A hundred years earlier, Susannah Faulconer would have been considered a great beauty, but her finely chiseled, elongated features were too subtle to compete with the bold cover-girl faces of the seventies. Her nose was thin and long but exquisitely straight; her lips narrow but beautifully arched. Only her eyes had a modern look about them. Wide-set and well-shaped, they were a light gray. They were also unfathomable, so that occasionally during a conversation, the person with whom she was speaking had the uncomfortable sense that Susannah simply wasn't there, that she had withdrawn to a place no one else was permitted to see.

For the past hour, the cream of California society had been arriving for the wedding. Limousines swept up the tree-lined drive and into the cobbled motor court that formed a crescent in front of Falcon Hill, the Faulconer family estate. Falcon Hill looked very much as if it had been part of the hills south of San Francisco for centuries, but it was barely twenty years old—built in the posh community of Atherton by Susannah's father, Joel Faulconer, not long after he had taken over control of Faulconer Business Technologies from his own father.

Despite differences of age and sex, there was a sameness about the guests who sat in the carefully laid-out rows of lacy white wrought-iron chairs. They all looked prosperous and conservative, very much like people accustomed to giving orders instead of taking them—all except the beautiful young woman who sat toward the back. In a sea of Halston and Saint Laurent, Paige Faulconer, the bride's younger sister, was conspicuous in a maroon thrift-store dress from the thirties draped at the shoulders with a funky, pink marabou boa.

As the music of the processional swelled, Susannah Faulconer turned her head slightly and spotted the cynical smile on her sister's pouty mouth. She resolved not to let her old conflicts with Paige spoil her wedding day. At least her sister had decided to attend the ceremony, which—after everything that had happened—was more than Susannah had expected.

Once again she was conscious of the tight pearl choker. She made herself forget about Paige and take in the beauty of the gardens instead. Marble statuary carved in Vicenza, and sparkling fountains purchased from a chateau in the Loire Valley, gave the gardens an old world look. Dozens of urns containing rose bushes heavy with white blooms had been strategically placed throughout the greenery. Gardenias floated in the fountains, and festoons of white ribbon blew gently in the June breeze. Everything was perfect, exactly as she had arranged it.

She concentrated on Cal, who was waiting for her beneath the pristine white canopy that had been constructed in front of the largest of the stone fountains. With his upper-crust good looks, Calvin Theroux reminded her of the men in magazine ads for expensive Scotch. At the age of forty-two, he was one of the most influential men in the Faulconer corporation. Despite their seventeen-year age difference, she and Cal were considered to be a perfect match. They had everything in common. Both had been raised in prosperity—she in San Francisco, he in Philadelphia. They had gone to the most exclusive private schools and moved in the best circles. Of course, Cal hadn't been kidnapped when he was seven, but then, neither had most people.

The choker tightened around her throat. She heard the distant sound of a riding mower and imagined her father's displeasure when he realized that the gardener at the neighboring estate had chosen this particular hour on a Saturday afternoon to cut the lawn. He would be annoyed that she hadn't thought to send the neighbors a note.

Cal's arm brushed against her own as she reached the altar. "You look beautiful," he whispered. The suntanned creases at the corners of his eyes deepened as he smiled.

The minister cleared his throat and began. "Dearly beloved . . ."

She knew she was doing the right thing by marrying Cal. She always did the right thing. Cal loved her. He was mature and thoughtful, and he would be a perfect husband. But the knot of misery that had been growing inside her refused to ease.

"Who gives this woman to be married to this man?"

"I do." Joel Faulconer's strong, handsome features were softened by the intense expression of fatherly pride that lurked about his mouth as he transferred her hand from his own arm to Cal's. He stepped away, and she could hear him taking his place in the second row of chairs.

The sound of the lawn mower grew louder.

Her maid of honor took the bridal bouquet, and Susannah's hand slipped discreetly to her neck. She looped her index finger just over the top of the Bennett family choker and eased it away from her skin. Cal was listening intently to the minister's words and didn't notice.

"I, Calvin James Theroux, take thee, Susannah Bennett Faulconer . . ."

The noise of the mower had grown so loud that others had begun to notice. Cal's nose twitched as if he had just caught a whiff of something unpleasant. Susannah stood quietly, her eyes steady, her mind unsettled.

And then she realized that the sound wasn't coming from a mower at all but from something else entirely.

She sucked in her breath and all the blood drained from her head. The minister was talking to her now. She couldn't concentrate. The noise was coming closer, moving around the side of the house and heading directly for the gardens. Cal turned to look, the minister stopped talking. Susannah could feel her skin growing damp beneath her breasts.

And then it happened. The peaceful gentility of the Faulconer gardens was shattered by the loud, vulgar roar of a big, black, twin-engine Harley-Davidson motorcycle shooting into view.

The bike barreled across the manicured lawn and cut past a statue of Andromeda. The rider's cry rang out over the noise of the engine, a primitive, atavistic cry.

"Suzie!"

With a choked exclamation, she spun around. The pulse at the side of her throat began to throb.

Her father leapt to his feet, knocking his chair askew. Cal curled his hand protectively over her wrist. The bike came to an abrupt stop at the far end of the aisle runner she had so recently walked along. Its front wheel crumpled the pristine fabric.

No, she thought. *This isn't real. It's only a nightmare. Just another nightmare.*

"Su-zie!"

He wore a black leather jacket and blue jeans that were taut across his thighs as they straddled the motorcycle. He had the dark, snapping eyes and high flat cheekbones of a full-blooded Comanche, although he was more Mediterranean than Native American. His skin was olive, his mouth thin, almost cruel. The breeze blowing off San Francisco Bay caught his shoulder-length black hair and tossed it away from his face. It blew long and free like a flag.

"What's the matter, Suzie? Forget to send me an invitation?" His voice rose over the roar of the Harley, and his dark, mesmerizing eyes speared through her skin.

A murmur went up from the guests, an expression of outrage, astonishment, and horrified delight at being present to witness such an outrageous scene. Could this *person* be one of Susannah's friends? None of them could imagine it. One of Paige's flings, perhaps, but certainly not Susannah's.

In the background, Susannah was dimly aware of her maid of honor muttering "Ohgod, ohgod, ohgod" over and over like a mantra. She found herself holding onto Cal's arm as if it were her lifeline. She tried to speak, but the proper words wouldn't form. She began to pull at the choker, and her long, aristocratic fingers shook as she attempted to free it from her neck.

"Don't do this, Suzie," the man on the bike said.

"See here!" her father shouted as he tried to disengage himself from the row of wrought-iron chairs and the rope garland that cordoned off the seats.

She was so anguished that she couldn't even think about the embarrassment she was suffering in front of her guests, the personal humiliation of what was happening. Stay in control, she told herself. No matter what happens, stay in control.

The man on the bike held out his hand toward her. "Come with me."

"Susannah?" Cal said behind her. "Susannah, who is this person?"

"Call the police!" someone else exclaimed.

The man on the Harley continued to hold out his hand. "Come on, Suzie. Climb up on the back of my bike."

The Bennett family choker gave way under Susannah's fingers, and heirloom pearls tumbled down onto the white cloth that had been laid for the ceremony, some even rolling off into the grass. It was her wedding day, she thought wildly. How could such a vulgar, untoward event happen on her wedding day? Her grandmother would have been prostrate.

His arm slashed the air in a contemptuous gesture that took in the garden and the guests. "Are you going to give cocktail parties for the rest of your life, or are you going to come with me and set the world on fire?"

She pulled away from Cal and pressed her hands over her ears—a shocking, awkward gesture from proper Susannah Faulconer. Words erupted from her throat. "Go away! I won't listen to you. I'm not listening to you." And then she began moving away from the altar, trying to separate herself from all of them.

"Follow me, babe," he crooned. "Leave all this and come with me." His eyes were hypnotizing her, calling to her. "Hop on my bike, babe. Hop on my bike and follow me."

"No." Her voice sounded choked and muffled. "No, I won't do it."

He was a ruffian, a renegade. For years she had kept her life under perfect control. She had done everything properly, followed all the rules, not stepped on a single crack. How could this have happened? How could her life have careened out of her control so quickly?

Behind her stood safe, steady Cal Theroux, her twin, the man who kept the demons away. Before her stood a street-smart hustler on a Harley-Davidson motorcycle. Impulsively, she turned away from both of them and looked toward her sister, only to see the frozen shock on her face. Paige wouldn't help her. Paige never helped.

Susannah clawed at her neck, but the pearl choker was gone. She felt the old panic grip her, and once again she found herself being drawn back to the horror of that spring day in 1958—the day when she became the most famous child in America.

The memory washed over her, threatening to paralyze her. And then she grew aware of her father freeing himself from the row of chairs, and she summoned all of her strength to shake away the past. She had only an instant, only an infinitesimal fragment of time to act before her father took control.

Calvin Theroux stood to her right, promising love, security, and comfort. A messiah on a motorcycle stood to her left, promising nothing. With a soft cry, proper Susannah Faulconer chose her destiny.

BOOK
ONE
· ·
THE
VISION

Whatever you can do, or dream you can, begin it.
Boldness has genius, power, and magic in it.

—Goethe

1

....

Susannah's real father wasn't Joel Faulconer, but an Englishman named Charles Lydiard, who met Susannah's mother when he visited New York City in 1949. Katherine "Kay" Bennett was the beautiful socialite daughter of a recently deceased New York City financier. Kay spotted Lydiard on the afterdeck of a friend's yacht, where he was leaning against the mahogany rail smoking a Turkish cigarette and sipping a Gibson. Kay, always on the lookout for handsome unattached men, immediately arranged an introduction, and before the evening was over, had fallen in love with Lydiard's finely chiseled aristocratic looks and cynical world-weary manner.

Kay was never the most perceptive of women, and it wasn't until a year after their marriage that she discovered her elegant husband was even more attracted to artistic young men than he was to her own seductive body. She immediately gathered up their two-month-old daughter and left him to return to her widowed mother's Park Avenue penthouse, where she threw herself into a frantic round of socializing so she could forget the entire unsavory incident. She also did her best to forget the solemn-faced baby girl who was an unwelcome reminder of her own lack of judgment.

Charles Lydiard died in a boating accident in 1954. Kay was in San Francisco when it happened. She had recently married Joel Faulconer, the California industrialist, and she was much too preoccupied with keeping her virile young husband happy to dwell on the fate of a disappointing former husband. Nor did she spare any thoughts for the three-year-old daughter she had left her elderly mother to raise on the other side of the continent.

Susannah Bennett Lydiard, with her gray eyes, thin nose, and auburn hair tightly confined in two perfect plaits, grew into a solemn little mouse of a child. By the age of four, she had taught herself to read and learned to move soundlessly through the high-ceilinged rooms of her grandmother's penthouse. She slipped like a shadow past the tall windows with their heavy velvet drapes firmly drawn against the vulgar bustle of the city below. She passed like a whisper across the deep, old carpets. She existed as silently as the stuffed songbirds displayed under glass domes on the polished tables.

Her Grandmother Bennett was gradually losing her mind, but Susannah was too young to understand that. She only knew that her grandmother had very strict rules, and that breaking any one of them resulted in swift and terrible punishment. Grandmother Bennett said that she had already raised one frivolous child, and she didn't intend to raise another.

Twice a year Susannah's mother came to visit. On those days, instead of walking around the block with one of her grandmother's two elderly servants, Susannah went to tea with Kay at the Plaza. Her mother was very beautiful, and Susannah watched in tongue-tied fascination as Kay smoked one cigarette after another and checked the time on her diamond-encrusted wristwatch. As soon as tea was over, Susannah was returned to her grandmother, where Kay kissed her dutifully on the forehead and then disappeared for another six months. Grandmother Bennett said that Susannah couldn't live with her mother because Susannah was too wicked.

It was true. Susannah was a horribly wicked little girl. Sometimes she touched her nose at the dinner table. Other times she didn't sit up straight. Occasionally she forgot her pleases and thank-yous. For any of these transgressions, she was punished by being imprisoned for not less than one hour in the rear closet. This was done for her own good, her grandmother explained, but Susannah didn't understand how something so horrible could be good.

The closet was small and suffocating, but even more terrifying, it held Grandmother Bennett's old furs. For an imaginative child, the closet became a living nightmare. Dark ugly minks brushed at her pale cheeks, and gruesome sheared beaver coats rubbed against her thin arms. Worst of all was a fox boa with a real head forming its grisly clasp. Even in the dark of the closet she could feel those sly glass fox eyes watching her and she sat frozen in terror, her back pressed rigidly against the closet door, while she waited for those sharp fox teeth to eat her up.

Life took on dark, frightening hues for such a small child. By the time she was five, she had developed the careful habits of a much older person. She didn't raise her voice, seldom laughed, and never cried. She did everything within her limited powers to stay out of the terrifying feral depths of the closet, and she worked so diligently at being good that she would probably have succeeded if—late at night when she was sound asleep—her body hadn't begun to betray her.

She started to wet herself.

She never knew when it would happen. Sometimes several weeks would go by without incident, occasionally an entire month, but then she would awaken one morning and discover that she was lying in her own urine. Her grandmother's paper-thin nostrils wrinkled in distaste when Susannah was brought before her. Even Susannah's wicked mother Katherine had never done anything so odious, she said.

Susannah tried to hide the bedding, but there was too much of it and she was always discovered. When that happened, her grandmother gave her a stinging lecture and then made her wear her soiled nightgown into the closet as punishment. The acrid scent of her own urine mingled with the camphor that permeated the old furs until she couldn't breath. Furry monsters were all around her, ready to eat her up. She could feel their sharp teeth sinking into her flesh and their strong jaws snapping her tender bones. Bruises, like a string of discolored pearls, formed down the length of her spine from being pressed so hard against the closet door.

At night she struggled against sleep. She read books from her grandmother's library and pinched her legs to keep awake. But she was only five years old, and no matter how hard she tried, she eventually slipped into unconsciousness. That was when the fox-eyed monster crept into her bedroom and dug his sharp teeth into her flesh until her small bladder emptied on the bedclothes.

Each morning she awakened to fear. Afraid to move. Afraid to inhale, to touch the sheets. On those occasions when she discovered that the bed was dry, she was filled with a sense of joy so sharp it made her queasy. Everything about the day seemed brighter—the view of Park Avenue from the front windows, the shiny red apple she ate with her breakfast, the funny way her solemn little face was reflected in her grandmother's silver coffeepot. When the bed was wet, she wished she were old enough to die.

And then several days after her sixth birthday, it all changed. She was huddled in the closet with the smell of urine stinging her nostrils and fear clogging her throat. Her wet nightgown clung to her calves, and her feet were tangled in the soiled bedclothes her grandmother had ordered be put into the closet with her. She kept her eyes fixed, staring through the darkness at exactly the spot where she knew the fox head was hanging.

Her concentration was so intense she didn't hear the noise at first. Only gradually did the piercing sound of her grandmother's voice sink into her consciousness, along with a deeper male voice that was unrecognizable. She knew so few men. The doorman called her "little miss," but the voice didn't sound like it belonged to the doorman. There was a man who fixed the bathroom sink when it leaked, the doctor who had given her a shot last year. She saw men on the street when she took her walks, but she wasn't one of those dimple-cheeked little moppets who attracted the attention of adults, so few of them ever spoke to her.

Through the thick door she could hear the male voice coming closer. It was loud. Angry. She sprang back in fear and the furs caught her. The mink, the beaver—their dead skins swung against her. She cried out as the grisly fox head struck her cheek.

The door flew open, but she was sobbing in fear and she didn't notice.

"Good God!"

The angry male voice penetrated her consciousness. Panicked, she pushed herself deeper into the suffocating depths of the furs, instinctively seeking a known terror instead of an unknown one.

"Good God," the voice repeated. "This is barbaric."

She stared into the malevolent face of the fox and whimpered.

"Come here, sweetheart," the voice said, speaking more softly this time. "Come here."

Slowly she turned, blinking against the light. She turned toward that soft, crooning voice, and her eyes drank in their first sight of Joel Faulconer.

He was big and golden in the light, with powerful shoulders and a large, handsome head. Like a magic prince in one of her books, he smiled at her and held out his hand. "Come here, sweetheart. I'm not going to hurt you. I won't let anyone hurt you."

She couldn't move. She wanted to, but her feet were tangled in the wet bedcovers, and the fox head was butting against her cheek. He reached for her. She winced instinctively and drew back into the coats. He began crooning to her as he pulled her free of the furs. "It's all right. It's all right, sweetheart."

He lifted her into his strong arms and held her against his chest. She waited for him to recoil when he felt her damp nightgown and smelled her acrid scent, but he didn't. Instead, he clasped her tightly against his expensive suit coat and carried her into her bedroom, where he helped her to dress. Then he took her away from the Park Avenue penthouse forever.

"That stupid, stupid bitch," he murmured as he led her from the building.

Not until much later did she realize that he wasn't talking about her grandmother.

*　*　*

15

Joel Faulconer wasn't a sentimental man, so nothing in his experience had prepared him for the surge of emotion that had overtaken him when he had seen Susannah huddled like a frightened animal in his mother-in-law's moth-eaten furs. Now, six hours later, he glanced over at her strapped into the airplane seat at his side and his heart turned over. Her enormous gray eyes were set in a small, angular face, and her hair was skinned into braids so tight her skin seemed as if it might split over her fragile bones. She stared straight ahead. She had barely spoken since he had taken her from the closet.

Joel took a sip of the bourbon he had ordered from the stewardess and tried not to think about what would have happened to Susannah if he hadn't given in to the vague impulse that had taken him to his mother-in-law's doorstep that morning. Kay didn't like her mother, so he had only met the woman a few times in social settings and had never spoken with her long enough to realize that she was mentally ill. But Kay should have known.

As Joel thought about his wife, he felt the familiar combination of disgust and arousal she always managed to produce in him. She hadn't even disclosed that she had a daughter until several months after their wedding—about the same time he had begun to have second thoughts concerning the wisdom of his marriage. Kay had assured him that the child was better off with her mother, and not being anxious to take on the burden of another man's offspring, Joel hadn't pressed her. She went to see the child whenever she was in New York, and he had assumed that Susannah was well cared for. By the time Kay had given birth to his own child, he had nearly forgotten the existence of the other one.

He swirled the bourbon in his glass and stared blindly out the window. What kind of woman could conveniently forget she had a child? Only someone like Kay—a woman who was too silly and shallow to see what would be perfectly obvious to anyone else. He should have taken it upon himself to investigate long ago.

He turned his head to study the little girl at his side. She sat straight in the seat with her hands clasped neatly in her lap. Her head was beginning to wobble a bit, and he suspected the noise of the airplane engines would soon put her to sleep. As he watched, her eyelids, like fragile eggshells, began to drift downward, and then they abruptly snapped back up.

"You're sleepy," he said.

She turned to look at him, and he felt another pang of sympathy as he saw that her eyes were huge and stricken, like those of a fawn caught before a hunter's gun. "I—I'm fine," she stammered.

"It's all right. We won't be in California for hours. Go ahead and take a nap."

Susannah stared helplessly at the magic, golden prince who had rescued her. It would be unthinkable to disobey him, yet if she slept, the fox-eyed monster was certain to find her. Even in this great silver airplane, he would find her and make her wet herself, and then her prince would know how bad she was.

Joel caught her hand and gave it a soft squeeze. "Just shut your eyes."

His voice was so gentle that she could barely control her tears. "I—I am unable," she said.

He gave her all his attention, as if she were an important adult instead of only a child. "Why is that?"

"Because it's unwise. Sir." She added the courteous form of address belatedly and hoped he wouldn't notice her extraordinary lapse of manners.

"I don't know very much about six-year-old little girls. I'm afraid you'll have to explain it to me."

Those blue eyes speared through her, sympathetic but demanding. He had a dent in the center of his chin, and she wished she could push the tip of her finger into it to see what it felt like. Her mind raced as she tried to find a polite way to explain. Bathroom talk was vulgar and unacceptable. There was never an excuse for it. "I rather suspect—" she said. "It's quite possible—"

He chuckled.

Alarmed, she looked at him. He gave her hand another squeeze. "What a queer little bird you are."

"Yes, sir."

"I don't think you can keep calling me 'sir.'"

"No, sir. What would you like me to call you?"

17

He was thoughtful. "How about 'Dad'?" And then he smiled. "On second thought, let's make it 'Father' for the time being. Somehow I think you'd be more comfortable with that."

"Father?" Her heart soared. What a wondrous word! Her own father was dead, and she desperately wanted to ask this golden prince if that meant she would now be his little girl. But it was dreadfully impolite to ask personal questions, so she held her tongue.

"Now that we have that settled, why don't you tell me why you can't fall asleep?"

She stared ahead miserably. "I'm rather a-afraid that I might—not on purpose, of course—purely by accident . . . I might commit an unfortunate mishap on the airplane seat."

"Mishap?"

She nodded her head miserably. How could she explain something so terrible to this shining man?

He didn't say anything for a moment. She was afraid to look at him, afraid of the revulsion she would see on his face. She stared at the woven back of the airplane seat ahead of her.

"I see," he finally replied. "It's an interesting problem. How do you think we could solve it?"

She didn't move her eyes from the back of the seat ahead of her. He seemed to expect her to say something, so she made a tentative offering. "You could pinch my arm, perhaps, if I began to fall asleep."

"Uhm. Yes, I suppose I could do that. Except I might fall asleep, too, and then I wouldn't notice. I think I have a better idea."

She cautiously turned her head to look at him. His fingertips were pressed together and his forehead knitted in concentration.

"What if . . ." he said. "What if we both just shut our eyes and took a small nap. Then, if you woke up and found out you'd had an unfortunate, uh, mishap, you could nudge me in the arm. I'd ask the stewardess for a glass of water, and when she gave it to me, I'd accidentally spill it over your skirt and onto the seat."

It took Susannah's quick mind only a few seconds to

absorb the staggering brilliance of his plan. "Oh, yes," she whispered on a rush of expelled breath. "Oh, yes, please."

She slept for hours. When she awoke, she was dry, rested, and happier than she could ever remember.

Her happiness carried her through those first few California days in the place called Falcon Hill. The house was as big as a castle and full of sunshine. She had a pretty, pink three-year-old baby sister named Paige who let Susannah play with her, and she saw her beautiful mother every day, not just for tea at the Plaza. Every night her new father came into her bedroom and left a glass of water for her so she could spill it on the sheets if she had a mishap. Susannah loved him so fiercely it hurt.

From the time he was fifteen, Joel Faulconer had fed on the lore of Tom Watson, the founder of IBM. He had watched avidly as Watson had molded his company into one of the most successful corporations in the world. He wanted the same to happen with Falcon Typewriter, the company his father Ben and his uncle Lewis had founded in 1913. Being good wasn't enough for Joel Faulconer. He had to be the best.

Returning from World War II with big dreams, Joel presented his father and his uncle with audacious strategies for expanding the company. Selling typewriters was small-time, he told them. They needed to attack IBM in its own territory by expanding their product line to include accounting machinery. They should be going after government contracts and upgrading their sales force.

His uncle, Lewis Faulconer, with his flashy suits, Havana cigars, and two-toned shoes, dismissed all of his nephew's suggestions. "Your father and me made ourselves millionaires a couple of times over, buddy boy. What do we need more money for?"

"To be the best," Joel replied, tight-lipped and seething with frustration. "To give Watson and IBM a run for their money."

Lewis's gaze slithered from Joel's well-cut hair to his Stanford class ring. "Shit, boy. You're not even wet behind the ears and you're trying to tell your daddy and me how to run the company we founded."

Ben Faulconer, who had gained more social polish over the years than his brother, was intrigued by Joel's ideas, but still cautious about making the sweeping changes his son insisted the postwar economy mandated. Still, Joel was certain he could manage his father, if only he could get rid of his uncle Lewis.

In a move that was to prove prophetic, Joel snatched up patents from the infant computer industry. At the same time, he began a systematic courtship of the high-ranking officers of the company, and with very little effort maneuvered his uncle into an escalating series of blunders. It took two years, but he finally succeeded in uprooting Lewis Faulconer.

On Lewis's last day with the company he had helped found, he confronted his brother in Ben's comfortable, paneled office. "You let a fox in the hen house, Benny," he warned, his words slurred because he no longer had any reason to wait until noon to take his first drink of the day. "Watch your ass, boy, because he'll be after you next."

Nonsense, Ben had thought to himself, secretly proud of Joel's cunning in ridding the company of a man who had become an embarrassment. The very idea of worrying about the security of his own position seemed ridiculous to Ben. He was chairman of the corporation—an untouchable. Besides, Joel was his son.

One year later, at the age of thirty, Joel Faulconer had forced his father into early retirement and taken over the helm of the newly renamed Falcon Business Technologies—or FBT, as it was being called. The company immediately began to prosper beyond anyone's imagination.

Two weeks after Susannah's arrival in California, FBT was marking the eighth anniversary of Joel's ascendancy to the chairmanship with the dedication of their new corporate headquarters near Palo Alto. Officially named the FBT Center of Corporate Activities, it had already become known simply as the Castle. Joel was secretly pleased with the nickname. After all, what better place for a king to live than a castle?

Not that he actually thought of himself as a king. But in the kingdom of Falcon Business Technologies, he certainly had unlimited power. Even the President of the United

States was answerable to the people, but Joel was only answerable to himself and a handpicked Board of Directors. He was proud to have accomplished so much at such a young age. At thirty-eight, he was one of the most influential men in American industry. If only he had as much control over his own household.

As he shot a pair of onyx cuff links into the sleeves of his dress shirt, he glanced impatiently at his wife. She was sitting at her dressing table and applying lipstick to the full mouth that had ministered so effectively to his body such a short time before. At thirty-three, she was just entering the prime of her beauty. Her breasts strained seductively against the bodice of her slip whenever she leaned toward the mirror. She worked with utter concentration, as if the simple act of applying lipstick took every ounce of her intelligence—which wasn't far from the mark, he thought.

"You're going to be late again, Kay," he snapped. "You know how important tonight's affair is. You promised me you'd be on time."

"Did I?" she said vaguely. She screwed the lipstick down into its tube and then began looking about for the jeweled cap. Wisps of light brown hair from her short Italian cut feathered her cheekbones, softening features that were already pleasantly blurred. Her mouth was too full for fashion, but he had always liked it. Too much, perhaps. It was more a trollop's mouth than the sort of mouth that belonged on the wife of a powerful man.

"Don't be angry, darling," she said. "Ever since you got back from New York, you've been so angry with me."

"Do you blame me? I knew you were stupid, but I never imagined that even you could have been this stupid."

Kay reached for a cigarette and smoothed the thin arch of her eyebrow with her little finger. "Don't start shouting at me again, Joel. I've explained that it wasn't my fault. Whenever I went to see Susannah, she was well-dressed. How was I to know anything was wrong?"

Joel bit back a retort, knowing that he would only end up making his feather-headed wife later than she already was. What a terrible marriage he had saddled himself with. Still, he refused to dwell too critically on the sensual side of his nature that drew him to women like Kay—seductive high-born kittens who were marvels in bed but inept at the business of daily living. After all, powerful men were allowed a few weaknesses of the flesh. He had toyed with the idea of divorcing her, but that sort of scandal was dangerous for someone in his position. Instead, he blamed her for not becoming the efficient sort of wife a man of his stature needed.

"Have you seen my earrings, darling? The sapphires?" She poked ineffectively at the clutter on her dressing table in hopes her expensive jewels might be lurking among the Max Factor bottles and cubes of Ayds diet candy.

"God, Kay, if you've misplaced those sapphires again, I'm going to take them away from you. Do you have any idea how much they cost?"

She absentmindedly picked up her lipstick tube again. "A fortune, I'm sure. I remember now. I took them off in the living room and tucked them in a drawer of the secretary so I wouldn't lose them. Be a darling and get them for me."

He stalked from their bedroom and went downstairs. As he walked into the living room, he didn't see Susannah sitting like a quiet little mouse in the corner chair, her legs drawn up under the skirt of her new calico nightgown, her eyes bright with adoration as she caught sight of him.

"Damn!" The drawers of the walnut secretary held the usual clutter of Kay's possessions, but no earrings. He banged them shut one by one. "Dammit to hell. Where could she have put them?"

"Can I help you, Father?" Susannah slipped from the chair and walked toward him, her voice quietly deferential. Joel had forbidden anyone to braid her hair, so it hung loose and bone-straight. As she stood before him, she looked so anxious that his heart turned over in his chest. Because he was so powerful himself, he felt her absolute helplessness and total dependence on him even more acutely. She was so solemn, so quiet, so overly polite with her old woman's vocabulary and desperate obsequiousness. He could not ever remember feeling so protective of another human being—not even his own daughter. Baby Paige had an army of caretakers to watch out for her well-being. This ancient little girl had no one but himself.

"Your mother left some earrings here."

"Earrings? Might they be blue?"

"Yes. They're sapphires. Why? Have you seen them?"

"Yesterday I saw Mother put some earrings in that bowl on the mantel."

Joel went over to the bowl and pulled out the sapphires. He smiled at her. Her lips curled in response. It was a trembling, uncertain attempt at a smile, but it was a smile nonetheless.

"What a good girl you are," he said softly. "What a very good girl." And then he hugged her.

Without either of them realizing it, six-year-old Susannah had taken the first step toward becoming the efficient wife that Joel Faulconer so badly needed.

2

The next year was magical. Joel legally adopted her so that she was now his real daughter—no longer Susannah Lydiard, but Susannah Faulconer. She went to school for the first time, and the teacher praised her because she was the smartest student in the class. She stopped wetting the bed and began to smile more. Everyone except her mother seemed to like her.

Although Susannah tried hard to please her mother, nothing seemed to work. She kept herself as neat as a shiny new penny and did everything that was asked of her, but Kay still complained.

"Don't sneak up behind me like that!" Kay shrieked at least once a day. "I've told you a hundred times! It gives me the creeps!"

Susannah perfected a quiet little cough when her mother was around so Kay would always know she was there.

Kay liked Paige much more than she liked Susannah—not that Susannah could really blame her. Paige was so adorable that Susannah immediately made herself a willing slave to her baby half sister. She fetched toys for her, entertained her when she was bored, and placated her when she had a temper tantrum. The sight of her sister's chubby

24

pink face crumpled in tears was more than she could bear.

"You're spoiling her," Kay complained one afternoon as she looked up from the society pages and flicked her cigarette ash. "You shouldn't give her everything she wants."

Susannah reluctantly withdrew her new Barbie doll from Paige's destructive grasp. Paige's blue eyes darkened and she began to howl in protest. The howls grew louder as she ignored all of Susannah's attempts to distract her with other toys. Finally, the newspaper snapped closed.

"For God's sake!" Kay screeched. "Let her play with your Barbie. If she breaks it, I'll buy you another one."

Only her father remained immune to Paige's charms. "Paige has to learn that she can't have everything she wants," he told Susannah in his most severe voice after observing several of these exchanges. "You need to start exercising some judgment. God knows your mother won't."

Susannah promised him she would try to do better, and the very next day she walked out of the room when Paige threw a temper tantrum, even though it nearly broke her heart.

By the time Susannah had finished first grade, the wounds inside her were beginning to mend. Ironically, Kay's criticism proved to be nearly as healing as Joel's affection. From Kay Susannah learned that she wouldn't be shoved in a closet simply because her mother didn't like her. As the world became a safer place that summer, she gradually began to relax her diligence and behave like a normal child.

It was a terrible mistake.

Falcon Hill was set at the end of a long tree-bordered drive sealed off at the entrance with iron gates. In the late afternoon when the adults gathered on the terrace behind the house for martinis, Susannah developed the habit of wandering down the drive to the gates where she played with a doll or climbed up on the filigreed ironwork to extend her view. After having spent so many years being restricted to prescribed walks around the same city block, she found her new freedom dazzling.

She was jumping rope at the bottom of the drive one June afternoon when the balloon man appeared. Even though she was seven years old, jumping rope was a new skill for her—one requiring all her concentration—so at first she didn't see him. The soles of her leather sandals scuffed on the blacktop as she counted softly under her breath. Her fine auburn hair, neatly secured back from her face with a pair of barrettes shaped like cocker spaniels, lifted off her shoulders each time the rope snapped.

When she finally looked up and saw the balloon man, she didn't find his presence along the narrow residential road unusual. A magician had entertained at Paige's birthday party, and an Easter Bunny had personally delivered their baskets. California was an enchanted place where all sorts of magical things could happen.

Tossing down her jump rope, she stepped up on the bottom rung of the gate and watched his approach.

"Balloons for free!" the man called as he came nearer.

He was wearing dusty brown shoes along with a workman's gray pants and gray shirt. Unlike a workman, however, his face was covered by a merry clown mask with a cherry nose and fuzzy purple hair.

"Balloons for free! They never pop, they never stop. Best balloons around."

Balloons that didn't pop? Susannah's eyes widened in amazement. She hated the angry noise balloons made when they broke, and she was entranced with the idea of possessing one that wouldn't frighten her.

As the man approached, she pushed a small hand through the fence and, gathering her courage, said, "Could I please have one of your free balloons, sir?"

He didn't seem to hear her. "Balloons for free. They never pop, they never stop. All my balloons for free."

"Excuse me," she repeated politely. "Might I have a balloon."

He still didn't look at her. Maybe he couldn't see her through his clown mask, she thought.

"All my balloons for free," he chanted. "Come and follow me."

Follow him? Although no one had ever spoken to her

about it, she wasn't certain she was permitted beyond the gates. She gazed longingly at the multicolored bundle of balloons dancing on their strings, and their beauty made her feel giddy.

"All my balloons for free. Come and follow me."

The balloon man's chant seemed to sing in her blood. Her parents were drinking martinis on the terrace, and by the time she ran back to ask for permission, the balloon man would be gone. It seemed silly to lose her chance to own one of these magical balloons, especially since she was certain her father wouldn't mind. He kept telling her to have fun and not to worry so much.

"All my balloons for free. Come and follow me."

She pulled the gate key from its hiding place in a little tin box tucked inside one of the stone urns. Precious seconds elapsed while she fit it into the lock. "Wait," she called out, afraid the balloon man would disappear. She caught her bottom lip between her teeth and concentrated on making the lock work. The key finally turned. Planting the heels of her sandals firmly on the blacktop, she dragged open the gate far enough to slip through.

She felt enormously pleased with herself as she began running beside the high row of hedges that had been planted next to the fence to give the estate privacy from the road. "Please wait for me!" she cried.

It was a warm June day. The hem of her bright yellow sundress slapped her legs and her hair skipped out behind her head. In the distance the balloons bobbed on their strings, gay splashes of color spangled against the open sky. She laughed at the beauty of them, at the distant music of the balloon man's cries, at the joyous feeling of being a child and running free along the narrow road. Her laughter sounded strange and wonderful to her ears. Although she was too young to articulate it, the heavy weight of her past no longer seemed so burdensome. She felt happy, secure, and wonderfully carefree.

She was still laughing when a strange man jumped out from a stand of sycamores and grabbed her.

Fear coagulated in her throat, and she made a horrible animal sound as his fingers dug into her arms. He had a big, fleshy nose and a bad smell. She tried to scream for her father, but before she could utter a sound, another man—the balloon man—came up beside her and pressed his hand over her mouth. Just before he covered her with a blanket, he yanked off his mask and she caught a glimpse of his face, as thin and sly as the head of a fox.

They shoved her down on the floor of a paneled van. One of them kicked her and told her to be quiet. The heavy weave of the blanket snagged a cocker spaniel barrette and pulled a clump of her fine hair from its roots. She bit through her bottom lip to keep from crying out. The heat inside the blanket was suffocating and her cramped position agonizing. But it was fear rather than pain that finally forced her into unconsciousness.

Hours later, the harsh jolting of the van awakened her. She tasted the rusty blood in her mouth and knew she was going to die, but she didn't make a sound. The van jerked to a stop. Her body began to tremble. She curled tighter, instinctively protecting the fragile organs that supported her life. The hinges of the rear doors squealed like a dying animal as they opened. The blanket was snatched away and she squeezed her eyes shut, too young to look bravely at what she feared.

They dragged her from the van. The cold night air hit her skin, and she gazed hopelessly at the flat desert landscape around her. The darkness was as thick as the inside of her grandmother's closet, its blackness penetrated only by a thin icing of stars and the dim glow of the van's interior light.

The sly-faced balloon man had her in his grasp. As he carried her toward a wooden shack, her instinct for survival took over and she tried to free herself. She screamed over and over again, but the emptiness of the desert absorbed her little girl's cries as if they were nothing more significant than the whisper of a few grains of blowing sand.

The man with the fleshy nose unfastened a padlock on the door of the shack and thrust her inside. The interior smelled like dust and rust and oil. Neither man spoke. The only sounds were her own broken whimpers. They wrapped a heavy chain around her neck as if she were a dog and bolted the other end to the wall. Just before they left her alone, one of them thrust the bundle of balloons inside. But the balloon man had lied. By the second day the heat in the shed had popped every one of them.

Newspapers all over the country carried the story of the kidnapping of little Susannah Faulconer. The police guards found a ransom demand for a million dollars in the mailbox. Kay sealed herself in her bedroom with Paige and refused to go near the windows, even though the draperies were tightly closed. Joel was wild with fear for the small, solemn stepdaughter he had grown to love so deeply. As he paced the rooms of Falcon Hill, he asked himself how something like this could have happened. He was an important man. A powerful man. What had he done wrong? She meant more to him than any person on earth, but he had not been powerful enough, he had not been *ruthless* enough, to protect her.

On the third day of the kidnapping, the FBI received an anonymous tip that led them to the shack on the edge of the Mojave Desert. The agents found Susannah chained to the wall. She was curled on the floor in her soiled yellow sundress, too weak to lift her head or to realize that these men were friends instead of enemies. Her arms and legs were raw with scrapes, and the strings of a dozen broken balloons were wrapped through her dirty fingers.

Susannah was so severely dehydrated that there was some concern among her doctors about brain damage. "She's a fighter," Joel said over and over again, as if repetition would make it true. "She'll make it. She's a fighter." Holding her hand, he willed his strength to pass into her small body.

The men who had kidnapped Susannah were betrayed by a former cellmate, and less than a week after Susannah's rescue, they were caught at a roadblock. The balloon man pulled a gun and was killed instantly. The other man hung himself in his cell with a length of twisted bed sheet.

To Joel's joy and Kay's relief, Susannah's body gradually grew stronger. But her spirit didn't heal as quickly. There had been too much evil in her young life, too many battles to fight. Weeks passed before she would speak, another month before Joel coaxed a smile from her. If she had been kidnapped when she had been living with her grandmother, the effect might not have been as devastating. But kidnapping a child who had finally begun to feel secure enough to behave like a child left permanent scars.

Every school morning for the next ten years, she was driven in a securely locked limousine from Falcon Hill to the portals of one of San Francisco's most exclusive girls' academies. She grew tall and coltish. The other girls respected her because she was always willing to help them out of whatever scrape they might have gotten themselves into, and she never spoke badly of anyone. But she was too reserved to make easy friendships, and so serious that she sometimes reminded them uncomfortably of their mothers.

Kay found Susannah's quiet efficiency and perpetual composure irritating, but Susannah spared her so many tedious burdens that she developed a detached affection for her oldest daughter. Still, she couldn't understand how it was possible for Joel to favor his adopted daughter over his own flesh and blood. Unfortunately, the more he criticized Paige, the more rebellious her second daughter became. Without Susannah to act as a shield, Kay knew that her beautiful child would have constantly been at the mercy of her father's displeasure.

By the time Susannah was seventeen, she had become as indispensable to Joel as one of his senior vice-presidents. She kept track of his social schedule, dealt with his servants, and was the perfect hostess—never making her mother's mistake of greeting someone with the wrong name. With Susannah sitting capably at the helm of his household, Joel was spared the more disastrous effects of Kay's incompetence.

As Joel's kingdom grew, so did his arrogance. Not even Susannah escaped the chill of his displeasure when something wasn't arranged to his satisfaction, but this only made her try harder. She pleased him by becoming the most successful debutante San Francisco had seen in years—at least in the eyes of the social matrons who arranged the events. They were enraptured by her reserve and graciousness. The old ways weren't dying, they agreed—not with a young woman like Susannah Faulconer to carry forth the torch.

Susannah loved mathematics, and her excellent academic record would have guaranteed her admittance to any university in the country, but she enrolled in a local college so she could continue to manage the household at Falcon Hill. From the beginning her grades suffered because she missed so many classes while taking business trips with her father and tending to her ever-increasing responsibilities at home. But she owed Joel Faulconer everything, and the glow of living in the warmth of his approval more than compensated for setting aside her own vague dreams of independence.

When she was twenty, she fell in love with a thirty-year-old investment analyst and they began to discuss marriage. Free love floated in the air of the early seventies like oxygen molecules, but the man was so intimidated by her father that he attempted no more than chaste kisses. When she finally gathered enough courage to tell him that she wasn't averse to deepening their relationship, he said he had too much respect for her to sleep with her and she would only hate herself afterward. Several months later she discovered that he was sleeping with one of Paige's friends, and she ended their relationship.

She tried to accept the fact that she was the sort of woman to inspire respect rather than passion, but as she lay in bed at night, she lost herself in sexual fantasies. Not proper fantasies with soft music and romantic candlelight, but raunchy scenarios involving swarthy desert sheiks and brutally handsome white slavers.

And then Kay developed lung cancer, and nothing else mattered. Susannah dropped out of college to care for her mother and tend to her father's increasing demands. Kay died in 1972, when Susannah was twenty-one. As she watched her mother's coffin being lowered into the ground, she experienced both grief and the terrible foreboding that her own young life had just ended with as much finality as Kay's.

On a sunny April day in 1976, two months before her wedding to Calvin Theroux, Susannah met her sister Paige at a small, weathered restaurant tucked away from the city's tourists on one of San Francisco's commercial fishing piers. It was an unusually busy day for her, but she didn't appear either rushed or flustered. Her sage-green suit looked as fresh as if she had just put it on minutes before, instead of at seven that morning. She wore simple gold clips at her ears, and her auburn hair was pulled back into a soft French twist that was a bit severe for a woman who had only the month before turned twenty-five.

Although Paige was already ten minutes late, Susannah didn't fidget as she waited. She gazed at Russian Hill in the distance and mentally rearranged her schedule.

Paige's voice interrupted her reverie. "I've got a million things to do, so this had better not take long."

As she looked up at her sister, Susannah firmly repressed her irritation. Paige was prickly at best, and it would do no good to antagonize her before they'd even had a chance to talk. Her mind flashed back to the time when they were young children, and she had smuggled Paige small toys and chocolate-covered cherries after Joel had punished her. But then one day Paige had told him what Susannah was doing, and Joel had put a stop to any more errands of mercy. Susannah still didn't understand why her sister had tattled.

Paige tossed her knapsack on the floor and took the opposite chair. While she was getting settled, Susannah studied her sister's appearance. Even in worn blue jeans and a faded Mexican cotton top, Paige was extraordinarily beautiful. Her nose was petite, her lips as pouty as Kay's had been. She had Joel's blue eyes, and lush blond hair that fell halfway down her back and always managed to look as if some lusty young man had just rumpled it with vigorous lovemaking.

At the age of twenty-two, Paige was as modern as Susannah was old-fashioned. She was tough and cocky, with a longshoreman's mouth and apparently unlimited self-confidence. Susannah ignored the familiar stab of envy that always passed through her when she was with her sister. She gestured toward the menu. "The abalone is really wonderful here. Or you might enjoy the avocado stuffed with crab."

"I'll have a hamburger," Paige replied indifferently.

Susannah placed her own order for mahi mahi, a fish she'd grown fond of during her frequent trips with Joel to

Hawaii. As the waiter moved away, she broached the subject of their meeting.

"Did you think about what I said on the phone? Tonight is Father's fifty-eighth birthday party. I know it would please him if you were there."

"Did King Joel tell you that?"

"He didn't have to. I'm certain of it." Susannah was certain of no such thing, but she had to end this estrangement between them. Right now her sister was living in a shabby one-bedroom apartment with a would-be rock singer named Conti Dove.

Paige impatiently pushed her hair away from her face. "Don't you ever get tired of running around playing Miss Goody-Two-Shoes? Fuck off, will you?"

Susannah's impassive expression gave no hint of how much she disliked hearing those tough, ugly words coming from her sister's lovely mouth. At the same time, she thought how exciting it would be if, just once in her life, she could toss those rude words at somebody. What would it be like to be so free? What would it be like to have life stretching ahead like a blank canvas—unplanned and waiting to be filled with bold, exciting strokes from one's very own brush.

"He's your father," Susannah said reasonably, "and this estrangement has gone on long enough."

"Exactly twenty-two years."

"That's not what I mean. I'm talking about your leaving home."

"I didn't leave, Susannah. His Highness kicked me out. Not that I wasn't getting ready to split anyway, so you can wipe that pitying look off your face. The best thing that ever happened to me was getting out of that mausoleum." Paige pulled a cigarette from a pack she had tossed on the table and lit it with a cheap plastic lighter. Susannah looked away. Cigarettes had killed their mother, and she hated seeing Paige smoke.

"Look, you can stay around and play Queen of the Castle to Daddy's King if you want—waiting on him hand and foot, giving him birthday parties, taking all the shit he hands out—but that's not my scene."

Definitely not, Susannah thought. Within the space of

eighteen months, Paige had flunked out of college and had an abortion. Joel had finally lost patience and told her she wasn't welcome in the house until she was ready to start acting like a responsible adult.

The waiter arrived with their food—broiled mahi mahi for Susannah, a burger and fries for Paige. Paige sank her teeth into her hamburger. As she chewed, she refused to look at the creamy amandine sauce that covered Susannah's fish, refused to think about how wonderful the mahi mahi must taste. Since her father had ordered her out of Falcon Hill, Paige couldn't remember having eaten anything more exotic than an anchovy pizza. The bite of hamburger she had just swallowed settled heavily in a stomach already churning with years of resentment from growing up in the shadow of an older sister who was perfect—an outsider who had taken her place in her own father's heart when she had been too young to defend herself.

Paige watched as Susannah delicately set her fork on her plate. Susannah had begun to remind her of those nineteenth century portraits she had studied in her art history class before she'd flunked out of college—portraits of thin, juiceless women who spent their lives languishing on chaise longues after giving birth to small blue-lipped infants. A deceptive image, Paige admitted to herself, since Susannah seemed to have an endless supply of energy, especially for good works such as saving her younger sister from a life of rock 'n' roll and sexual debauchery.

Paige could barely resist the urge to reach across the table and rumple that always-tidy auburn hair, rip away that carefully tailored suit. If only Susannah would scream or yell once in a while, Paige might have been able to get along with her better. But Susannah never lost control. She was always calm and cool, Daddy's paragon of a daughter. Susannah always said the right thing, did the right thing, and now she was capping her accomplishments by marrying exactly the right man—Mr. Calvin Stick-Up-His-Ass Theroux.

Paige was absolutely certain that Susannah was still a virgin. A virgin at twenty-five! What a joke. An image flashed through her mind of the bride and groom climbing into bed the night of their wedding. She saw Cal Theroux flashing that spectacular smile of his and easing up Susannah's nightgown just to the top of her thighs.

"Pardon me, darling, but this won't take a second."

Paige imagined Susannah picking up her reading glasses along with the latest issue of *Town and Country* from the bedside table and speaking in that quiet, carefully articulated voice of hers. "But, of course, dear. Just tap me on the shoulder when you're finished."

Across the table Susannah spotted the cynical smile on her sister's face but decided to ignore it. "The party starts at eight," she told Paige. "All his old friends will be there, and I know they'll think it's strange if you don't show up."

"Tough shit," Paige snapped. "Get off my ass, will you?"

"Paige—"

"Look, you're not my mother, so stop acting like you are."

Susannah hesitated. "I know you still miss her. I don't mean to nag."

"He won't even notice that I'm not there." Paige tossed down her half-eaten hamburger and stood. "Listen, I've got to go. See you around sometime." She snatched up her knapsack from the floor and made her way through the dining room. Her swaying blond hair, along with her tight-fitting jeans, attracted the attention of most of the male diners. She favored several of them with a seductive smile before she walked out the door.

As Susannah watched Paige disappear, she wished for the thousandth time that the two of them could have the close loving relationship other sisters shared. It would be so wonderful to have someone to confide in—to be silly with.

But then Susannah was never silly with anyone. For her the daily business of living required great seriousness. As she paid the check, she remembered how often she had listened to Paige giggling with her friends, and she felt another stab of envy toward her rebellious sister.

"I hope everything was satisfactory, Miss Faulconer?"

"Excellent as always, Paul. Thank you."

Susannah slipped her credit card back into her purse and

got up from her chair. As she left the restaurant, her posture was perfect, her movements contained and graceful. She bore no resemblance at all to the little girl who had once been so enchanted with a bundle of dancing balloons that she had unlocked the protected gates of her own life and—for a few glorious moments—run free.

3

Falcon Hill had been built in the style of an opulent French manor house. In addition to marble bathrooms and polished teak floors, it contained five fireplaces with Louis XV mantels, an oval-shaped morning room, and a well-stocked European wine cellar. Susannah paused inside the arched entryway to the dining room to check the last-minute arrangements for her father's birthday celebration. The handpainted wallpaper was softly illuminated by a matching pair of antique chandeliers sparkling with a waterfall of crystal prisms. Sprays of white flowers spilled from the low Georgian silver bowls. The antique linen tablecloth and twenty matching napkins had been purchased at auction in London a decade earlier. Each piece bore the gold-embroidered crest of Czar Nicholas I.

Susannah had just finished adjusting one of the floral arrangements when she heard Cal's voice in the foyer. She went out to greet him and to straighten his tie, just as she had straightened her father's tie a short time before. Cal and her father were alike in so many ways. Both were commanding presences, both utterly self-assured.

"You look lovely, darling," Cal said, openly admiring her black evening gown. It had an off-the-shoulder neckline surrounded by a wide white organdy ruffle. When she'd put it on, she had thought the combination of the frothy neckline and her bare shoulders made her look as if she had just climbed naked out of a vat of whipped vanilla nougat.

He chucked her under the chin. "You look like a beautiful, graceful swan."

Just her luck, she thought. Cal ate vanilla nougat, but she had never known him to eat a swan.

She turned away abruptly and led Cal toward the living room. He kissed her again—a neat kiss, precisely on target, as neat as the crease in his trousers, as exact as the part in his hair.

"Do you remember me telling you about the problems I was having with Harrison's region?"

He kept his voice low in case there were any eavesdroppers lurking about, and without waiting for her answer, launched into a detailed account of his latest success at work. She needed to speak to the cook, but she listened patiently. Serving as Cal's audience wasn't something she minded. In public, her fiancé was both discreet and modest to a fault, and it was only when he was with her that he dropped his natural caution. Sometimes she thought he didn't really enjoy his triumphs until he had spread them out before her.

After the guests arrived, dinner progressed agreeably. She had seated Cal and her father close together. Although only forty-two, Cal was a senior vice-president, and insiders considered him Joel's probable successor, especially in light of his upcoming marriage to Susannah.

She noticed how handsome the two men looked sitting at the other end of the table. At fifty-eight, Joel was nearly as lean and fit as her fiancé, and his ice-blue eyes hadn't lost a bit of their sharpness. Age had given his face more character than it had possessed on the day he pulled her from her grandmother's closet. The cleft in his chin had deepened, and his square jaw was sharper. Although his blond hair had darkened at the top and grayed at the temples, it hadn't thinned, and he was still vain about it.

Cal's triangular face was much narrower than her father's, broad at the forehead but tapering from the cheekbones down to the jaw. A gray streak, like a lightning bolt, cut a dashing path through the center. He was always tan from sitting behind the helm of his French-made racing sloop, and he had a ready smile that flashed white teeth and oozed confidence.

"Wonderful dinner, Susannah," Joel said, lifting his glass in her direction. "You've outdone yourself." He gave her their private smile, and she felt as if someone had tossed a shower of gold stars over her head. Her father could be difficult and autocratic sometimes, but she loved him deeply.

The plump, aging Italian countess at her side finished a generous wedge of chocolate truffle cake. "You thin girls are so lucky," she said in heavily accented English as she gazed at the barely touched piece of cake on Susannah's plate. "I have to watch every bite I put in my mouth."

"No one would ever know it," Susannah replied graciously. "You have a wonderful figure. Tell me about your gown? It's Italian, isn't it?" Skillfully, she deflected her guest from worries about her waistline to a rapturous description of Valentino's last collection.

She heard her father's laughter at the other end of the table. By tilting her head ever so slightly, she could observe Joel sharing a joke with Cal. She nodded agreeably at the countess's description of a two-piece dinner ensemble, and at the same time noted Cal's hand resting lightly on the stem of his wineglass. His fingers looked sun-browned and strong. She could see the starched edge of his shirt cuff showing beneath the sleeve of his dinner jacket. He was wearing the monogrammed gold cuff links she had given him, and his fingers were sliding up and down the stem of the wineglass. She felt a hot rush of sexual excitement.

"You're absolutely right, Countess," she said. "The Italian designers have been so much stronger this year."

She remembered the first time she and Cal had made love. She had been so excited, so pitifully grateful that she had finally found a man who would relieve her of her burdensome virginity. But it had been over with quickly and wasn't nearly as thrilling as she had thought it would be. It was her fault, of course. After indulging in so many lewd fantasies, was it any wonder that Cal's all too human touch had seemed vaguely antiseptic and somehow perfunctory?

She remembered her embarrassment afterward.

"You nearly poked my eye out, darling," he had said. "I didn't imagine you would be quite so . . . athletic." And then he'd smiled, as if a smile could take the sting out of his words. "Not that I'm complaining, mind you. Just rather surprised, that's all."

He had made her feel as if her passion were a breach of etiquette, and she'd been more restrained ever since. Now the bedroom was one more place where she had to mind her manners.

She took a small bite of truffle cake and nodded at the countess. While she chewed she envisioned herself licking a line from the hollow at the base of Cal's throat down his chest and over his hard belly. She saw herself using the tip of her tongue as a sharp, pointed dart, making little stabs at his skin and then softening her tongue to dip lower and lick again.

"More sherry, Countess?" she inquired.

"That would be lovely, dear."

With the barest tilt of her head, Susannah caught the attention of one of the waiters she had hired for the evening to supplement her regular staff. The glow of the candles glimmering in her fine auburn hair touched the strands with gold just as candlelight had illuminated the gracious heads of women of wealth and privilege for centuries.

Another burst of laughter rang out from the head of the table, and Cal called down to her, "Susannah, your father is telling lies about you."

She smiled. "My father never lies. He just colors the truth to suit his purpose."

Joel chuckled and gazed at her fondly. "Not this time, Susannah. I was telling Cal about your hippie period."

Her fingers clenched in her lap, but no trace of agitation was evident in her voice or in the calm, smooth line of her brow. "Be careful what you say, Daddy. You'll scare poor Cal away before we get him to the altar."

"He's made of stronger stuff. He won't be frightened by a little mushy-headed liberalism."

Susannah took a sip from her wineglass, maintaining her

cool, careful smile even though she was having difficulty swallowing.

"I can't imagine Susannah going through a hippie period," Paul Clemens said. He was FBT's Vice-Chairman of the Board and Joel's oldest friend.

"She wasn't wearing beads and living in a commune," Joel quickly interjected. "But when she was twenty, she came to me and—with great solemnity, mind you—announced that she was thinking about joining the Peace Corps."

There was a momentary silence, and then the sound of several chuckles. *Please don't do this, Daddy,* Susannah silently pleaded. *Please don't trot out my confidences for dinner party conversation.*

She touched her napkin to the corner of her lips, smearing her lipstick on the gold crest of Czar Nicholas I. "I'm certain no one wants to hear about my boring youth," she said.

The flicker of a frown passed briefly over Joel's features, and she knew her interjection had displeased him. He disliked it enormously when anyone interrupted one of his stories.

Madge Clemens, Paul Clemens's wife, turned toward Susannah. "Why on earth did you want to join the Peace Corps? It's so—I don't know—*bacterial* or something."

"I was young," Susannah replied with a trace of a smile and a casual shrug. "Young and idealistic." Her fingers tightened in her lap.

"You little rebel." Cal winked at her as if she were a mischievous ten-year-old.

Joel leaned back in his chair, the worldly-wise patriarch protecting foolish females from their silly little mistakes. "A stern lecture on the political facts of life from Old Dad put an end to it, of course. But I haven't stopped teasing her about it."

The smile never left Susannah's face. No one watching her could guess at the humiliation she felt.

"If everyone has finished," she said smoothly, "let's have our after-dinner drinks in the living room."

Everyone was finished, and the party moved on.

An hour later one of the waiters came up behind her as she stood chatting with several of the FBT wives while a string quartet from the San Francisco Symphony played discreetly in the background. The waiter whispered, "There's a man who wants to see Mr. Faulconer. He wouldn't leave, so we put him in the library."

What now? she wondered. She excused herself from the group before her father became aware that there was a problem and headed for the library. As soon as she opened the doors she saw the worn soles of a pair of motorcycle boots propped on top of Joel Faulconer's massive walnut desk.

"Un-fucking-believable," a male voice murmured.

For a fraction of a second she thought he was talking about her, and then she realized his head was turned upward toward the hand-embossed copper ceiling that had come from an old French tavern.

"May I help you?" she asked, her voice cool and distinctly unhelpful.

Somewhat to her surprise, he didn't jump up in embarrassment when she spoke. Although he swung his boots to the carpet, he remained seated as he studied her.

He was so obviously foreign to her world that she felt a combination of unease and fascination. He wore an old leather motorcycle jacket over a black T-shirt, and his hair was long. It wasn't the fashionable length of a young executive's hair, but Apache-long, falling straight as the blade of a knife until it curled up on the shoulders of his jacket. He was perhaps a year or so younger than she was, and brash—she saw that, too. His cheekbones were high and flat, his mouth thin. But it was his eyes that ultimately held her attention. They were hard black marbles flecked with amber. And they were incredibly vulgar.

It wasn't a lecherous vulgarity she saw there. He didn't try to undress her visually or make an exploratory trip down her body. Instead, she saw the vulgarity of too much intensity of expression for too short an acquaintance.

"I'm going to have to ask you to leave," she said.

"I want to see Joel Faulconer."

"He's unavailable."

"I don't believe that."

Why did he keep looking at her as if she were some sort of

exotic species on exhibit at the zoo? "If you'd like to meet with him, I suggest you call his office for an appointment."

"I did that. The bitch who answers his phone keeps brushing me off."

Her voice passed from cool to cold. "I'm sorry, but there's nothing I can do."

"That's bullshit."

A small pulse began to throb in her throat as he slowly rose from the chair. She knew she should call for help, but she had grown so very tired of talking to overweight countesses and gouty vice-presidents. Would it be so terrible —not to mention dangerous—to wait just a few more minutes and see what the outspoken stranger who had invaded her father's library had in mind?

"Saying you can't do anything is bullshit," he repeated.

"I'm asking you to leave."

"You're what—his wife, his daughter? You can do anything you want." He snapped his fingers in the air in front of her eyes. "Just like that, you can arrange for me to see him."

She raised her head ever so slightly, so that she was looking down the length of her nose at him in the deliberately hostile fashion her father employed so effectively. "I'm his daughter Susannah, and he's entertaining tonight." Why had she told him her name? Whatever had possessed her?

"Okay. Tomorrow, then. I'll meet him tomorrow."

"I'm afraid that won't be possible."

"Christ." He looked at her with disgust and shook his head. "When I first saw you—those first few seconds—I had this feeling about you."

He fell silent.

It was as if he'd tapped out the initial seven notes of Beethoven's Fifth, but left off the eighth. She waited. The white organdy ruffle rose and fell over her breasts. She was frightened so badly that her palms had begun to perspire. Frightened, but excited, too, and that frightened her even more. She knew all too well that disaster could appear from nowhere—on the sunniest of June days, from behind the merry mask of a clown. Still, she couldn't seem to force herself to break away from him and go for help. Perhaps it was the aftereffect of her meeting with Paige, perhaps it was

43

simply a reaction to spending too many evenings with people who were so much older than herself.

"What kind of feeling?" The words seemed to have left her mouth of their own volition—she who never spoke impulsively.

He walked around to the front of the desk, those dark, amber-flecked eyes never moving from hers. When he spoke, his voice was low and intense, barely more than a whisper. "A feeling like maybe you'd understand."

She heard the sounds of the string quartet playing another world away. Her mouth felt dry. "Understand what?"

Now his eyes did roam over her, suggestively, unapologetically, as if he alone could see the red-hot wanton who was hidden beneath her composed exterior. An erotic image flickered unbidden through her mind of his hand reaching out and lowering the bodice of her dress. The image lasted only a second, but the effect was almost unbearable— flooding her body first with heat and then with self-disgust.

He grinned—as if he had read her mind—and his brash young lips parted. She became aware of a tapping sound and followed the noise with her eyes. He was bumping the toe of one of his motorcycle boots against an old leather sample case that was leaning against the side of her father's desk.

"Do you know what I've got in here?" he asked, still tapping his toe. His voice was intense; his eyes blazed like an Apache warrior about to take a scalp. Unable to draw her gaze away from him, she shook her head.

"I've got the key to a new society in here."

"I—I don't understand." The stammer was back. She hadn't stammered since those first few years after her kidnapping. It was as if her unconscious were sending her danger signals.

Unexpectedly, his face shattered into a grin that was charming, boyish, and completely disarming. He whipped the sample case from the floor and laid it on the highly polished surface of Joel's desk, paying no heed at all to the neat stacks of papers he sent flying. He patted the case with the flat of his hand. "I've got the invention of the wheel in here. The discovery of fire. The first steam engine. The cotton gin. I've got the genius of Edison and the Wright

Brothers, Einstein and Galileo. I've got the entire fucking future of the world in here."

His casual obscenity barely registered as he mysteriously telegraphed his fervor to her.

"This is the last frontier," he said quietly. "We've built condos in Alaska and McDonald's in Africa. China sells Pepsi. Blue-haired old ladies book weekend trips to Antarctica. There's only one frontier left, and I've got it."

She tried to keep her expression cool and guarded—revealing nothing of what she was thinking—but for the first time in as long as she could remember, she couldn't quite pull it off.

He came closer until they stood nearly eye to eye. She felt the vitality of his breath on her cheek and wanted to trap it in her own lungs for just a few moments to see what all that energy would feel like.

"The frontiers of the mind," he whispered. "There's nothing else left. And that's what I've got in this case."

For a moment she didn't move, and then his words gradually penetrated the cool, logical part of her brain. At that moment she finally realized he was making a fool of her, and she felt both cheated and angry. "You're a salesman," she said, overwhelmed with the irrational notion that a bright, shining star had been snatched from her fingers. He was only a salesman. All this time she had stood here and let herself be conned by the Electrolux man.

He laughed. It had a youthful sound to it, rich and full, much different from the subdued masculine chuckles she had grown accustomed to. "I guess you could say that. I'm selling a dream, an adventure, a whole new way of life."

"My father doesn't need any more life insurance." The sarcastic bite to her words felt good. She was hardly ever sarcastic. Her father didn't approve.

He rested his hips against the front edge of the desk, crossed his ankles and smiled at her. "Are you married?"

The question took her by surprise. "No, I—I'm engaged. That's really none of your business, is it?" There was no reason for her to be stammering. She had been handling difficult social situations for as long as she could remember, and her awkwardness unsettled her. She hid her discomfort behind cool hostility. "Let me give you some advice, Mister . . ."

"Gamble. Sam Gamble."

A perfect name for a con artist, she thought. "It will be nearly impossible for you to get to my father. He keeps himself well insulated. There are, however, other people at FBT—"

"I've already seen them. They're turkeys. Real three-piece suit deadheads. That's why I decided to crash your party tonight. I have to talk to your old man in person."

"He's entertaining guests."

"How about setting up an appointment for me on Monday, then? Would you do that?"

"Of course not. He'd be quite angry—"

"You know, you're really starting to piss me off." His mouth tightened with irritation and his hand flattened on the leather sample case. "I don't know whether I'm going to show you this or not, even if that's the only way I can get to your old man. I'm just not comfortable with who you are."

His brashness dumfounded her. "*You're* not comfortable with who *I* am?"

"I mean, it's bad enough that I have to come to a reactionary company like FBT with my hat in my hands."

Heresy was being uttered in Joel Faulconer's library. It should have made her furious, but instead it gave her a strange thrill of excitement. She beat the emotion away and paid penance for her disloyalty. "FBT is one of the most progressive and influential corporations in the world," she said, sounding nearly as pompous as her father.

"If it's so progressive, how come I can't get anybody in the whole, deadhead organization to talk to me?"

"Mr. Gamble, your obvious lack of credentials might explain the difficulty." Along with your leather jacket, she thought. And your motorcycle boots and long hair. And those jeans that show off far too much.

"Credentials are crap." He picked up his sample case and, looking edgy and restless, ran his hand through his hair. "Listen, I've got to sleep on this. You're sending me mixed signals, and I'm still not sure about you. I'll tell you what. If I decide you're okay, I'll meet you in the rotunda at the

Palace of Fine Arts tomorrow around noon. If I don't show, you'll know I changed my mind." And he began to walk toward the library door.

She stared in astonishment at the back of his leather jacket. "I'm not going to meet you anywhere."

He stopped walking and slowly turned to her, one corner of his mouth lifting in an engaging grin. "Sure you are, Suzie. You wouldn't miss it for the world. And you know why? Because underneath that pretty upper-class poker face of yours, you think I'm sexy as hell. And guess what? I think you are, too."

She stood without moving as the door closed behind him. The skin on her scalp felt as if it were burning. The mounds of her breasts were hot. No one had ever called her sexy. No one—not even Cal, her lover.

And then she was filled with self-disgust for having been taken in—even for a moment—by macho swagger. Did Sam Gamble actually imagine she would meet him tomorrow? A feeling of satisfaction shot through her as she pictured him arriving at the Palace of Fine Arts only to discover that he had been stood up.

With her posture so erect she might have been wearing a whalebone corset from another century, she returned to her guests. For the rest of the evening, she determinedly ignored the faint echo of a long ago chant ringing in her head.

All my balloons for free. Come and follow me.

When Sam Gamble got home, he saw that the lights in the garage were still on. That wasn't unusual. Sometimes the lights didn't go off until five or six in the morning. He set the sample case on the kitchen table. It was an old table—gray Formica with curved chrome legs. There was a sad-looking spider plant hanging in the window. An empty can of Pringles sat on the counter next to an ugly ceramic cookie jar. He lifted the jar's lid and tossed in the small electronic device that he had used to trigger those fancy iron gates at Falcon Hill. She had been so shaken up, she hadn't even asked him how he'd gotten past them.

Walking over to the refrigerator, he opened the door and propped one hand on the top as he bent down to look inside.

"Shit. The spaghetti's gone." He pulled out a can of Coke instead and opened it. After he took a swig, he picked up the sample case and walked outside to the garage.

A man was standing at a lighted workbench with his back to the door. He didn't turn as Sam came in.

"I just met the most incredible woman I've ever met in my life." Sam sprawled down on a dirty floral couch. "You should have seen her. She looks like that actress I was telling you about who did that play on PBS a couple of weeks ago—Mary Streep or somebody—except she's prettier. And cool. Christ, is she cool. Snooty on the surface. High-class. But there was something about her eyes . . . I don't know. She pulled this bitch routine, so I knew it wouldn't do any good to show it to her right then. But I wanted to. Damn, I really wanted to blow her mind."

Breathing in the pleasant smell of hot solder, Sam lay back on the couch and propped the can of Coke on his chest. "I never saw anybody move like she does. She's *still,* you know what I mean? A still person, even when she's in motion. You can't imagine her ever raising her voice, even though I could tell I was really pissing her off."

He sipped his Coke for a while and then got up and wandered over to the workbench. "I have to talk to her old man—show him what we've got—but every time I try to get to him, somebody stands in my way. I think if I could catch her interest—get her on my side—she might arrange a meeting. I hate the idea of selling out to FBT, but we don't seem to have any other choice. I don't know. She might not show up. I'll have to think about it."

He watched the other man's hands—the precision of his touch, the sureness of his movements—and shook his head in admiration. "You're a genius, you know that, Yank. An honest-to-shit genius."

And then he threw his arm around the man's shoulders and gave him a wet kiss on the cheek.

The man named Yank jerked around indignantly, splashing a trail of hot solder on the surface of the workbench. "What the heck's wrong with you?" He hunched his shoulder to his cheek, wiping off the kiss. "Why the heck did you do that?"

"Because I love you," Sam said with a grin. "Because you're a goddamned genius."

"Well, heck, you don't have to kiss me." Again, he wiped at his cheek with his shoulder. Finally, calming, he looked around the garage, studying it as if he'd been gone for a very long time. "When did you get back? I didn't hear you come in."

Sam's grin broadened. "I just got here, Yank. Just this second."

4

$\bullet\ \bullet$

Conti Dove, born Constantine Dovido, was dumb, sweet, and sexy as hell. A few months earlier a girl had told him that he looked like John Travolta, and he had been talking to Paige about it ever since. Conti had dark hair and a Jersey accent, but as far as Paige could see, the resemblance ended there.

Paige almost loved Conti. He treated her well and he wasn't astute enough to see what a fake she was.

"Does that feel good, doll?" he asked, using his fingers on her like he used them on the strings of his Gibson.

"Uhm, yes. Oh, yes." She moaned and writhed, putting on a top-notch, first-class, all-star performance so Conti would never suspect that his hot little mama could barely stand to have him touch her.

Nothing was specifically wrong with Conti's lovemaking. He pushed all the right buttons and didn't fall asleep the minute he was done. It was just that Paige found sex to be a drag. She did it, of course, because everybody did, and she liked being held. But most of the time she didn't enjoy it very much. Sometimes she really hated it.

When she was sixteen, she had been raped by a college boy she had met at a rock concert in Golden Gate Park. She had never told anybody about it. Either people would feel sorry for her or they'd say she had it coming.

While she waited for Conti's lovemaking to be over, she clutched his bare arms, cupping the biceps he had developed so spectacularly by working out with the weights they kept in the corner of their bedroom. The bedroom was as clean as she could make it because she hated dirt, but it was painfully ugly. It had a cracked ceiling, mismatched furniture, and a double mattress on the floor. Paige wouldn't sleep on the mattress unless Conti was beside her, because she was always afraid a mouse would run over her head and get tangled in her hair.

"Tell me how good it feels," he crooned in her ear. "Tell me it's good."

"It's good, Conti. It's good."

"Doll . . . doll . . . God, I love you. I love you so much." He pushed himself inside her and began pumping away to the rhythm of "I Can't Get No Satisfaction" that kept playing over and over in her head.

It was the song that the Doves did best. Paige sang backup, Jason was on bass, Benny at the drums. Mike played the keyboard while Conti sang lead, banging his Gibson and thrusting his hips to the rhythm.

I can't . . . get no . . . satis . . . faction

Conti dug his fingers into her buttocks, tilting them higher to receive him, plunging deeper. She let her mind slip away from what was happening, to a beautiful, pure place—a country garden with hollyhocks and larkspur and an old iron pump in the center. She imagined the sound of birds and the scent of honeysuckle. She saw herself lying back on a homemade quilt under a shady old tree. And at her side a plump, rosy-cheeked baby kicked happily and batted the air with its fists. Her baby. The baby she had lost when she'd had her abortion.

I can't . . . get no . . .
I can't . . . get no . . .

Conti let out a low, strangled moan and buried his mouth in her neck. As he shuddered, he seemed so vulnerable to her that she felt a foolish need to protect him. She stroked his back, giving him a sad kind of comfort. How many men had shuddered over her like this? More than a dozen. A lot more. Her friend Roxie said a girl wasn't really promiscuous until she'd hit triple digits, but Paige had felt promiscuous ever since she'd been raped.

When Conti had calmed, he drew back and gazed down at her. "I love you so much, doll."

Tears glistened in his eyes, and to her surprise she felt her own eyes fill. "I love you, too," she replied, even though she knew she didn't. But it seemed unspeakably cruel to say anything else.

Their bedroom romp had made them late, and they had to hurry. All five members of the Doves waited tables at a club called Taffy Too, named after the original owner's dog, who presumably had been Taffy One. They received no salary and only half their tips, but the Doves put up with it because the owner let them play a one-hour set at eleven o'clock each evening.

Taffy's was a third-rate club located in the heart of one of San Francisco's less picturesque neighborhoods, but occasionally some big shots slumming it would end up sitting at a front table. Conti thought the Doves might get discovered that way. In Paige's more depressed moments she thought that perhaps Conti was the only member of the Doves talented enough to perform any place better than Taffy Too's, but generally she repressed such thoughts. She might not be the world's best singer, but somehow she was going to make a success of herself and rub it in her father's face.

They had almost reached the alley that led to the back entrance of Taffy's when Conti lifted his arm and yelled out, "Yo, Ben, my man!"

Paige winced at the loudness of Conti's voice. Benny Smith, their drummer, approached. He was small and thin, with a short Afro and light brown skin.

"Hey, Conti. What's happenin'?"

Conti slid his hand up under her hair and wrapped his fingers around the back of her neck like a high school jock with his cheerleader girlfriend. "Nothin' much. You hear anything more about that dude from Dee-troit Mike was telling us about?"

"Dude's disappeared," Benny replied. "But I hear some dudes from Azday Records showed up at Bonzo's last night."

"No kidding? Maybe they'll come over to Taffy's."

Paige didn't think that was too likely. Unlike Taffy's, Bonzo's was a semirespectable club that booked better acts. She listened as Benny and Conti continued to trade rumors, acting as if each day held a golden key that would open the door to their success. She no longer remembered what that sort of optimism felt like.

They had a thinner crowd at Taffy's that night than normal, so the latecomers who arrived in the middle of the Doves' third Stones number were even more noticeable. Paige, wearing a cheap blue sateen jumpsuit with flashy metal studs, was beating her tambourine against her thigh when the two men took their place at the front table. One of the men was in his early fifties, the other younger. They both looked prosperous. Their suits bore the unmistakable sheen of silk and she caught the glint of expensive watches at their wrists.

Benny nearly knocked over his drums when he spotted them. As they finished "Heart of Stone," he whispered, "Those are the dudes from Azday records. I recognize the old guy—he's Mo Geller. Come on, everybody. Don't fuck up! This is it!"

Conti looked over at her, a panicked expression on his face. She felt surprisingly calm, given the importance of the event, and she gave him a reassuring smile. Benny hit the downbeat and the band kicked in. As she felt the beat of the song, she whipped her head to the side, letting her hair fly. It caught the lights so that it looked as if shimmering golden flames were leaping up from her head. She shook it again. Conti turned toward her as he sang. A wildness seemed to hit him, and he laughed at her—a sexual dare. She caught his mood as he picked up the beat. His hips moved and she laughed back at him—then stuck out her lip in a sexy, taunting pout. He came over to her, not missing a beat of the music, and leaned into her. She whipped him with her hair. They did a frenzied, dirty dance while the other band members called out encouragement. When the number ended, they got more applause than they had received in months.

The two men stayed through the rest of the set, and afterward bought them all drinks. "You kids generate a lot of excitement," Mo Geller said, clinking the ice cubes in his glass. "Got any material of your own?"

Benny assured him that they did, and the Doves took the stage again, performing two songs that their bass player had written. When they were done, Mo handed them one of his cards. "It's early to be talking about a contract, but I'm definitely impressed. We'll be in touch."

All of the Doves went to Conti and Paige's place afterward to celebrate. They smoked grass, told stupid jokes, and drank cheap wine. Conti started to talk about how much all of them meant to him and dissolved into sentimental tears. They were giddy and silly, high on pot and their first brush with success. By the time dawn lightened the sky, the men had curled into various corners of the apartment and fallen asleep. Paige, however, was sitting wide awake in a chair by the window.

At six o'clock she slipped out of the apartment and made her way down the littered hallway to the pay phone that hung near the front door. Digging a coin from the pocket of her jeans, she pushed it into the slot and, after a few moment's hesitation, dialed. Susannah would still be in bed, and the housekeeper shouldn't be in until eight. Unless her father was out of town, he would pick up the phone himself.

"Yes?" He answered brusquely, as if he were speaking into his office intercom.

She tangled the dirty, stretched-out telephone cord through her fingers. "Daddy, it's Paige."

There was a moment's silence. "It's six o'clock, Paige. I'm just getting dressed. What do you want?"

"Look, I'm sorry I couldn't make it to your birthday party. I—something came up."

"I wasn't aware that you'd been invited."

Her mouth twisted bitterly. She should have known that Saint Susannah was responsible for the invitation. "Yeah, well, I was."

"I see."

She turned to face the grimy wall. Her words came quickly, fiercely. "Listen, I just thought you might like to know that a man from Azday Records came to hear us play last night, and he wants to talk to us about a contract."

She squeezed her eyes shut, barely breathing as she waited

for his response. She wanted to frame the words for him so he would say what she needed to hear—words of enthusiasm, of praise.

"I see," he repeated.

Leaning her forehead against the wall, she gripped the receiver so tightly that her knuckles turned pale. "It's no big deal or anything. Azday is an important company. They listen to a lot of bands, and it might fall through."

Joel sighed. "I don't know why you've called to tell me this, Paige. You surely don't expect my blessing. When are you going to start acting like an adult?"

She winced and set her jaw. "Hey, Joel, I'm having fun. Life's too short for all that shit." Silent tears began to slide down her cheeks.

His reply was stiff with disapproval. "I have to dress, Paige. When you're willing to start acting responsibly like your sister, I'll be more than willing to talk to you."

A harsh click traveled over the line as he ended the conversation.

Paige stood perfectly still, holding the receiver to her ear. Her wet cheek lay pressed against the wall where her tears smeared the carelessly scrawled obscenities and abandoned phone numbers of a decade. "Don't go," she whispered. "I never meant to cause you so much trouble. I just wanted you to notice me, to be proud of me. Please, Daddy. Just once be proud of me."

A door slammed and a kid in his early twenties came out into the hallway on his way to work. She banged the receiver down and straightened so quickly that her spine might have been shot through with an injection of liquid steel. Lifting her chin, she swept past him, her hips swaying in an easy, carefree manner.

A long, low wolf whistle sounded from behind her.

She tossed her hair. "Fuck you, shithead."

Susannah pulled the silver Mercedes sedan her father had given her for her birthday into the parking lot at the Palace of Fine Arts. The rotunda rose like a Baroque wedding cake over the other buildings in San Francisco's Marina District. A light drizzle had begun falling when she'd reached the city. Her hand trembled as she turned off the windshield wipers and the ignition. There was still time to go back, she told herself. She nervously touched her neatly coiled hair, then she slipped the keys into her small leather shoulder bag.

As she got out of the car, she felt as if a stranger had taken over her body—a restless, rebellious stranger. Why was she doing something so out of character? Guilt gnawed at her. She was getting ready to commit exactly the sort of irresponsible act she criticized her sister for.

She walked across the parking lot toward the main building, thinking about the Palace's history so she wouldn't have to think about her own behavior. The Palace of Fine Arts had been constructed in 1913 as part of the Pan-Pacific Exposition to celebrate the opening of the Panama Canal. It had been restored from near ruin in the late 1950s and now held the Exploritorium, a hands-on science museum that was a favorite of the city's children. Joel had served on the Board of Directors until recently, when she had taken his place.

Bypassing the Exploritorium, she walked along the path that took her to the rotunda, which was set next to a small lagoon. The rotunda, open to the elements, had massive columns and a dome that was circumscribed by a classical frieze. It was raining harder now and the building was damp, chilly, and deserted.

As she stared through the columns out toward the dreary, rain-pocked lagoon, she crossed her arms over her chest and hugged herself. Although she had on wool slacks and a cable-knit sweater, she wished she had chosen a warmer blazer. Nervously, she fingered her engagement ring. With the exception of a thin gold watch, it was her only piece of jewelry. "Less is more," her grandmother used to say. "Remember, Susannah. Less is always more." Sometimes, though, Susannah thought that less was less.

Misery settled over her. She shouldn't be here. She was uneasy and guilt-ridden. She wanted to believe that she had come today only because she was curious about what Sam Gamble carried in his leather case, but she didn't think that was true.

"I was right about you."

Startled, she spun around and saw him walking into the rotunda. Drops of rainwater beaded on his jacket and something silver glimmered through his dark hair. With a jolt she realized that he was wearing an earring. Her stomach knotted. What kind of woman slipped away from her father and her fiancé to meet a man who wore an earring?

He set the leather sample case next to a sawhorse and some wooden crates being used for repair work. She could smell the rain in his hair as he came close. Her eyes fastened on a few dark strands that were sticking to his cheek, then moved to his silver earring, which was shaped like one of the primitive heads on Easter Island. It swayed back and forth like a hypnotist's watch as he spoke. "I usually expect too much from people, and then I'm disappointed."

She slipped her hands into the pockets of her blazer and prepared to keep silent, as she frequently did when she was uneasy. Ironically, these silences had earned her the reputation of being totally self-possessed. And then—as if she had fallen under the spell of that hypnotically swaying earring— she heard herself saying exactly what she was thinking. "Sometimes I don't think I expect enough from people."

For her, it was an uncharacteristically bold piece of self-revelation, but he merely shrugged. "I'm not surprised." His eyes moved over her face with an intensity that further unnerved her. And then his lips curved into a cocky grin. "You want to take a ride on my Harley later?"

She looked at him for a moment and, amazingly, felt herself beginning to smile. His question was so unexpected, so wonderfully startling. No one had ever asked her such a thing.

"I'm not exactly the motorcycle type."

"So what? Have you ever ridden one?"

For a moment she actually considered the idea. Then she realized how ridiculous it was. Motorcycles were dirty and unsafe. She shook her head.

"It's great," he said. "Incredible. Straddling the bike. Feeling all that power between your thighs—the vibration, the surge of the engine." His voice dropped and once again his eyes caressed her face. "It's almost as good as sex."

She was a world champion at hiding her feelings, and not by a flicker of an eyelash did she betray the effect his words had on her. All too clearly, she saw what a mistake she had made by coming to meet him. Something about him fed those inappropriate erotic fantasies that plagued her. "I was under the impression that you asked me to come here today to discuss business, Mr. Gamble."

"I thought redheads were supposed to have hot tempers. You don't look like you ever get mad."

She felt strangely defensive. "Of course I do."

"Have you ever gotten royally pissed off?"

"I get angry like everyone else."

"Have you ever thrown anything?"

"No."

"Hit anybody?"

"Of course not."

A mischievous smile tilted the corner of his mouth. "Have you ever called anybody an asshole?"

She started to make a properly stuffy response, only to feel that treacherous smile once again tugging at the corners of her mouth. "I've been much too well brought up for that sort of thing."

He lifted his arm and, without warning, gently scraped the backs of his knuckles over her cheek. "You're really something, Suzie. You know that?"

Her smile faded. His hand felt slightly rough, as if the skin were chapped. Cal's hands were so smooth that she sometimes didn't realize he'd touched her. She eased her head away from him. "My name is Susannah. No one ever calls me Suzie."

"Good."

Discomfited, she slid her fingers along the leather shoulder strap of her purse. "Perhaps you should tell me why you wanted to meet me here today?"

He laughed and lowered his arm. "Other than a couple of English professors I had in college, you're the only person I know who can use a word like 'perhaps' and not sound like a phony."

"You went to college?" Somehow, it didn't fit his wild biker's image.

"For a couple of years, and then I got bored."

"I can't imagine anyone getting bored with college."

"Yeah, well, I'm pretty restless." Without asking permission, he clasped her arm and led her over to one of the wooden crates the workers had left. "Sit down here. I want to show you something." She sat and crossed her hands in her lap as he lifted his case to the spot beside her.

"I like challenges, Suzie. Adventure. Maybe you'll understand who I am when you see this."

She found herself holding her breath as he pressed the latches. What secrets did this biker medicine-show man carry with him? Her imagination conjured up a panoply of ridiculously romantic images—yellowed treasure maps, precious jewels bearing ancient curses, sacred scrolls from the caves by the Dead Sea.

With a dramatic flourish, he flipped open the lid.

For a moment he was silent. When he finally spoke, his voice held the whispered awe of someone in church. "Did you ever see anything so beautiful in your life?"

She stared down into the contents of the case and was overwhelmed with disappointment.

"The design is so elegant, so damned efficient, it makes you want to cry. This is it, Suzie. You're looking at the vanguard of a whole new way of life."

All she saw was an uninteresting collection of electronic parts mounted on a circuit board.

"It's a computer, Suzie. A computer small enough and cheap enough to change the world."

Her feeling of letdown was almost palpable. This was what she got for sneaking around like a cat burglar. It must be the pressure of the wedding that had made her act so irresponsibly. She twisted her engagement ring so the diamond was straight and slipped back into her polite, cool shell. "I really don't know why you're showing me this." She began to rise, only to have a hard hand settle on her shoulder and push her firmly back down. It startled her so much she made a small exclamation.

"I know what you're thinking. You're thinking this is too small to be a computer."

She wasn't thinking any such thing, but perhaps it was better to pretend she was than to let him suspect how jumbled her real thoughts were. "FBT has been a pioneer in computers since the 1950s," she said evenly. "I've been around them most of my life, and they're much larger than this."

"Exactly. Even the so-called 'mini' computers are nearly as big as a refrigerator. But this is still a computer, Suzie. The heart and guts of one. A *micro* computer. And Yank's improving it every day."

"Yank?"

"He's an electronic genius—a born hacker. We met when we were kids, and we've been friends ever since. He can design the sweetest pieces of integrated circuitry you've ever seen. It's a point of pride with him to come up with a design that uses one less chip than anybody else's. With an established company behind this computer, it could be on the market before the end of the year."

By "an established company," he meant FBT, she thought. How could she have lost sight of the fact that he wanted to use her to get to her father?

He had made her feel foolish, so she was deliberately unkind. It wasn't like her, but then, neither was slipping away from home to meet a street-smart biker. She gestured dismissively toward the unimpressive batch of electronic parts that obviously meant so much to him. "I can't imagine anybody wanting to buy something like this."

"You're kidding, aren't you?"

"I never kid."

She saw his impatience and once again found herself staring at him, almost mesmerized as she watched him try unsuccessfully to contain his emotions. Unlike her, he didn't seem to conceal anything. What would it feel like to be so free?

"You don't get it, do you?" he said.

"Get what?"

"Think about it, Suzie. Most of the computers in this country are million-dollar machines locked up in concrete rooms where only guys in three-piece suits can get to them—guys with ID cards and plastic badges with photos on them. Companies like FBT and IBM make these computers for big business, for government, for universities, for the military. They're made by fat cats to serve fat cats. Computers are knowledge, Suzie. They're power. And right now the government and big business have all that power locked up for themselves."

She tilted her head toward the collection of electronic circuits. "This is going to change that?"

"Not right away. But eventually, yes, especially with a company like FBT marketing it. The board needs expanding. Everything has to be self-contained. We need a terminal, a video monitor. It needs more memory. But Yank is coming up with new hacks all the time. The guy's a genius."

"You don't seem to have much respect for FBT. Why are you offering them your design?"

"I don't have enough money to manufacture it myself. Yank and I could make a few of these and sell them to our friends, but that's not good enough. Don't you see? A giant like FBT can make it happen. With FBT behind Yank's design, the world will have a computer that's small enough and—even more important—one that's *cheap* enough so that people can buy it for their homes. A person's computer. A home computer. Something to stick on top of a desk and hack around on. In the next couple of years, we're going to turn those big fat cat computers into dinosaurs."

There was something so charismatic about the fire in his eyes, the energy charging through his body, that for a few moments she actually found herself caught up. "How does it work?"

"I can't show you here. It has to be hooked up. You need a power supply. The memory has to be loaded in. You have to have a terminal—like a typewriter keyboard. A television for video display."

"In other words, this doesn't do anything."

"It's a computer, for chrissake!"

"But it can't do anything unless you attach all these other things to it?"

"That's right."

"I think you're wasting your time, Sam. My father won't be interested in something like this. I can't imagine anyone wanting to buy it."

"Everyone in the entire frigging world is going to want to buy it! Before too many years have passed, a home computer will be another everyday appliance—like a toaster or a stereo. Why can't you see that?"

His antagonism jarred her, but she forced her voice to

remain smooth yet strong, just as it was when she needed to make a point at a hospital auxiliary meeting. "Maybe in the twenty-first century, but not in 1976. Who would actually buy something like this—a machine that doesn't do anything until you hook up a dozen other things to it?"

"For the next few years, mainly hobbyists and electronics junkies. But by the 1980s—"

"There can't be enough hobbyists to make something like this profitable." She forced herself to glance at her watch so he could see that she had more important things to do than sit here chatting about his quixotic vision of computer-filled households.

He shook his head and regarded her with thinly disguised hostility. "For someone who looks intelligent, you're really out of touch. Do you spend so much time planning dinner parties that you can't see what's happening all around you? This is California, for chrissake. You're living on top of Silicon Valley. The electronics capital of the world is right at your feet. There's a whole universe of people out there who've been waiting all their lives for something like this."

As Joel Faulconer's daughter, she had spent most of her life in a world where high technology was served right along with the soup course. She wasn't ignorant, and she didn't like his condescension. "I'm sorry, Sam," she said stiffly, "but all I see is a briefcase full of electronic parts that don't do anything. I'm certain you're wasting your time. My father won't agree to see you, and—even if he did—he would never be interested in anything this impractical."

"Talk to him for me, Suzie. Convince him to see me. I'll take care of the rest."

Her gaze took in the leather jacket, the length of his hair, the earring. "I'm sorry, but I can't do that."

His thin lips twisted and he looked past her toward the lagoon. It had begun to rain harder and the surface of the water was gray and rippled. He shoved his hands in the pockets of his jacket, making the leather rustle. "Okay, then here's something you *can* do. Come to a meeting with me next week."

She was alarmed. Meeting him once was bad enough—twice would be unforgivable. "That's impossible."

"You just think it's impossible. Loosen up a little. Take a risk for a change."

"You don't seem to understand. I'm engaged. It would be unseemly for me to meet you again."

"Unseemly?" His eyebrows shot up. "I'm not asking you to sleep with me. I just want you to meet some people I know. Do it, Suzie. Throw away your etiquette book for a change."

She tried not to let him see how badly he had shaken her. Gathering up her purse, she stood—straitlaced Susannah Faulconer wrapping propriety around her like a maiden aunt's crocheted shawl. She opened the catch on her purse and pulled her car keys from one of the neatly arranged compartments. "What kind of people do you want me to meet?" She asked the question coolly, as if a guest list were the only really important thing on her mind.

Sam Gamble smiled. "Hackers, honey. I want you to meet some hackers."

5

·························

They were the nerdiest of the nerds—bespectacled California boys of the sixties, who grew up in the suburbs of the Santa Clara Valley south of San Francisco.

In other parts of America, baseball and football reigned unchallenged, but in the Santa Clara Valley electronics permeated the air. The Valley harbored Stanford and Hewlett-Packard, Ames Research Laboratory and Fairchild Semiconductor. From the moment they woke up to the moment they fell asleep, the boys of the Valley breathed in the wonders of transistors and semiconductors.

Instead of Wilt Chamberlain and Johnny Unitas, these boys of the sixties found their heroes in the electrical engineers who lived next door, the men who toiled in the laboratories at Lockhead and Sylvania. Electronics permeated the air of the Santa Clara Valley, and to the bespectacled boys of the suburbs, the engineers with their slide rules and plastic pocket protectors were modern-day Marco Polos, adventurers who had unlocked the exotic mysteries of electron flows and sine waves.

The boys grew adept at barter. They did odd jobs in exchange for the surplus parts the men culled from the storerooms of the companies for which they worked. The boys washed cars for boxes of capacitors, painted garages for circuit boards, and every spare penny they earned went into buying parts for the transistor circuits and ham radio receivers they were building in their bedrooms.

In actuality, there wasn't much else for these boys to do with their money. Most of them were still too young to drive, and the older ones had no need to save their money for dates because no self-respecting California schoolgirl would have been caught dead with any one of them. They were the nerdiest of the nerds. Some were so overweight that their stomachs bulged from beneath their belts, others so underweight their Adam's apples seemed larger than their necks. They were pimply, myopic, and stoop-shouldered.

As they grew older, they went to college. Despite their impressive IQ's, some of the most talented never graduated. They were too busy having fun hacking around in their university's computer lab to go to their thermodynamics class or study for an exam in quantum mechanics. They programmed the big mainframes to play games they invented—games with galaxies exploding in dazzling patterns of starbursts and jets streaking across screens spattered with constellations that actually moved. They could only get time on the machines at night, so they slept during the day and hacked until the graduate assistants kicked them out in the morning. They ate junk food to the point of malnutrition and lived their lives under the blue flicker of fluorescent lighting. Like vampires, their skin turned pasty and white.

They were always horny. When they weren't hunched over a terminal, they were dreaming of feelable, kissable, suckable breasts and sweet little miniskirted asses. But they lived at night, it was hard for them to meet women, and when they did, they ran into trouble. How could anyone talk to a person who didn't understand the joy of spending an evening with a DEC PDP-8 writing a subroutine to solve quadratic functions?

They were the nerdiest of the nerds, and their encounters with women frequently didn't go well.

Most of them were too caught up in the excitement of an interesting hack to think about the fact that they might hold the keys to a new society in their heads. Although they yearned for small, inexpensive machines they could use freely at any time of night or day instead of having to sneak into a computer lab at three in the morning, most of them didn't let their thoughts go much further than ephemeral daydreams. They were having too much fun writing elaborate sine-cosine routines that would make the games they had invented run better. They were hackers, not visionaries, and they didn't think too much about the future.

But the visionaries were around. With rebellious young eyes uncorrupted by old knowledge, they saw what was happening at places where the nerds got together, places like the Homebrew Computer Club. The visionaries saw, and they understood.

Sam Gamble impatiently paced along the walkway leading to SLAC, the Stanford Linear Accelerator Center. Susannah was late. Maybe she wouldn't come. He pushed his hands in the back pockets of his jeans and encountered his wallet. It was thicker than normal because he'd gotten paid that day. He'd bought two books—Clarke's *Profiles of the Future* and Minsky's *The Society of Mind*—along with a new Eagles tape.

Sam hated his job. He worked as a technician at a small semiconductor company in Sunnyvale. He was competent at what he did, but since he didn't have a degree, it was basically dead-end work. Yank didn't have a degree either, but Yank was an electronics genius and he had a good job at Atari. A job that would probably end soon, Sam reminded himself. Yank tended to be chronically unemployed because he would get involved in some incredible hack and forget to go to work. Sam had come to the conclusion that the modern corporation—even one as freewheeling as Atari— wasn't designed for guys like Yank. In his opinion, time clocks were one of a million things wrong with the way businesses were run in this country.

After Sam had dropped out of college, he'd bummed around the country for a while on his bike. It was fun. He'd met a lot of people, slept with a lot of women, but he'd finally gotten tired of the aimlessness of it all. When he'd come home, he'd fallen in with Yank Yankowski, who'd just flunked out of Cal Tech. He and Yank had known each other since they were kids, but Yank was a year older and they'd run in different crowds. Sam had been a hell raiser, while Yank was almost invisible—this weird skinny kid who hid away in his family's garage and built strange gadgets.

The sound of a well-tuned German engine caught Sam's attention. He watched the silver Mercedes pull into the parking lot, and the efficient, no-nonsense design of the car gave him a visceral rush of pleasure. There wasn't any reason in the world Detroit couldn't build a car like that—no reason except greed and a lack of imagination.

As Susannah came up the walk, she looked like all the women in the world he'd ever wanted but had never been able to have. It wasn't either her money or her looks that primarily attracted him. He'd slept with rich women before, and he'd certainly slept with prettier ones. But Susannah was different. He took in the way she moved, that discreet mouth, the simple design of her belted cashmere coat. It was classic, just like the car she drove. Just like Susannah Faulconer.

Susannah walked toward him, her spine as straight as the yardstick her grandmother had strapped to her back when she was a child. All day she had been telling herself she wouldn't come here tonight, but then she had been on the phone with Madge Clemens, discussing a luncheon program for the wives of the FBT regional presidents. Madge was debating whether Susannah should invite someone to do the women's colors, which was the very latest thing, or whether they should have a guest speaker. Madge had been going on about how nice it would be to have a personalized packet of fabric swatches when she'd suddenly changed her mind and told Susannah that they simply had to invite this wonderful doctor her sister had heard speak.

"He's marvelous, Susannah," Madge had said. "I know everyone will get a lot out of his presentation. He brings slides and everything. And all of us are interested in menopause."

Susannah hadn't said a word. For a moment she had sat without moving, and then she found herself slowly lowering the receiver to the cradle and hanging up right in the middle of Madge's sentence. It was unforgivably rude, but her arm had seemed to move of its own volition. Ten minutes later she was on her way to Palo Alto.

"I—I'm sorry I'm late," she said to Sam. "There was a lot of traffic and I—"

"You lost your guts?" He ambled toward her, his walk slightly bow-legged, as if he were still riding his Harley.

"Of course not," she replied stiffly. "I just didn't leave myself enough time."

"Sure." He stopped in front of her and his gaze was openly admiring as it traveled over her coat, although what he found so fascinating about her old cashmere wrap-around, she couldn't imagine. "How old are you?" he asked.

Fifty years old. Fifty-five. Ready for menopause; ripe for estrogen supplements. "I was just twenty-five last month," she replied.

He smiled. "That's great. I'm twenty-four. I knew if you were too much older than me, you'd have all kinds of hang-ups about the two of us. You look closer to thirty." He took her arm and began drawing her toward the building, apparently unaware of how rude his comment was. He must have felt her resistance because he stopped. At first he looked puzzled, and then he scowled.

"You're not used to people who say what they're thinking, are you, Suzie? Well, I don't go for any dishonest bullshit. I'm real. That's one thing you have to learn about me."

"I'm real, too," she countered, which was a perfectly ridiculous thing to say. She unsettled herself even further by adding, "Nobody seems to understand that." She was appalled. Why did she keep making these personal revelations to a man she barely knew?

He studied her with his intense dark eyes. "You're something, do you know that? Classic, elegant, efficient—like a great piece of design."

She took a shaky breath, forcing herself to speak lightly so she had time to pull back into her shell. "I don't know if I like the idea of being compared to a piece of design."

"I appreciate quality. I may not have any money, but I've always appreciated the best."

And then, unexpectedly, he slipped his arm around her

shoulders and pulled her body close to his. The contact dazed her. He stared down into her face, his eyes touching her forehead, her nose, her mouth.

"Please," she whispered. "I don't think—"

"Don't think," he said, leaning forward to nuzzle her neck with his lips. "Just feel."

He was a seducer, a tempter, a peddler of patent medicines hawking his wares from the back of a Harley-Davidson, a tent-show evangelist delivering the promise of eternal life, a salesman in a sharkskin suit selling shares in the Brooklyn Bridge. He was a *hustler*. She knew all that. She knew it without question. But still she couldn't make herself draw away.

He tilted his head, and his mouth settled on hers. His lips were moist and warm, alive with activity. He was so lusty, so young, his skin so fresh and rough. Her hand crept upward until she rested her open palm on his jacket. She felt starved for the touch and taste of him. Her fingers constricted, grasping at the leather, and her lips parted involuntarily.

Their tongues tangled—hers tentative at first, his quicksilver and full of magical promises. She forgot about good manners, about reserve and dignity. She even forgot about being afraid as youth churned in her veins—springtime green and callow. Her blood was young and abundantly fed. She felt its surge. She grew weak beneath the spurt of rich new hormones flowing through her veins. He opened her mouth farther, slipped his hands inside her coat, pushed them under her sweater to touch her skin. He made love to her with his tongue. She moaned and leaned toward him.

It was he who finally pulled away.

"Christ," he muttered.

Appalled, she pressed her wrist over her lips. She had lost control again—just like the first time she and Cal had made love. Just like that long-ago June day when she'd slipped through the safe iron gates of Falcon Hill to chase a bundle of balloons.

"Relax, Suzie." His voice was soothing as he observed her consternation. "Don't get so uptight about everything. Take it easy."

"I can't take it easy. I'm not like you." With shaking

fingers she reached into her coat pocket for her car keys. "I can't do this anymore, Sam. I'll—I'll talk to my father and ask him to meet with you. I can't do anything more."

And then, because she was frightened and couldn't think clearly, she did something incredibly stupid. It was a reflex, the involuntary response of someone who has attended too many formal receptions. Before she turned to leave, she extended her hand to him.

He looked down at it and laughed. She started to snatch her hand back, but he caught it, lifted it to his mouth and bit down hard on the ends of her fingers.

She gave a small exclamation of pain.

He sucked where he had bitten, and then kissed the tips of her fingers. "You crack me up," he said huskily. "You really do."

She wanted to bolt, but before she could get away, he caught her arm in a firm grip. "Not yet, honey. I'm not letting you leave yet."

Holding her tightly, he steered her up the steps and into the breezeway that led to the building. "I really have to go," she protested.

"You don't have to do anything you don't want to. And right now, you want to stay with me."

He led her across the lobby to the auditorium doors. Without giving her time to recover, he pulled them open and thrust her into the very epicenter of nerddom—the Homebrew Computer Club.

Her thoughts still weren't coherent, and it took her a few moments to calm her breathing pattern enough so she could adjust to the activity taking place around her. She saw several hundred people gathered in clusters about the auditorium and vaguely noted that they were an odd mixture. As her head cleared, she saw that almost all of them were male—most of them in their twenties, although some were obviously teenagers. A few wore the shirts and ties of respectable businessmen, but the majority were scruffy—many of them leftovers from the counterculture. She saw unshaven cheeks and long ponytails draping the backs of faded blue work shirts. Groups huddled around electronic equipment set up on card tables placed near the stage and across the back wall of the auditorium. Directly in front of her, a pimply-faced boy who couldn't have been more than fourteen or fifteen was engaged in a hot argument with a group of men who were twice his age.

An obese character with polyester pants belted above his protruding stomach passed in front of her. "Who's got an oscilloscope?" he called out. "I need to borrow a 'scope for a couple of days."

"You can borrow mine if you've got a logic probe."

Electronic parts were being passed back and forth. Schematic drawings exchanged hands. Sam gestured toward an unkempt-looking man with a sharp nose and tangled hair. "That's John Draper. He's Captain Crunch—probably the most famous phone phreak in the world."

"Phone phreak?"

"He discovered that the toy whistles packed in Captain Crunch cereal produced the same 2600 Hertz tone that the telephone company was using to move long distance calls over its lines. He dialed a number, blew the whistle into the mouthpiece, and the call went through free. Then he started mapping telephone access codes, bouncing from one trunk line to another—hitting communications satellites all over the world. He got a kick out of taking the longest possible route to call himself—sending the call through Tokyo, India, South Africa, about four or five other places—all to make a second phone ring on the table right next to him. With the time delay, he could actually talk to himself."

Susannah couldn't help but wonder what he had to say.

"Captain Crunch knows more about building illegal blue boxes to make free telephone calls than anybody here. Just mention his name and the phone company goes nuts."

"I can imagine."

"He's on probation now."

She smiled, although she shouldn't have, because she was on close terms with several members of the Bell System's Board of Directors.

"A lot of these guys really get off on exploring the telephone system."

"Because of its elegant design?" she inquired, feeling as if she was starting to catch on.

71

"The best. Fantastic."

"Your design's shit," an acne-scarred kid told a man in a wheelchair. "A bucket of noise."

"I worked on that design for six months," the other man protested.

"It's still a bucket of noise," the kid replied.

Sam steered her toward one of the card tables where a group of onlookers was gathered around an untidy-looking man in his early twenties with a beard and thick-lensed glasses. He was peering intently at a moving pattern on a television screen. "That's Steve Wozniak. He's the only engineer I know who's as good as Yank. He works as a technician for Hewlett-Packard, and he and a buddy of his—a guy named Steve Jobs—are putting together a single-board computer, sort of like the one Yank and I have made. They've named theirs Apple. Pretty weird name, huh?"

Weird wasn't the word for it, she thought as she looked around at the strange assortment of people clamoring for information. Despite the fact that she didn't understand most of the technical references flying around her, she felt their excitement just as Sam had said she would.

"Everything is open here. Everybody shares whatever they know. It's part of the hacker heritage from the early 1960s—free exchange of information." He pointed toward the young kid arguing with three older men. "At Homebrew, people are judged by what they know, not how old they are or how much money they make. A lot different from big corporations like FBT, isn't it?"

A shadow passed across his face, and she knew that even while he urged her to set up an appointment with her father, he was regretting the necessity of dealing with FBT. His prejudice rankled.

"Let me introduce you to Yank."

As he led her toward the front of the auditorium, he called out greetings to various club members. Just like Steve Wozniak at the back of the room, Yank Yankowski was at the center of a group gazing down at a television set hooked up to a circuit board that looked like the one Sam had been carrying around in his case.

"It'll take me a few minutes to get his attention. Sometimes when he gets involved, he's—" Sam broke off as he

72

stepped in front of her and spotted the design flashing across the television screen. "Holy shit," he said, his voice full of wonder. "Yank's got color! He did it. He actually got color." He immediately forgot about her and pushed through the men clustered around the card table so he could make his way to Joseph "Yank" Yankowski.

Yank was one of the more noticeable figures in the room, Susannah decided. Probably four or five inches over six feet, he stood half a head taller than Sam. He wore thick-lensed glasses with black plastic frames and sported a short dark brown crew cut. Thin almost to the point of emaciation, he had a high sloping forehead, prominent cheekbones, and a long nose. His spare torso ended in a pair of pipe-stem legs. With twenty extra pounds of flesh, a decent haircut, contact lenses, and some clothes that didn't look as if they'd been slept in, he might have been moderately attractive. But as it was, he reminded her of someone Paige would have dismissed as a complete nerd.

Susannah watched as the demonstration continued. Sam had apparently forgotten she was there. He kept throwing questions at Yank and studying the machine on the card table. She took one of the aisle seats and watched the way his hair curled up on the shoulders of his jacket. Her father wouldn't listen to a word Sam had to say once he caught sight of that hair, not to mention the Easter Island earring. Why had she promised Sam that she would try to set up an appointment?

She didn't want to think about her father, so she concentrated on the lively chaos in the auditorium. The confusion made her remember tours she had taken through the research and development labs at the Castle. Everything was always orderly in the FBT labs. Men with neat hair and necktie knots showing at the top of their white lab coats stood at well-defined work spaces. They spoke to each other respectfully. No one shouted. Certainly no one ever called a coworker's design "a monumental piece of shit."

What she saw in front of her now verged on anarchy. Vehement arguments were still breaking out. People were climbing up on chair arms and calling out the name of a piece of equipment they wanted to borrow. She remembered the plastic ID badges she had seen on those white FBT lab coats, the special pass even her father had to display. She remembered the locked doors, the uniformed security guards, and she thought about what Sam had said concerning the hacker heritage. Here in the environment of the Homebrew Computer Club, no one seemed to have any secrets. Everywhere she looked, she saw a free exchange of information. Apparently, none of them thought about holding back what they knew for personal profit.

Sam appeared in the aisle at her side. "Susannah, come on over and meet Yank. That crazy son of a bitch got color without adding any more chips. At the last meeting, he and Wozniak talked about running it off the CPU, but nobody really believed either one of them could do it."

"Incredible," she said, although she had only the vaguest idea what Sam was talking about.

"It might take me a minute to get his attention." Sam led her forward. "Yank, this is Susannah. The one I was talking about."

Yank didn't look up from his screen.

"Yank?"

"The son of a gun still won't synch up." Yank's eyes remained glued to what he was doing.

Sam looked over at her and shrugged. "He gets pretty involved when he's working."

"I can see that."

Sam tried again. "Yank?"

"Why the heck won't it synch up?"

"Maybe we should save introductions for another time," Susannah suggested.

"Yeah, I guess so."

As they began walking toward the back of the auditorium, she wished she hadn't spoken as if they had a future. There wouldn't be another time. After what had happened between them outside, she couldn't possibly see him again.

"So what do you think?" he asked.

"It's definitely an interesting group."

"It's not the only one, either. There are others all around the country—hundreds of hardware hackers getting together to build small computers." He studied her face for a moment. "Can't you see what's happening here? This is the vanguard of the future. That's why it's so important for me to talk to your father. Did you mean it when you said you'd set up that appointment?"

"I'll try," she said reluctantly, "but he may not agree."

"I'll give you my phone number. Call me when you arrange it."

"*If* I arrange it." She hesitated, knowing he would probably laugh at her, but also knowing her father too well. "There's one thing more . . ."

"What's that?"

"If I can make the appointment, you'll—you'll be careful how you dress, won't you?"

"Afraid I'll show up like this?"

She hastily denied the truth. "Oh, no. Of course not."

"Well, you're right. I will."

Her forehead creased with alarm. "Oh, no. I'm afraid that would be a terrible mistake. My father's from another generation. He doesn't understand people who don't wear a business suit. Or men who wear earrings. And you'll need to get your hair cut." Even as she spoke the words, she felt a stab of regret. She loved his hair. It seemed a part of him—free and wild.

"I told you, Suzie. I don't go in for any bullshit. This is who I am."

"If you want to do business with my father, you'll have to learn to compromise."

"No!" He spoke the word so loudly that even in the chaos of the Homebrew Computer Club, people turned to look. "No. I don't make compromises."

"Please, not so loud."

He grabbed her arm, his fingers digging through her sleeve. "No compromises. Don't you see, Suzie? That's why people fail. It's why this country is so fucked up—why businesses are so fucked up. That's what I love about computers. They're as close as we can get to a perfect world. There aren't any compromises with computers. Something is either black or white. Octal code is absolute order. Three bits of ones or zeros. Either a bit *is* or it *isn't*."

"Life's not like that," she replied softly, thinking of all the compromises she had to make.

"That's because you won't let it be. You're a chickenshit, Suzie, you know that? You're afraid to get passionate about anything."

"That's not true."

"You pull this class A con job trying to keep anybody from seeing how scared you really are. Well, it's a waste of time when you're with me, so don't bother."

He glared at her for a moment, and then his expression softened. "Look, stop worrying about business suits and haircuts. Just get your old man to talk to me. He was a pioneer in the fifties when he whipped up those early computer patents. I know I can make him understand. I'll make him see the magic. Damn, I'll make him understand if it's the last thing I do!"

As Susannah watched the fire of his vision burn in Sam Gamble's young eyes, she almost thought he would succeed.

6

•••••••••••••••••••••••

As Sam drove north toward the FBT Castle, he didn't need to remind himself how important today's interview was. For months, doors had been closing all over Silicon Valley.

At Hewlett-Packard Steve Wozniak had shown his bosses the Apple motherboard he had designed and asked if they were interested. Hewlett-Packard had said no.

At Sam's insistence Yank had approached Nolan Bushnell at Atari with his board, but the company was too busy trying to stay on top of the video-game market. Atari had passed.

On the East Coast Kenneth Olsen, president of Digital Equipment Corporation, the leading minicomputer company in the world, couldn't understand why anyone would want a computer at home. DEC had passed.

And in Armonk, New York, mighty IBM dismissed the microcomputer as a toy with no business application. IBM saw no market. IBM passed.

One by one, all of the Big Boys had shaken their heads. All but FBT. Today, Sam was determined to make certain recent history didn't repeat itself.

The engine was pinging on the Plymouth Duster he had borrowed from Yank, and the muffler needed to be replaced, resulting in a combination of noises that was driving Sam crazy. How could Yank tolerate owning a car that was such a total piece of garbage? Sam hated the way Detroit had given up quality for the fast buck.

The upholstery on the seat next to him was torn, fast-food wrappers were scattered everywhere, and several old motors were tossed in the backseat, along with the guts from a Zenith television set. Most mysterious of all, a shoe box full of vacuum tubes lay like excavated dinosaur bones on the floor next to him. Sam couldn't imagine why Yank was carrying around a box of vacuum tubes. They'd been obsolete for two decades, ever since Bardeen, Brattain, and Shockley had taken advantage of the semiconducting qualities of silicon and invented the transistor. That invention had changed both the history of the Santa Clara Valley and Sam's life forever.

By the sixties, electronic circuits microscopically etched on tiny chips of silicon had pushed the cattle and the fruit orchards out of one of the most perfect agricultural climates in the world. Now electronics was the cash crop. Sam frequently heard the adults clucking their tongues over how the Valley used to be, but he liked living in a place that harvested semiconductors instead of apricots. He loved being part of the age of electronic miniaturization—an age where a computer circuit that would once have filled an entire room with thousands of inefficient, heat-producing vacuum tubes could now be contained on a silicon chip no larger than one of those soapy little Sen-Sen's he used to pop into his mouth when he was a kid.

He jammed the Duster's reluctant accelerator to the floor and switched lanes. It didn't take a crystal ball to see that the continuous miniaturization of electronics would inevitably lead to a small computer, so why were the established companies so apathetic? Not after today, he told himself. Thanks to Susannah's intercession, he had his audience with Joel Faulconer.

He rubbed his thumb along the steering wheel as he thought about Susannah. When he'd walked into that Homebrew meeting with her, he'd felt like a goddamned prince. But being with her wasn't just an ego trip. There was something else. When he was with her, he heard this click in his head. It was weird. This weird *click*. Like maybe some of his missing parts had just slipped into place.

The idea was odd, and he shook it off as he exited the freeway just west of Palo Alto and drove into the hills. It wasn't long before he spotted the entrance to the Castle. The FBT complex occupied 125 acres of land. Sam turned into the palm-lined drive and approached the central building. His lip curled in distaste. If he had built the place, he would have done the whole thing differently. That phony Greek revival style belonged on Wall Street, not in Northern California. And there were too many columns, too much marble. Total crap.

After a hassle with the security people over the sample case containing the computer motherboard, Sam was escorted across the lobby to the elevators. His aesthete's eye gave high marks to the paintings on exhibit in the lobby at the same time that his idealist's heart attempted to ignore the plastic visitor's badge that protruded from the pocket of his leather jacket. Once again he found himself torn between his determination to give Yank's beautiful design to the world by selling it to FBT and his distaste at the idea of turning it over to such a huge, impersonal corporation.

The receptionist on the top floor was young and attractive. Her mouth tightened at his appearance, so he let his eyes slide insolently to her breasts. Fuck her. He didn't have any use for women like her—phony sophisticates who thought that class was something they could buy at a high-priced boutique. After he gave her his name, she checked an appointment book, then led him down a corridor. He grew increasingly contemptuous. The interior decor might be first-class, but the atmosphere at the FBT offended him—the guard-dog secretaries, the elitism of the closed doors, the sterile, hushed silence. With every step, he yearned for the rowdy openness of the Homebrew Computer Club. If only he and Yank had enough money to start their own company. If only they had more options.

Susannah was sitting in a wing chair in the reception area outside Faulconer's office. As he spotted her, he heard that click in his head again. That strange, comforting click. Her auburn hair was neatly brushed back from her face and arranged in a French twist. She looked composed and costly in a beige wool dress with a single strand of pearls at her throat. The sight of her gave him a rush. He wanted to touch her, to hear the soft tones of that expensive private-school voice.

Susannah lifted her head as Sam approached. Her heart plummeted to her stomach and then catapulted back into her throat. She felt breathless and disoriented. The effect he had on her was so strong that several seconds passed before she could take in his appearance, and then she was barely able to hide her consternation. Despite what he'd said, she hadn't actually imagined that he would show up in jeans and a leather jacket for his meeting with her father. Her gaze lingered on those jeans and the intimate way they cupped him.

The secretary disappeared. She remembered how displeased Joel had been when she'd asked him to meet with Sam. He had insisted she be present for the meeting, and she suspected it was a subtle form of punishment for imposing on him. With a sinking dread and an awful exhilaration, she rose and stepped forward.

"Hello, Sam."

His eyes swept over her appreciatively, and he nodded.

She tucked her purse under her arm. As she spoke, she tried to hide the fact that her pulse was racing out of control. "My father's not pleased about this, I'm afraid. He doesn't approve of family interference in business, and he probably won't be very receptive to you."

"I'll make him receptive."

His arrogance maddened her. How could someone who was only twenty-four have so much self-confidence? "I told him you were a friend of one of the new board members at the Exploritorium." It wasn't entirely untrue. *She* was a new board member.

"I won't lie to him about us."

She gripped her hands together. Why was he being so unbending? He had catapulted into her life without invitation and upset everything. "There isn't any *us*," she said stiffly. "And sometimes lies are a kindness."

He looked at her for a moment, and then the hard lines of

his mouth softened. "Trust yourself, Suzie. Don't be so afraid of everything."

No other person had ever accused her of being afraid. Even when she was a child, people had told her how brave she was for surviving her kidnapping. How could Sam know these things about her?

Joel's secretary appeared and led them through paneled doors into her father's private office. He rose from behind his massive desk with its polished malachite top. Not by a flicker of an eyelash did he betray any reaction to Sam's long hair and informal attire. Yet even as he graciously extended his hand, Susannah felt as if she could hear his contemptuous, unvoiced scorn.

Sam took his time moving forward to return Joel's handshake. Susannah experienced an uneasy combination of dread and admiration. What kind of man wasn't intimidated by Joel Faulconer?

"Thanks for agreeing to see me," Sam said. "You won't be sorry."

Susannah inwardly winced.

"My pleasure," Joel replied.

Not waiting for an invitation, Sam began talking about Yank's design and the future of the microcomputer at the same time that he was tossing his sample case onto a chair and flipping open the latches. "I'd like to have been able to give you a full demonstration of the machine in operation, but apparently you didn't have the time." Did he linger on the last word deliberately, she wondered, or was that vaguely insulting emphasis accidental?

Susannah turned toward the wall of windows that overlooked the manmade lake outside. A series of seven stone fountains shaped like obelisks rose from the water. They represented the seven continents of the world, all of them part of the FBT empire. As she watched their spray shoot high into the sky, she wished she were anyplace but in her father's office. She hated being in a tension-ridden atmosphere. She always thought it was her responsibility to somehow make things better.

Sam took out the motherboard and pushed aside a neat stack of reports to set it on the desktop in front of Joel.

"This is the wave of the future. The heart and guts of a revolution. This machine will shift the balance of power from institutions to individuals."

Without waiting for an invitation, he launched into a technical explanation of the efficiency of the design. Her father asked a number of quietly uttered, overly polite questions. She retreated to a leather chair on the far side of the room.

"FBT has never been inclined to enter the consumer products market," Joel said mildly.

Sam dismissed this with a disdainful wave of his hand. "Haven't you been following the Altair 8800?"

"Perhaps you should fill me in."

Sam began pacing in front of the desk, filling the office with his restless energy. Even from her safe perch at the side of the room, she could feel his intensity. "A year and a half ago, *Popular Mechanics* ran a picture on its cover of the Altair 8800, this small computer about half the size of an air conditioner that can be built from a kit. The only way to get information out of it is by reading a panel of lights flashing octal code. The machine doesn't have any memory, so it can't do much, and all anybody gets for his money is a bag of parts that have to be assembled. But within three weeks the company that was manufacturing it went from near bankruptcy to having $250,000 in the bank."

Joel's eyebrows lifted, but Sam was so wrapped up in his enthusiasm that he didn't notice. "Two hundred and fifty thousand dollars! They got more orders than they could fill. People were sending money for add-on equipment that was only in the talking stages. One guy drove all the way to Albuquerque and lived in a trailer outside the company's offices while he waited for his machine."

"My, my," Joel said, shaking his head. And then he looked thoughtful. "Two hundred and fifty thousand dollars, you say?"

Sam planted his hands on the edge of Joel's desk, then leaned forward eagerly. "In only three weeks. There's an incredible market, especially when you consider the fact that the Altair is primitive compared to what Yank has designed."

Joel gazed down at the motherboard in front of him with admiration. "Yes, I can see that. And how much are you and Mister—is it 'Yankowski'? How much are the two of you asking for this design?"

Sam sat down, hesitating. "We'd want some assurance that FBT would aggressively market the machine."

"I understand."

"And we'd like to be involved with the process."

"Ah, yes. Heading up the project team, perhaps? Something like that?"

Sam looked a bit surprised, but then he nodded.

"And the price tag?" Joel inquired.

Sam leaned back in his chair and crossed one ankle over his knee. Susannah could almost see him pulling the number from the top of his head. "Fifty thousand dollars."

"I see." Joel picked up a stainless-steel letter opener. "And how much yearly revenue do you think your computer could generate for FBT once the product was established?"

"A few million, I'd guess," Sam said cautiously.

"Ah." Joel looked thoughtful. "Could you be more specific?"

"Maybe two and a half million."

"Two and a half million? Are you sure about that number?"

Sam had begun to grow wary. "I haven't done any research, if that's what you mean."

"Could it be less?"

"I suppose."

"More? Perhaps three million?"

"Possibly."

"Two point eight million?"

Sam stared at Joel for a few seconds and then slowly stood. "You're jerking me off, aren't you?"

Susannah made a soft, barely audible gasp and rose from her chair.

"Jerking you off?" Joel looked puzzled, as if he were trying to understand the meaning of the expression. "Now why would you think that?"

Sam's jaw jutted forward. "Just answer my question."

Joel scoffed. "Why would I be jerking someone off who wants to make this company two million dollars a year? That's nearly what FBT pays to have its garbage collected."

Sam's complexion turned chalky.

"You don't have the slightest idea what you're talking about, Mr. Gamble. You have no idea of the value of what you're selling or of its worth to this corporation. It's obvious that you haven't done your homework, because if you had, you certainly wouldn't be wasting my time with this meeting."

Joel had been toying with a panel of switches set into the top of his desk, and now he began to press them. Slowly he turned his head to look out the window. Sam followed the direction of his eyes and watched as the seven columns of water rising from the stone fountains outside began to still, one by one. Like God, Joel Faulconer could command the forces of the universe. The show of power wasn't lost on Sam.

As the last column of water disappeared and the lake grew still, Joel resumed speaking. "I have no interest at all in someone who comes to me with a story about a bankrupt company making a profit of $250,000. I'm not even interested in a profit of two million dollars. Now if you had said you were going to make me a hundred million, I might have listened."

"You son of a bitch."

Joel's hand moved and all seven fountains once again sprang to life. "I'm not turning you down because you're crude and arrogant. I'm not even turning you down because you didn't have the common courtesy to get a haircut before you came to see me. I'm turning you down because you don't think big enough. Good day, Mr. Gamble."

For a few seconds Sam didn't move. Then he snatched up the motherboard and began walking toward the door. Before he got there, however, he stopped and turned back to Joel. "I almost feel sorry for you, Faulconer. You're even stupider than I thought you'd be." Then he left the office.

The blood had drained from Susannah's face and her skin was ashen. As Joel turned to her, he could clearly see her distress, but he didn't take pity on her. "I don't care how many favors you owe your friends. Don't ever impose on me like this again."

"I—I didn't mean to impose," she said shakily. "I know he was unforgivably rude, but—" Joel's eyes gave her a look so imperious that she faltered. How could she defend Sam after what he'd said? But her father had been rude, too—deliberately baiting Sam.

"It's just—you were rather hard on him," she finished lamely.

"Are you actually defending him?"

"No, I—"

He tilted back his head so that he seemed to be looking at her from a great distance, and the acute hostility in his expression made her feel ill. She'd had the audacity to question her father's authority, and now she would be punished.

Without saying another word, he punched a button on his intercom. "My daughter is leaving now. Would you please see her out."

The endless winter of Joel Faulconer's disapproval had begun.

Susannah had watched others endure her father's icy silences, but she had seldom had to endure one herself—and never one of this duration. As the weeks passed and the time for the wedding drew nearer, Susannah began to feel as if someone had placed a curse on her. Despite her repeated apologies and her attempts to restore her father's good mood, he remained silent and condemning.

Cal had to be in Europe for several weeks on business, so he wasn't around to act as a buffer, and each day seemed to bring another last-minute crisis with the wedding arrangements. Twice she picked up the phone to call Sam Gamble and tell him how she felt about the way he had behaved, but both times she hung up before she dialed. It was infinitely better not to talk to him again. Infinitely better not to think about either his rudeness or his crazy enthusiasm for putting computers in people's houses right along with their stereos and television sets.

Her father finally forgave her, but only after he delivered a stinging lecture about imposition and disrespect. A newly cynical voice inside her whispered that he wouldn't have relented so quickly if he hadn't needed her to accompany him on a week-long trip to Paris. It would inconvenience him to entertain French cabinet members without an official hostess at his side.

In Paris they stayed at Joel's favorite hotel, the Crillon, an imposing graystone edifice on the northwest corner of the Place de la Concorde. The evening they arrived, Cal appeared at their suite to escort them to a reception at the American embassy, located nearby on the Avenue Gabriel. Since Joel was present along with several of his aides, her reunion with Cal was warm but restrained. They had little time to talk during the reception at the embassy, but as they were leaving, Cal gave her a mischievous I've-got-a-secret smile.

"We have some celebrating to do tonight," he said. "I've made dinner reservations for us at the Tour."

Tour l'Argent was one of the most famous restaurants in the world, but as Susannah settled into the limousine, she felt restless and suggested they go someplace that wasn't quite so formal. Her mind drifted back to a rainy afternoon she had spent in Paris some years ago.

"Would you mind going to La Coupole in Montparnasse? I know it's just a brasserie and we're overdressed, but it'll be fun."

He gave her one of those skeptically indulgent looks she sometimes received from her father. "You're not in one of those crazy Montparnasse sort of moods, are you?" The creases at the corners of his splendid blue eyes deepened as he teased her.

She sensed that he was excited about something, and she smiled back. He undoubtedly had a story he'd been saving for her about some brilliant maneuver he had pulled off in his negotiations with the French manufacturers. He was so handsome, so perfect. Despite the difference in their ages, he was everything she could possibly want in a husband. They had common interests, similar backgrounds.

Impulsively, she leaned over and pressed her lips to his in a fierce, possessive kiss. He returned the kiss for only a moment before he drew away and gave her a meaningful glance toward the back of the driver's head. Patting her on the knee, he began to speak about an incident that had happened at the reception.

His rejection hurt her. Cal was a stickler about appearances, and most of the time she didn't mind. But they were in Paris. Couldn't he let down his guard just for the evening? As the neon sign of La Coupole came into view and Cal chatted about the embassy reception, she envisioned Sam Gamble sitting beside her in the limo. Sam—pushing her down on the plush seat and slipping his hands up under the skirt of her gown. Sam, discovering that she was naked beneath—naked, open, ready to receive him. With Sam, she could be another sort of woman, someone sexy and sultry, loose and wild.

She firmly pushed the image from her mind. A few minutes later, as they walked into La Coupole, the conversation that floated between them was as light and aimless as a cloud of soap bubbles.

For half a century La Coupole had attracted a diverse group of artists, intellectuals, students, and assorted eccentrics. Henry Miller had played chess with Anaïs Nin beneath its lofty ceiling. Jean-Paul Sartre had eaten a late lunch with Simone de Beauvoir at the same corner table nearly every day. Chagall and Picasso had dined there, as had Hemingway and Fitzgerald. But as Susannah took her seat across from Cal, she thought of the legends she had heard of the brasserie's nascent days during the 1920s, when Kiki de Montparnasse, Paris's premier playgirl, had stuck a rose between her teeth and cavorted nearly naked in the fountain that sat in the center of the dining room.

"The fountain was turned into a giant flower vase decades ago," she said. Cal looked up from the menu he had been studying. She smiled self-consciously and nodded toward the center of the room. "That giant flower vase was originally a fountain, but the restaurant had to drain it because the patrons kept swimming in it."

He nodded politely and asked her if she would prefer lamb curry or fish. "Honestly, Susannah, I can't believe we're giving up duck at the Tour for such ordinary food."

"The lamb curry will be fine," she replied quickly. As they waited for their order to arrive, she gazed around her, but the magic was gone and she could no longer recapture La Coupole of her imagination. Now she saw only a noisy dining room full of ordinary people. There was no sign of a Modigliani or a Camus. No one who resembled Josephine Baker was walking through the door leading a pet lion cub on a diamond-studded leash. Where are you, Kiki de Montparnasse? she thought. I wish I could see a woman free enough to jump into a fountain without thinking about what people would say.

Cal reached across the table to take her hand. "I had planned a more romantic setting to tell you this, but I may not have another chance." With his thumb, he covered the diamond on her engagement ring. It was exactly one carat because both of them had agreed that a larger stone would be ostentatious. Less is always more.

"It's actually your father's surprise, and you're going to have to pretend to hear it for the first time when he announces it, but it's so extraordinary that I wanted to give you a chance to prepare yourself."

"Our mysterious wedding present?" she asked. He nodded and his smile broadened.

Ever since the engagement, Joel had been hinting at a spectacular gift. She had overheard part of a telephone conversation he'd had with one of his attorneys, and told Cal that she suspected Joel was deeding them the charming vacation house he owned on Maui. It was a valuable piece of property, and both of them had been moved by the possibility of such generosity.

"You were right about the house," he told her.

"I thought so."

"Except you picked the wrong one."

"Oh?" She took a sip from her wineglass. "It can't be London. He needs that for business. It must be the house at Pebble Beach, although it's hard to imagine him parting with it. He loves living on the golf course."

"It's not Pebble Beach." Cal clasped her hand between both of his. She could not remember seeing him look so pleased. He chuckled and his blue eyes gleamed with triumph.

"Susannah, Joel is giving us Falcon Hill."

7

● ●

The next evening over thin stalks of white asparagus and glasses of finely aged Vouvray, Joel made the announcement that he was deeding them Falcon Hill as a wedding gift. He told them that he wanted to spend more time at Pebble Beach, that he no longer needed such a large house. And then, casually, he suggested that Susannah convert the guest house at Falcon Hill into something comfortable for him when he was in town.

She had barely slept the night before, and now her heart felt as if it were shrinking in her chest. He was trapping her. Until that moment she hadn't realized how much she had been looking forward to living independently from her father. Why hadn't she guessed that he would want to continue to have her at his beck and call? Now, by giving them Falcon Hill as a wedding gift, he had made certain that her marriage wouldn't inconvenience him, that she would still be available to do his bidding.

And then she was filled with guilt at her selfishness. Joel Faulconer had given her everything. He was the shining prince who had rescued her. How could she be so ungrateful? Throughout the rest of the meal she found herself thinking about debts of love and wondering how they were ever repaid. She loved her father very much, but did she owe him her life?

Later that evening, when Cal took her to her suite, she tried to discuss her feelings with him. He drew her into his arms and rubbed her back as if he were comforting a child. "I think you're overreacting, darling. I know he can sometimes be domineering, but I'll be there to make certain he doesn't take advantage of you. Let's not cast a shadow over such an extraordinary gift. Falcon Hill is worth millions."

"Is that all you can think about? How much Falcon Hill is worth?"

He stepped away from her, his face mirroring his surprise at her outburst. And then his eyes grew as chilly as the silver streak that shot through his hair. "You've deliberately chosen to misunderstand me. I don't appreciate being snarled at."

She pressed her fingertips to her temple. "I'm sorry. I guess I'm just tired."

"I'm tired, too, but I don't snap at you."

"You're right. It was unforgivable."

But Cal refused to accept her apology. Giving her a stony look, he stalked from her suite. Susannah felt the familiar tightness in her stomach as one more male chose to punish her with silence.

She returned to San Francisco feeling as if something hard and cold had taken up permanent lodging inside her.

After his confrontation with Joel Faulconer, Sam had jumped on his bike and headed for San Diego. Although he had a couple of friends there, he made no effort to contact any of them because he didn't want company. Instead, he played Breakout in the arcades, slept on the beach, and woke up at night with the cold sweats. All he could think about was what a prick Faulconer was. No matter how hard he tried, he couldn't blot out the image of Susannah standing there watching her father make an asshole out of him.

Day after day he got angrier with Yank. This was Yank's problem, not his. Sam was tired of playing father and mother to a guy who couldn't drive three blocks without getting lost. Yank should be out hustling his own design. But

Yank couldn't see any further than his next hack, and Sam knew that his friend didn't have the most rudimentary understanding of the significance of what he was doing. And then one night while Sam was playing his dozenth game of Breakout, he saw Yank's hands in his mind—the incredible genius of those hands—and his anger dissolved.

That was when he realized that Joel Faulconer was right about him. He hadn't even started to think big enough. He'd been so wrapped up in the idea of selling Yank's design to somebody else that he hadn't listened to the voice inside him telling him that handing Yank's genius over to a fat-cat company went against everything he believed in.

He got on his bike that same night and headed north. He was going to start his own company. No matter what it took, no matter what sacrifices he had to make, he was going to do it.

And the closer he got to San Francisco, the more he found himself thinking about Susannah. He kept remembering all those leggy San Diego girls with their short shorts and those skimpy halter tops that outlined their nipples. Wherever he went, they had given him sexy come-ons, but even though many of them were more beautiful than Susannah, he kept thinking about how cheap they looked.

He hated imitations. All of his life he had been surrounded by inferiority—the shoddy little house he had grown up in, the incompetent public school teachers with no tolerance for a sullen, gifted rebel who had asked all the wrong questions, the father who spent every evening staring at the television screen and telling his son that he was a loser. For as long as he could remember, Sam had dreamed of surrounding himself with beautiful objects and exceptional people. And now, making the best microcomputer had become inexorably linked in his mind with having the best woman. By the time he reached the Valley, he was convinced that if he could have Susannah Faulconer, he could also have everything else that was missing from his life.

The next day he quit his job and packed up the computer board, the television—everything he needed to demonstrate Yank's machine. That same afternoon he began to make the rounds of Silicon Valley electronics shops. No one was interested.

By the second day, he was seething with frustration. "Just let me set it up," he told a Santa Clara store owner. "Let me give you a demo. It'll only take a few minutes."

"I don't have a few minutes. Sorry. Another time maybe."

The following day he had his first piece of luck. One of the store managers agreed to watch Sam's demonstration and even marveled over the elegance of Yank's design. Then he shook his head. "It's a neat little machine, no doubt about it. But who'd buy it? People aren't interested in a little computer. What are they going to do with one?"

The question drove Sam crazy. People figured out what to do with a computer—that was all. How could he explain something so rudimentary? "Hack around," he said. "Play some games."

"Sorry. Not interested."

On the fourth day the machine never made it out of the trunk of Yank's Duster because Sam couldn't find one store owner who would agree to see it. "Let me just show you what it can do," he pleaded. "Look, it'll only take a few minutes."

"Listen, kid. I'm busy. I got customers."

In an electronics store near Menlo Park, Sam finally lost his temper. He slapped his hand down on the countertop so hard he knocked a box of switches to the floor. "I've got a machine here that's going to change the future of the world, but you're telling me that you're too goddamn busy to spare a few lousy minutes to look at it!"

The owner took a quick step backward. "Get out of here before I call the cops!"

Sam drew back his boot and kicked a hole through the side of the counter. "I don't give a fuck! Call them! Let's see if you're smart enough to dial the fucking telephone!"

Then he stalked out.

Two weeks before Susannah's wedding, some of the FBT executive wives gave her a shower. It was nearly midnight when she got home. She swung the Mercedes around the east wing of the house toward the garage. The trunk was loaded with bridal lingerie and monogrammed towels. With the exception of a nymphet third wife, Susannah had been the youngest person there, yet they had all treated her as if she were their contemporary. Several of them had started talking about the movie stars they'd had crushes on when they were young—Clark Gable, Alan Ladd, Charles Boyer. They'd all looked at her strangely when she'd mentioned Paul McCartney.

As she reached up to punch the garage door control that was attached to the visor, she found herself longing for the days when her fantasies had starred a chubby-cheeked Beatle instead of a long-haired biker. She jabbed the control again. The garage door refused to budge, and she remembered that it had stopped working the day before and been disconnected. Her head was aching, and she rubbed her temples. If only she were sleeping better, she wouldn't be so edgy. But instead of sleeping, she kept staring at the ceiling and replaying every encounter she'd had with Sam. She reconstructed from memory exactly what he'd said to her and what she'd said in return. But most of all, she remembered the way he had kissed her.

Sagging back into the seat, she pressed her eyes shut and let that forbidden image wash over her. Once again she felt his brash young mouth settling over her own. Her bottom lip grew slack as she relived the moment his tongue had entered her mouth. She expanded the memory from what had happened to what had not, and imagined the feel of his naked chest against her bare breasts. Her breath made a soft rasping sound in the quiet interior of the car.

With a great strength of will, she forced her eyes open and fumbled for the door handle. She had to quit doing this. She was becoming obsessed with him, and she had to pull herself together. As she got out of the car and walked toward the garage door, she promised herself that she would stop dwelling on what had happened. She would stop thinking about him at all.

A rustling noise in the trees penetrated her thoughts. She glanced uneasily over her shoulder, but the outside lights hadn't been left on and she couldn't see anything. Walking a little faster, she stepped into the path of the Mercedes headlights and reached for the garage door handle.

"Enjoy your party?"

She gasped, and spun around in time to see Sam coming out of the shadows, both thumbs tucked into the side pockets of his jeans. Blood coursed through her veins at the sight of him. She pressed her hand to her throat and took a deep breath. "What are you doing here? You scared me."

"Good."

"How did you get through the gates?"

"Gadgets are a hobby of mine," he said sarcastically. "Or have you forgotten?"

"Sam, I—I'm tired. I don't want any confrontations."

He scowled at her. "How was your wedding shower? I've been reading about all the festivities in the papers. Why the hell haven't you put a stop to it?"

"Put a stop to it?" It was as if he had suggested she grow another head. Didn't he understand that once something like this was set in motion, there was no turning back? She was trapped. No, not trapped. Of course she wasn't trapped. She wanted to marry Cal. Cal was perfect for her.

"It's not right," he exclaimed. "You're locking the door on the two of us before we've had any chance at all. God, you're a chickenshit. If my own guts weren't aching so bad, I'd almost feel sorry for you."

"There isn't any two of us," she said fiercely. "You asked me to help arrange a meeting with my father. I did. That's all."

"You're a liar." He walked over to the Mercedes, then ducked his head inside and turned off the ignition. His hand lingered for a moment on the leather upholstery before he straightened to face her. She thought uneasily of her father. His bedroom was in the far wing of the house, but what if he heard them?

"I'm going to start my own company, Suzie, and I want you with me."

"What?"

"Any day now I'll get the first order. It's starting. Everything's starting right now."

"I'm glad for you, but—"

"It's starting. *Right now!*" Each part of his face had gone rigid with intensity. "Stop being so scared. Build my dream with me. Forget about your wedding. We can change the world. You and me. We can do it together."

"What are you talking about? I want you to leave. Don't you see? We're not anything alike. We don't understand each other." Even as she said it, she knew the words were a lie. He could read her mind. He saw inside her when no one else could.

"Don't you think I'm good enough for you? Is that it?"

"No! I'm not a snob. I'm just—"

"I need you. I need you to help me get my company started."

He speared her with his dark, exacting eyes. She wanted to weave her fingers through his hair, touch his silver tongue with her own. Desperately, she tried to make him understand. "I'm getting married. And I don't know anything about starting a company. Why would you want my help?"

He could barely explain it to himself, let alone her. "I feel good when you're around. You remind me of what it's all about. Quality, elegance, classic design."

"Is that all I am to you? A piece of design?"

"That's only part of it. There's something between us— something strong and right. Get rid of that deadhead you're engaged to. If you loved him so much, you wouldn't have turned into a firecracker when I kissed you. There's a whole world out there. Don't you want a little bit of it?"

"You don't know anything about my life."

"I know that you want a hell of a lot more from it than you're getting."

"I'm getting a lot," she retorted, determined to hurt him. "Like that Mercedes that you keep touching. And Falcon Hill. My father is giving us this house as a wedding gift."

"Is the house going to make good love to you at night?"

Stunned, she stared at him.

"Is it, Suzie?" His voice dropped, grew low and husky. He walked closer to her, and she took an involuntary step back, only to bump into the garage door behind her. "Both of us know how much you want that, don't we? Will the house love you real good? Will it hold you at night and fill you up and make you moan?" Reaching out, he pushed his hand inside her jacket and rubbed the skin at her waist through the soft knit of her dress. "Will the house make you cry out real deep in your throat? Have you ever cried out like that for a man? Fast little pants? Whimpers?"

"Stop. Please don't."

"I could make you cry out like that for me."

He pushed his hips into hers and pressed her against the garage door. She saw the flicker of the silver earring through the strands of his hair and felt that he was hard. The dark eroticism she no longer seemed able to control swept through her like wildfire. "Don't," she whispered. "Don't do that."

He leaned forward to brush his lips along her neck. She turned her head to the side, moaning softly. His hand moved upward over her rib cage and cupped her breast through the dress. He laughed softly and touched the nipple. "Can that house make you come?"

It was too much. With a cry that came from the deepest part of her, she pushed away from him. "Don't do this to me! Leave me alone!" And then she fled into the house.

She moved through the next few days in a daze. Her father and Cal seemed to attribute her distraction to bridal nerves, and both were exceptionally considerate. One morning as her father was leaving for an overnight business trip, he hugged her and said, "You know how much I appreciate all the ways you help me, don't you? I know I don't say it often enough, but I love you, sweetheart."

Her eyes misted at the tenderness in his voice. She thought of her secret meetings with Sam, the way she had deceived him, and was overwhelmed with guilt. At that moment, she silently vowed to be the best daughter in the world.

But the vow was easier made than kept. With only a week left until her wedding, Susannah lay in the darkness and watched the illuminated numbers on her digital clock flip to 2:18. She couldn't eat, she couldn't sleep. Her chest felt heavy, as if a great weight were pressing down on her.

Without warning, the phone on her bedside table jangled. She snatched it up and held it to her chest for a moment. Then she cradled it to her ear. "Hi," she whispered, grateful to have a partner in insomnia. "You couldn't sleep either?"

But it wasn't Cal. It was Conti Dove—Conti, Paige's lover, calling to tell Susannah that Paige had been arrested several hours before at an all-night grocery store and he didn't have enough money to bail her out of jail. Susannah pressed her eyes shut for a moment, trying to imagine what else could go wrong. Then, being careful not to wake her father, she threw on the first clothes she could grab and left the house.

Paige was being held at a downtown police station on the fringes of San Francisco's crime-infested Western Addition. Conti was waiting by the front door. Susannah had only met him once before, but she had no trouble recognizing him. Low-slung chinos, sleepy bedroom eyes with lids at half mast, wiry dark hair. He didn't look like a candidate for Mensa, but he was definitely sexy in an earthy sort of way.

He slipped his hands from the pockets of a red Forty-Niners' windbreaker and walked toward her. "Uh, yeah—listen, I'm sorry I had to bother you. Paige'll probably kill me when she finds out, but I couldn't leave her in jail."

"Of course you couldn't." Shouldering her purse, Susannah followed him into the station, where she posted Paige's bond, handling everything as efficiently as if she did this kind of thing all the time. She was courteous to the police officers and did what she could to keep the arrest from ending up in the newspapers. She made polite conversation with Conti, but all the time she wanted to cry from a combination of exhaustion and rage. Her sister had been arrested for shoplifting. Her beautiful sister, child of one of the wealthiest men in California, had been caught slipping two cans of cat food into her purse.

"Why, Conti?" she asked, as they took their seats on a scratched wooden bench that lined one wall of a claustrophobically narrow hallway. "Why would Paige do something like this?"

"I dunno."

Normally, Susannah would have let it go at that, but something had happened to her in these past two months that had made her impatient with polite social evasions, so she pressed him. "If she needed money, I would have given it to her."

He looked embarrassed. "She doesn't like to take money from you." Shifting his weight on the bench, he crossed his ankle over his knee and then uncrossed it. "I dunno. We thought we was going to get this contract with Azday Records. Paige was all excited. And then a couple of weeks ago, this guy, this Mo Geller, backed out. He heard another group play and he said they had a better sound. Paige took it pretty hard."

Susannah asked several more questions, but Conti was uncommunicative. Finally, they lapsed into silence. Fifteen minutes passed. Conti got up and wandered over to a water cooler. Half an hour went by. Susannah had to go to the bathroom, but she was afraid to leave the hallway. Conti bummed a cigarette from an empty-faced teenager.

"I'm not supposed to smoke, you know," he finally said. "My voice."

"Yes. I understand."

"They got her in this holding cell."

"I know."

"You don't think there would be, like, guys or anything in there with her? Givin' her trouble."

"I don't think so. I'm sure they separate men and women." Why was she so sure? She had never been in a police station.

"She stole cat food," he said suddenly. "She's in jail because she stole two cans of cat food."

"Yes. That's what they said."

He dropped his cigarette and ground it into the linoleum with the toe of a leather sneaker. When he lifted his head, he looked as baffled and unhappy as a child. "See, the thing of it is—we don't have a cat."

At that moment, Paige came through the door. Her jeans were ripped at the knee. Her pretty blond hair hung in tangles around her face. She looked tired, young, and scared. Conti rushed toward her, but before he got there she spotted Susannah. Paige's shoulders stiffened. She lifted her head defiantly. "What's *she* doing here?"

"I'm sorry, hon," Conti said. "I—I couldn't pay the bond."

"You shouldn't have called her. I told you never to call her."

As Susannah stood, she found herself remembering the chocolate-covered cherries she had tried to smuggle to Paige when she got in trouble as a child.

"I don't need you here," Paige said belligerently. "Go back where you came from."

The hostility in her sister's face made Susannah feel ill.

Why did Paige hate her so much? What did everyone want from her? She tried so hard to please them all, but whatever she did never seemed to be enough. She slipped her hand into the pocket of her trench coat and squeezed hard, digging the nails into her palm so she wouldn't lose control. "Paige, come home with me tonight," she said calmly. "Let me put you to bed. We can talk in the morning."

"I don't want to talk. I want to get laid. Come on, Conti. Let's get out of here."

"Sure, honey. Sure." He looped his arm around her shoulders and pulled her protectively to him. With her upper body turned into Conti's chest, she walked awkwardly.

Susannah stepped forward. She meant to tell Paige that they had to talk, that they couldn't just forget something like this had happened. She would be logical, reasonable, choose her words carefully. But the soft words that came from her mouth weren't the ones she had planned at all.

"Paige, I don't know if you remember, but I'm getting married on Saturday. It would mean a lot to me if you were there." At first Susannah didn't think Paige had heard. But then, just before Conti led her through the door, her sister gave a nearly imperceptible nod.

The electronics shop was located in Cupertino just off Stevens Creek Boulevard. Sam thought he knew every shop in the Valley, but Z.B. Electronics was new. As he pulled up outside, he spotted a group of three teenage boys approaching the shop. He immediately tagged them as "wireheads" —the name high school kids gave to the boys who spend all their time in the school electronics lab. When Sam was in high school, he had hung out with both the "wireheads" and "freaks," the kids who were caught up in the counterculture. The fact that he didn't stick to one group had confused everybody.

Acting on impulse, Sam got out of the car and opened the trunk of the Duster. He called out to the boys, "Hey, help me carry this stuff inside, will you?"

A pudgy, long-haired kid detached himself from the group and walked forward. "What do you have?"

"A microcomputer," Sam replied casually, as if everybody in the Valley drove around with a microcomputer in the trunk.

"No shit! Hey, guys, he's got a micro in his trunk." The kid turned to Sam and his face was alive with excitement. "Did you build it?"

Sam handed him one of the boxes of equipment and picked up the heavy television himself. Another boy slammed the trunk lid. "I helped a friend of mine design it. He's the best."

As they walked toward the shop, the boys began peppering him with questions.

"What kind of microprocessor did you use?"

"A 7319 from Cortron."

"That's shit," one of them protested. "Why aren't you running it off an Intel 8008 like the Altair?"

"The 8008 is old news. The 7319 is more powerful."

"What do you think of the IMSAI 8080?" the pudgy kid asked, referring to a new microcomputer that was rapidly challenging the Altair's supremacy.

"IMSAI's nothing more than a rip-off of the Altair," Sam said derisively. "Same old stuff. Have you ever taken one apart? Total shit. A bucket of noise."

One of the boys rushed in front of Sam to open the door. "But if you're using another microprocessor, none of the Altair equipment will work with it."

"Who cares? We've done everything better."

As they walked inside Z.B. Electronics, an enormously obese man with yellow hair and pink watery eyes glanced up at them from behind the counter. Sam stopped in his tracks. As he looked past the man, his stomach did a flip-flop, and the television in his arms suddenly seemed as light as a box of microchips. No wonder the kids were attracted to this store. On two rows of shelving directly behind the man's head rested a dozen Altair microcomputers.

Sam Gamble had hit pay dirt.

"Chamber of Commerce weather," Joel kept saying the morning of the wedding. "It's Chamber of Commerce weather."

Susannah forced herself to take a bite of dry toast while she stared through the dining room window at the sun-spangled June day and watched the gardeners tying the last of the white ribbon festoons in the trees.

Her father glanced up from his newspaper, a man in complete command of his world. "Could I have more coffee, dear?"

As she refilled his cup, she felt tired and worn, like an old lady with all the drama of life behind her.

The woman who was coordinating the wedding arrived shortly before noon, and for the next few hours she and Susannah busied themselves double-checking arrangements that had already been triple-checked. She sat for the hairdresser who arrived at two, but the style he arranged was too fussy. After he left, she brushed it out and made a simple coil at the nape of her neck. At three o'clock she put on her antique lace dress and fastened a little Juliet cap to her head. While she secured the Bennett family choker around her neck, she watched through the window as the guests arrived. And then, when it was time, she went downstairs.

"My little girl," Joel whispered as she approached. "My perfect little girl."

Moments later the trumpets sounded, heralding the beginning of the ceremony.

Cal was smiling at her as she approached. The minister began to speak, and she tugged surreptitiously on the pearls. Why couldn't she breathe? Why was the choker so tight?

The ceremony continued, and the noise of the lawn mower that had been bothering her grew louder. People were turning their heads and Cal's eyebrows drew together. The minister had just begun to address her when she finally recognized the sound for what it was. Her gasp was drowned out by the noise of the Harley shooting into the garden.

"Suzie!"

She spun around and saw his black hair flying in the breeze like a pirate's flag. He looked magnificent and appallingly dangerous—a dark angel, a wicked messiah.

"What's the matter?" he called out. "Forget to send me an invitation?"

As he taunted her from the seat of his Harley, the long-ago chant of the balloon man began to beat in her ears.

"Come on, Suzie. Climb up on the back of my bike."

She pulled away from Cal and pressed her hands over her

ears. "Go away! I won't listen to you! I'm not listening to you!"

But Sam was a man with a vision, a child of the middle class, immune to the rules of upper-class propriety, and he paid no attention to her entreaty. She stumbled away from the altar, trying to distance herself from all of them.

"Follow me, babe. Leave all this and come with me."

She wouldn't do it. She wouldn't go to the end of the drive. She wouldn't unlock the iron gates. She was a good girl. Always a good girl. She wouldn't ever, ever again run off with a clown-faced balloon man.

All my balloons for free. Come and follow me.

Her father was untangling himself from the rope garland that cordoned off the end of his row, coming to rescue her, to protect her and keep her. To keep her at Falcon Hill. To keep her with Cal. She saw Paige's shocked face, Cal's appalled one. She clawed at her neck so she could breathe, but the choker was no longer there. A sprinkling of pearls had scattered over the toes of her wedding pumps.

"Hop on my bike, babe. Hop on my bike and follow me."

She felt the pull of his sun, the light of his vision, the blazing glory of his challenge. A yearning for freedom burst inside her like a rocket-born rainbow. She heard the rage of proper angels in the outbursts of the people around her, but the call of a leather-clad devil spurred her on. No more. No less is more. Not ever. From now on more is more.

She began racing toward him, flying along the pristine white runner and crumpling it beneath her feet. One of her shoes came off. She kicked off the other. The little Juliet cap blew away, tugging free her careful hair.

Paige's voice rang out over all the rest. Paige—proper Paige—calling out in horror at the unforgivable act her sister was committing. "Susannah!"

Joel shouted her name and rushed forward. Paige cried out again.

Sam Gamble threw back his head and laughed at them all. A strand of black hair blew in front of his mouth and stuck to his bottom lip. He gunned the Harley. Held out his hand. Come on, babe. Come-on, come-on, come-on.

She lifted the lace skirt of her dress high up on her thighs, revealing long thin legs and a flash of garter blue. Her auburn hair flew out behind her. She reached for him. Reached for her destiny and felt his tight grip pulling her into the future as she straddled the Harley.

She wrapped her arms around his waist and pressed her breasts against his jacket. The Harley roared to life between her thighs, its vibrations shooting high up inside her, filling her full to bursting with new life.

At that moment she didn't care if all the balloons in the world would someday burst around her. She only cared that she was finally free.

8

●●●●●●●●●●●●●●●●●●●●●●●

For several moments the wedding guests stood frozen like well-dressed figures in a modern *tableau vivant*. Cal Theroux was the first to move. White-faced and humiliated, he shoved a path through the crowd and disappeared. Joel, looking neither right nor left, made his way to the house with rigid dignity.

Paige was too stunned to move. The breeze picked up a cluster of feathers from her boa and blew them against her cheek, but she didn't feel anything. Her world had tilted, shifting everything it contained so that it could never resettle in the same position.

She shook her head slightly as she tried to reconcile all that she knew about her cool, perfect sister with the woman who had just fled her wedding on the back of a Harley. As she stared at the crumpled aisle runner and the place where the grass had been trampled down, she realized that she hadn't known her sister at all.

The idea terrified her. She immediately shoved it away and let a clean, pure surge of anger take its place.

Susannah had lied to all of them. She had a secret life, a secret self that none of them had ever suspected. That image of cool perfection had been a sham. How clever her sister was, how deceitful. She had manipulated them so that she remained the favored daughter while her younger sister was the outcast.

Paige nurtured her anger, clasping it to her breast and hugging it close. She let it fill every pore so that there was no room left for fear, so that no place remained inside her where she might hide other lies—lies about herself.

Sounds began to work their way into her consciousness—exclamations, muted conversation. The guests had formed animated groups, and at any moment they would begin to descend on her. They would ply her with questions she couldn't answer and pour buckets full of pity over her head. She couldn't bear it. She had to get away.

Her battered VW was parked in the motorcourt among the Jags and Rollses, and she wove her way along the perimeter of the garden toward it. But before she slipped around the corner of the back wing, she slowed and looked back.

The groups were still huddled together. Heads were moving back and forth as everyone offered an interpretation of what had just happened. She waited for the men to reach for their pens so they could calculate the effect that this might have on the price of FBT stock.

As she watched them, she could feel the blood rushing through her veins like a river on a rampage. Her ears were ringing. This was it! This was what she'd been waiting for. All her life she'd been waiting for this chance.

Hesitantly, she slipped her tawdry boa from her shoulders and let it fall behind an urn of roses. Then, with her heart in her throat, she began moving toward the guests. When she reached the nearest group, she gathered her strength and spoke.

"It seems a shame for all this food to go to waste. Why don't we move toward the reception tent?"

Everyone turned to her, surprised.

"Why, Paige!" one of the women exclaimed. "Poor dear. What an awful thing."

"None of us can believe it," another interjected. "Susannah, of all people."

Paige heard herself replying in a smooth, careful voice that sounded a bit like her sister's. "She's been under a lot of pressure lately. I— We can only hope she gets the professional help she needs."

An hour later, with the small of her back aching from the tension of fielding their questions, she said good-bye to the last of the guests and entered Falcon Hill. The house enveloped her—comforting and suffocating at the same time. She walked through the deserted rooms on the first floor in search of her father and then climbed the stairs. The door to her old bedroom was shut. Nothing was there for her and she felt no temptation to go in.

Susannah's room was neat as always. The suitcases for the honeymoon waited by the door like abandoned children. Paige stepped into the adjoining bath. The marble tub and sink were immaculate. No auburn strands of hair clung to the sides, no smears of makeup spoiled the ebony surface. It was as if her sister never used the room, as if she somehow managed to emerge into the world clean and perfect— without any effort on her part.

Her father's bedroom was as orderly as Susannah's and just as empty. She found him in a small study at the back of the house, which overlooked the gardens. He was standing at the window, staring down on the shambles of his daughter's wedding.

Her stomach pitched. "Daddy?"

He turned his head and gave her a calm inquisitive stare, as if nothing of any import had happened. "Yes, Paige?"

Her fragile self-confidence deserted her. "I—I just— wanted to see if you were—were all right."

"Of course. Why wouldn't I be?"

But as she looked more closely, she could see his pallid complexion and the harsh brackets at the corners of his mouth. His weakness gave her a sudden spurt of strength. "Would you like me to fix you a drink?"

He gazed at her for a moment as if he were making up his mind about something, and then he nodded stiffly. "Yes, why don't you do that?"

She turned to leave, only to have him speak again.

"And Paige. That dress is quite ugly. Would you mind changing it?"

Her first reaction to his criticism was the familiar defensive surge of anger, but almost immediately the anger faded. He wasn't sending her away. He wanted her to stay. Now that Susannah was gone, she wasn't an outcast anymore.

It took her only seconds to make her decision. Slipping out into the hallway, she went to Susannah's room and removed the thrift-shop dress. Five minutes later she descended the stairs wearing one of her sister's soft Italian knits.

The world flew past Susannah's eyes like a carousel spinning out of control. The wind tore at her hair, snarling it around her head, whipping it against Sam's cheeks. Her dress had ridden up, and the tops of her legs chafed against the rough denim of his jeans, but she didn't notice. She had moved to a point beyond simple sensation. As she clung to his waist, she prayed the wild ride would never end. The motorcycle was a magic chariot that held time at bay. As long as the machine kept moving, there was no yesterday, no today, no tomorrow.

Sam seemed to understand her need to fly. He did not take them due south, but zigzagged across the peninsula, showing her a familiar world from a different perspective. The San Andreas Reservoir flashed by, and later the bay. They roared through quiet neighborhoods and ran with the wind along the highway. Eighteen-wheelers sped by them, tossing grit and belching blast-furnace gusts of air that stole her breath. Car horns blared at the lace-clad runaway bride perched so incongruously on the back of a Harley-Davidson. She wanted to ride forever. She wanted to race through time into a different dimension—a world where she had no name. A world where actions bore no consequences.

South of Moffet Field, Sam pulled off the highway. Before long, they were passing industrial parks and strip malls. Then he began to slow. She pressed her cheek against the back of his shoulder and closed her eyes. Don't stop, she prayed. Don't ever stop.

But he did. He kicked off the engine, and the bike became still between her thighs. Turning, he pulled her close against him. "Time to get a move on, biker lady," he whispered. "Your man is hungry."

She made a breathless, frightened sound. Was he her man? Oh, God, what had she done? What was going to happen to her?

He let her go as he got off the bike, and then he held out his hand. She grasped it as if his touch could save her.

"It's a new world," he said. "We're walking into a new world."

More accurately, they were walking into a Burger King.

Susannah's eyes flew open as she became aware of where they were. The asphalt of the parking lot was warm beneath her stockinged feet. She was barefoot. Oh, God, she was barefoot in front of a Burger King! A hole had formed in her silk stockings over one knee, and a small circle of skin pushed through like a bubble on bread dough. Sam pulled her forward, and she saw faces gaping at them from the window.

Her frightened reflection stared back at her—rumpled lace wedding dress, auburn hair hanging in rowdy tangles, thin nose red from the wind. Panicked, she grabbed at his arm. "Sam, I can't—"

"You already have."

With a tug on her hand, he thrust her through the door into the burger-scented heart of middle America.

A gaggle of teenage boys interrupted a burping contest to stare at them from an orange booth. She heard laughter at the spectacle she was making of herself. The soles of her stockings clung to a sticky spot on the tiled floor. A group of six-year-olds celebrating a birthday party looked up from beneath crooked cardboard crowns. One of them pointed. Throughout the restaurant, patrons abandoned their french fries and Whoppers to stare at Susannah Faulconer. She stood there and tried not to let the enormity of what was happening sink in.

Good girls didn't get themselves kidnapped. A society bride didn't flee her wedding on the back of a Harley-Davidson. What was wrong with her? What was she going to do? She had humiliated Cal. He'd never forgive her. And her father . . .

But what she had done was too monstrous, and she couldn't think about her father. Not now. Not yet.

Sam had stopped at the counter. He turned to her and studied her for a moment. "You're not going to cry, are you?"

She shook her head, not able to speak because her throat had closed tight. He didn't know her well enough to know that she never cried, although at that moment she very much wanted to.

"You look great," he whispered, his eyes sweeping over her. "Loose and sexy."

A thrill shot through her, the sensation so intense that she forgot for a moment where she was. No one had ever called her such a thing. She drank in the sight of his face and wondered if she would ever get her fill of looking at him.

He gave her a crooked grin and glanced up at the menu board. "What're you going to have?"

Abruptly, she remembered where she was. She tried to take courage from his complete disinterest in the opinions of the people watching them. He had called her loose and sexy, and with those words she wanted to become a new person, the person he was describing. But words weren't enough to make her into someone else. She was still Susannah Faulconer, and she hated the spectacle she was making.

He ordered and picked up their food. Numbly, she followed him to a table by the window. Her appetite had deserted her, and after a few bites she abandoned any pretense of eating. Sam reached for her hamburger.

As she watched his strong white teeth rip through the bun, she tried to tell herself that no matter how frightened she was, anything was better than dying a slow death of old age at twenty-five.

Susannah had somehow imagined Sam living in a small bachelor apartment, and she wasn't prepared for the fact that he still lived with his mother. The house was one of the small mass-produced ranches that had sprung up in the Valley during the late fifties to house the workers who had flooded to Lockheed following the launching of Sputnik. The front was faced with green aluminum siding, the sides and back with dingy white stucco. Tarpaper topped with fine gravel covered the roof. It sparkled faintly in the fading sunlight.

"The light's not on," Sam said, gesturing toward the garage that sat off to the side along with a ragged palm. "Yank must not be here."

"Does he live here, too?" she asked, growing more nervous by the minute. Why couldn't Sam have lived by himself? What was she going to say to his mother?

"Yank has an apartment on the other side of town. Mom's in Las Vegas with a girlfriend for the next couple of weeks. We have the place to ourselves."

That, at least, was a relief. She walked behind him to the front of the house. Next to the door stretched a long opaque window with vertically ridged glass. The caulking around it had loosened and cracked. Sam unlocked the door and went inside. She followed, stepping across the threshold and directly into the living room. She caught her breath.

The decor was a monument to bad taste. Ugly gold shag carpeting covered the floor. An aquarium filled with iridescent gravel sat next to a Spanish sofa with dark wood trim, brass nail heads, and red velvet upholstery. Sam flipped a wall switch, turning on a lamp made up of a wire bird cage filled with plastic philodendrons. Nearby, occupying what was obviously a place of honor, hung a full-length oil painting of Elvis Presley wearing one of his white-satin Las Vegas outfits and clutching a microphone with ring-encrusted fingers.

Susannah looked over at Sam and waited for him to say something. He returned her stare, his expression belligerent as he waited for her to make a comment. The look of challenge in his eyes and the stubborn set to his jaw touched her. She wanted to go to him and lay her head against his shoulder and tell him she understood. A man with so much passion for elegant design must find it unbearable to live in such a place.

She asked to use the bathroom. Decals of fat fish were stuck to tangerine tiles. She took off her torn stockings and stuffed them into a plastic wastebasket. A smaller painting of Elvis done on black velvet regarded her from the wall behind the toilet. LOVE ME TENDER was written in glitter script across the bottom, except some of the letters had worn off so that it read LOVE ME TEN. Not one, she thought as she washed her hands, avoiding her reflection in the mirror. Don't love me two or three. Love me *ten*.

She found Sam in the kitchen. He offered her a can of Coke and a pair of gold sandals with a plastic daisy at the apex of each thong. "They're my mother's," he said. "She won't mind."

She slipped into the sandals but politely refused the Coke. He studied her for a moment, then picked up a handful of hair next to her cheek and closed it in his fist. She felt dizzy with his closeness, as if she were racing toward the edge of a cliff.

"You have beautiful hair," he whispered. He brushed his thumb over her lips. Her breath quickened. The amber flecks in his eyes glowed like the fireflies she had once trapped in a jar as a child. When Susannah wasn't looking, Paige had opened the lid and dumped the insects on the ground, then squashed them with the soles of her sneakers so that their crushed bodies left a yellow phosphorescent streak in the grass. Afterward, Paige had cried so hard that Susannah had thought she would never stop.

The expression in Sam's eyes told Susannah that he wanted to make love to her, and the tissues in her body began to feel loose and fluid, as if she'd had too much wine. There had been so much emotion that day, so many feelings rushing through her. She wanted to live out all her fantasies, but she was frightened. This was the final step in her emancipation, and she wasn't ready.

She pulled abruptly away from him and walked back into the living room. Elvis, soul-eyed and sullen, looked down at her from the wall. Did she love Sam ten? she wondered frantically. She didn't even know what love was anymore. Was this love or was it simply lust? She loved her father, and look what she'd done. She'd been pretending to love Cal, and that had resulted in disaster. And Sam? Had she gone crazy succumbing to the sexual fantasies this amber-eyed renegade aroused in her? Had she thrown away everything familiar for sex?

"Come on out to the garage with me," he said from behind her.

She whirled around and saw him standing in the archway between the kitchen and living room.

"I want you to see what we're doing," he said. "You're going to be part of it now."

He led her toward the back door, talking all the time. "I told you it was starting for us, Suzie, and I meant it. Last week I got an order for forty circuit boards from this guy named Pinky at Z.B. Electronics. Forty! And this is just the beginning."

As Joel Faulconer's daughter, it was difficult for her to work up much excitement for such small numbers, but she tried to respond enthusiastically. "That's wonderful."

She felt the plastic petals on the daisies of her sandals scratch at her toes as she crossed the backyard. Sam pointed toward the garage with his can of Coke. She studied his hand as it curled around the can. It was a working man's hand. His fingernails were clean but uneven, and an untidy white scar marred his thumb.

"Garages are good luck in the Valley. Bill Hewlett and David Packard started Hewlett-Packard in a garage in Palo Alto, and we're going to start our company in this one. Right now, half the guys in Homebrew have projects going in garages. Do you remember Steve Wozniak from the Homebrew meeting? I pointed him out to you."

"He and his friend are the ones building that single-board computer with some sort of fruit name."

Sam nodded and stopped in front of the side entrance to the garage. "They're working out of Steve Jobs's parents' garage in Los Altos. I heard that Mrs. Jobs is driving Woz crazy by running in and out all the time to use her washer and dryer." Sam grinned and opened the door. "Yank has it even worse."

Susannah didn't understand what he meant until she stepped inside the Gamble garage. It was roughly divided into two sections. The back section held shelves of electronic equipment, a long lighted workbench, and a faded floral sofa. The front of the garage was partitioned off with blond paneling. Susannah walked through a narrow doorway set in the paneling and saw a shampoo bowl, a beauty-shop chair, and several hair dryers. Where the garage door should have been stood a wall of gold-flecked mirrored tiles.

At that moment a phone sitting on a small desk next to an appointment book began to ring. An answering machine clicked on and a woman's voice announced, "This is Angela at Pretty Please Salon. I'm closed for the next two weeks while I try my luck in Vegas. Leave a message and I'll get back to you."

There was a pause and then a beep. "Hi, Angela. It's Harry Davis at Longacres Funeral. Old Mrs. Cooney passed away during the night. I wanted you to do her before the first viewing on Monday, but since you're not going to be around, I'll get Barb. I'll call you with the next one."

The answering machine gave its final beep. Susannah turned to Sam and said weakly, "Your mother does the hair on corpses?"

"She does them when they're alive, too, for chrissake," he retorted belligerently. "She works with one of the nursing homes. When the old ladies finally croak, the funeral home calls her. It drives Yank crazy."

"The funeral home?"

"The old ladies. The nursing home buses them over here to get their hair done. Sometimes when he's working, they peek through the door and start asking him questions." He took a swig of his Coke and gestured with his thumb toward the other side of the partition. "Come on. Let me show you what we're doing."

She left the Pretty Please Salon to follow him into the other section of the garage. The guts of a Sylvania television along with the computer circuit board, a keyboard, and a cassette tape recorder sat on a workbench. He flipped on the overhead work light and began to fuss with the equipment. In front of her, the picture tube started to glow. He put a tape in the cassette recorder, and before long a message appeared in block letters on the screen.

WHAT IS YOUR NAME?

"Go on," Sam said. "Talk to it."

She walked forward and hesitantly typed, "Susannah."

"Now push this key." She did as Sam directed, and another message appeared.

HI, SUSANNAH. I'M HAPPY TO MEET YOU. I DON'T HAVE A NAME OF MY OWN YET. DO YOU HAVE ANY IDEAS?

She was struck by the oddity of having a machine address her by name. "No," she typed.

THAT'S TOO BAD. LET ME TELL YOU ABOUT MYSELF. I AM BEING RUN OFF A 7319 MICROPROCESSOR FROM CORTRON. I HAVE 8K BYTES OF MEMORY. WOULD YOU LIKE TO KNOW MORE?

"Yes," she typed.

The machine responded with more technical information and then, to her surprise, flashed the question, ARE YOU MALE OR FEMALE, SUSANNAH?

"Female," she typed.

ARE YOU PRETTY? it asked.

Sam reached around her and typed, "Yes."

ARE YOU STACKED?

She smiled for the first time that day. "This machine has a naughty mind."

"Don't blame me. I didn't program it."

She entered the word no on the keyboard.

THAT'S TOO BAD. WOULD YOU GO TO BED WITH ME ANYWAY?

She chuckled and entered the word no.

DARN. I NEVER HAVE ANY LUCK WITH WOMEN. I THINK MY MICROPROCESSOR IS TOO SMALL.

She laughed. "What would the machine have done if I'd said yes?"

Sam's hand slid up along her spine. "It would have told you to stand in front of the screen and take off your clothes."

She shivered. His fingers rose above the mandarin collar of her wedding dress and touched the skin at the back of her neck. She didn't move as he held his hand there. He rubbed the skin lightly with his thumb while he pointed out other features on the small computer. She was barely listening.

She wanted to lean back into his chest and press so tightly against him that her body dissolved into his. She envisioned her spine slipping through his skin, her ribs locking with his. And once he had absorbed every part of her flesh and sinew and bone, she would be able to feed from the very source of his spirit. His energy would become her own. She would feast on his brashness and arrogance, on his daring and certainty, on all of those qualities that were missing in her but that he possessed in abundance. By absorbing Sam's spirit, she would make herself complete. And reborn, she would finally be able to march boldly into the world, fully armed against all of the boogeymen, protected against evil, so that nothing bad could ever happen to her again.

He took her hand and led her from the garage. They walked back across the small yard to the house. The scent of someone's backyard barbecue was heavy in the evening air, and a group of kids were playing flashlight tag in the next yard.

When they got inside, Sam gestured toward the kitchen table. "Have a seat. I'll take care of dinner tonight. You can do it tomorrow."

Her stomach was no more ready to handle food now than it had been earlier. "We just ate a couple of hours ago."

"Yeah, I know, but I'm hungry again." He went over to the refrigerator and looked inside. "I'm funny about food. I'll go for a couple of days without eating much of anything, and then I'll eat everything in sight." He pulled another Coke from the refrigerator, shut the door and leaned back against it, apparently not having found anything else that suited him.

He took a swig. The expression in his eyes was so piercing that she had to look away. "You seem to drink a lot of Coke," she said nervously.

"I'm addicted. I got hooked on Coke when I stopped smoking pot." He wandered over to a sliding pantry door, opened it with his foot, and after contemplating the shelves for a few moments, pulled out half a loaf of white bread, a jar of Jif peanut butter, and a plastic squeeze bottle of honey. He grabbed some utensils and sat down next to her.

"Gourmet fare," she said lightly, trying to relieve the awful tension that had taken hold of her.

He didn't smile. "I've got other things on my mind besides food."

"Such as what?" Oh, God. What a stupid question. What an incredibly stupid question. He had sex on his mind. Sex with her.

He squeezed a drop of honey through the bright yellow nozzle onto his index finger. His eyes never left hers as he sucked it off. "Can't you guess?"

A wave of desire curled through her, starting in the center of her chest and moving down through her body into her legs. She tried to tell herself to get up and move away, but she felt as if she were paralyzed. What if sex was all that he wanted from her? She knew that he was a daredevil. What if he was only interested in the challenge that she presented? She realized that she could not let anything else happen between them until they had talked. They needed to understand each other better before they did something that could never be taken back.

He tilted his head, and the ends of his hair formed a dark pool on top of his left shoulder. She snatched up the jar of peanut butter as if she were suddenly ravenous and began clumsily unscrewing the top while she framed the words that needed to be spoken.

He gave her a slow smile and took the jar from her. "I said I'd do the cooking."

She watched as he spread peanut butter on a piece of bread, set it down on the table, and picked up the honey bottle. He gazed at her for a moment. She realized she was holding her breath. His arm seemed to move in slow motion as he reached for the silk-covered buttons on the front of her wedding dress. She needed to tell him to stop, but she couldn't speak.

He paused only when he reached a point well below her breasts. The dress was fully lined, so she wore no slip. He brushed the bodice aside to reveal her bra. It was filmy, part of a bra and panty set she had bought to light a fire in the stodgy soul of Cal Theroux.

He hooked his finger over the front clasp and tugged on it but made no real effort to open it. "Scared?"

She was terrified. Staring at the honey bottle he still held in his hand, she felt her mouth go dry with fear. If only she could reach through his skin and draw out his brashness. "Of—of course not," she stammered. "Don't be ridiculous."

He moved his thumb roughly over the top curve of her breast. "Maybe you should be scared. Because, baby, you can't imagine what I'm thinking about doing to you."

Rockets went off inside her. The edges of her fear evaporated in the strength of her desire. *Do it!* she wanted to scream. *Do it! Please!* She gripped her hands tightly in her lap to keep herself under control. Despite the fact that she had run away from her wedding on the back of a motorcycle, despite the fact that she wore sandals with a plastic daisy stuck between her toes and had gone to the toilet in front of a portrait of Elvis Presley, she was still Susannah Faulconer. And a well-bred young woman didn't scream *Do it,* not even to a man who set her on fire.

He let go of her bra clasp and squeezed a honey spiral over the surface of the peanut butter he had spread for her. Then he lifted the bread to her mouth. She looked at it. Her jaw wouldn't move.

"Open up," he whispered.

She was accustomed to obeying a man's orders, and she did what he said. After she had taken a small bite, he bit into the other side. "Is it good?" he said.

She nodded. He pushed the bread toward her for another bite. They ate without speaking, chewing slowly, looking into each other's eyes.

He picked up the honey bottle and lifted the yellow plastic nozzle to her mouth. For a moment, she thought he was going to feed it to her like a baby's bottle. Instead, he squeezed a curl of honey on her narrow bottom lip. She felt it hanging there, lush and heavy. Before it could drop, he leaned forward and sucked it off himself.

"I love honey," he murmured against her mouth.

His tongue stroked her lip. She whimpered and closed her eyes, knowing she was losing the battle for control of her body. He kissed along the curve of her throat, leaving a sticky trail. "Do you love honey?" he whispered.

"Yes. Oh, yes."

He pulled open her bra and pushed the fabric out of his way. The cool air feathered her skin; his fingers brushed against her. She could barely keep from crying out. She felt a rough scrape. Her eyes flew open in time to see him deliberately rubbing the yellow plastic nozzle back and forth over her nipple. As she watched, he squeezed a droplet of honey onto her pebbled flesh.

She cried out as his head descended and his mouth closed over her, sucking her clean.

The cry released her. She could no longer hold herself in check. She could no longer be a good girl—a pristine princess with deadened breasts and tightly seamed legs. She caught his hair in her fists and crumpled it, then she brought her fists to her mouth and tasted the long rough strands. She wanted to eat him, to devour his hair, his strength, his audacious courage.

With a wicked laugh, he lifted her from the table and pressed her against the ugly wallpaper. She caught the back of his head in her hands and pulled his mouth to hers. Opening wide, she took him in. The kiss was hot and bold, rich with peanut butter and honey.

He pulled the bodice of her dress farther down over her shoulders, so that she had to lower her arms. She reached for his buttocks and clutched him through the seat of his jeans, pushing the heels of her hands into the caves formed in the sides of his hard, young man's cheeks.

He began to murmur naughty words, dirty little phrases, what he would do to her, what she would do to him, crude, filthy, fabulously inventive sonnets of obscenity. As he talked, he pushed up her dress and tugged at her silk panties. Her bad-mannered hands rushed to his zipper. Because he was so hard, she had to struggle with it.

"I'm going to . . ."

"I'll make you . . ."

"Before I'm done, you'll . . ."

To everything he suggested, she cried yes.

And then he had her on her back. The ugly kitchen spun around her as she splayed her legs to act out her naughty girl dreams. His long bad boy's hair tickled the insides of her thighs just as she had imagined it would. His mouth encompassed her. She couldn't breathe. She was going to die. Only the smallest fragment of time passed before she shattered. She heard her voice as if it belonged to someone else, moaning and crying out again and again.

As she settled back to earth, she knew that this was what she had been missing. But her feeling of completion dissolved as she remembered the abandonment of her behavior. Whatever would he think of her? She would have to apologize, try to explain.

He kissed the soft flesh on the inside of her thigh. "You're starved, aren't you?" he said. "Poor starved baby."

A feeling of lassitude stole through her as he began to croon, "I'll take care of you, poor baby. I'll feed you." And then he pressed his mouth to her and did it again.

She had barely finished crying out the second time when he shifted his weight. "I want it like this," he said to her or to himself—she wasn't sure which. "I want you like this."

And then he thrust inside her. He was young and randy, fundamentally selfish, dangerously impatient. He plunged himself between her well-bred thighs and took her with all the vigor of a brash, blue-skies thinker for whom no part of life—not even sex—would ever be enough.

She cried out with every thrust, digging her hands into his flesh and begging for more. They rolled over and over on the hard floor, knocking away a chair and banging up against the cupboards. Her hair tangled with his, her long thin legs clutched his darker ones. When he spilled himself within her, he let out a roar of satisfaction.

Afterward, he let her rest for a while. She played with his hair and took the silver Easter Island earring into her mouth so she could avoid talking.

He made her get up to take off the rest of her clothes. She glanced nervously toward the kitchen window. He laughed at her as she pulled away from him and slid the café curtain closed on its phony wooden rod.

"There's nobody back there," he said, brushing his brown hand over his pale, flat stomach. "No one can see."

"Better safe than sorry," she said inanely.

He emitted a bark of laughter and consumed what remained of their peanut butter sandwich in one bite. With his mouth stuffed full, he said, "You crack me up. You really do."

Then he picked up the plastic honey bottle and came toward her again.

9

In contrast with the rest of the house, Sam's bedroom was almost monastic in its simplicity. It contained a sturdy antique chest and a simple bookcase holding a top-quality stereo system. The walls were painted stark white and were unadorned, and the top of the chest was swept clean of any knickknacks.

Susannah tossed restlessly in the double bed. Her hair, still damp from the shower she and Sam had shared a few hours before, tangled around her throat. The world she lived in had been turned upside down, and she was dizzy with the upheaval. Her logical brain—the brain that had made her excel at science and mathematics when she was in school—refused to let her sleep. It kept ticking off the crises that she faced.

She had no clothes and no money. Her bank accounts would be closed by morning. She loved her father, and how could she ever make him understand what she had done? How could she ever make him forgive her? She turned her head toward the man for whom she had given up everything. Even in sleep he looked driven. His forehead was furrowed, his lips compressed. She should never have let him make love to her until they'd had a chance to get to know each other better.

But even the logical part of her brain couldn't make her regret what had happened between them. Their joining was everything she had imagined lovemaking should be. For the first time in her life, a man had praised her passion so that she felt joy in her sexuality instead of shame. It was a gift so precious she could barely absorb it.

He stirred at her side and reached out—lusty, insatiable, just like all the demon lovers she had ever imagined. He whispered her name. His eyes drifted open and he smiled at her.

She knew then that she loved him. It was more than lust that had made her turn her back on her family for this man. When she met him, she had been dying inside. Her attraction to him was as primal as a drought-starved plant drinking in a summer rain shower. She needed his wildness, his youth, his delirious optimism. She needed his freedom from fear.

Turning to him, she touched the earring that lay against his jaw. Within minutes, they were making love again.

The bed was empty when Susannah awakened. She found one of his T-shirts lying across the footboard along with a wraparound denim skirt he must have appropriated from his mother's closet. She lifted the T-shirt to her nose for a moment before she put it on, but it held the scent of laundry detergent instead of his skin.

After she had dressed, she went into the kitchen to look for him. No one was there, but through the window she could see into the garage. The side door was open, and she spotted him standing at the workbench. Part of her wanted to race across the yard just so she could touch him for a moment. Instead, she went over to the kitchen telephone. Her hands shook as she dialed the number for Falcon Hill. The line was busy. She hung up, grateful for her reprieve. She told herself that she had to try to reach Cal and offer some sort of apology. But she simply couldn't bring herself to call him.

After drinking a small glass of orange juice, she headed out to the garage. As she crossed the yard, she heard the distant sound of Sunday morning church bells and watched as a beat-up Plymouth Duster pulled into the drive. The engine ground to a stop and Yank Yankowski got out. He came toward her, all knobby wrists and bony face, rather like a stork wearing eyeglasses. His hair looked even worse than she remembered. He didn't have one of those tough, Marine Corps, go-to-hell crew cuts, but something that looked more like David and Ricky Nelson permanently trapped in the fifties.

His forehead was knotted in concentration. As he came nearer, she could make out his eyes through the lenses of his glasses. They were light brown and vague. She hadn't known until that moment that a pair of eyes could appear so completely unfocused.

"Hello." She held out her hand politely. "I don't believe we were ever formally introduced. I'm Susannah Faulconer."

He walked right past her.

Startled, she watched him disappear through the garage door. One of his socks was navy, the other white. What a curious person, she thought.

A few seconds later she entered the garage. He and Sam were engaged in a technical discussion. She waited for Sam to turn and catch sight of her. When he finally did, she searched his face for some sign that last night had changed him. He looked no different, but in the seconds that flashed by before he spoke, she imagined that he was remembering what had passed between them.

"Yank's invented a new game, Suzie. Come on over here. It's great! You've got to play."

She needed no prodding to move closer to him, and she soon found herself shooting at speeding targets while the men called out instructions. She was so absorbed in Sam's nearness that she barely noticed Yank. His comments were all impersonal, directed toward the game. Despite the fact that he was actually speaking to her, she had the sense that he still didn't really see her. She was only a disembodied pair of hands manipulating his precious machine.

"The other way," Yank said. "Go to the left!"

"There!" she cried. "I got one!"

"Watch out! You're going to get hit."

It really was fun, she decided, but that was all. Nothing more than a few hours' clever entertainment. She couldn't understand Sam's obsession with this impractical little toy.

"Come on, give me a turn," Sam said.

She waved him off. "In a minute. Let me play one more game."

Yank finally took the game away from them so he could do some troubleshooting on the circuit board. While he worked, Sam gave her a lesson in basic electronics. He pointed out components of the single-board computer to her—integrated circuits and multicolored resistors, tubular capacitors, a power transistor with a heat sink. He talked about miniaturization, and painted a picture for her of a future in which today's tiny microchips would be viewed as large and cumbersome. Some of it she already knew, much of it she didn't. It was a fascinating world, made beautiful by Sam's gift for creating word pictures.

When Yank asked for Sam's help, she watched them work for a while and then reluctantly slipped back into the house to try to call Falcon Hill. The line was still busy, and after several more tries, she concluded that the phone had been left off the hook. She thought about her father's battles with Paige and felt a wrenching inside her as she tried to imagine living without his love. In some families love was given unconditionally, but not in hers.

She called Cal but got no answer. Eventually she sat down and wrote him a letter, asking forgiveness for the unforgivable.

Sam came inside for her and announced that he was taking her to a Chinese restaurant for dinner. Susannah was about to say that she needed a few minutes to change her clothes, but then she remembered that she had nothing to change into.

As they walked out the back door, she spotted a dark blue Ford Pinto that had pulled in behind Yank's Duster. "Shit," Sam said.

"What's wrong?" Had Angela Gamble returned ahead of schedule? What was she going to say to Sam's mother?

Sam didn't answer her question. Instead, he stalked toward the garage like a man with a deadly mission. Reluctantly, Susannah followed him.

To Susannah's relief, the woman standing next to the workbench was about her own age—certainly not old enough to be Sam's mother, although her polyester blouse and navy skirt combined with a bad permanent made her look older. She had a pear-shaped build—narrow shoulders, small bust, plump hips. Her skin was beautiful—pale and unblemished—but the faintest shadow of a mustache hovered above her top lip. It wasn't a gross mustache, merely the sort of thing that a stylish woman would have taken care of with a monthly application of depilatory.

". . . all the food groups, Yank. I left you my three-bean salad, but did you eat any? No you didn't. Not one bite. Kidney beans are a wonderful source of protein, but all you eat are chocolate chip cookies. Well, I'll tell you something, mister, I'm not making you any more chocolate chip cookies. No, sir. Not until you start eating right."

"Leave him alone, Roberta."

The woman had been so engrossed in her lecture to Yank that she hadn't heard them come in, and she jumped when Sam spoke. Susannah watched as her face filled with color. "Sam. I—I didn't— That is—"

He walked slowly forward. With his low-slung jeans and bow-legged biker's gait, his advance bore more than a trace of menace, and Susannah didn't blame Roberta for moving back a few steps. He tucked one of his thumbs into a belt loop, and she felt a primitive sexual thrill at the expense of the hapless Roberta.

"I guess I wasn't clear enough when we had that little chat a few days ago," he said.

"Now, Sam. I—I just stopped by for a minute."

"I don't want you here, Roberta. I don't like the way you nag him."

Roberta attempted to gather herself together. "I can come here if I want. Yank likes to have me around. Don't you, Yank?"

Yank picked up a roll of solder and bent over the circuit board.

Sam leaned against the side of the bench. "Like I said. Stay away from here. If Yank wants to sleep with you, that's his business, but keep away from him when he's working."

Roberta glared at Sam, obviously trying to summon her

courage to argue with him, and just as obviously failing. With dismay, Susannah saw the woman's chin start to tremble. She hated unpleasant scenes and couldn't help but do her best to put an end to this one.

"Hello, I'm Susannah." The Faulconer name was well-known, and she instinctively withheld it.

The woman, obviously grateful for the intercession, came toward her with awkward haste to return the greeting. "I'm Roberta Pestacola. Like Pepsi Cola, but with a 'pesta' instead.

"You're Italian."

Roberta nodded. "On both sides of my family—not just one side like Sam."

Until that moment Susannah hadn't known that Sam was Italian.

"I'm Yank's girlfriend," Roberta went on. "We're practically engaged." She told Susannah that she was a hospital dietitian and that she did ceramics as a hobby. When she finally paused, it was obvious that she was waiting for Susannah to offer some information about herself and her relationship to Sam.

"How fascinating," Susannah replied.

Sam stepped forward and took Roberta's arm. "I'll walk you to your car, Roberta. I'm sure you've got some food groups that you need to go balance."

Roberta's hand shot out and she gripped the vise on the end of the workbench, less from a desire to stay, Susannah suspected, than from uneasiness at the thought of being alone with Sam. Once again, her distress won Susannah's sympathy.

"I'll walk to the car with you."

But Sam wasn't having any of it. "Stay out of this, Susannah. Roberta and I need to have a little chat all by ourselves."

A soft voice pierced through the tension. "Roberta, get that trouble light for me, will you?" Yank lifted his head and blinked a few times as if he had just awakened from a long slumber. "Hold it so I can see what I'm doing."

Roberta dashed eagerly forward, breaking Sam's grip as she snapped up the light.

Sam looked at Yank with disgust and turned his attention back to Roberta. "You'd better not start nagging him. I mean it, Roberta. We've got an order for some boards, and Yank has to work out the last of the bugs. I don't want you here when I get back."

Sam stalked out of the garage with Susannah following him. "God," he said. "That's the worst case of sexual desperation I ever saw in my life."

Susannah wasn't exactly certain whether he was talking about Yank or Roberta, since neither of them struck her as any kind of prize.

"I know it's practically impossible for Yank to get a woman to go to bed with him, but I can't imagine being desperate enough to stick it to old Roberta. I'll bet you anything she makes him disinfect it first."

Their intimacy was still new, and his comment flustered her. "Yank doesn't seem like the sort of person who would be very interested in sex."

"He's interested, all right. He's the one who wrote that raunchy computer program. But Yank's a lot better with machines than he is with women." Sam threw his leg over the Harley and gave her his cockiest grin. "I—on the other hand—am fantastic with both."

They ate at a seedy Chinese restaurant where Sam consumed all of his cashew chicken and three quarters of hers. Then they munched on fortune cookies and he felt her under the table. She grew so aroused, she had to beg him to stop.

On the way home he wheeled the Harley into a deserted school playground. As they dismounted, he held out his hand for her. "Tonight's going to be the last vacation either of us has for a while. We might as well make the most of it."

He led her over to a free-form structure made of tractor tires and she sat on top of one of them. The area was lit by a pair of floodlights that threw exaggerated shadows of the equipment across the playground. It was chilly, and she zipped the windbreaker Sam had given her. As she looked up, she saw that the stars were obscured by either clouds or smog, she wasn't sure which.

Sam saw something quite different in the night sky.

"We're going to unlock the power of the universe, Suzie. You and me. Not just for the big honchos in their ivory towers, but for everybody. We're going to give ordinary people the power of the gods."

She shivered. "I don't know if I want that kind of power."

"That's because you're still afraid of your own shadow." His voice grew quiet. "Do you know what Yank's machine is going to give you? Do you know?" He gazed at her so searchingly, she felt as if she had no secrets left. "It's going to give you courage."

She gave a shaky laugh. "Just like the cowardly lion in *The Wizard of Oz.*"

"Just like that."

"I don't think you can get courage from a machine."

"You can from this one. If you want it. But you've got to want it bad, Suzie." He leaned back against one of the tractor tires. "The order for the forty boards doesn't just mean we're in business, you know that, don't you? It gives us a chance to put ourselves to the test. Not many people get that kind of chance. We have to get more orders, run some ads. And we're not going to make the same mistake MITS is making with the Altair. We're not offering any kits. Every board we sell is going to be fully assembled and top quality."

His plans were so unrealistic that she was deeply disturbed. It was all very well to talk about the power of the gods, but the truth of the matter was that he had a machine nobody knew they wanted, and it was being built in the garage of a woman who did the hair on corpses. How could he stake his future on something like that? How could she stake *her* future?

"Parts are expensive," she said noncommittally. "What will it cost to build forty boards?"

"With discounts, price shopping—I figure around twelve thousand. Then we have to have cases made. Something plain, but sturdy. I've already got a guy working on a printed circuit board to make the assembly easier. Have you ever seen one?"

"I think so. I'm not certain."

"It's a fiberglass board covered with a thin layer of copper. The copper gets etched away until only narrow paths of it are left on the fiberglass—like tiny wires."

"Copper conducts electricity," she said. "At least I know that much."

"Right. And fiberglass doesn't. The components fit into slots on the board. The right components, elegant design, and you've got a single-board computer. I figure we should be able to complete each board for around three hundred dollars. Pinky's going to pay us five and sell them for seven. We'll plow the profits into more boards, and before long we'll be able to produce a self-contained computer—terminal, monitor, the works. One of these days we're going to blow FBT right out of the water."

"Do you have twelve thousand dollars?"

"Yank and I have about two thousand between us, but I had to use some of that as a deposit for the printed circuit boards. A guy I know offered me eight fifty for my stereo system. That's about it."

With three thousand dollars, Sam thought he could take on FBT. She loved him, and so she concealed her dismay. "Did you try the banks?"

"The banks are run by morons. They don't have any vision. They're fossils. Monumental dinosaurs."

He had obviously tried the banks.

She lifted up her sandal and let the sand that had collected under her toes drift out. "What are you going to do?"

He gave her a searching look. "It's what are *we* going to do, isn't it? You're part of this. Or are you planning to run home to daddy and Calvin?"

The schoolyard lights caught the amber flecks in his eyes. She shivered. "That isn't fair."

"I don't give a shit about fair. I want to know. Are you in or out?"

"I want to be with you, Sam."

"That's not what I'm asking."

He was backing her into a corner, and she was frightened. Awkwardly, she slid down off the tire and looked beyond him to the dark borders of the playground. "I don't have any money. In case you were counting on it, you should know that I can't help you. My father controls everything."

"I don't expect money from you," he said angrily. "That's not why I want you with me. Goddammit! Is that what you think I want from you?"

"No, of course not." But just for a moment, she had thought exactly that. "I don't have anything, Sam—no clothes, no money, no place to stay."

"I didn't ask for a frigging dowry! We'll get you some clothes and you're staying with me. Are you in or out, Suzie?"

He was so certain, always so certain. The darkness at the edge of the playground suddenly seemed to be full of menace. "I told you. I want to be with you."

"You can't be with me and not be part of this."

What was she going to say? She was a practical person. The only impractical thing she had ever done in her adult life was fall in love with Sam Gamble. "It's not that simple." She turned away from him, but he came right up behind her.

"Bullshit. I want to know!"

"Don't bully me!"

"I want to know, dammit! Don't keep throwing up all these artificial barriers. Do you have the guts to go through with this or not? Do you have the guts to put yourself to the test?"

She spoke rapidly, pushing out the words before he could stop them. "It's not just a matter of guts. I have to be practical. I need to support myself."

"That's not the most important thing! Supporting yourself isn't the most important thing. You don't need money or clothes. Those are just excuses. It's your soul. That's what's important. That's all anybody really has. Don't you see? If you want your soul to survive—if you want it to grow and thrive instead of shriveling up and drying out like it was doing in that mausoleum at Falcon Hill, you have to dare. You have to give the world the finger, and you have to dare."

How he could talk. How this man could talk. She hugged herself against the night and the chill and the menace at the edge of the playground.

He caught her arm. His eyes blazed. "Suzie, listen to me. We're living on the threshold of a new society—a whole new way of doing everything. Can't you feel it? The old ways don't work anymore. People want information. They want control. They want power! When you look at Yank's circuit board, all you see is a collection of electronic parts. But what you should be seeing is a wave—this little wave way out in the water, far away from shore. This little hump of water that's just starting to form. But this little hump of water keeps coming closer. And the closer it comes, the more it starts to pick up speed. And then, pretty soon you look up and—Christ!—its not a little hump any longer but a great big wall of water that's risen up so high you can see it looming against the sky. You can see a white crest starting to form on the top like a crown. And that white crest is getting bigger and it's starting to churn and curl over at the top. And then you hear the noise. This tidal wave of water is picking up speed and it's starting to roar. And before long it's gotten so loud you have to hold your hands over your ears. That's when you start stepping backward. You don't want the wave to knock you down, and you're stepping backward faster and faster. And then—that's when you realize it. That's when you realize that no matter how fast you run, that motherfucker is going to slam right down on top of you. It's going to slam right down on top of everybody in the world. That wave is the future, babe. It's the future, and it's Yank's machine. And once that wave hits, none of us will ever be the same again."

He was filling her with his words just as earlier he had filled her with his sex. He was filling up her body and taking it over. The words caught her, heaved her about in their undertow and made it hard for her to breathe. But for all his talk, Sam didn't really understand what it meant to dare. He had nothing to lose. He lived in an ugly little house with a painting of Elvis Presley on the wall. He owned a stereo system and a Harley-Davidson. When Sam talked about not being afraid to dare, he wasn't risking anything. She—on the other hand—was risking it all.

He touched her. He cupped her face in his hands and stroked her cheeks with his thumbs. The wave washed her up on shore, and she experienced that helpless feeling women throughout the centuries have known when they realize that loving a man means loving his vision as well, that it means traveling across oceans, across continents, that it means being uprooted from family and giving up the safe for the unknown. "I—I need to think about this. Tomorrow, while you're at work, I'll think about it."

"I'm not going to work tomorrow."

"Why not?"

"I quit. I'm *in,* Suzie. I'm in all the way."

"You quit your job?" she said weakly.

"Last week. Now how about you? Are you in or out?"

"I—I don't know."

"Not good enough."

"I need time."

"There isn't any."

"Don't do this, Sam. Please don't badger me like this."

"I want to know, Suzie. Right now. Make up your mind. Are you in or out?"

She felt as if she were eons older than he was instead of only a year—millennia older in experience. A lifetime of dinner-table conversations drifted back to her. She saw hurdles he couldn't imagine, difficulties his visionary's eyes hadn't begun to glimpse. Everything she had learned from the day she was born urged her to tell him she couldn't help him and then to run back to Falcon Hill and beg her father's forgiveness.

But she loved him, and she loved the new spark he had ignited inside her—a spark that had been lit by his reckless energy, a spark that wanted to grow brighter and become stronger. A spark that was urging her to follow this restless young man she had so unwisely fallen in love with right off the edge of the earth.

When she finally spoke, her voice was shaky and barely audible. "I'm in."

10

. . . .

Yank's Duster coughed like an emphysema victim as Susannah drove north to Falcon Hill several days later. She had owned high-performance automobiles all her life, and until this moment she hadn't realized a car could behave like this one. She thought about using the car as an excuse to go back, but then imagined how Sam would scoff at her if she returned without getting the things she needed.

Each day it had grown more difficult for her to live without her possessions. Sam had given her money to get a new prescription filled for her birth control pills, and although that had been her most pressing need, it was only one of them. She needed her reading glasses and her driver's license. She needed clothes to replenish her borrowed wardrobe. No matter how much she wanted to avoid it, she hadn't been able to postpone going home any longer.

The gates loomed ahead of her. Sam had given her the small electronic gadget he had used to release the locks, but she didn't need it. It was Thursday morning and the gates were open for a grocery delivery. As she turned into the drive, she remembered the newspaper gossip column from last Sunday's paper that she had stumbled upon. It had contained a sly account of what had happened at her wedding and was accompanied by a picture of herself and

Cal "in happier times." Sick at her stomach, she had tried once again to reach her father, this time at his office. His secretary had pretended not to know who she was and informed her that Mr. Faulconer was currently out of the country.

Her trepidation grew as she parked the Duster in the motorcourt and climbed the front steps to the house. While she waited for someone to answer the bell, she wished a familiar household retainer would appear—one of those mythic housekeepers of fiction who would welcome her home with a tart scolding and a warm plate of cookies. In reality, Falcon Hill's current housekeeper had a small tattoo on the back of her hand and had only been with them a few months.

The slim hand that opened the door, however, bore no tattoo.

"Paige?"

"Well, well, the runaway bride returns."

Susannah was astonished to see her sister, but even more surprised to see that Paige was wearing one of Susannah's own silk dresses instead of her customary blue jeans. Antique gold earrings glimmered through her hair. They were the ones Joel had bought Susannah as a high school graduation present.

A smirk distorted Paige's pretty mouth. "I can't believe you have the nerve to come back."

"What are you doing here?"

Paige's eyes skimmed Susannah's tidy hair and untidy outfit, then flicked to the battered Duster in the driveway. "Falcon Hill is my home, too. Or have you forgotten that?"

There was an expression of such smugness on her sister's face that Susannah felt sick. "I'm just surprised, that's all. Is Father home?"

"Luckily for you, no. You've been declared persona non grata for the rest of your natural life. He's left orders that your name is no longer to be spoken in this house. You're being disinherited, spurned—I actually think he's trying to find a way to un-adopt you. Right out of the Old Testament."

Susannah had known it would be bad, but not this bad.

Like someone deliberately probing a sore tooth, she inquired, "What about Cal? How is he?"

"Oh, he's just peachy—considering the fact that he's been publicly humiliated. It's a miracle the newspaper story hasn't gotten bigger play, but you've still managed to make him look like the Bay Area's biggest asshole."

Susannah didn't want to think about what a terrible thing she had done to Cal. She couldn't bear any more guilt.

"Actually, it's been pretty interesting around here. It's starting to feel as if you never existed. As if you never came into our lives."

Susannah didn't want to hear any more. She moved forward, ready to slip past Paige and get what she needed, but Paige sidestepped, blocking the way. "You can't come in, Susannah. Daddy's forbidden it."

"But that's ridiculous. I need to get some of my things."

Triumph glittered in Paige's eyes. "Maybe you should have thought of that before you ran off with your stud."

"He's not a—"

"I thought you were a virgin. Isn't that a hoot? If you had to have a toy boy, Susannah, you could at least have been nice enough not to wave him in Daddy's face."

Susannah mustered her dignity. "I didn't mean to hurt anyone. I just couldn't help it."

"Don't tell me you couldn't help it!" Paige's smugness dropped away, and for a few moments she looked as befuddled as a child. "I thought I knew you, but that's not true at all. The person I knew wouldn't have run off like that. God, Susannah . . ." And then her hostility slipped back into place like the click of a lock. "Not that I care."

Susannah tried to make her understand. "I couldn't stand it any longer. I love Father, but I felt as if he was choking me to death. And Cal was becoming an extension of him. They were making me feel old. I'm only twenty-five, but I felt like an old lady. I didn't really expect either of them to understand, but I thought you would."

"I don't understand any of it. All I know is that perfect Susannah isn't so perfect anymore. For the first time in my life, Daddy has stopped waving all those unlimited virtues of yours in my face. Do you know how long I've waited for this? He talks to me at dinner now. He tells me about his day. He doesn't even miss you, Susannah!"

Susannah felt weak under the strength of Paige's antipathy. A bittersweet image passed through her mind of a crayon picture Paige had drawn when she was in kindergarten. The two of them had been holding hands and standing together under a rainbow. Whatever had happened to those two little girls?

"We're sisters," Susannah said. "I've tried to watch out for you."

"Half sisters. And you're not the only one who knows how to play Lady Bountiful. Wait for me here. I'll put some of your things together and bring them out to you."

Before Susannah could react, the door to Falcon Hill had been firmly slammed in her face.

Paige delivered Susannah's possessions in two shopping bags from Gump's. She had included the reading glasses and driver's license as well as miscellaneous pieces of clothing, none of it Susannah's best. There was no jewelry, nothing of monetary value. When Susannah returned to the Gamble house, she put the clothes neatly away in Sam's closet and tried not to dwell on Paige's vindictiveness.

While the printed circuit boards were being finished, Sam had been trying to raise money to buy the parts they needed. He brought his former coworkers to the garage and enveloped them with his rhetoric, speaking of a new society in which ordinary people would have the power of the universe at their fingertips. Exactly what they were to do with that power, he never defined. Gradually Susannah realized that he had only the vaguest idea himself what ordinary people would really do with a computer.

Even as she stood mesmerized at his side, she found herself growing increasingly uneasy. Not only didn't they have a definable market for their product—they couldn't even tell future customers what to use it for. By the weekend he had raised less than eight hundred dollars. It was only a fraction of what they needed.

She spent all of her spare time at the local library reading everything she could find about starting a small business.

She wanted to learn as much as possible so that she could set her discoveries before him as small gifts of her love. But it didn't take her long to discover that they weren't doing anything right. They had no money, no defined market for their product, no experience. None of them were college graduates. Every piece of evidence pointed to the fact that they could not possibly succeed.

She read about venture capitalists—that unique breed who made fortunes from financing risky new businesses. But she couldn't imagine interesting any reputable venture capitalist in backing a three-person operation being run out of a garage that was partially occupied by the Pretty Please Beauty Salon.

In the evenings while the men worked, she curled up on the old floral sofa in the garage and made her way through one business- or economics-related book after another. Occasionally they needed an extra set of hands and she was called upon to fetch a part or hold a light. When Yank wanted something from her, he tended to call her Sam.

"Hand me that jumper, Sam," he would say. Or, "Sam, how about a little more light."

The first few times she had corrected him, but he had looked at her so blankly that she had finally given up. He couldn't seem to comprehend the simple fact that she existed, let alone that she had become a fixture in his life. He was the strangest person she had ever met—so absorbed in his work that he seemed to inhabit an entirely different dimension of reality from everyone else.

Another week slipped by. The printed circuit boards were to be ready the next day. They had enough money to pay for them, but that was all. Where were they going to find the thousands of dollars they needed to purchase parts for forty boards? Without collateral, Sam couldn't get credit from any of the suppliers, and none of the banks would talk to him.

"They're all morons," he complained to Susannah as he paced back and forth across the garage, growing more agitated by the minute. "They wouldn't know a good idea if it hit them on the head."

It was past midnight and she was tired. Still, she tried to

make him see the situation realistically. "Sam," she said gently, "you can't really expect them to lend you money. Setting aside the issue of collateral, all they see when they look at you is a wild-eyed biker."

He shoved his hand impatiently through his hair. "Don't start with all your uptight crap again, all right? I'm not in the mood."

His attack was unfair and it hurt, but she had no idea how to defend herself, so she retreated like a turtle ducking into its shell. As she picked up the book on production efficiency that she had been reading, she tried to make excuses for him. He had been working hard. He hadn't meant to attack her. But the words on the page in front of her wouldn't focus. She kept remembering the night at the playground when Sam had asked her if she had the guts to put herself to the test. Did she have the courage to stand up for herself or was she going to spend the rest of her life nodding her head in agreement to the opinions of every man she met?

Hesitantly, she closed the book. "I think it's important for us to deal with reality. The world as it actually is—not as you think it should be." Her voice sounded tentative instead of assertive, as she had intended.

He spun on her. "What's that supposed to mean?"

"It means that appearances are important. I love the way you look and the way you dress. I love your hair. It's part of you. But hard-headed businessmen don't tend to have much patience with nonconformists."

His lips tightened scornfully, the lips that had kissed her so passionately that morning. "Appearances are shit, Susannah. They don't mean anything. Quality means something. Ideas. Hard work. That's all that counts."

Her brain was calling out alarms and her stomach had begun to twist into its familiar knots, but still she forced herself to press on. "Appearances mean something in the business world."

"Maybe in that phony FBT world, but that's not what I'm about. I want success, but I goddamn well won't sell my soul for it. That's your territory, not mine."

Failure pressed in on her. Some people were good at confrontation, but she wasn't one of them. Her fingers crept toward her book and her lips began to frame a retraction. But Sam hadn't finished with her.

"You know, you're really starting to piss me off. You're a goddamn snob. If you want to go around looking at the labels in people's clothes before you talk to them, that's your business, but don't expect me to buy into it. And another thing—"

"These decoder chips are out of tolerance, Sam," Yank said from the workbench.

Susannah felt a rush of gratitude for the timeliness of Yank's interruption. Although he had been standing right in front of them all evening, she had once again forgotten he was there. As Sam went to help him, she quickly gathered up her book and retreated to the house. She would pretend to be asleep when he came in so she wouldn't have to deal with any more conflict. She had tried to hold her ground, but Sam was like a steamroller mowing her down.

Ever since she had moved in with him, she had slept nude, but now she found an ugly cotton nightgown Paige had packed for her and she slipped into it. As she went into the bathroom to brush her teeth, she thought of her father's icy silences and Cal's cold withdrawal. She tried to find comfort in the fact that at least Sam expressed his anger openly.

The bathroom door banged open. "What the hell happened to you?" he inquired angrily.

She spun around, her hand flying to her throat. "I—I was tired. I decided to go to bed."

"The hell you did. We were in the middle of a goddamn fight, and you ran away." He pushed himself into the small room. She waited for the tiled walls to bulge outward from the strain of trying to contain all the energy that he brought with him.

"Arguing never solves anything."

"Who says? Who comes up with shit like that?"

"I don't want to fight."

"Why not?" He glared at her belligerently. "Are you afraid you won't win?"

"I'm not a fighter. I don't enjoy conflict."

"You're an asshole."

She was stunned by his attack. Nothing in her life had

prepared her for this kind of overt hostility. A surge of anger, dark and ugly, began to creep through her. She didn't deserve this. She loved him, and he had no right to say these things to her. Her anger frightened her as much as his attack, and she realized that she couldn't deal with either one. She had to get away from him. She had to escape before something terrible happened. Rushing to the door, she tried to push past him.

He caught her arm and pulled her around. His lips had narrowed into a hard line, and his expression was tight with anger. "You're a real chickenshit, you know that? A little mouse afraid of her own shadow."

"Let me go!" Her own anger was growing bigger and stronger, taking over her body like a foreign virus.

"No. I don't like scared little rabbits."

"Stop it! Let me go!"

"Make me."

"Don't do this!" she shouted. "Don't you treat me like this. I don't deserve this and I won't stand for it, and you can just go to hell!"

He laughed and dropped his head to her mouth. "Better. That's lots better." Her lips were already parted in indignation and he slammed his teeth against hers.

She couldn't breathe. She tried to shove him away, but he pinned her against the vanity. She struggled, pushing at his chest with the heels of her hands. And then something strange began to happen inside her. A heat was building there, a dark excitement. She parted her lips and thrust her tongue into his mouth.

The heat turned to fire. He pushed up her cotton nightgown. It bunched around her waist as he lifted her onto the edge of the vanity. He opened her legs and stepped between them. She felt him fumbling with the front of his jeans, and she began pressing hard against him. He grabbed her knees from behind and lifted them higher. She cried out as he thrust inside her, then she locked her legs around his waist so she could take him all.

Their lovemaking was wretchedly uncomfortable and she didn't have an orgasm, but she reveled in the ferocity of it. Afterward he took her to bed and made love to her all over again. That night she lay spent next to him, exhausted from an outpouring of so much emotion, and yet filled with triumph. She had gotten angry, and her world hadn't come to an end.

Her mind churned with so much activity that she couldn't fall asleep. The light patterns shifted on the ceiling. She repositioned her pillow, but it didn't help. Taking care not to wake Sam, she slipped out of bed and headed toward the kitchen so she could get a drink of water. As she passed naked beneath Elvis's full-length portrait in the living room, she glanced uncomfortably at the singer's image. She should have put on a robe, but all her robes were back at Falcon Hill.

The fluorescent stove light in the kitchen was on, emitting a blue-white glow. Her bare feet padded across the floor. She crossed to the cupboard and reached for a glass. At that exact moment she heard a thump.

She spun around, all her senses alert, and watched in horror as the back door began to swing open.

A dark form loomed on the threshold. It took her only a few seconds to recognize the tall, thin figure as Yank Yankowski's. What was he doing here? she thought wildly. It was nearly three in the morning and she was stark naked. What was she going to say?

The chill night air he had brought with him raised goose bumps on her bare skin. Her nipples were puckered, the hair on her arms standing up. He still hadn't seen her. As he pushed the door shut, she glanced desperately around for a place to hide. She wanted to vanish into the walls, get swallowed up by the floor. If she tried to make a dash for the living room, he would see her.

He crossed directly in front of her, passing not more than five feet away but still not looking at her. The edge of the kitchen counter dug into the small of her back as she tried to smear herself into a film as thin as the aluminum coating on a wafer of silicon. The rubber soles of his sneakers squeaked on the floor. He stopped in front of the refrigerator with his back toward her. Her hand snaked along the counter, frantically groping for something to cover her nakedness.

At that moment the kitchen was flooded with light. In her

imagination, it seemed as if thousands of watts of electricity had been let loose, but in reality Yank had only pulled open the refrigerator door and activated the small appliance bulb.

She made an audible gasp and then froze, afraid he had heard her. But he didn't turn. He stood in front of the refrigerator staring inside. Seconds passed. Half a minute. The tips of her fingers bumped against a pot holder lying on the counter. She clutched it like a fig leaf in front of her, feeling more embarrassed, more ridiculous by the minute.

Why didn't he move? For one wild moment she thought that maybe she was still asleep, that this was all a silly dream like the ones where she was presiding naked over a committee meeting.

He kept one hand clamped to the refrigerator handle, the other hung at his side. What was wrong with him? Why didn't he move? He was dead, she thought frantically. He had died standing up.

She inched to her right and stepped out of the direct path of the refrigerator light into the glow from the stove light. Maybe she could get to the back door and slip outside. She could hide behind the house until he left. But what if she got locked out?

He turned so abruptly that she made a small, startled sound. It reverberated in the quiet of the kitchen. Finally, he was facing her.

She froze like an animal caught in the beam of a car's headlights. His torso was silhouetted against the open refrigerator, and the stove light had silvered the lenses of his glasses so that she couldn't see his eyes clearly. But there was no doubt about the direction in which he was looking. Those glasses were pointed right at her.

Her hand was clammy around the pot holder. She hunched her shoulders forward, trying to cover her breasts with her upper arms. Her upbringing had prepared her for every conceivable social situation, but she couldn't imagine what to say in this one.

Yank continued to stare at her. She had to do something! Without taking her eyes from him, she began inching toward the living room door, the pot holder clutched over her pudendum so that she looked like Eve fleeing the

Garden. As she passed in front of the stove, her body temporarily blocked the stove light and the reflection in his glasses disappeared. For the first time, she could see his eyes.

They were completely blank.

She was so surprised that she stopped moving and looked at him more closely. She had never seen eyes so vague, so unfocused. She took another step to the side. His head didn't move; his gaze remained firmly fixed on some mysterious point to her right. She couldn't believe it. What kind of man was he? Slowly she lowered the pot holder.

She almost laughed. *He didn't see her!* Once again, Joseph "Yank" Yankowski was too enmeshed in some complex internal electronics problem to be aware of what was happening around him. He was so lost in thought that he didn't see a naked auburn-haired woman standing directly in front of him.

She slipped from the kitchen and made a dash for the bathroom, where she locked the door and indulged in the first honest laughter she could remember in weeks.

Meanwhile, in Angela Gamble's kitchen, Joseph "Yank" Yankowski remained just as Susannah had left him. The refrigerator door was still open and he hadn't moved from his position. Only his eyes were different. Beneath the lenses of his glasses, the lids were squeezed tight while inside his skull billions of interconnected nerve cells churned with activity. Thalamus, hypothalamus, the fissured moonscape of cerebrum and cerebellum—all the parts of Yank Yankowski's genius brain were at work, accurately reconstructing from memory each separate micron of Susannah Faulconer's pale naked flesh.

Even though she hadn't slept well, Susannah awakened early the next morning refreshed and full of energy. The encounter with Yank had amused her, and the confrontation with Sam had given her courage. She decided that a woman who could stand her ground in an argument with Sam Gamble was capable of anything. Even while she slept, her mind had been working, and as she stepped into the shower, she once again heard the voice that had whispered to her in her dreams. *Appearances. Appearances are everything.*

Sam came into the kitchen a little after eight o'clock. She had already dressed and she was standing at the sink drying the dishes from the night before. Normally, he teased her about her tidiness, but this morning he didn't seem to have the heart for it. She didn't need to ask why he was so quiet. They were due to pick up the printed circuit boards in an hour. But what good were circuit boards when they didn't have the money to buy the components that went on them?

He walked over to the refrigerator and pulled out a carton of orange juice. Without bothering to fetch a glass, he tilted the container to his lips. She wiped off the counter with the dish towel and then hung it away neatly. Appearances, she told herself. Appearances were everything.

He turned, really seeing her for the first time. "What are you all dressed up for?"

She wore square-heeled leather pumps and a black and white checked suit that was several years old and had never been one of her favorites. Still, it was good quality, and it was the only professional-looking outfit Paige had included. Her hair was neatly coiled at her neck with the pins she had borrowed from the Pretty Please Salon. She stepped forward. Sam had said that Yank's machine could give her courage. It was time to find out if that was true.

"We've tried it your way," she said. "Now I want to try it mine."

Spectra Electronics Warehouse was exactly the sort of place most women hated. It was a vast electronics junkyard of a building with concrete floors and towering shelves filled with cardboard cartons reinforced by wire strapping. An open ceiling supported a network of pipes and jaundiced neon lights. Thick parts catalogues with dog-eared pages were mounted next to a long wooden counter plastered with Fly Navy bumper stickers. The place felt cold and smelled like metal, plastics, and old cigarettes. It was so different from the sorts of places Susannah normally patronized that she might actually have liked it if she hadn't been paralyzed with fright.

"Hey, Sam. Howzitgoin'?" The man behind the counter looked up from a pile of invoices.

Sam swaggered forward. "Not too bad, Carl. How about you?"

"All right. No complaints." Carl pulled a pen from an ink-stained plastic pocket protector and returned his attention to the invoices. Sam was obviously not regarded as a customer important enough to warrant any more of his time.

Sam looked at her and shrugged, telling her without words that this had been her idea and she was the one who could see it through. The piece of toast she had eaten for breakfast clumped in her stomach.

When Sam saw that she wasn't moving forward, he came to the proper conclusion that she had lost her nerve and gave her a look of disgust. She wanted to show him that he was wrong—that a socialite could teach a silver-tongued hustler a few things, that she was good for something more than planning cocktail parties. But her feet felt as if they were glued to the floor and she couldn't seem to unstick them. He wandered over to thumb through a parts catalogue, separating himself from her.

Without quite knowing how it had happened, she found herself moving forward. Carl looked up. He seemed vaguely perplexed. Women in Chanel suits—even suits that were five years old—weren't frequent patrons of Spectra Electronics.

She extended her arm for a handshake, then tightened her grip when she realized it wasn't firm enough. "Faulconer," she said, introducing herself with her last name for the first time in her life. "I'm Susannah Faulconer. Sam's business partner."

Her hand was clammy. She withdrew it before he noticed and gave him a bright red business card with SysVal boldly printed in black. As she passed it over, she prayed that the ink was dry.

SysVal stood for "Sam Yank and Susannah in the Valley," the name she and Sam had been arguing over all morning, right up to the time they stood at the counter of a print shop that guaranteed business cards in an hour. Sam had wanted to give the company an antiestablishment name like General Egocentric or Hewlett-Hacker, but she had stubbornly resisted. He had yelled at her right in front of the clerk at the print shop, but their confrontation the night before had stiffened her resolve not to let him have his way when she knew he was wrong. She still could barely believe that the name on the card was the one she had chosen.

"Faulconer?" Carl said as he eyed the card, which had her name written in the bottom corner incongruously placed in front of Sam's and Yank's and—even more incongruously— with the bold title "President" printed after it. "You have anything to do with FBT?"

"Joel Faulconer is my father," she said, "but I'm currently on sabbatical from FBT." That was vaguely true.

She turned her head as if she were knowledgeably survey- ing her surroundings, when actually she was just trying to slow down her heartbeat. From Sam's briefing, she knew Carl was the person they had to deal with, but what did she know about someone who owned an electronics warehouse? The building was cool but she was perspiring. She would never be able to carry this off. She was a socialite, not a businesswoman.

And then she saw the respect in his eyes generated by hearing her last name, and she found the courage to plunge ahead. "Sam tells me that you're the best dealer in the area. He's a severe judge, and I'm impressed."

Carl was pleased by her praise. "We try," he said. "We've been here for ten years. In the Valley that's a long time." He began telling her in some detail about his business.

"Interesting," she said as he wound to a close.

He gestured toward a cloudy Pyrex pot sitting on a hot plate. "Can I get you a cup of coffee, Miss Faulconer?"

He seemed to have forgotten Sam's existence, and for the moment that was fine. Off to the side, she could see Sam thumbing through the catalogues, but she knew that he was taking in every word of this exchange.

"Thanks, but I'm afraid I don't have time. I have another appointment." She gave her wrist a brisk glance only to remember, too late, that she wasn't wearing a watch. All of her watches were in her dresser drawer at Falcon Hill—or on her sister's wrist. She surreptitiously tugged down the sleeve of her jacket before Carl could notice.

"You're obviously competent at what you do. Reliability is important to me." Her knees were starting to feel weak, but she plunged on before she lost her nerve. "For some time I've been interested in helping develop small companies outside the FBT umbrella. I've been looking for ventures that excite me—new products, new concepts, fresh people. When Sam showed me the computer that he and his associate had designed, I knew I'd found exactly what I'd been looking for."

"Sam's a good guy," Carl said, belatedly remembering who had brought her here. "He's got good instincts."

"I think so, and I'm not easily impressed." She couldn't believe the man wasn't seeing right through her, but he continued to listen. "We're lining up suppliers now, which is why I'm here. We think this new computer marks the wave of the future. I've made the decision to commit myself and all my resources to SysVal." That was true anyway. Carl didn't have to know just how nonexistent those resources were.

"I'll be happy to help you in any way I can."

"Good. I want to make certain you'll give Sam everything he needs."

"He's got it," Carl replied enthusiastically.

"And time is important. We need reliable parts and we need them quickly."

"I understand."

She put out her hand and shook his, her grip much stronger this time. "I know you're busy, and I won't take up any more of your time. You have my business card." She hesitated at the exact moment when she wanted to appear most in control. Hoping she hadn't already betrayed herself, she said firmly, "Use that address for billing. Thirty days, normal terms."

For the first time, Carl looked doubtful. She had expected this to happen, but now that it had, she couldn't remember what she had planned to do about it.

"If we're dealing with a new company," he said, "we generally ask for payment in advance."

Out of the corner of her eye, she saw Sam's head lift from the parts catalogue. This was it. Now the socialite had to turn into a hustler. Whatever had made her think she could pull this off? She raised her eyebrow, hoping she looked vaguely annoyed instead of sick to her stomach. "In advance? How odd. That's really going to drive my accountants wild."

"Nothing personal, Miss Faulconer. It's normal procedure."

"Of course. I understand. I should have realized this would be a problem. FBT is accustomed to working with much larger suppliers."

Deliberately, she turned her back on him and walked over to Sam. "I know that you want to get your parts here, Sam, but I'm afraid it's not possible. You have to see that this is going to cause all sorts of difficulties for me."

Sam looked properly annoyed. "The prices are better here at Spectra," he said. "You'll end up paying more somewhere else."

She managed a stiff shrug. "Cost is relative. The larger suppliers can accommodate themselves better to our accounting system. From my perspective, this is a relatively small order—"

"Now, Miss Faulconer—" Carl practically leaped around the counter. "I'm sure we can work something out."

The blood had started to roar so loudly in her ears that she was surprised he couldn't hear it. She risked glancing at her wrist again. Two hairs past a freckle. She remembered that saying from her childhood. What time is it? Two hairs past a freckle. "I'm quite late already. I really don't—"

"We'll take care of it," Carl insisted. "Don't worry. Thirty days will be fine."

It took all her self-control not to break out in a huge smile. "Are you certain? I don't want to inconvenience you."

"No inconvenience at all," Carl replied. "Now you go on to your appointment. Sam and I'll get started on your order."

She could barely restrain herself from leaping into the air like a child. She wanted to jump and shout and scream with joy at how clever she had been, how brave, how absolutely unconventional! Instead, she smiled at Carl and began walking toward the door.

As she stepped outside, she promised herself that she would do whatever she must to pay him back. She might have hustled him, but she wouldn't cheat him.

That evening Angela Gamble burst into the garage like the rhythm section of a street band—charm bracelets jangling, stiletto heels tapping, Gypsy coin earrings tintinnabulating.

"Sammy Bammy! I'm back!" She stretched out her arms and dashed forward—a hot pink flash in a gauze jumpsuit cinched at the waist with a metallic fish-scale belt. Her shoulder-length cloud of black, sprayed hair barely moved.

"Hi, Mom." His smile didn't quite reach his eyes as he half-heartedly returned her hug.

She gave him a loud kiss on the chin and smacked his face with the flat of her hand. "That's for all the trouble you probably got into while I was away." Without stopping to catch her breath, she raced toward Yank, grabbed his rear end in both hands and squeezed hard. "Gotcha, hot cheeks. Miss me?"

Yank turned and blinked. Susannah, who had been unpacking a box of parts when Sam's mother had burst in, watched in astonishment as a smile slowly spread over his face. "Hi, Angela."

At the age of forty-two, Angela Gamble was slim and small. Only an inch over five feet tall, she was pretty despite her gaudiness, and fiercely engaged in a battle against encroaching middle age. She stretched up onto her tiptoes and planted a solid kiss on Yank's mouth. Then she slapped him across the face even harder than she had slapped her son. "That's for all the trouble you *didn't* get into while I was gone."

Yank rubbed his cheek absent-mindedly, gave her another smile—this one a bit vague—and reached for his logic probe.

She turned to Susannah. "Hi, honey. I'm Angela Gamble. You Sammy's new girlfriend?"

Susannah stepped forward and introduced herself.

Angela gazed at her curiously. "You look so familiar to me. Sammy, why does she look so familiar?"

Sam, busy sorting capacitors, said offhandedly, "She looks like that actress we saw on PBS a couple of months ago."

"I never watch PBS. I can't stand foreign accents. It's your hair. I don't ever forget a hairstyle. Not too many women still wear it in a bun like that."

Susannah felt vaguely apologetic. "I don't always wear it like this. Sometimes I wear it down."

"I'd take some of that weight out of it if I were you. Cut it just below your jaw line. Soften it with long layers so it stays full but isn't fussy. You don't look like the fussy type."

Her suggestions were delivered so good-naturedly, Susannah couldn't take offense. "I'll consider it."

Angela's scrutiny continued. "What did you say your last name was again?"

"Faulconer," she said hesitantly.

Angela looked thoughtful for a moment and then she let out a squeal. "I don't believe it! I read a story about you in the newspaper, didn't I? You're the daughter of that big shot. You're the one who ran away from her wedding! Ohmygod! Sammy, do you know who this is? This is Susannah Faulconer. She was getting married to this guy, and then right in the middle of this swank society wedding this other guy shows up on a Harley and—" She stopped in mid-sentence. Her jaw dropped as her eyes flew from Susannah to Sam. "Oh my God," she said breathlessly. "Oh my God! It was you!"

Without warning, she began to squeal in delight and pound her heels up and down on the concrete floor like a pint-sized flamenco dancer. "Sammy! I should have known. When I read that story, I got this shiver up my spine. I should have known right then. You're just like your old man! God, if he could only hear about this one."

Sam stiffened. Then he stepped forward. "Susannah is staying with me for a while."

"That's great! Oh, that's just great! If I'd known about this, I would have come back last week. Vegas was dead anyway. The town just isn't the same when Elvis isn't headlining. And then I had to listen to Audrey going on and on about how fat he's gotten. Fat or not, the King is still the King."

Sam interrupted abruptly. "You feel like making some spaghetti or something? I know it's late, but we're all pretty hungry."

Susannah looked at him curiously. She had just offered to make him something to eat, but he had refused.

"Sure, baby." Angela gave him another slap on the jaw and hugged Susannah. "You stay as long as you like, honey. And if Sammy gives you any trouble, you tell me about it. Between the two of us, we'll keep him in line." She jingled-jangled as she left the garage.

Susannah moved into Angela's sewing room that same night, despite the fact that Sam's mother had made it more than clear that she wasn't a prude. Susannah's desertion upset Sam, and he gave her another lecture about how uptight she was, but she was incapable of sharing his bed while his mother slept on the other side of the hall. They weren't married. They weren't engaged. They hadn't even discussed the possibility.

The next morning Angela caught her in the kitchen before Sam was awake. "Come on, honey," she said. "We're going to do something about that bun."

Ignoring Susannah's protests, Angela propelled her out to the garage and pushed her down in the shampoo chair.

For the next twenty minutes, Angela chattered as her silver scissors snipped, snipped, snipped. She cut Susannah's hair in long, fluffy layers, lifting the length so that the ends no longer quite touched her shoulders. She could still put her hair in a French twist or pile it on top of her head, but now feathery tendrils softened the angular lines of her face and curled along her neck. The style wasn't so different that she felt uncomfortable, but much looser and more untidy than anything she had ever worn. She knew that Cal Theroux wouldn't have approved of the change, but she felt as if she had been freed from an old, burdensome weight.

Sam rolled over in bed and reached out for Susannah. He frowned as he realized she wasn't there. He didn't like it when she slipped out of bed before he got up, before he could enjoy the feeling of her bottom pressed into his stomach and inhale the light floral scent of her hair. Sometimes he propped himself next to her and watched her sleep. She was always tightly curled, with her knees drawn up and her clasped hands pressed beneath her chin. There was something sad about the way she slept, as if she were trying to compress herself into a target so small that the demons of the world would fail to notice her.

He got out of bed and, after a quick shower, went to the garage, where he found her in the beauty shop with his mother. Both were so engrossed in studying Susannah's new hairstyle in the mirror that they didn't see him standing in the doorway. As he watched them, he wished that some of Susannah's class would rub off on his mother.

As usual, being near Angela made him tense. Why couldn't she be like other mothers? Why did she have to dress like a hooker and decorate her house like the world's worst garage sale? When he was a teenager, she had flirted with all of his friends, humiliating him in a way that he still couldn't forgive. She had no taste, no class, and no interest in acquiring either one. On the other hand, she had been his relentless defender through all the battles of his childhood. When the world seemed to be crashing around him, she had stood up to his father, to school officials, and to anyone else she believed was harming her son.

Susannah lifted her head and caught sight of him in the mirror. His chest expanded with pride. He had wanted this elegant woman, and now she was his. The thrill of conquest beat like a drum in his brain. She was going to make all the difference in his life. Her stillness would calm him and help him focus his energy. Her breeding would soften his rough edges. Her grace and timeless beauty would expand him in the eyes of others. With Susannah at his side, life no longer held any limits for him.

Her eyebrows drew together, and he realized that she was waiting for his reaction to her new haircut. He loved the way his opinion mattered to her. Just as he opened his mouth to tell her how terrific she looked, Angela interrupted.

"What do you think, Sammy? I haven't lost my touch, have I?"

Without a word he turned away from his mother and went back into the garage. As he reached the workbench, Susannah came through the doorway, her gray eyes regarding him with solemn intensity. Jeezus, it was sweet to have a woman like her look at him that way.

She frowned, and he realized that his failure to comment on her hair had made her mad. She pushed back her shoulders and set her jaw, practically daring him to make a derogatory remark. He almost laughed. She was learning. All he'd had to do was point the way, and she'd caught on real fast.

He reached out and took her into his arms. "It looks great."

Her annoyance fell away, and she beamed with pleasure. "You really like it?"

"Yeah, I really do." He kissed her fiercely. She leaned into him just like always and moaned softly against his mouth. Reluctantly, he drew away.

She sighed and looked over at the boxes of parts. "You're going to put me to work now, aren't you?"

"I promise you can take a coffee break sometime next week."

She laughed, and then, together, they settled down to begin the laborious process of assembling forty single-board computers.

The task involved "stuffing" every one of the printed circuit boards by hand. Sam showed her how to insert the wires on each of the small components through tiny holes in the copper pathways that ran through the circuit board. After all the components were in position, each wire had to be permanently soldered to the board and clipped. The job was both monotonous and demanding. If everything wasn't done exactly to specifications, he made her do it again.

When Susannah had finished assembling a board, Sam tested it and then put it in a long wooden "burn-in" box where it would be left on for forty-eight hours. Parts generally failed within a short period of time or not at all.

Susannah's fingers were sore at the end of the first hour, but she didn't complain. She was too conscious of the ticking of the clock and the fact that they had only thirty days to repay Spectra Electronics.

Joel dreamed that a dog was chewing on his shoulder. He was trying to get to Susannah, to save her from something horrible, but a wild dog had sunk its teeth into his shoulder and he couldn't move.

He awoke with a gasp. The dream was so vivid that he could still feel the pain. And then he realized the pain was real. As he clumsily lifted his hand to his chest he felt his pajamas soaked with sweat.

He would never forgive Susannah for doing this to him. He had given her everything, and look how she had repaid him.

The pain in his shoulder began to ease and his breathing steadied. It wasn't the first time he had experienced this tight, cramping ache. Perhaps he should see a doctor, but the idea of revealing his personal problems to anyone, even a medical professional, repelled him. He simply needed to get a grip on himself. He hadn't worked out since all of this had happened. He should get back into his old routine, set up a golf game. There was nothing wrong with him that some old-fashioned self-discipline wouldn't fix. Self-discipline and getting his daughter back.

Unaccountably, his heart began to pound again. Two weeks had passed. She should have returned long ago. The awful thought that she might not come back was never far from his mind. What would he do without her? She meant everything to him.

The darkness in the room grew oppressive. His hand trembled as he reached out for the lamp at the side of his bed. He bumped against a vase of garden flowers that Paige had left on the table and knocked it over. He swore as he flipped on the light. Dirty flower water had soaked his papers as well as the cookies that had been lying on a china plate next to the vase. Every night Paige left a snack by his bedside, like a child putting out a treat for Santa Claus. He never ate the snack—food before bedtime didn't agree with him—but still she put it out.

Joel stared down at the sodden cookies and wondered why he couldn't love the child of his own flesh as much as he loved his adopted daughter. But emotional introspection made him uncomfortable, so he got out of bed and crossed the floor to the window. Facts were all that mattered, and he acknowledged the simple, indisputable fact that Susannah had long ago become the most important person in the world to him. He had to get her back.

As he gazed out into the darkness, he chided himself for not having taken her last telephone call. She must have realized by now what a horrible mistake she had made, and he should have given her the opportunity to beg his forgiveness.

His hand closed over the edge of the windowsill. He had always been a man of action, and it wasn't in his nature to let events slip so far from his control. He had been patient long enough. Tomorrow he was going to see her. He would point out how reprehensibly she had behaved, and after he had laid out a few conditions of his own, he would relent and let her come back to Falcon Hill.

For the first time since the afternoon of her wedding, some of the darkness inside him lifted. He walked from one window to the next, envisioning their meeting. She would cry, of course, but he mustn't give into any emotional manipulation on her part. After everything she had put him through, he wouldn't make it easy for her. He would be tough, but he wouldn't be unreasonable. Eventually, Susannah would thank him for treating her so compassionately. Years from now they might even be able to smile about what had happened.

Feeling much more like himself, Joel returned to his bed. As he sank back into his pillow, a sigh of satisfaction slipped from his lips. He had been too emotional about all of this.

By this time tomorrow night, he would have his daughter back. And then everything would be all right.

The afternoon was unusually hot for Northern California. Susannah had propped the garage door open, but only an occasional breeze managed to make its way inside. Even though she had pulled her shorter hair into a ponytail with a red rubber band from the morning newspaper, her neck was damp. She looked up from the board she was stuffing to study Sam. He had a bandanna wrapped around his forehead so he didn't drip sweat onto the boards. For a moment she let her gaze linger on the muscles bunched beneath his T-shirt.

"I sure as hell hope Pinky doesn't decide to renege on the deal," he said abruptly. "I've met guys like him before. They're hardware freaks—seduced by the last piece of equipment they set eyes on. Half the guys in Homebrew must have discovered his place by now, and I'll bet some of them are trying to sell him their boards. If we don't get ours to him fast, he might strike a deal with someone else and then back out on us."

Susannah rubbed the small of her back where it was aching from having been bent over the assembly table for so long. "It seems to me that we have enough real problems without inventing unlikely ones." She stretched, trying to work out the kinks. "Remember that we have a contract and the others don't."

The muscles she had been admiring beneath his T-shirt grew unnaturally still. Slowly, she laid down her soldering iron. "Sam?"

He didn't say anything.

A warning bell went off in the corners of her mind, and she pushed herself up from the table. "Sam, you do have a written contract with the man, don't you?"

He became unbelievably busy with the board he was putting into the burn-in box.

"Sam?"

He turned on her belligerently. "I didn't think about it, all right? I was excited. I just didn't think about it."

She pulled off her reading glasses and rubbed her temples.

Suddenly she felt very tired. Her love for him kept blinding her to the fact that he was only a kid. A wild kid with a silver tongue. And she was an uptight socialite, and Yank was a hopeless nerd, and none of them knew what they were doing. They were goofing around, playing at being grown-ups. Why was she even surprised that he hadn't thought to draw up a contract? At that moment, she realized how insurmountable their problems really were. They were deeply in debt. It was only a matter of time before this house of cards they were building came crashing down around them.

"Look, don't worry, okay?" he said. "I told you the guy's a hardware freak, and we've got the best piece of hardware in the whole Valley."

She wanted to yell at him and tell him that it was time to grow up. Instead, she said wearily, "No more oral agreements, Sam. From now on everything has to be in writing. We can't ever let this happen again."

"Since when did you start giving orders?" he retorted. "You're sounding like a real bitch, you know that?"

Perhaps it was the effect of the heat, or the ache in her muscles, but her customary patience deserted her. A surge of righteous anger swept through her, and she slapped the flat of her hand down on the table. The sound reverberated through the garage, startling her as much as it did Sam. For a few seconds she stared down at her hand as if it belonged to someone else, and then, incredibly, she found herself slapping it down again.

"You're the one who made the mistake, Sam. Don't you dare attack me. You're the one who messed up! Not me."

He looked at her for a moment and then wiped the back of his forearm over his sweat band. "Yeah, you're right. Okay."

She stared at him. Was that all there was to it? Had she actually won an argument with him?

He grinned at the expression of surprise on her face and began to amble toward her, running deliberately lecherous eyes over her body. Susannah experienced a moment of deep pleasure, a sense of the strength of her own womanhood that was new and wonderful. Without thinking about what she was doing, she hooked her index finger over the snap on his jeans and tugged. When he came up against her, she gave him a trashy kiss, open-mouthed and deep.

"Would you be a doll baby and do a shampoo for me? I hate to interrupt, but I'm really backed up."

Susannah pulled abruptly away as Angela came through the beauty shop door. Sam whirled around. "She's not your shampoo girl, for chrissake!"

Susannah interceded. "My back hurts and I need to stretch for a few minutes. I don't mind. Yank will be here before long, and Roberta's coming over this evening to help."

Sam's lips tightened at the mention of Roberta, but since he was the one who had called her and told her she had to help assemble the boards, he couldn't really protest. Susannah suspected he would have made the elderly women in Angela's beauty shop stuff boards if they had better eyesight.

A blast of cool air from the window air conditioner hit her as she stepped through the door of the beauty parlor. One elderly woman was under a hair dryer, and Angela was giving another a perm. Susannah ushered the third to the shampoo bowl and supported her as she leaned back. She didn't mind helping Angela. Sam's mother was so good-natured it was impossible not to like her. Besides, when Susannah was helping out, she felt less guilty about the fact that she wasn't contributing anything toward her room and board.

As she gently worked the lather through the elderly woman's thin hair, she thought about how badly she needed money. All her life she had been dependent on her father, and now she was dependent on Sam and Angela. She had even been forced to ask Sam for money to buy a box of Tampax. He had given it to her without comment, but she still found the experience demeaning.

"Well, h-e-l-l-o there." Angela's voice, flirtatious and sassy, rose over the sound of the water running in the shampoo basin. Susannah glanced up, then sucked in her breath as the walls of the small shop seemed to tilt in crazy directions.

Joel Faulconer stood in the doorway, aloof and out of

place in a hunter-green polo shirt and crisply creased khaki slacks. He had put on some unneeded weight since she had last seen him, and his golfer's tan had faded. It was probably only her imagination, but he seemed older than she remembered.

He gazed around him without saying anything. In the past few weeks, Susannah had grown accustomed to her surroundings, but now she saw it all again through his eyes— the garish mirrored tiles, the plastic plants and ugly photographs of overly elaborate hairstyles. She saw herself— cheap and common in a man's T-shirt and a pair of threadbare slacks she had once worn for gardening. She could almost read his mind as he watched her shampoo the hair of a woman who was wearing blue bedroom slippers with slits cut in the sides to accommodate her bunions.

Susannah heard a cry of pain and realized she had dug her fingers into the poor woman's scalp. "I'm sorry," she apologized, releasing her. Her hands shaking, she finished rinsing out the woman and wrapped her head in a towel. Then she went over to her father. Angela looked on, making no attempt to hide her curiosity.

"I—I tried to call you," Susannah said.

"So I understand." Joel's eyes flicked over her clothing, revealing nothing except distaste.

Angela's charm bracelets had stilled, and Susannah could feel the curious eyes of her customers. Making an awkward gesture with her hand, she indicated that Joel should follow her into the workshop. It was empty. Sam must have gone to see someone about the cases to house the computer boards.

The burn-in box gave off a warm plastic smell that mingled with the sharp scent of perm solution. The garage seemed unbearably hot and airless. She hugged herself. "Would you like me to get you some iced tea? There's a pitcher in the kitchen. It'll only take a moment."

Ignoring her, he wandered over to the workbench and looked at the board that was sitting on it. He snorted contemptuously.

"I can fix you a drink if you'd rather," she said quickly.

He turned and stared at her so coldly, she couldn't believe that he had ever regarded her with tenderness. She couldn't bear it. Her throat tightened as she gazed at the man she had loved for nearly as long as she could remember, the golden prince of her childhood who had slain her dragons and loved her when no one else would. "Don't hate me," she whispered. "Please."

"Surely you didn't expect me to forget all the pain you've caused."

"Let me try to explain. Let me explain how I felt."

"*Now* you want to tell me how you felt," he scoffed. "Fascinating. Now that it's all over, and hideous damage has been done, you decide you want to settle in for a cozy father-daughter chat."

He was so cold, so accusing. "I just want you to understand that I never meant to hurt you."

"I'm afraid the time for confidences has long passed. Why didn't you talk to me before that debacle of a wedding? Tell me, Susannah, when did I turn into such a monster? Did I beat you when you were a child and you came to me with your troubles?"

"No," she said miserably. "No, of course not."

"Did I lock you in a closet every time you did something wrong?"

"No, it's not—"

"When you wanted to confide in me, did I push you aside and tell you I couldn't spare the time?"

"No. You were wonderful. You never did any of those things. It's just—" She struggled to find the words. "When I displeased you, you were always so cold to me."

His eyebrows shot up. "I was *cold* to you. Well, of course. Why didn't I think of that? In the face of such terrible parental abuse, who in the world could fault you for what you've done."

She bit her lip. "Please. I didn't mean to hurt you." The words seemed to be squeezing through a microscopically tiny passageway in her throat. "I didn't mean to hurt Cal. I just couldn't stand—I just couldn't stand being perfect any longer."

"Is that what this is about?" he said scathingly. "Your perfection? I wish you'd told me, so I could have disabused you of the notion long ago. You were never perfect, Susannah."

"I know that. It's just—I felt as if I had to be perfect or

you wouldn't love me. I felt as if I always had to do what everyone expected of me."

"You certainly chose a dramatic way to prove otherwise, didn't you?" he said contemptuously. Walking over to the assembly table, he gazed down at the assorted parts with distaste. When he looked back up at her, his features were rigid. "Now that you've had a taste of real life, I suppose you're going to beg me to let you come back to Falcon Hill?"

His statement caught her unaware. "You're my father. I—I don't want to be cut off from you."

"I'm supposed to forget everything that has happened and take you back? It's not going to be that easy, Susannah. You've hurt too many people. You can't just return to your old life and expect everything to be the way it was."

"I don't want my old life back," she whispered.

"If you expect Cal to be waiting with open arms, you'll be sadly disappointed," he went on, not hearing her. "He'll never forgive you."

Cold was seeping through her skin into her bones. "Daddy, I don't want Cal. I want to help Sam build his computer. I want to stay here."

Joel's entire body stiffened and his face grew ashen. For a moment he seemed to be fighting to catch his breath, and when he finally spoke, his voice was hoarse. "Are you telling me that you would rather live in this sordid place with that hooligan than come back to your family?"

"Why does it have to be one or the other?" she cried. "Daddy, I love you! But I love Sam, too."

"I don't think this is about love," he retorted. "Your relationship with that man—it's about sex."

"No, it's not—"

"Cal was a decent man, but apparently he wasn't *hot* enough for you."

Susannah wanted to cover her ears against Joel's venom. "Don't talk to me like this. I won't listen."

"I can only guess what your particular fetish is," he lashed out. "Leather? Motorcycles?"

His expression had grown so ugly, she hardly recognized it. Was this vindictive, hateful man really her father? In the background she heard the hum of a hair dryer and Angela's chatter. She clasped her arms around her body and tried to hold herself together.

Joel's complexion looked gray and unhealthy beneath his fading tan. "What do you get from your stud? Does he beat you? Are you that sort of woman?"

A sneering voice came from the outside doorway. "Naw, Faulconer, you got it all wrong, man. She's the one who beats me. Don't you, Suzie?"

Sam swaggered forward, every step insolent. One thumb was tucked in the waistband of his jeans, the other in his pocket. His blade-straight hair fell from beneath his sweatband and pooled on his shoulders. The silver earring glimmered through the black strands.

He stopped just behind her and slipped his hand possessively around her waist. "Your little girl is a wild cat with a whip."

Joel made a choked exclamation and took a menacing step forward. "You insolent—"

"That's right," Sam drawled. "I'm insolent, I'm crude, I'm stupid. I'm so stupid that I stole your precious daughter from right under your nose." He pulled Susannah tighter against his body, her back to his chest. Then he deliberately slid his thumb up onto her breast. "Does this give you any idea what I plan to do to your company?"

"Stop it, Sam!" Susannah couldn't bear it. He had no sense of caution. No sense at all. She pulled away from him and stepped toward her father. "I didn't mean to hurt anybody. I'm sorry for that. I just— I just couldn't help it."

Joel turned away as if he could no longer bear looking at her. His eyes returned to the workbench and the cluttered assembly table. When he spoke, his voice was frigid. "You've made a poor bargain, Susannah. You've tied your future to a hoodlum and a toy that no one will ever want. If you hadn't betrayed me, I could almost feel sorry for you."

"I didn't betray you. I—I love you."

"You've turned into a tramp. An ungrateful, cheap little tramp."

His words struck her like small, deadly pellets. She wanted to protect herself against them, but she had no defenses left. A deafening silence filled the small garage.

163

They all stood without moving, as if they had nowhere else to go.

"Don't you think you might be getting a little carried away here, Mr. Faulconer?" The jingle-jangle of charm bracelets came from the doorway of the Pretty Please Salon.

As Angela came into the garage, Joel gave her a look so malevolent that most women would have retreated. But Angela was a sucker for great-looking men, no matter how foul their dispositions, and Joel Faulconer was great-looking, even if he was a son of a bitch—a fact she intended to point out.

"Your daughter is one of the finest young ladies it's ever been my pleasure to meet. And as for what you said about my son—calling him a hoodlum—I want you to know that I don't appreciate that one bit."

Sam took a step toward his mother. "Stay out of this. This doesn't have anything to do with you."

Angela held out her hand. "Just one minute, Sammy. I haven't had my say yet."

Joel stared at Angela as if she were a particularly loathsome reptile, and then his eyes made a path from her swaying plastic earrings to her gold-lamé sandals. "By all means let your mother speak. She's obviously a woman whose opinion deserves to be heard."

Sam's arm shot back and his breath released in a hiss. Susannah leaped forward to put herself between him and her father. "No, Sam! You're only going to make it worse." She spun on Joel. "The problems between us don't have anything to do with Mrs. Gamble."

Angela planted her hand on her hip. "Let me just tell you one thing before you go, Mr. Faulconer—"

"Mom! Don't say any more."

Angela waved Sam off and concentrated all her attention on Joel. "Let me just tell you that you might want to think twice about casting aspersions at my son, since you don't know who he really is."

The threatening tone in Sam's voice grew stronger. "Don't do this, Mom. I'm telling you."

Angela lifted her chin, more than willing to take on the chairman of FBT. "My son—the one you called a hoodlum —the one you think isn't good enough for your daughter—"

"Stop it, Mom!"

"My son happens to be the only male child of Mr. Elvis Presley!"

The garage went completely still. Sam's face looked as if it had been carved from stone. Susannah's lips parted in astonishment. For several moments Joel Faulconer didn't move. When he finally turned to Susannah, his expression was haggard.

"I will never forgive you for this," he hissed. And then he left.

Susannah started to run after him, but Sam caught her arm and hauled her up short before she could take a step. "Don't you dare," he snarled, pushing her down at the assembly table. "You stay right here! Godammit, don't you even think about going after that bastard."

Without a word of explanation, Angela returned to her elderly ladies. Sam waited for Joel's car to leave, and then he stormed from the garage. Susannah rubbed her arm where he had grabbed her and reached out to pick up the soldering iron. But her hand was shaking so badly that she couldn't manage it. She sat in silence for some time while she waited for the pain to go away.

Sam still hadn't returned by dinner time, although Yank and Roberta had shown up several hours earlier. Roberta's mindless chatter coupled with Yank's unrelenting silence strained Susannah's frazzled nerves to the breaking point. When she couldn't stand her thoughts anymore, she retreated into the kitchen and began assembling ingredients for a salad. As she tore apart a head of lettuce, Angela came inside.

"It'll probably just be you and me for dinner, Susannah. I wouldn't count on Sammy showing up for a while." Angela squirted some dishwashing liquid into her hands and washed them under the kitchen faucet. "Let me cut up some cheese and salami and we can have ourselves a big chef salad—ladies' night special."

"All right."

Angela's bracelets clinked against the refrigerator door as she opened it to pull out several deli packages. "You like olives?"

"Olives are fine." Susannah fumbled for the paring knife.

"I'm really sorry about that awful scene with my father. It's bad enough that I'm mooching off you all the time without putting you through something like that."

Angela waved away her apology. "You're not responsible for your father. And I like having you here. You're a real lady. You're good for Sammy. The two of us—you might have noticed—we don't get along too well. He's ashamed of me."

A polite denial sprang to Susannah's lips, but she bit it back. If Angela had the courage to be honest, she wouldn't insult her with well-meaning evasions. "He's still young," she said.

Angela's face softened. "Young and a rebel. What a time I've had with him."

The pain of her confrontation with Joel had overridden her curiosity about Angela's strange revelation. Now she remembered it. "His father . . . ?"

"Frank Gamble was a decent man, I guess. But he didn't have any imagination."

Susannah's hand stilled on the lettuce. She hadn't expected to hear about Frank Gamble. What about Elvis?

Angela began unwrapping the deli packages. "I had to marry him because I was a good Italian girl who had gotten herself in trouble, if you understand what I mean. But we didn't have too much in common. And when Sammy was a teenager, Frank was always screaming at him about being a hippie and a bum, and Sammy kept running away. It was terrible. I loved Sammy a lot more than I ever loved Frank. When Frank left me for another woman a few years ago, I was actually relieved, although whenever I went to Altar Society meetings, I pretended I was broken up about it since I'm Catholic."

"I see." Susannah quartered a cucumber as she tried to put it all together.

"Of course, it was hard having Frank run off with somebody in her twenties, especially when my boobs were starting to sag and my face didn't look as good as it used to. I was so pretty when I was in my twenties," she said dreamily. And then she gave a self-conscious laugh. "Listen to me. You'd think I was ready for the grave instead of just hitting my prime. You want to know about Elvis, don't you?"

"Not if you don't want to tell me."

"I don't mind. It's just— Sammy hates it when I talk about him. I know I should have kept my mouth shut out there in the garage, but your father was—pardon my French—acting like a real bastard."

"He's not like that all the time. I'm afraid I've hurt him pretty badly."

"Sammy hurts me all the time, but I don't ever go after him like that."

Tears welled in Susannah's eyes. She blinked them away and briskly rinsed off a tomato. "When did you meet Mister—uhm, Elvis?"

"Every once in a while during the fifties, I used to drive down to L.A. and work as an extra. I got a job on *Love Me Tender*. It was Elvis's first starring role, and every female extra in the world wanted to work on that film. Luckily, I had this friend in the business who had a friend. Anyway, it all worked out." She nibbled absentmindedly on a sliver of Swiss cheese. "All I have to do is shut my eyes and I can see him right now singing the title song." She began humming "Love Me Tender."

Something didn't seem right to Susannah. Sam was twenty-four. He had been born in 1952. Surely Elvis wasn't starring in movies that early. "When was that film made?"

"I'm not too good with dates. I met him for the first time much earlier than that anyway. In—I guess—'fifty-one. I went to Nashville with a girlfriend. Elvis was called the Hillbilly Cat then, and he was getting ready to sign his first record contract. You should have seen him. Young and sexy, with those eyelids drooping down and his hair all greased back. Don't get me wrong, Susannah. I was a good girl. I always went to mass. I even thought about being a nun for a while. But with Elvis, it was sort of holy anyway. Do you want hard-boiled egg in your salad?"

"Fine—anything," Susannah said distractedly.

"You really love him, don't you?"

For a second Susannah thought Angela was talking about Elvis, and then she realized the subject had shifted back to Sam.

"Yes. Yes, I do."

"You're not too much alike."

"I know."

"Suzie, be careful with Sammy. He's different. He doesn't see the world the same way as everybody else. You're really a nice girl, and I don't want him to hurt you."

Angela's warning made Susannah uneasy, but when she went out to the garage a few hours later and found Sam hard at work, she was so glad to see him that she pushed it to the back of her mind. They worked side by side for a while. Finally, she asked him about Angela's claim that he was Elvis Presley's son.

"It's a lie," he said brusquely. "Something she invented around the time she got divorced. Whenever she talks about it, her story changes. The dates never match up. Just forget about it, will you? I don't want to talk about it anymore."

She didn't press him, and sometime around midnight, he pulled her into the deserted interior of the Pretty Please Beauty Salon, where they made love in the shampoo chair. Afterwards, Susannah realized that neither of them had thought to lock the door, but since Angela had gone to bed hours before, she supposed it didn't really matter much. Yank was still in the garage, of course, but Yank didn't count. He wouldn't have noticed if they had made love right on top of his workbench.

12

• •

The old man's playing with his toys again."

The two FBT grounds keepers, one plump and soft, the other thin and wiry, leaned on their shovels and gazed over at the seven obelisk-shaped fountains in the reflecting pond at the Castle. One by one, they stopped sending their silvery streamers of water into the air. But before the ripples in the pond had stilled, the columns of water began flowing again, rising systematically from the first fountain to the last.

"Man, I'd like to have his job," the heavier of the two men commented as he watched the water catch the light, recede, and then catch the light again. "Sit around in an air-conditioned office all day, play with a bunch of fountains, and pull in a couple million a year."

They began digging again, only to stop and look curiously back at the reflecting pond. Instead of the systematic ebb and flow they were accustomed to, the fountains had begun going on and off in a quirky, random fashion neither had witnessed before. The effect was eerie and vaguely disquieting, turning the smooth pond water choppy and gray.

"The old man must be having a bad day."

"What's he got to feel bad about? Shit, man. If I had his money, I'd be dancin' in the streets."

The center four fountains abruptly stopped, as if someone had slammed a fist in the middle of the panel of control switches. The grounds keepers watched for a moment and then went back to their shovels.

Joel swiveled his desk chair so that he was no longer looking through the window at the reflecting pond. He had once been so proud of the FBT fountains. When he had controlled the switches, he had felt as if he were somehow controlling the continent each fountain represented: Europe brought to life with a flick of his hand, South America firmly under his rule, North America beating at the heart of his mighty kingdom. Even Asia had seemed to fall under his power. He had felt like a king in command of the world.

Now he merely felt tired.

The nagging pain in his chest was back. He could barely comprehend what had happened in that squalid little garage. She should have been repentant. She should have begged him to take her back. Instead she had asked him to *understand.* As if he could understand something so sordid.

The buzz of the intercom interrupted his thoughts, and his secretary announced Cal. Joel straightened in his chair at the same time that he pretended to turn his attention to the papers on his desk. It wouldn't do for Cal to see that anything was wrong. Not that Joel didn't trust Cal. He did. Cal was like the son he'd never had—smart, ambitious, and just as ruthless as he had been himself at that age. But the basic rule of maintaining power was not to let anyone, no matter how close he might be, see your weakness.

"I need to go to Rio next week," Cal said after they had exchanged greetings. He took a cup of coffee from Joel's secretary and, settling into a comfortable leather wing chair across from the desk, began to fill Joel in on their negotiations with the Brazilians.

As Joel listened, he was acutely conscious of Cal's appearance. The younger man was professionally attired in the FBT uniform: a dark blue suit, custom-made white shirt, and silk rep tie. His wing tips were polished to a sheen, his hair neatly trimmed. Joel had always found the white streak that ran through the center of Cal's hair too flamboyant, but he couldn't really blame Cal for that. All in all, he couldn't help comparing him to the long-haired thug who had carried off his daughter on the back of a motorcycle, a man who was purported to be the illegitimate offspring of Elvis Presley. He raged against the humiliation of Susannah keeping company with a person like that.

The discussion came to an end. Joel toyed with the edge of one of the binders on his desk. "I had our security people make some inquiries about Susannah," he said carefully, "and then I went to see her yesterday." He couldn't bring himself to mention that she had been shampooing hair.

Cal's jaw tightened, but other than that he showed no reaction. His self-control made Joel uneasy, perhaps because he no longer felt as much in command of himself as he used to. But his uneasiness might have been caused by something else, some wayward sense of protectiveness toward his ungrateful daughter, which Cal's barely repressed hostility was triggering. The thought infuriated him, and his voice hardened.

"She and that hoodlum she's living with have actually found someone naive enough to order that ridiculous machine they're working on—an electronics dealer in the Valley. It's a small business with shaky credit."

"I see." The room grew quiet. Cal's cup clinked delicately against his saucer. "From what you've told me, they don't sound much more professional than kids running a Kool-Aid stand." The leather seat cushion of the chair wheezed softly as he shifted his weight. "Amateurs run into so many catastrophes when they do business with each other."

It was exactly the tack Joel had expected Cal to take, but he still couldn't suppress a growing feeling of uneasiness.

Cal went on. "If their operation is that tenuous, the smallest setback will finish them. This fellow who ordered their little toy, for example. If he backed out, they would find it impossible to recover."

"*If* he backed out."

"It's difficult to imagine what someone like that might not be prepared to give up for a chance to do business with FBT."

Cal had finally made his point—one that Joel had already considered. He was surprised at the vehemence of his response. "No. I don't want any interference. None, do you understand?"

A muscle ticked just beneath Cal's cheekbone. "I'm a bit surprised."

"That's because you're not quite as perceptive as I thought you were. You didn't understand how unhappy Susannah was, for example."

Cal's expression grew wooden. Joel's attack had obviously surprised him, but not nearly as much as it surprised Joel. Was he actually making excuses for Susannah? He immediately backstepped. "Not that I'm blaming you, of course. Still, I don't want any interference."

For the first time, Cal let his bitterness show. "You're obviously more forgiving than I. I suppose that isn't surprising. You're her father, after all."

Joel thought of the way Susannah had let Gamble put his hand on her breast, and a rush of righteous outrage hit him anew. "Forgiveness has nothing to do with it. By God, Susannah is going to suffer the consequences of what she's done! Judging by what I saw yesterday, it's only a matter of time before they fail. But when it happens, I want her to know she did it to herself. Do you understand me? We do this my way, Cal. I won't give her a convenient scapegoat. I don't want her to be able to believe for one minute that she could have succeeded if we hadn't interfered."

Some of Joel's tension eased. Susannah just needed more time, that was all. It had only been a few weeks. By going to see her yesterday, he had rushed things. Once the reality of her sordid new life set in, her desire to rebel would fade and she would come running back to him.

He saw that Cal still looked wary. Did Cal sense his ambivalence where Susannah was concerned? He returned Cal's gaze steadily and steered the conversation into safer waters.

"Paige said you invited her to dinner at the yacht club on Saturday."

"Yes," Cal replied smoothly. "I'm enjoying her company very much."

I can't . . . get no . . . sa tis . . . fac tion . . .

Paige kept her eyes shut, waiting for it to be over. It was creepy being in bed with Cal. She didn't even know why she had let it get this far, except Conti had called her today to tell her he was going back East, and he had cried on the phone.

Cal stiffened, then relaxed. For a moment, she wondered what was wrong, then she realized that small spasm had marked his orgasm. He had made no sound—he had barely inconvenienced her. Apparently Cal was always well-behaved, even when he came.

As she eased herself out of bed and went into his bronze and gold bathroom, she was grateful that he had gotten it over with quickly. Maybe Cal didn't enjoy sex any more than she did. It was a tantalizing idea, and later, when they were dressed and he was driving her home, she decided to test it.

"I don't think it's a good idea for us to sleep together again, Cal. It's a little too weird."

The headlights from an approaching car caused an angular pattern to pass over his face. "You're quite sensitive, Paige. I never realized that until tonight." Incredibly, he reached over and patted her knee. The gesture was comforting rather than sexual. "I don't want to speak out of turn, but I know it can't be entirely easy for you at Falcon Hill. I respect Joel more than any man in the world, but he's not the easiest man to please."

His sympathy and understanding touched her. "No, he's not." Then she said bitterly, "Especially since I'm not his precious Susannah."

His expression stiffened as it always did when she mentioned her sister's name. Sometimes she did it deliberately, just so she could watch the way his lips tightened.

"Susannah manipulated him," he said. "But then, she manipulated all of us, didn't she? When I think how she used to talk about you . . . the lies and distortions she spouted behind your back. The worst of it is, I believed her." He glanced over at her. "I'm sorry for that, Paige. I feel as if I owe you something. If we're not going to be lovers, at least I'd like for us to be friends. Do you think that's possible?"

Paige was cynical about men. She knew that Cal wanted to stay close to Joel, and from his viewpoint, one daughter was probably as good as another. But he had been so kind, so sympathetic, and she needed someone to care about her. "What about—sex?" she asked. "You're not mad?"

Once again, he patted her knee. "I've never been particularly interested in carving notches on my bedpost. Don't misunderstand me. I enjoy sex, but it's not the most important thing in my life. Right now I need a friend more than a lover." He extended his hand. "Friends?"

He was so sincere that she let her guard down. "Friends," she repeated as she took his hand.

They chatted easily the rest of the way to Falcon Hill. Gradually, she found herself relaxing. Cal understood how unfair Joel had always been to her, and for the first time since her mother had died, she had someone on her side. By the time they reached home, she felt better than she had in ages—like a battered ship that had just sailed into a safe harbor.

Sam delivered the forty computers to Pinky at Z.B. Electronics precisely on schedule. Each machine was neatly encased in a wooden box with the words SysVal and the Roman numeral I visible on the front in gold rub-on letters that Susannah had finished applying just before dawn that morning.

To her relief, Pinky paid his bill on time and she was able to settle up with Spectra. But they were only out of debt for a day before Sam ordered more parts on credit and the cycle began all over again. Only this time they didn't have a committed buyer for the new boards.

During the next few weeks, Pinky sold several of their single-board computers to hardware freaks like himself, but the machines weren't flying off the shelves, and she was frantic with worry. They had taken out several ads in hobbyists' magazines and a few orders had trickled in, but not many. Yank had already started work on the prototype of the self-contained computer they wanted to build, but if they hoped to survive long enough to begin manufacturing it, they needed to buy themselves time. And they needed money. Big money. Susannah decided to swallow her pride and see if she could find it.

Every day for a week, she put on her old Chanel suit and, borrowing either Yank's Duster or Angela's Toyota, went to see acquaintances from what she had begun to think of as her former life. She didn't waste time trying to contact Joel's friends or any FBT people. Instead, she phoned members of Kay's old social circle and people who had sat with her on the boards of charitable organizations. Almost all of them agreed to see her, but she quickly discovered that they were far more interested in confirming the gossip they had heard about her than in investing in SysVal. When the subject of money came up, they shifted uncomfortably in their seats and remembered urgent appointments.

Each day, she returned tired and discouraged. At the end of the week, she went out to the garage and told Sam that she had run out of names. He pressed the half-empty can of Coke he had been drinking into her hand and said, "We need to find a venture capitalist who's willing to pump a few hundred thousand into the company. Then we could get serious about moving beyond the hobbyists' market and building the computer we really want to build." He lifted a board from the burn-in box and began putting it in its wooden case.

She rolled the lukewarm Coke can between her hands. "No respectable venture capitalist will pay any attention to us. We don't look *serious.*"

At that moment the buzzer that Yank had rigged over the workbench went off. She sighed, set down the can, and rushed from the garage and across the yard toward the kitchen door.

Generally she made it to the phone on its fifth ring, but today she stumbled on the step and lost time. As she lifted the receiver to her ear, she yearned for the day they could afford to have a separate telephone line in the garage instead of being forced to use the kitchen phone. She knew that it sounded more professional to have a woman answer, but sometimes she resented the fact that she was the one who always had to make the dash across the yard.

"SysVal. May I help you?"

"Yeah. I got a question about the voltage levels at the I/O interface."

At least this phone call was from a customer instead of one of Angela's friends. "I'm sure we can answer that for you. Let me put you on hold while I connect you with our Support Services Department." She flipped on the portable radio they kept tuned to a rock station and set the receiver in front of it, then she rushed back outside and gestured for Sam, who was watching at the garage window. He hurried across the yard to take the call.

Appearances, Susannah kept repeating to herself. *Appearances are everything.*

That same night she and Sam enjoyed the luxury of being able to sleep together, since Angela had taken an overnight trip to visit a friend in Sacramento. But even lovemaking couldn't push their business problems far from their minds.

"I've been thinking," Sam said, his lips resting against her forehead. "We need to take on one more partner. Someone who understands electronics and knows about marketing. A person with a sharp mind, who hasn't bought into the system." He rolled over on his back. "Someone inventive. And he can't be an asshole. We need to hire somebody like Nolan Bushnell at Atari."

"I think he already has a job," Susannah said dryly. She twirled a strand of his hair through her fingers.

"Or—this would be great—one of the big guys at Hewlett-Packard."

Susannah rolled her eyes. Hewlett-Packard, with its progressive management style, seemed to be the only American corporation that Sam admired. "Why would anyone leave H-P to come work with us in a garage for no money?"

"If they had vision they would. Hell, yes. We wouldn't even want them if they didn't have vision."

This was what she both loved about him and despaired over. "It would be impossible for us to attract anyone with an important name to this company."

"Will you stop telling me what's impossible? You do that all the time. Start telling me what's possible for a change."

"I'm just being practical."

"You're just being negative. I'm getting sick of it. I can't work like that." He pushed himself from the bed and went out into the kitchen.

Her stomach churned, but she forced herself not to go after him. She was determined not to settle back into her old patterns of conciliation. Sam's anger burned hot and fierce, but it was over quickly. Still, she didn't fall asleep until several hours later, when he slipped back into bed.

Not long after their conversation, Sam began cornering

Hewlett-Packard vice-presidents in the company parking lot. Several of them thought they were being mugged and locked themselves in their cars, but a few of them actually came to the garage to see their operation and to offer advice. On one rainy evening, Sam even managed to corner Bill Hewlett himself.

Hewlett was pleasant but firm. He wasn't quite ready to leave the billion-dollar company he had helped found and follow Sam Gamble's silver tongue to the land of small computer nirvana.

After that, Sam lost all respect for Hewlett-Packard.

Labor Day weekend marked the first small computer trade show. It was being held in Atlantic City, and Sam announced that they were going. "We need to establish ourselves as a national company instead of a local one," he said.

Susannah agreed with him philosophically, but felt that the expense of the trip for a company that hadn't sold even all forty of its original single-board computers made it impossible. He rode roughshod over every one of her objections, and when she saw she couldn't change his mind, she made a condition of her own. If they were going to exhibit at the trade show, they would do it her way.

Atlantic City, by the summer of 1976, was a faded hooker about to succumb to a variety of social diseases. Legislation was afoot in Trenton to allow legalized gambling, but until that happened, the city that had once been the gayest spot on the Atlantic seaboard had lost all vestiges of its former beauty. The boardwalk was decaying and their hotel seedy. By the time they had checked in, Susannah was convinced the trip was doomed, but she still hustled her partners over to the convention hall to set up their booth.

To her relief, the worst of her nightmares hadn't come true—the crates that held what Sam called "Susannah's Goddamn Folly" were undamaged, and he began unpacking.

She concentrated on how great his rear end looked when he bent over instead of on what he was saying. The booth had ended up costing nearly a thousand dollars—far more than they could afford. But she had wanted them to look like a much larger company than they were, and so, over Sam's strident objections, she had ordered it built. If she was wrong, she would have to shoulder the blame alone.

But as it turned out, she wasn't wrong. By noon the next day, several hundred people were wandering through the exhibits, and all of them were drawn to the SysVal booth. While the companies surrounding them displayed their products on crudely draped card tables bearing identical white tagboard signs printed with the company's name, SysVal showed off its machine in a brightly colored booth with dramatically angled walls and the company name spelled out in illuminated crimson letters. Only MITS, the manufacturers of the Altair, and IMSAI, their closest competitor, had more elaborate displays. Without a word being spoken, Susannah's booth made SysVal look like the third largest single-board computer company exhibiting, when in fact they were one of the smallest. Her triumph made her feel wonderfully cocky and full of herself.

Toward the end of the first day, she glanced up and saw Steve Jobs standing in front of their machine. Since their situations were similar, she had been interested in watching the two Steves—Wozniak and Jobs—as they tried to stir up interest in their Apple single-board computer.

Jobs was only twenty-one and Woz twenty-five, and like her own partners, neither was a college graduate. Compared to Steve Jobs, however, Sam was a fashion plate of respectability. Jobs was unkempt and unwashed, with dirty jeans and battered Birkenstock sandals. Sam had told her that he was a vegetarian and a Zen Buddhist who had traveled to India in search of enlightenment. He was still thinking about returning to become a monk.

Instead of looking at the computer they had on display, Jobs was studying Susannah's booth. He and Woz were selling their Apples from a card table on the other side of the convention hall. She watched Jobs as his alert eyes took in the multicolored backdrop and the brightly lit name. He knew the SysVal operation was just as small and eccentric as his own, but he could see that they had made themselves appear bigger and more important. He looked at Susannah, and she felt a moment of recognition pass between them—a moment that leaped across the barriers separating a San

Francisco socialite and an unkempt Silicon Valley hippie. Jobs understood what she had done. She suspected that the little Apple Computer Company—if it survived—would never again make the mistake of showing up at a trade show with their wares displayed on a card table.

Late Monday night, after the trade show had closed, Susannah, Sam, and Yank left Atlantic City and headed for the Philadelphia airport with fifty-two new orders in their pockets. Their success had even made Yank talkative, and they boarded their flight with a sense of celebration.

As Sam slid into his seat, he pulled a copy of the *Wall Street Journal* from the seat pocket in front of him. "Now that I'm going to be a tycoon, I'll have to change my reading habits," he joked. He made a great play out of opening the newspaper and busily arranging it in front of him. He was trying to be funny, but Susannah couldn't manage much more than a polite smile. She had seen her father's head buried in the same newspaper too many times.

An array of feelings, bittersweet and painful, swept over her. Several moments passed before she realized that Sam had fallen silent next to her. She glanced over and saw that his face had grown rigid.

"Sam?"

He abruptly folded the paper and stuffed it under his arm. "We've got to get off the plane."

"What?"

"Come on."

"Sam?"

"Hurry. They're getting ready to close the door."

His air of urgency alarmed her, and she found herself rising from her seat. He planted his hand in the small of her back and pushed her ahead of him. "Sam? What are you doing? Where are we going?"

He directed her past a stewardess. "We've got to get off. Hurry up."

She glanced over her shoulder at their partner, who was still seated, his eyes vaguely puzzled beneath his glasses. "What about Yank?"

"Somebody'll take care of him."

Within minutes, Susannah found herself standing in the boarding area while her few remaining clothes took off for

San Francisco. Three hours later, she and Sam were on their way to Boston in search of a man named Mitchell Blaine.

Blaine lived in an expensive English Tudor located in Weston, one of Boston's more prestigious suburbs. The afternoon sun filtered through the maple trees and sparkled on the ivy that climbed the walls of the house. As Susannah and Sam walked up the antique brick pathway toward the front door, she found herself hoping that the owner was on vacation in Alaska someplace. Although that certainly wouldn't stop Sam. He would probably insist they board the next plane to Fairbanks.

On the flight to Boston, she had studied the article in the *Wall Street Journal* that had caught Sam's attention, and she'd learned as much as she could about the man they had come to see. Mitchell Blaine was one of the wunderkinds of Route 128, the high-tech area that had formed around Boston and was the East Coast counterpart to California's Silicon Valley. A midwesterner by birth, he had a Bachelor's degree in Electrical Engineering from Ohio State, a Master's Degree from MIT, and an MBA from Harvard. But it was his ability to combine technological know-how with a wizardry for marketing that had made him a multimillion-aire.

During the late sixties and early seventies, he had quickly risen through the ranks of several of Boston's most aggressive young high-tech companies and at the same time wisely taken advantage of their early public stock issues to begin amassing his personal fortune. By 1976 he had a reported net worth nearing five million dollars—insignificant compared to the world's great fortunes, but respectable money for someone who'd been orphaned at the age of seven. Business analysts had targeted him as one of the bright new leaders who would direct the course of high-tech industry as it moved into the 1980s.

And then, four days earlier, his meteoric career had come to an end. In a tersely worded one-paragraph press release that had sent industry analysts reeling, he had announced his retirement from the business world. He was only thirty-one years old.

The article had given no explanation for his decision, but that hadn't stopped Sam, who had immediately invented his own. "The man's bored, Susannah. He's only thirty-one. He wants a challenge. SysVal is going to be just what he needs."

Try as she might, she could find no evidence in the article to support Sam's conclusion. The article told the facts about Blaine's life but nothing about the man himself.

She caught his arm as they approached the front steps of the house. "Sam, this is awful. We have to call first."

"And give him an opportunity to brush us off? Not a chance. Besides, you don't think we can just ring up information and get Mitchell Blaine's private phone number, do you? It was hard enough for you to find out where he lived."

She didn't want to think about how embarrassed she had been to rouse one of FBT's Boston executives out of bed at six-thirty in the morning with a preposterous story about needing Blaine's address for her father's social calendar. "We can't just show up on his doorstep," she insisted. "It simply isn't done."

Sam jabbed the door bell. "If you're afraid you'll get kicked off the Social Register, it's too late. Our little escapade on your wedding day took care of that."

"Damn it, Sam!"

"Wow. Miss Goody-Goody is swearing. She's going to have to sit in the corner." He punched the door bell a second time.

He was being unbearably nasty, but she understood him well enough to suspect he was merely trying to distract her from the fact that he knew she was right.

"What are you going to say to him? How are you going to explain our presence?"

"I'm not. You tell him who you are and get us in the door. After that, I'll do all the talking."

That was what she had been afraid of.

He rang the bell several more times, but nothing happened. "No one's here, Sam. Let's forget—"

"Just keep ringing, damn it!" He disappeared around the side of the house.

She violated every rule of etiquette she had ever learned by ringing two more times. Just as she was turning away, Sam reappeared. "There's a television on in the rear of the house. Let's go."

"No, Sam! It might be the maid."

"He's here. I know it."

She stumbled over a sprinkler head as he dragged her through a hedge of yews. A shaded flagstone patio lay directly in front of them. As they stepped up on it, a security alarm went off.

"We're going to get arrested!"

"Not until we've seen Blaine." Without releasing his grip on her, Sam steered her across the patio to the back door and began to pound it with his fist.

"Hey, Blaine!" he shouted. "I know you're in there! I want to talk to you. I've got Susannah Faulconer here. FBT Faulconer. Joel Faulconer's daughter. She doesn't like being left on the goddamn doorstep. Let us in."

"Shhhh!" she hissed. "Be quiet! Will you be quiet!" She imagined Blaine huddled inside his house in terror while he waited for the police to rescue him from the madman who was storming his house. "He's going to think we're here to murder him!"

No sooner had the words left her mouth than one of the patio doors slid open and they had their first sight of their quarry.

In those initial few seconds, Susannah came to the rapid conclusion that Mitchell Blaine probably didn't care whether he was about to be murdered or not. As Boston's young high-tech marketing whiz stumbled out onto the patio, she realized that he was too drunk to care much about anything.

Even drunk, he was formidable. She had been around the exclusive brotherhood of powerful corporate men all her life, and although Blaine was only thirty-one and obviously not at his best, she knew at once that he was a member in good standing. But if she had been pressed to define exactly why she was so certain, she would have had difficulty. Members of the brotherhood reveled in their power too much to drink to the point of oblivion, as Blaine had done. And although he was wearing the proper uniform—a custom-tailored white dress shirt and well-cut gray trousers —the garments looked as if they had been slept in.

His straight, sandy hair was conservatively cut by a barber who had been well-trained to meet the precise requirements of the brotherhood. But the regulatory side part was uneven, and instead of being combed neatly back from his forehead, the hair at the front tumbled forward in a manner acceptable only after a set of tennis.

His body wasn't quite right, either. Although he was imposingly tall, his build was a bit too muscular for a member of the corporate elite and his abdomen a little too taut. But the directness in those wide-spaced, light blue eyes was familiar, as well as the chilling contempt in his blunt, slightly irregular features.

She caught her breath as Blaine came toward Sam. "Get the hell off my property."

Sam formed the peace sign, a gesture that would have amused Susannah if she hadn't been so appalled at the rudeness of their intrusion. "We just want to talk," Sam said, refusing to back off by so much as an inch. "We've come a long way to talk to you."

"I don't care how far you've come. You're trespassing, and I want you out of here!" Blaine took an uneven step forward.

Sam was starting to get angry, managing by some incredible sleight-of-mind to turn himself into the wronged party. "Listen. We've busted our asses finding you, and the least you can do is hear us out."

"The least I can do is kick you out of here."

Gathering her nerve, Susannah pushed herself between Sam and the formidable Mr. Blaine. "Let's go inside and I'll fix you a cup of coffee, Mr. Blaine. You look like you could use it."

"I don't want any coffee," he said with angry precision. "I want another drink."

"All right," she replied stubbornly. "I'll fix you some coffee to go along with your drink."

Fortunately, the relentless whine of the security alarm had begun to bother him even more than their presence. He turned back toward the house, and at that moment she knew why she had recognized him as one of the elite brotherhood of the powerful. Even though he was staggeringly drunk, he had been able to dismiss them with cruel accuracy as persons of no consequence to him.

He moved with surprising grace for a man in his condition, although he did manage to stub the toe of his expensive black leather wing tips on the step. Sam refused to wait for an invitation that he knew wouldn't be forthcoming. Grabbing Susannah, he pulled her through the patio door after him.

They walked into a family room complete with timbered ceiling and a soaring Old English fireplace that looked large enough to roast an ox. The green and red plaid design in the carpet held indentations showing that couches and tables had been in place quite recently, but many of the items themselves were missing. The few pieces of furniture that remained were obviously expensive, but dark and heavy.

When Blaine finally realized they had followed him, he looked annoyed, but not alarmed. She spotted the glass that he had been drinking from. Ignoring her conscience, she snatched it up and handed it to him. While Sam studied their surroundings, she adopted the deferential manner of one of Joel Faulconer's secretaries and managed to convince Blaine to deactivate the alarm and call off his security company.

When the house was finally quiet, Sam spoke. "I've got a proposition for you, Blaine . . ."

She went into the kitchen to make coffee. While she was waiting for the water to boil, she spotted a nursery school calendar hanging crookedly by a magnetic clip on the side of the refrigerator along with a collection of crayoned art work. Children had obviously occupied this house until fairly recently, but where were they now?

As she returned to the family room with the coffee, she saw that Blaine had refreshed his glass with three fingers of something that looked like straight scotch. Sam was waving a can of Coke in the air and talking, talking, talking. ". . . is the most incredible, extraordinary machine you've ever seen. Simple, elegant—it'll blow you away."

Blaine turned as he spotted Susannah. "So you're Joel Faulconer's daughter?" His consonants were slightly blurred at the edges.

"Yes, I am."

"He's a son of a bitch."

She shrugged noncommittally and held out a coffee mug, which he ignored. Taking a mug for herself, she sat in one of the remaining chairs. Something poked her in the hip. As

Sam resumed speaking, she reached behind her and pulled out a toy truck. For a moment she studied it, and then she quickly pushed it back where it had come from. The fresh indentations in the carpet and the evidence of the recent presence of children all pointed to the fact that Mitchell Blaine had marital problems, probably fairly recent ones, if she were to judge by his intoxicated condition.

Sam had been nervously passing his Coke can from one hand to the other while he spoke, and now he turned to her. "Mitch agreed to fly to San Francisco with us this afternoon."

"I did?"

"That's what you told me, Mitch," Sam replied. "Remember how anxious you are to see our computer."

Susannah rose quickly to her feet. Sam was lying. This was another one of his monumental bluffs. "Sam, I don't think—"

"Call the airlines and make certain the tickets are taken care of, will you? I want to leave as soon as possible."

Blaine drained his glass. "I'm not going anywhere until I have another drink."

Susannah was normally impatient with drunks, but something about Blaine touched her. Maybe when Sam realized that this man was in pain, he would leave him alone. She studied the fresh dents in the carpet and asked softly, "Has your wife been gone long?"

Blaine's expression closed up tight. "That's none of your business."

"I'm sorry. I'm sure this is a difficult time for you."

He reached for the scotch bottle. She realized that he was determined to drink himself into oblivion, and was equally determined that it be a solitary journey. As she watched the care with which he was performing each simple movement, she felt an unexplainable sense of protectiveness toward him. Even blindly drunk, he hadn't lost a shred of dignity.

She could tell that Sam was growing impatient, but for the first time that summer, the needs of a man other than Sam Gamble had caught her attention. "I don't think drinking is going to help," she said. "Perhaps I could call one of your friends."

Sam shot her a warning glance. Then he pushed her out of

the way and took the bottle of scotch from Blaine's hand. "You don't want to see any of your friends right now, do you, Mitch? Bunch of stiffs. The California climate will fix you right up. And once you see our computer, you won't even think about your wife anymore."

Susannah began to protest, but Sam gave her a look so murderous that she fell silent.

Two hours later they were on their way back to San Francisco with a nearly comatose Mitchell Blaine slumped in the seat between them. Every time he began to wake up, Sam ignored her protests and poured another drink for him. Long before they reached San Francisco, a terrible foreboding had taken hold of Susannah. Drunk, Mitchell Blaine was formidable. She couldn't imagine what he would be like when he was sober.

13

●●●●●●●●●●●●●●●●●●●●●●●●

Blaine was not a happy man when he woke up the next morning. He staggered from Sam's bedroom into the hallway, where he bumped into Angela Gamble, who was wearing only a fluffy bath towel and nail polish. Angela was so startled that her towel slipped, which didn't bother her nearly as much as the fact that she hadn't had time to do her hair.

Blaine groaned and slumped into the wall, his solid body making a noisy thwack. In the kitchen, Susannah heard the sound and snatched up a water glass along with three aspirin before she raced back to the hallway.

He was still in the rumpled clothes he'd been wearing the day before. His jaw was covered with rusty stubble, his eyes bloodshot. Angela's towel was once again anchored under her arms, and she looked at Susannah quizzically. Since she had been asleep last night when Sam and Susannah had returned, she had no idea who her newest house guest was. Susannah gave her an I'll-tell-you-later-look and extended the aspirin and the water glass toward Blaine. He fumbled for them.

"Good morning," she whispered. As soon as he had swallowed, she gestured toward the bathroom. "I'll put some clean clothes out for you while you take a shower. There's a razor on the sink."

He gave her a bleary, hostile look. "Who *are* you?"

"We'll talk as soon as you've had your shower."

She gently steered him toward the bathroom and quietly shut the door. She wondered what he would think of Elvis.

After giving Angela a brief summary of the events of the last few days, she laid out a set of clean clothes from Blaine's overnight bag, which she had packed herself before they had ushered him out of his house the afternoon before. Then she returned to the kitchen, where she began frying bacon. She and Sam had decided it would be best if she fed Blaine to help him over the initial pain of his hangover and then brought him out to the garage. At the time, their plan had seemed logical, but now she dreaded the idea of dealing with Blaine by herself. Unfortunately, both Sam and Yank were busy setting up a crude version of the prototype of the self-contained computer that Yank had been working on, and she didn't have any choice.

Very little time passed before Blaine walked into the kitchen. A distinct feeling of dread settled over her at the difference in his appearance. All those liquor-softened edges had hardened. His jaw was smoothly shaven and rigidly set. Although his sandy hair was still damp from the shower, it had been precisely parted and combed into unquestioning obedience. His clothing was impeccable. Even after spending the night in a suitcase, neither his pale yellow sport shirt nor his expensively casual trousers had the nerve to retain a single wrinkle. His hangover had to be deadly, but he gave no sign that he was suffering. He was stiff and starchy, sternly correct, and coldly furious.

"How do you like your coffee?" she asked nervously, as she filled a mug.

"Black." He bit the word out, snapped it off, tossed it away.

She handed him a full mug and arranged the food she had prepared for him on a plate. She wasn't much of a cook and the eggs were a little too brown at the edges, but he didn't comment. Once again, she thought about fleeing to the safety of the garage, but she forced herself to pour a cup of coffee and carry it over to the table. To her astonishment,

Blaine stood and pulled out her chair. Instead of easing her mind, the display of courtesy was so chillingly correct that she grew even more uncomfortable.

She nervously sipped her coffee and observed his impeccable table manners. When Blaine was drunk, she had felt some sympathy for him, but now that he was sober, he reminded her too much of the men she had run away from.

He showed no inclination to speak, so she carefully reintroduced herself. He studied her for a moment, and she received the definite impression that he disliked everything he saw. Turning his attention away from her, he gazed intently out the dinette window. She could almost feel the effort of his self-control, and she braced herself for the inevitable.

"What is that, Miss Faulconer?" he asked coldly.

She followed his gaze. "Where?"

"In the corner of the yard."

"Do you mean the palm?"

"Palm?" He pressed his thumb against his temple and said sarcastically, "Palms don't grow in the state of Massachusetts, do they, Miss Faulconer?"

"No. No, they don't."

"Where *do* they grow, Miss Faulconer?"

She shifted uncomfortably in her seat and silently swore at Sam for abandoning her like this. "In California. You're near Menlo Park, south of San Francisco."

"Silicon Valley?" Each syllable was laced with hostility.

At that inauspicious moment, Angela came tripping into the kitchen, her heels clattering on the linoleum, her silver bangle bracelets jangling so loudly that he winced. She greeted Blaine and turned to Susannah. "Mrs. Albertson died yesterday, and I need to tint her hair before the viewing. Be a dear, will you? If Mrs. Leonetti croaks this morning, too, call me right away at the funeral home so I don't have to make an extra trip. They use the same color."

No sooner had she left the kitchen than the back door opened and Yank ambled in. He was holding a voltmeter in one hand and his shoe in the other. "The interface card," he announced to no one in particular. He limped past them and went into the living room.

Susannah didn't have to meet Blaine's eyes to read his

189

reaction. He was not the sort of man to tolerate personal eccentricities. She quickly rose from her chair. "Let me take you out to the garage so you can meet my partner. Actually, you met him yesterday, but—"

"I'm not going anywhere with you, Miss Faulconer." Blaine stood, his square, blunt features hard-edged and rigid. "I don't know what you did to me yesterday, and I'm not staying around this loony bin long enough to find out." He walked over to the telephone and snatched the receiver off the hook. His movements were relentlessly efficient as he dialed information, pulled a credit card from his wallet and called the airlines. While he was on hold, Susannah tried to explain to him as professionally as possible what they were doing. He ignored her.

Yank reappeared while Blaine was making arrangements for a limousine. She grabbed his arm and pushed him back into the living room. "Tell Sam I need him right away."

Yank looked blank.

She dug her fingers into his arm, barely restraining herself from rapping him on the head with her knuckles. "Get Sam. Do you understand what I'm saying, Yank? I need Sam. Do you understand me?"

"I'm not retarded, Susannah," he said quietly. "Of course I understand you." He went back outside.

Blaine had gone to fetch his suitcase. She followed him to the bedroom. "Please, Mr. Blaine, at least take a few minutes to see our computer. You won't regret it. I promise you."

"You're the one who's going to regret it, Miss Faulconer. I'm just beginning to realize that I have a legal case for breaking and entering and probably a few dozen other felonies." He snapped the lock on the suitcase she had packed for him the day before. "I don't know what sort of games you're playing, but you picked the wrong man. I've never liked your father and I don't like you."

"I don't like her old man, either," Sam said from the doorway, "but Suzie's okay."

Okay? She was only *okay?*

Sam sauntered into the room and leaned against the doorjamb. In comparison to Blaine's starchy demeanor, he looked wonderfully free and uninhibited.

"Look, Blaine," he said, "I know you're pissed, and if I was you, I would be, too. But the fact is, you don't have a damn thing waiting for you back in Boston except a bottle of scotch and a houseful of self-pity, so why don't you hear me out."

Every muscle in Blaine's body went rigid. He whipped the suitcase from the bed and stalked to the door, only to find that Sam had blocked it.

"Get out of my way."

Sam's eyes narrowed. "I've got the adventure of a lifetime out in that garage. A chance to change the world, to put your mark on the future, to paint your name across the sky in indelible ink. What you've done up till now is small-time compared with what I've got waiting for you. We're adventurers, Blaine. Soldiers of fortune and missionaries rolled into one. We're taking a joy ride into the future. A rocket-propelled rainbow right through the stars."

Blaine was not a man with a poet's soul, and his jaw clenched. "What in the hell are you talking about?"

"I'm talking about the fact that we've got a mission here. Maybe the final mission. A handful of American adventurers have been carving their names in the history books since the middle of the nineteenth century—the railroad barons, the oil men, the industrialists. They were renegade capitalists, and they weren't afraid of hard work, of risk, of daring. Men like Carnegie, Ford, Rockefeller. And do you know what, Blaine? We're going to be the last of them. Yank, Suzie, and me. We're going to be the last buccaneers of America's twentieth century."

Susannah wanted to press her hands to her head to keep it on her neck. She felt as if parts of herself were spinning. Where did Sam get these ideas? Where did he find the words?

Blaine seemed stunned. "You're nuts."

Sam bristled with hostility, then jerked back from the door. "Get the fuck out of my house."

"Sam . . ." she said warningly.

His lips thinned with contempt. "We're looking for somebody with guts and vision. I thought you might be that man, but I was obviously wrong."

She realized that Sam wasn't bluffing. Mitchell Blaine

hadn't lived up to his expectations, and—just like that—Sam was finished with him. She watched with consternation as Sam turned on his heel and left the room. Panic bolted through her—a panic that had little to do with their current situation. What a dangerously impatient man she had chosen to fall in love with—quick to judge, quick to dismiss. The kitchen door banged.

Blaine pushed past her and headed for the living room. "I'll wait for my limo outside," he said brusquely.

At that moment Yank stepped forward. Susannah hadn't seen him standing across the room near Elvis's portrait. Had he been listening to them all along, or was he merely caught up in the midst of some complex internal calculation? As she tried to think of what to say to Blaine, Yank walked over to him and took his suitcase. "I'll carry it for you," he muttered.

"You don't have to."

Yank paid no attention. He opened the front door. She followed them both outside, still frantically searching for some last-minute argument that would save the situation. Yank bumped into one of Angela's green ceramic frogs as he went down the front step. She saw the flash of a brown sock and then a blue one. He turned right and cut across the grass. Blaine made an inarticulate exclamation as Yank and his suitcase headed up the drive toward the garage.

"Hey!"

Yank didn't seem to hear. The corner of the suitcase hit the Duster.

Blaine turned to look at her, his expression incredulous. "Are all of you crazy?"

Susannah thought for a moment and then reluctantly nodded.

"Christ," he muttered. "Hey, you! Bring that back."

Yank continued toward the garage, his forward motion as immutable as the laws of physics. He and the suitcase disappeared inside.

Sam was standing by the workbench staring at the crude prototype when she and Blaine entered. Yank set down the suitcase, picked up a tattered manual and began looking through it as if he were all alone.

Blaine bent to reclaim his suitcase. "I don't know where

you people get your gall, but—" His words snapped off as he spotted the dazzling color patterns spreading across the screen. His fingers relaxed on the handle of the suitcase, and he slowly straightened.

"I thought you told me you were building a single-board computer," he said gruffly.

Sam didn't respond for a moment. He seemed to be making up his mind whether or not he would acknowledge the comment. Finally he replied, "We are."

Blaine gazed at the screen intently. "You can't get color like that on a single-board computer."

"We're running it off the CPU," Sam explained.

His suitcase forgotten, Blaine walked toward the workbench, every part of him focused on the machine in front of him. "I don't believe you. Open it up."

Sam gave Blaine a long, searching gaze, and then reached for a screwdriver. As he removed the case, Blaine began bombarding him with questions. Sam answered him tersely at first, and then became more animated as he warmed to the subject. The conversation quickly grew so technical that Susannah lost the thread, and before long even Sam began to have trouble providing the specific answers Blaine wanted. Yank stepped in, giving quiet, measured responses.

Susannah heard a horn honking, but none of the rest of them noticed. She hesitated for only a moment before she slipped outside and dismissed the limousine.

For the rest of the day, she sat at the assembly table stuffing the boards for the new orders they had picked up in Atlantic City and listening to the men talk. At one point she fetched drinks for them, and later she made sandwiches. By early afternoon, Blaine had a logic probe in his hand. As she set aside the board she had just completed, she looked over at the activity at the workbench and shook her head in bewilderment. Starchy, conservative Mitchell Blaine was a hardware freak just like her partners.

By seven o'clock Sam and Blaine were awash in male camaraderie. "Do you like pizza, Mitch?" Sam asked. "Or do we have to take you someplace with tablecloths?"

Blaine smiled good-naturedly. "I like pizza just fine."

Sam pointed his Coke can at Blaine, challenging him with it as if he held a six-gun. "How about rock and roll?"

"To tell you the truth, I'm more a country western man."

"You're kidding."

"A little tolerance for us old folks, Sam. We all have our foibles."

"Yeah, but country western is really pushing it."

Ten minutes later they were backing out of the driveway with Sam behind the wheel of the Duster and Blaine in the passenger seat. In the back Susannah held a spool of coaxial cable on her lap while Yank straddled an oscilloscope. They drove to Mom & Pop's, a pizza and burger place located in a strip mall between a dry cleaners and a Hallmark shop. The restaurant served beer by the pitcher and had video games, which made it a favorite of Sam's and Yank's. As they went inside, the uneasiness that had been building inside Susannah all afternoon grew stronger. She felt like an outsider, someone whose only function was fetching food and caring for the creature comforts of men.

They piled into the largest of the circular green vinyl booths, leaving her the place at the end and then steadfastly ignoring her. As Sam spoke, his dark eyes glittered with excitement. Even as her resentment toward him grew, she could feel that familiar core of warmth building up in the deepest parts of her body.

Just as the waitress arrived with their pizzas, Roberta slipped into the seat next to her. "I don't know why Yank and Sam like this place," she whispered, dabbing at the top of the nearest pizza with a paper napkin. "Everything is so greasy."

While the men talked electronics, Susannah listened to Roberta detailing her latest sinus infection. Her resentment fed on itself until she couldn't stand it any longer. Sam and Mitchell Blaine were acting as if they had known each other for years instead of two days. She decided she wasn't going to let them shut her out any longer, and when the next lull occurred in the conversation, she addressed Blaine. "Could you tell us what you know about attracting venture capital?"

Once again she received the impression of a chilling dislike. What had she done to this man? Why was he behaving so warmly toward Sam and treating her with such antipathy?

To her astonishment, Blaine turned to Sam as if her question had come from him. "Venture capital is tricky, Sam. You don't want to go after it until you absolutely have to. If you're not careful, you'll end up giving away the store."

"Does that happen very often?" she asked, refusing to be ignored.

Again he addressed Sam. "When Ken Olson and Harlan Anderson founded Digital Equipment Corporation in 1957, they gave up seventy percent of the business for a $100,000 investment. DEC is projecting a billion dollars in sales next year, so nobody's hurting, but it was still a lousy deal. Do you have a business plan?"

"I'm working on it," Sam replied.

Susannah stiffened. She was the one working on the business plan.

Using the information she had painstakingly gathered, Sam began discussing the specifics. Only when he forgot a statistic or some important fact did he turn to her. But as soon as she had supplied the information he needed, she ceased to exist.

"Come on, Susannah, let's go to the little girl's room." Roberta caught her arm in a death grip and began pulling her from the booth. Susannah had no choice but to accompany her, but she fumed inwardly as Roberta maintained a steady stream of chatter all the way to the rest room. Yank's girlfriend was a college graduate. Couldn't she, just once, make it to the rest room by herself?

As they walked through the swinging door, Roberta said, "Mr. Blaine seems really interested in SysVal. He's just what the guys have been looking for."

"Not just the guys," Susannah replied sharply. "I'm part of SysVal, too."

"Well, sure you are, Susannah. So am I. But it's different with us. We're in it because of them. I mean, I'm in it because of Yank and you're in it because of Sam. Right?" Roberta slipped into the stall. "Although to tell you the truth, I'm starting to get a little impatient with Yank. I'm not getting any younger, and I think it's about time we got married."

As Roberta babbled on, Susannah stared at herself in the

mirror. Was it true? Was she only part of SysVal because of Sam? Would she still want to pursue this impossible crusade if she weren't so desperately in love with him?

Her hand spun the faucet and water splashed from the bowl onto the front of her slacks. SysVal was hers, too, dammit! She had bought into Sam's dream. Somehow, along the way, she had begun to believe that it could happen. Sam had called them the last buccaneers of America's twentieth century. She wanted it to be true, and she wasn't going to let them take it away from her.

Leaving Roberta still chattering in the stall, she went back out to the booth, determined to make some sort of stand, but only Yank was there, scribbling a diagram on the back of a napkin. Blaine and Sam were playing video games. She watched as Sam let out a whoop and Blaine slapped him on the back, the uptight millionaire executive suddenly as carefree as a teenager. She could almost feel the affinity developing between them, that mysterious attraction of opposites as Mr. Establishment met Easy Rider.

She planned to talk to Sam when they got home—to tell him how she felt about being closed out—but he and Blaine sat up until dawn weaving futuristic fantasies of how everyday life might be reshaped by a small, affordable computer. They were still talking when she finally excused herself to go to bed.

The next day Blaine rented a car and moved into a hotel, but except for a few hours of sleep at night, he spent all his time with Sam. The kinship they had developed continued to exclude her. Although they argued frequently, and Blaine steadfastly resisted all of Sam's efforts to get him to commit to SysVal, the bond between the men grew daily. Each seemed to provide something the other lacked. Sam was attracted to Blaine's greater knowledge and breadth of experience—Blaine to Sam's vision and poetry.

When she was finally able to corner Sam alone, she tried to talk to him about how she felt, but he shrugged her off. "He's used to working with men, that's all. He's not ignoring you. You're making a big deal out of nothing."

But she didn't think so. Blaine's aversion to her seemed to run deeper than a general prejudice against women.

The next afternoon, while she was doing a shampoo for

Angela, she heard Blaine and Sam on the other side of the partition discussing the prototype. "The SysVal I is only a toy for hobbyists, Sam. If you want to build a company, you're going to have to base it on that self-contained computer. Ordinary people aren't going to want to hook up a television set and all sorts of other equipment to make their computer work. Everything has to be in one piece, and it has to be simple. As soon as you get the funding lined up, you have to get that machine on the market."

They talked about possible markets for the computer, and then Sam asked Blaine what he thought they should name it.

"The most obvious name is the SysVal II," Blaine replied.

"Yeah, I suppose. I just wish we could come up with something more dramatic."

Sam had never asked *her* about a name for the new computer. Her resentment gnawed deeper. She went to the library for a few hours to get away from both of them, but only ended up reading everything she could find about Mitchell Blaine. What she discovered depressed her further. In addition to being an outstanding engineer, he was considered a brilliant marketing strategist, respected by some of the most important business analysts in the country. He was everything they could have hoped for and more. Except there was no "they" as far as Blaine was concerned —only Sam and Yank.

"You can't go back to Boston," Sam told Blaine the day before he was planning to leave. "Boston's old history, man."

But the change of environment seemed to have healed some of Blaine's personal wounds, so that he was thinking more clearly. "I don't mean to insult you, Sam, but I can get a top position in just about any corporation in America. No matter how much fun I'm having, I'd be crazy to give that up to work with a couple of kids trying to run a company out of a garage. And I'm definitely not crazy."

Sam continued to badger Blaine all the way to the airport. Susannah sat in the backseat and listened as Sam asked Blaine the same question he had once asked her. "Are you in or out? I want to know."

Blaine gave Sam a good-natured slap on the back. "I'm out, Sam. I've told you that from the beginning. Do you have any idea what I was getting paid before I resigned? I was making almost a million dollars a year, plus stock options and more perks than you can imagine. You can't touch a package like that."

"Money's not everything, for chrissake. It's the challenge. Can't you see that? Besides, the money will come. It's just a matter of time."

Blaine shrugged him off. "I'm thinking about moving back to the Midwest. Chicago, probably. But I want to keep in touch. You helped me over a pretty bad time, and I won't forget it. I'll give you as much advice as I can on an informal basis."

"Not good enough," Sam persisted. "I want one hundred percent. And if you don't give it to me, you're going to regret it for the rest of your life."

But Mitchell Blaine didn't prove as easy to badger as Susannah had been. "No sale," he said.

14

∙∙∙∙∙∙∙∙∙∙∙∙∙∙∙∙∙∙∙∙∙∙∙

Blaine was a fast reader with an almost photographic memory, and he devoured the printed word like other people consumed junk food. But he had been looking at the same page in *Business Week* since he had left San Francisco on the Boston-bound 747, and he didn't have the slightest idea what he had read.

He kept thinking about Sam and Yank and what they were doing in the garage. He couldn't remember being so excited by anything in years. They were doomed to fail, of course. Still, he couldn't help but admire them for making the attempt.

The flight attendant serving the first-class passengers was covertly studying him. She bent forward to speak to a passenger in the row across from him and her straight skirt tightened across her hips. As a married man, he had always been scrupulously faithful, but his days of being Mr. Straight Arrow were over, and he imagined those hips beneath his own.

She turned toward him and asked him if he needed anything. The whiff of her perfume killed his arousal as effectively as a cold shower. She was wearing an old-fashioned floral scent reminiscent of his aunts' bathpowder.

He had smelled like that bathpowder himself for years—not because he had used it, but because the scent clung to everything in that rambling old house in Clearbrook, Ohio.

He shut his eyes, remembering the bathpowder and his aunts, and the oppressive, cloying softness of his upbringing.

"Mi-*chull!* Mi-*chull!*" Every afternoon at four-thirty one of his aunts stood on the front porch of the house on Cherry Street and called him inside for piano practice.

Their names were Theodora and Amity. They were his father's relatives, and the only ones willing to take on the responsibility of raising an asthmatic seven-year-old boy after his parents were killed in a fiery automobile accident one Easter Sunday.

They were maiden ladies. Although they insisted they were unmarried by choice, not because they disliked men, in actuality there were only three males in the town of Clearbrook of whom they entirely approved—their pastor, their assistant pastor, and Mr. Leroy Jackson, their handyman. From the moment they set eyes on the small boy who had come to live with them, they were determined to make little Mitchell Blaine the fourth male in Clearbrook to receive their unqualified approval.

It was all a matter of civility.

"Mi-*chull!*"

He dragged his eleven-year-old feet reluctantly up the sidewalk. Behind him, he heard Charlie and Jerry calling out taunts just loudly enough so that he could hear, but Miss Amity Blaine couldn't.

"Sissy boy. Sissy boy. Run home and get your diapers changed."

They always said that about the diapers. They knew he couldn't play sports because of his asthma, and they knew that he had to go home to practice the piano, but they always said he was going home to get his diaper changed. He wanted to curl up his fists and smash their faces, but he wasn't allowed to fight. Fighting might make him wheeze, and the aunts got scared when he started to wheeze. Sometimes, though, he thought that his aunts might be using the wheezing as an excuse to keep him clean, because more than anything in the world, they hated dirt. They also hated name-calling, dogs, sweat, scabby knees, sports, television, curses, and everything else that went along with being a boy growing up in Clearbrook, Ohio, in the 1950s.

His aunts loved books and music, church bazaars and crochet. They loved flowers and beautiful manners. And they loved him.

The hinge on the gate squeaked as he opened it. Everything in the old house squeaked, rattled, and clucked.

"Mi-*chull,* Mi-*chull.*"

Aunt Amity reached out for him as he hit the steps. He tried to make a fast dodge to the side before she grabbed him, but she was too quick. She blocked the doorway with her bony, birdlike body and drew him into her arms. While Jerry and Charlie watched in the distance, she planted a kiss on the top of his head. He could hear their derisive hoots in the background.

"You've been running again, haven't you?" she said, tidying his already tidy hair, straightening his pristine white shirt collar, fussing over him, always fussing. "Dear, dear, Mitchell. I can hear that wheezing. When Theodora discovers that you've been running, I'm afraid she won't let you go out to play tomorrow after school."

That was the way they disciplined him. One of them would catch him in a misdemeanor and blame the punishment on the other. The punishments were always gentle and unimaginative—no play after school, sentences to be written fifty times. They thought it was the effectiveness of their methods that had turned him into the best-behaved boy in Clearbrook. They didn't understand that he tried desperately to please them because he loved them so much. He had already lost the mother and father he adored. In the deepest part of him, he was afraid that if he wasn't very, very good, he might lose his aunts, too.

He washed his hands without being prompted and settled himself behind the piano, where he stared at the keyboard with loathing. He had no musical ability. He hated the songs that he had to practice about sunshiny days and good little Indians. He wanted to be out with the other guys playing ball.

But he wasn't allowed to play ball because of his asthma. The wheezing didn't bother him much anymore—not like when he was a real little kid—but he couldn't convince the aunts of that. And so, while the other guys were out playing ball, he was playing scales.

But the scales weren't the worst. Saturday mornings were the worst.

The Misses Amity and Theodora Blaine supported themselves by teaching piano and giving deportment lessons. Every Saturday morning at eleven o'clock, the daughters of Clearbrook's best families dressed in their Sunday frocks and donned white gloves to knock politely on the Misses Blaines' front door.

Wearing a suit and tie, Mitchell stood miserably in the hallway next to his aunts and watched the girls enter. One by one they dropped a small curtsy and said, "How do you do, Miss Blaine, Miss Blaine, Mitchell. Thank you so much for inviting me."

He was required to bend neatly from the waist in front of girls like fat little Cissy Potts, who sat behind him in his sixth-grade class and wiped her boogers on the back of his seat. He had to say things like, "How delightful to see you again, Miss Potts."

And then he had to take her hand.

The girls settled in the living room, where they were instructed in such skills as the proper method of performing an introduction, accepting an invitation to dance, and pouring tea. He was their guinea pig.

"Thank you, Miss Baker, I'd love a cup of tea," he said.

Snotty little Penelope Baker would pass him his cup of watered-down tea and stick her tongue out at him when the aunts weren't looking.

The girls hated the Misses Blaines' deportment class, and they hated him in turn.

He spent his Saturday mornings gracefully balancing thin china saucers on his knee and taking himself to faraway places where no females were allowed. Places where a man could spit in the dirt, scratch himself, and own a dog. While he took Mary Jane Simmons's hand and led her to the center of the living room rug for a dance, he dreamed of feeling his legs fly out from under him and his hip hitting hard against the dirt as he slid into home plate. He dreamed of going up for a slam dunk and hanging off the hoop. He dreamed of hunting rifles, fishing rods, soft flannel shirts, and blue jeans. But the aunts' cluckings and warnings and sighings held him in gentle, unbreakable bondage.

Only in the classroom was it possible to let himself go, and no matter how much the other boys taunted him, he refused to rein in his quick mind. He answered questions in class, did extra-credit projects, and got the best marks in sixth grade.

Teacher's pet. Teacher's pet. Diaper Boy is teacher's pet.

When he was fourteen, his voice dropped and his muscles thickened. Almost overnight, he shot up until he towered over his aunts' small, birdlike bodies. His wheezing disappeared, but they continued to pet him. They made him wear a white shirt and tie for his first day of high school. Freshman year brought academic brilliance and gut-wrenching, aching loneliness.

The summer before his sophomore year, he was walking home from helping his aunts teach Vacation Bible School when a moving van and a paneled station wagon pulled up to the white clapboard house next to his own. The doors of the station wagon opened, and a man and a woman got out. Then a pair of long, suntanned legs emerged, followed by frayed denim cutoffs. He held his breath and watched as a beautiful girl close to his own age appeared before him. Her hair was arranged in a sprayed blond bubble kept neatly back from her face with a madras headband. She had a pert nose and soft mouth. A man's blue work shirt clung to a pair of high pointy breasts.

She turned to study the neighborhood and her eyes fell on him. He waited for the condescending sneer, the look of superiority, and could barely believe it when she gave him a shy smile. He walked closer, wishing the bible and curriculum book he was holding at his side would become invisible.

"Hi," she said.

"How do you do?" he replied, and immediately cursed himself for not being more casual. But he didn't know how to be easy like the other guys.

She looked down at the sidewalk. He spotted a little speck of dandelion fluff caught in the top of her blond bubble, and had to fight back a nearly irresistible urge to brush it away. As she continued to stare at the sidewalk, he realized that she was shy, and he felt a great surge of protectiveness toward her.

"I'm Mitchell Blaine," he said, using the skills that had become second nature to him after nearly a decade of deportment classes. "I live next door. Welcome to the neighborhood."

She looked back up at him. Only a dab of soft pink lipstick remained at the bow of her upper lip. She had eaten the rest away. "Mitch?" she inquired.

No one had ever called him Mitch except the parents he barely remembered. He was Mitchell. Mitchell–Mitchell–Diaper Boy.

"Yes," he said. "My name is Mitch."

"I'm Candy Fuller."

They stood on the front sidewalk and talked awkwardly. Candy and her family were from Chillicothe, and she would be a sophomore at Clearbrook High that September, part of the class of '64, just like he was. Candy had been a junior varsity cheerleader at her old school, and she wanted to cheer for Clearbrook this year. When they finally parted, Mitch felt as if his life had begun all over again.

For the rest of that summer they met every evening after dinner on the old metal bench beneath his aunts' grape arbor. Candy had to wash the dishes before she could come outside, and she always smelled like Joy detergent. They sat on the bench with the flat dark grape leaves curling about their heads and they talked.

Candy spoke of the friends she had left behind in Chillicothe and her worries that she might not be able to make the varsity cheerleading squad at Clearbrook High. Mitch talked about how he'd like to have his own car and whether or not he would be able to get a scholarship to college. He kept the darker bitterness of his life hidden away, out of fear that her affection for him would turn to disgust.

The adoration in Candy Fuller's deep blue eyes grew stronger every evening. Her reaction left Mitch breathless. No girl had ever looked at him that way. His stomach cramped as he remembered that Candy was from Chillicothe. She didn't know about the sissy boy, the diaper baby who wasn't allowed to play sports. All she saw when she gazed at him was a tall, lean fifteen-year-old, with sandy hair, light blue eyes, and a broad, handsome face.

They lived in splendid isolation through those dog days of summer, drenched in the scent of grapes and Joy and the infinite, unspoken promise of young love. The night before school started, they were quieter than normal, each sensing the changes that the next day would bring. Candy scratched a thin white line in the suntan on the top of her thigh.

"I don't hate moving here anymore, Mitch. This month, it's been special. Meeting you. But I'm scared about tomorrow. I'll bet all the girls at school are crazy about you."

He shrugged, trying to act cool, although his heart was thumping so hard it was painful.

She studied the toe of her once-white sneaker and her voice began to quiver. "I'm afraid you won't still like me after school starts."

He couldn't believe it. This soft, pretty, bubble-haired cheerleader with her sweet mouth and pointy breasts was afraid that she would lose him. The stirring of emotions that gripped his chest was the sweetest pain he had ever experienced. "I'll still like you tomorrow," he murmured. "I'll always like you."

She tilted her face up to him, and he realized that she wanted him to kiss her. Closing his eyes, he leaned forward and touched that sweet Candy-scented mouth with his own. Although dark, sexual thoughts of her had tormented him for weeks, the kiss was pure. It was a gesture of adoration, a symbol of promise, a farewell to summer.

"Will you walk me to school tomorrow?" she asked when they finally drew apart. Her eyes were large and beseeching, as if she still wasn't certain that he cared for her.

"Of course," he replied. He would have walked with her to the moon.

And then they kissed again. This time it was different. Their mouths met hungrily. Their young bodies joined with a raw, untried passion. He felt the thrusts of her young breasts against his chest and the small bumps of her spine beneath his fingertips. Dark longings raced through his body and heated his blood. A man's need surged through him, its urgency blocking out everything but the feel of Candy's body pressed next to his.

"You can touch my chest if you want," she whispered.

He couldn't believe he'd heard her right. For several seconds he did nothing, and then he gingerly slid his hand between their bodies. The well-worn fabric of her blouse was soft beneath his palm. When she didn't stop him, he let his hand creep upward, still staying outside her blouse. He felt the bump that marked the bottom edge of her bra and waited in agony for her to push him away.

But she didn't move. He slid his fingers higher until he touched the slope of her breast. Through the fabric of her blouse and the sponginess of her padded bra, his hand closed over her. He groaned and held the soft mound as if it were a fragile baseball. They kissed and he gently kneaded it. The Fuller's back porch light snapped on and they sprang apart.

Her eyes were misty with the depth of her feelings for him. "I never let a boy do that to me," she whispered. "Don't tell anybody."

He shook his head and silently pledged to keep the precious gift she had given him their secret forever.

At seven-thirty the next morning, she met him on her front porch. He could see that she was embarrassed about what had happened between them the night before, and he was overwhelmed by her fragility. She was so vulnerable, so needful of his protection. As he watched the tip of her tongue flick nervously over her lips, he determined to shield her from all the spiteful demons at Clearbrook High.

"Do I look all right?" she asked, as if her entire future depended on his response.

He took in her white blouse with its gold circle pin on the collar and her pleated green plaid skirt. "You'll be the prettiest girl in the sophomore class," he replied earnestly.

They walked to school hand in hand, her small fingers curled through his bigger ones. He felt the morning sun warming his face, and shortened his strides so she could keep up. His shoulders drew back. A slight swagger appeared in his walk. With Candy Fuller walking at his side, he was no longer Mitchell Blaine. He was Mitch. Mitch the Indestructible. Mitch the Mighty. Mitch the Manliest of the Manly.

"Do you think the other kids will like me?" she asked.

An uneasiness passed through him, a vague foreboding. But he was Mitch the Fearless, Mitch the Brave, and he shook it off. "You shouldn't pay too much attention to what the other kids think."

He could see that his response mystified her, and he remembered that she was a cheerleader—part of a group that was dedicated to conformity. His uneasiness grew.

"Don't you think they'll like me?" Anxiety had crumpled her brow.

"Of course they will."

The American flag cracked in the morning breeze as, hand in hand, they walked into the school. They were in different homerooms, and he had promised to stay with her until second bell. As they walked down the main hallway, he was lulled by the joy of entering Clearbrook High with Candy Fuller at his side, and so he wasn't prepared when he rounded the corner by the sophomore lockers and the taunts began.

"Here's Mi-*chull*," the boys clucked, imitating his aunts. "Mi-*chull*, Mi-*chull*." There were five of them leaning against the metal locker doors, five scrubbed-up would-be rebels made omnipotent by banding together.

"Who's that you got there, Mi-*chull?* Hey, baby, come on over here and meet some real men."

Candy looked first at the boys and then at Mitch. She was bewildered by their behavior. None of the boys was as good-looking at Mitch, none as tall and well-built. Why were they taunting him?

Mitch tried to appear tolerant, as if they were children and he was a world-weary adult. "Why don't you guys grow up?"

They hooted with laughter and catcalls, pounded their fists in merriment against the locker at his absurd attempt to defy them.

Candy grew more befuddled. She gazed at him, accusation and betrayal beginning to form in her eyes. She had thought he was one of the special, one of Clearbrook's chosen. Now she realized that wasn't true. She had somehow managed to ally herself with an outcast.

He felt her fingers slackening in his and panic filled him. She wanted to get away from him, to distance herself. In those few seconds, everything changed. Without knowing any of the facts, without understanding a single detail of his past, she understood that he was a social pariah and that she should not have let herself be seen with him. He was going to lose Candy Fuller, and with that knowledge came the certainty that he didn't want to live anymore. If he couldn't be Mitch the Brave with Candy Fuller at his side, he didn't want to be anyone.

The girls had gathered around the boys, and they were laughing, too. Their amusement was easy and untroubled. Mitch had been the target of their jokes for so long that their attacks upon him were inspired more by habit than venom. They even felt a distant sort of fondness for the boy who had been the source of so much amusement over the years.

Candy was pulling at his hand now, trying desperately to get away from him, to take the small steps that would transport her from the land of the untouchable to the arena of the acceptable.

"Mi-*chull*, Mi-*chull*," Charlie Shields called out in a high, good-humored falsetto. "Come here and get your diapers changed."

A blue-black vortex of rage and pain consumed him. The rage caught him in its grasp and sank its talons through his flesh. A cry built inside him as he let that small, sweet hand go, a roar of outrage at this loss of his fresh new manhood. And with that roar, years of dilligent self-control gave way inside him.

He launched himself at the boys. They were five and he was one, but he didn't care. It was a suicide attack, a kamikaze mission with no hope for personal survival, but only a distant yearning for some posthumous dignity of the spirit. They laughed as he came toward them. They catcalled at the hilarity of Mitchell Blaine attacking them. But then they saw the expression on his face and their mockery died.

He began to throw wild, vicious punches. The girls

screamed and a crowd gathered in response to the invisible radar that instantly detected a hallway fight.

Charlie Shields shrieked in pain as Mitch's fist snapped the cartilage in his nose and sent blood spurting out. Artie Tarpey gave a grunt of agony as he felt a rib crack. Mitch was indiscriminate with his violence, propelled by a rage that had been building inside him for nearly a decade. He hit anything he could touch, and barely felt the blows he suffered in return. Two of the boys were finally able to pin him long enough to slam him into a locker. He smashed the thin metal door with his body and then hurled himself back at them.

The boys had fought among themselves since they were children, and there were unwritten rules of conduct they all followed. But Mitch hadn't been part of their fights, and he didn't know their rules. Now the boys found themselves the targets of a vicious, single-minded attack that was outside their realm of experience. Mitch brought Herb McGill down with a flying tackle and pinned him to the tiled floor. Charlie, holding his broken nose and whimpering with pain, tried to rescue Herb, but Mitch shook him away.

It took three male teachers to put an end to the violence, and even then Mitch didn't give up easily. As the men dragged him away to the principal's office, he refused to meet the eyes of Candy Fuller.

The aunts were summoned. They cried when they saw him slumped forward on the office bench with his bruised elbows propped on his thighs, bloody hands dangling between his splayed knees. His white starched shirt was torn and gore-spattered, his eye swollen closed. He looked up at their frail, birdlike frames and saw their fear for him.

Aunt Theodora recovered before her sister and advanced like a brigadier general upon the principal. "Explain this outrage at once, Jordan Featherstone. How could you allow something like this to happen to our Mitchell?"

"*Your* Mitchell just sent three of his classmates to the emergency room at the hospital," Mr. Featherstone replied sharply. "He's suspended for the next two weeks."

The aunts listened in horror to the details of their nephew's hallway brawl. They gazed at Mitch, first with bewilderment and then condemnation. Amity's eyes grew fierce behind her wire-rimmed spectacles. "You will come home with us at once, Mitchell," she ordered. "We will deal with this in private."

"We are extremely disappointed in you," Theodora exclaimed. "Extremely!"

He could see them conjuring up their most terrible punishment. A stern lecture, a hundred sentences instead of fifty. His heart contracted with love for them and regret at the distress he had inflicted. "Go on home," he said gently. "I'll be there in a little while."

Flabbergasted, they repeated their commands. He shook his head sadly. When they saw that they couldn't sway him, Amity tried to tidy the torn shoulder seam of his shirt, and Theodora told Jordan Featherstone that his school was full of hooligans.

Mr. Featherstone began to lecture him, but Mitch had something else to do. He apologized politely to the three adults. "I'm sorry," he said. "I don't mean to be rude, but there's something I have to do."

He walked out of the school and made his way on foot to the emergency room at Clearbrook Memorial Hospital.

There he found Artie Tarpey, Herb McGill, and Charlie Shields, who was holding an ice pack to his nose. Mitch sat quietly with them while they waited their turn to get patched up. They talked about the Warrior's football team and whether they had a shot at division finals. They talked about the sophomore teachers and the tunes on the Top Forty. None of them mentioned the fight.

That fall Mitch broke forever his aunts' gentle domination. He landed a part-time job at a local television repair shop and fell in love with the relentlessly masculine world of electronics. When his school suspension was over, he patiently endured all of their cluckings and twitterings, then kissed them affectionately on their papery cheeks and went out to train with the football team. Although the squad had already been chosen, his dogged persistence won him the admiration of the coaches, and by the end of the season he was playing.

In the next two years Mitch Blaine re-created football at Clearbrook High. No one had ever seen a boy play the game like he did. He wasn't the fastest wide receiver in the state, but he was so strong, so ferocious in his concentration, so single-minded in his race for the goal line, that it was almost impossible to stop him. The college scouts began sending him love letters.

Off the playing fields, Mitch was still the most well-behaved boy in Clearbrook, Ohio—quiet, polite, conservatively dressed, academically brilliant. The girls who had once laughed at him left notes in his locker and fought with each other for the right to ask him to a turnabout dance. One of those who fought for his attention was Candy Fuller. He was consistently courteous to her and relentlessly unforgiving.

In a cabin on the shores of Lake Hope, he and Penny Baker lost their virginities together. The experience was better than anything he had ever imagined, and he determined to repeat it as often as possible.

"Would you raise your seat back, Mr. Blaine? We're getting ready to land."

The flight attendant who smelled like his aunts' bathpowder stood next to his seat. He still missed those dear old ladies. They had died a few years ago, Amity passing on within three days of Theodora.

The flight attendant leaned over him deferentially. "Is Boston home, or are you here on business?"

"Home," he replied, although it no longer felt that way.

She chatted with him for a few minutes and couldn't quite hide her disappointment when he didn't ask for her phone number.

Mitch had long ago accepted the fact that he had a strong effect on women, but he hadn't given the matter much thought since his undergraduate days at Ohio State. He still didn't understand that the contrasts in his nature were what fascinated them. Women were drawn to his quiet courtesy and impeccable manners, but it was the juxtaposition of those gentler qualities with an almost ferocious masculinity that had made so many of them fall in love with him over the years.

Mitch didn't worry about his masculinity any more. He didn't have to. But when he had graduated from high school, it had been very much on his mind. He remembered leaving his aunts behind for his freshman year at Ohio State, and then he remembered his sophomore year, when he finally found the father figure he had been seeking for so long—Wayne Woodrow Hayes, the Buckeyes' legendary football coach.

Mitch smiled and shut his eyes. While the plane circled Logan Airport, he thought back to those Saturday afternoons when he had carried the football to glory in the horseshoe-shaped stadium on the banks of the Olentangy River. Even now he could hear the chimes of "Carmen Ohio" ringing in his mind. But most of all, he remembered Woody.

Everybody called the Buckeye football players dumb. A lot of them *were* dumb. Woody knew that. But he didn't like everybody else knowing it. When Woody first saw the hard-hitting, clean-living boy from Clearbrook, Ohio, in action, his eyes got misty. Not only did Mitch play the kind of single-minded, no-holds-barred football that Woody had invented, but he was carrying a 3.7 grade average in Electrical Engineering to go along with it.

Not Phys Ed.

Not Communication Arts.

Electrical Engineering.

Woody was a scholar, and he loved intelligent minds. His hobby was military history, and he laced his pregame speeches with references to his favorite men—Napoleon, Patton, and General Douglas MacArthur.

Mitch Blaine knew who they were.

Every Buckeye football player who wore the scarlet and gray respected and feared Woody Hayes, but that didn't keep them from joking about his old-fashioned sentiments behind his back. Mitch saw the humor in Woody, but he still loved listening to him talk. Woody believed in God, America, and Ohio State, in that order. He believed in back-breaking hard work and a strict moral code. And, gradually, Woody Hayes helped define for Mitch what it meant to be a man.

Mitch grew close to the crusty coach. Even after he was graduated from Ohio State and had gone on to MIT for his master's degree, he still telephoned him. One evening in the summer of 1969, Mitch called with the biggest news of his life.

"Coach, I've decided to get married."

There was a long silence on the other end of the phone. "That red-haired young lady you brought over for me to meet the last time you were in Columbus?"

"Yes. Louise."

"I remember." Woody seemed to be collecting his thoughts. "She's from a rich family, you told me."

"Her people came to Boston with the Pilgrims."

Another long silence, and then Woody delivered his verdict. "She has thin blood, son. I advise you to reconsider."

Like a fool, Mitch hadn't listened.

Mitch's house smelled damp and empty when he let himself inside. He set his suitcase down and wished it could all be different, that he could walk upstairs and find David, his five-year-old son, and Liza, his three-year-old daughter, curled beneath the covers in their bedrooms. But those bedrooms were empty now, stripped of their furniture and the sweet scramble of toys he used to stumble over when he kissed them good night.

His housekeeper had cleaned up the mess from his alcoholic oblivion. As he carried his suitcase upstairs, he felt a curl of disgust in his gut from all that self-pity he had been wallowing in. During the first few weeks after Louise had left with the children, he had been able to function normally. But the house had been so empty at night that he had begun keeping company with a bottle of scotch, not the best companion for someone who had never been much of a drinker. Eventually, he had conceived an alcohol-inspired plan to stop working, buy a boat, and sail around the Caribbean for a while. He had managed to implement the first part of his plan, but the second and third parts had required too much energy. And then Sam Gamble had kidnapped him, and the small wonders he had seen in that garage in Silicon Valley had forced him to rejoin the world.

As he stripped off his clothes and turned on the shower, he

reminded himself that Sam Gamble hadn't been his only kidnapper. His mouth tightened with displeasure as he thought of Susannah Faulconer. Of all the women Sam could have taken up with, Susannah Faulconer had been the worse possible choice. Mitch knew from experience, since he had married a woman just like her. Susannah and Louise even looked a little alike. Both were tall and slender. They had discreet private-school voices and carried themselves with that special air of composure that only those born into privileged families seem to possess. And both obviously got a kick out of slumming with men who were their social inferiors.

He had even considered warning Sam about Susannah, but Mitch hadn't listened to Woody, and Sam wouldn't listen, either. Only experience would teach Sam that women like Susannah Faulconer were dilettantes. They were fascinated by men who weren't part of their upbringing, but that fascination faded in the day-to-day drudgery of living.

"I'm tired of being married to you, Mitch," Louise had said one evening a month ago, when he'd come home from work. The sight of his cool, sophisticated wife sitting on the couch toying with a set of car keys was imprinted on his mind forever.

"We don't have anything in common," she had gone on. "You like to work. I like to go to parties. I want to have fun some place other than in the bedroom for a change."

Mitch had refused to admit even to himself that he no longer loved her. Their marriage had its roots in a youthful attraction of opposites instead of commonality of interests, but it was too late to remedy the mistake. They had children, she was a good mother, and marriage was forever.

"If you're unhappy, we'll make changes," he had said immediately. "We're a family, Louise, and we made vows to each other. If we have problems, let's get some counseling to help us work them out."

"Why bother?" she had retorted. Then she had told him that she had already taken the children to her mother's and she was on her way to join them. Picking up her purse, she had left the house without another word.

And that was what he couldn't forgive. She had simply

walked out, abandoning a seven-year marriage without making any effort to solve the problems between them.

Mitch understood bored socialites like Susannah Faulconer. He knew what they could do to a man, and he pitied Sam Gamble for what lay in store for him. But at the same time, he couldn't stop thinking about the excitement taking place in that Silicon Valley garage.

15

Susannah was sitting at the assembly table soldering some connections on the board she had just finished stuffing when Mitchell Blaine walked back into her life. It had been nearly a month since he had returned to Boston, and although he and Sam had talked on the phone a number of times, Mitch had shown no signs of changing his mind about joining them. Now, as he gave her a coldly courteous nod, she experienced an uneasy combination of hope and dismay.

Sam was obviously glad to see him, but he refused to give anything away. His lip curled as he surveyed Mitch's conservative navy-blue suit and maroon tie. "Somebody die? You look like a fuckin' pall bearer."

"All of us don't have your flair for fashion." Mitch gazed with distaste at Sam's ragged jeans and a faded T-shirt that was stretched nearly to transparency over Sam's chest.

Sam grinned. "So what are you doing out here?"

"I had an interview this morning. I thought I'd stop by to invite you and Yank for dinner. There's a French place in Palo Alto, or we could go into the city if you prefer."

Susannah's grip tightened on her soldering iron and she glanced sharply at Sam to see how he would react to the fact she had been neatly cut from the picture.

Once again Sam let his eyes rove over Mitch's business suit. "Let's make it Mom and Pop's."

She waited for him to say more—to mention her—but he didn't. Mitch agreed to Sam's choice of restaurant. They chatted for a while and looked over the latest work Yank had done on the prototype.

Susannah confronted Sam as soon as Mitch left, but he shrugged off her indignation. "Give him time," he said. "Once he gets to know you, he'll change his mind. You're too sensitive." He reached for her, ready to quiet her protests with kisses, but a new stubbornness took hold of her, and she resisted him. For some unfathomable reason Mitch disliked her, and he was giving no indication that he intended to change his mind. Getting up stiffly from the table, she went into the house so she could collect her thoughts. Sam didn't follow her.

That evening, she took her clothes into the bathroom and got dressed. She told herself she wouldn't let them dismiss her without a fight, but courage still didn't come easily, and she fumbled with the button at the waistband of her skirt, and then snagged her hair in the inexpensive loose-knit mauve sweater she had bought at Angela's favorite outlet store. Brushing her hair to the nape of her neck, she tied it back with a scarf. Angela came into the bathroom and fluffed the curls that had formed around her face.

"Don't let them push you around, Suzie," she said, attuned as always to what was happening around her. "Stick to your guns." She clipped a pair of beaded pink and purple triangles to Susannah's lobes. "I won fifty dollars at the slots when I was wearing these in Vegas last June. They'll bring you luck."

Susannah smiled and gave her a fierce, impulsive hug. She felt closer to Sam's mother than she had ever felt to her own.

Yank and Sam were both in the kitchen. Sam looked surprised when she walked in, as if he hadn't expected her to come with them. The sharp corners of the pink and purple triangles banged into the hollows beneath her ears.

"I don't know why you're making such a big deal of this," he said defensively. "It's just a meeting."

Instead of replying, she walked out to the car.

Mitch was already at the restaurant when they arrived. He had traded in his suit for dark brown slacks and a gold sport shirt. A Rolex gleamed in the sandy-brown hairs at his wrist. He stood as she approached, but made no attempt to hide his displeasure at her appearance. The men slid into the booth on each side of him. She took the seat on the end, keeping her back as straight as Grandmother Bennett's yardstick.

"This is supposed to be a business meeting, Sam," he said, nodding in her direction.

"That's why I'm here," she replied before Sam could answer.

The jukebox began to play a Linda Ronstadt hit. "Roberta isn't coming," Yank said abruptly.

Susannah gave him a sharp glance. Yank was hardly given to idle chatter, so he obviously wanted to make a point, but she had no idea whether he was indicating that she shouldn't be here either or whether he was making a distinction between the two women in her favor.

He began to draw an abstract figure in the moisture on the beer pitcher—another one of his diagrams. Did he design circuitry even in his sleep? she wondered. For the moment, it was easier to watch Yank's finger than deal with the tension that permeated the booth.

A circle appeared. A transistor maybe?

Two dots. A curve.

Yank had drawn a happy face.

"So . . . did you take a job with IBM yet?" Sam's voice snapped with sarcasm.

"I've been asked," Mitch replied as the waitress approached with the pizzas he had ordered. "Actually, I've had a number of interesting offers in the past few weeks. A lot of high-tech companies, naturally, but Detroit, too. And the soft drink people have been pretty persuasive." As they ate, he detailed several of his offers, including one from Cal Theroux at FBT.

Sam listened with increasing impatience, then pushed away his pizza and leaned back in the booth. "Sounds safe. Safe and predictable."

Mitch gave him a long stare. "It's a miracle that you've managed to keep SysVal alive this long. You don't know anything about selling a product. You don't have any organization, any definable market. Your company is so eccentric that it's a joke." He went on and on, detailing their shortcomings until Sam's mouth had tightened in a grim line and Susannah felt as if someone was banging her head into the wall. Yank drew three more happy faces.

Finally, Sam had had enough. He wadded up his paper napkin and tossed it down on the table. "If we're such a joke, then why did you come back, you son of a bitch?"

For the first time, Mitch seemed to relax. A smile spread slowly over his broad, good-looking face. "Because you hooked me. You hooked me good. SysVal is all I've been able to think about since I went back to Boston. I told myself I needed a vacation. I've tried to take some time off. But nothing's worked."

Sam sat slowly upright, his expression cautious, afraid to hope. "Are you telling me—"

"I'm in." Mitch shook his head. "For better or worse, I'm in all the way."

Yank smiled. Sam let out a whoop that startled one of the waitresses so badly she dropped a pie.

"That's great! God, that's really great!"

"We have to deal first," Mitch said, holding up his hand. "I have some conditions."

Sam could barely contain his excitement. "Name them."

"I want an equal partnership with you and Yank. Each of us takes one third of SysVal. In return, I'll guarantee a $100,000 line of credit at the banks. That'll keep us away from the venture capitalists for a while." He opened a leather folder he had brought with him and pulled out a gold pen. "Yank, you have to leave Atari. The SysVal I is only a toy. Our future is locked up in that prototype you're building, and you have to commit to it full-time."

"I like Atari," Yank said. "I have this new game coming out in a couple of months."

"Are you crazy?" Sam exclaimed. "This is a hell of a lot more important than a goddamn video game."

"I don't know about that, Sam," Yank replied earnestly. "It's one heck of a good game."

Sam rolled his eyes to the ceiling and turned to Mitch. "I'll take care of him. I promise."

Mitch began to discuss contingencies, eventual strategies for venture capital, a marketing plan, but Susannah didn't hear anything more. All the muscles in her torso seemed to have contracted into tight, painful bands. At the same time, her legs were rubbery and her pulse was beating much too fast. On and on they went—their exclusive male chatter cutting her out and pushing her aside like a whore who has been well-used and is no longer wanted. She drew herself up and tried to calm her heartbeat, but her voice was unsteady. "What about me?" she said.

Sam immediately grew cautious. "Let's talk about this later."

No scenes, Susannah. Be good. Be polite. The voices of the past whispered their earnest cautious messages. But she had learned brashness from Sam Gamble, and she pushed the voices away. "No. I think we need to talk about it now, since this concerns everyone here."

Mitch crossed his arms over his chest and looked irritated. "Another item on my list of conditions, Sam. Keep your woman troubles away from the company."

Susannah could feel her cheeks burning. Sam put all his weight on one hip and pulled Yank's car keys from his opposite pocket. "Look, Suzie. Take the car. I'll meet you at home in a couple of hours and we'll go over this."

"No!" She found herself on her feet, standing at the end of the booth and glaring down at the three of them. A pulse throbbed in her neck beneath skin as tight as a drumhead. She was dizzy and reckless with anger, uncaring of the scene she was creating for the people in the neighboring booths. "None of this is satisfactory to me, Mr. Blaine. None of it."

He waved his hand dismissively. "Miss Faulconer, I—"

"I've got the floor now, and it's my turn to talk. Sam seems to have forgotten to give you one important piece of information. If you intend to work with him, you need to know that he's quite brilliant in defining the big picture, but abysmal when it comes to details. He should have told you that tending to the details has been my job. Like finding the money to build those first forty boards. And paying our bills. And making certain dealers took us seriously when we went to Atlantic City. The fact is, Mr. Blaine, SysVal wouldn't exist today if it weren't for me."

She looked first at Sam and then at Yank, daring them to contradict her. Sam was scowling and Yank was studying the beer pitcher. Neither of them said anything.

"Vision isn't enough to run a company, and neither is genius. A company needs somebody to do the work, somebody to see to the everyday details, somebody to get the job done. That person has been me. And if any of you—if any *one* of you—thinks he's going to cut me out now, he's grossly mistaken."

Sam looked down at the table, refusing for the first time since she had known him to meet her eyes. Only Mitch met her gaze directly. He was tough. She could see that. And his stiff, starchy exterior hid the instincts of a street fighter.

"Aren't you being a little melodramatic, Miss Faulconer? Perhaps you'd better separate your romantic difficulties from company business." His voice was silky with condescension.

She had no one to help her. Only herself. Her intelligence and her guts. If she didn't stand up to this man right now, he would gun her down and leave her for dead. "This has nothing to do with my personal relationship with Sam. You've deliberately ignored me from the beginning, but you're not going to do it again. I told you that Sam wasn't good with details, so I'm not surprised that he seems to have forgotten to discuss one of those details with you."

"And what's that?"

"SysVal already has a binding three-way partnership agreement. And I'm one of those three partners."

Sam's head shot up. She saw consternation in his face, and realized that he had actually forgotten about the piece of paper she'd thrust under his nose that afternoon before they'd gone to Atlantic City.

"We all signed it, Mr. Blaine—even though one of us seems to have forgotten." She didn't mention that the paper hadn't been witnessed, that it probably wasn't legal at all, that the socialite was once again trying to pull a hustle.

"I see."

Her voice had begun to shake ever so slightly. "I'm not just Sam's tootsie, Mr. Blaine, as you seem determined to believe. Whether you like it or not, I'm the president of SysVal."

"That title doesn't mean anything!" Sam exclaimed. "We were just using the Faulconer name on those business cards. It was your idea."

"And without my name on those business cards, we wouldn't exist today."

Sam's arm shot out across the table. He grabbed her wrist and pulled her roughly down on the seat. His eyes were hard, glittering with anger. "You're going to ruin this for us, you know that? You're going to fucking ruin everything. What difference does it make how we divide things up? If you and I get married, what difference does it make?"

The pain was so sharp, she had to close her eyes for a moment. A knife, diamond-edged and lethal, sliced through her. She wanted to buckle over and curl into a tiny ball. Whenever she had wanted to talk about their feelings for each other—about their future together—he had evaded her. Now he was using marriage as a bargaining chip to manipulate her, as a carrot to dangle in front of her so she would do as he wished. Her body managed to feel both cold and hot at the same time. For the first time, she wondered if SysVal was worth it.

Yank spoke, apropos of nothing. "If I leave Atari, I won't have any health insurance."

His interruption gave her the chance to steady herself. Later. She would think about Sam's emotional betrayal when she was alone. For now she would force herself to separate the personal from the professional, just as men had been doing for centuries. Like a child playing in a sandbox, she would bury every one of her feelings to be retrieved later.

Sam's fingers had loosened on her wrist. She drew away from him, then crossed her hands on the table to keep them steady. She forced herself to forget about Sam, to concentrate only on Mitchell Blaine. "You have the reputation and the experience we lack. On the other hand, we have something you need. I've studied your career, Mr. Blaine. Sometimes you've been a bit too bold for your employers, haven't you? It must be frustrating to have some of your most innovative ideas curbed by men who are more conservative than you."

She thought she saw a flicker of surprise, and she pressed

her point home. "At SysVal, you'll find the aggressive, creative climate you've been looking for—something to relieve that boredom that's been bothering you. Because of our inexperience, we don't have preconceived notions of how things have to be done. We have a chance to build a humane, progressive company from the bottom up—a company that cares about people as well as its product. The three of us would very much like to have you as a fourth partner, Mr. Blaine; however, as president of this company, I have some conditions of my own."

Sam made a small exclamation, but she ignored him. "Your offer of a $100,000 line of credit with the banks is generous, but not quite generous enough if you want an equal partnership. I handle the books, Mr. Blaine, and we're going to need double that if we want to put the self-contained computer on the market without going to the venture capitalists right away. I'd also like to see you toss in $25,000 of your own money as soon as possible to show good faith and get us out of our immediate cash bind." She turned to Yank. "Is that agreeable with you?"

Yank nodded vaguely.

"Sam?" She forced herself to look at him.

He had clamped his teeth together so tightly that a pale rim had formed around his lips. "What the hell do you think you're doing? Mitch is holding all the cards. We're not in any position to bargain with him."

"That's not true. This is our company. As much as we may want him to be part of it, we have the final say. Isn't that correct, Mr. Blaine?"

"Up to a point, Miss Faulconer. But only to a point." His voice was soft, barely above a whisper, but it conveyed a cold authority. "Without me, you won't have a company much longer."

"Without you," she said quietly, "Sam will find someone else."

Silence fell over the table. For the first time since their confrontation had begun, Mitch had lost some of his composure. She continued to press her advantage. "Don't make the mistake of underestimating him. Sam is brash, arrogant, and lousy with details. But he has a gift. It's a gift few people have and even fewer know how to use, but he happens to be one of them. Sam has the ability to make sensible people do impossible things."

"Sensible people like you, Miss Faulconer?"

"And like you, Mr. Blaine."

For a moment he looked at her thoughtfully, and then he rose and tossed some bills down on the table. Without saying another word to any of them, he left the restaurant.

The air outside was chill. Mitch picked up his steps as he crossed the parking lot, the soles of his loafers slapping angrily on the pavement. He prided himself on his analytical mind, his ability to make decisions without being influenced by emotional overtones. But he had blown it badly in that restaurant tonight.

She wasn't anything like Louise. He couldn't imagine the woman who had gone into battle with him tonight abandoning a seven-year marriage without making any effort to confront her husband with her grievances. Despite her distant air, she was a fighter and not quite the dilettante he had imagined.

But then, maybe he was wrong. Maybe he was still so shell-shocked from his impending divorce that he couldn't judge women anymore. He slipped the key to his rental car out of his pocket and fit it in the lock. What would happen if she got her way? Would she grow bored and start looking for a new diversion?

"Mr. Blaine."

He reluctantly turned his head.

Although she was walking toward him quickly, she gave no real appearance of haste. He had noticed that about her from the beginning—the restraint in her movements, the stillness about her, the closed, cool facial expression. Those mannerisms reminded him of someone else. Louise, of course. But no, that wasn't quite right. Now that he had watched Susannah in action, he realized that she wasn't like Louise at all. She was like someone else. But who?

She stopped next to him. He drew his eyes away from her and removed the key from the door lock. "Haven't you finished raking me over the coals yet, Miss Faulconer?"

She started to speak and then stopped, no longer quite the confident woman she had been a few moments earlier. Her hesitation pleased him. He didn't enjoy finishing second place to a woman, and certainly not to one who was a neophyte.

"Just one more thing," she said. "I'd like to know why you dislike me so much. It's because of my father, isn't it?"

She was so earnest, so proper. Once again he experienced that twinge of familiarity, the nagging sense that he had met her before. "I don't like your father, but I respect him. He has nothing to do with this."

He saw that his response had thrown her off balance, and he was pleased.

"Then what? Have I done something specific? I know it can't be because of what I said tonight. You've disliked me from the beginning, haven't you?"

She was determined to press him, and he was equally determined not to put himself at any further disadvantage. He certainly wasn't going to tell her about Louise. "Do you mind if we just let this discussion go?"

She caught her bottom lip between her teeth, and he knew she hadn't finished with him. To his surprise, he heard himself saying, "Whatever my original opinions were, you've changed them this evening."

The slow smile that captured the corners of her mouth was hesitant, but so winsome that he felt his own lips begin to curve in response.

"Is that actually a compliment?" she asked.

"It's a compliment, Miss Faulconer. Definitely a compliment."

And then he realized what it was about her that seemed so familiar. The perfect manners, the quiet courtesy, the steely determination. She didn't remind him of Louise. She reminded him of himself.

The realization floored him, and then, unexpectedly, he felt his spirit lighten. In that moment, he made his decision, knowing even as he said the words that he had set his life on a new and dangerous course. "I'll accept your terms, Miss Faulconer. But don't feel too confident, because I'm going to be looking over your shoulder every minute."

"Fair enough, Mr. Blaine. Because I'll be looking right back."

He laughed. In her own way, she had as much gall as Sam Gamble, but she packaged it so much more discreetly.

Pulling the car door shut, he pressed the button to lower the window. "Tell our business partners that I might have a better name for our new computer than the SysVal II."

"Oh?"

"Maybe we should name it after you."

Her eyes widened in surprise. "After me?"

"Yeah." He leaned out the window. "Maybe we should call it the Hot Shot."

She laughed, a lovely sound, like the tinkle of antique bells. "Hot shot? Me?"

He drew in his head and slipped the car into reverse. "You, Miss Faulconer."

Susannah watched him pull his car out of the parking lot. She was still smiling as he turned out onto the highway. Imagine anyone calling her a hot shot. It was ridiculous, of course. But nice.

She heard footsteps approaching from behind, and her smile faded. Sam's hand touched her shoulder. He sounded more weary than angry.

"Just what in the hell do you think you're doing? God, you're the last person in the world I would have ever expected to have hang-ups about power."

She wanted to make some scathing retort that would hurt him as he had hurt her, but all the spirit she had summoned for her confrontation with Mitch faded. She followed Yank to the Duster, which was parked at an awkward angle in the next row.

Sam stayed on her heels. "This company isn't going to work if you pull any more power plays like that. That's not what we're about. It isn't going to frigging work!"

Yank began tapping his pants pockets in search of his keys. An eddy of cool night wind whipped Sam's hair up from his neck. Her heart ached. Why did he have to be so fierce? So driven?

"You've blown this deal, Suzie. I mean you have destroyed everything. Everything we've been working for. Everything we've tried to do. It's like you deliberately set out to sabotage us."

Yank tapped his shirt pocket and said in a distracted voice, "She didn't blow it, did you, Susannah?"

"No," she replied. "I didn't blow it."

"She didn't blow it, Sam."

Sam stared at both of them, and then at her. "What do you mean? Did he say something to you? What are you talking about?"

Without bothering to consider how Yank had known what would happen, she managed to say, "Mitch has accepted. He's joining SysVal as our fourth partner."

Sam's face shattered as if a sunlit prism had broken apart inside him. "He told you? He's accepted? That's fabulous! I mean, that is freaking fabulous!" He grabbed her and pulled her to his chest. But the moment of shared joy that should have been perfect had been ruined for her.

He released her and threw his arms into the air. "This is going to be fantastic!" With his neck arched, he began drawing word pictures of the revolution they were about to begin. He wasn't as tall as either Yank or Mitch, but as he sliced the air with sweeping gestures and spangled the night with his grandiose dreams, he seemed so much bigger than either of them.

She could feel his energy pulling at her, that indomitable force of will tugging her up toward his personal rainbow. She wanted to go with him on his climb, but this time something within her resisted. Only when he saw how rigidly she was holding herself did he grow quiet. After studying her for a few moments, he said, "Yank, Suzie and I are going to take a walk. Wait for us, okay?"

Yank began searching the ground at his feet. Sam extracted the Duster keys from his own pocket and tossed them over. "We won't be long."

He caught her arm and began drawing her back toward the row of stores. "You're still too chicken to fight with me, aren't you? You're incredibly pissed, but you're going to sulk instead of fight."

Some of her spirit began to come back. Was it his touch? Did he have a magical way of passing his energy through his skin and into hers? "I'm not afraid of fighting with you," she said. "But right now, I'm just not certain you're worth it."

Even as the words were slipping from her mouth, she couldn't believe she was uttering them. His steps faltered, and she knew that she had hurt him. It was a strange feeling to realize she had any power over him at all. She moved up onto the sidewalk. An ice cream cone lay deflated in an ugly brown puddle on the pavement. They walked past the door of Mom & Pop's. She stopped in front of the dry cleaners and stared blindly at a wedding gown entombed in a windowed cardboard box. Once again, she reached deep inside herself to find the courage to say what she must.

"Don't ever try to cut me out again, Sam," she said quietly.

"Is that what you think I was doing?"

"Yes. You excluded me and then used marriage as a bargaining chip to keep me in line."

"You're getting paranoid. I assumed we'd get married one of these days. You're not the sort of woman who's going to be happy shacking up for very long." He slipped one hand out of his jacket pocket and laid it over her shoulders. "Suzie, I'm sorry. I wasn't trying to pull any sort of power play. I just didn't understand you were so hung up about crossing all the t's and dotting the i's."

"To me, it was more than crossing t's."

"But I don't see it that way. You and I are a couple, aren't we? What one of us has, the other has."

He was so earnest, so persuasive, but this time she wouldn't let herself be swept away. "Then why didn't *you* drop out?" she asked gently. "Why didn't you say, 'I'll step aside. Let Susannah be your partner. What she's got, I've got'?"

He pulled his arm from her shoulders. "That's ridiculous! It's not even logical. This whole thing was my idea. SysVal means everything to me."

"I lost my father, Sam. SysVal means everything to me, too."

The harsh glare faded from his features as he took in the significance of what she was saying. Slowly he smiled—a rueful, apologetic smile. Some of the ice inside her began to melt. He tilted his head toward her and touched her forehead with his own. Her eyelids drifted shut. They stood like that for a moment, with their eyes closed and foreheads touching.

"I'm sorry," he whispered.

She knew that she was near tears, and she forced them

back so that she didn't sound self-pitying. "I want to be as important to you as the company."

"You and the company are all mixed up together in my mind."

They stood like that for a few moments with only their foreheads touching. Then their noses brushed, and their mouths. Although their lips were together, they didn't kiss.

"I love you, Suzie," he whispered, his voice sounding young and scared. "I know I get crazy sometimes, but you've got to promise me you'll stick with me. Please, babe. I need you so much. Oh, God, I love you. Promise me you'll always be there for me."

He gripped her hands at her sides so tightly he seemed to be trying to couple their flesh. At that moment, she realized how fiercely she loved him. Her throat had constricted and she couldn't talk—she couldn't force out the words he needed to hear. Instead, she parted her lips and gave him a dark, desperate kiss.

16

●●●●●●●●●●●●●●●●●●●●●●●●●

Slap some paint on his shirt, Susannah," Sam said three weeks later, as he placed a two-by-four over a pair of sawhorses. "I'm embarrassed to be in the same room with him."

Mitch looked down at his crisply pressed work shirt and a pair of dark blue jeans with razor-sharp creases. "What's the matter with the way I look? We're building a wall, for Pete's sake, not going to a fashion show."

Sam snorted, and Susannah smiled to herself. Building the partition to separate the assembly and storage areas in their new office space was the first job the four of them had done together, and despite the fact that Sam and Mitch had been trading jibes all morning, the wall was taking shape rapidly.

She had spent the first two weeks of October scouring the Valley for office space, but it had been difficult finding something that was adequate and yet met their limited budget. With Mitch as a partner, they had easily secured a bank loan. Each of them was now drawing a minuscule salary, and their cash flow problems had temporarily eased. But they all knew the loan was only a temporary stopgap, and in order to postpone going to the venture capitalists, they had to scrimp wherever they could.

She had finally found office space at a reasonable rent in the back of a tilt-up, one of the low rectangular buildings that filled the Valley's industrial parks. It wasn't a large area, but it was bigger than the garage and, with a few additions, would meet their needs. They had begun constructing the dividing partition the day before.

"I'll bet you go to a tailor to get your underwear made," Sam said to Mitch as he held the board for Yank to cut.

"My tailor doesn't make underwear," Mitch replied. And then, "I've heard there's a market in the Orient for human hair, Sam. It occurs to me that if you'd sell yours, we could buy this building instead of just renting it."

Susannah groaned. "Tell them both to be quiet, will you, Yank? They're giving me a headache."

"You didn't have a headache this morning." Sam leered at her, and then swung the two-by-four around so that it gently slapped her rear.

She absolutely refused to blush. If she were going to work with men all day, she at least had to pretend to be one of the guys. "That's true," she countered sweetly, "but I'll certainly have one by tonight."

Mitch smiled. Although she knew he was still watching everything she did and waiting for her to take a misstep, their relationship was at least superficially cordial.

She went over to help him support a joist he was nailing into place. "Boy, are you lucky you joined up with us. They wouldn't have let you do work like this in Boston."

He looked down at her from his perch on the ladder, with a hammer in his fist and a satisfied expression on his face. "This is great, isn't it? I haven't had so much fun since I was in college."

She grimaced as she tried to ease the cramp in her shoulders. "You were supposed to be the sane person in this partnership. Now you're as crazy as the rest of us."

On the other side of the room, Yank was driving Sam wild by insisting on measuring every board to the sixteenth of an inch. Finally Sam couldn't stand it any longer. "We're not doing brain surgery, for chrissake! It doesn't have to be exact. Just saw the son of a bitch in half."

But Yank, with his engineer's passion for precision, didn't know how to compromise. By afternoon, Sam refused to work with him any longer, and Susannah was forced to take his place.

As Susannah worked, her eyes followed Sam. She kept wondering when it would wear off, this need to touch him every moment they were together. She knew that he was arrogant and frequently self-centered, but he was also the most compelling person she had ever met. He waved challenges in her face like red flags, and pushed her into another universe with his lusty lovemaking. With Sam, she could be bold and strong. Without him— But she couldn't bear to think about life without Sam. Left on her own, she would probably crawl back into her proper hollow shell and stay there until she died.

She realized that the events the night Mitch had joined the company had changed their relationship. Both of them sensed that they had nearly lost something precious. Ironically, Sam was the one who had begun to press the idea of getting married. Being Sam, he had painted word pictures for her of what their marriage could be—the endless *possibilities* of a union both spiritually and physically sublime, the *power* of that sort of synergy, the *unlimited potential* of the joining of matched minds. As always, his rhetoric had mesmerized her. They had even gone so far as to apply for a marriage license and to get their blood tested. But then Susannah had found office space and everything else stopped.

They christened the wall with a six-pack of beer that evening and spent the next day moving in. At ten that night, dirty and exhausted, they made their way to Mom & Pop's.

Mitch had been talking for some time about the need for a formal organizational chart. Yank had said that he wouldn't accept any title except Engineer, but even Sam knew that the rest of their responsibilities had to be better defined. After the waitress had taken their order, Mitch pulled a neatly folded piece of paper from his pocket and slid it toward the middle of the table. Even before he opened it, Susannah suspected that it was the organizational chart he had been talking about.

It was illogical to hope that she could retain her position as president. Mitch had far more experience and was the better choice to head the company. But although she was reconciled to the fact that she would be demoted, she wasn't going to let Mitch give her an empty title. If it meant another fight, then so be it.

Mitch unfolded the paper and straightened it with his fingers. It was the roughly drawn chart she had expected, and her eyes first fell on Yank's name written in neat block letters slightly below center. He was listed as Head Engineer.

Sam gave a hoot of laughter and pointed to his own name. "Chairman of the Board. Yeah, I like the sound of that."

And then, to her astonishment, Susannah saw she was listed as President and Chief Operating Officer, while Mitch had appointed himself Executive Vice-President of Sales and Marketing.

Mitch took in the expression of surprise on her face. "Being president sounds impressive, Susannah, but it'll be mainly dirt work for a long time. I hope you're up to it."

"But you're far more qualified. Why—"

"Marketing technical products is what I do best, and it's why you recruited me. I don't want to be distracted with day-to-day operations. You've said that you're a detail person. Now you're going to have to prove it."

Her mouth felt dry. Even though this was what she had wanted, she was frightened. They weren't operating out of a garage anymore. What did she know about running a real company?

Mitch called for a vote, and before the pizzas arrived, she had been officially elected SysVal's first president.

On a warm and sunny afternoon just before Halloween, Susannah was in the Gamble garage packing up the last of the equipment. Mitch had been right, she thought, as she slapped a pile of tools in the carton with a little more force than necessary. Being president sounded a lot more impressive than it was. Everyone had gone off and left her to do the final cleanup. Yank was working on the prototype, and Mitch had flown to Boston to see his children. Sam was supposed to be helping her, but he had run off a couple of hours ago and not returned.

In the past two weeks she had been able to handle most of the emergencies that had popped up, and the company was still running. Although Yank continued to grumble about the way the three of them had strong-armed him into leaving Atari, the work on the prototype for the self-contained computer was now progressing much faster. They had hired a talented engineer from Homebrew to design the power supply, and spent hours debating what they would name the machine. All of them had discovered they liked images that had to do with heat and fire. After much discussion, they voted to name the machine the Blaze.

Sometimes as she studied its emerging circuitry, Susannah found herself remembering the evening at the playground with Sam. *Do you know what Yank's machine is going to give you?* he had told her. *It's going to give you courage.* In a funny way, Sam's prophecy had come true.

As if she had conjured him with her thoughts, he poked his head in through the garage door. His hair was even longer now than when they'd met. At night, when she was naked, she liked to comb it through her fingers and pull the inky strands across her breasts.

"It's about time," she said grouchily.

He grinned like a kid who'd just gotten away with something. "Sorry. Things to do."

"I'll bet. You've probably been out joy riding."

Removing the wrenches she was holding, he cupped her bottom and pulled her hips forward so that their jeans rubbed together. Then he kissed her. "You're sounding like a nagging wife. Come to think about it, that's not a bad idea. Go get your face washed. We're getting married in half an hour."

Her head shot back. "What?"

He grinned. "It's all arranged. Mom just left to pick up Yank, and they're meeting us at the tire playground. I like the idea of doing it there. The guy who's marrying us is the brother of this guy I know. He's got another ceremony at one o'clock, so we sort of have to rush."

She stared at him.

He stepped back, tilted his head to one side and gave her that cocky I-dare-you look. A police siren whined in the distance. She could see him waiting for her protests, waiting for her to give him a long list of all the sensible reasons they couldn't do something this impulsive. She thought of the hundreds of phone calls and endless rounds of appointments that had gone into the preparations for her wedding to Cal—all those intricate, elaborate, ultimately useless preparations.

Although she had known him only six months, her mind refused to consider the possibility of a future without Sam. She needed to touch his skin and breathe his air for the rest of her life. "All right," she said breathlessly. "I'll do it."

He let out a whoop of delight and drew her back into his arms. "God, I love you." He pulled her into the house, where he barely gave her five minutes to comb her hair and dab on a few cosmetics. She substituted a purple gauze blouse for her T-shirt, but before she could unfasten her jeans to exchange them for slacks, he was dragging her back outside toward the Harley.

They arrived at the playground just as Yank and Angela climbed out of Angela's red Toyota. Yank was at his worst, so distracted he didn't seem to have the vaguest idea what was happening. Angela was talking a mile a minute and dabbing her eyes with tissue. To Susannah's surprise, Sam pulled a florist's box from the bike's saddlebag. Inside was a bridal bouquet of yellow roses.

The minister, whose name was Howard, appeared in a Grateful Dead T-shirt and told Sam how cool he thought all this was. Neighborhood children playing on the tires and riding along the bike path came over to see what was going on. Susannah felt as if she had been thrown back to the sixties.

They stood in front of a dome made of tractor tires, with Yank on Sam's right and Angela, sniffing and holding a rosary, on Susannah's left.

"Listen, you guys," Howard said as he began the ceremony. "I don't know either of you, so what I have to say isn't important. Why don't you just look at each other and make the promises you think you can keep. Sam, you go first."

Sam turned to her and squeezed her hand. "I promise to give you everything it's in my power to give, Susannah. I'll be honest. I'll speak the truth for both our sakes. And I won't be afraid to walk into the future with you."

They were strange vows, but they stirred threads of emotion deep inside her because they were so typical of Sam, so exactly right.

It was her turn. She gazed into his eyes and tried to find words to express the inexpressible. "I promise to give you my best, Sam, whatever that may be." She paused and the traditional wedding vows of love and honor passed through her mind. She searched for a new way to say them, a way that would reflect the passion and joy she felt in his presence, but her silence lasted too long, and Howard spoke before she could finish.

"That's cool. That's really cool." He picked up both their hands in his and squeezed them. "The law says that you're married, but only the two of you know what that really means." He then went on to ruminate about the universal powers of light and harmony and concluded with the words, "Be groovy."

The children on the playground giggled as Sam kissed her, and then Angela kissed them both. Yank and Sam shook hands, and Howard hugged everybody, including the kids. Sam made a mad dash over to a set of playground rings suspended from a heavy chain and pulled himself across them, hand over hand. When he dropped to the ground, he threw back his head and laughed. He was exultant, as if he had claimed some priceless possession. Together, they raced to his bike.

Angela had not been able to find a box of rice in Yank's kitchen cupboards and had grabbed a box of elbow macaroni instead. She quickly distributed its contents, and the motley assortment of wedding guests pelted the bride and groom with it as they roared away.

They took a wild ride into the hills. Sam's hair had come loose and it blew into her face, stinging her cheeks. She pressed her breasts to his back and held him tightly against the chill cut of the wind. They left civilization behind and climbed higher. Eventually he steered the bike onto a narrow, rutted road that soon dwindled to an overgrown path. When even that disappeared, he slowed and drove through the dry brush to the edge of a steep bluff. Only then did he stop.

The sound of silence was sharp after the roar of the engine. The Santa Clara Valley lay below them, its highways, industrial parks, and rectangular buildings laid out so that it look like an enormous integrated circuit. "I've put the world at your feet, Suzie," he said, his voice husky. "The two of us together—we can have whatever we want. By ourselves, we're not anything. But together, the Valley's ours. Yours and mine. We'll be king and queen."

There was a strange intensity about his words that made her uneasy. She broke the tension by saying lightly, "Queens are supposed to have crowns. I don't even own a baseball cap."

He smiled and the sunlight sparked silver lights in his black hair. She drank in the sight of the wild, free lover who was now her husband. "One of these days I'll buy you your own Harley," he said. "How about that? It'll be a royal Harley." He tugged her blouse from the waistband of her jeans and pressed his lips to her temple. "You'll ride it naked right down the middle of El Camino Real, just like Lady Godiva."

As he reached behind her for her bra clasp, she instinctively closed her hands over her breasts. Although the area was deserted, she was hardly used to taking off her clothes outside, and she laughed nervously. "It sounds uncomfortable. Won't I be cold?"

He gave her a sexy, half-lidded look and pushed her hands away. "Baby, I'm going to keep you so hot that you'll never be cold again."

Her bra fell to the ground. He gazed at her breasts and used the tip of his finger to draw a line down the center of one. She had a crazy desire to lift her arms high over her head and display herself to him.

He tugged down her jeans and her panties at the same time and pulled them off along with her shoes. The air was crisp and chill on her skin, the ground cold beneath her feet, but she barely noticed.

For a moment he rested the flat of his hand over his stomach. Then he lowered the zipper. The denim fell open in a deep V. Her lips parted slightly as she saw his bare stomach and the line of dark, crisp hair and realized that he wore no briefs beneath.

"You ever done it on a bike before, Suzie?"

"A thousand times," she said breathlessly.

"Big talk." He cocked his head toward the black leather seat. "Straddle it."

Her mouth had grown dry. Once again he was daring her, testing her, pushing her beyond the safe boundaries of her experience. Without taking her eyes from his, she did as he said, keeping her back to the handlebars so she was facing him. The black leather was chill against her bare buttocks and the soft insides of her thighs.

His mouth cocked insolently. Facing her, he swung his leg over the seat and slipped his hands under her knees. Lifting and spreading them, he pushed his own legs beneath her. The inside of her bare calves rubbed against the outside of his denim-clad ones, the underside of her thighs lay over the top of his. He looked down at her. Through her excitement, she thought how vulnerable her position made her to him. She was open and assailable while he was a hard, strong, denim-encased ridge hidden beneath her.

"You're going to be a great queen." He played with her breasts until she moaned, and then he indented her nipples with his thumbs as he pressed her back against the handlebars. She tilted her neck and looked at the sky. Her hair tumbled over the tachometer and the headlight. Thin blue-white clouds skidded across the sky while he pulled at her nipples until they turned into hard, swollen buds.

Finally, he moved the flat of his hand down between her breasts and over her abdomen, skimming her body as the clouds skimmed the sky. His hand came to rest on her tight, auburn curls. "Snooty and cool on the outside . . ." He moved his fingers. "Hot on the inside."

She moaned and drew up her feet. Her toes curled over the rear pegs as he caressed her. She felt as if she were moving out of her body into the sky. The Northern California sun came from behind a cloud and struck her skin. Her hands clutched his calves. She arched her back and turned her breasts upward like some primitive human sacrifice offered for the pleasure of a god.

Beneath her hips he opened his jeans the rest of the way and released himself. His boots were still on the ground, steadying the bike as he shifted his hips, poised himself, and entered her. She clutched his calves harder, arched higher. But as he began to move inside her, she couldn't get enough of him.

She pulled herself up to straddle his lap. Her hair fell over his shoulders and down his back, the auburn strands drifting like fine silk over the tough black leather. She was the aggressor now. She impaled herself deeper on him and made him adjust his rhythm to hers. A lock of his hair brushed her lips. She took it in her mouth. Wrapping her arms around his neck, she arched her waist and took him all.

He groaned. "That's good . . . That's so good."

Tears stung her eyes as she moved upon him. "Oh, yes. Yes."

"More . . . Give me more."

"I love . . ." she cried. "I love you . . ."

"Harder . . . More . . . Yes . . . more."

Her orgasm was quick and shattering. ". . . love you so much," she sobbed as she died upon him.

He dug his fingers into her buttocks and thrust himself hard up into her. As she felt him reach his crisis, she pressed her damp cheek to the top of his head and willed him to speak the love words she craved.

His cry was hoarse and strangled deep in his throat. "More," he demanded. "Give . . . me more."

17

The SysVal offices were sparsely furnished. Three battered steel desks sat in separate corners of the open room, and two long worktables occupied the fourth. A few rock concert posters and a fold-out Harley-Davidson ad hung on the wall. As Mitch walked through the door, he couldn't help but compare the posters to the Helen Frankenthaler canvas that had hung in his last office.

Although it was only a little after seven on Monday morning, Susannah was already sitting at her desk. Her feet were tucked under her, and she had a pencil stuck behind her ear. As he walked inside, she looked up from her notepad and smiled at him.

"I know all about the early bird and the worm," she said, "but don't you think you should have gone home to get some sleep first?"

"I slept a little on the plane."

"How was Boston?"

"Fine."

She didn't press him, and he was glad. He still felt bruised from having left his kids last night. Liza's dark curls had smelled like baby shampoo when he'd kissed her good-bye. David had locked his arms around his neck and begged him not to leave. Mitch blinked his eyes and headed for the coffeepot.

Susannah spoke hesitantly. "I don't want to pry, but I know having your children so far away can't be easy on you. If you need a friend . . ."

"Yes, thank you." He spoke briskly, pushing away her concern so that she would know his personal life was off limits. He took care of his own troubles, and he didn't need anyone's sympathy.

As he carried the coffee mug over to his desk, he glanced at the oversized calendar that hung on the wall. "Did anything come up this weekend?"

"Nothing much. I processed some new orders, took care of the mail, washed my hair, got married. Nothing really."

He spun around, sloshing coffee onto the floor. "You got married?"

She laughed. For the first time he noticed that she was carrying her own private glow with her. Her skin was luminous and her features seemed to have blurred at the edges, as if they were being photographed through a Vaseline-smeared lens.

"We've been talking about it for some time. You know Sam. He gave me half an hour's notice."

As she told him about the playground ceremony, his hands convulsed around his coffee mug. He was furious. He must have been crazy to have left his children on the other side of the continent for this.

When she finally paused, he set down his cup and regarded her steadily. "Quite frankly, I can't believe you've done this."

Some of her glow faded. He felt like a schoolyard bully, but he pushed away any remorse. He should have seen this coming, but he had been too caught up in the risk and excitement of their venture to dwell on the relationship between Sam and Susannah. Besides, he certainly hadn't envisioned Sam as a family man.

He watched her gather her dignity about her. "You know how Sam and I feel about each other."

"Didn't it occur to either one of you that we should have discussed this first?"

"We don't need your approval, Mitch."

"You may not need my approval, but you're damned well going to need a lawyer. Have you thought about what this marriage does to our partnership agreement?"

She was smart, he'd give her that. It didn't take her long to see that she and Sam had neatly managed to take control of half the company. "I—I'm sorry. I didn't think— We'll get it all ironed out with an attorney this week. You surely realized that neither of us was trying to pull any sort of power play."

She was probably telling the truth, he thought. That's what was so incredible. He had known from the beginning that he was getting involved with amateurs, and he had no one to blame but himself. Her expression was so stricken that he softened. "Is the lucky bridegroom in the back room?"

She cautiously accepted his peace offering. "Still in bed."

"I saw his bike outside. I thought—" He broke off at the self-satisfied expression that had begun to form on her face. "You rode the Harley over here by yourself?"

She smiled. "It was wonderful, Mitch. I beat the morning traffic, so I was only slightly terrified."

He tried to imagine his ex-wife jumping onto a motorcycle and failed abysmally. But then, he had given up the notion weeks ago that Louise and Susannah were anything alike.

Her laughter faded, and she gave him a look so earnest that his anger began to dissolve. "Be happy for us, Mitch. Sam and I need each other."

He didn't want to be on the receiving end of any intimate confessions. Taking a sip of his coffee, he nodded his head toward her hand. "No wedding ring?"

She smiled slightly. "An antiquated symbol of enslavement."

"That sounds like Sam talking, not you."

"You're right. But I'm the one who made the decision to keep my own name instead of taking his."

"Not all of the old traditions are bad ones."

"I know. But my name is my last link with my father." She hesitated. "I guess I'm not ready to give that up."

By now he had heard the story from Sam of the way Joel

Faulconer had turned his back on her. He tried to imagine doing something like that to his own daughter, but he couldn't.

"How does Sam feel about your not taking his name?"

"He harangued me for at least an hour. But I think it was more a training exercise than a sign of real conviction. He wanted to make certain marriage hadn't turned me into a yes-woman."

"Sam definitely likes a good fight."

Susannah's expression turned serious. "I'm not afraid to fight with him, Mitch. Just because we're married doesn't mean I'll rubber stamp his opinions. When it comes to SysVal, I'm my own woman."

We'll see, he thought to himself. *We'll see.*

By the end of the following week, they had taken the legal steps necessary to protect the company in the event that Sam and Susannah's marriage failed. Documents were drawn up to make certain that partnership shares couldn't change hands in a divorce settlement and upset the balance of power. If either Sam or Susannah found it depressing to sign papers that dealt—theoretically, at least—with the end of a marriage that had just begun, neither of them commented.

As fall slipped into winter, Mitch watched for signs that Sam and Susannah's marital relationship was affecting their business decisions. Finally, he was forced to admit that, more frequently than not, he and Susannah joined forces against her husband.

While the SysVal partners were growing accustomed to their new office, the little Apple Computer Company continued to operate from the Jobses' family garage in Cupertino. Its founders were also at work on a prototype of a self-contained computer, which they were calling the Apple II. One night early in December, over video games at Mom & Pop's, Mitch discovered that Yank had openly discussed his work on the Blaze with Steve Wozniak. His expression grew incredulous as he absorbed this casually offered piece of information.

"Are you out of your mind?" he exclaimed, angrily

confronting Yank, who was standing at the next video machine. "Your designs are this company's most basic asset. You don't share them with a competitor. Don't *ever* let anything like this happen again! Ever!"

Yank was completely mystified by Mitch's anger. "Woz and I like each other's work," he said in his reasonable, logical voice. "We've always helped each other out."

Sam and Susannah had been playing Super Pong together when the eruption occurred. Observing the curious stares of a couple in a nearby booth, she moved her body slightly, hoping to block some of the confrontation from public view while Sam tried to calm Mitch.

"Look, it's a different world out here," Sam said. "Yank's a hacker. Hackers can't even understand the *concept* of proprietary information."

Mitch's expression grew fierce. "Listen to me, all of you. We're not playing games with SysVal. From now on every piece of information on the Blaze design is proprietary— right down to the number of screws holding on the case. This is not debatable! No one talks publicly about anything, do you hear me? No one!"

Yank turned away from Mitch to gave Sam a long, piercing gaze, and then he said distinctly, "This is crap."

It was the first time Susannah had ever heard him use a vulgarity. Without uttering another word, he stalked away from the three of them and left the restaurant.

Mitch was as angry as she had ever seen him. Sam, in his impulsive manner, wanted to deal with the situation in the middle of Mom & Pop's, but she hustled both men outside and they drove to Sam and Susannah's apartment.

The apartment was small and dingy, with a view of the trash Dumpster, but Susannah loved having a place of her own and didn't mind its shabbiness. They had neither the time nor the money to improve it, which was probably just as well because Susannah had finally admitted to herself that domesticity had never interested her. When it came to a choice between spending her time working on the development of the Blaze prototype or picking out living room draperies, the Blaze won hands down.

Sam grabbed a beer from the refrigerator for Mitch and a

Coke for himself and then began to pace the floor. Susannah took a seat in the room's only armchair. Mitch, whose outrage over Yank's breach of security hadn't eased at all, sat on the couch and scowled. They were in the positions they usually occupied late at night when the three of them got together to refine their business plan and define exactly what they wanted their company to be.

How many nights had they spent like this, with Sam painting word pictures of a company that had glass walls, open doors, and rock music playing, while Mitch countered with his own, more pragmatic vision—one centered on swelling market share and snowballing profits instead of a Utopian working environment? Despite the friendship between the two men, they were frequently at loggerheads, and Susannah had to act as mediator. She realized that this night would be no different.

Sam planted his hands on his hips and looked over at Mitch. "You've got a Master's from MIT, but Yank and I are Valley kids. We weren't trained in colleges. Our roots are in the suburbs—in garages. For hackers, the rewards come in breaking codes and in getting into closed systems—in showing your design to someone who's smart enough to understand the dazzle of what you've done. When you tell a hardware hacker like Yank that he can't show off a brilliant piece of design to one of the few people he knows who can really appreciate it, it's like you've cut off his oxygen supply."

"Then we have a serious problem," Mitch said coldly.

Silence fell between them.

Susannah sighed in frustration. Why couldn't either of them ever see the other's viewpoint? Once again she found herself wanting to bang their heads together. Mitch grounded everything in reality, Sam in possibility. She alone seemed to understand that only with the melding of both philosophies could the true vision of SysVal emerge.

She slipped into her customary role of mediator as if it were an old, comfortable bathrobe. "Don't forget that while Yank is showing off the Blaze, he's also looking at the Apple II. Surely there'll be some benefits in that."

"That's nuts," Mitch protested. "What if—by the grace

of God—we actually manage to make a success out of this ridiculous company? We can't function indefinitely with our newest technology flying out the window all the time."

"You're right," she said, "but in this case being right doesn't make any difference, because Yank simply won't pay attention." She had already given the matter some thought, and now she shared her ideas with them. "As soon as we're able, we need to begin surrounding him with the most brilliant young engineers we can find—eccentric thinkers like he is. We have to create the Homebrew environment internally."

Sam's head snapped up, his eyes grew bright. "That's no problem. The best people in the world will be standing in line to work for us. There won't be any time clocks. No assholes in three-piece suits telling people what to do."

"But everything will be directed," Mitch said. "Everybody will be working together toward a common goal."

"The goal of giving the world the best small computer ever made," Sam said.

"The goal of turning a profit," Mitch replied.

Susannah smiled and took a sip of tea. "You're absolutely right."

December passed—sometimes a blur of activity, at other times painfully slow. Christmas was difficult for Susannah. While they exchanged presents around Angela's artificial tree, garishly decorated with plastic ornaments and ropes of pink tinsel, Susannah's thoughts wandered to the towering Douglas fir that would have been erected in the entrance hall at Falcon Hill, its branches glimmering with French silk ribbon and antique Baroque angels. Had Joel and Paige thought about her at all today? It had been foolish of her to cherish even a dim hope that the Christmas season would magically bring them all back together again. As she looked up at the plastic Santa on the top of Angela's tree, she felt unbearably sad.

She told herself she mustn't do it, but late that afternoon, while Sam and Angela were watching a football game on television, she slipped into the kitchen and dialed Falcon Hill. The phone began to ring, and she bit the inside of her lip.

"Hello."

Her father's deep, abrupt voice was so familiar, so beloved. Her own voice sounded thin in response. "Father? It's—it's Susannah."

"Susannah?" His voice lifted slightly at the end of her name, as if he might have forgotten who she was.

Her knuckles grew white as she gripped the receiver. "I—I just called to wish you a Merry Christmas."

"You did? How unnecessary."

She squeezed her eyes shut and her stomach twisted. He wasn't going to give in. How could she have let herself hope, even for a moment, that he would? "Are you well?"

"I'm fine, Susannah, but I'm afraid you've picked rather a bad time to call. Paige has planned a marvelous meal, and we're just sitting down to eat."

She was overwhelmed with memories of past Christmases —the sights and smells and textures of the season. When she was a little girl, her father used to lift her high up on his shoulders so she could put the angel on top of the tree. An angel for an angel, he had said. Now Paige would be sitting in her seat at the bottom of the table, and that special smile he had once reserved for her would be given to her sister.

She was afraid she was going to cry, and she spoke quickly. "I won't keep you, then. Please tell Paige Merry Christmas for me." The receiver hung heavily in her hand, but she couldn't sever this final connection by hanging up.

"If that's all?"

She hugged herself. "I didn't mean to interrupt. It's just—" Despite her best efforts, her voice broke. "Daddy, I got married."

There was no response. No words of acknowledgment, let alone expressions of affection.

Tears began to run down her cheeks.

He finally spoke, in a voice as thin and reedy as an old man's. "I can't imagine why you thought I'd be interested."

"Daddy, please—"

"Don't call me again, Susannah. Not unless you're ready to come home."

She was crying openly now, but she couldn't let him go. If she held on just a little longer, it would be all right. It was Christmas. If she held on just a little longer, there would be no more angry words between them. "Daddy—" Her voice broke on a sob. "Daddy, please don't hate me. I can't come home, but I love you."

Nothing happened for a moment, and then she heard a soft click. In that moment she felt as if the remaining fragile link between father and daughter had been broken forever.

In the kitchen at Falcon Hill, Paige held the receiver tightly to her ear and listened to the click as her father hung up the telephone on her sister. She replaced the receiver on the cradle and wiped her damp palms on her apron. Her mouth was dry and her heart pounding.

As she returned to the stove, she refused to give in to the memory of herself standing in a dingy hallway with a dirty telephone cord wrapped around her fingers while she tried to pry some words of tenderness from her father. She refused to feel sorry for Susannah. It was simply a matter of justice, she told herself as she turned the heat down under the vegetables and pulled the turkey from the oven. She had spent last Christmas stoned and miserable in a roach-infested apartment. This year Susannah was the outcast.

The servants had the day off, so she was responsible for Christmas dinner. It was a task she had been looking forward to. The turkey finished baking in the oven along with an assortment of casseroles. The counter held two beautiful fruit pies with an elaborate network of vines and hearts cut into the top crusts. In the past seven months she had received a surprising amount of pleasure from simple household tasks. She had planted a small herb garden near the kitchen door and livened up the corners of the house with rambling, old-fashioned floral displays, instead of the stiff, formal arrangements Susannah had always ordered from the florist.

Not that her father ever noticed any of her homey touches. He only noticed the jobs she forgot to do—the social engagement she had neglected to write down, the closets she hadn't reorganized, the plumber she had forgotten to hire—all those tasks her sister had performed with such relentless efficiency. As for the latest Ludlum thriller she had left on his bedside table, or the special meal waiting for him when he got back from a trip—those things didn't seem to matter.

"Do you need some help, Paige?"

She smiled at Cal, who had poked his head into the kitchen. She knew that Cal was an opportunist, and she doubted that he would have proven to be such a good friend if she hadn't been Joel's daughter. But he understood how difficult Joel could be, and he listened sympathetically to her problems. It was wonderful to feel as if she had someone on her side.

"Let me just set the turkey on the platter, and you can carry it in," she said.

Since there would only be the three of them for dinner, she had decided to forgo the huge, formal dining room with its long table for a cozy cherry drop-leaf set up in front of the living room fireplace, where they would be able to see the Christmas tree through the foyer archway.

When all the food was in place, she seated herself and removed the red and green yarn bow from her napkin. The center of the table held an old-fashioned centerpiece she had put together the day before with evergreen bows and small pieces of wooden dollhouse furniture she had unearthed in the attic. It had amazed her how many of her childhood toys had survived, even a few sets of tiny Barbie doll shoes. She couldn't believe those little plastic shoes hadn't been lost over the years, until she remembered how careful Susannah had always been with their toys.

While her father carved the turkey, old memories slipped over her. She saw Susannah's auburn hair falling forward in a neat, straight line as she dug out a tiny Monopoly house Paige had lost in the thick pile of her bedroom carpet. She saw Susannah in spotless yellow shorts stooping down on the brick terrace to rescue crayons her sister had left in the sun. Paige wouldn't use the crayons once the sweet, sharp points had worn off, but Susannah used them forever, patiently peeling back the paper until only a waxy nub was left. Unexpectedly, Paige felt a hollowness inside her.

Despite her careful preparations and Cal's attempt at conversation, the meal wasn't a success. Joel seemed tired and said little. Her own conversation was stiff. Paige didn't blame Cal for taking his leave not long after they had finished dessert. When she walked him to the door, he gave her a sympathetic glance and a friendly peck on the cheek. "I'll call you tomorrow."

She nodded and returned to the living room. Joel had seated himself on the couch with a book, but she had the feeling he wasn't really reading it. She felt even more lonely than when she was by herself.

"I think I'll go clean up the kitchen," she said abruptly.

Joel slapped down the book and jabbed his hand toward the remnants of their Christmas dinner. "I can't imagine what possessed you to crowd us around that ridiculous table when we have a perfectly good dining room that cost me a fortune to build."

Paige could barely keep herself from lashing out at him. She struggled with her hurt. "There were only three of us. I thought it would be cozier in here."

"Don't do it again. Susannah would never have—" He broke off abruptly.

She went cold all over. "Susannah isn't here anymore, Daddy. I am."

He seemed to be waging some kind of internal war with himself. It was the first time she could remember her father looking uncertain, and she felt a queer stab of fear prick at the edges of her hurt.

He rose from his chair and said stiffly, "I know you think I'm unreasonable, but I'm accustomed to having things done a certain way. I realize that may not be fair to you."

It was the closest she had ever heard him come to an apology. He began walking toward the door. Just as he passed her, he reached out and gave her arm a single awkward pat.

At least it was something, she told herself as she watched him disappear. She went back over to the window and looked out on the immaculate December gardens of Falcon Hill. An image formed in her mind of another sort of Christmas Day. She saw herself wearing blue jeans instead of a silk dress, and standing next to a Christmas tree decorated with construction paper chains rather than antique Baroque angels. She saw noisy, rumpled children tearing at wrapping paper, a long-suffering golden retriever, and a faceless husband in a sloppy sweatshirt pulling her into his arms.

Angry tears stung her eyes. "Fucking Norman Rockwell," she muttered in disgust.

18

We can't afford it," Mitch protested, dropping a heaping teaspoon of sugar into his coffee.

"We can't not afford it," Susannah countered.

Sam grinned, thoroughly enjoying having someone besides himself deal with Miss Appearances-Are-Everything for a change.

It was March, and they had been in their new offices for nearly five months. The three of them were sitting in a booth at Bob's Big Boy, where they had gotten into the habit of meeting for breakfast most mornings so they could coordinate their activities for the day.

Sam took a swig of Coke. "You might as well save your breath and give in, Mitch. Susannah's still a socialite at heart. She's almost always right about this crap."

"It's not crap," she said, planting the heels of her hands on the edge of the table and getting ready to dig in. "The two of you think anything that's not immediately quantifiable is unimportant. That's the problem with you technical types. You're either punching calculators or walking around with your head in the clouds."

She settled back in the booth and waited for her jibe to pierce through their early morning grogginess. Neither man was at his best until ten o'clock. She, on the other hand, jumped out of bed full of ideas.

"You've got to control her better, Sam," Mitch said earnestly. "There's a definite pattern developing here. Have you noticed how she always picks mornings to attack?"

Susannah gave Mitch a smug smile and turned to her husband. "He's joking, Sam. The way we know that Mitch is joking is that his jaw is in its unclenched position. God knows, if we waited for the man to crack a smile, we'd be here forever."

Mitch shook his head sadly over his coffee cup. "Vicious personal attacks at seven-thirty in the morning."

"Stop distracting me," she said. "You know I'm right."

Mitch grunted and took another swig of coffee.

They had decided to unveil the Blaze at the First West Coast Computer Faire to be held next month at San Francisco's Civic Auditorium. This trade show, capitalizing on its California location, promised to be larger than the one in Atlantic City, although no one was exactly certain how many disciples of small computers would attend.

Unfortunately, the Blaze wasn't ready. They were still having difficulties with the power supply, and Yank wasn't satisfied with the cassette tape version of BASIC that would be used to operate the machine. In addition, the cases for the two models they intended to have on display had been delayed. And they were nearly broke.

Susannah had done her best to push the large, unsolvable problems to the back of her mind and focus on those she could solve. Foremost in her mind was making certain that the launching of the Blaze wasn't overshadowed by all the other products that would be on display at the Faire.

She picked up half a slice of toast that Sam hadn't eaten and renewed her attack. "This is going to be a huge show. Our booth is impressive, but the Blaze could still get lost. To make sure that doesn't happen, we invite the press and the most important members of the trade to a private party the night before. They'll all be in town for the Faire. We'll give them something to drink, some food, and we'll show them the Blaze then instead of waiting for the next day."

"Sorry to side with the enemy, Mitch," Sam said. "But I

like Susannah's idea. We'll be able to jump start all the competition."

Susannah was grateful for Sam's support. She never knew which side of an issue he would come down on. But then, Sam was unpredictable about everything. Being married to him was like existing on a constant adrenaline high. Although it was frequently exhausting, she had never felt so alive in her life. Alive, but on edge, too. He wanted something more from her, something that she wasn't giving him. But she couldn't imagine what it might be.

Mitch threw up his hands. "All right. I admit it's a good idea. But you know our financial picture as well as I do, Susannah. You have to do everything on a shoestring."

"A thread," she promised, crossing her heart. "I'll do it on an absolute thread."

Susannah arrived early at the downtown restaurant where they were holding the party to launch the Blaze. Her clothing budget still limited her to shopping at Angela's outlet stores, but she wasn't displeased with her inexpensive black crepe trousers and the tunic top she had spruced up with a sequined appliqué from a fabric shop. Her hair was pulled away from her face and confined at the nape of her neck with a silver metallic scarf. She was alone. The men had been working on the software and she hadn't seen them since early afternoon.

She paused just inside the doorway of the private party room to take in the effect of the decorations. Bunches of balloons in lipstick red and lacquer black—the colors of the new Blaze logo—gave everything the festive atmosphere of floral arrangements, but without the expense. At one end of the room, a dais dramatically displayed the only two fully assembled Blaze computers in existence.

Behind the computers hung an enlarged reproduction of the spectacular new logo. The Blaze name, in curving letters that were black at the bottom and gradually turned into hot red at the top, rose in a stylistic pyramid of flames with the central A forming the apex. SysVal was neatly printed beneath.

Walking forward, she stopped in front of the machine that held the key to all of their futures. The physical design of the

Blaze had been Sam's. From the beginning he had known what he wanted—something small and sleek that would look comfortable in people's homes, a friendly machine with rounded edges instead of sharp corners and a soft ivory-colored case that didn't fight its surroundings.

As Susannah gazed down at the Blaze, she saw the embodiment of Sam's dream. The computer and the keyboard were one harmonious unit. Instead of duplicating the shape of a typewriter, the Blaze keyboard was wide and shallow with keys contoured to fit the fingers. She ran her hand over the flat top that housed Yank's genius compacted onto only sixty-six chips, an incredible engineering feat.

Someone entered the room behind her. "Hi, baby. It's beautiful, isn't it."

She turned, then sucked in her breath as the man she loved walked toward her.

"Oh, Sam . . . What have you done to me?"

His beautiful hair was gone—that wild black biker's hair she loved to crush in her hands when they made love, the long, dark strands that sometimes slipped between her lips when he drove high and hard inside her, his rebel's hair, the hair that had snapped in the breeze like a pirate's flag the day he had stolen her from her father's care.

It still hung bone-straight, brushed away from his ears, but the back didn't even reach the top of his white shirt collar. White shirt collar, dark blue necktie, sport coat. Each item was more loathsome than the last. Those were Cal's clothes, her father's clothes, not the clothes of a blue-skies thinker who dreamed of changing forever the dying days of the twentieth century.

Only the jeans were familiar, but even they weren't right. The denim was new, the seams dark and tightly stitched instead of soft and frayed. The stiff zipper lay nice-boy flat over his crotch, the prim new denim de-sexing him.

She hated it. She hated every bit of it. Her eyes returned to his hair. It swept back from his temples, revealing two ordinary ears unadorned by a swaying silver Easter Island head. They were the respectable ears of an IBM salesman, of an FBT vice-president. How could those ears belong to a small computer evangelist who sold the future instead of bibles?

Behind her the gay red and black balloons bounced forgotten, and her palm left a sweaty imprint where it had rested on the top of the Blaze.

"What have you done to me?" she whispered again.

Sam looked at her quizzically, but before he could say anything, the door swung open again and Mitch walked in with Yank. Mitch was unbearably smug as he slapped Sam on the back and patted his lapel. "Doesn't your boy look great, Susannah? He and I went on a little shopping trip. He changes his tune when you dangle a three-hundred-dollar imported Italian sport coat in front of him."

Yank was wearing his version of dress-up, a wrinkled brown corduroy suit with a narrow, mustard-colored tie hanging askew. The underside of the tie extended barely three inches below the knot.

Mitch shrugged apologetically at Susannah. "I only had so much time. Do something, will you?"

She busied herself reknotting Yank's tie. As she worked, she tried to calm her inexplicable feeling of panic. Sam was Sam, she told herself. Cutting his hair and putting on a sport coat didn't change anything for either one of them. Besides, she had said from the beginning that he needed to look more like a business man, and now she had her wish. She glanced over at him busily loading the Blaze display programs. They were married, but marriage didn't feel the way she had always imagined. She had no sense of safety or stability. Instead, every day was an adventure full of new battles to be fought. Sometimes, she was almost overwhelmed with the intensity of just being alive on the same planet with Sam Gamble.

The guests began to arrive, and she had no more time for personal ruminations. She had sent out over a hundred invitations to members of the press and other influential people in the trade, and she watched nervously as they critically circled the two machines, guzzling beer, munching on pizza and firing questions at all of them. Before long, they were watching in fascination as the large television monitors began to display the games and programs that had been designed to show the little computer's awesome power.

More than one skeptic pulled up the bright red cloth that draped the display table in search of the larger computer they were certain was hidden beneath. They shook their heads in amazement when they found only electrical cords and cardboard cartons.

"Amazing."

"Son of a bitch."

"This is freaking fantastic!"

The SysVal founders were hackers at heart, and it wasn't long before Sam slipped the case from one of the prototypes. (Neither he nor Yank had even considered designing a computer that couldn't be opened up.) Within minutes, a hundred guests were craning their necks to see the internal poetry of Yank's wondrous machine. By midnight it was evident that the launching of the brash little Blaze was an unqualified success.

The restaurant finally forced them to disband at two in the morning. The men loaded the equipment into Mitch's car, and the four partners headed for the hotel where they had booked rooms for the night. Sam and Mitch were still wired from the excitement of the evening, and neither wanted to sleep, even though they had to be at the Civic Auditorium in a few hours to set up. But Susannah was exhausted, and she declined an invitation to go to the bar with them for a drink. Yank also refused, and they crossed the lobby together.

In many ways Yank still remained a mystery to her. Angela had told her that Yank's ability to shut out the world when he worked had begun when he was a child growing up in the Valley. His mother and father had fought bitterly, but as good Catholics, they wouldn't divorce. From a young age he had learned to immerse himself in electronic projects so that he could transport himself to another world, where he wouldn't have to listen to the ugly sounds of their arguments. His parents had retired to Sun City several years ago and apparently still fought as bitterly as ever. He seldom saw them.

As they stepped into the elevator, Susannah made a stab at polite conversation. "Roberta wasn't at the party. She's not sick, is she?"

"Roberta?" Yank didn't seem quite certain who Susannah meant.

Normally Susannah would have been amused, but despite

the enthusiastic reception the Blaze had received at the party, she was on edge, and her tone was unnaturally sharp. "Roberta Pestacola, your girlfriend."

"Yes, I know."

Susannah waited. The elevator doors opened. They got off together. After a few steps Yank stopped walking, stared for a moment at a fire extinguisher, then began walking again.

She was suddenly determined to have a normal conversation with him. "Is anything wrong between you and Roberta?"

"Roberta? Oh, yes." He began patting his pockets for a room key.

They continued down the corridor. Although she was tall, he topped her by a good seven inches. Thirty more seconds of silence passed. Susannah was exhausted from the evening and still unsettled over the changes in Sam's appearance. Her already frayed nerves snapped. "The purpose of conversation is to exchange information. That's difficult to do with someone who hardly ever finishes his sentences and never seems to have the vaguest idea what anyone is talking about. It's really irritating."

He stopped walking and looked down at a point just behind her right ear. "It's probably not a good idea to take out your frustration on one person when you're really upset with someone else."

She stared at him. How did he know she was upset about Sam? He shifted his gaze and looked directly at her.

She nearly winced. His eyes were so clear and so strongly focused that she had the feeling he could see the smallest cells inside her.

"Roberta and I are no longer together, Susannah. I'm not proud of staying with her for as long as I did, since I wasn't too fond of her even at the beginning. But it's difficult for me to attract women, and I like having sex very much. This means I sometimes make compromises. Is there anything else you want to know?"

Susannah actually felt herself flush. "I—I'm sorry. It's none of my business."

"No, it isn't."

Embarrassed, she fumbled in her purse for her own room key, and managed to drop it just as they reached her door.

Yank stooped over to pick it up off the carpet. As he straightened, he once again looked at her with that penetrating gaze she found so disconcerting.

And then, more quickly than she could have believed possible, she lost him to the gods of genius. His eyes grew vague and his face emptied of all expression. Muttering something that sounded like "zany diode," he began moving off down the hallway as if she didn't exist.

Black sock.
Brown sock.
Black sock.
Brown sock.

None of them were prepared for what happened the next day. By early that morning thousands of computer enthusiasts had formed five lines that wrapped around both sides of the block-long Civic Center. No one had expected so many people, but despite the crowded conditions, everyone was good-natured and enthusiastic.

Throughout the day loudspeakers blared out announcements, computer-generated music played, and printers clattered. Lines formed to attend the event's workshops and people stood four and five deep at the booths. They could get their biorhythms charted at the IMSAI exhibit and play a game on the Sol at the Processor Technology display. Many companies—some actually larger than SysVal—were still showing their products on draped card tables with hand-lettered signs, but they were dwarfed by exhibitors like Cromemco, MITS, and even the tiny Apple Computer Company, which had apparently learned its lesson about appearances at Atlantic City. Even though they had only moved out of their garage a few months ago, they were introducing their Apple II in an impressive booth complete with a backlit plexiglass sign bearing their new brightly-colored Apple logo.

While Mitch spent his time making contacts with distributors and dealers and Yank wandered the hall to survey the competition, Sam and Susannah, along with several teenage employees they had recently hired to help manage the increasing workload, manned the SysVal booth. Sam was everywhere at once, holding four separate conversations at the same time and telling all who came within the sound of his voice about the miraculous little micro called the Blaze. Yank's splashy graphics display was a big hit with the crowd, as well as a target-shooting game people were standing in line to play.

Susannah distributed hundreds of expensively printed color brochures, smiled until her cheeks ached, and began taking orders for the Blaze almost immediately. As she discussed memory expansion, switching versus linear power supply, and eight-slot motherboards, she realized how far she had come from a woman who had once regarded her most strenuous challenge to be finding a good caterer.

At the end of the weekend, when one of the Faire's organizers announced that thirteen thousand people had been in attendance, a huge cheer went up from the crowd. Trade shows had been held in Atlantic City, Trenton, and Detroit, but the overwhelming success of the West Coast Computer Faire had put all of them to shame. On this April weekend in 1977, California had finally taken command of its own small computer kingdom.

Sam caught Susannah in his arms as the attendance was announced. "We've made history today! This is our Woodstock, baby. A digital love-in for a new generation."

That night, when they headed back to the Valley, they had orders for 287 Blazes in hand.

19

· ·

By August the hills of the Santa Clara Mountains were brown from lack of rain. Joel Faulconer squinted at the sun through the windshield of his tan rental car and wished for the winter rains. He was finding it difficult to breathe. There was too much dust in the air.

He had parked the car so that he had a clear view of the single glass door that led into the SysVal offices, but the van parked on one side of him made the car barely noticeable to anyone walking through the lot. Over the past six months, Joel had learned to choose his locations carefully. He rented inconspicuous cars, and he always brought a newspaper with him so that if Susannah should appear unexpectedly, he could block his face.

The indignity of what he was doing was something he refused to dwell on. He didn't think of it as spying on his daughter. He tried not to think of it at all. Coming here was necessary. That was all. He had to find a way to get her back.

In an hour he was due in his office for an afternoon meeting with one of the most important industrialists in Japan. It was the kind of encounter that had once sent adrenaline pumping through his veins. Now what he really wanted to do was take a nap.

He continued to have difficulty sleeping at night, and last night had been particularly bad. He should have been more honest with his doctor when he had finally gone to see him a few weeks ago, but he couldn't bring himself to confess to a medical lackey twenty years younger than himself that he was suffering from a depression so deep and so black that he didn't think he could ever climb out of it. The night before, he had spent hours locked in his library, gazing down at the Smith & Wesson revolver he kept in a mahogany case.

Sweat broke out on his body. For weeks now he had felt as if he were living on the jagged edge of something monstrous. He told himself not to think about it. He would be better soon. Any day now.

The door of the building opened and Sam Gamble walked out. Joel's stomach pitched. The bastard. Gamble moved across the parking lot toward the used Volvo he had bought a few months ago. His walk was cocky, as if he were a king instead of an arrogant upstart. Joel consoled himself with the thought that the Gamble car was merely another item that would fall to the bankruptcy court when this harum-scarum operation went belly up. He was both incredulous and frustrated that it hadn't already happened. Of course, he hadn't counted on Mitchell Blaine throwing his hat into their circus ring. Still, even Blaine couldn't work miracles.

Cal had been as bewildered as Joel when he had heard the news. "Why is Blaine doing something so bizarre?" Cal had asked.

Joel had kept his response casual. He saw no sense in letting the younger man realize how much the news had shaken him. "His wife left him. He's obviously not thinking clearly. But I don't believe we need to worry too much. Even Mitch Blaine won't be able to keep them afloat much longer."

Cal had pressed him to move more aggressively against SysVal, but once again Joel had demurred. Susannah was going to fail on her own. Only then—only when she had suffered defeat at her own hands—could he possibly take her back. He envisioned her remorse, the way she would beg him to let her return to Falcon Hill.

The sound of tires squealing distracted him from his thoughts. Gamble was just reaching for his car door when a small red Toyota shot into the parking lot and jerked to a stop near the Volvo. A woman jumped out and began rushing toward him. She wore a purple elasticized top, black jersey wrap skirt, and high heels with ankle straps. It took Joel only a moment to recognize her as Gamble's cheap little floozy of a mother.

Gamble had already spotted her. She had left the engine of her car running and the door open. He hurried forward in concern. She grabbed his arm and began to speak with enormous agitation. Joel could pick out a few isolated words but not the sense of what she was saying. Gamble looked as if he were growing angry. She clutched harder at his arms. He shook her off and went back to his car.

"Sam!" she cried.

Gamble jumped into the Volvo without sparing her another glance. Gunning the motor, he peeled out of the parking lot. She crumpled like a rag doll against the trunk of her car.

Joel watched her clutch her arms in front of her stomach and begin a slow rocking that sent her gold hoop earrings swaying. Her dark hair was mussed and her expression was full of despair. Perversely, the sight of her misery lifted his spirits as nothing had in weeks. It made him feel more in control of his own life, more like his old self. At the same time, curiosity piqued him. Anything that made Sam Gamble angry might be good news for him.

He hesitated for only a moment before he got out of the car and walked toward her. The pavement began to tilt under his feet. He wasn't feeling well, not well at all. Perhaps he should cancel his appointments this afternoon and go home. But no. Someone might discover that he wasn't feeling like himself. That wouldn't do at all.

Several moments passed before the woman seemed to recognize who he was, but even recognition didn't alter the misery on her face.

"Is there anything I can do?" he inquired. Despite his solicitous words, he felt no particular sympathy for her— she was cheap and common—and yet the strength of her misery gave him a peculiar sense of relief. No matter how difficult the past year had been for him, he hadn't once been reduced to this sort of excessive display of emotion.

"It's over," she said, a black trail of mascara running down her cheeks. "There's nothing anyone can do."

Once again he had the sense that the pavement was tilting beneath him. He concentrated on keeping his balance and on trying to decipher her words. What was over? Did she know something about SysVal? Was that why Gamble had been so angry?

"Have you ever lost someone?" she went on in a broken voice. "Someone important to you."

For a moment, he was afraid something had happened to Susannah, and fear rushed through him. Then he remembered Gamble's anger and realized it was something else. This woman had probably had a squabble with one of her aging boyfriends. All of this hullabaloo undoubtedly had its roots in a middle-aged lovers' quarrel.

"Part of me wants to die, too." She dabbed at her eyes with the back of her hand, leaving a dark smear on her first two knuckles.

"Nonsense," he replied sharply, wincing as a dull stab of pain went through his shoulder. He wanted to rub it, but he forced himself to keep his arm still. "It's ridiculous to make a fuss over trivialities. I suggest you go home and fix yourself a drink."

"I can't go home now. There's something I have to do. Someplace I have to go." She turned away from him and walked toward the front of the car.

He looked down at his watch and saw that if he didn't leave soon, he would be late for his meeting. And then the numbers began to waver in front of his eyes. He swayed and braced himself on the trunk of her car. His own car suddenly seemed to be miles away.

She bent to get into the Toyota. Pain gripped his chest. He leaned against the car trunk, using it for support. The pain didn't ease. For the first time it occurred to him that he might actually faint. The idea horrified him. What if Susannah found him helplessly crumpled in the parking lot? He had to sit down. He had to rest for a moment, but his car was so far away, and he didn't have the strength to get there. He took several awkward steps forward, moving along the side of the car to the open door.

She looked up at him curiously. His mind raced, but his

brain was dull with pain and he couldn't think what to say. He had to sit down. He couldn't stand any longer. "You—you need to go home," he stammered. "You're not—not in any condition to drive."

She reached for a pair of oversized sunglasses. "I can't go home. I have something I have to do."

He had begun to sweat profusely. In a breathless, choppy voice that didn't seem to belong to him, he said. "Not—not alone. You shouldn't go alone." His hand convulsed over the roof of the car. He couldn't faint. He couldn't let Susannah see him like this. "I'll—I'll go with you. Make certain you're safe."

"Whatever," she said dully. "It doesn't really matter."

He barely made it around the front of the car, but she was so caught up in her own misery that she didn't notice. As he slumped down into the passenger seat, he gasped for breath. The car began to move. He no longer cared about his meeting or the rental car he had abandoned in the parking lot. All he cared about was the fact that he hadn't crumpled like an aged fetus onto the asphalt where his daughter could see him.

They had begun to move out into the traffic on El Camino, and the pain was easing. He noticed that her fingernails were too long and covered with a garish purple-red polish. She pushed a tissue underneath her sunglasses to dab at her eyes. He thought about asking her what was wrong, but he didn't really care. He was too tired. His legs felt rubbery, his head hurt. He would just stay with her for a while, until he felt more like himself, and then he would call his driver to come and get him. Once again he shut his eyes. If he rested for just a few minutes, he would feel more like his old self.

When he awakened, the sun was sinking. He blinked with alarm and tried to get his bearings. They were moving fast. A road sign for Interstate 5 whipped by on his right. He saw a herd of cattle grazing and the ridges of the Sierra Nevada Mountains in the distance. They must be somewhere in the San Joaquin Valley.

The radio was playing softly, a pop tune. He looked down at his watch and was startled to see that it was nearly seven o'clock. "Where are we? Where are you going?"

She jumped as if she had forgotten he was there. Her

sunglasses were off, and the lap of her skirt held a collection of damp, wadded tissues. She tilted her head toward the radio. "I—I can't talk now. When the song is over."

The voice on the radio was familiar—a male pop singer. He dimly recognized the song, something about a child being born in a ghetto.

There were so many things he needed to do. He should tell her to get off at the next exit so he could call his driver. How would he explain this? Everyone would be alarmed because he hadn't shown up for his meeting. He had a full work schedule planned for tomorrow. He tried to arrange his thoughts in proper order, but he couldn't manage it. All he could see was the Smith & Wesson revolver lying in its mahogany case. His eyes drifted shut again, and he was consumed with a sense of his own helplessness. The song came to an end.

Her voice quivered. "They've been playing all-Elvis for hours. I—I still can't believe that he's dead. He was so young. Only forty-two."

His eyes shot open. "What are you talking about?"

"Elvis," she whispered softly. "Didn't you hear? Elvis Presley died today. August 16, 1977."

Was that what this was about? He wanted to roar his anger at her, but his brain felt foggy and his head seemed to have been wrapped in hot, wet wool. She stared straight ahead at the road. A tear dropped off her chin and made an amoeba-like stain on the front of her purple stretch top. No wonder Gamble had been angry with her in the parking lot. It was beyond Joel's comprehension that someone could be so distraught over the death of a celebrity when there were so many real problems in the world.

"I have to go to Graceland—in Memphis. I have to pay my respects." Her voice caught on a sob.

He couldn't believe he had heard her right. "You're driving to Tennessee?"

"I have to." She blew her nose, dropped the tissue into her lap, and picked up another. And then she said something that sent a chill slithering up his spine. "The King is dead. I can't believe it. I just can't believe that the King is dead."

He could feel sweat breaking out on his forehead. No! *He*

was the King! He had years ahead of him. Decades. He had so many things left to do and endless time in which to do them. The interior of the car was cool, but he couldn't seem to stop sweating, and he made a dash at his forehead with the sleeve of his suit coat.

Her mouth trembled. "I never imagined it. I thought he would live forever." She turned to look fully at Joel. Her face was stripped bare of makeup, her lipstick eaten off. "I'm only forty-three. That's not old. Only a year older than Elvis. It's just— How can I ever be young again if Elvis Presley is dead? How can any of us ever be young again?"

Joel no longer even remembered what it was like to feel young. He closed his eyes again, not to sleep, just to escape.

South of Bakersfield she exited to get gas. He went into the phone booth and called his secretary. He made up an excuse for his absence and began to tell her to get hold of his driver, but he ended up telling her to inform Paige he wouldn't be coming home tonight.

It was irrational. He was feeling better and he couldn't justify what he was doing. Even so, he couldn't seem to change his course. He decided to go just a little farther with Angela—only a few more hours. Then he would have her drop him at one of the hotels on the interstate, where he would spend the night. In the morning he would call his driver so he would be back in time for his meetings.

When he returned to the Toyota, Angela was sitting in the passenger seat holding two cans of soda pop and assorted packages of junk food. He got behind the wheel. She popped the top off one of the soda cans and handed it to him. He was thirsty, so he took a sip. It was overly sweet and awful. He couldn't remember the last time he had tasted soda pop. The second sip wasn't quite so bad.

His suit coat was mussed and damp. He took it off and turned to lay it carefully over the backseat. Then he started the engine and pulled back out onto the road. "I'm not going much farther."

"I don't even know why you're here."

The thought sprang into his head that he was there because he didn't want to die, but that made no sense. He wasn't old, only fifty-nine. And he was an important man.

He tried to distract the direction of his thoughts with a question. "Why are you doing this? Why is this so important?"

"Elvis is Sammy's father."

Joel snorted.

"You don't believe me, do you? Nobody believes me." He could see her marshaling her forces, but then she turned to stare out the window. Several long moments passed, and her shoulders slumped in defeat as if she had just given up something precious. "I wish he'd been Sammy's father. I wish I'd been able to meet him. They tell such lies about him. That he wasn't faithful to Priscilla while they were married, that he used drugs and acted strange. I never believed any of it. Elvis loved the little people. He cared about people like me. Going to Graceland to pay my respects is the least I can do for him."

She leaned back against the seat and eventually shut her eyes.

The rhythm of the interstate and the soft Presley ballads playing on the Bakersfield radio station began to lull him. It was growing dark, and he turned on the headlights. It had been years since he had driven any distance himself. Angela fell asleep next to him with her mouth slightly open. He yawned, feeling relaxed for the first time in ages. Driving was good for him. He would do more of it from now on. That was all that was wrong with him. He just needed to relax more.

The radio was fading, so that the words to "Kentucky Rain" were interlaced with static, but he didn't change the station. He noticed the St. Christopher medal affixed to the dashboard and a bottle of nail polish lying overturned on the floor. A litter bag advertising State Farm Insurance swayed from the cigarette lighter. He didn't feel sleepy, merely relaxed.

Next to him, Angela's breathing came in soft, sibilant puffs. Her skirt had ridden up above her knees. He noticed that her legs in their dark stockings were good, but nothing about her stirred him sexually. He had never liked cheap women, not even when he was young. By the time he reached Barstow, she had tucked her legs under her.

He had to stop again for gas around midnight. She woke up and took over the driving. He immediately fell asleep in the passenger seat.

They crossed Arizona during the night, shifting drivers whenever they stopped for gas. The next morning they had breakfast at a truck stop near Albuquerque. Angela went to the rest room to wash her face, and when she came out, she had reapplied her makeup. Her figure in its purple stretch top attracted the attention of some of the truckers, and they watched her over the top of their coffee cups. Joel was embarrassed to be seen with her. He took comfort from the fact that no one knew who he was.

When he went to the men's room to wash up, he saw a stranger in the mirror. His face looked bloated, his skin chalky and unhealthy, and his jaw was covered with stubble. Usually he shaved twice a day, so he wasn't reminded of the fact that his beard was mostly gray, but he didn't have a razor, so he splashed water on his face and looked down at the faucets instead of into the mirror.

He wasn't conscious of the moment when he made the decision to go all the way to Memphis with her. He simply couldn't make himself do anything else. The driving was good for him, he told himself. He needed a vacation.

As they approached the eastern border of New Mexico, Angela began to cry again. When he couldn't bear it any longer, he snapped at her. "Will you stop it, for God's sake. You didn't even know the man."

"I'll cry if I want to. I didn't invite you to come with me. You can get out any time." She reached for the radio and spun up the volume. Since morning she had been listening to news reports coming from Memphis.

". . . the twenty thousand mourners who were lined up along Elvis Presley Boulevard this morning have now swelled to fifty thousand, all of them hoping for a chance to view the body of the King of Rock and Roll as he lies in state in the drawing room at Graceland. Vernon Presley, the father of the singer, has ordered that doors to the estate be opened to allow as many of his fans as possible to file through and pay their respects. Thousands of floral tributes have arrived from all over the world since yesterday afternoon, many of them bearing the simple inscription, 'To the King.' All of the mourners share disbelief that the King is dead. . . ."

Joel snapped off the radio dial. He didn't want to hear about kings dying. He didn't want to think about . . .

Angela turned the radio back on. He gave her an icy glare—the glare that had intimidated heads of state and corporate presidents. She ignored it.

Outside of Amarillo they blew a tire. The service station was dry and dusty and the heat rose in waves from the cracked asphalt. They sat at a rickety picnic table in the sparse shade of a dying ailanthus tree while they waited for a new tire to be put on.

"Elvis gave so much to me," Angela said. "When I was upset or sad, when my husband Frank treated me like dirt, Elvis was always there. His songs made me feel at peace with myself. This might sound sacrilegious, but I don't mean it to be. Sometimes when I'd kneel in church to pray, I'd look up at the statue of Jesus. And then it would seem like it was Elvis hanging there. He sacrificed so much for us."

Joel couldn't think of a single thing Presley had sacrificed except dignity, but he didn't say so. The woman was crazy. She had to be. But then, what did that say about him?

"Did you go to high school, Joel?" she asked. It was the first time she had addressed him by name. He wasn't accustomed to women like Angela calling him by his first name. He would have preferred her to call him Mr. Faulconer.

"I went to a military academy," he replied stiffly.

"Did they have cheerleaders?"

"No. Certainly not."

"I used to be a cheerleader. I was one of the best." Softly, sadly, under her breath she began to chant, "We've got the team, we've got the steam, go fight. We've got the team, we've got the steam . . . I was so popular in high school. All the kids liked me because I was never stuck up, not like some of the other girls. I was nice to everybody. You know what I liked best about high school? Your whole life was ahead of you, and in your mind you made all the right choices. In your mind everything came out perfect. Not like real life, when you marry the wrong man and have trouble with your kid. Not like what's happened to you and me."

He jumped up from the picnic bench so suddenly that it tilted, nearly unseating her. "Don't you dare presume to speak for me. My life is perfect. I wouldn't have it any other way."

She gave him a look so sad that it cut right through him. "Then why are you going to Graceland?" she asked softly. "If your life is so perfect, why are you going with me to Graceland?"

He turned away from her. High, dusty weeds spoiled the polish on his expensive shoes. A coffee spot marred the spotless white of his custom-made dress shirt. "I've been tired, that's all. I needed to get away. I need a rest."

This time she was the one who gave a soft snort of disbelief. "Never kid a kidder, Joel. You're even lonelier than me."

He wanted to strike out at her for her presumption, but he couldn't summon up words that were cruel enough. She came up behind him. A hand settled in the center of his back and rubbed gently, like a mother comforting a child. His eyes drifted shut with the pain of her soft, soothing touch.

The service station attendant called out that their tire was ready. It was Angela's turn to drive.

"God has Elvis now," she said as she merged with the traffic in the right lane. "I keep trying to tell myself that."

"Do you really believe that?" he scoffed.

"Don't you?"

"I'm an Episcopalian. I give to the church. Sometimes I even attend, but—no—I don't believe in God."

"I'm sorry," she said sympathetically. "I think it must be harder for men like you to believe. You have so much power that you start thinking you're God, and you forget how unimportant you really are. Then, when bad times hit, you don't have anything to fall back on. With me it's different. I've never been important, and I've had faith all my life."

"God is nothing but a crutch for the ignorant."

"Then I'm glad I'm ignorant, because I don't know what I'd do without Him."

They continued their odyssey—Amarillo to Oklahoma

City, Oklahoma City to Little Rock, Little Rock to Memphis—two middle-aged people on their way to Graceland, one of them mourning the passing of her youth, the other on his way to see death so he could make up his mind if he still wanted to live.

They reached Memphis early Thursday morning. A crowd of several thousand had kept vigil at Graceland throughout the night, and it was already difficult to find a parking place anywhere near. Angela parked the Toyota in front of a fire hydrant some distance away. Joel badly needed a shower and clean clothes, as well as a decent meal. He thought of calling a taxi to take him to a hotel. He thought of a dozen things he could do, but he ended up walking to Graceland with her.

The day was already heavy with humidity. Helicopters circled over the mansion, and all the flags they passed hung at half mast. The sight of the flags deeply disturbed him. It seemed inappropriate to mourn a rock and roll singer so lavishly. Would the California flags be flown at half mast when he died? He shook off the thought. He didn't intend to die for a very long time. When he got back home, he would see his doctor and tell him how badly he had been feeling. He would tell him about the tightness in his chest, about the fatigue and depression. He would get some pills, watch his diet, start exercising again.

Although it was still early, souvenir hawkers plied the crowd that had gathered around Graceland's high brick walls and spilled out onto Elvis Presley Boulevard. Weeping mourners hugged Elvis T-shirts to their chests along with photographic postcards and plastic guitars made in Hong Kong. Joel found the vulgarity unspeakable.

The funeral cortege would be emerging through Graceland's famous music gate, and Angela wanted to be able to see it all. Joel moved her to the front of the crowd that had gathered in the shopping center directly across the street. It took some time, but despite his disheveled appearance, people sensed his importance and made way for them. He noted the heavy police presence and numerous first-aid stations set up to tend to those who were fainting from heat or hysteria. The city officials were obviously worried about

the temper of the crowd, which seemed to change indiscrim-
inately from a noisy outpouring of grief to almost carnival
gaiety. A woman in green rubber shower thongs told Angela
that at four o'clock that morning a kid in a white Ford had
jumped the curb and hit three teenage girls who were
keeping vigil. Now two of them were dead. Life seemed
increasingly arbitrary to Joel.

Cars began entering through the music gate for the funeral
service which was to be held inside the mansion. Angela
thought she spotted Ann-Margret in one of them. Another
bystander said he had seen George Hamilton, and there was
a rumor that Burt Reynolds had slipped in through the back.
It amazed Joel that these people actually cared about minor
motion picture celebrities, not one of whom could possibly
have been accepted for membership at his country club.

Joel could probably have gained entrance to the funeral
with nothing more than a few well-placed phone calls, but
the idea repelled him. He was not a participant, but an
observer of this plebeian carnival of loud voices and excessive emotions.

The morning dragged on, and the heat grew so oppressive,
breathing became difficult. He bought two rickety camp
stools from a vendor. They sat on them in sight of the gates
and waited for the funeral cortege to emerge.

"What's important to you, Joel?"

The question was presumptuous, so he remained silent.

She lifted her hair off her neck and fanned herself with a
flattened red and white cardboard popcorn box. "Sammy
and my friends are important to me. Your daughter. Going
to Vegas. Going to church. I like doing hair and being with
my girlfriends. The old ladies laugh at my jokes, and I make
them feel pretty again—I like that. But most important is
Sammy." She set down the popcorn box and studied one
fingernail where the purple-red nail polish had started to
chip. "I know I embarrass him—the way I look and the kind
of person I am—like telling a few people that Elvis is his
dad. But I won't change, not even for him. I tried changing
for Frank, and it didn't work. A person has to be what they
are. I like wearing flashy clothes and having a good time.
Otherwise, before you know it, you're fifty and you haven't
ever lived."

He was fifty-nine years old. Did she think she was talking about him? "I live on one of the most beautiful estates in California," he said coldly. "I have homes all over the world, cars, everything a man could possibly want."

"Despite all that, I feel sorry for you."

He was furious with her. Where did she get the audacity to pity him? "Save your pity for someone who needs it."

"You seem to be missing out on all the good parts of life." Once again she began to fan herself with the popcorn box. "You don't believe in God, and you won't make up with your daughter."

"You leave Susannah out of this!"

"She's a special girl. She's kind and sensitive, and Sammy's probably going to hurt her. You should be there for her."

"She doesn't deserve anything from me. She's made her own bed, and now she can damn well lie in it."

"Sometimes the best part of loving somebody is loving them even though they've hurt you. Listen to me, Joel. Any fool can love somebody who's perfect, somebody who does everything right. But that doesn't stretch your soul. Your soul only gets stretched when you can still love somebody after they've hurt you."

"Your husband for example?" he said scornfully. "You women are amazing. You let men walk all over you because you're too spineless to stand up to them, and then you hide your weakness under the cover of sacrificial love."

"Loving never makes you weak. It's being untrue to yourself that does that. It's like with Sammy. He wants to make me over into somebody like Florence Henderson. That's how he is. He buys me things like little pearl earrings and white cardigan sweaters. I always thank him, but those things aren't my style, and as much as I love him, I won't let him change me. That's how I stay true to myself. So I keep saying my prayers and hoping one day it'll be better between us. It should be like that with you and Susannah. Just because she did something you don't approve of doesn't mean you should cut her out."

His face was stony. "I refuse to have anything to do with someone who has betrayed me."

"She wasn't betraying you. She was just following her own star. It didn't have anything to do with you."

"It would be impossible for me to forgive her after what she's done."

"But, Joel—that's what makes it love. Otherwise it's just shaking hands."

He didn't want to think about what she'd said, but he couldn't help it. Was it possible that this cheap, gaudy woman knew something about life that had escaped him?

Suddenly the music gate opened. A limousine as white as Elvis's Las Vegas show costumes crept forward, followed by another. Next to him Angela gave a dry, broken sob. One by one, sixteen white limousines passed in a mournful parade through the gate. People were crying. Tough-faced men and overweight women let tears fall unashamedly down their cheeks. And then Angela clutched his arm as the white Cadillac hearse appeared—the hearse bearing the body of the King of Rock and Roll.

Angela took a deep, shattered breath and whispered, "Good-bye, E."

Joel watched the hearse turning slowly out onto the boulevard. He felt a sharp pain in his shoulder and rubbed it. He didn't want to ponder the fate of kings. He didn't want to think about his own mortality and why he had come on this strange odyssey, but suddenly the emptiness of his life pressed down on him with so much weight that he felt as if he were being pounded through the pavement into the dry, hot, Tennessee earth. He thought about what Angela had said—that the best part of loving was being able to love someone who had hurt you. He pressed his eyes shut and remembered just how badly Susannah had hurt him. But in the face of death and funerals, it no longer seemed to matter quite so much.

And then he finally admitted how badly he wanted her back. He wanted Susannah back, and he wanted to be able to love Paige the way a daughter should be loved. He envisioned his family gathered around him at Christmas dinner with rosy-cheeked grandchildren at the table and Kay at his side—silly, frivolous Kay, who used to make him laugh and helped him forget the pressures of holding power.

As he clutched his shoulder and struggled to breathe, he saw his faults stretched out in front of him like a long unbroken line on a sales graph. He saw his sins of pride and selfishness, he saw his small cruelties and his foolish belief that he could shape the world through the strength of his own will. He saw the arrogant way he had squandered the love of the people who cared for him.

The pain gripped him, traveling from his shoulder down into his chest, and he thought of the little girl he had pulled from her grandmother's closet so long ago. She had given him perfect, unconditional love—the most precious gift of his life—and he had thrown it away. Panic swept over him as he realized all he had lost. Was it too late? Could he have her back?

With astonishing suddenness, a wave of euphoria swept over him, riding right alongside his pain. It didn't have to be too late! As soon as he got back, he would tell her. He would fly home tonight and go to her. He would tell her that he forgave her, that he loved her. His life would once again have meaning. Everything would be all right again.

Angela's eyes were still on the white hearse, and her face, even in profile, looked stricken. "I know I'm not young anymore," she whispered, "but—do you think I'm still attractive, Joel?"

He clutched his chest, no longer able to draw a breath that wasn't pain-wracked. There was no more time. He felt the chill coming over him, the fading of light, and he knew he had to give something back quickly, something good and precious. With his last remaining bit of strength, he pushed out the words.

"You'll always . . . be quite . . . beautiful, Angela. . . ."

And then, in the shadow of the hearse bearing a king, another king slumped to the ground.

20

Susannah had just fallen asleep when the phone rang shortly after midnight. She groaned and rolled over, automatically reaching out for Sam before she remembered that he was still at work. She should be there, too, but she had been exhausted and had finally gone home.

She fumbled for the phone, wondering why her husband and her partners couldn't leave her alone for even one night. "Hello," she murmured thickly.

"Susannah?"

"Paige?" She was instantly alert to the strangled sound in her sister's voice. "Paige, what's wrong?"

"It's—it's Daddy."

"Daddy?" Her spine stiffened and she braced herself for something horrible.

"He's—he's dead, Susannah. He had a heart attack."

"Daddy's dead?" The words slipped from her lips, the syllables distorted as if they had been spoken underwater.

Paige was crying. It had happened in Memphis, she said. No one knew what he was doing there. Susannah gripped the sheet as her sister went on. The night closed around her like a small, tight box.

Paige hung up. Susannah continued to hold the telephone. She didn't want to replace the receiver. She didn't want to break her last fragile link with someone in her family. *Daddy,* she cried out silently. *Daddy, don't do this to me. I'm your sweetheart, remember? I'll be good. I promise. I'll never be bad again.*

A monster pressed down on her chest. Her golden prince had gone. There would be no more chances to win back his love. She began to cry—deep, wracking sobs that came from her soul. There was no more time left to receive her father's forgiveness. Her daddy was dead.

Sam heard the sounds when he walked in the door—soft, animal sounds. Fingers of fear shot through him as he ran toward the bedroom. Susannah was huddled in the far corner with her back smeared against the wall and her hands tangled in her nightgown. "Suzie . . ."

He rushed toward her, knelt down on the floor and pulled her against him. The expression on her face chilled him. Someone had broken in the apartment and raped her. He drew her closer, rage and fear shaking him. "It's all right, baby. I'm here. I'm here."

"Sam?" Her voice quivered like an old woman's. "Sam? Daddy's dead."

Relief coursed through him. She was all right. Nothing terrible had happened to her. Hearing the news of Joel's death didn't particularly trouble him, and instead of trying to offer her phony words of comfort about a man he had detested, he stroked her.

It felt strange to have her clinging to him so helplessly and to hear those broken little sobs coming from her. Their position on the floor was awkward. He lifted her and helped her over to the bed. Her body was naked underneath the thin nightgown, and as he lay down with her, he could feel himself starting to get hard. Jeezus, she would never understand that in a million years.

He hated anything that had to do with death. Once, he had heard a priest say that death was what gave life its meaning, but he didn't believe that. Death took away meaning. Death robbed life of any sense. When he was ten, the inevitability of his own death had struck him for the first time, and he had been consumed with a cold, gripping terror. For months afterward he had been afraid to go to bed at night, until, finally, he had told himself it wouldn't happen. The rules of the universe would change for him. Death was one more barrier to be smashed, one more hurdle to overcome.

He wished she would stop crying. He wished she hadn't brought death into their bedroom. He began stroking her breasts. In the midst of death, there is life. In the midst of death, there is—

"Sam." She pushed his hand away.

"No, Suzie," he whispered. "Let me. I'll make it better. I promise."

She continued to cry as he lifted her nightgown and pushed open her thighs. "I'll make it go away," he promised. "I'll make it all go away."

But he couldn't make it go away, and when he finally shuddered inside her, she felt even more alone.

For the next two days, he treated her tenderly, but when she awakened the morning of the funeral, he was gone. Frantically, she called the office, but neither Mitch nor Yank had seen him. Angela had been away for days and no one answered the phone at her house. Finally, she realized that he had deliberately disappeared and she would have to go to the funeral alone.

She picked up the keys to the old Volvo they had bought and squeezed them so tightly that the ridges bit into the palm of her hand. She needed Sam, and he wasn't here for her.

A dark maroon Cadillac Seville was pulling into the parking lot as she walked unsteadily from the apartment building. Mitch got out and came toward her. "Get inside," he said quietly. "I'm coming with you."

She nearly slumped against him with relief. He took her elbow and helped her into the car. As they drove toward Atherton, she stared blindly through the windshield. "Sam's afraid of death," she said numbly. "If he weren't afraid, he would have come with me."

Mitch made no response.

Solid, strong, and immovable, he stayed by her side throughout the ceremony. Sometimes it seemed as if only his presence was keeping her from flying apart. Spasms kept wracking her body, but he held tightly to her hand. She refused to cry. Once she started, she would never be able to stop.

Whenever she looked at the sleek black coffin, her teeth chattered. She tried to talk silently to her father. *It's not finished between us, Daddy. Nothing's finished. I love you. I still love you.* But no comforting messages came to her from the other side of the grave.

Cal sat with Paige, and when the ceremony ended, a crowd gathered around the two of them, offering their condolences. But hardly anyone spoke to her, not even people she had known for years. It was as if—in running away from her wedding and breaking the rules—she had betrayed them all.

As they left the church for the cemetery, she overheard a guest mutter, "Not his real daughter, of course. Adopted." The word was delivered as if it had been sucked from a particularly juicy lemon. Mitch heard it, too, and squeezed her hand.

The gravesite ceremony was mercifully short. As Mitch was leading her away, Cal approached. "Susannah?"

It had been a year since they had spoken. The eyes that had once gazed at her with pride were now full of venom. This was the man she had planned to spend her life with. Now his hatred struck her like a blow.

"I hope you're satisfied," he sneered. "You killed him, you know. He was never the same after you left."

Susannah felt as if she had been punched in the stomach. Mitch stiffened and took a menacing step toward Cal. "Get away from her, Theroux," he said harshly.

A soft touch penetrated Susannah's pain, the brush of a hand on her arm. It settled there only for a moment and then lifted away like a butterfly in flight. She turned numbly toward her sister.

Paige of the tight jeans and saucy walk was conservatively dressed in Kay's old pearls and a subdued black dress. Her rock and roll sister who used to whip her hair to the beat of the Stones looked as proper as an old dowager. Susannah waited for Paige to condemn her, too, but her sister wouldn't even meet her eyes.

"Come along, Paige," Cal said, his lips thin and tight. "There's no need for you to be subjected to her presence."

Mitch drove her home and offered to come inside with her, but she knew she couldn't hold herself together much longer and she refused. Before she got out of the car, she leaned over and pressed her cheek to his jaw. "Thank you," she whispered. "Thank you so much."

The radio was playing softly in the kitchen as she entered the apartment. She expected to see Sam there, but instead she found Angela washing dishes in the kitchen. She set down the dish she had been drying and opened her arms. "Poor baby."

Susannah felt something break apart inside her. She went toward her like a three-year-old running to her mother with a mortal wound. She cried in Angela's arms while Angela stroked her back and said, "I know. I know, baby."

Her nose began to run and tears dripped off her chin onto the shoulder of Angela's blouse. Her body no longer seemed to belong to her. What had happened to the woman who never cried?

"My father's dead," she said. "I won't ever see him again."

"I know, honey."

"I never—I never got to say good-bye. Now I'll never get the chance to put it right."

"You tried, honey. I know you did."

"I didn't think he would die. Not ever. He always seemed like God."

Angela led her to the living room sofa. She rubbed her arms and held her hands, but Susannah couldn't be comforted. "I loved him. I always loved him. He just didn't love me back."

Angela stroked her hair. "That's not true, honey. He loved you. He told me so."

Several seconds passed as her words penetrated Susannah's deepest misery. She looked up and saw Angela's face wavery through her tears. "He told you?"

Angela brushed Susannah's hair back from her wet cheeks, freeing the strands that were stuck there with the lightest scrape of her fingernail. "We were together at the end. Your father went with me to Graceland for Elvis's funeral."

"Graceland? My father?" Susannah stared at her without comprehension.

"I don't think he meant to come with me. But it just sort of happened."

Gradually, Angela unfolded the story of the trip. Susannah listened, stunned by what she was hearing.

"The day he died, he talked about you," Angela said.

Susannah went cold all over. "What did he say?"

"He didn't hate you, Susannah. I think he hated himself."

The horrid words Cal had assaulted her with kept punching at Susannah's brain. "I think I killed him," she whispered. "I did a terrible thing to him. If I hadn't run away, he would be alive today."

"Don't say that! Don't say that, honey. You weren't responsible." Angela spoke in quick, breathless tones. "Those last few hours, we were sitting on these camp stools across from the music gate, waiting for the hearse to come out. We started talking about both of you—about you and about Sammy. Just before the hearse came out, he looked me straight in the eye and he said, 'Angela, I've been wrong to cut Susannah out like I've done. She had to get away. I understand that now. I love her, and as soon as I get back to California, I'm going to tell her so.'"

Susannah held herself rigidly. "He told you that? He told you he loved me?"

"As God is my witness. He told me he was going to call you that very day."

Susannah pressed her eyes shut and tears slithered from beneath her lids. "Oh, Angela."

Angela took her in her arms once again. She was much smaller than Susannah, but she sheltered her. "I—I couldn't bear the idea that he went to his grave hating me."

"He loved you, honey. He went on and on about how much you meant to him."

Susannah pulled away, her forehead crumpling. "You're not making this up so I'll feel better, are you, Angela? Please. I have to know the truth."

Angela squeezed her hands tightly. "It's true. I'm Catholic, Susannah. If I didn't tell the truth about somebody's last moments on earth, it would be a mortal sin. He loved you so much. He told me again and again."

Angela's eyes were wide and earnest, and Susannah wanted desperately to believe her. But although grief had dulled some of her senses, it had sharpened others. As she gazed at her mother-in-law, she knew with absolute certainty that Angela was lying from the bottom of her loving, generous heart.

Sam came home that evening with an expensive hand-woven shawl she had admired in a boutique a few weeks earlier. He made no mention of his disappearance, and she was too drained to ask him about it. As she tucked the shawl away in a bottom dresser drawer, she told herself that no one was perfect and she had to learn to accept Sam's faults. But a fissure had been ripped in the fabric of their marriage.

Several weeks passed before she learned that she had been cut from her father's will and that he had left everything to Paige. Millions of dollars were involved as well as a huge block of FBT stock. But it wasn't the financial loss that devastated her. It was the additional evidence of her father's lack of forgiveness.

Sam argued with her for weeks because she refused to challenge the will. Even in death he hated for Joel to get the best of her. But she didn't want money. She wanted her father alive. She wanted another chance.

Sometimes Susannah thought it was only the overwhelming work load that kept her going through the next few months. She had little time to wallow in either grief or guilt, no time at all to try to decide how she would live the rest of her life, knowing that she could never be reconciled with her father. All of the hours that would have been devoted to introspection were occupied with keeping their small company alive; ironically, success was proving to be even more dangerous to SysVal than failure.

"Will you relax, for chrissake," Sam said, glaring at her as he paced the carpeted reception area of Hoffman Enterprises, one of San Francisco's most prestigious venture capital firms. "If they see how nervous you are, you're going to blow this whole deal. I mean it, Susannah, you could personally screw us up—"

Mitch slapped down the magazine he had been pretending to read. "Leave her alone! Susannah, why do you put up with his nonsense? If I were you, Sam, I'd worry about what I was going to say instead of giving her a hard time."

"Why don't you go fuck yourself?"

"Why don't you—"

Susannah whirled around. "Stop it, both of you! We're all nervous. Let's not take it out on each other." Mitch and Sam had always argued, but in the four months since her father's death, it had grown worse. While their relationship had deteriorated, her own relationship with Mitch had grown closer. She would never forget the way he had stood beside her when she had most needed it.

These past months had been unusually difficult. Not only had she been faced with a searing personal crisis, but SysVal was in deep trouble. Despite the fact that stacks of new orders were coming in every week for the Blaze, the company had run out of money.

Sam glared at her and resumed his pacing. Mitch continued to brood. She wandered over to the windows, where she stared at the view of the ocean, the Golden Gate, and the distant hazy outline of Marin beyond. The chill December rain that splashed against the skyscraper's windows matched her mood.

It bothered her that Sam always seemed to be at his worst when she most needed his support. Today, for example. This meeting meant everything to them. If they couldn't get the financing they needed, they simply wouldn't be able to survive. As orders poured in for the Blaze, they had been feverishly adding new staff, expanding their facilities, and searching out additional subcontractors to assemble the machines—all within the space of a few months. Now they simply couldn't pay their bills. The money was there on paper in future orders, but it wasn't in hand where they needed it.

They had known from the beginning that they were dangerously undercapitalized, but now she and Mitch estimated that their precarious financial balancing act was within thirty days of collapsing. They could no longer put off going after venture capital.

Mitch studied the straight line of Susannah's back as she

stood at the windows. He had grown to care very much for her in the past year, and he was worried. The strain of her father's death had taken an enormous toll, and the business of running SysVal grew more complicated by the day. God knew, Sam wasn't any help. The more Mitch watched them together, the more he saw that Sam was a user. He took everything Susannah had, but he gave very little back.

All of them knew how important this meeting was. Granted, there were firms other than Hoffman Enterprises they could have gone to for financing, but Mitch had both his heart and his head set on making this deal. Leland T. Hoffman was a wily old fox who had written the textbook on venture capital and financed some of the biggest success stories in American business. If Hoffman put his money behind SysVal, it would legitimize them in a way that nothing else could.

The general public was gradually becoming aware of the microcomputer. Commodore had introduced the PET. The TRS-80 was on display at Radio Shack stores all across the country, and both SysVal and the little Apple Computer Company had begun to find a small, but loyal following. But was that enough to convince a man of Hoffman's reputation to make a substantial investment in SysVal?

A secretary appeared to usher them into a conference room, which was furnished in lush art deco. Hoffman, white-haired and plump with prosperity, sat at the center of a burled walnut table and leafed through the folder of material they had prepared for him. None of the half dozen other men who were seated rose to greet them or acknowledged their presence in any way, an obvious intimidation tactic that Mitch hoped wouldn't rattle his partners.

Sam curled his lip at the opulent surroundings, then sprawled down in a chair. He tilted it back and stretched his legs out under the table like a sulky James Dean. Susannah smiled pleasantly, but fumbled with her papers as she sat. She smoothed the skirt of the conservative pale gray business suit that Mitch had asked her to purchase for the occasion. Mitch knew that Susannah was irritated with him for being so specific about her wardrobe, while he totally ignored the jeans that Sam was wearing with his sport coat.

But Mitch had a clear idea of the impression he wanted to give today, and his partners' manner of dress was all part of it.

Hoffman finally raised his head and studied Mitch over the top of his half glasses. Then he shifted his gaze to Susannah.

"Hello, Uncle Leland," she said.

Mitch nearly fell out of his chair. *Uncle* Leland?

Sam seemed to be as surprised as Mitch to discover that his wife knew Hoffman. Mitch wanted to strangle her for springing something like this on them.

"Susannah. It's good to see you again." Hoffman's tone was brisk and formal. "Now what can we do for you and your friends?"

Mitch's stomach sank. Hoffman wasn't taking them seriously at all. He hadn't agreed to meet with them because he was interested in backing SysVal, but merely as a courtesy to Susannah.

Mitch wanted to bang his head against the table in frustration. He forgot that only a few minutes before he had been worried about the strain Susannah was under. Now he wanted to kill her.

Susannah was to make the first presentation. She picked up her leather folder and proceeded to the front of the room. She looked so cool and composed that even Mitch, who knew better, was nearly fooled.

"Gentlemen." She gave all of them a polite smile. "I have to begin with an apology to my business partners for not telling them that we're meeting today before an old family friend. Although Leland and I aren't blood relatives, he was a longtime acquaintance of my father and has known me for nearly as long as I can remember. I didn't tell my partners about this acquaintance because I didn't want them to believe—even for a moment—that an old family connection would make Hoffman Enterprises magically open up its checkbook to SysVal."

Looking thoughtful, she took a step forward. "If I were a man—my father's son instead of his daughter—this old family relationship would almost certainly work to my advantage. But as a woman—my father's daughter—I find myself at a distinct disadvantage."

She smiled at Hoffman. "When I was growing up, Leland, you didn't watch me climbing trees and getting roughed up in football games. Instead, you saw me cutting out paper dolls and having tea parties. Although a grown woman stands before you now, in your mind you're undoubtedly scoffing at the idea of putting your money behind someone who once—and it pains me to admit this—came running to you for protection from an exceedingly ugly earthworm."

The men around the table chuckled, and Mitch felt himself beginning to relax. It was impossible to read Hoffman's expression, but Mitch had to believe that he was impressed by Susannah's good-humored introduction. His admiration for his business partner grew. She was really good at this. As he watched her, he realized that she had actually begun to enjoy herself.

"Women in the business of electronics are a rare species," she went on. "Ironic, isn't it, since women are destined to become major users of small computers? I regard being a female in this industry as an advantage, since I look at everything from a fresh viewpoint. But if my being a woman bothers any of you, I do offer some consolation." She nodded her head toward Sam and Mitch at the foot of the table, and grinned wickedly, "My partners have more than enough testosterone to put all of your minds at ease."

Even Hoffman smiled at that.

Now that she had them relaxed, she launched into her presentation. In her efficient, no-nonsense manner, she offered the business plan they had all labored over for so long, outlining market projections and five-year goals that were aggressive, but credible. As she spoke, her private-school voice and calm assurance gave their renegade company an air of old world stability, despite the fact that Sam had propped his motorcycle boots on the polished tabletop.

She finished her presentation and returned to her seat. Mitch noticed that the men were looking at the papers in front of them with a bit more interest.

Sam dropped his feet to the floor and rose slowly from his chair. "There are winners and losers," he muttered. "Fast buck artists, con men, bullshitters." He glared at all of them. "And then there are champions. And do you know what separates them?" He punched the air with his fist. *"Mission. Mission* is what separates them."

Brother Love's traveling salvation show was off and running. For the next twenty minutes he paced the room, tugging his necktie loose with one hand, shedding his sport coat with the other, jabbing a hand into the pocket of his jeans only to pull it out and shove it through his hair. With a spectacular display of verbal pyrotechnics and oral gymnastics, he painted a picture of a shining future with a Blaze microcomputer beating solidly as its heart.

Hallelujah, brother. And amen!

When it was all over, Mitch was exhilarated. His intuition had been right and he hadn't needed to speak at all. Together, Susannah and Sam had formed exactly the company image he wanted to present—rock-solid respectability countered with outrageous razzle-dazzle. Only a fool could resist them, and Leland Hoffman was no fool.

Although it would be several days before Hoffman got back to them, at least they knew they had given him their best. They went to Mom & Pop's that night to celebrate. Sam immediately claimed Victors, a new high-tech target game that all of them, with the exception of Yank, had decided was the best video game ever made.

Sam called her over. "Come on, Suzie. Cheer me on." Her earlier resentment had dissolved, and she went to join him. He kissed the corner of her mouth without taking his eyes off the screen. "I've got a good game going here. Give me a couple of minutes and then I'll let you play."

She slid behind him so that her breasts were pushed up against his back, and propped her chin on the top of his shoulder while she watched him maneuver the joystick. Her high-tech, whiz-bang husband. Her body began to feel hot, the way it did before they made love. She slipped her hands down onto his upper arms, conscious of the movement of his muscles on the controls through the sleeves of his T-shirt. Sometimes he made her feel as if she was tottering on the edge of a deep precipice. What if she fell off? Would he be the one who would catch her or the one who had pushed her? It was a disconcerting thought, and she shook it off.

Mitch was playing Space Invaders at the next machine.

Releasing Sam, she stepped over to watch him. He glanced longingly toward the Victors game. "Is Sam about done?"

"Forget it. I'm next."

"Are you open to negotiating for position?"

"Unless you're talking diamonds, forget it."

Mitch smiled. "At least I don't have to beat off Yank, too. I can't understand why he won't play Victors. He loves good video games."

"Who can understand what goes through Yank's head?"

Just as she spoke his name, the restaurant door opened and he walked in. She looked more closely and then let out a soft, incredulous exclamation. Distracted, Sam glanced up. "Jesus . . ." he murmured.

Mitch had fallen into a disbelieving silence.

Although Yank was walking toward them, he wasn't the one who had caught their attention. Instead, it was the woman sashaying at his side who had temporarily stunned them into speechlessness. She was a traffic-stopping redhead with crimson lips, elaborate makeup, and leopardskin pants that looked as if they had been tattooed on her hips. Overshadowing all that jutted a pair of breasts so spectacular that only a miraculous feat of engineering seemed to be holding them within the confines of her gold tank top.

"Maybe she's his wet nurse," Susannah whispered, unable to take her eyes off the monumental mammaries.

"Are you kidding?" Mitch whispered back. "He'd suffocate to death."

Yank walked up to them and nodded. He refused to have anything to do with the day-to-day business operations of the company; typically, he didn't ask about their meeting with Hoffman Enterprises, but about a problem they'd been having with their keyboards. "What'd the manufacturer say, Sam? Did you talk to them?"

"Uh . . . static." The woman's presence seemed to have robbed Sam of his capacity for coherent speech.

Yank looked irritated. "Of course it's static. We've known that for weeks. What do they intend to do about it?"

"Do?"

Susannah stepped in and extended her hand to Yank's companion. "Hi, I'm Susannah Faulconer."

"Kismet," the woman replied in a breathy, affected voice.

"I beg your pardon?"

"Kismet Jade. My numerologist picked it out. You're a Sagittarius, aren't you?"

"Actually, no." Susannah quickly introduced her partners, but Kismet barely spared them a glance. She was too busy cantilevering her left breast over Yank's upper arm.

"I'm hungry, Stud Man," she purred. "You gonna buy me something to eat, or do I have to work for my dinner?" She gave him a wicked, moist-lipped smile that clearly indicated exactly what sort of work she had in mind.

Yank calmly adjusted his glasses on his nose. "I'll be happy to get you something to eat. The pizza is excellent, but the burgers are quite good, too."

"Stud Man?" Mitch muttered at Susannah's side.

"I ordered some pizzas," Susannah said quickly.

Kismet walked two vermilion fingernails up the length of Yank's arm. "Play Victors with me while we wait."

"I'm sorry, Kismet, but I don't play Victors."

Kismet began to pout. "Why not? It's the best arcade game that's come out this year."

Yank looked genuinely distressed. "I'm awfully sorry, Kismet. I really don't like to play Victors. Sam is our champion. He's the best Victors player you've ever seen." He gave Sam a pleading glance. "Would you mind playing a game with Kismet?"

"Uh—sure. No problem."

Mitch abandoned Space Invaders and walked with Susannah to the table. "She certainly is a far cry from Roberta," he said. "Sam's going to have a hard time keeping his eyes on the screen."

"So would you," she pointed out as they slid into the booth.

Kismet released a giggling obscenity as Sam annihilated her before she even reached the second screen. She took the quarter Yank handed her.

Susannah studied them. "Have you spent any time at all thinking about what it will mean if this deal goes through?"

"That's about all I've done lately."

"I don't mean the company. I'm talking about how it will change us personally. On paper, anyway, each one of us will be worth a lot of money."

"I have money now. You've had it before. We know what it's like."

She studied Yank and Sam. "They don't."

"Nothing ever stays the same, Susannah."

"Uhm. I guess you're right." She picked up her beer and took a sip.

On the opposite side of the room, Kismet arched her arms around Yank's thin neck, pressed her lips to his, and thrust her long experienced tongue deep within his mouth.

Susannah experienced a moment both bittersweet and poignant. Mitch was right. Nothing was ever going to be the same again.

BOOK TWO

• •

THE MISSION

We have set out together on an adventure to give the world the best computer humankind can produce. We will support and stand by our products, placing quality and integrity above all else. We relish the adventure because it gives us the opportunity to put ourselves to the test of excellence.

Statement of Mission
SysVal Computer Corporation

21

• •

The money came rolling in. Slick, green, fast money. Hot money. New money. Money aching to be spent.

The seventies whirled into the eighties, and the greatest industrial joy ride of the twentieth century picked up speed. Silicon Valley was awash in electronic gold as capitalism struck its finest hour.

Home video games had already captured the imagination of the American family, and by 1982, the idea of having a computer in the house no longer seemed strange at all. Firms sprang up overnight. Some of them collapsed just as quickly, but others left their founders with almost unimaginable riches.

In the posh communities of Los Gatos, Woodside, and Los Altos Hills, the electrical engineers stepped out of their hot tubs, stuffed their plastic pocket protectors into Armani shirts, hopped into their BMW's, and laughed like hell.

By the fall of 1982, the nerds owned the Valley. The bespeckled, pimply-faced, overweight, underweight, dateless, womanless, goofiest of the goofy, were the undisputed, unchallenged kings of the entire freaking Valley!

Man, it was sweet.

Yank pulled his Porsche 911 crookedly into a parking space at SysVal's main building and then headed up the walk toward the main entrance. He nodded absentmindedly at the two female account executives who had stopped in mid-conversation as he approached and gazed wistfully at the retreating back of his leather bomber jacket. Once inside the lobby, he determinedly ignored the security guard stationed behind the elliptical-shaped desk.

Everyone else who worked at SysVal had to show a plastic security badge to be admitted. Even Sam wore a badge. But Yank pretended the badges didn't exist, and Susannah had left orders that the guards were to admit him on sight.

Logically, he understood that those golden days of Homebrew were gone forever—the days of free and open information, of one for all and all for one. It was September of 1982. John Lennon was dead, Ronald Reagan was in the White House, and Uncle Sam had just busted up AT&T. The world was changing, and the Valley was filled with industrial spies intent on stealing the latest American technology and selling it to the Japanese, the Russians, or even a new start-up in the next industrial park. SysVal's astounding success had made it a prime target for those roaches of humanity. Yank understood all that. But he still wouldn't wear a security badge.

As he headed down the hallway toward the multimillion-dollar lab that had been built especially for him, he had the nagging sensation that he had forgotten something very important. But he dismissed his worry. What could be more important than solving the problem with the trace lines of solder on their new circuit board? They were too close. He had an idea . . .

Ten miles away, in the gilt and brocade bedroom of his Portola Valley home, lingerie model Tiffani Wade's carefully arranged seductive pose was ruined by the frown marring her forehead. "Yank? Yank, you can come back in now. I'm ready."

She called out three more times before she realized that no one was going to answer, then she sagged back into the pillows. "You son of a bitch," she muttered. "You've done it to me again."

* * *

Susannah shut off the Blaze III that rested on the credenza behind her desk and stretched. Somewhere in the building one of the employees fired off an air horn. She barely noticed. At SysVal, people were always firing off air horns or calling out Bingo numbers over the loudspeaker system, just so no one ever made the mistake of confusing them with IBM or FBT.

As if someone had overheard her thoughts, the loudspeaker began to squawk. "Mayday, Mayday. The Japanese have just attacked the parking lot. All employees driving domestic cars should immediately take cover. This is not a drill. I repeat. This is not a drill."

Susannah rolled her eyes. God forbid they should ever have a real emergency. No one would believe it.

SysVal's employees were primarily men in their twenties, and they prided themselves on being bad. In the six years since the company was founded, Sam Gamble's personality had become their model. Even the whiz kids at Apple Computer weren't as raunchy, as brazen, as wild as the rowdy bunch at SysVal. At Apple they held Friday afternoon beer blasts, but at SysVal they showed stag movies, too. The boys of SysVal strutted their stuff—their youth, their audaciousness, their sense of destiny. They were the ones who had made the magical little Blaze available to the world and helped humanity learn the beauty of personal computing. Like their brash, charismatic founder, they were young, invincible, immortal.

Taking off her glasses, Susannah rubbed the bridge of her nose, then looked across her office at a much-abused dart board with the Apple logo painted on it. She thought about the five of them—Jobs and Woz, Sam, Yank, herself. All of them college dropouts. Freaks, nerds, rebels, and one overly polite socialite. In the five years that had passed since the West Coast Computer Faire, everything they touched had turned to gold. It was as if the gods had blessed them with youth, brains, and unlimited good luck. On paper, anyway, she and her partners were worth over a hundred million dollars each, while at Apple, Steve Jobs was worth more than three hundred million. Sometimes the enormity of their success scared Susannah to death.

The battered Apple dart board gave visual evidence of the

early rivalry between the two young companies, but in the past few years that had changed. With the dawning of the 1980s, the Big Boys had finally lifted their heads and realized that they had been left behind. Late in 1981, IBM had introduced the IBM-PC. Apple Computer, in a display of bravado that Susannah still wished SysVal had thought of first, had taken out a full-page ad in the nation's newspapers. The ad said, WELCOME IBM. SERIOUSLY. A paragraph of copy had followed in which the brash young upstarts at Apple had assumed the role of the wise old men of the industry and spelled out for Mighty IBM all of the glories of personal computing—as if IBM were too inexperienced, too stupid, too wet-behind-the-ears, to figure it out for themselves. The sheer audacity of it had kept the business community laughing for months.

A custom-designed radio-controlled car zoomed into her office, did a three sixty in the middle of her carpet and zoomed out again with no sign of a human operator. SysVal's engineers were entertaining themselves again.

Rubbing her eyes, she pushed a stray lock of hair away from her face. Her hair was shorter now, cut in a breezy style that feathered around her cheeks and softened the sharp, aristocratic features of her face. Since no important meetings were on her docket for that day, she had dressed informally in a coral cowl-neck sweater and tight, straight-legged jeans. Two slim gold bangles glittered at one wrist and a wide gold cuff hugged the other. The third finger of her right hand sported a two-karat marquis-cut diamond that she had bought for herself. More, she had definitely concluded, was better than less.

On impulse, she reached for her telephone and dialed the number that connected her directly with Mitch's private office. But before the phone could ring, he walked through her door.

"Mental telepathy," she said, some of her tension slipping away merely at the sight of his solid, comforting presence. "I was just calling you."

He slumped wearily into the chair opposite her desk. "Somebody left a bra in the hallway."

"As long as the person who lost it isn't running around bare-chested, don't complain."

Of them all, Mitch had changed the least. The blunt planes of his face had hardened a bit, and a few strands of gray had begun to weave through the sandy hair at his temples. But his body hadn't lost any of its tone. At thirty-seven, SysVal's Executive Vice-President of Sales and Marketing was still as solid as the Buckeye wide receiver who had won a place in Woody Hayes's heart.

Mitch was the most respectable corporate officer SysVal had, a wonderful piece of white bread who thought nothing of flying across the country to watch one of his kids play soccer, and was recently honored as the Bay Area Jaycees' Man of the Year for his civic contributions. Over the years, he and Susannah had developed a deep friendship.

She saw at once that he was exhausted. He had been driving himself for months, trying to win a multimillion-dollar contract with the state of California to install the Blaze III in hundreds of its state offices. The contract would provide the capitalization SysVal needed to finish up the work on the Wildfire and launch their new business computer ahead of the competition. Unfortunately, SysVal's competition for the contract was FBT, and Cal Theroux had been lobbying hard for the Falcon 101, FBT's new personal computer. Although the entry of giant corporations like IBM and FBT had legitimized the personal computer, it had also made things a lot tougher.

"Be honest with me," he said, as he stretched out his legs. "Do you think I'm stuffy?"

"You? Perish the thought."

"I'm not joking. I want to know."

"You're serious?"

He nodded.

"Yes. You're definitely stuffy."

"Well, thank you. Thank you so very much." He glared at her, a picture of offended dignity.

She smiled. "Does this sudden soul searching have anything to do with your relationship with the beautiful, talented, and terminally obnoxious Jacqueline Dane?"

"Jacqueline is not obnoxious. She is one of the finest actresses in this country."

"As she is quick to point out. Did you see that television interview she gave last week where she went on and on about the importance of making *serious* films and doing *serious* work? She kept pushing her fingers through her hair like she had mange or something. I have never yet seen that woman give an interview where she hadn't managed to work in the fact that she has a degree from Yale. She bites her fingernails, too."

He gave her his best stony-eyed gaze. "I suppose you would prefer it if I started dating bimbos like Yank does."

"You and Yank could do each other big favors by trading women for a few months. Yank needs to date someone with an IQ that's higher than the speed limit, and you need to find a woman who can lighten up a little. Honestly, Mitch, I can't believe Jacqueline had the nerve to call you stuffy. I think her face would crack if she ever tried to smile."

"You just said I was stuffy," he pointed out.

"I'm allowed to say that because I'm one of the best friends you have, and I adore you. She, on the other hand, only cares about dead philosophers with names no sensible person can spell."

"I had my fill of party girls when I was married to Louise. I like serious women."

Susannah shook her head in disgust. There was simply no reasoning with him. In the past six years, Mitch had had long-term relationships with three women, all brilliant, beautiful, and sober-minded. Susannah still couldn't make up her mind which one of them she detested the most. At heart he was a family man, and Susannah was afraid he might actually marry Jacqueline Dane. And if her suspicions were right, the actress would jump at the offer. Mitch had a funny effect on women. For someone who was basically a stuffed shirt, he certainly didn't have any trouble finding bedroom companions.

She knew she was beating a dead horse, but she plunged in anyway. "Why won't you let me pick out some women for you? Really, Mitch, I know just the sort of person you need. Someone who's intelligent, but warm. Someone who won't try to mother you, since I know you hate that. A woman with a sense of humor to make up for the fact that you have absolutely none." It wasn't true. Mitch had a wonderful sense of humor, but it was so dry that most people didn't appreciate it. "A woman without much libido, since you're getting older and you probably don't have the sex drive you used to."

"That's it." He stood and glared at her. "My libido isn't any of your business, Miss Hot Shot."

"Touchy, touchy." She tried to imagine herself joking with a man about his sex drive six years ago and failed. SysVal had changed them all.

He finally smiled. "Now that you're filthy rich, you've turned into a real brat, do you know that?"

"We're all filthy rich. And I'm not a brat."

She noticed the strain that had been evident when he had come into her office had dissipated. The company was a pressure cooker of activity with a new crisis popping up every hour, and she and Mitch had long ago discovered that baiting each other worked as well as anything else to relax them both.

An angry male voice blared through the loudspeaker. "Whichever son of a bitch took DP27E's new HP calculator had better get the fucker back to the office right now!"

Mitch's expression grew pained, and he lifted a disapproving eyebrow toward the speaker. "Susannah?"

She sighed. "I'll put out another obscenity memo." They had learned years ago that it was useless to lock up the loudspeaker controls. There was nothing the SysVal engineers loved better than breaking through anything that bore even a passing resemblance to a closed system.

She asked him about his visit to Boston. Over the years, Mitch's children had visited him frequently, and she had grown fond of them. She kept a framed picture nine-year-old Liza had drawn for her on her desk next to a paperweight David had made in his sixth-grade art class.

Mitch walked over to her window. "I finally met Louise's new husband. He and I had a couple of beers and talked about the kids. He said they were getting along well, and he wanted me to know that he wasn't going to try to take my place with them. He saw himself as a big brother, not a father, that sort of thing. Heck of a nice guy."

"You hate his guts, don't you?"

"I wanted to slam my fist right through his face."

She gave him a sympathetic smile. Not for the first time, it occurred to her that Mitch was a much better friend to her than Sam had ever been.

They chatted for a few more minutes, and then Mitch left. Her stomach rumbled and she realized she was hungry. Maybe she could talk Sam into leaving early tonight. It would be wonderful to have dinner at home for a change and spend an evening alone together—something they hadn't done in longer than she could remember.

She got up from her desk, deliberately pushing away the painful knowledge that Sam wouldn't want to spend an evening alone with her. She had made it a habit not to dwell on the problems in her marriage when she was at work, but it was difficult. As she walked out of the office, she forced herself to think about the company instead.

SysVal had become one of the most glamorous privately owned companies in the world. Thanks to Mitch's brilliant financial strategies, the original four partners had each held onto a whopping fifteen per cent of the company. Susannah didn't like to think about how much money they had. The amount was almost obscene.

As she turned the corner into the next hallway, she ran into two of the engineers who were playing with the radio-controlled car. She chatted with them for a few minutes and admired their toy. When she finally moved on, she wasn't aware of the fact that they still watched her.

Even though Susannah wasn't beautiful, there was something about her that drove the young engineers at SysVal slightly crazy. Maybe it was those tight jeans—those long slim legs. Maybe it was the way she moved—tall and proud. But physical appearance was only part of their attraction to her. There was the aphrodisia of her wealth and the ever-increasing influence she held in a male-dominated industry. All in all, at the age of thirty-one, Susannah was a potent combination of style, sex, brains, money, and power, qualities that were irresistible to the brilliant young men who came from all over the world to work for SysVal.

They joked about what it would be like to sleep with her, but behind their sexual bantering lay a genuine respect. Susannah was tough and demanding, but she was seldom unreasonable. Not like some people.

Sam wasn't in his office.

Susannah moved on. SysVal headquarters occupied three large buildings, grouped together in an informal campus arrangement. Her office was in the main building, the center section of which was open, with glass block walls and partitions that didn't quite reach the ceiling. A Joan Jett song blared from one of the labs, and she passed a group of video games that occupied a cranny in the brightly painted hallway. At SysVal, the boundaries between work and play were deliberately obscured.

Lights were coming from the left, and she took a sharp turn in that direction. Although it was after six o'clock, the New Product Team was still meeting to talk about the problems they were having with the Blaze Wildfire, the revolutionary new business computer they hoped to launch within a year.

For all the future promise of Sam's Wildfire project, the Blaze III was SysVal's workhorse, the bread and butter of the company. The Blaze III was the computer that America was buying for its kids, the computer that small offices were growing to depend on, and the computer that—along with its ancestors the I and II—had made them all rich.

Sam's voice punched the air and spilled out into the hallway from one of the conference rooms. She paused inside the doorway to watch him. Once just the sight of him had sent thrills of excitement through her body. Now she felt a sense of despair. Somehow she had to make things right again between them. But how could she do that when she wasn't even certain what was wrong?

He was straddling a chair backward, straining the fine woolen material of his charcoal slacks. His white shirt-sleeves were rolled to the elbows, his collar was unfastened, and the heels of his Italian loafers were propped up on the chair rungs. A dozen young faces sat cross-legged on the floor around him, gazing up at him as he spoke, their expressions rapt while they listened to Brother Love's new-age Sermon on the Mount. Blessed is the microchip, she thought, for its users shall inherit the earth.

The employees both loved and hated Sam. With his evangelist's zeal, he inspired them to do the impossible, but he had no patience for incompetence and was brutal in his criticism. Still, very few of them left, even after suffering one of his humiliating public tongue-lashings. He gave them the sense that they had a mission in life. They were soldiers in the final crusade of the twentieth century, and even those who had grown to detest him continued to scramble all over themselves to please him.

She frowned as she watched those young, eager faces soaking up everything he said. An aura of hero worship had developed around Sam that bothered her. It might be good for the company, but it wasn't good for Sam.

Her presence in the doorway caught his attention. He turned his head and frowned at the interruption. She remembered how his face had once softened when he caught sight of her. When had it begun to change? Sometimes she thought that it went as far back as her father's funeral.

She gestured toward the kitchen at the back, signaling him that she would meet him there. He returned his attention to the group without making any acknowledgment. She straightened her shoulders and walked on with quiet dignity. Just before she reached the kitchen, she passed a woman with two very young children on their way to the large cafeteria. All of them wore visitor's badges, and the mother was carrying a picnic basket.

Her depression burrowed in deeper. It wasn't the first time she had seen something like this. SysVal's employees worked such long hours that spouses—usually wives—sometimes showed up with their children so they could provide some facsimile of a family dinner. SysVal didn't hire anyone who wasn't a workaholic, and the long hours were taking a toll on family life—something Sam hadn't taken into account when he constructed his Utopian vision of their company. But then, families weren't important to Sam. She touched her fingers to her waist, feeling the hollowness inside. How much longer was he going to ignore this pressing need she had for a child? Just because she was SysVal's president didn't mean she wasn't a woman, too.

She made her way to the refrigerator in the back of the kitchen and pulled out a carton of yogurt. But as she began to peel off the lid, her fingers faltered and her eyelids squeezed shut. What was she going to do about her marriage? Far too many times, Sam felt like the enemy, like another person for her to please, another person with an invisible checklist of qualities she had to live up to.

He shot through the door, wearily shoving his right hand through his short black hair. "Susannah, you're going to have to get on Marketing again. I'm sick of their bullshit. They either have to buy into the Wildfire—and I mean total commitment—or they can take their asses over to Apple. They're like a bunch of goddamn old ladies . . ."

She let him rant and rave for a while. Tomorrow he would undoubtedly storm the Marketing Department and throw one of his famous temper tantrums. Then she would have to clean up after him. Sam was thirty now, but in many ways he was still a child.

He collapsed into one of the chairs. "Get me a Coke."

She went over to the refrigerator and pulled out a can from his private stock. The top hissed as she popped it. She set it in front of him, then bent forward and brushed his mouth with a soft kiss. His lips were cool and dry. After he had been speaking to a group, she was always surprised that they weren't red hot.

She began to knead the tight muscles of his shoulders with her thumbs. "Why don't we take off early Friday night and drive down to Monterey? There's an inn I've been hearing about. Private cottages, ocean view."

"I don't know. Maybe."

"I think it would do us both good to get away for a while."

"Yeah. You're probably right." Despite his words, Susannah knew that Sam didn't really want to get away. He fed off the furious pace of the company. Even when he was at home he was thinking, working, lambasting people over one of their seven telephones. Sometimes she thought that Sam was trying to outrun life.

Her hands grew still on his shoulders. "It's a good time of the month. Full moon, baying wolf, ripe egg."

He pulled abruptly away from her. "Christ. Don't start the baby shit again, all right? Just don't start. You can't even find time to help me look for that new Oriental rug for the dining room. How do you expect to take care of a kid?"

"I don't like picking out rugs. I do like children. I'm

thirty-one, Sam. The clock's ticking. SysVal is going to have on-site child care by the end of the year. That'll make a big difference to me and the rest of our female employees."

As soon as she had spoken, she wished she hadn't brought up the child-care issue. She had given him an excuse to divert their conversation from the personal back to the company, and she knew he would take advantage of it.

"I don't know why you act like this child care thing is all signed, sealed, and delivered. I'm not backing you, and I don't think Mitch will, either. It's not a corporation's responsibility to take care of its employee's kids, for chrissake."

"It is if the corporation wants to hang onto its female work force. I'm going to fight you on this one, Sam. I'll take it right to the Board of Directors if I have to."

"It wouldn't be the first time." He rose abruptly from his chair. "I don't understand you anymore, Susannah. You seem to fight me on everything."

It wasn't true. She still believed that of all of them, Sam had the truest vision of what SysVal could be. Because of him, the company had never been loaded down with hierarchies. The organization was fluid, lean, and profitable.

"I don't know, Susannah. You've changed. And I'm not sure it's all for the better." His eyes skimmed down over her clothing. He didn't like it when she wore jeans. He hated her shorter hair. If he overheard her swearing, he staged a major confrontation. She had finally realized that a big part of Sam wanted her back the way she had been when they had first met.

"Sam, we need to spend some time together without telephones ringing and people showing up at the front door. We have some problems we have to work out, and we need time alone to do it."

"You're turning into a broken record, you know that? I don't want to hear about it anymore. I've got enough on my mind without a load of crap from you."

"Excuse me. Uh—Sam?"

Mindy Bradshaw walked into the kitchen in such a gingerly fashion that the floor might have been covered with rattlesnakes. She was a thin, anemic-looking blonde, with baby-fine hair that fell like a veil over the sides of her face.

Mindy was one of the most recent additions to the New Product Team. Although she was bright, she lacked self-confidence and was frequently at the receiving end of one of Sam's more humiliating public tongue-lashings. Several times in the past few weeks, Susannah had seen her running from a meeting in tears, not exactly the behavior Susannah wanted to see from the company's minority female work force—a group of which she was fiercely protective. Despite Sam's abuse, however, Mindy continued to hang on to his every word and gaze at him as if—at any moment—he just might levitate.

Sam was obviously relieved at the interruption. "Yeah, Mindy, what is it?"

"Pete and I wondered— That is—"

"Christ, Mindy. Start all over, will you? Walk into the room like you own it for a change. Stand up straight, look me in the eye, and tell me to go to hell if you feel like it."

"Oh, no," she said breathlessly. "It's just—Pete and I have been crunching some numbers. We have some ideas about pricing on the BDI that we want to go over with you."

"Yeah, sure." He pitched his empty Coke can into the recycling bin and left the room without a backward glance.

Susannah walked listlessly back toward her office. These past few years had turned her into a fighter, but she didn't know how to fight this. On impulse, she took a detour that led to the east wing of the building. Maybe Yank was still working in his lab. Sometimes when she was rattled, she liked to drop in there and spend a few minutes with him. They seldom talked, but being with Yank was soothing. She enjoyed the quiet patience of his movements, the steadiness of his eyes when they actually focused on her. His presence settled her.

And then she hesitated. She wasn't going to get into the habit of using other people as a crutch simply because she couldn't solve her own problems. She returned to her office and flicked on her Blaze III. The light began to glow on the screen. For a moment, she regarded the machine with a mixture of love and bitterness. And then she lost herself in her work.

* * *

Long after midnight that same evening, Sam eased naked into the hot tub. The house that rose behind him was a stark ultramodern structure with a roof line that jutted at sharp angles like bats' wings against the night sky and held eighteen solar panels to provide energy. He and a team of architects had worked on the design for nearly a year, and it had taken another two years to build. Everything was the best. The interior held free-form couches upholstered in white suede and jagged-edged tables chiseled from rock-crystal selenite. The deck was made of marble and sculptured black granite. Rigidly geometric furniture constructed of cold-rolled steel glimmered faintly near the perimeter of the hot tub. The hot tub itself, made of black marble, was the size of a small swimming pool.

He had settled into a ledge contoured to fit his body. Although he was tired, he couldn't sleep. As the inky water swirled around him, he gazed down at the lights in the valley below and pretended that they were stars and that he was hanging upside down in the universe. He let himself float, concentrating only on the surge of the waters and the feeling of rushing through unexplored space.

He had more money than he had ever dreamed existed. He could buy anything he wanted, go anywhere, do anything. But something was missing. The water sucked at him and he raced deeper into space. *Find it,* a voice whispered. *Look around you and find what's missing.*

He was only thirty years old, and he didn't want life to be safe and settled. Where were the challenges? The thrills? SysVal wasn't enough anymore. And neither was Susannah.

A sound intruded on his thoughts. One of the doors that led out from the house to the deck had opened behind him. Susannah came into his line of vision. He watched with resentment as she pulled her silk robe tight and hugged herself against the night chill.

"You couldn't sleep?" she asked.

He settled deeper into the bubbling waters and wished she would go away.

"Would you like me to get in with you?" she said softly.

He shrugged. "Whatever."

She unfastened her robe and let it slide from her shoulders. She was naked beneath. There was a momentary shift in the rhythm of the water as she settled onto the ledge next to him.

"The water's hot."

"One hundred and two degrees, like always." He arched his neck and laid his head back in the water, closing his eyes to shut her out.

He felt her fingers on his arm. "Sam, I'm worried about you."

"Don't be."

"I wish you'd tell me what's wrong."

His eyes snapped open. "You're what's wrong! Why don't you leave me alone?"

For a moment she did nothing, and then she rose silently from the tub. Water glistened on her body. His eyes roved down over her small breasts, her waist, the soft auburn tuft. She didn't have any idea how hot she still made him. He grabbed her hand before she could move away and pulled her down. She lost her balance and landed awkwardly beside him.

He pushed her back onto the ledge. "Open your legs."

"I don't want to." She tried to twist away.

"Open them, damn it," he insisted.

"Sam, this isn't right. We need to talk. Sex isn't enough this time."

She started to get up. He clenched his teeth and moved on top of her. He didn't want to listen to her. He wanted to get the fire back, the challenge, the thrill of conquest. Wedging open her thighs, he thrust hard and buried himself inside her.

She wasn't ready for him and she winced, but he tilted up her hips and drove deeper.

She dug the heels of her hands into his chest, trying to push him away. "Dammit, Sam. Don't do this!"

He refused to let her up. The night-black water swirled around him like a witch's caldron. Steam rose from his shoulders as he arched his back and thrust again and again, cursing her in his mind. In the old days, she had made him happy . . . In the old days, life had been exciting . . . Everything had been new—the company—Susannah . . . In the old days, life had thrilled him.

He cried out when he came, shuddering violently and

falling heavily on her. With a hard shove, she pushed him off her body and rose from the tub.

"Susannah . . ."

She spun around, steam coming from her body. Her light gray eyes blazed with fury. "Don't you ever do that to me again."

Naked and fierce, she stood over him. She was silhouetted against the sky, her head in front of the moon, so that a halo of silver light had formed around her wet hair and spilled down over her shoulders. Water sluiced like quicksilver over her skin. As he stared at her, her entire body glowed with an eerie moon-induced incandescence. She looked both holy and profane.

He hated the strength he saw there. The strength and power and courage that hadn't been there when they had first met. When had she gotten ahead of him? How had she learned secrets he didn't know?

A dam of emotion burst from inside him, and he shouted at her. "Why should I worry about how you feel? You don't care about me!"

She stared down at him, the moonlight forming an unearthly aurora behind her. "You don't even know what you want."

He wanted that *click* he used to feel, that sense that she would fill in his missing parts, that she would give him some of her serenity, polish off his rough edges, soothe his impatience. He wanted her to take away his fear of death. He wanted her to relieve his boredom, offer him a fresh challenge. Make life exciting again. And she wasn't doing it.

He rose from the hot tub and angrily slicked the water from his body with the flat of his hand. "If you haven't figured out what's wrong by now, I'm not going to explain it to you."

"You'll have to make peace with yourself," she said flatly. "I can't do it for you."

His anger swelled. "I should have known you would try to make it my fault. What's happened to us is *your* problem, Susannah. Yours, not mine."

He turned to stalk away from her, but he hadn't finished punishing her for not being able to help him. Spinning back around, he made a final cruel attack. "I'm warning you right now. You'd better not be playing any games with those birth control pills."

Her hand spasmed at her side. "You bastard."

Water was glistening on her cheeks, but he didn't know if it was from the hot tub or because she was crying. "If you get pregnant, I'll leave you," he said viciously. "I mean it."

She spun away from him and stalked toward the house, her robe lying forgotten on the deck.

"Things had better start changing around here," he shouted after her.

But she had disappeared inside, and he was left alone with himself.

22

*F*BT had been caught with its pants down. All of its sophisticated forecasting tools, its graphs and charts and leather-bound strategy statements, its legions of MBA's and Ph.D.'s and decades of experience, hadn't been able to predict the public's growing fascination with the personal computer.

Personal computer. Just the name made the FBT executives cringe. What kind of name was that? It sounded like a douche, for godsake.

As the seventies had come to an end, the executives had kept themselves busy smiling and harumphing and doubletalking the press, referring to stable product line and the fickleness of the consumer products market. They had talked about FBT tradition, waxed poetic over the majesty of their giant mainframes and those eye-popping profits listed in crisp black ink in their annual reports. And the more they had talked, the more they had qualified and quantified away, the more the world's business community had laughed behind their backs at them for having been so woefully left behind by a bunch of wild-eyed kids.

For Cal Theroux it had been unbearable.

He was the one who had given FBT back its self respect with the launching of the Falcon 101 in January of 1982. It had been his baby from the beginning, and its success had given him the final leverage he needed to consolidate his power within FBT. Now Cal was riding the small computer's success all the way to personal glory.

On the other side of the office, his secretary was unpacking the last of his personal effects and arranging them in the bookshelves. She had been at the task for some time, and he was growing impatient. The ceremony that marked his appointment as the new chairman of FBT would begin in less than an hour, and he wanted a few moments to himself.

"That's enough for now, Patricia. When my wife arrives, send her in."

His secretary nodded and left.

Finally alone, Cal allowed himself the liberty of sliding back in his chair and contemplating his imposing surroundings. Some men were obsessed with sex, others with wealth. But for Cal, power had always been the ultimate prize.

He stroked the polished malachite top of the chairman's desk and touched the panel of switches that controlled the FBT fountains. Since the grounds were crawling with members of the press, he suppressed the urge to manipulate the switches as he had seen Joel do so many times. Even Paul Clemens had not been able to resist toying with those seven fountains during his reign as FBT chairman following Joel's death. They were the final symbol of command, and now they belonged to Cal.

The door opened and his wife Nicole entered. "Hello, darling." As she walked across the carpet toward him, her shoulders tensed almost imperceptibly. He knew she was awaiting his verdict on her appearance.

She looked reed-thin and stylish in a black suit with tan piping. Her dark hair fell in a smooth page boy that formed identical sickles over her ears and revealed the small diamond studs he had given her last week for their third wedding anniversary. Although she was only thirty-four, faint lines had begun to appear near her eyes. It would not be long before he would have to arrange plastic surgery for her.

"Take off the bracelet," he said, eyeing the silver bangle at her wrist with distaste.

She obeyed him instantly. Nicole's dedication to pleasing

him was one of the qualities he liked most about her. He had chosen well. Not only was she the daughter of one of the more prominent members of the FBT Board of Directors, but she had been in love with him for years, even when he was engaged to Susannah. At the time, however, Joel Faulconer's daughter had been the bigger prize. His jaw tightened. How he would love to see that bitch's face when he took office today as FBT's chairman.

"It's a zoo in the lobby," Nicole said. "Half the world has shown up to watch you take office." She gazed around her at the well-appointed office. "I can't believe this has finally happened. I'm so proud of you, darling."

As she chattered on, he watched the adoration glimmering in her eyes, and he could almost pretend that he loved her. But he wasn't a sentimental man, and he no longer believed that he was capable of that sort of emotion. The closest Cal had ever come to love had been with Susannah, and that had led to the greatest humiliation of his life.

Even after six years, his stomach still churned when he remembered standing at the altar and watching her run away on that motorcycle. Instead of easing his desire for revenge, the passing years had fueled it. He had been patient for so long. While Joel was alive, the old man had prevented him from doing what needed to be done. In the years after his death, during Paul Clemens's reign, Cal's position had been precarious and he hadn't been able to allow himself the luxury of taking even the mildest risks. But with the success of the Falcon 101, all of that had finally changed.

His intercom clicked on, interrupting the monologue Nicole had been delivering on the suitability of the dress she had chosen for the reception that evening.

"Miss Faulconer is here."

"Send her in."

He could feel Nicole's resentment, and he smiled inwardly. His wife made no secret of the fact that she detested Joel Faulconer's daughter. But that was all right. His long-term friendship with Paige kept Nicole on her toes.

The door burst open and Paige breezed in, carefree and beautiful, her skin golden from the sun. She greeted Nicole with a cool cheek-press and headed toward Cal. "I can't believe you made me come back for this hideous ceremony,

Calvin. One of the photographers goosed me on my way in through the lobby. He had a great ass, but even I draw the line at body odor." She slid into his arms. "No tongue, sweetie. Your wife is watching."

He brushed a suitably chaste kiss across her lips. Being with Paige was exhausting, but necessary. It was ironic that she, rather than Susannah, had provided the weapon that had allowed him to rise to his current position. From the beginning, Paige had hated the responsibilities that went along with the huge block of FBT stock she had inherited, and Cal had made certain he was always there to advise and comfort her. Within a year of Joel's death, Paige had given him her proxy so he could vote her shares in any way he wished. In return, he had promised not to burden her with the FBT responsibilities she detested. Heads, he won. Tails, he won.

"You know I wouldn't have asked you back today if it hadn't been absolutely necessary," he said.

She stuck out her lip in a playful pout. "But there are going to be speeches. I hate speeches."

"Really, Paige," Nicole said stiffly. "Life can't always be one of your parties."

"Who says?" Paige settled on the edge of Cal's desk and crossed her long legs. They were bare of stockings, he noted with disapproval. At least her raw silk suit was appropriate, although he doubted that she had bothered to put on a bra beneath it. He remembered with some nostalgia the time before Joel's death, when Paige had dressed conservatively and behaved with at least a modicum of dignity. That had changed within a year of her father's funeral—about the time he and Paige had made their agreement.

"I haven't bothered you for months," he said. "You know I wouldn't have asked you to fly in if it hadn't been absolutely necessary."

She regarded him evenly. "You couldn't miss having your picture taken with me today of all days, could you, Calvin? A photograph for all the world to see of Paige Faulconer symbolically passing on the mantle of her father's power."

Sometime Paige was smarter than he gave her credit for. He always tried to remember that.

Nicole fluttered near the doorway, obviously reluctant to

leave the two of them alone. "I'm supposed to meet Marge Clemens. I'm afraid I have to go."

"I'll be down in a few minutes," he told her.

She had no choice but to leave. As the door shut, Paige regarded him with cynical amusement. "Poor Nicole. Doesn't she realize that if we had wanted each other, we would have done something about it long ago?"

She slid down off the corner of the desk. In a manner that was too offhand, even for her, she said, "I'm cutting out of the FBT dinner early tonight."

"Any reason?"

"Susannah sent me an invitation for some sort of party SysVal is holding." She tucked a wayward strand of blond hair behind her ear and wouldn't quite meet his eyes. "I decided to stop by."

Cal kept his voice carefully neutral. "You've received lots of invitations from Susannah over the years. I don't remember that you've ever been inclined to accept one. Why now?"

"I'm in town."

"The only person who detests Susannah as much as I do is you. Why now?" he repeated.

She hesitated for a moment and then, withdrawing a folded white card from her purse, passed it over for him to read. It was an invitation to a party SysVal was holding to celebrate having reached half a billion dollars in sales for their fiscal year. Handwritten at the bottom of the invitation in Susannah's neat script was the message, "How long are you going to keep running away from me, Paige? What are you afraid of?"

Paige snatched the card from him and shoved it back in her purse. "Can you believe it? That prissy bitch actually thinks I'm afraid of her."

"She's very successful," he said calmly, even though the word tasted like poison in his mouth. "Probably the most prominent female executive in the country today."

"And I ended up with FBT and all of Daddy's millions. Well, tonight I'm going to rub every one of them in her face."

The enlarged Blaze logo that took up much of the back wall was the first thing that caught Paige's eye as she entered

316

SysVal's soaring lobby. As she stared at the logo, she thought of how much her sister had accomplished in six years, and she was so filled with envy that she felt dizzy. Her eyes darted through the crowd. When she saw no sign of Susannah, she forced herself to relax. If only she hadn't shown Cal the invitation, she could have backed out, but now it was too late.

A bar was set up off to the left. As she made her way toward it, she noted that SysVal's party guests favored denim and old running shoes. The beaded white satin gown that had looked so stunning at the FBT dinner she had just left was distinctly out of place here, but she didn't care. She had never been the sort of woman who needed to dress like everyone else to be comfortable.

Most of the guests were drinking beer, and the bartender had trouble finding the champagne she requested. While she waited, she thought about checking into a hotel instead of returning to Falcon Hill. The furniture was under dust covers and the house still bore the faint, sweet smell of death. Falcon Hill carried too many memories of that year when she had tried so desperately to make a home— running around baking pies and planting herb gardens like a demented Betty Crocker. She had even worn her sister's clothes. In the end it had been meaningless. She still hadn't been able to make her father love her.

She blinked her eyes hard and wished she hadn't come. After all of these years, why had she given in to the impulse to see her sister tonight? Maybe if she hadn't felt so rootless and alone after that horrible scene at her Malibu beach house three days ago, she would have tossed Susannah's invitation into the trash where it belonged.

She had actually thought she'd found Mr. Right. He was a documentary filmmaker, and they'd been seeing each other for six months. She should have realized that he was more interested in having her finance his new film than in everlasting love, but she had steadfastly ignored all of the warning signs. God, she was stupid. She had even been planning a wedding in her head.

The bartender finally handed her a glass of champagne. She decided to cancel her plans and leave tomorrow for her new villa in Sardinia. She could spend some time with Luigi or Fabio or one of the other minor Italian princes who drank Bellinis with her at the Hotel Cervo's piano bar in the evening and accompanied her back to her villa to spend the night. She had bought five houses in the past three years, each time throwing all of her energy into renovations and decorating, certain that this was the house that would finally make her happy. But happiness was proving to be one commodity that the millions her father had left her couldn't buy.

The lobby was crowded, but she found a spot along the side wall of windows where she could study the other guests. The men had already begun to notice her, which was predictable. It never took long. She looked through the windows toward the parking lot. In the reflection of the glass, she saw one of the party's male guests break away from his friends and come toward her. He had wild-looking hair, wire-rimmed glasses, and a knobby Adam's apple bobbing up and down in his throat. Terrific, she thought wearily. Just what she needed.

He planted the flat of his hand on the window next to her head, a cool operator leaving a big sweaty palm print on the glass. "I never forget a pair of beautiful eyes, and yours are gorgeous. My name's Kurt. Haven't we met somewhere before?"

"I doubt it, Kurt. I make it a practice never to talk to weenies."

He tried to smile as if she'd made a joke, but when her expression remained cool, his lips began to droop at the corners. "I, um, do you want me to get you a drink?"

She lifted her full champagne glass, making him feel even more awkward and stupid.

"Uh, how about some food? There's, uhm, some real good meat balls."

"No, thank you. But there is something you can do for me."

The muscles of his face lifted into an eager, puppy dog grin. "Sure."

"You can fuck off, Kurt. Would that be all right?"

He flushed and mumbled something before slinking away with his tail between his legs.

She bit down on the inside of her lip, making a little raw

place. He had been harmless, and she could have let him down easily. When had she become so unforgivably cruel?

"Quite a performance." A crisp, male voice spoke from behind her.

She never forgot a handsome face, and it didn't take her long to place Mitchell Blaine. The day of her father's funeral had been a blur, but she could still remember him standing at Susannah's side. He was blunt-featured, good-looking. And proper. God, was he proper. She bet he had a drawer full of perfect attendance Sunday school pins stuck away at home.

"Glad you liked it," she replied.

"I didn't like it at all. He's a nice kid."

Screw him. Screw everybody. Not a bad idea, as a matter of fact. She drained her glass. "You want to get out of here and go to bed with me?"

"Not particularly. I like women in my bed. Not children." His eyes were light blue, cold and unsmiling.

Anger rushed through her. "You bastard. Nobody talks to me like that. Do you know who I am?" Her words echoed in her ears—petulant and obnoxious. She wanted to erase them so she could say different words, words that would turn her into someone else, someone sweet and warm.

"I imagine you're Paige Faulconer. I was told that you'd been invited."

She maintained her lofty bitchy pose. "And doesn't that mean anything to you?"

"Just that the gossip I've heard is true."

"What gossip?"

"That you're a spoiled, rude little girl who should have been turned over somebody's knee a long time ago."

"Kinky. Want to give it a try?" She gave him a phony, moist-lipped smile.

"I think I'll pass. I already have two children, and I don't need another."

She didn't let him see by so much as a flicker of an eyelash how humiliated she felt. Instead, she let her words drip with condescension. "You're married. How unfortunate."

"Why? I can't imagine what possible difference that could make to you."

She swept her eyes down over his body, then lingered for

319

one long moment on his proper, gray-flannel-clad crotch. "I don't *do* married men."

To her astonishment, he laughed, a short bark of sound. "But I'll bet you *do* everybody else, don't you?"

His amusement infuriated her. Nobody laughed at her. Nobody. But before she could come up with a sufficiently cutting reply, he touched her chin with his index finger and said softly, "Ease up, honey. Life's good."

"Mitch?"

The expression that softened his blunt features as he turned his head toward the woman who had come up behind him was so warm and affectionate that Paige felt sick. She turned, too, and all the old emotions surged through her, making her bitterly regret giving into the loneliness that had led her here tonight.

She and Susannah had only seen each other a few times since their father's death, not enough for her to grow accustomed to the changes in her sister. Susannah's hair was shorter—barely reaching her jaw line—and her carriage was more relaxed. She looked free and funky, not at all like old uptight Miss Goody-Two-Shoes. Tonight she was wearing chunky gold hoops with a persimmon-colored blouse and beige slacks cinched at the waist with a fish-scale belt. But the expression on her face as she caught sight of Paige was the same as ever—tense, wary, overly conciliatory.

"Paige! No one told me you'd arrived. I'm so glad you came. Have you met my partner, Mitchell Blaine?"

"We've met," Mitch said.

Paige's lips curled in a sleek cat's smile. "I offered to go to bed with him, Susannah, but he turned me down. Is he gay?"

Susannah got that old tight look on her face, the one she use to wear every time Paige and Joel were trapped together in the same room. "Paige—"

"I'm not gay," Mitch replied. "I'm just discriminating." He brushed his lips against Susannah's cheek, squeezed her shoulder, and walked away.

"I wish you hadn't done that," Susannah said softly. "Mitch is a good friend—probably the best friend I have."

"If you don't want me to insult your friends, you shouldn't send me nasty little invitations."

"It got you here, didn't it?"

Paige lifted a glass of wine from the hand of one of the male guests who was passing and gave him a sexy smile as a reward. She tilted her head back toward her sister. "I don't think I've ever seen so many nerds gathered together in one place in my life."

"Talented nerds. Some of the most brilliant people in the Valley are in this room tonight."

"And you seem to fit right in. But then, you were always pretty much of a nerd yourself, weren't you, Susannah?"

Susannah smiled—patient, saintly Susannah. "You haven't changed, have you, Paige? You're still as tough as nails."

"You bet I am, sis."

"I wanted you to meet Sam, but he seems to have left."

Paige had avoided meeting Sam Gamble for six years, and she had no interest in doing so now. Besides, she had spotted him when she had first come into the lobby. He had been on his way out, and he had been surrounded by fawning people, just as Cal had been surrounded at the FBT reception. Although Gamble had acted as if he weren't aware of all the attention he was receiving, she hadn't believed it for one minute. Men like her sister's husband always knew exactly what they were doing. That's why they bored her.

"I recognized him when I first came in."

"He's very special," Susannah said. "Difficult, but special."

There was a burst of laughter, and someone began playing the Brady Bunch theme song over the loudspeaker. Quickly, Paige drained her wineglass. She couldn't handle this any longer.

"Sorry I can't stay, Susannah, but I've got to get back to Falcon Hill and count all the money Daddy left me."

Susannah flinched, but she didn't give up. "Let me show you around first."

"Don't take this the wrong way," Paige sneered, "but a company tour isn't exactly my idea of a good time."

Her sister stubbornly stayed by her side as Paige headed for the door. "Then let's get out of here," Susannah said, following her outside. "Come on. We'll go for a drive."

"Forget it."

"Afraid I'll eat you up?"

Paige came to a halt in the middle of the sidewalk. "I'm not afraid of you."

"Prove it." Susannah caught her arm and began steering her toward a late model BMW parked close to the building. "We'll take a drive, and I'll show you my house."

Paige jerked her arm away. "I don't want to see your house. I don't want to have anything to do with you."

Susannah stopped at the side of the car. The lights in the parking lot reflected off the hoops swinging at her ears and sent golden lights shimmering through her deep auburn hair. Susannah's new prettiness felt like another wound to Paige.

"You *are* afraid of me, aren't you, Paige?"

Paige gave a hollow laugh. "What is this? A grown-up version of I-dare-you? That was always my game, not yours."

Susannah opened the door on the driver's side and nodded toward the interior. "It's a good game. If you're not chicken, get in."

Paige knew that she didn't have to give in to Susannah's childish taunts, but she hated the smug look on her sister's face. The night stretched ahead like a hundred years, and she told herself that anything was better than going home alone to Falcon Hill. Shrugging indifferently, she got in. "Why not? I guess I don't have anything better to do at the moment."

Susannah carefully concealed her satisfaction as she pulled out of the parking lot. The more trouble she had with Sam, the more important it became to her to establish some sort of connection with her sister. Paige was her only blood relative, and surely they were both old enough by now to find new ground for a relationship. As she pulled out of the industrial complex onto the highway, she kept the conversation light. Paige answered in monosyllables or not at all. Some of Susannah's satisfaction began to fade. Paige's hostility seemed to be growing stronger instead of easing.

They left the highway and drove up into the hills. After several miles, Susannah turned into the drive that led to her house. A thick wall of shrubbery offered privacy from the road. Ahead of her the roof line rose in forbidding angles against the sky, and once again she realized how much she detested the harsh chill of this house. It was a cold temple dedicated to the worship of high technology, designed by a man who had always been obsessed with having the best.

"Cozy," Paige said sarcastically.

"Sam designed it."

"Didn't your big bad husband let you have any opinions?"

Susannah tried not to jump at the bait. "Houses aren't important to me."

Paige's evening gown rustled as she got out of the car. Instead of walking toward the pair of bronze doors that marked the entryway, she took the lighted path that led to the back of the house. Susannah followed, feeling increasingly uneasy. The beads on Paige's gown glittered like ice chips. Everything about her radiated hostility, from the stiff line of her neck to the harsh rhythm of her stride.

They cleared the side of the house and were met with the breathtaking view of the Valley. Paige stalked up the granite steps onto the bottom level of the deck and stared out at the lights. "I'll bet you're really proud of yourself, aren't you, Susannah?"

There was an ugly sneer in Paige's voice that made Susannah want to turn away. This had been a terrible idea. Why had she ever thought she could change the path of their relationship? "I've worked hard," she replied, trying to keep her tone neutral.

"I'll just bet you have," Paige spat out. "How much of that work did you do on your back?"

Susannah was stunned into silence by her sister's maliciousness.

"Now you can spend your days and nights counting your new money and laughing at Daddy in his grave."

All of Susannah's determination to renew their relationship disappeared, replaced by her own rage. "Don't say that. You know it's not true."

"It's true, all right," Paige retorted. "You showed him, didn't you? Too bad he's not still alive so you can throw your success in his face."

"I didn't do this because of him. I did it for myself."

"You're so goddamned sanctimonious. So smug and

self-righteous." Paige spoke with deadly quiet, but her words struck Susannah like small bursts of venom.

She gripped the keys she still held in her hand. "Stop right there, Paige. You're acting like a child, and I've heard enough from you."

But Paige didn't want to stop. The poison stored inside her bubbled to the surface and burst forth in short, caustic spurts. "You've always been perfect. Always right. So much better than everyone else."

"That's enough! I've tried for years to establish some sort of adult relationship with you, but I'm not going to try any longer. You're spoiled and selfish, and you don't care about anyone but yourself."

"How would you know?" Paige shouted. "You don't know anything about me. You were too busy stealing my father to ever try to understand me."

"Get out of here!" Susannah threw the keys at Paige. "Take my car and get out of my sight." Turning her back on her sister, she walked rapidly toward the door on the far side of the deck.

But Paige wasn't finished. Propelled by years of self-loathing, she came after her, running almost, ready to pummel Susannah with more hatred. Susannah couldn't bear anymore. She shoved the door open.

"Do you have any idea how much I've always hated you?" Paige shouted, rushing into the house behind her. "I'm his real daughter! Not you. But I couldn't compete with your perfection act. Do you understand that a day doesn't go by when I don't wish that you'd never been born."

Susannah stalked through the back hallway and down the steps. Paige was still at her side when she dashed into the living room.

"Why did you have to come live with us?" Paige cried. "Why did you have to be so much *better* than me?"

Susannah gasped and then the gasp turned into a soft, kittenlike mew.

On a white suede couch in the center of the room, Mindy Bradshaw was jerking her skirt down over her naked thighs, while Sam fumbled awkwardly with his trousers.

Susannah mewed again. She could feel her hands opening and closing at her sides. The world reduced itself to the scene before her and the awful mew of pain that kept rising from her throat. And then her lips began to move, to form words. They came out tinny, like the computerized voice of a robot.

"Excuse me," she said.

The apology was idiotic, obscene. Susannah staggered blindly out of the room. She knew her legs were working because the walls were moving past her. She walked up one ramp and down another, past the massive mantelpiece of stainless steel. After every four or five steps, that awful sound kept sliding out. She tried to stop it, tried to clamp her lips together, but it wouldn't be contained.

Someone touched her elbow. For a moment she thought it was Sam and tried to shake him off. Her arm was clasped more firmly, and she realized that Paige was at her side.

It was easier to concentrate on her sister than on the obscenity she had just witnessed. The lesser pain of Paige's hatred seemed almost a safe harbor in comparison to the starkness of Sam's betrayal.

Susannah felt her lips quivering again. Sam and Mindy. Sam was having sex with Mindy. Her husband. The man she had loved so blindly for so very long.

She realized she was in the kitchen. An awful pain traveled from her throat down through her stomach, a pain that crushed her heart and filled her breasts like bitter milk.

Paige spoke hesitantly. "Let's get out of here."

"Go away." Susannah shoved the words through a narrow passageway before her throat closed on a sob.

Paige's fingers grasped her arm. They were icy cold, distracting Susannah from her desperate need to draw another breath.

"Let me take you somewhere."

Susannah couldn't tolerate pity, especially coming from someone who hated her so much. "Just leave me alone," she said almost desperately. "I don't ever want to see you again."

Paige released her arm as if she had been burned and closed the keys Susannah had thrown at her in her fist. "Suit yourself. I'll send your car back in the morning."

Susannah stood at the kitchen windows and stared out into the darkness. Seconds ticked by. Paige's icy white dress whipped past. Before long, footsteps clicked on the floor behind her.

She kept her eyes on the blackness beyond the window. It was as dark as the inside of her grandmother's closet, as malevolent as a shed on the edge of the desert.

"The old silent treatment, Suzie? It's so goddamned typical of you, I don't know why I'm even surprised."

Her breath caught on a sob. He had gone on the attack. Why hadn't she realized that was what he would do? The pain was so fierce, she didn't think she could bear it. She gathered herself together as best she could and turned slowly to face him.

His black, straight hair fell over his forehead and stuck out near his ear just the way it did when she ran her fingers through it as they made love. Except this time it had been Mindy's fingers that had rumpled that beloved hair.

"I sent Mindy away," he said, as if that would make everything all right.

Tears were sliding over her lips. She tasted their salt and thought of how hard she had been fighting for her marriage, of the baby she had wanted so badly. "Was Mindy the first?" The question slipped out unwanted, but the moment she heard the words, she knew she had to have an answer.

He combed one hand through his hair. She could almost see him gathering his forces for the struggle—relishing the fact that there would be a struggle. This was what he did best—charging blindly at an insurmountable obstacle and pounding away until it gave. Her chest shuddered as she tried to hold back another sob.

"It doesn't make any difference. How many doesn't matter. Infidelity. Fidelity. Those are just words. That's not what you and I are about."

He was angry, defensive, electric with restless energy. He began to pace the kitchen, his body vibrating with tension as he dodged the black granite islands. "We've never tried to push our marriage into someone else's mold. That's why it's worked for us. We're smarter than that. We know what we want. . . ."

He talked and talked and talked.

". . . the two of us are bigger than convention. We can do

anything together. That's what's made us strong. What happened tonight is little shit, Suzie. Maybe I shouldn't have done it, but it's not important. Don't you see? It's little shit. It's not goddamned important!"

Her hands closed over a ceramic bowl on the counter in front of her. With a slash of her forearm, she sent the bowl crashing to the floor at his feet and expelled the questions that were killing her. "I want to know if she was the first! Were there others? How many others?"

Some of his belligerence began to fade in the face of her agony. For the first time he looked frightened.

"How many?" she screamed.

He was an idealist, a man dedicated to speaking the truth, and he kept to his code. "A couple of times on the road," he mumbled. "A girl I used to go with. What difference does it make? Don't you understand? This doesn't have anything to do with us."

"Yes, it does!" she screamed as she snatched up another bowl and threw it across the kitchen. "We're married. When people are married, they don't fuck other people!" She punished him with the tough, nasty obscenity that she knew he would hate.

"Stop it!" He lurched toward her, his expression vicious. "Stop doing this!"

She hissed with pain as he caught her shoulders and then, without warning, backhanded her across the cheek.

She slammed up against one of the counters. With a gasp of pain, she lifted her fingers to her face. Her nose was running. She dabbed at it with the back of her hand. As she drew it away, she saw a smear of blood.

He saw it, too. His eyes widened, stricken at what he had done. He took a step forward. "Suzie, I—"

The sight of her blood chilled her. She moved backward.

His face crumpled like a child's. "I didn't mean to hurt you. I—God, how could you do this to me? How could you make me do something like that?"

She walked past him with uneven steps, crossing the kitchen and making her way to the foyer. The closet was tucked behind a slab of polished granite that looked like a tombstone. She pulled out the small traveling bag she kept packed with basic necessities. Her cheek throbbed and her hands trembled as she snagged the strap, but a deadly calm had settled over her.

"Don't do this." Panic rang in his voice as he came up behind her. "Don't you leave me! I mean it, Suzie. If you leave, don't plan on coming back. I mean it, do you hear me?"

Tears were running down her cheeks. She turned toward him, and when she spoke, her voice was as rusty as an old saw. "You've made a mistake, Sam. Don't you see? I've turned into your vision of me. And the woman you've created won't put up with you any longer."

23

Susannah rushed from the house. Dimly, she remembered that she had no keys and that Paige had taken her car, but she didn't care. She would walk. Nothing could make her go back in that house.

She fled past a row of shrubbery and saw her car still parked in the drive. Paige sat behind the wheel, waiting like a vulture to pick the bones from her carcass. Susannah bit back a sob. She couldn't bear any more. Why hadn't Paige gone away? Didn't her sister have a speck of compassion left?

The front door banged open behind her. "Suzie!"

She heard his voice calling out to her just as he had the day he had stolen her away from her father. She stumbled, righted herself, and rushed awkwardly forward. He called out for her again. She saw Paige reach over from behind the steering wheel and push open the passenger door.

"Suzie!" he cried.

Paige's gloating seemed the lesser evil. Thrusting her traveling case into the car, she jumped in after it. Sam reached her just as Paige threw the car into reverse. She glimpsed his contorted face at the window, and then they hurled backward down the drive.

She knew Sam's ruthless determination, and she waited

with dread for him to run for his car and give chase. But he stood in the glare of the headlights without moving. She felt an absurd surge of gratitude that at least he was giving her this. Then she remembered Mindy and realized that Sam wasn't letting her go out of compassion, but because he had given Mindy his car.

The tires squealed as Paige spun onto the road and raced down the mountainside toward the highway. As times, she barely seemed to have the car under control. Maybe they would die. The prospect didn't seem so terrible.

As they moved out onto the freeway, a broken sound slipped from Susannah's lips. Her cheek still stung from his blow. Her throat was burning and her eyes were filled with hot tears. Small spasms began to wrack her body.

She had no idea how much time passed before they stopped. Numbly, she lifted her head and saw that they were at the airport. Paige walked around the front of the car and opened the door to pull her out.

"I can't— Please, Paige."

Paige gripped her arm firmly. "You'll do what I say."

Susannah tried to push her away, but her limbs had no strength. Although it was late, people were still milling around. She realized with paralyzing certainty that Paige was going to parade her in front of everyone in the airport and that she couldn't do anything to stop her.

She was wrong. Her sister led her into a private lounge and immediately brought her a cup of coffee. Her stomach rebelled at the smell and she pushed it away. Paige searched through her case and pulled out the passport that Susannah always kept there. She slipped it into her own purse, then went over to a phone bank and began making calls. A little later she returned.

"There's a British Airways flight leaving for Heathrow in an hour. I've booked us seats. We'll pick up a plane to Athens from there."

"Athens?" she repeated dully. "I can't go to Greece. I have a job."

"Your job will hold for a few weeks. I've got this house on Naxos." For the first time, Paige hesitated. "It's nice there. The sun's hot and everything's white and pure." And then her mouth grew sullen, as if she didn't really care whether Susannah accepted or not.

Susannah covered her cheek with her hand. "I can't possibly go away. I have responsibilities." Even as she forced out the words, she couldn't imagine going to work on Monday and facing Sam again.

Paige stared out into the middle of the lounge and plucked at one of the bead-spangled flowers on the skirt of her evening gown. "I have these cats. They're silly, really. Not pedigreed or anything. But I want to show them to you."

A strange combination of belligerence and yearning mingled in Paige's voice. She continued to pick at the beads on her skirt. Susannah stared across the lounge and tried to take in what had happened to her, but the pain kept her mind from working. Suddenly, it seemed perfectly reasonable that she should fly halfway around the world to see Paige's cats. At least she wouldn't have to go to work on Monday.

The rocky islands of the Cyclades lie spattered over the turquoise waters of the Aegean like so many pebbles flung by a giant fist. Birthplace of ancient myths and legends, the islands are a mecca for lovers of Greek antiquity. The spirit of Narcissus is said to have been reincarnated on Mykonos, Thira is suspected to be the lost continent of Atlantis, and Naxos was the refuge of Ariadne after she saved Theseus from the labyrinth of her father, King Minos.

Susannah had been to the Greek islands several times before, although never to the island of Naxos. As the battered jeep made its way inland from the dusty airstrip, a white-hot sun hovered in the bleached sky overhead. They had left the tourist town of Chora with its discotheques and Coca-Cola signs far behind and were crossing the heart of the island. Susannah was barely aware of the breathtaking contrasts around her—the stark moonscape of rocky hills silhouetted against the brilliant blue green of the sea. Squat windmills perched near slopes terraced with vineyards, fruit, and olive trees. The gears of the old jeep ground ominously as they made their way through the steep twisting streets of the villages, some so narrow that the driver had to stop and wait for a donkey to pass because there was not enough room for both animal and vehicle to travel side by side.

Susannah's eyes scratched like sandpaper against splintered wood and her body ached with exhaustion. They had been traveling forever. She was no longer even certain what day it was, and she couldn't remember why she had ever agreed to come on this trip.

Paige sat silently next to her. The fierce glare of the late afternoon sun turned her tumbled hair into tarnished silver. In her rumpled, soiled evening gown, she looked beautiful and dissolute, like a ruined playgirl left over from a Fitzgerald novel. She had handled passports and tickets, the delay at Heathrow, the complex arrangements to get to Naxos, all the business of traveling that Susannah normally managed so expertly. In all that time Susannah hadn't spoken a word to her.

It was evening when they reached the cottage on the eastern side of the island. Susannah stumbled numbly into the room Paige indicated. She was aware of the sound of the sea and clean lavender-scented sheets. Then she slept.

When she awoke late the next morning, sunlight was trickling through the closed shutters and throwing hyphens of light on the white stucco walls of the room. Her body felt heavy and sore as she made her way into the tiny bathroom. She showered, then slipped into a pair of seersucker shorts and a light blue halter top she found lying across the foot of the bed.

She winced as she stepped out into the rustic interior of the cottage's main room and a blaze of sunlight hit her full in the face. A sharp pain pierced her temple. She made her way over to the open screenless windows and saw that the white stucco cottage clung precariously to a barren hillside overlooking the sea. Even though she had vacationed on the Aegean several times before, she had forgotten the depth of the water's jewellike tones. It spread before her like a bottomless pool of azure tears.

She turned back to the room and tried to find some sense of peace in the simplicity of her surroundings. An earthenware bowl of peaches sat on the scrubbed wooden table, while a basket of geraniums caught the sunlight in one of the windows. The windowframes, shutters, and door were all painted the same bright cerulean blue as the Aegean, and the thick stucco walls of the cottage were so crisp and clean, they looked as if they had just been whitewashed. She felt as if she had been plunged into a world where only three colors existed—the dull gray-brown tones of the bare hillside, the blazing white of stucco and sky, and the rich, cerulean blue of sea, shutters, and doorway.

A fat tabby walked across the flagstone floor and rubbed against her ankles. "That's Rudy," Paige said, coming into the room from outside. "Misha's taking a nap on the patio."

Paige wore a faded bandanna top and a pair of cutoffs so threadbare that her skin beneath was visible in several places. Her feet were bare, her face free of makeup, and she had snared her hair into an untidy ponytail. Even so, she looked beautiful.

Susannah couldn't believe that she had put herself in the position of being dependent on Paige. She had to get out of here. As soon as possible, she had to leave.

"You look like shit," Paige said, picking up the blue and white striped dish towel that hung next to the stone sink in the kitchen and using it to pull a fragrant loaf of brown bread from the oven. "Go keep Misha company on the patio. The table's all set and breakfast is almost ready."

"You shouldn't have bothered," Susannah said coldly. "I've made a mistake. I have to get back."

Paige set a sweating pitcher of fruit juice on top of a tray that held two blue glass goblets. "Carry this out. I'll be there in a few minutes."

For the moment it was easier to do as she was told than to argue. Susannah stepped through the door onto a patio paved with smooth brown pebbles. She squinted while her eyes adjusted to the light and the breathtaking view of sky and sea below. An old olive-wood gateleg table holding handwoven place mats, ceramic plates, and cutlery was sheltered from the sun by a lacy network of jasmine trees growing up from the other side of the stucco wall. Wooden chairs sat at each end, their rush seats covered with plump blue pillows. Flowers spilled over the tops of fat pottery crocks, and the old stone head of a lion provided a spot of shade for a sleeping cat.

The animal looked up as Susannah set the tray on the table. Then he stretched, yawned, and went back to sleep. Paige began bringing out food: mugs of coffee, a bowl of eggs soft-boiled in their speckled brown shells, a majolica plate arranged with a sunburst of melon slivers. She cut the bread she had just baked into thick slices and then spread one with butter. It melted into little amber puddles as she held it out to Susannah.

Susannah shook her head. "I'm sorry. I don't feel like eating."

"Give it a try."

Susannah couldn't remember the last time she had eaten —not on the plane, certainly. She hadn't eaten at the party. Her stomach rumbled as the warm, yeasty scent pricked her nostrils. She took the bread, and as she bit into it, she discovered that the simple act of chewing provided a momentary distraction from the pain that wouldn't go away. She sipped at a glass of freshly squeezed orange juice and ate part of a melon slice. When her stomach began to rebel, she cuddled a mug of coffee and gazed out at the sea.

With the meal over, the awkwardness between them increased. In the past she would have broken it with inconsequential chatter, but she no longer cared enough about her relationship with Paige to make the effort. The fantasy of sisterly love had died along with everything else. Paige began to tell Susannah about the cottage and how she had restored it. Then she fetched a San Francisco Giants baseball cap for herself and a straw hat for Susannah and announced that they were going to walk down to the beach.

Susannah followed, simply because she couldn't summons the energy to do anything else. Paige led the way around to the side of the house where there was a gentler drop to the beach than the sheer cliff face that fell from below the patio. Even so, the descent exhausted Susannah. Paige walked over the rocks and hot sand to the water's edge, then dipped her toes in the sea.

"You didn't say anything about breakfast. How did you like my homemade bread?"

"It was delicious," Susannah replied politely. What had

she done wrong? her brain screamed. Why had Sam gone to other women?

Paige kicked at a wave. "I love to cook."

There was a long pause. Susannah realized that she needed to say something. "Really? I hate it."

Paige looked at her strangely. "You always took over the kitchen on the cook's days off."

"Who else was going to do it?"

Paige leaned over and picked up a small smooth stone. "I might have."

"Maybe," Susannah said bitterly. "Or maybe you would have just told me to go to hell."

It was the first time she could remember inflicting the initial blow, but Paige didn't respond. Instead, she pulled off her baseball cap and tossed it down on the beach.

Susannah gazed up the hillside. The cottage seemed miles away. "I think I'm going to climb back up and take a nap. Then I need to make arrangements to get back."

"Not yet." Paige unsnapped her cutoffs. "We're going to swim first."

"I'm too tired to swim."

"It'll do you good." Paige pulled off her cutoffs to reveal lacy white underpants. She slipped them down with her thumbs and then unfastened her top. "This is my very own nude beach. Nobody ever comes here."

As Paige discarded her clothes, Susannah looked at her sister's body. Paige's breasts were larger than her own. Her waist was trim and her stomach flat. She was golden all over. Sam would have liked Paige's body. He liked big breasts.

"Come on," Paige taunted, dancing backward into the waves. "Or are you chicken?" She slapped the water, sending a splatter of drops in Susannah's direction.

Susannah was pierced with a desperate longing. She wanted to forget what had happened, to be young and carefree and splash in the waves like her sister. She wanted to touch the childhood that had been denied her, to go to a place where betrayal didn't exist. Instead, she shook her head and climbed the hill back to the cottage.

That afternoon, Paige went off to the village on a battered moped while Susannah lay in the shade of the jasmine trees and punished herself. She should have cooked more meals for Sam. She should have shared his passion for that awful house.

A chill settled over her that even the Greek sun couldn't dispel. Hadn't these last six years taught her anything? Why was she so quick to assume blame for the problems in their marriage? Sam had been betraying her for a long time—and not just with other women. He had been passing judgment on everything she did and criticizing her when she didn't live up to his invisible spec sheet. He had scoffed at her need for a child, ignored her attempts to repair their marriage. And like a little boy, he had looked to her to fix all the problems he had within himself. She had endured Sam's bad temper, his arrogance, and his small cruelties. But if she endured his infidelity, he would have swallowed her whole.

They ate an early dinner and went to bed not long after dark. In the morning she told herself to make arrangements to return to San Francisco, but she dozed on the patio instead. One day slipped into the next. Paige fed her and made her walk down to the beach every morning, but otherwise she left her alone. Toward the end of the week, she produced a second moped and decreed that Susannah was riding into the village with her to help shop for dinner. Susannah protested, but Paige was insistent, so she did as she was told.

On the way, Paige pulled into a lovely old olive grove that had been part of the island for centuries. As they wandered silently through the trees, Susannah breathed in the fresh scent of earth and growing things. She rubbed her palm over her slim waist and pressed that barren flatness. The tears she had been repressing pricked her eyes. Now there would be no baby to grow inside her.

She stopped under a twisted old tree and stared off into the distance. Paige plopped down in the shade. The afternoon was so still, Susannah felt as if she had found the end of the world. If only she could locate exactly the right place, she might be able to drop off the edge.

After days of barely speaking at all, words began to tumble from her lips. "I didn't know he was sleeping with other women. I knew we had problems, but I thought our sex life was all right. I really did."

"It probably was."

Susannah turned on her. "It couldn't have been or he would have stayed faithful."

"Grow up, Susannah. Some people don't feel alive unless they're having sex with half the world." Paige's face took on a closed, hard expression.

"But he loves me," she said fiercely. "Despite everything he says and everything he's done, he loves me."

"What about you?"

"Of course I love him!" she cried, furious with Paige for asking the question. "I gave up everything for him. I have to love him!" She sucked in her breath as her words hit her. What was she saying? Did she truly love Sam or was she still caught up in an old, worn-out obsession?

"I'm definitely not an expert on love," Paige said slowly. "But I think there are lots of different kinds. Some are good and some are bad."

"How do you tell the difference?"

"The good love makes you better, I guess. Bad love doesn't."

"Then what Sam and I had was definitely good love, because he made me better."

"Did he? Or did you do it yourself?"

"You don't understand. Daddy wanted me to be his perfect daughter. Sam told me I should be strong and free. I listened to Sam, Paige. I listened to him and I believed him."

"And what happened?"

"A miracle happened. I discovered that Sam's vision was right for me. It was a perfect fit."

"That should have made him happy." Cynicism edged Paige's words.

Susannah blinked against the sting of tears. "But it didn't. A big part of Sam liked the old Susannah Faulconer. Deep inside, I don't think he wanted me to change at all."

"I like the new Susannah."

The unusual softness in Paige's voice pierced through Susannah's misery, and she looked at her sister as if she were seeing her for the first time. Against the sunlight, Paige's profile was as soft and blurred as an angel's. "Did I treat you so terribly when we were growing up?"

Paige plucked at a blade of grass. "You treated me

wonderfully. I hated you for it. I wanted you to be awful to me so I could justify how awful I was to you."

Something warm opened inside Susannah like a loaf of her sister's bread. The awful chill that wouldn't go away thawed a little.

"I thought if you were out of the way, Daddy would love me," Paige said. "But he never did. Not really. You were everything to him. Even after you left, he let me know I couldn't compete. The irony of it was that I did so many things better than you—the meals were more imaginative, the house prettier. But he never saw that. He only saw the things I didn't do well."

Paige's unhappiness touched a chord inside Susannah. "After the way you've taken care of me, I can't imagine you not doing anything well."

Paige shrugged off the compliment. "Look at my checking account some time. And I'm completely disorganized. I hate everything connected with FBT business. Daddy should never have left the company to me. I don't know what I would have done without Cal."

Susannah looked away.

"He's been a good friend to me, Susannah," Paige said earnestly. "You really humiliated him."

"I know that. And the selfish part of me doesn't care. Isn't that awful? I'm so glad to have escaped marrying him that I'm willing to feel guilty about what I did to him for the rest of my life."

"Even though escaping Cal meant that you married Sam?"

Susannah stared at the dappled shadows on the ground. Nothing had changed, but some of the turmoil inside her seemed to have eased. "I could never regret having had Sam in my life. In a funny way, he created me, just like he created the Blaze. In the end I guess his vision of me wasn't right for him. But it was right for me."

"Are you going back to him?"

The pain that was never far away spread through her again. She was a fighter, and she didn't take her marriage vows lightly. In the deep quiet of the olive grove, the vow she had made on her wedding day came back to her as clearly as if she had just spoken it. *I promise to give you my best, Sam, whatever that may be.* As the words echoed in her mind, she knew that she had done exactly that, and she finally understood the time had come to begin fighting for herself.

"No," she murmured. "No, I'm not going back."

"That's good," Paige said softly.

For dinner that night, Paige fixed a cheese pie with fresh marjoram and tossed a handful of pine nuts into a dish of green beans. As Susannah ate her sister's wonderful food, she began to feel at peace with herself. Something important had happened in the olive grove. Maybe she had finally completed the task she had begun when she'd run away from home. Maybe she had found herself.

The next morning after breakfast, Paige once again dragged her down to the beach. As she stripped off her clothes, she said, "This time you're going in the water. No more excuses."

Susannah began to protest, but she stopped herself. How much longer was she going to wallow in self-pity? Reaching for the tie at the back of her neck, she unfastened her halter top, then pulled off her clothes until she was as naked as her sister.

"I've got bigger boobs than you," Paige called out in a deliberately taunting voice as Susannah waded into the surf.

"I've got longer legs," Susannah retaliated.

"Giraffe legs."

"Better than duck legs."

The water was sun-warmed and wonderful, the surf gentle. Susannah bent her knees and settled down so that the water covered her shoulders. The sea was gentle and soothing. For a while, anyway, it made her feel well again.

"You can't stay out too long," Paige said, flipping over onto her back. "You're a real paleface. Not to mention other parts of you." A wave passed in a swirl of foam beneath her. "What should we have for dinner tonight?"

Susannah turned on her back to float. "We just finished breakfast."

"I like to plan ahead. Lamb, I think. And a tomato and

cucumber salad with feta crumbled on the top. Stuffed eggplant— You're starting to drift out. Come back in."

Susannah obediently did as she was told.

That evening they worked together in the kitchen. Paige opened a bottle of Skeponi, a local wine, and poured two glasses for them to sip while they worked. "Slice that cucumber thinner, Susannah. Those things look like hockey pucks."

"I'm not enjoying this," Susannah grumbled after she produced another slice that was too thick to meet her sister's approval. "Why don't you cook while I straighten out your checkbook?"

"You're on," Paige said, laughing.

Five minutes later, both sisters were happily occupied— Paige with a hollowed-out eggplant and a mixture of pine nuts, herbs, and currants; Susannah with her pocket calculator and what she quickly labeled "the checkbook from hell."

Just as they were getting ready to eat, Susannah heard the sound of a moped approaching the cottage. Paige stiffened. The moped stopped, and several seconds later someone knocked. As Paige opened the door, Susannah glimpsed a handsome young Greek with thick curly hair. Paige immediately stepped outside, but Susannah could hear bits of conversation through the open window.

". . . in village today. Why you not come to me?"

"I have company, Aristo. You shouldn't have come here."

The conversation went on for several minutes. When Paige reentered the cottage, the old hard look had settled over her face. "One of my legion of lovers," she said tightly, picking up the last of the serving dishes and carrying them to the old kitchen table.

Susannah brought over the wine bottle and poured them each a second glass. "You want to talk about it?" she asked cautiously.

Paige's tone immediately grew caustic. "What's there to say? Unlike you, I've never been Miss Pure and Innocent."

It was Paige's first attack. Susannah set down her wineglass. "What are the new ground rules between us, Paige?"

"I don't know what you mean."

"If it weren't for you, I'd probably be curled up in a ball someplace. You've taken care of me in a way no one else ever has. But does that mean we can only get along if I need you? Not if you need me?"

Paige toyed with one of the wrinkled oily olives in her salad. "I like taking care of people. I just never get the chance."

"You're getting the chance now, and I'm not ready to give it up." Her voice broke a little. "I feel battered, Paige. You've given me sanctuary. I'm not used to needing people, and it scares me to think about how much I need you right now."

Paige's eyes filled in response. "I always wanted to be just like you."

Susannah tried to smile, but couldn't quite manage it. "And I wanted to be like you—a rebel giving the world the finger."

"Some rebel," Paige scoffed. "I don't want my life to be this way. I'm tired of running all over the world and having sex with men I can't stand."

"Then why do you do it?"

"I don't know. Sex lets me connect, you know. Except I don't connect at all, and that makes me hate myself."

And then she told Susannah about the boy who had raped her when she was sixteen. She spoke of Aristo and Luigi and Fabio and the string of lovers who existed like spoiled meat everywhere she went. She talked about the filmmaker she had imagined she was in love with and the abortion she couldn't quite forget.

Afterward, they were silent. Susannah thought of the roles they had been assigned from the time they were small children. Paige played the rebel daughter while she took the part of the obedient conventional one. But all along it should have been the other way around. They were like two sisters who had gotten their parts mixed up at some cosmic version of Central Casting.

Paige abruptly shattered the silence. "I'm starved."

Their dinner had long grown cold, but they fell on it

anyway, both of them suddenly lighthearted from the connection they had made with each other.

"You know what I really want?" Paige said, stuffing a gooey chunk of eggplant into her mouth with her fingers. "I want to mother the whole world. Sort of like a slutty version of Mother Teresa."

Susannah, who hadn't imagined she would even be able to smile again, burst out in laughter. They drank more wine and Paige told terrible jokes and they cleaned up the dishes together. Afterward, Paige moved a small lamp into the center of the kitchen table. She gave Susannah her old mulish look. "I bought something for us in the village. If you start laughing again, I won't speak to you for the rest of my life."

"All right. I won't laugh."

"Promise?"

"I promise."

Paige reached into one of the cupboards and pulled out a cheap coloring book along with a brand new package of Crayola crayons.

Susannah hooted with laughter. "You want us to color?"

Paige gave her a snotty look. "Do you have a problem with that?"

"Oh, no. I think it's a wonderful idea." Without thinking about what she was doing, she swept her sister into her arms and hugged her so tightly that Paige let out a yelp.

They settled down at the table, chairs butted up next to each other as the two Faulconer sisters bent their heads over the coloring book. Susannah worked on the left page, her sister on the right. Paige fancifully shaded her cartoon cow in pinks and roses, then added a comically oversized hat. Her artistic eye held no regard for the thick black outlines of the drawing, even as her homey soul craved strong, respectable borders.

Susannah neatly outlined all the separate parts of her lady pig before she dutifully filled in the blocks of color. Constriction was fine in coloring books, she discovered, but it wouldn't do at all in real life.

"Not fair, Susannah. You wore the point down on the blue crayon. I can't stand it when the points aren't sharp."

And because Susannah cared more about pushing life to its limits than she did about crayons, she gave Paige the sharp ones and used the dull, blunt nubs herself.

It was an arrangement that made them both blissfully happy.

24

●●●●●●●●●●●●●●●●●●●●●●●●●●●

Mitch stood at the edge of the patio and gazed down at the secluded beach from behind a pair of silver-rimmed aviator's sunglasses. A sweat stain had dared to form a patch on the back of his pale blue knit shirt, and his gray slacks were rumpled from the long plane trip. But fresh clothes were the furthest thing from his mind as he watched the two women playing in the surf below.

Paige's body, with its full centerfold breasts, was the more voluptuous, but it was Susannah's lean, thoroughbred form that held his attention. Water glittered like crystals on her shoulders, her breasts, and the flat plane of her belly. It slithered down the small of her back and glossed her small, sweet ass as she waded at the edge of the waves.

He knew he shouldn't watch, but the sight of her held him in a grip that was so powerfully erotic, he couldn't turn his head away. Thou shalt not covet thy partner's wife, a voice whispered. But he had been coveting his partner's wife for a very long time.

He didn't know exactly when in the past few years friendship had turned to love or affection had become desire. There was no specific moment he could point to and say—now! Right now I know that Susannah Faulconer is the woman I've been looking for my entire life. He certainly hadn't wanted to fall in love with her. It was messy. Inconvenient. It absolutely violated his moral code. But just the sight of her filled him with a piercing sweetness that transcended anything he had ever felt for a woman.

Except now that her farce of a marriage was finally over, that sweetness had been distorted by anger. For years he had kept his emotions firmly leashed when he was around her. He had never slipped, not once. But when he had heard what had happened, something inside him snapped. He wanted to shake her for her stupidity, for all those wasted years she had held on. He wanted to shake her until he rattled loose whatever it was inside her that had made her an emotional slave to Sam Gamble.

And now he would have to comfort her. He would have to be good old Mitch, patting her back and pretending to be sad right along with her. He would have to be her compassionate and understanding friend when he didn't want to be a friend at all, when he wanted to kick up his heels and shout, "Good riddance."

That's what he wanted her to do, too. He wanted her to look up into his eyes and say, "Thank God that's over. Now you and I have a chance."

But Susannah wasn't frivolous with her emotions, and he knew that wouldn't happen—not for a very long time, if ever.

The recent turn of events at SysVal made everything more complicated. As he remembered the crisis that had arisen so abruptly, he wondered what he would do if she weren't ready to go back with him.

Paige looked up at the cottage, interrupting his thoughts. He could tell by the way her body grew still that she had spotted him, but he didn't back away. Susannah continued to play in the waves, so he knew that her sister hadn't shared the news that they had an observer. If Paige wasn't going to tell, neither would he. He continued to watch.

Susannah was astonished to see the back of a man's head and shoulders rising above one of the patio chairs as she came up from the beach. He turned and smiled at her, the sun glinting off the metal rims of his aviator glasses as he stood.

"Well, if it isn't SysVal's lost lady."

"Mitch! What are you doing here?"

"I was in the neighborhood."

She rushed toward him and then remembered that she was naked beneath her beach towel. Clutching it more tightly in her fist, she leaned forward and kissed a jaw that bore an uncharacteristically rakish stubble.

His hand pressed flat against the small of her back for a moment and then he released her. "I've been worried about you. It's been three weeks."

Had it been so long? September had slid into October and she had barely noticed. "You came this far just because you were worried?"

To her surprise, the corners of his mouth tightened in the subtle sign that indicated he was upset. "You could have telephoned, Susannah. You must have known—" He broke off as something just behind her caught his attention.

Susannah turned her head to investigate, and to her dismay saw Paige standing on the edge of the patio, the beach towel wrapped low on her hips, her breasts as brown and bare as one of Gauguin's Tahitian women.

"Well, well, well," Paige said. "If it isn't Mister—Black, is it?"

"Blaine," he said. He gazed at her for a moment, and then dropped his head so that it was obvious he was deliberately staring at her breasts through his sunglasses. "You're looking well, Paige."

Susannah was embarrassed. And then she wondered why she should be uncomfortable. These two were both pros. Mitch certainly knew what he was doing, and Paige had to work out her devils in her own way.

Paige looked over at Susannah, obviously expecting her to intercede in some way. Susannah lifted an eyebrow. *You got yourself into this, sister mine. Now you can get yourself out.*

She could see Paige begin to grow flustered. Mitch stubbornly refused to redirect his gaze. Paige made an elaborate show of yawning as if all this were too, too boring for words. "I'm thirsty," she said. "I guess I'll go get us something to drink."

Susannah had to suppress the urge to applaud her sister's

feistiness. Paige knew she had lost the battle, but she was going down fighting.

Paige, however, had one final salvo to deliver. "You really should have come swimming with us, Mr. Blaine, instead of standing up here spying. It would have been so much cooler." With a smug glance at her sister, she disappeared inside the cottage.

Susannah rounded on Mitch. "You were spying on us?"

He slowly pulled off his sunglasses and folded in the stems. "Not spying exactly."

"Then what, exactly?"

"Just sort of watching."

"I don't believe this! Mitch, how could you do something so slimy?"

"Aw, come on, Susannah. Ease up, will you?" He stuffed his glasses in his shirt pocket. "What would you have done if you were a healthy heterosexual male who just happened to stumble on the sight of two beautiful naked women cavorting in the water?"

She saw his point, but she didn't have too much fondness for any member of the male sex at the moment, and she refused to give in. "I'm not beautiful, and I'm not a woman. I'm your business partner."

"Ri-i-ght. And for a business partner, you've got a ter-rific—"

He broke off as he found himself on the receiving end of one of the more chilling of her glares—the glare that, five years ago, she had reserved for anyone who had the audacity to ask SysVal to pay its bills on time.

He studied her for a few moments and the teasing light faded from his eyes. Once again, she observed an almost imperceptible tightening at the corner of his mouth. "Are you okay?" he asked.

She shrugged, then sat down on one of the rush-seated chairs, keeping her towel tucked securely beneath her arms. With the tip of her finger, she traced a bright terry-cloth stripe that ran across the tops of her thighs. "Did you know, Mitch?"

He wandered over to the stucco wall and looked down at the sea. "Know what?"

"About Sam and Mindy? About the others?"

The breeze lifted his hair as he turned back to her. He nodded.

She felt as if she had been hit with a new betrayal. "Sam's infidelity was common knowledge, wasn't it? Everyone knew but me."

"I wouldn't say it was common knowledge, but . . ."

Slowly she rose from the chair and gazed at him. "We're friends. Why didn't you tell me?"

He studied her and said quietly, "I thought you knew."

She felt sick at her stomach. Was this the opinion Mitch had of her? Did everyone see her as some spineless creature who turned a blind eye to Sam's wanderings? "Don't you know me better than that?"

"Where Sam is concerned, I don't know you at all."

He seemed to be condemning her, and she resented it. "You're blaming me, aren't you?"

"Sam is one of the greatest visionaries in our business, but when it comes to personal relationships, everyone knows he's pretty much a loser. I guess what I don't understand is why you're the only one who was really surprised. Why is that, Susannah?"

Hurt welled inside her. She couldn't believe that Mitch was attacking her. "I didn't ask you to come here, and I don't want you prying into my life."

He glared at her, the corners of his mouth growing tighter by the second. And then something seemed to give way inside him. "Aw shit." He closed the distance between them in two long strides and wrapped her in his big, bear arms.

She needed his comfort, and she was more than willing to forgive him. Wrapping her own arms around his waist, she laid her cheek against the solid wall of his chest where she could hear his heart pumping beneath her ear. "I loved him, Mitch," she whispered. "I loved him and I didn't want to know."

He drew her closer, rubbing his hands up and down her back through the towel. "I know, honey," he murmured, his voice sounding slightly hoarse. "It'll be all right."

As he spoke, the motion of his chin scraped her temple. His fingers rose above the top edge of the beach towel and touched her skin. She closed her eyes, drawing comfort from his presence in a way she had never been comforted by Sam.

And then something changed. His body began to grow tense. The muscles in his arms hardened until she felt as if she were being imprisoned instead of sheltered. A warning bell went off inside her. His leg pressed against the center line of her thighs as if he were trying to push them apart. She had never been so aware of his greater strength, never before felt threatened by it. This was Mitch, she told herself. It was only Mitch. And then he crushed the beach towel in his fists.

"Mitch!" She rescued the towel and pushed herself away at the same time.

He let her go so abruptly that she stumbled. She trapped the towel before it could fall and righted herself. "Mitch, what—" But as she raised her eyes to his face, she couldn't remember what she had been about to say.

"Yes, Susannah?" he asked calmly.

He looked as solid and unflappable as ever. She began to feel stupid. What was wrong with her? Mitch didn't present any threat. Was this going to be another legacy that Sam had left her—the sense that all men were dangerous?

"Hors d'oeuvres, anyone?" Paige appeared with a tray of cheese, black olives, and crackers.

Her head had begun to ache, and she was grateful for her sister's interruption. Excusing herself, she went into the cottage to shower.

Paige—out of pure mischievousness, Susannah was certain—insisted Mitch stay with them in the cottage. That evening she outdid herself with a meal of plump prawns sautéed in butter and herbs, rice pilaf, Greek salad, and a chewy loaf of fresh, warm bread. Mitch was effusive with his compliments, and Paige's cheeks took on a rosy flush. Neither of them paid much attention to Susannah.

Over bowls of apple cobbler drizzled with cream, Mitch entertained them with a story about Yank losing his new Porsche at a shopping mall. He was so amusing that before long Susannah relaxed and joined in. The tension between Susannah and Mitch dissipated, and they were soon trying to top each other, telling Paige stories about Yank. When they began describing Yank's habit of misplacing his girlfriends, Paige accused them of exaggerating. "Nobody's that much of a nerd."

Susannah and Mitch looked at each other and laughed.

But Susannah's lighter mood vanished after dinner when Mitch broached the subject of her return to California. She knew she couldn't stay here forever—she had already been away much too long—but the thought of returning made her insides twist. "I'm not ready. I can't go back yet."

His brow furrowed and he looked as if he were about to say something more, but he merely took a sip of coffee and asked Paige about the island. The strain between them was back.

For the next two days, Mitch and Paige baited each other until Susannah wanted to slap them both. Mitch continued to bring up the subject of Susannah's return, but she refused to discuss it. He began to make vague allusions to a new problem at SysVal. She ignored him. For the past six years she had dedicated herself to the company. Someone else could take over for a while.

By the third day, Mitch could no longer postpone his departure. "We need you in California, Susannah," he said once again, as he handed over his suitcase to the driver of the jeep that was taking him to the airstrip in Chora. "Come with me. We can get a later plane." Once again, she had the sense that he was holding something back.

"Soon," she replied quickly. "I won't stay much longer."

"When? Damn it, Susannah—"

Paige quickly intervened, jumping into the fray like a mother bear defending her cub. Using tactics that were distinctly her own, she brushed her small body against Mitch's big one and gave him her poutiest smile. "So long, Mitch. Look me up whenever you decide you're man enough to go skinny dipping with me."

Instead of ignoring Paige's baiting, he smiled. For a moment his eyes flicked to Susannah, and then he cupped Paige by the back of her neck and gave her a long, deliberate kiss.

When Susannah saw his tongue slip into her sister's mouth, she looked away. She was well aware that Mitch had a strongly sexual nature tucked away beneath his endless supply of navy-blue suits, but it made her uncomfortable to witness it.

Mitch pulled back and slapped Paige's rear. "Keep it warm for me, lamb chop. One of these days, I just might run out of interesting things to do and take you up on your offer."

He brushed Susannah's cheek with a friendly kiss and climbed into the jeep. Paige shaded her eyes with her hands and watched the vehicle disappear. "Mitch Blaine is definitely one hell of a man."

It was the first time Susannah had ever heard her sister speak about any male without cynicism. She suppressed a stab of jealousy because Paige was forming a relationship with Mitch while her own friendship seemed to be showing mysterious signs of strain.

"I should have gone back with him," she said stiffly. "I don't know what's wrong with me. I can't stay here forever."

Paige draped a comforting arm over her sister's shoulders. "Give yourself a little more time."

Time didn't help. Another week passed, but whenever Susannah thought of returning to California, her heart began to race. One afternoon, she stood at the stone sink washing up their luncheon dishes while Paige went into the village, and as she dried a serving bowl, she told herself she had to do something soon. It wasn't fair to impose upon Paige much longer. For the first time, she let herself think about leaving SysVal and going to another company. Her misery was so encompassing that she didn't hear the jeep pulling up outside the cottage.

Yank hated to travel. He could never find his tickets and his boarding passes disappeared. He picked up the wrong luggage and always seemed to end up next to crying babies. Occasionally he became so absorbed in his thoughts that he missed his boarding call altogether and the plane took off without him. As a result, SysVal had an unwritten policy that he was never to be sent on a business trip alone. But Mitch hadn't been able to retrieve Susannah, and they certainly couldn't send Sam. That meant Yank had to do the job.

His coworkers would have been surprised to know how efficiently he had managed the complicated trip to the island of Naxos. They still didn't understand that he was able to function quite well when he chose to. It was just that most of the time he didn't choose to.

As he got out of the jeep in front of the cottage, he made a precise currency conversion in his head and then tipped the driver exactly fifteen percent of the fare, counting out the drachmas and organizing them into precise piles in the palm of his hand. When he was done, he carefully slipped his wallet back into his pocket so he wouldn't lose it and picked up his suitcase. It was leather and monogrammed with matching Y's. A former girlfriend had given it to him as a present for his thirtieth birthday. Later, his accountant told him that she had charged it on one of Yank's own credit cards.

While he walked up the path to the cottage, he organized his thoughts and mentally prepared himself for the task of retrieving Susannah. This was a job he couldn't afford to bungle. It was too important to all of them.

She answered the door after his first knock. She appeared so tired and sad that Yank wanted to hug her, but of course he didn't. All the feeling he had held for her since the evening Sam had brought her to the Homebrew meeting rushed through him like a bombardment of electrons.

"Yank!" Susannah's mouth grew slack with astonishment. She glanced past his shoulder to see who had brought him. He could almost feel her dread that it might be Sam.

"Hello, Susannah." He watched as she tilted her head to the side to look behind him again. "I'm alone."

"Alone?"

He nodded.

Her forehead wrinkled. "Did someone come part of the way with you?"

"I came all the way alone."

"All the way to Greece?"

"Could I come in, Susannah? And if it isn't too much trouble, I'd very much like something to drink."

"Of course." She stepped aside to admit him, but she couldn't resist one last peek outside before she shut the door.

"I think we have some Greek beer," she said. "But—Why are you here, Yank?"

"I've come to get you," he said simply. "I've come to take you home."

The sun was in Paige's eyes, so for a moment she thought the man standing with his back to her on the patio was Mitch. A flash of pleasure washed through her at the idea of engaging in another round of sexual dueling with the delectably stuffy Mr. Blaine. But then she realized that the man looking out toward the sea was much leaner than Mitch and even taller—maybe four or five inches over six feet.

As he turned toward her, she caught her breath. What an incredibly arresting man! His brown hair was side-parted and well-cut. His features were unusually sharp: bladed cheekbones, a thin straight nose, finely chiseled lips—all of it topped by a pair of light brown eyes that were widely spaced and compelling. He was casually dressed in a charcoal shirt with a pair of chinos and a webbed belt. A nearly empty bottle of Greek beer was clasped in his hand, and a gold watch with a leather strap encircled his wrist. All in all, he was an extremely tempting piece of male flesh.

She took a step toward him and stopped as a prickle of unease traveled up her spine. He was looking at her so strangely, almost as if he were taking her apart and examining the separate pieces—the iris of an eye, the curl that brushed her cheek, her chin, a breast. He shifted his gaze to her other breast, regarded it with great concentration, and then moved his eyes down over her torso to her hips. Instead of being insulted, she felt curiously flattered.

"Should I turn around so you can see the rest?"

"Not unless you'd like to." His voice was so deep and soft that it almost seemed to have blown in off the sea.

The door of the cottage opened and Susannah came out with a glass of ice water. She looked tense and frazzled. "Paige, you're back. I didn't hear the moped."

"Just got here." Paige set down the string bag of produce from the market and once again glanced curiously toward their visitor.

"Paige, this is Yank Yankowski. Yank, my sister Paige."

Paige nearly choked. This was Yank? This was the dopey

genius that Susannah and Mitch had told her all those stories about? Had Susannah gone blind or had she simply lost her mind?

Paige let her gaze drift appreciatively over Yank. "No wonder big business fascinates you, Susannah. Do you have any more male partners tucked away?"

Susannah looked at her blankly.

Paige returned her attention to Yank and saw that his eyes had grown unfocused. He began patting his pockets, muttering something indecipherable, and then—without a word to either of them—walked past them into the cottage.

Paige watched him with amazement. "What on earth—"

"He's working on something. He does that all the time." Susannah took a sip of her ice water and set it down. Her hand shook ever so slightly. "Paige, don't let him take me back."

"What are you talking about?"

"Yank's come here to take me back. I—I'm not ready yet."

Paige regarded her curiously. "Then don't go. I've told you that you can stay as long as you like."

"You don't know the way he is. When he has his mind set on something, it's impossible to distract him. He's like Sam, except different. He's so gentle. Kind. It's difficult to explain."

"That's ridiculous, Susannah. He can't take you back unless you decide to go with him."

Susannah didn't look convinced. "I never expected him to show up here. Yank doesn't travel by himself. He can't manage things."

"He seems to have managed things just fine." Paige shook her head in amusement. "I can't believe that's the same man you and Mitch were telling me all those dopey stories about. Susannah, he's incredibly sexy."

Susannah seemed vaguely startled. "Well, he's changed a lot since we started the company. He's certainly a lot better looking than he was when I met him. All the women he's had in his life these past few years have put him together. I guess it happened so gradually that those of us who are with him all the time barely noticed."

"What do you mean, 'put him together'?"

"They've done his clothes shopping for him and thrown out the awful stuff he used to wear. He had this terrible crew cut right out of the 1950s, and these ugly black glasses with Coke-bottle lenses. His girlfriends cleaned him up, organized his wardrobe, and made him get contacts—that sort of thing. But it's all surface cosmetics. Yank is still Yank. And—" She shivered slightly. "Sometimes he can be scary."

It was the first thing Susannah had said about Yank Yankowski that made any sense to Paige.

As she had done with Mitch, Paige invited Yank to stay the night and fed him a delicious dinner. To Yank's credit, he managed to keep up his end of the conversation throughout most of the meal and only faded out on them a time or two. After the dishes were cleared, he asked Susannah to show him the beach.

She made a great play out of pushing the cork back into a bottle of wine they hadn't quite finished. "Let's do it tomorrow. I'm a bit tired tonight."

"I'd very much like to see the beach now," he said quietly.

"It's late, Yank. And it's a steep climb."

"There's a full moon. We can see quite well."

Susannah shot Paige a pleading glance, and her sister's maternal instincts took over. She set down her dishrag and touched Yank's arm lightly. "Beach tours are my specialty. If you treat me right, I might even let you cop a feel behind the rocks."

Susannah's hands stilled on the cork as Yank's mouth curved in a slow sleepy smile that was almost mesmerizing. Paige was right. Yank had turned into an incredibly attractive man, and she had barely been aware of it.

Paige wove her fingers through his and pulled him toward the doorway. "Don't wait up for us," she called over her shoulder. "I'm not letting him back until I've had my way with him."

For all her bravado, Paige felt awkward the moment the cottage was behind them and they were alone. There was something spooky about him—as if he knew all sorts of things other people didn't. She didn't like being put at a disadvantage with Yank, but she wasn't quite certain how to take control.

The moon lit their way, shining silver on the harsh rocks

as they headed down the path to the beach. The night was warm and still, and the waves lapped softly at the shore. She walked to the edge, pretending to be mesmerized by the water, while she tried to ignore the fact that Yank was studying her quite openly.

His scrutiny made her increasingly uncomfortable. She fell back on her old tricks. "Did anyone ever tell you that you're incredibly sexy?"

"Yes."

"Susannah thinks you're a nerd."

"I know."

"Doesn't that bother you?"

"Do you think it should?"

"How would I know? If you want to go through life having everyone think you're weird, I guess that's your problem."

He laughed softly.

His amusement irritated her. It suggested that he understood something she could not even begin to perceive. In retaliation, she reached for the tail of her T-shirt and began to pull it up over her bare breasts. "Let's go in for a swim."

He caught her hands, stilling her movement in a surprisingly firm grip. "No, I don't want you to take off your clothes in front of me."

"God, not another one. First Mitch and now you. What are you? A couple of Buddhists or something?"

"Maybe Mitch understands, too. Seducing either one of us isn't the right thing for you to do. Not now."

"Who made you God? How do you know what's right and wrong for me?"

"I just know, that's all. It occurred to me at dinner exactly how all this might turn out. If we're very, very lucky, of course."

"How what will turn out? What are you talking about?"

He brushed the side of her cheek with his hand in the gentlest gesture she could ever remember receiving from a man, and she looked into eyes that were as wise and compassionate as the eyes of a dime-store Jesus. "You mustn't give yourself to anyone for a while, Paige. Not sexually. It's quite important."

She slapped away his gentle touch with the flat of her hand. "I'll 'give myself' to anybody I like! God, you really are a nerd! From now on, you mind your own goddamn business, do you hear me? Fuck you, mister. Just . . . fuck you."

He gave her a sweet sad smile and turned away to watch the waves.

Susannah made certain she was in bed before Yank and Paige returned from the beach. She couldn't bear the thought of another discussion about leaving. As she plumped her pillow, she remembered Paige's astonishing reaction to Yank's appearance. Her sister's sexual sparring with Mitch hadn't been at all surprising—Mitch was an incredibly attractive man—but Paige had seemed just as captivated with Yank.

She shut her eyes and tried to relax so she could sleep, but her eyelids kept jumping open. To distract herself, she began to imagine what it would be like to make love with Yank. Try as she might, all she could picture was Yank getting distracted at the crucial moment.

And then, to her utter shame, she felt a flash of desire. For the first time it occurred to her that sexual frustration was something she would have to learn to live with. She was a sensual woman, and that part of her wouldn't go away just because she no longer had a husband to satisfy her. At the same time, she was so bruised that she couldn't imagine ever again making the deep emotional commitment that she needed before she could go to bed with someone.

A picture of Sam hovering over her as they made love took shape in her mind. The pain that accompanied it was so sharp she bit down on her lip. *Don't think about it,* she told herself. *Think about someone else.*

She pondered the bleak sexless years ahead. Once again she tried to envision herself with Yank, but the picture wouldn't take hold. Another picture took its place, one of herself and Mitch. Fantasy was a harmless pursuit, so she gave herself permission to strip off the black trunks that he had worn on the beach. She imagined his shape and size, and her limbs began to feel pleasantly lax. She let him pick her up and lay her down on a blue silk sheet. She conjured up the scent that he carried with him of starched shirt and clean skin. Her body felt heavy and languid.

She groaned and buried her face into the pillow. As her eyelids squeezed shut, Sam's mouth took shape in her mind. Sam's mouth—hard and determined—whispering a life-long litany of traitorous love words.

She got up very early the next morning, still groggy from her awful night. Holding her sandals in her hand so she wouldn't make any noise, she slipped across the front room toward the door so she could get away before Yank awakened. Later she would be ready to face him, but not yet.

"Susannah?"

She moaned with frustration as Yank slipped out of his bedroom. His hair was tousled and he had pulled on the wrinkled chinos he had been wearing the night before. The rest of him was uncovered. She didn't realize until that moment that she had never seen Yank without a shirt. His chest was lean almost to the point of boniness, but there was a tautness about his flesh that made his thinness appealing.

"I'm going into town," she said, anxious to get away before he stopped her. "I thought I'd get some pastries for breakfast."

"We don't actually need any pastries." He walked over to the kitchen table, where he picked up a ripe peach from a bowl of fruit and bit into it. He chewed slowly, then looked down at the peach as if he had never seen one before. "It would be easiest on you, Susannah, if you simply resigned yourself to going back with me this afternoon."

"This afternoon? That's impossible."

"Would you prefer to wait until tomorrow morning?"

"No, I—"

"This afternoon, then." He made the statement with ominous finality.

"Yank, I don't want to go back. Not yet. Don't press me on this."

"Someone has to press you. I was very disappointed with Mitch. He should have brought you back last week."

"I'm not a piece of cargo! Listen to me, Yank. The thought of facing Sam— I just can't do it yet."

"Of course you can. You're quite strong, Susannah. You need to remind yourself of that."

She didn't feel at all strong. She felt like a little girl with a string of broken balloons woven through her fingers. "Being

358

forced to face Sam a dozen times a day is a little more than I can handle right now."

"The company depends on you."

She threw down her sandals. They skidded across the floor and banged into the leg of a chair. "Forget about the company! I'm sick of hearing about it. If we believe the Gospel according to Gamble, SysVal is just as important as Christianity. I don't buy that anymore. We're making a computer, for God's sake. A machine. That's all." She waved her hand toward the ceiling. "See! The sky didn't fall. I spoke blasphemy and nothing happened."

Yank looked strained, as if being near such an outpouring of emotion had exhausted him. He dropped the peach pit into the waste basket. "SysVal isn't three kids in a garage anymore. It's a company filled with people who have to pay their mortgages and support their families."

"I'm not responsible for that. All those people aren't my responsibility."

"Yes, they are. You're essential to SysVal."

"I'm the most replaceable of the partners, and you know it."

"You're the least replaceable. I'm surprised you don't realize that. From the very beginning, you're the only one of us who has always been able to see the whole picture. The rest of us only see parts."

"That's ridiculous. Mitch sees it all."

"Better than I do. Better than Sam, maybe. But Mitch's business background has given him biases you don't have. And Mitch and Sam give each other energy, but they don't really understand each other. Without you interpreting for them, they can't even talk."

It was a long speech for him. He began to stare off into space, and she assumed that he had worn himself out. But he was merely taking a few moments to arrange the rest of his thoughts properly. "You're not a visionary like Sam or a marketing strategist like Mitch. You can't design like I do. But you understand people, and you're the one who keeps us on track. If it weren't for you, SysVal would have been lost in chaos long ago. You have this way of keeping order."

The part of her that wasn't miserable was gratified that Yank thought so highly of what she did. Somehow, his praise meant more to her than any compliments she had ever received from either Sam or Mitch.

"Mitch wants you to come back when you're ready, Susannah. He told me quite explicitly that I was not to force you to return."

"I'm a free human being," she said with what she hoped passed for conviction. "You can't force me."

"That may be, but freedom is relative. I have information that Mitch has ordered me not to divulge. If you knew this information, you would immediately return."

Although she had known Mitch was keeping something back from her, for the first time she grew alarmed. "What information? What are you talking about?"

"It's quite disturbing, Susannah."

"Don't you dare do this to me! If you know something I should know, tell me. I don't care what Mitch says."

"Oh, I intend to tell you. I was quite surprised that Mitch thought he could bully me like that."

"What's happened, Yank? What's this all about?"

Yank wandered over to the window and looked out at the view for a few moments. Then he turned back to her. "A few days after you left, Sam began to lobby our Board of Directors."

"That's not unusual. Sam is always lobbying the board for something."

"This time his goal was quite different."

Susannah felt a chill of apprehension deep in the pit of her stomach. "What do you mean? What's he done?"

"Susannah, I'm sorry to have to tell you this, but Sam is trying to convince the board to sell SysVal."

25

When Paige awakened, Susannah told her what had happened and tried to convince her sister to return to San Francisco with them. But Paige shrugged her off, insisting she had already made plans to go to Sardinia. She immediately began the business of closing up her cottage and arranged for a jeep to come and get all three of them. Their relationship was still so fragile that Susannah was reluctant to press her. At the same time, she felt so emotionally intertwined with her sister that she didn't want a lengthy separation. What if they fell back into their old antagonistic pattern?

Their parting at the airport wasn't as difficult as it might have been because Yank disappeared at the last moment and both of them had to set off after him. Paige found him with a group of passengers ready to board a flight to Marrakech. She took him back to the proper gate just as Susannah had given up all hope of locating him.

He absentmindedly passed his ticket and boarding pass over to Susannah, then turned back to Paige. "Please remember that request I made when we were on the beach. It's very important."

Susannah looked at them curiously, trying to figure out what Yank was talking about.

Paige ran her fingers along her purse strap. "What's it worth to you?"

"Worth?"

"Yeah. Are you willing to put your money where your mouth is?" Her eyes swept over him insolently. "And I'll just bet your mouth has been in some very interesting places."

Yank flushed. "You're suggesting I make the same agreement?"

"Why not? Misery loves company."

"I hadn't thought that far ahead."

"Maybe you'd better."

"You have a point. Although—"

"Do you agree?"

He considered her question for a few moments and then nodded.

Susannah was mystified by the conversation, but her speculation was stopped short as the loudspeaker announced the final boarding call. Neither she nor Paige seemed to know quite what to say. Susannah smiled shakily. "Thanks. Thanks so much for everything."

Paige shrugged off Susannah's gratitude. "I owed you one."

Yank had begun to wander away. Susannah grabbed him and steered him toward the gate. Just before they passed through, she gave Paige a final wave.

Paige stood in the middle of a bustling crowd of tourists and watched her sister and Yank Yankowski disappear. As they slipped out of sight, a deep ache passed through her like a dark wave on her private beach. Something important was slipping out of her life, and she didn't have the faintest idea how to get it back.

On the trip from Athens to Heathrow, Yank told Susannah what he knew about Sam's sudden determination to sell the company. He offered the details in his customary systematic fashion, laying out the facts as he knew them and refusing to speculate on anything he wasn't certain of.

Sam wanted to sell SysVal to Databeck Industries, an international conglomerate. Databeck had offered to buy SysVal a year ago, and at the time Sam had scoffed at them, even though several of the board members had urged that the offer be considered. No matter how hard she searched, she could find only one explanation for Sam's change of heart. He wanted to get back at her for leaving him. The idea that he would sacrifice the company that meant everything to him just to punish her sent a chill to the very marrow of her bones. How could she have thought she knew someone so well and not have known him at all?

They had to lay over for several hours at Heathrow before their plane left for San Francisco. When they finally boarded, Yank fell asleep quickly, but Susannah couldn't rest. Instead of concentrating on the crisis at SysVal, she kept imagining herself walking into the lobby. Everyone would be watching her. She envisioned the pity in their faces, imagined the whispers behind her back. The images were unbearable, and she forced herself to concentrate on the implications of Sam's turnabout.

They all had been so certain that nothing like this could ever happen. The four partners each held fifteen percent of the company, giving them a controlling sixty percent. The other board members held the remaining forty. They had always felt so safe with this arrangement. But if Sam could unite the board, and if he then threw his fifteen percent in with them, nothing that she, Yank, or Mitch could do would keep the company from being sold.

They arrived in California at six in the morning. Even though it was early, Susannah asked Yank to drop her at Mitch's house. He lived in a charming California-style ranch that sprawled over several acres in Los Altos Hills. As he opened the door, she saw that he was clad only in a pair of running shorts. Sweat gleamed on his arms and darkened the pelt of sandy hair on his chest. He looked surprised to see her, but he was so hard to read that she wasn't certain whether he was pleased or not. The strange, erotic fantasy she'd had about him when she was in Greece slipped back into her mind, and for a moment she couldn't quite meet his eyes.

"Welcome home," he said, stepping aside to admit her. "I just got back from my run." He took her traveling case and led her into the living room. Normally it was one of her favorite places in the house, a happy hodgepodge of American Southwest and French Riviera. Chairs and couches were upholstered in nubby, neutral-colored fabrics brightened up with throw pillows printed with colorful geometrics. The stucco walls held large canvases splashed with tropical flowers, and tables with curly wrought-iron legs were placed at convenient intervals. But the pleasure she usually felt at being in such cheerful surroundings eluded her.

He set down her case next to one of the couches. "Give me a minute to take a shower and then we'll talk. There's a pot of fresh coffee in the kitchen."

She stopped him before he could leave the room. "You should have told me what Sam was doing when you came to Naxos." She hadn't intended to sound so condemning, but there still seemed to be some mysterious strain between them and she couldn't help it.

"You had plenty of chances to ask questions," he replied. "I don't remember hearing any."

"Don't you play games with me, Mitch. I expect better of you."

He picked up a wadded T-shirt from one of the end tables and began to rub his damp chest with it. "Is that an official reprimand, Madame President?"

A month ago she could't have imagined being intimidated by him, but now there was something so forbidding about the way he was looking at her that she had to force herself to hold her ground. "You can take it any way you want."

He yanked his T-shirt on, then pulled it down over his chest. "I tried every way I knew to talk you into coming back, Susannah, but I wasn't going to force you if you weren't ready. We've got a big fight ahead of us, and your personal problems are going to make it more complicated. If Yank and I couldn't have one hundred percent from you, I wanted you out of our way."

He was acting like she was an encumbrance. "That wasn't your decision to make," she snapped. "What's wrong with you, Mitch? When did you turn into the enemy?"

Some of his stiffness faded. "I'm not your enemy, Susannah. I don't mean to be abrupt. Sam's called an informal meeting of the board tomorrow at three o'clock. My guess is that he intends to tighten the screws."

"Forget it," she said fiercely. "He can call any meeting he

wants, but his partners aren't going to be there to see the show. I'm not going to meet with anybody on the board—formally or otherwise—until I've had a few days to ask some questions. Without us, they can't have much of a meeting."

"We have to confront the board sooner or later."

"I know that. But I'm taking the ball into my court for a while. Make sure that you're unreachable tomorrow afternoon at meeting time. I'll take care of Yank."

Mitch seemed to be thinking over what she'd said. "I'll give you a couple of weeks, Susannah, but no more. I don't want anyone to think we're running. That'll hurt us nearly as badly as what Sam is doing."

She didn't like the fact that he was questioning her judgment, but at least some of his stiffness had dissipated. What was happening to the two of them? She'd grown to take Mitch's friendship for granted, and she couldn't imagine losing it, especially now when she felt so fragile. The burst of adrenaline that had kept her going had begun to fade, and she sat down on the couch.

He saw that she was exhausted, and went to get her a cup of coffee. As she sipped it, he told her he had reserved the town house SysVal owned for its traveling executives so she had a place to stay until she got resettled. He had also reclaimed her car from the airport and stored it in his garage. His thoughtfulness made her feel better.

Forty-five minutes later, she climbed the stairs to the town house's second floor, slipped into the freshly made bed and fell into a troubled, dream-ridden sleep. She awoke around noon and telephoned home to make certain Sam wasn't there. When she received no answer, she dressed and drove over.

She half expected to find the locks had been changed, but her key worked without any difficulty. The house looked the same—cold and uninviting. She went into the bedroom with its steel-framed furniture and gray suede walls. Everything was exactly as she had left it. Everything except—

Her eyes widened as she saw a small oil painting hanging on the wall between their matching bureaus. It was a seascape in soft feminine pastels that were at odds with the room's cold gray interior. She had found the painting a year ago in a gallery in Mill Valley and immediately fallen in love with it. But Sam had hated it and refused to let her hang it. This was the first time she had seen it since she had come home from a business trip and discovered that he had sent it back.

She sagged down on the side of the bed and stared at the painting. Tears welled in her eyes. How could he be taking the company away from her on one hand and, at the same time, giving her this painting? The pastels blurred through her tears, swimming together so that the painting seemed to be in motion. The waves of the seascape heaved toward the shore in watery blue and green swells.

She thought of Sam's wave—the wave of the future he had told her about all those years ago. That wave had swept over them just as he had promised, and just as he had promised, they had been changed forever. She stared at the painting, and the great vat of grief that had been sealed shut inside her opened up, sending dark eddies through every part of her. She hugged herself and stared at the painting and rocked back and forth on the edge of the bed while she truly mourned the death of her marriage.

And with the death of her marriage, she mourned the death of the child she had hoped to bear, that dark-haired, olive-skinned child of feisty spirit and soaring imagination who would never be born. She hugged that child to her breast and loved it with all her might, pouring years of maternal care into a few brief moments. She cried it a bleak lullaby, that unconceived child of her imagination, and let her heart tear apart as she laid it in its grave.

When she left the house, she felt as old and empty as a hollowed-out stone.

• •

Walking into SysVal that same afternoon was one of the hardest things Susannah had ever done. She wore an unadorned black knit, garbing herself in its severe lines as if it were a suit of armor. As she flashed her pass at the front desk, the security guard wouldn't quite meet her eyes. A group of jeans-clad workers conversing in the lobby stopped talking as she came toward them. They looked down at the floor; they looked at the walls. The company grapevine was powerful, and Mindy Bradshaw obviously hadn't kept her mouth shut. By now every SysVal employee must know that Susannah had walked in on Sam and Mindy making love.

As she moved through the halls, several of the men called out cautious greetings, as if she were a terminal cancer patient and they didn't know what to say. She nodded graciously and kept walking—spine straight as a ramrod, posture so perfect she would die before she bent. She had been San Francisco's Deb of the Year in 1965. She had been trained in the old ways to retain her dignity regardless of provocation and to hide her emotions behind a mask of serenity.

As she neared her office, her palms began to perspire, but she didn't lower her head by so much as a fraction of an inch. Ahead of her a technician ducked into an office so he could avoid the embarrassment of having to greet her. The corners of her mouth began to quiver, and she realized then that she couldn't carry it off. She was no longer San Francisco's perfect socialite or SysVal's efficient president. She was a woman who had learned to feel and bleed and care. Her steps faltered. She couldn't do it. She simply couldn't go through with this.

Her muscles were so tightly wound that she jumped when a voice sounded over the loudspeaker. It was a voice that had never before been heard over the SysVal system because it belonged to the man who had been trying for several years to have that same system disconnected. It was Mitch, clearing his throat and speaking in the dry, businesslike fashion of someone whose idea of fun was spending an evening reading sales forecasts.

"Ladies and gentlemen, the security desk has informed me that our president and chief operating officer, Susannah Faulconer, has just arrived back in the building. I feel compelled to address all of you today and set the record straight. The rumors that Ms. Faulconer has been hiding out in Las Vegas and dancing in a nude review are absolutely untrue, and anyone repeating such rumors will be dismissed at once. We have it on good authority that Miss Faulconer was not nude. She was respectably clad in a leopardskin G-string." And then the music of "The Stripper" blared out.

Heads popped out of offices. A hoot of laughter went up around the building. Susannah wanted to kill Mitch, to kiss him. He had known how hard it would be for her to come back, and this was his strange—and typically SysVal way—of making it easier. After the strain of their encounter that morning, this gesture of friendship meant everything to her.

Mitch's announcement pushed away the awkwardness and gave people something to say to her. For the next few hours, everyone teased her unmercifully. But there was still an edge of caution to their laughing remarks. Normally when she was away from the office for even a day, Sam's name would have come up a dozen times within an hour of her return. Now no one mentioned him.

More than anything, she wanted to put off seeing him. But she knew she couldn't hide away forever, and the longer she postponed meeting with him, the more difficult it would become. When Helen, her secretary, brought in the most urgent of her mail, Susannah forced herself to look up from her notepad and ask as coolly as she could manage, "Is Sam in today?"

"Gee, I— Yes, I think so."

"Good," she said briskly. "Call his office. I'd like to see him as soon as he can get free."

She forced herself to concentrate on her work. So much urgent business had piled up while she was gone that it was difficult even to prioritize it. And there were small irritations. When she turned in her chair to flick on the Blaze III she kept on her credenza, she was annoyed to discover that it had been replaced with a newer III. The machines were identical, but she had a sentimental attachment to her old Blaze. It was one of the thirteen original test models that Sam had insisted be put into use for a few months before the Blaze III was released to the general public, so that all the bugs could be worked out ahead of time.

When she asked Helen what had happened to her old computer, she was told that a technician had come for it. "He transferred all of your files to the new machine, so it shouldn't be a problem."

"Get hold of him and tell him I want my old Blaze back," she said. She didn't care if she was being illogical. She'd had enough changes forced upon her in the past month, and this was one she could control.

Helen nodded and then told her she had a call from Mitch. Susannah picked up her phone. "A nude review? Couldn't you have done better than that?"

"I'm an engineer, not a poet. I thought I told you not to come in to work until tomorrow."

"Too much to catch up on."

He hesitated. "Susannah, I'm afraid I've got more bad news. I don't like hitting you with everything on your first day back, but I just got a call from Sacramento."

She rested her forehead on the tips of her fingers, bracing herself for the next disaster.

He said, "The people we're dealing with in the state government got wind of the rumors that SysVal is up for sale, and that tipped the scales in favor of FBT and the Falcon 101."

She rubbed her temple with her thumb. A multimillion-dollar contract was lost; Sam wanted to sell the company. A month ago they had been sitting on top of the world. Now everything was coming apart.

She spent the next two hours on the phone to Sacramento, talking to everyone she could reach and trying to convince them that the rumors were untrue. The officials were polite but unbending. They had made the decision to go with FBT's Falcon 101 instead of the Blaze III, and that decision was irreversible. She turned to her computer and began crunching numbers, trying to determine how this financial setback would affect the new Blaze Wildfire project.

Sam came to her office around five. She sensed his presence in the doorway before she looked up.

"Hi, Suzie."

For so many years every part of her had jumped alive whenever she caught sight of him, but now she felt numb. She swiveled slowly in her chair and for a few brief moments saw him as others did, those who hadn't fallen under his spell. He looked tired and nervous. He needed a haircut, and his slacks and shirt were wrinkled, as if he'd fallen asleep in them.

"Did you go over to the house?" he asked as he walked into her office.

"I stopped in to pick up my things."

"You can't run away if we're going to get this worked out."

Now that she had left him, he finally wanted to work out their problems. She could almost have predicted this would happen, so why was it so hurtful? "We're not going to get our problems worked out. It's over, Sam. I've had enough."

He drove his hand through his hair, plunged his fist into the pocket of his slacks. "Look, Susannah. I'm sorry. I fucked up real bad. I know that. But it doesn't have to be the end of everything. If I'd known it was going to be such a big deal to you—"

"I don't want to talk about it!" She fought for composure. Years of bitter experience had taught her how easy it was to get caught up in Sam's twisted logic, and her emotional control was too fragile for her to argue with him now. "These are business hours, Sam, and we're going to talk business."

Rising from behind her desk, she forced herself to come around to the front. "Mitch just told me that we lost the contract with the state of California because they heard a rumor that we're going to sell SysVal. Tell me why you sandbagged us like this."

He flopped down in a chair, stretching his legs out and hunching his shoulders like a sullen schoolboy. "It's obvious, isn't it? It's time for us to sell. The economy is heading for a recession, and companies are going belly-up all over the Valley. We've been lucky, but I don't think we should push it. That contract with the state was fool's gold, anyway."

"And so, without consulting any of your partners, you took it upon yourself to approach the rest of the board about selling SysVal."

"What was I supposed to do?" he replied belligerently. "You'd run away, remember? How was I going to consult you?"

She wouldn't let him draw her into a fight. "What about Mitch and Yank? They didn't run away."

"Mitch and Yank don't understand things, not like you do. Listen, Susannah, this may seem like it's come out of nowhere, but everything's going to be okay. We can take all that we've learned and start a new company—something a lot better than SysVal. We've gotten too big too fast. This time, we'll keep ourselves even leaner and trimmer. Think how much we know about manufacturing. We can automate everything. Robotics is exploding. We'll save millions in labor costs. With our track record, we'll have every investor in the country standing in line to back us."

He was saying the right words, but the energy wasn't there. His eyes weren't shining with any mystic vision of the future. She sensed that he was throwing up some sort of elaborate smoke screen. Stalling for time, she walked over to the window and gazed out on a small, grassy courtyard. It was pretty, but uninspired compared to the elaborately landscaped grounds at FBT's Castle.

"What's this really about, Sam?" she asked quietly. "Are you trying to get back at me? Is that what you're doing?"

"No! God, don't you know me any better than that? What kind of a shit do you think I am?"

She didn't say anything.

He got up from the chair, looked down at the carpet and jabbed the leg of her desk with the toe of one of his custom-made Italian loafers. "Suzie, don't do this. Don't throw everything away because of what happened. I got rid of Mindy. I didn't think you'd want her around, so I fired her. And I went back to the shop and got that painting you wanted."

He was laying small gifts in front of her like a child who had misbehaved and wanted to make up with his mother. The betrayed wife in her felt a vindictive satisfaction that Mindy had been fired. The female corporate president noted the injustice and knew she would have to correct it right away.

She wasn't going to discuss their marriage, and she certainly wasn't going to discuss Mindy. "Why do you want to sell SysVal?"

"I told you. We've made a fortune, and we need to get out now. You have to listen to me, Suzie. It's all going to crash down. I can feel it. We need to get out while we can."

The old passion was back in his eyes, and it stirred a sense of apprehension within her. "You know something that you're not telling me."

"When did you get so goddamn suspicious? There aren't any hidden secrets here, Susannah. Just look at the fucking economy."

"We're not selling SysVal."

"The hell we're not. The rest of the board will go along with me. They're bean counters, Susannah. They don't like it when I get nervous. In the end, you won't have any choice. You'd better trust me on this, because if you don't, you're going to end up looking like a fool."

"I don't think so. I think you're the one who'll look like a fool."

"We went into this together, and I'm going to see to it that we go out together." He strode past her toward the door. "Don't fight me on this one, Susannah. I'm warning you. If you fight me, it'll be the last big mistake you make with this company."

* * *

At three o'clock the next afternoon, when SysVal's Board of Directors convened, Mitch, Susannah, and Yank were conspicuously absent. Sam paced the floor of the board-room while one of his assistants scurried to locate them. The assistant returned with the news that Mitch had made an emergency trip to Boston and that Susannah and Yank were nowhere to be found. The board overruled Sam's objection and voted to postpone their meeting.

Sam stalked out into the corridor. He couldn't believe she was defying him like this, that she was being so goddamn stubborn about everything. He should have known she would freak if she ever found out he slept with other women. She didn't understand that sort of shit didn't mean any-thing. She didn't understand that she was the only woman he wanted to spend his life with.

When he reached his office, he pushed through the line of people waiting in the reception area to see him and told his assistants they had fifteen minutes to find out where she was. Then he shut himself in his private office. She wanted a baby. Okay, he'd tell her a baby was okay. Maybe having a kid was what he needed. Maybe it would settle him down.

He realized he was sweating. Jesus, he was scared. Every-thing was happening so fast. Somehow he had to convince his partners to sell SysVal. And he had to get Susannah back. Not because of the company, either. Because of him.

Now that he was seeing things a little more clearly, he realized that it wasn't all her fault he wasn't happy. Maybe most of it was his fault. But she knew how crazy he got sometimes. She should have understood that he was just going through a hard time. She knew he loved her. He needed her. And if she left him, she was going to take all his missing parts with her.

"I don't mind coming with you, of course," Yank said to Susannah as they explored the empty bedroom of a newly built, multimillion-dollar luxury condominium that came complete with indoor pool, solarium, and a spectacular view. "But I don't need a babysitter. I wish you had trusted me to make myself unavailable this afternoon."

Susannah glanced at her watch. It was four o'clock. The

meeting should have broken up by now. She gave Yank an apologetic smile. "I couldn't afford to take a chance that you'd get distracted today and forget the time."

He didn't return her smile. He merely gazed at her, his expression inscrutable.

Feeling uncomfortable, she looked away. There was something so mysterious about Yank. She never knew what he was thinking. She doubted anyone did.

The realtor had left them alone so Susannah could go through the house a second time. This afternoon had seemed as good an opportunity as any to find a permanent place to live. She gazed unenthusiastically through the arched windows to the mountains beyond. "I guess this is all right."

"It seems adequate. Furnishings will add a lot, of course."

Susannah thought of the gaudy gilt and brocade interior of Yank's house, a decorating scheme favored by one of his early girlfriends.

A noise sounded below—the bang of the door being pushed open and then slammed shut. She caught her breath as she heard a pounding on the stair treads. Yank frowned.

Sam burst into the room. "I can't believe this. It's like I don't know who to trust anymore."

Susannah's control snapped. "Don't you talk to me about trust."

"You have a house, Susannah!" he exclaimed. "My house. Our house. You don't need another one."

"I don't want to talk about this now, Sam. I want you to leave."

He stalked toward her. Yank stepped forward, moving without any appearance of haste, but effectively blocking Sam before he could reach her. "You'd better leave, Sam," he said quietly. "Susannah doesn't want you here."

"Get out of my way!" Sam punched at Yank's chest, trying to push him aside. But Yank was wiry, and although he swayed to the side, he didn't budge. A vein in the side of Sam's neck began to pulse as he shouted, "I thought you were my friend. You should have been at the board meeting today. Instead, you were helping my wife leave me."

"Yank came with me because I asked him to," Susannah said. Sam's rage was embarrassing. Once again she had a sense of detachment as she studied him, a feeling that she was seeing him with newer, wiser eyes.

"I'll just bet he jumped all over himself trying to help you out," Sam retorted nastily.

Yank pressed his eyes shut and his mouth twisted with pain. "I think I'm going to have to give up on you, Sam. Susannah and I—we're both going to have to give up on you."

Sam winced and for a moment his face seemed to crumple.

"I saw a lawyer this morning," she said quietly. "Nothing you do now will make any difference." Clearing a wide berth around him, she walked out into the hallway.

"Don't do this, Susannah," he called from the doorway. "Come home with me right now."

But she wasn't going into battle with him, and she walked away.

Instead of returning to SysVal, Sam found himself driving to his mother's house. She was sunning herself in the backyard, wearing a bikini in some shiny bronze fabric that didn't look as if it had ever seen water. The headset of a Walkman was strapped over her ears, and her eyes were closed beneath a pair of sunglasses with the gold script letters A.G. glued to the bottom of one lens.

Even though he had offered to buy Angela a new house anywhere she wanted, she had refused to move out of the old neighborhood. She said she liked living here because she knew all the neighbors and her old ladies depended on her. He'd told her that she didn't have to work anymore—he had more money than he knew what to do with—but she said she liked her independence. He'd even offered to buy her a first-class salon that she could run any way she wanted, but she'd said she didn't want to work that hard.

As he reached down and shut off the Walkman, her eyes snapped open. "Hi, baby." She pushed her sunglasses on top of her head and sat up a bit. Her stomach wrinkled a little as she moved, but she still had a great body for someone who was forty-nine.

"Don't you look snazzy," she said, as she always did. "If anybody had told me when you were eighteen that you'd be running around someday in eighty-dollar neckties, I'd have told them they were crazy."

He took the webbed chair next to her, noticing as he sat that rust had formed around the screws on the arms. "Clothes aren't important."

"Try giving them up."

He stretched out his legs, looked up at the sky and closed his eyes. "Did you talk to Suzie?"

"She called me yesterday."

"She's got this stupid-ass idea that she's moving out."

"Uh-huh."

"Well?"

"You want some spaghetti?"

"So what did you tell her?"

"I didn't tell her anything. Suzie's a grown woman."

"So what did she say to you?"

"She said she's leaving you, Sammy."

He pushed himself out of the chair. "Yeah, well that's what she thinks. See, she wants a kid."

"I know. She wants a husband, too. You're getting what you deserve, kiddo. I've been trying to tell you that for a long time."

"You know, you really piss me off. You're my mother, not hers. You're always taking her side. Right from the beginning."

"I'm my own woman, Sammy. I call it like I see it."

He splayed his hand on his hip and glared at her. "Yeah? Well, you see it all wrong. She's important to me, you know. I need her."

Angela sighed and reached out to touch him. "Oh, baby. You're so hard to love."

"Databeck tendered an excellent offer, Susannah," Leland Hayward said over lunch at a pretty café in Ghirardelli Square. The venture capitalist was still one of SysVal's most influential board members. In addition to Hayward and the four founding partners, SysVal's board consisted of bankers and investors who had been brought in as they needed expansion capital. They were, by nature, conservative men, and as Susannah had visited privately with each one over the past four days, she had been dismayed to discover how nervous they were. Even Hayward, who was accustomed to taking risks, was worried.

He sprinkled Sweet'N Low into his coffee and shook his head. "You have to understand that when someone who's as much of a wildcatter as Sam starts getting cold feet and says we should sell, I have to listen."

"The company is solid," she insisted. "There's no reason to sell."

"You're behind schedule on the development of the Wildfire. You've just lost the contract with the state of California. That doesn't seem so solid to me."

"We only lost the contract because of the rumors about the sale."

"Maybe. Maybe not."

Susannah understood only too well. If she or Mitch had expressed worry over the financial state of the company, the board members would have been concerned, but not frightened. But when a swashbuckler like Sam said he wanted out, the board was thrown into a panic.

They finished their coffee and prepared to leave. As Leland rose from his chair, he frowned. "By the way, Susannah, I'm not too happy with your service people right now. They picked up my computer a few weeks ago when I was on vacation, and they haven't returned it or brought me a replacement."

Susannah pulled out the small notebook she kept in her purse and jotted a reminder to herself. SysVal policy dictated that any employee who received a complaint was responsible for following through on it. No one at SysVal— from the Chairman of the Board to the newest member of the typing pool—was exempt.

"I liked that machine," Leland went on. And then he chuckled. "Having one of those Blaze III test models made me feel like a pioneer."

Susannah looked at him curiously. "You had one of the test models?"

"Sam gave it to me. He found out I hadn't been using a computer and said I was a disgrace to the company. It took me a while to get used to it, but now I can't get along without it."

Susannah thought of her own missing computer and

wondered if someone in Engineering had pulled in all thirteen of the original test models to troubleshoot them. She reassured Leland that she would have a replacement machine sent over that afternoon, and once again asked him to reconsider his position.

"I've learned to trust my instincts," he said. "And right now my instincts are telling me that SysVal is in trouble."

She returned to her office frustrated and depressed. Her secretary handed her a pile of phone messages and she flicked through them, hoping to find something from Paige. For days, she had been leaving messages with the maid at Paige's villa in Sardinia, but so far she had heard nothing.

She was still thinking about her sister the next morning when Lydia Dubeck, an eager young MBA from Harvard who was one of the company's newest directors, poked her head into her office. "It's the darndest thing, Susannah. No one in Engineering seems to know anything about a recall of those thirteen test models. There aren't any work orders, and no one has heard about any problems. I guess that's good news."

Susannah was still troubled. "Sam's assistants should have a list of all the people who have one of those computers. Have someone get hold of it and find out the status of every machine."

But when Lydia caught up with her late that afternoon, she looked tired and irritated. "I don't know what the big deal is. Sam's apparently the only one who has a list. You'd think it was some sort of state secret. None of his assistants will give it to me, and he was in one of his moods when I finally ran him down."

Susannah didn't have to ask what that meant. Lydia had obviously received one of Sam's famous tongue-lashings. She thought for a moment, and decided that it was unwise to go into battle with Sam over something that was probably trivial, especially when a much bigger fight loomed ahead. "Thanks for trying, Lydia. Forget it for now."

She spent the rest of the afternoon in meetings. When the last one broke up at six, she decided to see if Mitch was still around so she could run some new ideas about financing the Wildfire past him.

His office was more formal than any of his partners'

offices. The windows were draped in a cream and maroon stripe, the chairs deep-seated and comfortable. Various civic awards hung on the walls, along with framed photos of his children.

He was deeply engrossed in a meaty-looking report lying open on his desk, and she paused for a moment to study him. Gold cuff links glimmered discreetly at his wrists. His collar button was securely fastened, his necktie neatly knotted. As he looked up at her, the lenses of his horn-rimmed glasses flashed in the light of his desk lamp. For a moment she tried to reconcile this bastion of corporate respectability with the man who had soul-kissed her sister.

"You want to go get some dinner?" she asked.

"Sorry. I'm meeting Jacqueline." He quirked an eyebrow as she made a face at him. "You're welcome to come with us, Susannah. Jacqueline enjoys your company."

"Thanks, but I think I'll pass. I'm not in the mood to discuss dead philosophers tonight." She settled down in the chair across from his desk and kicked off her heels. "Are you going to marry her?"

He immediately turned stuffy. "Really, Susannah."

"Well, are you?"

The loudspeaker crackled in the hallway outside. "Attention everyone. We have a lost pig in the building. Anyone spotting a two-hundred-pound porker answering to the name of Yoda should notify security at once."

Mitch sighed and Susannah cast her eyes to the ceiling. "Oh, Lord, I hope they're kidding," she said.

"Around here you never know."

Susannah's smile died on her lips as she thought how much this company meant to her, especially now that her marriage was over. "God, I love this place. I don't want to lose it, Mitch."

He took off his glasses and slowly folded in the stems. "I don't want to lose it, either, but it's not the worst thing that could happen. If we sold SysVal, we'd all end up with more money than we could spend in six lifetimes."

Susannah had refused to think about defeat herself, and she hated the idea that Mitch had even considered it. "This isn't just about money. We've built a wonderful company, and nobody is going to take it away from us."

"Sam has a lot of support, Susannah. Don't try to kid yourself about that."

"We have support, too. You know as well as I do that most of the board members don't even like Sam."

"Maybe not. But when he starts screaming 'fire,' they certainly start thinking about running for the nearest exit."

She poked her feet back into her shoes. Not for one moment had she considered the possibility that Mitch might change sides, but now she was no longer so certain. "I'm getting the feeling that you have some sort of contingency plan in mind, and I don't like it. We're not going to lose this company."

"That's emotion speaking, not logic. We have to be ready for anything. As much as we may want to deny it, we need to face the fact that we might not win."

She jumped up from her chair. "You face the fact. You and that computer brain of yours. I'm going to be too busy trying to keep us together."

"Susannah, you're overreacting."

The fact that he was right didn't make her any more conciliatory. She had imagined Mitch fighting at her side forever. Now she realized that might not happen. If at some point Mitch decided that the battle wasn't winnable, he would regroup. And that might very well put him on the other side.

Her fingers closed tightly around the papers she was carrying. "You're either with me or you're against me, Mitch. There's no middle ground. If you're with me, don't waste my time waving yellow flags. And if you're against me—then you'd better stay the hell out of my way, because this is one fight I'm not going to lose."

He slapped down the report he had been reading and stood. "SysVal isn't life and death, Susannah. It's only a company."

"No! It's an adventure." She threw SysVal's Mission Statement in his face, speaking Sam's words from the depth of her heart. "'We have set out together on an adventure to give the world the best computer humankind can produce. We will support and stand by our products, placing quality and integrity above all else. We relish the adventure because it gives us the opportunity to put ourselves to the test of excellence.' I believe it, Mitch. I believe every word."

"Don't confuse rhetoric with real life."

"It's not rhetoric. We have to have standards. Not just as a corporation, but as human beings. Otherwise, we've wasted our lives."

She stalked out the door and down the hallway. The tight bonds of their partnership seemed to be unwinding in front of her. She found herself heading for Yank's lab. It was late, but he would probably still be there. She would only stay a few minutes so she could watch him work. Just a few minutes in Yank's presence would steady her.

• •

27

The SysVal town house where Susannah was staying was located at the end of a narrow road and tucked away on a hillside thick with redwood and oak. She had just carried her first cup of Saturday morning coffee out onto the small private patio to enjoy the solitude when she heard her door bell ring. Setting down the cup, she went inside to answer it. As she crossed the small kitchen on her way to the foyer, she found herself hoping it was Mitch. Sometimes he stopped by on Saturday mornings, and she needed a chance to mend her fences with him, especially after their argument last week. But when she opened the door, she found her sister standing on the other side.

"Paige!"

"Don't slobber. It's only been a couple of weeks."

Susannah pulled her sister into the small foyer and gave her a hug. "Long weeks. I missed you."

Paige hung in her arms a moment longer than necessary, then pushed herself away. "Sardinia was a bore. I flew in last night." She tossed the strap of her purse over the banister, then glanced around at the foyer and into the living room. "This place is a dump."

The town house wasn't palatial, but it was hardly a dump.

Even so, Susannah didn't argue. "Temporary housing. I can't find anything I want to buy. How did you find me?"

"I called Mitch. What's wrong with him, anyway? He sounded funny on the phone."

"He was probably in bed with Jacqueline Dane." Susannah was surprised at how sharp she sounded. "Come on into the kitchen. You can fix us some breakfast."

"Me! I'm company."

"I know, but you're a better cook than I am."

Paige grumbled the entire time she was preparing their breakfast, but Susannah noted that she still made the effort to hunt through the shelves for cinnamon to add to the French toast, and that she refused to put the bread slices on the griddle until they had soaked in the egg batter a full ten minutes.

Susannah sank her teeth into the first bite. "Ambrosia. It's almost worth putting up with your nasty temper just to taste your cooking."

Paige ate a few bites, then set down her fork. Her hair tumbled forward, spilling like rumpled silk over the shoulders of her expensive designer blouse. She looked deeply unhappy.

"What's wrong?" Susannah said, putting down her own fork.

"Nothing, really. Nothing and everything. I don't know. What happened between you and that bastard you married was awful, but those weeks in Greece . . . They were nice, that's all."

Paige wasn't demonstrative, and Susannah knew this was the closest she could get to a statement of affection. "You're right," she said. "They were nice." She toyed with the handle of her fork while she chose her words carefully. "Paige, all that time we were together in Greece, you played the big sister and I got to be the little sister. I loved it. But right now I need to be the big sister again for a few minutes."

"Terrific," Paige said scornfully. "This is just what I need after traveling halfway around the world."

Susannah reached out and cupped her sister's arm. "You have a gift that's in short supply these days, kid. You're a natural-born nurturer. But you keep turning your back on that gift, acting like it's not important. And I think that's why you're so unhappy. Why don't you give yourself a chance?"

"A chance to do what?" she said fiercely. "I don't have a husband or kids. Men are jerks. The ones who aren't gay are sex maniacs."

"Paige, it's 1982. Marriage isn't the only way you can fulfill yourself. Why don't you stop whining about how awful your life is and start looking around you? There are hospitals full of sick children who could use a little of your attention. There are schools that need teacher aides, community centers looking for volunteers."

"I'm one of the richest women in California, Susannah. I can't just call up the Girl Scouts and tell them I want to help sell cookies."

"I don't know why not. Money should give you freedom instead of hemming you in. Figure out for yourself what you want to do and then do it."

Before she could go on, the telephone rang. She went over to the counter to answer it.

"Hi, baby doll. It's me."

At the sound of Angela's voice, Susannah smiled. She was grateful that her estrangement from Sam hadn't marred her relationship with his mother. Angela had changed very little in the past six years. She continued to fight off her birthdays as if each one were a lethal dose of poison, and she was having a high-voltage relationship with a man nine years younger than herself who adored her.

"Sorry to bother you, honey, but I had a broken water pipe in the garage sometime last night—one of the pipes that goes to a shampoo sink. Anyway, a neighbor got the water turned off, but everything's a mess."

Susannah was puzzled. It wasn't like Angela to worry her with household emergencies. She listened as Angela detailed her problems getting a plumber.

"Is there something I can do to help?" she asked.

"I tried to get hold of Sam, but he didn't answer."

If Sam wasn't home this early on a Saturday morning, he obviously hadn't spent the night in his own bed. This time the ache was less noticeable.

Angela went on. "I just thought someone should know

about it because of all those computers that are stored on the other side of the wall. I'm afraid the water might have gotten to some of them."

"What computers?"

"The ones Sam sent over a few weeks ago. Part of a new project or something. He was worried about security."

Susannah had no idea what Angela was talking about. Why would Sam be storing SysVal equipment in a garage? She reassured Angela that she would take care of it. They chatted for a few more minutes. Susannah hung up, then began punching in the number of SysVal's switchboard.

Her finger stalled before she completed the call. Something wasn't right.

"Paige, I have to run out for a while. It can't be any fun for you staying alone at Falcon Hill, and there's a perfectly good extra bedroom here. Why don't you pack a suitcase and move in with me for a few weeks?"

"You just want a free housekeeper," Paige grumbled. But Susannah could see that she was pleased with the invitation. By the time she left for Angela's, Paige had started making out a grocery list.

Angela let Susannah into the garage and left to meet a friend in the city. The garage smelled damp from the broken water pipe, but still familiar. A rush of nostalgia came over her as she remembered the hope and excitement of those early days. This part of the garage was now used only for storage. Boxes of beauty supplies took up the shelves that had once held those first SysVal computer boards. The abandoned burn-in box housed crimped rolls of old hairstyle posters. Her eyes swept from the burn-in box to the dusty workbench and then to the wall that divided the beauty shop from the rest of the garage.

Two rows of cartons marked with the Blaze logo had been stacked there. She carefully counted them. There were thirteen.

Flipping on all the lights so that she could see better, she stepped through a shallow puddle of water and made her way over to the boxes. The flaps weren't sealed. Pulling them back, she saw a silver-gray computer inside. It wasn't packed in molded Styrofoam like a new machine, but had been stored unprotected. With some effort she wrested it from the carton and set it on the floor. Although she could see that it had been used, she didn't have a list of serial numbers, and she had no way of knowing for certain if it was one of the thirteen test models or not.

Pushing up the sleeves of her sweater, she opened the next carton and continued to unpack the machines. Perspiration formed between her breasts and tendrils of hair stuck to her damp cheeks. She was breathing heavily by the time she maneuvered the eleventh computer from its box.

Her eyes swept over the case and then stopped as she found what she had been looking for—a brightly colored sticker mounted crookedly on the side of the metal housing. In hot pink letters it announced BOSS LADY. One of her assistants had put the sticker on the machine as a joke. This was her missing computer.

She called Yank from the telephone in the beauty salon. He was awake but vague. She repeated her instructions twice, hoping he would follow them. Then she sat down in the quiet garage along with the ghosts of her past and waited.

He arrived more quickly than she had expected. Without asking any questions, he set four of the computers on the workbench, including Susannah's old machine, and turned them on. Two of the machines were completely dead, and their screens remained dark. Two of them, including her computer, responded normally.

He tilted one of the nonfunctioning machines onto its side and unscrewed the case. "Somebody's been here first," he said. "The board is missing."

Susannah peered inside and saw that the printed circuit board that held many of the computer's components had been removed.

Yank moved the two machines that were still working over to the old burn-in box and left them running. Then he turned his attention to the computers on the floor. "Let's see what we've got here. One by one."

By the time they were finished, they discovered six dead machines and seven that still worked. Two of the dead machines still contained their circuit boards. Yank removed them and began testing them.

She pulled up one of the old metal stools and watched

him, taking care not to disturb his concentration, even though she itched to question him. Eventually her back began to ache. Slipping off the stool, she went into the Pretty Please Salon, where she made a pot of coffee.

She was walking back into the garage with two steaming mugs in her hand when a banging noise erupted from one of the working computers that had been plugged into the burn-in box. Startled, she moved closer, only to realize that the awful noise was coming from her old machine. It sounded as if the disk drive head was slamming back and forth. Coffee splashed over the side of the mug and spilled on the back of her hand as the noise grew worse. Instead of behaving like a sweetly engineered piece of high-tech equipment, her beautiful little Blaze was banging away like an old Model T.

Abruptly, the machine grew quiet and the screen went dark. A tiny wisp of smoke curled from the case.

"Interesting," Yank murmured, with typical understatement.

"Interesting? My God, Yank, what happened?"

"It died," he said.

She wanted to scream at him to be more specific, but she knew it wouldn't do any good.

He pulled her old machine from the burn-in box and carried it to the workbench. As he tilted it onto its side, he said, "Why don't you go on? This is going to take a while."

She hesitated, then decided she would go crazy just standing around watching Yank and waiting for him to say something. When Yank knew what was wrong, he would tell her. Until then, not even the threat of torture could pull an opinion from him.

She picked up her purse. "Work on this by yourself, Yank. When you find out what's happening, report to me directly. Don't talk to Sam. And don't talk to Mitch, either." She felt guilty for cutting Mitch out, but she wanted a little time to absorb the facts first before she told him what was happening.

He studied her closely, but didn't comment.

She had an appointment with her attorney that afternoon to discuss the divorce. Paige went with her, and afterward they did some shopping together. Although Susannah enjoyed her time with her sister, her mind was back in the Gamble garage trying to sift through what she had seen.

Only one moment of tension marred their afternoon together. As they were driving back to the town house, Susannah, in an attempt to encourage her sister to look for organizations where she could be useful, mentioned some of the local charities SysVal had involved itself with over the past few years. Perhaps it was because she was so worried about what she had discovered in the garage that she didn't guard her tongue carefully enough.

"I don't know whether or not you're aware of it, Paige, but ever since Father died, FBT has been doing a lousy job of getting money into the community. It's gotten even worse lately. Cal's great on high-profile grants—museums, symphonies—but he won't involve the company with drug programs, alcoholism, the homeless—anything that's down and dirty."

Paige's expression grew distant. "I won't talk about anything that has to do with Cal. He's the one subject that's off limits between us. There aren't very many people on this planet I owe any loyalty to, but Cal stood by me when I didn't have anyone else, and he's one of them."

Susannah didn't say anything more.

When they got back to the town house, Susannah found a message from Yank asking her to come to the garage at seven that evening. Paige had already made plans for dinner with a friend. Susannah did some chores around the town house and then drove to Angela's.

The lights were on in the garage when she got there. As she let herself in, she saw that Yank was still hunched over the workbench, his shirt pulled tight across his back. For a fraction of a moment the years flew away and she was a runaway bride again, watching a skinny egghead genius at work. But then Yank turned toward her and the illusion slipped away. The face of the man before her was strong and arresting, full of character and an almost unearthly sweetness. This man was self-confident in the deepest, most private way.

"The others will be here soon," he said quietly.

She stopped in her tracks. "Others?"

"We're partners, Susannah. We have to solve this together."

She experienced a disturbing combination of anger and guilt. "I gave you a direct order, and you chose to disregard it."

"Yes."

"I told you not to talk to anyone until you'd talked to me."

"It was an improper order, Susannah. Mitch should be here soon. I didn't call Sam, however, until just a few minutes ago. It will take him a while to get here, so the three of us will have a little time to talk first."

Headlights flashed through the side window as another car pulled in. Moments later Mitch stalked through the door. "What's this about?" he asked abruptly.

"We have a problem, I'm afraid," Yank replied.

Mitch's eyes roamed the garage, taking in the computers, the workbench, and coming to rest on her. She hoped he didn't guess that he was here at Yank's invitation, not her own.

Yank cleared his throat and began to speak. "We produced thirteen test models of the Blaze III because Sam wanted the computer in use for at least four months before it went on the market."

She could almost see Mitch mentally counting the machines scattered around the garage. "I remember. They've performed like champions. A few of the employees had them. Some of our customers. A couple went to elementary schools."

"Susannah had one in her office," Yank continued, "but it disappeared while she was in Greece. When she tried to find it, she discovered that hers wasn't the only one missing."

"Why didn't you tell me about this?" Mitch asked.

"In light of our other problems, I didn't think it was that important."

"Our test models disappear, and you don't think it's important?"

"It wasn't like that." She didn't like the way he was putting her on the defensive, so she recited the sequence of events coldly.

After she told of her phone call from Angela, Yank took

over and described what he had found. He mentioned the missing circuit boards on some of the machines and recounted the failure he and Susannah had witnessed in her computer. "It was an amazing piece of luck for me to actually be able to watch Susannah's machine fail. If that hadn't happened, it would have taken me much longer to understand the problem. All of the trouble has its source in one of the ROM chips."

ROM—standing for "read only memory"—was a custom microchip containing instructions that allowed the computer to perform automatically a specific set of tasks. Susannah listened carefully as Yank detailed how he had pinpointed the source of the trouble.

While Mitch questioned him more closely, Susannah mentally reconstructed the process of making a ROM chip. First the SysVal engineers decided what specific jobs the chip was required to perform. Then they wrote a list of instructions for those tasks in machine language. When the instructions were complete, the listing was sent to a ROM chip manufacturing firm where the chip was produced. For years, SysVal had used an Oakland-based firm named Dayle-Wells. The firm was efficient, reliable, and stood by its work.

"We've had chip failures before," Mitch said, when he was finally satisfied with Yank's explanation. "It's not something we take lightly, but it certainly doesn't justify all this secrecy."

Susannah had been thinking the same thing. Each tiny Sen-Sen-sized microchip was housed in a rectangular casing about an inch long. The casing had always reminded her of a caterpillar because it had a series of pointed legs at the bottom that fit into miniscule slots on the computer board. It was a relatively simple matter to unplug a faulty chip and plug in a good one.

Once again Mitch turned his attention to Susannah. "I assume Sam is behind this. Do you think this is related to his rush to sell the company?"

"I can't imagine what the link is, but it's difficult for me to believe this is coincidental."

Mitch gestured toward the computers. "But why all the

subterfuge? Just because one batch of chips fails doesn't mean that they're all bad. It's a problem, but it's not unsolvable."

"Remember that we're dealing with a ROM chip that contains software," Yank said, "and the possibility that I find alarming—"

But whatever Yank was about to say was cut short as Sam slammed into the garage. He looked wild, like a man on the brink of losing control. "Is it coincidence that I'm the last person here, or did my invitation have a different time printed on it from everyone else's?"

Mitch's features hardened. "You're lucky you got an invitation at all."

Sam turned on Susannah. For a moment, she almost thought he would strike her. Mitch must have thought so, too, because he took a step forward.

"This is your fault," Sam shouted. "You pick away and pick away without the slightest goddamn idea of what you're doing—always second-guessing me, thinking you know better."

"That's enough," Mitch interrupted. "Why don't you just cut through all the crap and tell us what's going on here."

Sam looked around at the empty cartons and the machines scattered everywhere. The tendons of his neck were stretched taut, his eyebrows drawn so close together they looked like a single line. "You should have done it my way. All of you should have trusted me. I was willing to take the responsibility. You should have let me do it. Why didn't you let me do it?"

"Because it's not your company," Susannah retorted.

His arm slashed the air. "It's not going to be yours, either, for very long because it's going up in smoke."

"A chip failure is hardly the end of the world," she countered.

"Oh, no? How many Blaze III's have we shipped since we introduced the machine?"

"Nearly two hundred thousand. But just because we have a bad part in the test models doesn't mean the ROM chip in every III we've manufactured is bad."

"Wrong again," Sam sneered.

"How can you know that?" she asked. "You can't possibly—"

"They're all bad. Every III we've shipped is going to fail after one thousand hours of use. Statistically, that'll average out to about a year—less time under office use, more time under home use."

"One year!" She caught her breath while Mitch swore softly. She wanted to reject Sam's conclusion, but she couldn't. He would never have predicted something this dire if he weren't absolutely certain.

She tried to sort through the facts logically. They'd faced recalls before, but never one this massive. She began thinking aloud, hoping to reassure herself as she reassured them. "It'll be a huge headache, but we can deal with it. Dayle-Wells is a reliable firm. If they've made a bad chip, they'll take financial responsibility for it." In her mind, she was already envisioning the logistics of this kind of recall. Once the outer case was opened, the actual replacement of the ROM chip was a relatively minor procedure. The old one was simply unplugged from its slots and a new one inserted. But the sheer number of machines involved made the recall complex, and it had to be done before the faulty chip physically destroyed the computer by smashing the disk drive head.

"Little Miss Pollyanna," Sam scoffed. "Always looking for the bright side. Well, babe, this time there isn't one. Dayle-Wells isn't responsible for the bad chip. We are."

Mitch's head shot up. Susannah felt as if a cold fist had clutched her spine.

Sam began to pace. "The ROM listing Dayle-Wells received from us was buggy."

Mitch spun around. "That's impossible. We have a dozen safeguards built in to keep that sort of thing from happening."

"Well, it happened this time. Five lines—just five lousy lines of bum code out of a hundred—but those five lines programmed a time bomb into the machines. Every Blaze III we've shipped will work for exactly one thousand hours, and then it will fail. The disk drive slams its head back and forth. It destroys itself and burns out the power supply.

After that—nothing." His voice had a harsh, raspy edge. "One thousand hours from the date the computer is first turned on, every one of those III's is going down."

Yank spoke thoughtfully. "The first of those failures will be showing up any day now, if they haven't already. Others are going to take years."

Dates and numbers spun like a roulette wheel in Susannah's head. They had charts that were amazingly accurate at predicting computer-use time. At best, they had only a few months to prepare. Once again, she began to think aloud. "We can handle the recall. It'll be expensive—it'll definitely hurt—but it won't kill the company."

"Susannah's right," Mitch said. "We can set up some sort of centralized system. Move a few hundred of our people into temporary service positions and send them out into the field. Thank God it's just one chip. We take out the old one, plug in the new one. We can do it."

Sam hunched his shoulders and turned his back to them.

Yank's voice was strained. "No. No, I'm afraid we can't. Come here and take a look."

With a sinking sensation in the pit of her stomach, Susannah got up from the arm of the couch and walked to the workbench. Mitch fell into step beside her. Sam stayed where he was with his back turned away from them. Whatever Yank was about to show them, Sam had already seen.

Susannah gazed down into the orderly, internal world of the Blaze III. Its microchips were laid out like rows of miniature houses on the neat little village streets of the green printed circuit board. With the tip of a pair of long-nosed pliers, Yank singled out one microchip. Susannah leaned forward to take a look.

"This is the bad chip," Yank said. "Look. It's soldered. The chip is permanently soldered to the board." He paused a moment, giving his words time to sink in. "We can't do a simple little chip swap. This particular part was designed to be permanent. That means we have to replace the whole circuit board on every Blaze III we've ever made."

Susannah's bones seemed to have lost the ability to support her. She felt as if she had just been punched in the belly. They couldn't afford to replace the circuit board on every machine they had manufactured. The cost would be prohibitive.

They didn't look at each other. Susannah stared down at the circuit board, Mitch at the litter of tools on the workbench. Silence ticked away like a doomsday clock. All of them knew that Yank had just pronounced their death sentence.

28

....

The four of them sat silently around Angela's kitchen table. Mitch held his reading glasses between his fingers and folded one stem in and out. Sam rolled an empty can of Coke between his open palms. Susannah rubbed her right temple with the pad of her thumb. She had just done the unthinkable. She had made the phone call that shut down the Blaze III assembly line.

Yank stared off into space. He had taken himself to a place so far away he might not have been with them at all.

Mitch finally spoke. "I can't even conceive of how many hundreds of millions this is going to cost."

No one said anything. Even a giant company like IBM or FBT would have difficulty recovering from this sort of financial catastrophe, and a young company like SysVal simply didn't stand a chance.

Susannah's hand curled into a fist. If only *some* of the III's had been bad, they could have handled it, but the fact that the machines they had shipped last week, yesterday, the ones that had come off the line that very morning—the fact that *all* of them were bad—made the situation so hopeless her mind could barely absorb it.

Yank slowly re-entered their world. "Who wrote the bad code?"

The Coke can slapped between Sam's palms. "I don't know for sure. My guess is that it was one of the engineers who was working on the instructions for the chip. A guy named Ed Fiella. He only worked for us about six months, then he quit."

"Did you try to find him?"

"Yeah, but he disappeared, so I let it go. I couldn't ask too many questions or people would have been able to figure out that something was wrong."

"No one else knows about this?" Mitch asked sharply.

Sam shook his head. "Until today, I was the only one who had all the pieces."

Susannah rubbed the pulse in her temple. "How could you keep something like this secret?"

"I used a couple of independent engineers in Boston to run a few tests, some guys in Atlanta—people who weren't likely to bump into each other while they were out jogging. And I didn't let any of them know this involved anything more than a couple of prototypes."

Yank looked searchingly at Sam. "You realize that these failures aren't accidental. Everything happens too specifically. The machine works for a thousand hours and then it stops. And when it fails, it does it spectacularly. All that noise—the disk drive banging. That's too bizarre to be accidental."

"You're saying someone—this Fiella, probably—deliberately planted a bug in the ROM chip?" Susannah asked.

Sam nodded. "Just five lines of code, but that's all it took."

"We have so many checks and balances built into our procedures," she said. "A test team, code reviews among the engineers. How could this happen?"

"Maybe Fiella somehow managed to switch the listings at the last minute." Sam walked to the refrigerator and pulled out another Coke. "You know, I'm almost glad you found out. I was getting tired of having all of you look at me like I was Benedict Arnold or somebody."

Mitch slipped his glasses back on. "This is why you started pressuring the board to sell the company."

"If Databeck buys SysVal," Sam said, "the board swap is

their problem. We're out clean and we have the money in our pockets to start a new company. Databeck is a big conglomerate. The loss will hurt them, but they can stand it."

"There are laws against that kind of thing," Susannah said wearily. "Once those machines start to die, they'll sue us for fraud."

Sam slammed his unopened Coke can down on the counter. "No they won't. That's the beauty. It'll be months before we see anything more than a few isolated failures, and I haven't left any loose ends. They couldn't even come close to proving that we had any previous knowledge of the defect."

Susannah dropped her eyes to the tabletop. "So we dump the company on them, take the money, and run."

"Something like that," Sam replied with a shrug.

She looked up from the table and stared him straight in the eye. "That's shit, Sam. That's really shit."

He gave her the black scowl he always used whenever she uttered a vulgarity. She looked away in disgust.

Mitch's tone was cool and impersonal. "We at least need to discuss the possibility of selling out to Databeck."

Susannah felt a prickling along the back of her neck, and she turned toward him angrily. "The only way Databeck will buy SysVal is if we don't tell them about the bug."

"They have a lot more resources than we do," he said calmly. "There's a slim possibility that they could save SysVal. We already know that we can't."

Her skin felt cold. Mitch was going to betray her, too. Her friend had become a stranger. She thought she knew him so well, but she hadn't known him at all. Feeling as if she had just lost something precious, she turned toward Yank. When she spoke, her voice trembled. "Yank, what do you think?"

He returned to her from a very distant place. His eyes met hers and his expression was deeply troubled. For a moment he did nothing, and then he gently, almost accidentally, brushed the tips of her fingers with his own. They tingled slightly, as if she had been touched by a greater power. "I'm sorry, Susannah," he said softly. "I'm still processing the information. I'm sorry, but I'm not ready to offer an opinion yet."

"I see."

"I'm not offering an opinion, either," Mitch said firmly. "I'm merely pointing out that we need to discuss all the options."

She didn't believe him. Mitch was a black-ink man, a homebred, bottom-line capitalist. They could discuss all the options in the world, but in her heart of hearts, she was certain he would eventually side with Sam.

Sam began to pummel them with facts and figures. Mitch grabbed one of Angela's scratch pads and took copious notes, filling up one page and then quickly flipping to the next.

Susannah listened and said nothing.

Eventually her silence grew oppressive to Sam. He planted the flat of his hand on the table and leaned down. "We've already seen what happens when we splinter, Susannah. For chrissake, we have to work together on this as partners. We have to speak with one single voice."

"And I'll bet you think that voice should be yours," she snapped.

"That's crap, Susannah. Why don't you stop taking potshots for a while and start acting like a team player?"

"All right." She stood up and walked over to the kitchen counter. "All right, I'll be a team player. I'll reduce all this discussion to one simple question—the only question. Are we going to tell Databeck about the bug or not?"

Mitch looked down at his notepad and drew the outlines of a box. He traced the border over and over again with his pen.

As always, Sam declared a spade a spade. "Databeck would snatch that offer back in a second if they knew about these machines. Unless we keep quiet, there isn't any offer."

"Then that makes our decision simple, doesn't it? Are we liars or aren't we?"

Mitch slammed down his pen. "Susannah, I have to tell you that I resent your condescending tone. You don't have any special pipeline to heaven."

"We had a mission," she said, her voice catching on the last word. "We set out on an adventure together, and we've always been true to it. We didn't lie. We didn't cheat or steal or take shortcuts. And we made money beyond our wildest dreams. But making money was never what the adventure was about. It was only part of it. The adventure was about pushing ourselves and finding our own excellence."

Mitch stood up. "Those are wonderful words, but we're trying to decide the future of thousands of people here."

"They're not just words!" she exclaimed, her heart pumping in her chest, as she tried desperately to make them understand. "We've been put to the test."

Mitch made a dismissive sound and scowled.

"People are put to the test everyday," she declared. "Just not as dramatically as it's happened to us. A clerk puts too much change in your hands. Do you give it back? A friend tells a racist joke. Do you laugh? Are you going to cheat on your taxes? Water down the liquor? When does a person take a stand? When do we say, 'Stop! That's enough! This is what I believe in, and I'll stand by it until I die.'"

The corners of Sam's mouth twisted sardonically. "Don't you love this? Listen to the rich girl talk. Only someone who has never been poor could be so morally pure."

The muscles in the back of her neck ached with tension and her palms were damp as she pleaded with them to understand. "Don't you see? We've slammed right up against the morality of our own lives."

"This is business," Mitch said. "We're merely discussing a business deal."

"No," she retorted. "It's a lot more than that."

He gazed at her with a combination of pain and wonder. "You want us to hang on even if those beliefs are going to take us on a death ride?"

"Yes. Yes, I do." She walked closer to him, until only the corner of the table separated them. "Ever since I was born, people have been telling me what the rules of life are. My grandmother, my father." She gazed over at the man who was still her husband. "And you, Sam. You, most of all. But none of those definitions ever seemed quite right to me. Now—today—right at this moment—I know exactly who I am. I know what I believe in. And I believe in our mission. I've always believed in it. Our mission statement isn't just what SysVal is about. It's what life is about. Quality, excellence, honesty, taking pride in what we do no matter what that might be, and standing by it. That's what makes life good."

Sam's face had grown rigid and Mitch looked shaken. She turned toward Yank so she could judge his reaction, and saw that his expression was as blank as a sheet of white paper. While she had been spilling out her soul, he had been in a world of his own, not paying the slightest bit of attention.

Sick at heart, she moved away. The edge of the counter dug into the top of her hip as she sagged against it. They were going to end the adventure. She could sense it. Their brave and daring adventure was going to be transformed into something loathsome and unclean. She wanted to hurt them for what they were doing, and the only way she could hurt them was to make them speak the truth aloud about themselves.

"I'm calling for a vote." Her voice was hollow. "Are we going to tell Databeck the truth or not?"

"A vote between the four of us means nothing," Mitch said. "It's obvious that we're going to be splintered."

"No! I want a vote. I'm putting all of us to the test. Right now. Right this moment. We've slammed against the wall, and each one of us has to take a stand. We have to declare what we believe in."

Mitch reached out toward her. The gesture was awkward, almost as if he thought he could stop her flow of words with his hand. She moved past his reach, determined to see this through to the end.

"Yank, how do you vote? Do we tell Databeck the truth about the machines or not?"

Yank blinked and looked faintly befuddled. "Well, of course we tell them. It would be dishonest not to."

She stared at him and absorbed his absolute certainty. At that moment, comprehension swept over her, an awareness so new and yet so old she couldn't believe that she hadn't understood it long go. The vision of excellence and integrity that Sam carried like an evangelist into the world had come from Yank. Sam had merely found the words to define everything that Yank believed in.

She gave Yank a shaky smile and looked at her husband.

As she stared into his eyes, one part of her still yearned to reach out to him, but she understood with absolute certainty that was no longer possible. "Sam? Please, Sam."

"Sometimes the end justifies the means," he muttered.

"What about our mission? Please," she begged him. "Think about our mission. Think about what it means."

"Too many people depend on us," he said flatly. "Too much money is involved. I vote no."

Some precious spark of optimism, a naive belief in the invincibility of the human spirit, died within her. Her throat felt tight and swollen as she turned to Mitch and uttered his name.

His face was pale, his words clipped. "This is ridiculous, Susannah. Completely meaningless. There are complexities here, subtleties that need to be examined and discussed."

All the confused emotions she felt for him were choking her. "I'm putting you to the test, Mitch," she whispered. "Do we tell them or not?"

He dropped his head. Stared down at the floor. As she saw the stoop to those broad shoulders she had so often leaned upon, she was overcome with a sense of her own arrogance. Who was she to hold Mitch up to judgment? He was a good man. She had no right to do this to him.

He spoke, his voice low-pitched and sad. "Yes. Yes, we tell them the truth."

A rush went through her—hot and cold at the same time, the birth of something new and strange.

Sam slumped against the wall. His shoulders hunched forward, his head sagged. Everything about him spoke defeat. She walked over to him, her sneakers making soft little squeaks on the floor, and this time she touched him, the lightest brush of her fingers against his hand. "We have a few months," she whispered. "Help us make a miracle."

"No," he said belligerently. "No, there aren't going to be any miracles."

She laced her fingers through his and squeezed them, trying to pass her strength to him as he had once passed it to her. "You can find one if you want to. You can do anything. I believe it, Sam. I've always believed it."

"You're a fool. A stupid, self-destructive fool." He

dropped her hand and gazed at her with bleak angry eyes. "You'll have my letter of resignation on your desk Monday morning."

A murmur of protest slipped through her lips.

"I'm quitting," he said. "The terms of our partnership agreement give the three of you sixty days to buy me out. I'm going to hold you to it."

She wanted to be angry with him, but instead she experienced a splintering sensation of separation. Lifting her hand, she cupped the cheek of the man she had once loved so well and so unwisely. "Don't do it, Sam. Don't walk away from us. The adventure isn't over. Stay and fight with us."

But no sparks flashed in those deep dark eyes. Something essential had left him. He stood before her—a visionary with no vision, a missionary who had lost his faith. Gently, he removed her hand from his cheek. Then he turned on his heel and left them alone.

29

$\bullet$

Susannah was cold with fear. She couldn't imagine SysVal without Sam. He *was* SysVal. He was the energy that propelled them, the force that guided them. Yank was gathering up his tools, and Mitch absentmindedly fingered his car key. She couldn't stand to have them leave her. "Come back to my house. I filled the freezer yesterday. We can find something to eat."

Apparently they were no more anxious than she to be alone, because they immediately agreed to her suggestion.

They drove separately. Mitch and Yank parked in front, while Susannah drove into the single-car garage. As she came in through the kitchen, she heard Paige's throaty laughter in the foyer.

"Well, well, well. If this isn't my lucky day. Tell me. Have you boys ever considered a sexual threesome?"

Susannah quickly made her way toward the foyer. She heard Mitch give a chuckle that sounded thin at the edges. "Sorry, cupcake, I only work solo."

"It figures. I'll bet you leave your socks on, too."

Susannah arrived in time to see Paige sauntering over to Yank. "Feeling left out, slugger?" She began to move closer, only to have him shoot out his hand and grasp hers, giving it a solid shake that effectively kept her at arm's length.

"It's good to see you again, Paige."

Paige's presence proved a welcome distraction. She picked up their somber mood, but she didn't ask any questions. Herding them into the kitchen, she began putting together a platter of cold cuts and making sandwiches.

Paige's position as a major FBT stockholder prevented them from discussing the crisis that was uppermost in their minds, but all of them seemed to welcome the respite. The next day would be soon enough for them to pick over the bones and see what they could salvage.

Yank was quiet and distracted throughout the meal. In contrast, Mitch teased and bantered with Paige as if he hadn't a care in the world. Once again Susannah wondered what it was about her sister that produced such a transformation in her stodgy partner.

Over scoops of vanilla ice cream smothered with home-made butterscotch syrup, Paige shifted her attention to Yank. She gave him a mischievous smile. "Do you know why female pygmies don't like to wear tampons?"

"Oh, Lord," Susannah groaned, losing interest in her ice cream.

Paige waved her to be quiet while Yank appeared to think over the answer. When nothing was forthcoming, she leaned toward him. "They trip on the strings."

Mitch chuckled. Yank's forehead wrinkled as if he were trying to sort out the physics of the whole thing.

"Paige, that's gross," Susannah protested.

The three of them gave her varying looks of disapproval, until she felt like an old maid schoolteacher with a prim mouth and chin whiskers. Slapping down her napkin, she got up from the table. "You people can party all night if you want to, but I'm going to bed. There's a cleaning lady coming in the morning, so leave the dishes."

Mitch stood up. "It's getting late. I think I'd better be getting to bed, too."

Paige lifted one eyebrow mischievously. "Why not climb in with Susannah? Now there's a combination of live-wire personalities guaranteed to set the sheets on fire. I'll bet the two of you could bring up the temperature of a bedroom—oh, maybe one and a half degrees."

"Paige, shut up, why don't you?" She scowled at her sister

and escorted Mitch to the door. Even though she knew it was silly, Paige's taunt had made her self-conscious. "In my office at eight on Monday, okay?"

He nodded and deposited a chaste kiss on her forehead. "You take care, hear? We'll work things out."

She shut the door behind him and walked upstairs to her bedroom. If only it were that easy.

In the kitchen below, Paige made a great show out of clearing the table. With far more force than was necessary, she snatched the dessert bowl out from under Yank.

He gently clasped her wrist. "You were rude to your sister."

"I'm always rude to Susannah. She wouldn't recognize me if I turned nice."

He maintained his grasp on her wrist. To punish him, she deliberately dropped down into his lap, where she wedged herself between the edge of the table and his thin, wiry body. "How's the celibacy trip going, lover boy? Ready to break your fast yet?" She wiggled the tip of her fingernail in between two of the buttons on his shirt and lightly scratched his bare skin.

He removed her hand.

She sighed dramatically and extracted herself from his lap. "Whenever I'm around you, I feel like Mary Magdalene trying to tempt Jesus."

"It's not the right time, Paige."

"And you're not the right man." She had intended to say the words lightly, but they came out with a sharp, vicious edge. She tried to cover up with a laugh, but it rang hollow.

He came up behind her as she walked over to the sink. "Please don't worry."

"Who me? Not a chance."

"Everything's quite difficult now. We have a crisis."

"Not my problem, slick. And by the way, our deal is off as of right now."

"That's not a good idea."

"Stick it, okay? I'm serving notice. Before the month is over, I'm going to tumble your good-looking buddy into a big double bed and screw his brains off."

He stood absolutely still. "You want to go to bed with Mitch?"

"Wouldn't any woman in her right mind?"

She waited for some reaction, prayed that he would yell at her or shake her or tell her he'd lock her in a room before he'd see her go back on the promise she'd made. Instead, he regarded her with great seriousness. And then to her astonishment, he leaned back in his chair and smiled in the deeply satisfied manner of a man who has the world under his absolute control.

"As long as it's Mitch, it's all right."

She wanted to slap his geeky, nearsighted face. He might just as well have stabbed a fingernail file right through the center of her heart. At that moment, she hated him, and so she gave him her bitchiest cat's smile. "Wanna watch?"

For a moment he looked so thoughtful that she wondered if he was actually considering the idea, but then he patted her arm and, as he got up to leave, told her she needed a good rest.

That night as she climbed into the guest-room bed, she heard the echo of the devil's laughter.

I can't get no . . .
I can't get no . . .

Sam's resignation lay on Susannah's desk when she arrived at work Monday morning. She stared down at it, unwilling to touch it with her fingers. The neat black and white letters swam in front of her eyes. She pushed the paper away and covered it with a folder. For now, at least, she would pretend that it didn't exist.

She managed to postpone the board meeting for another week while she brought in her key security people to begin tracing Edward Fiella, the engineer Sam suspected of being responsible for the bad code. Stressing the need for secrecy until they made a public announcement about the failures, she also had checks run on every employee at both SysVal and Dayle-Wells who had had any contact with the faulty ROM chip.

She spent the weekend preparing for the board meeting she had called for the following Monday. In hopes that bad news might be received better if it came in a brightly colored package, she dressed that morning in a hot pink suit draped at the neck with a boldly patterned Matisse scarf she had bought in the gift shop at San Francisco's Museum of Modern Art.

Mitch met her as she was walking toward the boardroom and fell into step beside her. "I just talked to Yank. Sam gave him his proxy."

Susannah didn't know what to say. Although she was glad that one of them had the proxy, she wished Sam had chosen Mitch. She would have trusted Yank with her life, but he was definitely a wild card when it came to a roll call. The men took their seats, and Susannah broke the news to them as calmly as possible. She might as well have detonated an atomic bomb in the middle of the conference table.

Leland Hayward's complexion turned gray, and he jumped up from his chair. "This is outrageous! How could something like this happen?"

"My investors are going to be wiped out," cried another board member as he fumbled in his suit pocket for a container of nitroglycerin pills. "What am I supposed to say to them?"

Mitch tried to calm the outbursts that had erupted around the table. "We have several months. Susannah and I remain hopeful that we can find at least a partial solution to our difficulty."

"Difficulty! This isn't a difficulty! It's a goddamn disaster."

They raged on, and Susannah made no effort to quiet them. For many of these board members, their jobs rode on the wisdom of their investment decisions, and the dramatic failure of SysVal would mark the end of their careers. They subtly let it be known that the partners should have kept the news of the computer failures to themselves and let the sale to Databeck go through.

"That's not what this company stands for," Susannah said. "You knew that about us from the beginning."

"Sam was going to let the sale go through," Hayward said in an accusatory voice. "Why didn't you let him do it? The board couldn't have been held responsible because he hadn't informed us. And where is Sam? Why isn't he here?"

She had dodged their previous questions about Sam's absence, but she could do it no longer, and she informed them of his resignation.

The absolute silence that fell over the table was worse than the men's anger. The news seemed to extinguish any dim hope they might have cherished of finding a way out of their disaster. The men didn't like Sam, but they believed in him.

The same emotion of despair had gripped her when she had seen Sam's letter of resignation lying on her desk, but something about their hangdog expressions sparked her anger. Sam wasn't superhuman. He didn't possess any special powers to save the company. There were other bright, inventive minds at SysVal, and one of those minds was her own.

Without clearly thinking through what she had to say, she rose from her chair and faced the board members squarely. "From the beginning, all of you knew that the SysVal adventure was one of high risk. But you were eager to go on that adventure as long as you could delude yourself into believing that the four founding partners were keeping the path safe for you. You were making so much money that it served you well to delude yourself. And so you told yourselves lies about us."

"What are you talking about?" Leland snapped. "What lies?"

"The lies that kept you comfortable so you could enjoy the fortunes you were making," she said angrily. "The lies about who we were. For all the faith you have in Sam's mystical abilities to solve any crisis, he's always frightened you. You didn't like that fear, and so in your minds you tried to overcome it by mentally transforming Mitch and Yank and myself into safe, conservative business partners who could balance out Sam's unpredictability. You didn't look at the three of us individually, only as we related to Sam. His arrogance disturbed you, so you found solace in my respectability. His inexperience terrified you, so you concentrated on Mitch's experience. When his flair for theatrics embarrassed you, you took comfort in Yank's solid silences. Always, it was Sam you turned to, Sam you believed in, and Sam you feared. You ignored the stories that I had run away from my wedding on the back of a motorcycle. You passed over any doubts you might have had about the stability of a man with Mitch's background throwing it all away to take up with three kids working out of a garage. You ignored Yank's radical genius and convinced yourself he was merely eccentric. Sam was the wildcatter. Sam was the swashbuckler. From the very beginning, you never understood that all four of us were the same. You never admitted to yourself that all four of us were renegades."

The board members were stunned by the passion of her words. Mitch leaned back in his chair and began to applaud, a lone set of hands clapping in the quiet room. Yank looked down at the notepad in front of him, a vague, satisfied smile tugging at the corners of his mouth.

"The adventure is not over, gentlemen," she said quietly. "We don't promise you that we can save this company. But we do promise you that no one—not Sam Gamble, not God Himself—has a better chance of saving SysVal than the three of us."

The meeting adjourned in a somber mood. As the members filed out of the room, Mitch came over to her and squeezed her shoulder. "Nice going, Hot Shot. What do we do now?"

"Now we get to work," she said.

SysVal teemed with the upheaval. Sam Gamble had disappeared, the Blaze III assembly line was shut down while a new ROM chip was being produced, and—incredibly—all work on the Wildfire project had been suspended. Everyone knew that something calamitous had happened, but no one was certain exactly what. The loudspeaker system was ominously silent.

Susannah and Mitch immediately went on the attack. To keep the public's confidence high in the Blaze III so that customers would continue to buy new machines, they had to move boldly. They drafted a series of newspaper ads in which they openly admitted that they had a problem with the old machines and assured their customers that a recall would be handled in a timely fashion. Before they could run the ads, however, they had to be honest with their employees.

Two days after the board meeting, Susannah appeared on SysVal's closed-circuit television system and told their employees exactly what had happened. Looking directly into the camera lens, she affirmed SysVal's intention to stand behind its product. Then came the most difficult part—announcing salary and hiring freezes and acknowledging that layoffs were inevitable. Speaking from the depths of her heart, she reminded them of SysVal's heritage and the absolute necessity of standing behind their product.

"This is a company that has always thrived on turmoil," she concluded, addressing the single camera in the small, high-tech studio. "Turmoil brings pain, but it also brings growth. Instead of complaining about our fate, let us welcome this crisis as an opportunity to dazzle the world. If we face this test valiantly, we will have taken another giant step along the continuing path of the SysVal adventure."

As soon as she had finished, the studio telephone rang. Her assistant announced that Mitch was on the line.

"Good speech," he said when she took the receiver. "Life's strange, isn't it? You sound more like Sam all the time."

She tightened her grip on the telephone receiver. "Sam is part of all of us. I just hope we got the best part of him."

The expression on Sam's face when she had last seen him continued to haunt her. She had tried to call him several times, but there was never an answer and no one knew where he was. Angela had gone over to the house, but it was empty and she was clearly worried. That night, as Susannah was getting ready to pull out onto El Camino, she decided to investigate for herself. Her marriage was over, but she couldn't turn off six years of caring.

The house smelled stale as she let herself inside. The bronze lamps shaped like Egyptian torches that sat in the foyer were dark, the living room cold and vaguely malevolent, with its sharply angled ceiling. Once again she realized how much she hated the harsh planes and unyielding materials of this building.

The telephone let out a shrill ring and she jumped. It rang again and again, scraping at her nerves. She stood motionless until it stopped and the house was once again quiet, then she moved through the empty rooms.

The heat pump clicked on. As she entered the vaulted hallway that led to the back of the house, she saw a wedge of weak gray light lying across the black granite floor. She walked closer and pushed on the partially opened door.

Sam lay on top of the rumpled bedcovers. He was unshaven, his chest was bare, and his jeans were open in a vee at the waist. One elbow was crooked behind his head. His other arm lay listlessly at his side while he stared up at the ceiling with hollow eyes.

On the side of the bed, a young woman sat in bra and panties filing a fingernail with an emery board. She was dark-haired and beautiful, with full breasts and long thin legs. She saw Susannah before Sam did. As she jumped up from the edge of the bed, her emery board hung in midair like a conductor's baton. Sam's gaze traveled from the ceiling to Susannah. He didn't show a flicker of expression.

She breathed in the thick, stale scent of marijuana and sex. Her stomach curled. A layer of dust covered the black lacquered furniture. The blinds were shut tight against the outside world. On the floor around the bed abandoned food cartons were mixed with dirty dishes. The painting Sam had bought her leaned with its face against the wall, a hole the size of a fist punched through the canvas.

"Get out of here," she said harshly to the woman.

The woman opened her mouth to protest, but apparently decided Susannah was too formidable to oppose. She glanced hesitantly toward Sam. He paid no attention to her; his gaze remained fixed on Susannah.

Susannah was dimly aware of the woman scrambling to get into her clothes and stumbling past her. Only when she heard the sound of the front door closing did she step farther into the room. "What are you doing to yourself?"

He turned his head to the ceiling.

She kicked away a damp bath towel. "Hiding is a coward's game. It won't solve anything."

"Unless you want to fuck, get out of here."

She didn't flinch from his vulgarity, even though the thought of going to bed with him repelled her. It wasn't just that he was sleeping with other women; she simply could no longer bear the idea of his touch. "Your mother is worried about you. We're all worried."

"Sure you are."

He sounded like a surly little boy. Whatever lingering elements of respect she had held for him crumbled away. His childishness, his infidelity, his self-pity had all diminished him.

"Are you going to spend the rest of your life sulking because you didn't get your way?"

For a moment he didn't move, but then he began to lever himself slowly out of bed. The dim light coming through the windows cast a blue-black shadow over his unshaven jaw. His hair was tousled, his arms hung at his sides. He began moving toward her, and she could feel his rage. She told herself not to underestimate him.

"You're not anything without me," he sneered.

"Do you have any idea how tired I am of dealing with your hostility?"

His nostrils flared and his hard dark eyes glittered with anger. "You're *nothing,* you hear me? You were an uptight socialite when I met you, and that's still what you are. Except now you're an uptight socialite playing at being a working girl."

The words hurt. She told herself they weren't true—she didn't believe them—but she was insecure enough that they still pricked.

"Madam President," he scoffed. "You think you've made so many contributions to SysVal. What a fucking joke. SysVal was always mine! You were so goddamn laughable the other night, I could hardly believe it. Talking about 'mission' and 'adventure' like you invented the words. Jesus, I wanted to puke."

She opened her mouth to defend herself, only to discover that she had no urge to do so. He was as pathetic as an overindulged child.

"I came to see if you were all right," she said. "Now that I know it's just self-pity bothering you, I'm leaving."

She turned to go, but he snatched her arm. "You got one more chance. I'm giving you one more chance to come with me."

"On a new adventure?" she shot back scornfully.

"Yeah. A new one. A better one. As soon as the word got out that I was leaving SysVal, every investor in this country wanted a piece of me. They're standing in line begging me to take their money. I'm the golden boy, babe. The goddamn dream child of capitalism."

His words sounded like braggadocio, but she knew they were true. An investor had even tried calling her that morning in hopes of locating him. She shook off his grasp. "You don't have the vaguest idea what the real adventure is. It's not just starting something—that's for kids. The real adventure is seeing it through. You bailed out at the toughest part, Sam. In your marriage and in your job."

For a moment she thought he was going to hit her, but she didn't flinch. Sam was a bully, and bullies had to be faced down.

"Get out of here," he said contemptuously. "Get out of here and learn what life's all about. Maybe then I *might* take you back."

She stared at him for one long moment. "I'm not coming back. Not ever."

Turning away from him, she left the house. As she stepped out into the cool, eucalyptus-scented air, she felt a sense of release. Whatever bonds of love and need had been tying her to Sam were finally destroyed. She was done forever with loving little boys.

30

• •

Hal Lundeen, SysVal's head of security, was one of the company's few employees over the age of forty. A former Oakland city cop, he was a confirmed pessimist who believed that no matter how bad a situation was, it could only get worse. The hunt for SysVal's saboteur was proving his adage.

It was December now, and he had been driving himself hard since October, when Susannah Faulconer had first called him into her office and told him about the sabotaged ROM chip. Every piece of evidence Lundeen had been able to gather pointed to Edward Fiella. He even thought he knew how the switch had been made. Fiella had apparently spilled a cup of coffee just as the messenger had arrived to pick up the ROM chip instructions that were to be delivered to Dayle-Wells. That's when the substitution had taken place. Unfortunately, finding Fiella had proved a lot more difficult than any of them had ever imagined.

Lundeen looked uncomfortable as he took a seat and gazed at the woman behind the desk. She wasn't going to be at all happy with what he had to tell her. "I'm afraid I've got some bad news about Fiella."

"Terrific," she muttered. "Did you lose him again?"

"Not exactly. We finally traced him to Philadelphia. Unfortunately, we were about ten days too late."

"He took off again?"

"No. Uh . . . he's dead."

"Dead!"

"Yeah. He was killed in an auto accident ten days ago."

"Oh, no." She rubbed her forehead with the tips of her fingers. "What happened?"

"A couple of drunk teenagers ran a stop sign. He was dead when the cops pulled him out of his car. Just one of those things."

"We can't seem to buy a piece of luck, can we? Did you find out anything else about him?"

"Yeah. The car the cops pulled him out of was a Mercedes 380 SL convertible. He bought it new a few weeks after he left SysVal."

"That's an expensive car. I didn't see any mention of it on his credit report."

"Funny thing about that. He paid cash."

She slid the pen between her fingers as she took in the implications of what he had said. "That pretty much eliminates the possibility that he was just a hacker sabotaging the chip for kicks, doesn't it?"

"I'd say so, Miss Faulconer. I'd say it blows that theory right out of the water."

Since only a founding partner could purchase another founding partner's shares, she, Mitch, and Yank had been forced to buy Sam out. The Blaze III recall had severely depressed the price of Sam's fifteen percent, but the buyout was still costing each of them millions.

Susannah had been hit the hardest because she couldn't tap into any of the assets she and Sam owned jointly until her divorce was final. As a result, she was forced to deplete all of her financial reserves. She replaced her BMW with a Ford compact, and was staying in SysVal's town-house condominium on a semipermanent basis because she couldn't afford to buy anything else for a while. It was the way of the Valley, she joked ruefully to Mitch. A millionaire one day, a pauper the next.

But it was no joke. Before all this had happened, her net worth—on paper, anyway—had been close to a hundred million dollars. But as the new year arrived and she continued to pour every dollar she could lay her hands on into their dying company, she was practically broke.

The dreary, rainy months of winter slid into early spring. What had begun as a trickle of computer failures turned into a deluge. The company was hemorrhaging money. They sold off all nonessential assets—a conference center near Carmel, warehouses, land they had bought for expansion— but it was like trying to stop the flow of blood from a bullet wound with a wad of toilet tissue. By the end of June, Susannah felt as if each day they survived bankruptcy was a miracle.

As she drove home late one June evening, she wondered if Mitch and Yank would be at the town house when she arrived. Her partners had gotten into the habit of dropping by several evenings a week. Ostensibly, they met there so they could talk without the interruptions that plagued them during the day. But Susannah knew the real reason they showed up so frequently on her doorstep was simply because they knew there was a good chance Paige would be there, and Paige helped all of them forget their troubles.

She was their beautiful, blond-haired den mother. She pampered them and clucked over them, feeding their spirits as well as their bodies. When they felt too battered to go on, she restored them with her lively chatter. She was the major stockholder of their fiercest competitor, but they had stopped worrying about divulging company secrets in front of her. Paige had no interest in the business discussions that raged around her, merely in what everyone wanted to drink and eat.

Susannah's hands tightened on the car's steering wheel. She was torn between her love for Paige and the jealousy that had begun to grow inside her these past few months. If Mitch was there when she got home, he would be trading sexual innuendoes with her sister and grinning like an idiot. Frankly, she was getting sick of it. The two of them were just too revoltingly touchy-feely. Even a blind fool could see that they were ideal for each other. Yin and yang. The perfect mating of opposites. So why didn't they just get it on and put an end to her misery?

But she didn't want them to get it on. Even though she loved them both and saw how good they were for each other, the thought of them together made her insides feel raw. She hated her selfishness, but she couldn't seem to help it. She wanted her friendship with Mitch back the way it used to be, and his growing closeness with Paige was shutting her out.

She had been so upset about the situation that she had actually tried to talk to Yank about it a few weeks ago. He had given her his inscrutable smile and told her that everything had its proper time and she should be patient. She had wanted to slap him silly.

When she arrived home, she heard three voices coming from the dining room. Paige was feeding her partners just as she had expected. Susannah stood well back in the hallway and watched unobserved for a few minutes as Paige fussed over the men. She hopped up to go to the sideboard and choose special tidbits for their plates, fishing out mushrooms because Yank didn't like them, adding black olives because Mitch did. She was June Cleaver packaged in the body of the Playmate of the Month. As much as Susannah loved her, Paige's soft womanliness had begun to make her feel sexless. Paige was every man's fantasy woman—mother and sex goddess combined. How could she compete with that? Susannah wondered.

Not that she wanted to compete. It wasn't as if she were in love with Mitch or anything. She had already experienced the great love of her life, and look where that had ended up. It was just that she'd started to look at Mitch a little differently. Which was certainly understandable. She was a sensuous woman. Her body wasn't accustomed to celibacy, and Mitch was an incredibly attractive man. The past eight months had added more gray to his temples and deepened the brackets around his mouth, but, if anything, the changes had made him more appealing, certainly too appealing to be running loose around a woman who hadn't been intimate with a man for nearly a year.

He leaned back in his chair and stretched like a well-fed cat. She felt a peculiar giddiness creep over her as she watched his dress shirt stretch over his chest.

"Too bad we can't package you and put you up for sale, Paige," he said. "We'd make millions."

Paige crossed her arms on the table and leaned forward so that her breasts were propped up on them. "Exactly what part of me would you want to package? My cooking or my . . . other skills."

Mitch grinned, something he hardly ever did with anyone except her sister. "We're buccaneer capitalists. Whichever will bring us the best profit."

"Probably Paige's cooking," Yank said quietly.

Mitch shook his head in comic bewilderment. "I think you'd better start going out with women again, Yank. Ever since you quit dating, you've been losing your perspective."

"Holy men don't date." Paige's voice was silky. "Isn't that right, Yank? Holy men don't need women. They're above all that slipping and slopping around."

Yank gave her the sad, patient look he wore so frequently when they were together, and then mentally withdrew to his accustomed position on the sidelines. The bantering Paige directed toward Yank wasn't nearly as good-humored as her comments to Mitch, Susannah had noticed. Maybe that wasn't so strange. Yank and Paige were definitely from separate planets.

"Would it be possible for me to have another cup of coffee?" Yank asked.

Paige hopped up, her blond hair flying. Both men followed her round blue-jean-clad bottom as she rushed over to the coffeepot on the sideboard. As Susannah shrugged off her coat, she couldn't suppress another petty stab of envy. Even though she knew it was demeaning, she wished one of them would look at *her* bottom that way.

If only she could forget about the crisis at SysVal for a while and just be a woman. While she hung her coat away, she played a little fantasy in her mind in which she had her sister's breasts and they were barely covered by a black lace negligee. She saw herself sashaying up to Mitch and saying something sultry like, "Hey, big guy, remember me? How's about you and me go make ourselves some whoopie?"

But this particular fantasy wouldn't work. She kept seeing Mitch's face going pale with embarrassment. She heard his self-conscious throat clearing. "Susannah, I wouldn't hurt you for the world. You know how much I value your friendship. But Paige and I . . ."

"Could I have a little more coffee, too?" Mitch held out his cup for Paige to refill. He had glimpsed Susannah skulking about in the hallway, but he was pretending he didn't know she was there. Paige leaned over him and poured. He smiled at her. She was so damned good for his bruised ego. He loved having that sweet small body racing around catering to him. He enjoyed trading jibes with her smutty little mouth. There wasn't one morsel of honest sexual chemistry between himself and Paige, but apparently Susannah didn't realize it, and for the time being that was fine with him.

Susannah's feelings toward him seemed to be changing now that he had stopped playing Mitch the Buddy. He hoped so. It was about time he started getting under Miss Hot Shot's skin. Although she might not know it, he had declared war and was banking on her love of a challenge. He prayed he wasn't miscalculating. How much longer would it be before she began to understand what he had known for so long—that they were kindred spirits, like personalities who viewed the world in the same way and fit together exactly the way a man and woman should fit?

Her divorce wouldn't be final until the end of the summer, and he intended to use every moment of that time to pry her eyes open. Maybe it wasn't fair for him to play games with her when they were in the middle of such a devastating crisis, but he didn't care about fairness anymore. It was obvious by now that SysVal couldn't survive the summer. He was going to lose his company and his money, but he wanted to make damned sure that he didn't lose Susannah, too.

The only thing that worried him was Yank. Susannah kept disappearing into his lab to watch him work. It was a habit she had developed whenever she was upset about something. Mitch thought her feelings for Yank were brotherly rather than romantic, but he wasn't absolutely certain. And Yank was impossible to read. What if he was in love with Susannah? Being forced to compete with Yank wasn't something he could take lightly. The rest of the world might underestimate his partner, but Mitch had never made that mistake.

"Suze! I didn't hear you come in." Paige had spotted her sister in the hallway. "Sit down. I'll fix a plate for you."

Susannah greeted all of them and took a seat at the table. Within seconds, she was served a glass of chilled white wine and a fragrant helping of chicken provençal. Paige did everything but plump a cushion behind her back. Susannah's spirits sank lower. She felt like the world's lowest life form for being jealous of someone who took such good care of her.

"My kids are flying in the second weekend in July," Mitch announced. "I thought I'd have a barbecue for them that Saturday. You're all invited."

"Sorry, lover," Paige said. "Big bad duty calls. That's the night I have to hostess FBT's annual party at Falcon Hill. Not that I wouldn't rather spend it with you. God, I hate those things."

"Then why do it?" he asked.

"Cal does so much for me that when he asks something in return, I try to accommodate him."

Mitch and Susannah exchanged a glance. Neither of them approved of the amount of power Paige had transferred to Cal Theroux. Since he was a forbidden subject between the sisters, Susannah had asked Mitch to urge Paige to take more interest in FBT affairs and reclaim her voting rights. Paige had told him to mind his own business.

That evening after the men had left, Paige propped herself on the living room couch with a magazine, and Susannah carried her briefcase over to the armchair. When she opened it, she discovered a fat manila folder she had thrown in just as she was leaving. For a moment she couldn't remember what it was, and then she realized it was the file on Edward Fiella that the security department had finally returned to her office that day. She had tossed it in her case so she could give it one last perusal before it was put away.

She settled back in the armchair and then noticed that Paige was staring off into space, her expression troubled.

"What's wrong?"

Paige snapped back to reality. "Nothing."

"I thought we weren't going to shut each other out anymore. Are you having problems at the shelter?" For months now Paige had been volunteering her services at a shelter for battered women. She loved her work there, but sometimes being in the presence of so much suffering got to her.

Paige shook her head, then set down her magazine. "Nothing that noble. I was just wondering . . . How come you haven't started dating anybody? It's been nearly a year since you left Sam. Your divorce will be final before long."

"There hasn't been much time. Besides, I'm not exactly the world's best company these days. It's hard to be cheerful when you've just laid off another seven hundred people."

"But don't you miss being with a man?"

"I'm with men all day long," she replied, deliberately sidestepping the issue.

"That's not what I mean."

Susannah knew exactly what her sister meant, but she certainly wasn't going to tell her that she had been having embarrassing sexual fantasies about Mitch. Instead, she told her part of the truth. "It takes all of my energy just getting from one day to the next. I don't have anything left at the moment for an emotional involvement."

"What about sex? Don't you miss it?"

"I miss it a lot."

Paige looked deeply unhappy. "I know it's stupid, but in Greece Yank made me promise not to sleep with anybody for a while. I don't know why I agreed, except you know how he is. Right after I got back, I got mad and told him I was going to sleep with anybody I wanted. But I didn't. And last month when I flew over to Paris for a few days, I was definitely planning on having a good time. I have a friend there. He's a playboy, but he's nice. Anyway, I never called him. God, Suze, it's been forever."

"Celibacy must be catching. Even Mitch seems to have given up all those dreary women he used to date." The moment the words were out, Susannah wished she hadn't brought up his name. Of course Mitch had stopped dating. He was moving in on her sister. She recovered quickly. "Maybe you just needed some time off from men for a while."

"I guess. But I'm starting to think about sex a lot. Which is really ironic, because I didn't use to like it very much."

And then Paige got up from the couch, almost as if she wished she hadn't said so much. "I—I think I'd better sleep at home tonight. I have to meet with Cal early tomorrow about the FBT party. If I stay at Falcon Hill, I won't have to fight rush-hour traffic."

Susannah nodded. She knew she wasn't the best company right now and she didn't blame Paige for taking off. They walked to the door together. Paige grabbed her purse and jacket, kissed Susannah's cheek, and left the town house.

It was a beautiful night. The moon was full, the air sweet. As Paige drove home, she tried to concentrate on how pretty the sky was so that she wouldn't start to cry. But she had barely reached the highway before the tears were dripping down her cheeks. She hated to cry. It was weak and stupid and completely infantile. But from the time Yank Yankowski had walked into her life, it seemed as if she had been doing a lot of it in her private time. God. She had been like a crazy woman for months. Every time she opened Susannah's door and she saw him standing there, she felt as if someone had shot heroin straight into her veins.

All she had to do was shut her eyes and she could see him. She tried to read messages into every change of his expression, and to transform those short cryptic statements he uttered into complex sonnets of passion, but it never worked. She was too much a realist. Of all the jokes God had played on her, this was the biggest. She, a woman who could chose among the most fascinating men in the world, had fallen in love with the nerdy, absentminded geek who was so obviously in love with her stupid, blind sister.

Susannah carried the file on Edward Fiella upstairs. She decided that she might as well do some work, because she certainly wasn't going to fall asleep easily, not with all those dirty dreams waiting for her. After she had gotten ready for bed, she propped herself into the pillows and flipped open the file. She had been through this material months before, and she didn't really expect to find anything new, but she still wanted to take one last look.

There was a coffee ring on the first page, which held a copy of his employment application. She skimmed through the rest. They had hired Fiella right out of college. He had been with them six months and then left. She knew that he had a degree from San Jose State, and she glanced through his college history. No fraternities. No professional associations. The summer before he had graduated, he had taken a job programming the computer billing system at the Mendhan Hills Yacht Club.

Her eyes stopped moving at the reference to the yacht club. Why had she never noticed that before? She had visited the Mendhan Hills Yacht Club many times. Although it was a small club, it was one of the Bay Area's most prestigious.

And Cal Theroux had been a member for as long as she had known him.

Her pulse was racing. Moments before, the bedroom had seemed cool, but now she was burning up. Don't leap to conclusions, she told herself as she threw off the covers. Cal wasn't the only high-ranking FBT official who was a member of the club, and she couldn't make assumptions just because a former SysVal employee had been in the same room with a competitor. She reminded herself that FBT and SysVal hadn't been rivals until the Falcon 101 had gone on the market. Even then, winning the contract with the state of California had been far more important to SysVal than to FBT.

But all of the logical arguments in the world weren't enough to convince her. Snatching up her telephone, she called Hal Lundeen and told him what she had discovered.

It took two days for Lundeen to report back with the information she needed. He flipped open his notepad. "You definitely stumbled on to something, Miss Faulconer. Cal Theroux headed the committee at Mendhan Hills Yacht Club that put in the computerized billing system Fiella worked on. The two of them definitely knew each other."

Susannah's hand tightened around the pen she had been holding. Now she felt free to acknowledge her instincts. The moment she had seen the reference to the yacht club in Fiella's file, she had known in her guts that Cal was responsible for sabotaging the Blaze. She thought of all that hatred festering inside him for so many years. Had she really imagined he had forgotten what she had done to him? That he wouldn't, at some point, strike back at her?

"We need something that will stand up in court," she said. "It'll have to be more substantial than this."

"Give me a few more days, and let's see what I can dig up. The more I find out about your Mr. Theroux, the more I think he's a pretty slippery operator. He's left a lot of dead bodies at FBT on his way to the top."

As soon as Lundeen left her office, she called a meeting with Mitch and Yank and told them exactly what she had discovered. But both men had been trained in the scientific method, and neither was impressed with her conclusions.

"These are serious accusations," Mitch said, "and everything you have is circumstantial. If you're not careful, we'll be facing a lawsuit for slander on top of everything else. Unless Lundeen comes up with something more definite, I don't see how this will help."

"He'll come up with something," she said. "He has to."

But a week later Hal hadn't unearthed anything more than unpleasant anecdotes from former colleagues about Cal's ruthless but effective climb to the top of FBT.

Susannah stopped sleeping. She couldn't eat. The first week of July slipped into the second, and the weekend arrived. She spent all of Saturday at her desk. Mitch's children were in town, and he had taken them to a Giants game. Because Paige was committed to hostessing the annual FBT party that evening, Mitch had postponed the barbecue he had planned until the next afternoon. Susannah looked forward to seeing the children, but she dreaded watching Paige and Mitch together.

By seven that evening she was exhausted, but she didn't want to go home. She got up from her desk and wandered through the empty hallways. Many of the corridor lights were permanently dimmed, the offices unoccupied. She remembered when Saturday nights had been full of activity. Now her footsteps echoed hollowly on the tile floors. She peered into laboratories that only a year ago had been bursting with brash young engineers eager to strut their stuff. Now they were idle. No one announced loose pigs in the hallways or warned of Japanese invasions over the loudspeaker system. It was as if the whole brilliant, brazen world of SysVal had been an illusion.

She rested her cheek against the cool green wall. The adventure had come to an end. A sense of defeat settled over her so all-encompassing, she wanted to sink down along the wall and curl up against it. Cal Theroux had beaten her. Right now the party would be beginning at Falcon Hill. While he extolled FBT's accomplishments, he would be secretly celebrating SysVal's destruction.

She thought of the bright young kids who had arrived from all over the country to work at SysVal, of the thousands of lives his vengeance had upset. And in her mind, she kept seeing Cal dancing in the gardens of Falcon Hill.

She squeezed her eyes shut. From the beginning Mitch had called her Hot Shot, but she had never felt less deserving of that nickname. A real hot shot wouldn't stand by and let all the people she was responsible for be destroyed by a bastard like Cal Theroux. A real hot shot would do something, have some sort of plan. A real hot shot would—

Her eyes sprang open. For a moment she stood without moving, barely breathing. Then she looked at her watch and began to run.

31

The library at Falcon Hill was unchanged. Her father's heavy mahogany desk still dominated the room. Susannah stood next to it clutching the telephone receiver in her hand while she waited for someone to answer the phone ringing in the pool house near the gardens. She was dressed in a slim scarlet chiffon evening gown with a rhinestone-banded bodice. As she waited, she remembered the night she had walked into this same room and found Sam seated behind the desk staring up at the embossed copper ceiling. A party had been going on then, too.

"Yes?" The voice that answered the pool-house telephone was male with a foreign accent. Probably a waiter.

"One of the guests is needed in the library immediately," she said. "Mr. Cal Theroux. It's an emergency." She repeated Cal's name for the waiter, reiterated the fact that the matter was urgent, and hung up the telephone.

She took several deep breaths and fidgeted nervously with the rhinestone border on the long scarlet scarf that accessorized the gown. The library faced the side of the house, so she couldn't see the party going on in the gardens at the back, but she could hear the lush sounds of an orchestra playing. She glanced toward the antique humidor on the corner of the desk to reassure herself that the small tape recorder hidden within couldn't be seen.

Less than two hours had passed since she had left SysVal. In that time, she had tested the powerful little machine to make certain it was working properly, dressed in her evening clothes, and driven to Falcon Hill. Using one of the side entrances, she had made it to the library without running into her sister, or anyone else for that matter, since the staff was working out of the pool-house kitchen and the main house was deserted. Now all she had to do was wait.

She wandered restlessly over to the bookcases, reviewing what she planned to say to Cal. He wouldn't be expecting to see her, and she needed to use the element of surprise to her advantage. Once again, the socialite had to pull a hustle. She wished she had been able to reach Mitch so she could tell him what she planned, but he had been out with his children and hadn't answered the phone.

The door behind her opened. Slowly she turned. "Hello, Cal."

Surprised flickered over his features when he saw who was waiting for him, and his eyes narrowed. "What are you doing here?"

"Enjoying your party?" she asked, deliberately sidestepping his question. He was tanned and elegant in his tux, but his appearance repelled her. How could she ever have considered spending her life with this unscrupulous man? She wondered if his antiseptic lovemaking made his wife feel as unwomanly as she had once felt.

"What do you want, Susannah?"

She stepped forward, making no effort to conceal her hostility. "I want to see you sweat, you bastard."

He hadn't expected a direct attack. The woman he remembered had been obedient and aristocratic. She would never have dreamed of challenging him like this. "What are you talking about?"

"I didn't realize you were responsible until a few weeks ago," she said bitterly. "Isn't that ironic? It never occurred to me that you were capable of doing something so horrible."

He had regained control of himself. "I have no idea what you're talking about."

"I'm talking about my computers, you bastard.

"What—"

"I'm talking about the Blaze III and a sabotaged ROM chip."

"You're ridiculous."

"I'm talking about thousands of lives that have been disrupted. About innocent people who have lost everything. I'm talking about a man so twisted that he didn't care who was hurt as long as he could get even with the woman who ran away from him."

She saw it then. A flicker of satisfaction crossed his features before he could hide it. "SysVal's problems are well-known," he said. "I suppose it's even understandable for you to look for a scapegoat. After all, it's easier to blame some mysterious saboteur for your troubles than to blame your own inept management."

Her stomach curled. "You're enjoying dancing on our grave, aren't you, Cal? How can you sleep at night knowing what you've done?"

"I sleep very well. Probably just as well as you slept after you decided to humiliate me in front of all my friends and business associates."

"I didn't run away from our wedding out of malice. What you've done is obscene."

He walked over to a chest that held an assortment of crystal decanters and poured himself a small brandy. There was a smugness in his every gesture, a sense of absolute confidence. He took a sip, then smiled, showing perfect white teeth. "I heard you left your husband. Sorry it didn't work out."

"Oh, it worked out. Not forever, I admit. But I wouldn't trade those years with Sam for anything."

He didn't like her response, and his jaw set. "There's a certain vulgarity about you, Susannah, that I didn't notice when we were together. I suppose I should be grateful that our wedding ceremony was never completed. I can't imagine having been forced to live with you."

"No," she said. "I can't imagine it, either. And now after all these years have passed, you finally have what you've been waiting for. I'm sure you know that SysVal is on the verge of bankruptcy."

He smiled, a sly fox's smile that made the hair prickle on the back of her neck. "Unfortunate."

"Unfortunate for both of us."

He swirled the liquor in his glass. "I doubt that it's going to affect me very much. Except in profits on the 101, of course."

"You're wrong. It's going to affect you quite a lot." She paused for a moment and then said softly, "I don't have anything more to lose, Cal. So I'm going to take you down with me."

The room grew quiet. Only the distant sounds of the orchestra penetrated the silence. He set down his glass. "You're bluffing. You can't hurt me."

Hustle, a voice inside her screamed. *Hustle, hustle, hustle.* "Oh, I can hurt you very badly. All of those people out there in the garden. All of the FBT executives and board members. The United States senators and newspaper publishers. All those important people." Her voice dropped to a whisper as she began her lie. "I'm going to go out there in just a few minutes and entertain them with a little story about treachery."

His face took on a grayish hue beneath his tan. "Susannah, I'm warning you—"

"I'm going to move from one group to the next. I'm going to tell them about the Mendhan Hills Yacht Club and your connection with a man named Edward Fiella. I'm going to tell them about that brand new Mercedes Fiella bought after he did his dirty little job for you. I'm going to lay out every piece of evidence we've gathered."

His features hardened. "You can't prove anything."

"It's a party, not a courtroom. I don't have to prove anything."

"That's slander. I'll ruin you."

"You already have."

Silence fell thick and heavy between them. She knew that she needed something more definite on the tape. He pulled an immaculate white handkerchief from his pocket and pressed it to his forehead before slipping it back into his pocket. She could almost see the wheels turning in his head as he tried to find a way out. He couldn't know her threat to expose him to the people in the garden was a bluff. She intended to bring him to justice legally, not through gossip. But he needed to incriminate himself for her tape recorder before that would be possible.

"They'll think you're crazy." A small muscle had begun to tic near his eye. "No one will believe you."

"Some of them won't. But you've made enemies, Cal. A lot of them are out there right now. Your enemies will believe me."

His mouth twisted with suspicion. "Why are you warning me? Why not just do it?"

"I told you at the beginning. I want to watch you sweat. I want you to know what's going to happen to you. Just like I've known what would happen all these months while I've watched my company die."

"You little bitch." He gritted out the words.

"That's right, Cal. I'm the most vicious bitch you've ever met."

"I won't let you do this."

"You won't be able to stop me."

His forehead was damp with perspiration, and once again he pulled his handkerchief from his pocket.

"Did it feel good to ruin me?" she asked.

"I'm warning you—"

"Did it make your heart pump faster?"

"Shut up, Susannah!"

"Is that how you make yourself feel like a man?"

"God damn you!"

"We both know you don't get your kicks from women. Is that how you turn yourself on?"

"You goddamn bitch!" His face was full of venom as he lashed out at her. "It felt better than anything I've ever done in my life. I'm almost glad you found out. I wanted you to know. I wanted you to know exactly who was responsible for what was happening to you."

He had driven the crucial nail into his coffin, but she couldn't let him see her jubilation. She wouldn't make the mistake of celebrating until she held the tape in her hand.

"Enjoy your revenge while you can, Cal," she said quietly. "You don't have much time left." She began heading toward the door.

He followed her, just as she had anticipated. "Don't you walk away from me," he ordered.

"I don't have anything more to say to you." She wanted him to accompany her back out to the garden. He would stay at her side while she mingled with the guests, and when she didn't say anything incriminating, he would think she had lost her nerve. As soon as she was certain it was safe, she was going to return to the library and fetch the tape. Tonight she would make copies to mail to every member of FBT's Board of Directors.

She was reaching for the doorknob when she heard the sound of his breathing behind her. It was labored, as if he had run a great distance. A chill chased along her spine as his hand clasped her shoulder.

"Susannah . . ."

She shook him off and tried to take a quick step backward, but he caught her by the wrist. "You can't do this, Susannah."

Spinning around, she saw the panic in his eyes. It frightened her, and she tried to pull away. "Don't touch me."

He tightened his grip. "You're not going to do this!"

She had never known Cal to lose control, and the desperation in his face sent a cold shock through her. "Let go of me!" Balling her fist, she lashed out at him.

He caught her arm before she could connect, grabbing her so roughly that her neck snapped. She opened her mouth to scream, but the sound died as he pinned her against his body and grabbed her by the throat.

"Stop it!" he commanded.

She clawed at his arm and let out a terrible, garbled cry. The fact that she couldn't draw a deep breath intensified her panic. She kicked at him and jabbed him with her elbows, fighting for survival with an animal instinct.

"I'm not going to let you ruin me!" he exclaimed, sounding increasingly frantic.

Twisting her neck, she sank her teeth into his upper arm.

With a muffled cry, he struck her on the side of her head. The blow dazed her. She whimpered and sagged back against him, barely staying conscious as he dragged her out into the hallway.

431

"You can't . . . do this." His words came to her in a choppy, disjointed fashion, like the late night signal from a faraway radio station. She had the vague sense that he was talking to himself as much as to her, making up his plan at the same time he dragged her down the hall. "No . . . you can't . . . I won't . . . I know . . . I know what you'll do. . . . You're going . . . to commit . . . suicide."

She gasped out a mutated version of his name, but she needed all of her energy to draw air into her lungs, and the sound didn't carry. He was strong, so incredibly strong. She remembered how proud he had always been of his body, how hard he had worked to keep himself in shape.

"What better place . . . to kill yourself . . . than the house where you were raised?" His breathing was heavy as he pulled her down the hallway. "Your company . . . is going bankrupt, your marriage is over." She kicked weakly at him, trying to break his powerful grip, but she was too dazed to do any damage.

"Paige told me she's been . . . worried about you. Everyone will understand."

She pushed another cry through the narrow passageway in her throat. He increased the pressure on her windpipe, but she continued to make as much noise as she could, even though the sounds were too feeble to carry out into the garden. She had never been so aware of the vastness of the house, and she prayed for someone to come inside.

The back door that led into the garage tilted in front of her. Keeping one arm around her throat, he tore several sets of car keys from the pegboard. She clawed at his arm, gasping for breath and trying to stay conscious. He dragged her down the steps into the garage and pulled the door shut behind them.

They were in the far wing of the house, well away from the gardens. Her old bedroom was above them, several guest rooms, parts of the house that hadn't been occupied in years. Even if she could scream, no one would hear her. Please God, she prayed, digging her fingernails into his arm. Let someone come to the garage. Please God.

Two cars were parked inside—Paige's Mercedes and a Chevy that the housekeeper used. The Chevy was the closest, and he pulled her toward it, snatching up a pair of work gloves on the way. Her muscles turned liquid with fear. Why did he need gloves?

The pressure on her throat eased. She coughed. "Cal . . . Don't . . ."

He began to drag her toward the Chevy. A fresh rush of terror gave her new strength. She lashed out at him, summoning every bit of energy she had left. She fought with vicious determination, using fists and teeth and feet. He cursed and wrenched her around. Before she could protect herself, his arm shot back and he struck her again.

An angry black whirlpool sucked at her, drawing her inexorably toward its viscous center. Someone was pulling at her, moving her body about. No! She wouldn't be shut in the closet. The fox head was there. The balloon man. She tried to fight, but something was happening to her arms. She couldn't lift them, couldn't move them. There were furs all around, suffocating her. Garish balloons swam in front of her eyes in a slow drifting dance. She wanted to watch them, but someone was breathing harshly in her ear. Her arms. Why couldn't she move her arms?

Scarlet and the glitter of rhinestones swam before her eyes. Her head sagged forward and then back. Gradually she realized that she was behind the wheel of a car. The housekeeper's old Chevy. The scarlet and rhinestone pattern swimming in front of her came into focus. It was the long scarf from her evening gown. Cal was wearing the work gloves and tying her wrists to the steering wheel with the scarf from her dress.

"No . . ." she gasped. She tried to move, but her limbs wouldn't work and something was wrong with her legs. Her ankles were tied.

Cal's breath rasped in her ears. He was leaning in through the open car door to secure her wrists. She saw the gray lightning bolt that shot through his hair, and struggled to stay conscious. Her wrists were throbbing and the rhinestones on the scarf were cutting into her skin. He had tied the scarf much too tight. Why was he tying her wrists? He had said she was going to commit suicide.

"Don't do this . . ." she murmured, her words slurred.

He stepped back to survey his work. And then, in a gesture that seemed almost tender, he pushed her hair back into place and straightened her dress. When he was satisfied, he rolled down the car window and shut the door.

Her throat was dry, her tongue felt swollen. She was still dazed from the blow and she had difficulty speaking. "Cal . . . don't do this."

"It didn't have to happen," he whispered. She heard remorse in his voice, but the wildness was still in his eyes. "I never intended to let it go this far. But I can't have you ruin me."

"I won't . . . tell. I promise."

"I'm sorry. Truly." He checked the scarf. Her hands had begun to cramp painfully, and they twitched when he touched them. "I'll come back and untie you," he murmured gently. "Afterward."

Afterward. After she was dead. Before anyone discovered her body. They would think she had killed herself. "No," she moaned.

He turned on the ignition and the Chevy's engine sprang to life. Helplessly she watched as he went over to Paige's Mercedes and turned it on, too. The powerful German engine roared. He stood by the car and straightened his tuxedo. For a moment the scene looked to her like a slick magazine ad. Expensive car. Expensive clothes. Expensive, evil man.

She screamed and began to struggle against the knots, trying to slide her wrists along the steering wheel so she could reach the gear shift. But the knots were too tight and her struggles were pushing the sharp prongs of the rhinestones deeper into her flesh. He walked toward the door that led into the house, returned the gloves to the shelf, and then removed his handkerchief from his pocket. Using it to turn the doorknob, he disappeared.

She refused to go silently to her death, and she cried out until her throat was raw. How long did it take to die of carbon monoxide poisoning? Maybe someone would come into this wing of the house. Maybe someone would hear her.

Her wrists wouldn't move. Sobbing, she began to throw herself against the steering wheel, trying to sound the horn. But it was recessed and she couldn't reach it with her body.

Her struggles were forcing her to consume the tainted oxygen at an alarming rate. She cried out as she saw blood beginning to seep through the scarf, and she realized that the rhinestones had cut into her flesh in a dozen places. She tried to hit the gear shift with her legs, but the rope around her ankles made it impossible for her to maneuver.

While she struggled, the automobile engines roared away in a death chorus. As she watched her blood seep in rusty patterns through the scarf, her life had never seemed more precious. She didn't want to die. When the police saw the blood on her wrists, they would know she hadn't committed suicide. And sooner or later someone would find the tape recorder. But bringing Cal to justice no longer seemed to matter.

Mitch's face swam in front of her eyes. As she faced death, she knew that she loved him. She had loved him for years, but since she was married, she had made herself believe it was merely friendship. He was good and kind and strong, everything a man should be. And the fact that he loved her sister didn't diminish her feelings for him at all.

The monster engines continued to spew out their poison. The blood trickled from the wounds in her wrists. How much time had passed? Was she starting to get sleepy? Please God, no. Don't let me get sleepy.

She wanted a baby. She wanted to tell her sister that she loved her. She wanted to bask in the light of Yank's gentle eyes. She wanted to see Mitch again. Even if she couldn't have him, she wanted to watch that wonderful face soften in a smile. Please, God, don't let me die.

And, gradually, a sense of peacefulness came over her. Her head wobbled and her forehead dropped against the top of the steering wheel. She needed to rest. Just for a little while. Just until she felt stronger.

And then she heard her father's voice.

Wake up, sweetheart. Wake up right now.

She saw Joel standing before her, holding out his arms. His face was as young and as golden as a prince's. He was real. He wasn't dead. He didn't hate her.

Her eyelids fluttered. *Daddy? Daddy, where are you?*

His smile faded and he looked angry with her. Just like the

day she had run away with Sam Gamble. So fierce and angry.

Your arms, he shouted. *Move your arms!*

No. She didn't want to move them. She was too tired. But he kept calling out to her over and over again.

Your arms! Move your arms!

The scarves were too tight. Her wrists were bleeding and she was sleepy. But he looked so angry—she didn't want to make him angry—he looked so angry that she tried once more. Gathering the small amount of strength she had left, she struggled against her bonds. For the last time, she pulled at the knots.

And her wrists began to move in their slippery path of blood. Pain clawed at her as she tried to slide them down along the steering wheel. Everything was spinning. She had to rest. She had to make the pain stop. Just for a moment.

Her fingers bumped against the gear shift, but she could no longer remember why it had been so important to reach it.

Wake up! Joel shouted. *Wake up now.*

She tried to focus, tried to remember what she had to do. With a rasping breath she tugged on the gear shift and awkwardly maneuvered the car into reverse.

But she had expended the last of her energy, and there was nothing left.

Your feet, he cried. *Lift your feet.*

He expected too much of her. He had always expected too much. Her feet were heavy. Much too heavy to lift.

Now! Now!

She pushed her clumsy feet against the accelerator.

The oxygen-eating engine roared. Her neck snapped as the car shot backward. It crashed through the garage door and catapulted out onto the driveway.

The slap of fresh, pure oxygen acted like a shot of adrenaline. She sucked the life-giving air into her lungs. Several minutes passed. Strength began to flow back into her body, and with the strength came agonizing shards of pain in her wrists.

She began to sob. Blood was smeared all over the steering

wheel, and she couldn't loosen the knots that held her wrists. How much longer before Cal discovered her and finished what he had begun? The faint sounds of the orchestra drifted in through the window. The music sounded more beautiful than anything she had ever heard. Biting her lip against the pain, she worked the car into drive. Then she once again slammed her feet on the accelerator.

The car shot down a small bank and onto the side lawn. With her wrists tied, it was almost impossible to steer, but she wrenched the wheel to the right and rounded the back of the house. On the opposite side of the grounds, she could see a striped party canopy and white paper lanterns swinging from the trees. The car rocked violently as the right wheels rode up on the terraced slope of the hillside. For a moment she thought she was going to flip, and then she gasped as the wheels steadied on even ground.

A low wall of shrubbery loomed ahead. The car careened wildly as she plowed through it. She could see the people more clearly. They were turning toward her. A heavy urn planted with topiary scraped the side of the car. The vehicle shuddered but didn't stop. One of the garden's marble statues appeared on her right. She wrested her arms to the left, just missing it. Men in tuxedos and women in glimmering gowns watched in horror as she raced closer.

She lifted her legs to hit the brake, but her foot caught beneath the peddle. The fountain materialized ahead along with well-dressed party guests who were scattering in alarm. She sobbed as she freed her foot and slammed on the brake.

Stones flew up from the tires. The car fishtailed on the gravel path and skidded into the side of the fountain. Her body jolted as the engine shuddered to a stop.

She heard a woman screaming, the sound of people running, a man's voice, loud and incredulous. "It's Susannah Faulconer!"

Someone was struggling with the door on the passenger side and then crawling over the seat to help her. Hands touched her wrists and tugged at the knots on the scarf. She whimpered with the pain.

More voices.

"She's tied. Why is she tied?"

"I'll call an ambulance."

"She's bleeding."

"Don't move her. You shouldn't move her."

But her arms and legs were free, and she was being taken from the car. Held in someone's arms.

Mitch. Mitch had come to help her.

Her eyelids fluttered. She wanted to thank him. Tell him she loved him. She forced her eyes open and saw a lightning bolt of gray hair.

"Don't try to talk," Cal murmured as he held her against his chest. "Don't try to talk." And then in a louder voice. "I'm going to take her inside. She's in shock."

Susannah tried to cry out, but she was dazed. He was moving more quickly. The paper lanterns flashed by in the trees overhead. A scream rose inside her, but the only sound that passed through her lips was a weak whimper. "Paige . . ."

A flash of pink appeared at her side, a cloud of blond hair. "I'm here, Suze. I'm here. Don't try to talk. Oh, sweetie, don't try to talk."

"Stop him . . ." Susannah tried to force out the syllables. Cal's fingers dug more deeply into her ribs. "Don't let him . . . take me . . . inside," she gasped.

Paige stroked her head. "Stop who, sweetie? It's all right."

"She's in shock." Cal picked up his pace. He was at the back of the house, stepping onto the patio. "See to the guests. Make certain no one was hurt."

"Stop . . . him. He tried . . . to kill . . ."

"What's she saying, Cal?" Her sister brushed her arm. "Suzie, I can't understand you."

"She's hysterical, Paige."

"What's wrong, honey?" Paige murmured. "We'll take care of you."

Susannah pushed the words out. "He . . . tried to kill me."

"Don't listen—"

Paige's voice was flat. "Stop for a minute, Cal."

Cal kept moving. "She's been hurt. I have to get her inside. Go see to the guests."

"I said to stop!" Paige threw herself at him, the mother lioness protecting her cub.

Men appeared at her side. Cal let Susannah go, and Paige pulled her down onto a patio chaise. The world gradually steadied.

A crowd was forming around her. Through a breach she saw the buffet tables covered in rose-colored linen. Ice falcons with their wings spread in flight dripped into silver trays. Nicole Theroux, frightened and bewildered, was standing at Cal's side. Cal looked frantic, and people were staring at him. He tried to disperse the crowd, but no one moved. Susannah recognized several of the FBT board members and their wives, many of the same people who had witnessed her disastrous wedding.

Paige held her bleeding wrists and told her to lie down, but there was no time. Susannah turned to Paul Clemens, her father's friend. "Paul . . ." Her voice was as weak as an old woman's. "In the library. There's a tape recorder . . ." She told him where she had hidden it. The effort exhausted her.

Cal started toward the back door.

"You stay right here," Paul said sternly.

The men at the gathering were accustomed to taking command, and without a word being spoken, they began to step forward in a silent cadre. Cal looked at them, his face haggard as he tried to comprehend the fact that his world was being ripped apart. Before they could get close to him, he broke away and dashed toward the side of the house.

Several of the men gave chase, but Cal was running with a strength born of desperation, and he eluded them.

Paul had fetched the recorder, and he rewound the small tape. No one in the crowd spoke. Susannah held her sister's hand as the tape began to play.

Later there was a doctor and the police. Paige tucked Susannah into Joel's old bed, murmuring over the white bandages that encircled her wrists. The doctor had given her a sedative, but Susannah struggled to tell Paige something before she fell asleep.

"I saw him."

Paige gently stroked the damp, clean hair back off Susannah's forehead. "Who did you see?"

"Daddy." Susannah's eyes clouded with tears. "He came to me when I was dying. Oh, Paige, Daddy came to me."

Paige patted Susannah's hand. "Go to sleep, Suze. You go to sleep now."

32

• •

I'm going to kill her!"

Pain had taken over every part of Susannah's body. She squeezed her eyes tight and wished that whoever was making so much noise in the hallway would be quiet. The sedative was powerful, and it took her a while to realize it was Mitch talking. Only a faint gray light seeped through the window. Why had he come to visit so early?

"How could she have done something so stupid?" His voice sounded like a jackhammer at dawn. "I mean it, Paige. As soon as she wakes up, I'm going to kill her."

"Shhh," Paige hissed. "You're acting like a wild man. Yank, make him be quiet."

After Mitch's angry bellow, Yank's murmurings were like a soft breeze. Susannah drifted back to sleep.

When she awakened several hours later, bright sunlight was streaming through her window. Intermingled with the stiffness in her muscles was a piercing sense of joy. She was alive for a new day.

The mattress sagged. She turned her head and saw Yank lowering himself to sit next to her. His clothes were wrinkled, his hair rumpled, his face lined with worry. At the sight of that dear sweet face, everything inside her broke apart. "Oh, Yank . . ."

Mitch had his hand on the doorknob when he heard Susannah's moan. His eyes were bloodshot, his hair standing in spikes on his head. He had been by her bedside all night and had just stepped out for a moment to help Paige deal with an overly aggressive reporter. Now he yanked open the door, overwhelmed with the irrational notion that her soft moan was a death rattle. He shouldn't have left, not even for a moment. He hadn't watched her carefully enough, and now she was going to die.

As he rushed into the bedroom, the scene in front of him gradually came into focus. She was curled up against Yank's chest as if he were the only man on earth. Mitch felt as if someone had given him a sucker punch right in the gut.

Yank lifted his head and saw him. He smiled his gentle smile. "Susannah's awake."

"Yes," Mitch said, his voice cracking with emotion. "Yes, I see."

Susannah stiffened against Yank. He laid her back on the bed. She turned toward Mitch.

"Hi, Hot Shot," he said, trying to make it easy for her by keeping his voice light.

She held out her hand. "Mitch."

He walked over to her, sat down on the side of the bed and curled her fingers through his. At the sight of the bandages on her wrists, he wanted to weep.

"I didn't think I'd ever see you again," she murmured.

He squeezed her hand tighter, pressed his eyes shut. "No more detective work, honey. Promise me."

Paige came into the bedroom leading a housekeeper and maid, all of them carrying trays ladened with food. "The police picked Cal up at a private airfield an hour ago, and the house is surrounded with three more television crews. No one is talking to anybody until everybody's had breakfast."

They didn't feel like eating, but none of them had the nerve to argue with Paige when the feeding urge was upon her.

In the aftermath of the scandal, FBT had a public relations nightmare on its hands, while Susannah became the Valley's Joan of Arc. Before a month had passed, her face had appeared on the cover of three national magazines. She sparred with Ted Koppel on *Nightline* and appeared on all three network morning news shows.

Would you buy a new computer from this woman?

You bet.

The publicity brought in an avalanche of orders for the Blaze III, and SysVal scrambled to get back to full staff to process them.

In the meantime, FBT struggled to extract itself from a public relations nightmare. Having its former CEO in jail waiting to go on trial for industrial sabotage and attempted murder definitely wasn't good for a company's image, and the corporation's stock tumbled to the price of a haircut. The state of California canceled its contract for the Falcon 101 and ordered the III. Investment money poured in to SysVal, as well as the initial payment on a huge financial settlement from FBT.

Although it was early evening, the SysVal parking lot was still half full as Sam pulled in. He turned off the ignition and sat in the car for a few minutes without moving. Six weeks had passed since Theroux had tried to kill Susannah. Sam had stayed away from SysVal while the worst of the media circus had gone on, but time was running out, and he had to make his move.

Since early spring he had devoted every minute to launching his new company. The concept was so beautiful, he couldn't believe he hadn't thought of it years ago. One night he had been handing over his credit card at a restaurant when it had hit him. He had stared down at that slim piece of plastic and felt as if the top of his head had blown off. What would happen if credit cards were embedded with microchips?

Aw, man . . . He had almost started to cry as he envisioned the beauty of it. The way the world did business would change forever. Ideas had flashed through his mind like lasers at a rock concert. An electronic credit card could handle bank transactions, dial a telephone, take care of parking meters and vending machines. A person's entire credit history could be stored on the card, their medical history, their fucking *life* history. The card could function as a door key, an ignition key, a security pass. His head had reeled. Jeezus . . .

He had more investors waiting in line to bankroll him than he needed. Money was no problem, but people were. He had gone on a raid, picking up some of the bright youngsters that SysVal had laid off, stealing a few programmers from Bill Gates at MicroSoft, a top executive from Intel. He had seduced a marketing whiz away from Apple. The Valley was churning with bright, young talent, and he had gone after the best. By mid-summer, he had money and he had a staff.

Now he needed Yank.

As he pocketed his keys and began to walk across the lot toward the building, he thought how sweet life had turned for his former partners. Hardly a week passed without another story in the newspapers about them. He tried not to resent the fact that the press had cast him as a villain because he'd bailed out of SysVal when it was in trouble. Since he'd sold his partnership at a deflated price, the bail-out had cost him millions, but he'd still made a fortune and he didn't care. Money wasn't the game. The game was vision. SysVal had gotten old and respectable. He wanted a challenge, a new adventure. He liked to be in on the beginning of the game, not the end. Some people weren't capable of business as usual, and he was one of them.

God, he was glad to get out of there. He could feel his blood pumping again.

But he needed Yank working with him. He couldn't imagine going any further without Yank's engineering genius behind him. He knew he had to stay patient while SysVal rode the crest of its publicity wave, but before long the company would stabilize, and he could have everything he wanted. Yank would freak when he found out what Sam was working on, and as long as Yank was certain that SysVal was safe, Sam would have no difficulty convincing him to come to work for his new company.

But Yank wasn't all Sam wanted. As he approached the entrance, he shoved his hand impatiently through his hair. His divorce was going to be final soon, and he had to move quickly.

His heart began to beat faster. God, he loved a challenge, and this was going to be the biggest challenge of his life. He could get Susannah back. What was it she had once said about him? That he had the ability to make sensible people do impossible things. Now he had to convince her that he'd settled down. Life was exciting again. He no longer had anything to prove by screwing around with other women, and he was finally ready to cope with a kid. Those were his bargaining chips.

Maybe it was good that they'd had this time apart, because now he understood how much she meant to him. Before she'd left him, he had been bored, restless, and he'd blamed it on her. He'd lost sight of how smart she was, how sweet. He hadn't felt complete since the night she had walked out on him. She seemed to have taken part of himself with her.

The last few times he had tried to talk to her on the phone, she had brushed him off, so he had decided to use Yank to get to her. Drop in on him at work. Make it seem casual. He had to get more aggressive with Yank anyway. This way he could kill two birds with one stone.

He didn't have any trouble getting past the SysVal security desk. Even at seven in the evening, the halls were bustling with activity, and he shot the bull with some of his former engineers before he left to find Yank. Somebody said he was eating dinner.

As he made his way toward the small kitchen in the back of the building, the loudspeaker blared. "Whoever ordered thirty-six pizzas and a box of Milk Duds, pick your order up in the main lobby now."

He shoved his hand in his pocket. It felt good to be back. And then he scoffed at himself. That was the sort of nostalgic bullshit that kept people from moving forward.

As he approached the kitchen, he saw Yank and Susannah sitting across from each other at one of the blond wooden tables. A picnic basket was propped between them. Too fucking cozy for words.

Ever since he and Susannah had split up, he'd been worried about Yank's feelings for her. He knew that years ago Yank had had a crush on her, but he'd never taken it very seriously. He'd even gotten a kick out of the way Yank used to look at her. Now he wondered if he'd been too casual about the whole thing.

Susannah laughed and Yank smiled back at her. He looked like he wanted to eat her right along with the piece of chicken on his plate. Since when had Yank ever taken time out from the lab to eat dinner?

Susannah saw Sam first and her smile faded. Her lack of welcome hurt. Jesus, he still wanted her. She was part of him, for chrissake.

"Sam." Yank put down his fork, stood, and held out his hand. As Sam shook it, he sensed a wariness in Yank, and that hurt almost as much as Susannah's lack of welcome.

He heard someone moving behind him and realized they weren't alone. Susannah's sister Paige stepped forward opening a wine bottle with a cork screw. He had only seen her once before, the night she and Susannah had walked in on him with Mindy. He could tell right away that she was a real bitch.

"My, my. Don't you look spiffy with your pants on." She ran her eyes up and down his body.

He wanted to slap her right through the wall.

Susannah didn't reprimand her sister for the wisecrack, and that really pissed him off. It scared him, too. What if he couldn't make her care again?

"Have a seat, Sam," Susannah said. "I think we can come up with an extra piece of Paige's chicken."

He sat, but refused the food. As Susannah reached for her napkin, he saw the faint scars on her wrist and remembered what she had gone through the night Theroux had tried to kill her. He felt rage, and something else he didn't want to identify. Maybe some kind of guilt bullshit.

Yank asked Sam what he had been doing, and Sam began telling him about his new company. Before long, he had thrown off his sport coat and was pacing the room, his fingers splayed, his arms making arcs in the air as he talked and talked and talked.

Hallelujah and amen! Brother Love's traveling salvation show was back on the road.

Susannah watched him without much expression, but Yank hung on to his every word. When Sam finally stopped talking, he noticed that Yank's eyes had grown unfocused, and he could sense his old partner's excitement as he pondered the miracles of engineering necessary to transform a wafer-thin credit card into a tool that could interface with the world.

Even Paige had lost her superior look. She had set down her wineglass and was staring at him as if he had just dropped in from another planet.

Susannah had noticed Yank's reaction, too, and she immediately rounded on Sam. "What do you want? Why are you here?"

He had forgotten those hair-trigger reflexes of hers, and he realized too late that he had miscalculated by talking to Yank when she was present. God, she was feisty. He had only wanted to pique Yank's interest, not steal him away in front of her.

But he could feel his adrenaline pumping at the idea of going into a battle with her again. Jesus, he loved a good fight. He had too many yes-men around him now. Not enough scrappers like Suzie. She liked everything up front, so why not give it to her? Why not have his fight and let her know what he wanted? That way she couldn't ever accuse him of having gone behind her back.

"What do you think I want?" he asked, spinning around the only empty chair at the table and straddling it.

"Suppose you tell me."

"I want the best, babe. Just like always."

"You can't have him."

"Yank's a big boy. He should be able to make up his own mind."

"He has. He's staying here."

"SysVal's getting old and respectable. Yank likes new challenges."

Paige's eyes were going back and forth between the two of them as if she were watching a tennis match. Yank was regarding them thoughtfully.

Susannah threw down her napkin. "I heard you were making some personnel raids. I thought you'd have enough decency to know that Yank is off limits."

Sam turned to confront Yank. "Still letting other people do your talking for you?"

Yank gazed at him with those gentle, infuriating eyes. "I'm not the only person you want. Am I, Sam?"

For the first time, Sam hedged. "What are you talking about?"

"Susannah's been through enough," Yank replied. "When are you going to leave her alone?"

Sam propped his arm over the back of the chair, still keeping it casual. "I'm not trying to recruit her. I know Susannah won't leave SysVal."

"But that's not what you want from her, is it? You don't want her to work for your company. You want her back as your wife, your good luck charm."

Susannah pushed her plate away and stood up. "I want you to leave, Sam. We don't have anything more to say to each other."

But Sam barely heard her. All of his attention was focused on Yank. Yank, the nerd—the goofy genius. Yank, who forgot his socks and lost his women. How could Yank think—how could be even imagine that he had a chance—at a woman like Susannah?

Sam's lip curled. He wanted to be cruel, to slice them both to the quick. "If you think I'm going to play dead and leave the field clear for you, buddy, you'd better think again. All I need is one night in bed with her. One night in bed, and I'll have her back. Isn't that right, Suzie?"

Susannah tightened her hands around the back of the chair. "Get out of here right now."

"I'm afraid this can't go on any longer," Yank said abruptly. "Susannah, we have to put an end to Sam's delusions about you right now. He's obsessed with you, and it has to stop."

"The divorce will be final in a few weeks," she snapped. "That'll put a stop to it."

"A piece of paper doesn't mean shit." Sam knocked over the chair as he leaped to his feet. "Get a divorce! Get a million of them! I don't care. Marriage doesn't mean anything, and neither does divorce. I want you back with me. We belong together. That's the only thing that matters."

Susannah slapped her palms on the table. "That's enough! Get out."

"He isn't listening to you, Susannah," Yank said. "He

refuses to listen. Sam doesn't understand about divorce papers. But he understands how to make a deal. Don't you, Sam?" Yank leaned slightly back in his chair.

Paige's eyes were huge in her face as she took in the scene these lunatics were playing out in front of her.

For a moment, Yank stared at a spot in the air directly in front of him, and then he said, "What about a contest? A contest and a deal."

Sam was poised, all his senses alert. "What kind of contest?"

"A contest between you and me. The winner gets Susannah. The loser steps aside forever."

"Are you out of your mind?" Susannah exclaimed. "Are both of you crazy!"

Sam laughed. "Wait a minute. Let me get this straight. You want the two of us to have a contest? If you lose, you'll stay away from her forever?"

Yank nodded slowly. "And if you lose, Sam, you leave her alone for the rest of your life."

Susannah made a choking noise, but neither of them paid any attention.

Sam immediately began to pace, hammering out the fine points. "You can't stay away from her if you're working with her every day. That means you'll have to get another job."

"Yes. All right. I won't sell out my partnership, but I'll get another job."

Susannah gasped.

Sam pressed his advantage. "With me."

"That's not part of the deal. The deal's about winning Susannah."

"I'm not a piece of property!" she exclaimed.

Sam ignored her. "And tell me exactly what you mean. The winner *gets* Susannah. What does *gets* mean?"

"You said you could have her back if you spent a night in bed with her," Yank replied. "Susannah will make love with whichever of us wins. Is that agreeable to you?"

"I will not!" Susannah cried. "Yank, I can't believe you're doing this!"

Yank gave her a stony look. "That's the agreement, Susannah. Do you understand it?"

She was starting to feel desperate. Yank was so serious, so determined. He was spooky when he was like this. She loved him, but she didn't desire him, and she wasn't going to go to bed with him. "No! No, I don't understand at all."

Yank turned toward Sam, who had stopped his pacing by the door. "Susannah will make love with whichever of us wins. The other one of us will leave her alone forever."

Sam's grin spread all over his face. Another challenge to face. Another barrier to smash. "Yeah. Yeah, I like this. Okay. I agree. What kind of contest?"

Yank looked at Sam as if he were the most thick-headed person left on earth. "Why, a video-game contest, of course. How else would we compete?"

"What?" Susannah shrieked.

"Oh, Jeezus." Sam began to laugh, collapsing against the doorjamb. "We're going to play a video game for her? Oh, Jeezus, I love this. The last buccaneers of the twentieth century fight a video game duel over their lady fair. What game? What game are we going to play?"

For the first time, Yank hesitated. "Why don't you chose?"

As soon as the words were out of his mouth, Susannah knew what was going to happen. She told herself it didn't matter. It didn't matter because she wasn't going along with them anyway. But still, she took a quick step toward Yank. "No! No, Yank! He'll choose—"

"Victors," Sam said. "I choose Victors."

"Oh, God . . ." She sank back down into her chair. They were crazy. Both of them were crazy, and she was even crazier to sit here listening to them. Why should she care what game Sam chose? There was no reason for her stomach to have plummeted like that. Sam could beat Yank at Victors from now until doomsday, and she wouldn't get in bed with him. The game didn't matter. Sam's choice didn't matter. But what was Yank doing? Hadn't she gone through enough? Why was he putting her through this?

Next to her at the table, Paige sat stunned.

Both men headed for the door, Sam charged with energy, Yank moving at his customary deliberate pace. An old

Victors game had been put away in one of the small storage rooms. It was a dinosaur now. Its graphics were stone age, its sound primitive. But it was still a classic—right up there with Space Invaders and Pac Man. Victors was a classic. And Yank Yankowski had never played a single game in his life.

33

• •

The men wrestled the Victors game into an office near the storage room, then plugged it in and checked the controls to make certain it still worked. As Paige walked into the office, she saw that Susannah was already there. She had positioned herself as far away from the men as she could get and still be in the room with them. She looked shaken, as if these men really were deciding her future.

They said nobody could die of a broken heart, but as Paige looked from her sister to Yank, she didn't believe it. She was dying. And because she loved them both, she had to find the strength not to let either of them see it. The outcome of the video game might be meaningless as far as Susannah was concerned, but the fact that it was taking place at all had sent the dream world Paige had been building around herself crashing down.

For these past six weeks, ever since the night Susannah had almost died, Paige had been praying that she would fall out of love with Yank, but her heart continued to soar with joy whenever she looked at him. She was happy merely being in the same room with him, breathing his air and drinking in the sight of his gentle, dear face. She wanted to live every second of the rest of her life with him. Have his babies, wash his clothes, take care of him when he got sick. She wanted to sit next to him in a rocking chair when they were both old and hold his hand. She wanted to die with him and be buried next to him and believe in eternal life so she could be certain their spirits would live together forever. He was the only person who made her feel at peace in the deepest, most secret part of her soul.

Now, regardless of the outcome of this stupid video game, she had to accept the fact that she could never have him. Yank wanted her sister, and Paige had to get out of their way. The terror of knowing Susannah had almost been murdered was something Paige would never forget, and the guilt she felt for having placed so much trust in Cal had become a crushing burden. Since that night, Susannah had become even more precious to her. More precious to them all, Paige realized. Yank hovered at her side like a guard dog. Mitch had a haunted look in his eyes whenever Susannah was around. Poor Mitch. The tragedy had made him more serious than ever. He seldom smiled. He hadn't stopped by the house for weeks. All he did was work.

As Paige approached, Susannah gave her a wan smile. "I thought you'd gone home."

"No. No, I'm still here," Paige replied.

"This is crazy, isn't it? They're both crazy."

"Then why are you watching?"

"It's Yank. I can't—I can't understand why he's doing this."

"Because he loves you." The words stuck like great chunks of bread in Paige's throat.

Susannah shook her head. "That's not true. And he knows Sam will win. Why is he trying to push me back to Sam? I won't go, Paige. I don't care what Yank says or what he does. This time he won't get his way. I'm not going back to Sam."

Paige nodded numbly, unable to imagine any woman preferring a macho stud like Sam Gamble to a wonderful man like Yank.

The Victors game began to emit cheerful little beeps. Sam had unbuttoned his cuffs and was rolling up his white shirt-sleeves. "You'd better play a practice game, partner. I don't want you to say I didn't give you a chance."

Yank gazed at the game controls with distaste. "I don't think so. I don't like playing this game, Sam."

Sam slapped him on the back. "Tough shit, hombre. This was your idea."

Victors was the most complex of the early target games. It provided a miniature history of the development of weaponry, from the stone age to the atomic age. On the first screen, primitively shaped men threw stones at small four-legged creatures and dodged lightning bolts from the sky. On the second and third screens, they shot arrows at running men and then fired guns at a platoon of soldiers while they avoided return fire. The final screen featured a moving city skyline. The players controlled an airplane that dropped bombs down onto small targets as skyborne missiles moving in erratic patterns tried to blow up the plane. If the player survived all the screens, a mushroom cloud appeared with the final score and a message:

CONGRATULATIONS.
YOU HAVE SUCCESSFULLY WIPED OUT
CIVILIZATION.
NOW WHAT ARE YOU GOING TO DO?

That message had knocked everybody out.

Sam had none of Yank's reluctance about playing a practice game. As he stood in front of the machine in a white shirt and trousers, with his necktie pulled loosely down from his open collar, Susannah remembered all those nights at Mom & Pop's. Mom & Pop's was now a vegetarian restaurant called Happy Sprouts. They hadn't been there in years.

"Okay, I'm ready," Sam said. "High score wins. Let's toss to see who goes first."

"Go ahead," Yank said gloomily. "You're ready. You might as well play."

Sam limbered his fingers and gave Susannah a cocky grin. Then he turned back to the machine. "Come on, baby. Don't let me down."

Paige couldn't help it. She stepped forward to watch. Susannah seemed certain that Sam was going to win. Maybe when that happened, it would trigger something inside of Yank. Maybe he would fall out of love with Susannah and in love with her. Maybe they would get married and live at Falcon Hill. . . .

And maybe cows would fly over their wedding.

Sam Gamble was a superb video-game player, she'd give him that. He concentrated so intently on the screen and the controls moving beneath his hands that she doubted if anything could distract him. A lock of straight black hair tumbled down over his forehead as he moved through the first three screens with a ruthless efficiency. The machine beeped. The beeps got faster and faster. He hit the final screen. The muscles in his forearms spasmed as he maneuvered the controls. Missiles flew, bombs dropped. His face blazed with excitement.

Sam gave a victorious roar.

The mushroom cloud appeared and the screen flashed its message. He had scored 45,300 points out of 50,000.

He turned to Yank and grinned. "In my heyday, I made 48,000, but I guess I can't complain."

And then Paige watched while he ran his eyes over Susannah's body. The way he did it wasn't exactly creepy— Paige could see that, in his own way, he really did care about her sister. But still, the possessiveness in his appraisal made her skin crawl. Only someone who was entirely self-absorbed could be so arrogant. What a terrible man to have fallen in love with.

Yank, looking completely miserable, walked over to the machine. He sighed and stared at the screen. For a moment he did nothing, and then he turned back toward them as if he were about to say something. Apparently he reconsidered. Clamping his jaw tight, he returned his attention to the machine and pushed the button.

Sweet.

It was so sweet watching him work.

He kept his hands loose, his attention focused. Every motion was precise. He did nothing at random. One by one the screens surrendered to him. Every projectile found its target. Arrows flew, bullets whizzed. He dropped his bombs with deadly accuracy and dodged missiles before they even came close. It was as if he had envisioned every event before it could happen. Nothing was random. He was all-powerful, all-knowing. No man could be so perfect. Only God. Only the Mighty Creator Himself could play so perfectly.

Fifty thousand.

Fifty thousand perfect points.

"You son of a bitch," Sam said. Over and over. "You son of a bitch . . ."

"She's mine, Sam," Yank replied, looking even more miserable than before the game. "We have a deal, and you have to live up to it."

Sam stared down at the floor. Long seconds ticked by. He gazed at Susannah. "Do you really want him?"

"A deal is a deal," she whispered.

Paige could feel this great, awful sob rising up from the very bottom of her soul. She couldn't breathe for fear it would burst from within her. She had to hold it back and hide her grief in a deep secret place where it could never be discovered. Somehow, she had to find the generosity of spirit to give these two people she loved her blessing. And then she would disappear from their lives because she simply could not bear to watch them together.

"I love you, Suzie," Sam said hoarsely, with an expression of desperation on his face.

Slowly, sadly, Susannah shook her head.

Sam felt it then. Deep in his guts. He finally understood that he had truly lost her. That no sparkling oratory, no offensive he could launch, regardless of how brazenly conceived, how aggressively implemented, would ever bring her back. For the first time in his life, he had been defeated by a will greater than his own. And then he had a glimpse of something dark and unpleasant hovering on the edge of his unconscious. A glimpse of something Susannah had once tried to tell him—that vision wasn't enough. That it wouldn't stave off loneliness or keep old age at bay. That there was a kind of love in the world of which he was incapable. Susannah understood that love, but he didn't. And because he couldn't give it to her, he had lost her.

He blinked his eyes. Picked up his suit coat. Screw her. He didn't need Susannah. He didn't need anybody. The world of ideas stretched before him, and that was enough.

He ran the collar of his suit coat through his fingers. Then he lifted his eyes to Yank's. "Victors is your game, isn't it?"

Yank nodded slowly. "It was the last game I invented. Right before you made me leave Atari."

"Why didn't you ever tell us?"

"You all kept going on about it. I was embarrassed. I meant to tell you, but then I waited too long, and it got awkward."

Sam could have cried foul, but Yank was the greatest engineer he'd ever met, and he deserved respect. "It's a good game, Yank," he said huskily. "A real good game."

He turned to walk out the door.

And collided with Mitchell Blaine.

Mitch exploded into the office. His face was flushed, his blue dress shirt stuck to his chest with sweat. His light blue eyes held a savage, awful gleam none of them had ever seen before. "What in the goddamn everlasting *hell* is going on here?" he roared.

Paige's feet seemed to move of their own volition as she raced toward him and threw her small body into his arms. Safe, solid Mitch. He was as good as a daddy. The only force of stability in a world filled with familiar people gone crazy. She had telephoned him right away, as soon as she had realized they were actually going to play this crazy game. But he hadn't gotten here in time.

"You're too late," she said. "It's over."

Mitch circled Paige's shoulders and hugged her against him. His arm was strong and protective, like her father's should have been when she was a child. She wanted to cuddle up against him and let him keep the wolves away.

"Somebody'd better start talking fast," he hissed, hugging her close. "Right now. Susannah, tell me what happened."

She shrugged with all the nonchalance of SysVal's unshakable corporate president—the valiant female warrior who had taken on everything and everybody who had threatened her company. But as she watched her sister cuddled into Mitch's big arms, her bottom lip began to quiver. "Yank won me."

Mitch's eyes shot to Yank. He pierced him with an icy gaze as deadly as any of Victors' missiles. "What does that mean?"

"It's very simple, Mitch," Yank said. "Sam refused to accept the fact that Susannah no longer wanted him in her life, so he and I had a contest. Whoever won got to take her to bed. I won."

Somewhere in Mitch's solid thirty-eight-year-old body, the reflexes of an Ohio State wide receiver still existed. With a muffled roar, he released Paige, shot over the corner of the desk, and charged straight for Yank Yankowski.

Yank went down immediately.

Paige screamed, Susannah yelled, both women raced across the small office and threw themselves on Mitch, one of them pulling at his legs, the other at his arms.

"Get off!" Paige screamed, straddling his hips. "Get off, you'll kill him!"

Susannah grabbed a handful of blue Oxford-cloth dress shirt (light starch only) and pulled. "Stop, Mitch. No! Don't do this!"

Sam stood by the doorway and watched the four of them grappling on the floor. God, he was going to miss this place.

Susannah lost one of her high heels. Paige knocked a Rolodex to the floor and the cards went skidding everywhere. The glowing screen of the Victors game flickered above them.

Mitch shook off the women, pulled Yank to his feet, and slammed him against a dividing partition. The partition promptly collapsed, sending the men crashing into the next office.

Sam watched it all, took in the expressions on their faces, and finally understood how these people fit together. This was the vision that had escaped him, the one he had been too preoccupied to see. He shook his head at his own stupidity.

"Let him go, Mitch!" Susannah cried. She had a death grip on one of Mitch's arms. But something distracted her, a small movement in the periphery of her vision. She twisted her head and caught sight of Sam just as he was turning to leave the office.

He gazed back at her. She sucked in her breath as she saw the resignation in his eyes, and realized that he had finally let her go. "So long, babe," he said. "See you around."

For the briefest of moments, their eyes locked, and then she nodded her head in a final gesture of farewell toward her first true love. *Good-bye, Sam Gamble. Godspeed.*

His mouth curled in that old cocky grin, the grin of the motorcycle pirate who had stolen her away from her wedding and reshaped her destiny. Then he turned his back on all of them and set out to conquer another brave new world.

The loudspeaker began to play "Twist and Shout."

"Fight, dammit!" Mitch ordered. He sounded mean, but he was having difficulty summoning the will to smash in the face of an opponent who was proving to be so pathetically inept. "Fight me, you son of a bitch!"

But Yank was mystified when it came to physical violence. Although he found he rather liked the *idea* of finally being in a fight after all these years, he didn't really like *fighting.* There was no time to think anything through. No time to ponder or plan.

In actuality, Mitch was having more trouble with the women than he was having with Yank. The Faulconer sisters hung onto him like burrs. No sooner had he shaken off one than the other came back again. Paige had him by the neck, Susannah was pulling on his middle. His knee was starting to hurt, and he had banged up his elbow when the partition collapsed. What in the hell was he doing? He was thirty-eight years old, father of two, a member of the United Way Board of Directors. What in the sweet hell did he think he was doing?

He let go of Yank and loosened Paige's grip from around his neck. When Susannah realized he had stopped the fight, she relaxed the arm that had been clamped around his waist.

Yank was blinking his eyes. Mitch glared at him. "You're not taking Susannah to bed."

"No." Yank blinked. "No, I don't think that would be a good idea at all."

There was a long silence. Mitch stared at Yank. Then at Susannah. All the tension left his body like air from an overinflated balloon.

Yank continued to blink. "I'm sorry, but I seem to have lost my contact lens."

Then they were all down on the floor, relieved to have an

excuse to pull themselves back together while they crawled around to find Yank's lens. Paige located it, still intact, under one of the Rolodex cards. Mitch straightened his necktie and rubbed his sore elbow. Susannah looked for her shoe.

"It's difficult . . ." Yank said, after he had inserted his lens and inspected a scraped knuckle. "It's difficult to see exactly how we might extract ourselves from this. Sam and I had a deal. I'm not proud of the fact that I didn't behave in an entirely honorable fashion. I should have told him I'd invented Victors, of course. But in any case, two wrongs don't make a right. Sam and I had a deal, and I have a certain obligation."

Now Susannah was the one who wanted to smack him. She stalked toward Yank, wobbling because she still hadn't found her shoe. "Yank, will you let it rest? It's over. The contest was meaningless."

To her astonishment, Mitch began to yell at her. "Shut up, Susannah! You may be dynamite when it comes to running a corporation, but you're hopeless when it comes to organizing your love life. I've let all this go on far too long. For six weeks I've been walking around with my tail tucked between my legs waiting for you to stop looking like you're going to break in half. Well, I've had enough!"

"Don't you dare talk to me like that!"

"I'll talk to you any way I like. Right now, I'm in charge." He spun toward Yank. "Let's make a side deal."

"A side deal? Yes. Yes, I think that's a good idea."

Paige's heart began an arhythmic thumping against her ribs.

"How do you want to go about it?" Mitch asked, all business now that he was once again in control. "Your deal, your call."

Yank was thoughtful. "Perhaps you could make me a monetary offer for her. That should make it official."

Mitch had cut his teeth on making deals, and he knew how to go for a quick kill. "I'll give you five dollars."

"Five dollars!" Susannah lurched toward them. "Did you say *five* dollars?"

"That would be fine," Yank replied. "If you don't mind, I'd prefer cash. I lose checks."

Mitch reached for his wallet and flipped it open. "I only have a couple of twenties. Do you have change?"

Yank pulled out his own wallet and inspected its contents. "I'm sorry. I only seem to have a twenty myself. Paige?"

Paige nearly lost her balance as she scrambled for her purse. But her hands were trembling so much she couldn't find anything. In desperation, she emptied the contents out on the desk, sending lipsticks rolling and chewing gum flying. Frantically, she snatched up her wallet and pulled open the dollar-bill compartment, breathing so fast she was dizzy. "No, no, I don't," she sobbed. "Oh, God. I've only got a fifty. What good in the world is a fifty?" And then she turned to Mitch and screamed, *"For God's sake, give him the twenty!"*

Susannah had to make some attempt to reassert her dignity. In a voice as chill as the polar ice cap, she said, "If this is an auction, I'll put in twenty and buy myself back."

"It's not an auction," Yank said firmly. "That would be demeaning."

Paige started to choke. Yank tapped her gently on the back.

Mitch passed over the twenty. "I want my change back."

Yank nodded and drew Paige toward him. For a moment he closed his eyes as his bruised jaw came to rest on the top of her head.

Paige settled against his chest. And then she stiffened as she remembered everything he had put her through.

Yank had been fighting over Susannah. Three men had been fighting over her sister. Not one, but three! Didn't anyone remember that she was the pretty one? Didn't anyone remember that she was the one men went crazy over?

Yank remembered. He stared down at her, this beautiful blond creature he had fallen so desperately in love with. She was every girl who had passed him by, every girl who had laughed at his awkwardness and then ignored his existence. All his life he had stood on the sidelines and watched women like Paige Faulconer walk right past without even seeing him. But now that was over.

Who could ever have imagined that someone like Paige could have fallen in love with someone like him? And he knew she loved him. He had felt the way their souls matched up right from the beginning, that night on the beach in Naxos. But he had wanted the two of them to last forever, and so he had given her time and all the room she needed to adjust, even though from that very first evening he had wanted to bind her to him so tightly she could never get away.

And tonight he had frightened her to death. What he had done for Susannah had hurt her badly. She was in a huff. He could see that, all right. Now he had to make it up.

"Susannah, I won't be in to work for several days," he said. "Paige and I need some time alone together."

Paige curled her lip and flashed her eyes just like a prom queen who had been forced to dance with the ugliest boy in the class. "I wouldn't go anywhere with you if you were the last man on earth. You're a nerd! A complete and total nerd!"

Yank took his time to consider his options. He had a scientist's passion for the truth. Tricking Sam had made him miserable, even though he had done it for the best of reasons. He had offended his own moral sensibilities once tonight. He certainly couldn't offend them twice.

Could he?

"Very well, Paige," he said. "Susannah, would it be possible for you to drive me to the doctor's office? My arm is a bit sore. I'm certain it's not broken, however—"

Oh, Lord, he could hardly breathe as Paige cradled his arm and cooed over him and made him feel as if he were a bronzed California surfer god with sculptured muscles, a white zinc nose, and a brain too small to ever cause the slightest bit of trouble.

Susannah watched the two of them leave. They were wrapped together as if they'd been born that way. Silence hung thick and heavy in the office. Mitch stood by the doorway, one hand resting loosely on the hip of his navy-blue trousers, the other at his side.

Susannah was so nervous she could hardly think. For months she had been on a wild roller-coaster ride as she realized that she loved Mitch and tried to lock her feelings away because she thought he loved her sister. Now she wanted him to take her in his arms and speak all those tender phrases she yearned to hear. But he wasn't saying a word.

She filled up the silence with chatter. "There's not one thing wrong with Yank's arm. He's manipulating her. I swear, Yank's getting stranger all the time. And my sister . . ." Her voice faded. Didn't Mitch care for her? She told herself that he had to care, or he wouldn't have gone so crazy with Yank.

She studied a point on the wall just past his shoulder. "I thought you and Paige . . ."

Mitch didn't say anything. He just stood there and looked at her.

His look was definitely possessive. She remembered the five dollars, and she could feel her cheeks growing hot. Did he really think he'd bought her from Yank?

She lowered herself to the floor and made a great business out of looking for her shoe. Anything to avoid looking at Mitch. She peered under the desk, under the credenza, over by the doorway. Mitch's shoes were there. Unlike hers, they were on his feet. Polished black wing tips peeking out from between neatly creased navy-blue slacks.

The silence was growing more oppressive. Her cheeks still felt hot. She jumped as her shoe dropped in front of her.

Just as she picked it up, two strong hands pulled her to her feet. Mitch looked quite stern, perhaps a bit dangerous. "Your divorce isn't final yet. As soon as it is, you and I have an appointment in the bedroom."

At first she thought he said boardroom. You and I have an appointment in the boardroom. She was so shaken that she heard him wrong. And by the time she realized what he had actually said, he was on his way out of the office.

She gritted her teeth. Oh, no. It wasn't going to be all business. No way. If Mr. Stuffed Shirt thought it was going to be all business, he'd better think again. She flung her shoe at the door.

His reflexes were quick, and she hadn't been trying to hit him anyway, so the shoe missed him by a yard. That didn't seem to appease him, however.

He turned back to her, crossed his arms over his chest and said with a deadly quiet, "You've got thirty seconds, Susannah."

"For what?"

"To stop acting like a feather-headed female and decide what you want."

"I—I don't know what you mean."

"Twenty-five seconds."

"Stop bullying me."

"Eighteen."

"You're a real jerk, do you know that?"

"Fifteen."

"Why does it have to be me?"

"Twelve."

"Why can't *you* say it?"

"Ten."

"All right. I'll say it!"

"Five."

"I love you, you jerk!"

"Damn right, you do. And don't you forget it."

He still looked as mad as hell, but something warm and wonderful was opening inside of Susannah. She wanted to slide into his arms and stay there forever. What was it about Mitchell Blaine's arms that made a woman want to lose herself in them? Moving forward, she placed her open palms on his chest. She could feel his heart racing just as hard as hers. She shut her eyes and lifted her mouth toward his.

He groaned, caught her wrists and set her firmly away from him. "Not yet," he said hoarsely. "I bought you, and I'm in charge."

Her eyes snapped open. "You're kidding."

He gave her that narrow-eyed look he turned on competitors when he was bargaining for position. "Legally, you're still a married woman. And I'm not going to touch you until your divorce is final, because once I get started with you, I don't intend to stop."

She repressed a delicious shiver of anticipation, and then frowned. "It's going to be another month, Mitch. That's a long time."

"Use it well."

"Me?"

He gave her his best steely-eyed glare, but she saw these funny little lights dancing in those light blue irises. "You might as well know right now, Susannah, that I expect value for my money."

The sound that slipped through her lips was a garbled combination of laughter and outrage. She decided two could play his game. Recovering quickly, she sauntered back over to him and slipped her fingers underneath his necktie knot. "I know exactly what *I've* got to offer. You're the unproven commodity."

"Now *that* is exactly the sort of disrespect we're going to have to work hard to correct." His voice was as solemn as a judge's, but she wasn't fooled for a minute. "I want to see a change of attitude, Susannah. At least a semblance of subservience."

"Subservience?"

"I'm the man. You're the woman. As far as I'm concerned, that says it all. It had better be that way after we're married, too."

"Did you say married?"

"I'm considering it."

"You're considering it? Of all the arrogant—"

"First you pass the bedroom interview, Hot Shot. Then we'll talk about a contract."

As she sputtered for breath, his sober face shattered into the biggest grin she had ever seen. Before she could say another word, he walked away.

But she wasn't done with him. She rushed over to the doorway only to discover that he was already half way down the hall. "Stop right there, Mitchell Blaine," she called out. "Do you love me?"

"Of course," he replied, without losing a step. "I'm surprised you even need to ask."

Then, as she watched, he took three long strides forward, leaped off the ground, and faked a perfect jump shot at the ceiling.

His shirttail didn't even come untucked.

34

• •

Yank and Paige left for Reno without bothering to change their clothes or pack a suitcase. Somehow, Paige had never imagined herself getting married in a silk blouse and pair of gray slacks, but no force on earth could have persuaded either of them to wait a day longer. The ceremony took place not long after midnight in a tacky little chapel with one of Elvis's guitars on display in a glass case. Yank had stared at the guitar for a long time and then said it reminded him of a woman he loved.

Paige didn't understand why one of Elvis's guitars would remind Yank of herself, but the service was ready to begin, and she didn't have time to ask any questions.

The wedding suites in the better hotels were already booked, and they had to settle for a smaller hotel. The bellhop showed them into a room that looked like a nightmare version of the inside of a Valentine candy box. The walls were covered in fuzzy zebra-striped wallpaper, and white fake fur rugs as thick as dust mops stretched from wall to wall. Festoons of shiny red and white satin draped the heart-shaped bed and were reflected in the gold-flecked mirror that served as a headboard.

"This is nice," Yank said in admiration.

Normally Paige would have laughed, but she was too

nervous. What if Yank was disappointed in her? She had faked lovemaking with some of the best, but Yank was a lot more perceptive than most men. Still, she didn't envision lovemaking as being the most important part of their life together. Anybody who was as cerebral as Yank probably wasn't going to be the world's most competent lover, which was fine with her. She'd already gone to bed with the greatest, and it hadn't been all that wonderful.

Cuddling with him appealed to her the most—so warm and cozy. The cuddling and the cooking. She wanted to fill his thin body with her rich, wonderful food. Nurse his babies from her bountiful breasts. Unaccountably, her eyes filled with tears.

She had her back to him, but somehow he seemed to know she was crying. He gathered her in his arms and held her. "It's going to be all right," he said. "You mustn't worry."

She stood on her tiptoes and buried her face in his neck. "I love you so much. I don't deserve you. I'm not a nice person. I lose my temper. I swear too much. You're so much better than I am."

He tilted up her chin and stroked her blond hair back from her face with his fingers. His eyes were filled with wonder. "You're the most wonderful woman in the world. I still can't believe you're mine."

As he gazed at her, all the goodness in his soul infused her. And then he dropped his head and kissed her. Oh, so slowly. She had never been kissed like that. His lips touched hers so lightly that at first she could barely feel them. She was the one who deepened the pressure. She was the one who opened her mouth.

The kiss went on and on. He was a man of infinite patience, and he believed in doing a job well. He kissed her cheeks and her eyelids, laid her back on the bed and tilted her chin to the side so he could kiss her throat. He found the pulse that fluttered there and counted the beats with the touch of his lips.

She felt so languid, so warm. His lips trailed down the open vee of her blouse and lingered there. Her breasts began to throb, anticipating his touch. She wanted more of him. Her fingers worked beneath his shirt. He pulled her hands away and clasped them gently between his own.

"Would you like some champagne?"

She shook her head. She didn't want any champagne. She didn't want him to stop.

But he got up anyway. He went to the ice bucket and fiddled with the bottle. It took him forever to get it open. First he had to dry it with a towel, then he made a big deal out of removing the foil neatly. He unscrewed the wire cage as if he were working with a delicate piece of machinery. She wanted to scream at him to just open it, for Pete's sake, and get back to her.

While he poured a glass for himself, she propped herself up against the pillows. He asked her again if she wanted some.

"All right," she replied grouchily. "As long as you've got it open."

He brought the glasses over and stood by the bed looking down at her. The narrow gold wedding band looked beautiful on his long thin fingers. Her body once again began to grow warm and her irritation faded. The mattress sagged as he settled on the side of the bed and put the glasses on the nightstand.

"Don't drink yet," he said. "I want to think of a toast."

And he sat there.

She couldn't believe it. She wanted him to kiss her again and touch her breasts, but he was sitting there thinking up a dumb toast. And while he was thinking, he began doing this thing with the palm of her hand. Just lightly stroking it with his thumb. She had never had her palm stroked in that particular way. It was so unbelievably exciting. Before long, she began to squirm.

"Did you think of it yet?" she finally gasped.

"A couple more minutes," he said, transferring his touch from her hand to the sensitive skin of her inner arm.

She closed her eyes. Her lips parted. What was he doing to her? The stroking on her arm continued forever, and then his mouth brushed over hers again in another of his delicious kisses. This was good, she thought. Now they were getting back to business.

She moaned as he kissed the base of her throat. His fingers played with the top button of her blouse. After another few years had passed, he opened it. He kissed the spot of skin revealed there and then unfastened the next button. A button and then a kiss. A button and then a kiss.

Her breasts where they rose above the scalloped lace of her bra were covered in a rosy flush. When would he get to her bra? To her slacks?

He stopped. "I think I have the toast now."

She gritted her teeth. If he didn't get his mind back on what he was doing, she was going to toast him.

He handed her back her champagne glass. "To my wife, the most beautiful woman in the world. I love you."

It was sweet—really sweet—but hardly original enough to be worth the wait. She clinked her glass with his, downed her champagne, dropped her glass to the carpet and threw herself back in his arms.

He gently disengaged himself and slipped off her blouse.

She wanted to give a whoop of triumph. Yes! He finally had the idea. He'd finally remembered what he was supposed to be doing. Now the bra. Don't forget the bra.

He didn't forget. His agile fingers unfastened the clasp so smoothly it seemed as if it had dissolved in his hands. He slipped the lacy garment off her and laid her down on the bed.

And then he just looked at her. She lay back and he inspected her with his eyes. Her nipples grew hard and beaded under his scrutiny. He bent forward. She closed her eyes, waiting for the heat of his mouth on her breasts, and felt his lips settle . . .

. . . over the curve of her shoulder.

She gave a little sob of frustration. Her hands knotted into fists at her side while he played with her shoulder for another ten years. My breasts! she wanted to cry. Taste my breasts, my bubbies, my pretty pretty boobies.

But the booby she had married had discovered a patch of incredibly sensitive skin at the inside of her elbow and he was sucking on it.

"Your slacks are getting mussed," he said finally.

"Yes," she agreed. "Oh, yes." She began to unfasten them, but again he pushed her away. He slipped them down over her legs and started to fold them.

"It doesn't matter," she said. "Just throw them across a chair."

"They'll get wrinkled," he replied, as if a pair of wrinkled slacks were some sort of monumental crime against nature. Standing, he held them by the cuffs, snapped the creases, and began matching up the inseams with a geometric precision that would have made Euclid weep with joy.

Paige wanted to weep, but not with joy. Why couldn't he understand how difficult it was for her to get aroused? Her excitement could vanish any second. It always did. He needed to take advantage of her arousal before it slipped away. Didn't he understand that?

Apparently he didn't. He had to carry the slacks over to the closet and hang them up. And not just any hanger would do. It had to be a trouser hanger.

She whipped off her underpants while his back was turned and lifted one knee just a bit so that the sole of her right foot was pressed against the curve of her left calf.

When he turned around and saw that, his eyes opened wider. Determined to gain the upper hand, she let one arm fall languidly to the side of the bed and began rubbing the sole of her right foot up and down her calf. Yank walked back toward the bed. She caught her bottom lip between her teeth. He abruptly took a detour.

She shot up on her elbow. "Where are you going?"

He walked over to one of the tables and flipped on another lamp. "It's hard to see in here," he said. "I like to see what I'm doing." And then he returned to the foot of the bed. Sliding his hands up and down her calves, he gently pressed her knees farther open.

Her mouth went dry. She looked up at him.

His hands rose to his shirt. But instead of taking it off, he began slowly rolling up the cuffs.

Her eyes flew to his face. For the first time, she saw the amusement lurking at the corner of his mouth.

"You're doing this on purpose," she gasped.

"I think," he said, "that no one has ever taken enough time with you."

Paige lived through a thousand glorious lives that night. Yank had been trained in the lessons of patience, and he believed in careful craftsmanship. He liked to form hypotheses and then test them. For example, if he used his tongue here and his hand there . . .

He was an engineer, an absolute genius when it came to working with small parts. And every one of her small parts surrendered to his intricate inspection and exploded under his skillful manipulation.

Who could have imagined he would actually have to smother her cries of fulfillment with his mouth? Who could have imagined that this absent-minded genius could bring her the satisfaction that had been eluding her all her life?

When he finally came to her, his eyes were glazed and his breathing as heavy as her own. She was hardly capable of rational thought, but she dimly realized what his patience was costing him and loved him all the more for it.

Even as he poised himself to enter her, he took care. He was her husband, her lover. But above all, he was an engineer. And good engineers never forced parts together that were of unequal size.

"All right?" he murmured.

"Oh, yes. Oh, yes," she gasped.

"My wife. My love."

She cried out with joy and passion as he entered her. He caught her cries in his mouth and they began to move together, rushing in harmony toward a place of perfect fulfillment.

As dawn streaked the sky, they lay satiated in each other's arms. "Why did you act like it would be okay if I went to bed with Mitch?" she whispered.

"Because I knew Mitch wouldn't go to bed with you."

"He would, too," she said indignantly. And then she smiled. "No, I guess he wouldn't have." Her fingers played with the textures of his chest. "I thought you loved Susannah."

He stroked her cheek. "I do. The same way you love her." He didn't see any need to tell her it hadn't always been that way, that there had been a time when he had been very much attracted to Susannah. She had been so different from the women he knew.

"Susannah's happiness is important to me," he went on.

"That's why I had to make Sam understand that he couldn't have her back. But in terms of physical attraction . . ."

When he didn't go on, Paige probed. "What? Tell me."

He looked troubled. "Please don't take offense at this, Paige. I love Susannah and I admire her. But don't you think she's a bit—plain?"

Paige gazed around her at the tacky wedding suite that Yank thought was so attractive. She giggled with delight and hugged him to her breasts. "Absolutely, Yank. Susannah is definitely too plain for you."

Everything about Mitch had begun to irritate Susannah. His clothes, for example. How many perfectly tailored navy-blue suits could a man own? How many navy and red rep ties? Couldn't he take a walk on the wild side just once and wear paisley?

And she hated the way he tapped his pen when he was annoyed, the way he leaned back in his chair and tugged on his necktie knot when he wanted to make a point. He took notes on absolutely everything—she hated that, too. What did he do with all those yellow legal pads once he filled them up? Did he rent a warehouse somewhere?

She fumed as she watched his gold pen scratch across the paper. He probably had one of those yellow legal pads on his bedside table so he could take notes on a woman's performance after they'd made love.

But she couldn't let herself think about that, and so she thought about how crazy he made her in meetings. They would be sitting around a conference table and he would be reading from his ten zillionth computer printout and talking about shipments and quotas and sales forecasts. Then, right in the middle of a sentence, he'd slip off those stupid horn-rimmed glasses and look over at her. Just a look. Just this macho-stud look like she was some sort of marked woman. God, it was irritating. It was so irritating, she would lose track of where she was and stumble around and then everyone would start looking at *her.*

"Susannah?"

She blinked her eyes. Jack Vaughan, their vice-president of Research and Development, was staring at her. *Everyone* was staring at her. She'd done it again. Mitch smiled and leaned back in his chair, making this stupid church steeple with his fingers.

"Susannah?" Vaughan repeated. "Do you have any questions about our figures?"

"No, no. They're fine." She suspected that everyone at the table knew she didn't have the slightest idea what figures they were talking about. A giant clock seemed to be ticking away in her head, marking this last week until her divorce was final. Why did Mitch have to be so stubborn? Why did he have to drive her crazy like this? She wasn't sleeping well at night. All of this waiting had worn her nerves to the breaking point.

The loudspeaker snapped on. "Attention unmarried females. Free gynecological exams are now being given in Building C. Ask for Ralph."

Susannah jumped out of her chair. "That does it! I'm going to have somebody's *ass!*"

Mitch looked pained.

Jack Vaughan closed his folder. "I think our meeting is adjourned," he said quietly.

She stomped toward the door. Mitch intercepted her before she could reach it with another one of his new tricks. He simply stepped in front of her and blocked her path with his body. It was nothing more than a macho power play, a completely juvenile way of reminding her that he was bigger and stronger than she was. Real tough-guy stuff.

"What do you want?" she growled, ignoring the fluttering in her stomach and the wonderful scent of his starched shirt.

He leaned down and whispered in her ear. "One more week, Hot Shot. Then I take what's mine."

She swallowed hard. He was getting to her. He was really getting to her.

Her divorce became final on a completely ordinary Wednesday. She sat through a session with her East Coast marketing people, and met with the management team that headed up their Singapore plant. Paige had called and asked if she could drop by in the afternoon, and Susannah had rescheduled a conference call to accommodate her.

She finished drafting a memo and looked at her watch. It was nearly time for Paige to arrive. She hadn't seen Mitch all day. Which was perfectly fine with her. He'd put her through hell this past month, and she planned to make him suffer for it. If he thought he could just jump in bed with her now that she was officially a free woman, she would very quickly set him straight. She might be free, but she had no intention of being easy.

Paige stuck her head in the door. "Hi."

It was so good to see her sister that some of Susannah's tension faded. Since her marriage, Paige's skin actually seemed to glow with contentment. And whenever Susannah saw Yank, he had this goofy smile on his face.

The honeymooners had settled in at Falcon Hill. The idea of Yank Yankowski serving as lord and master of Joel Faulconer's home made her smile. *You might actually have liked him, Daddy,* she thought. *Once you got over the initial shock, of course. He's the best there is, and he's made Paige so happy.*

Susannah took in her sister's pale raspberry suit, the pearls at her throat, the chignon, and the gray lizardskin pumps. "My, my. I'm impressed. Did you get all dressed up for me?"

"No. I did it for Paul. He gets nervous when board members wear blue jeans."

"Paul?"

Paige stepped aside, and Susannah saw that she wasn't alone. Paul Clemens, Cal's predecessor as FBT chairman, was with her. Susannah got up to greet him. They chatted awkwardly for a few minutes.

Realizing that this was to be more than a sisterly chat, Susannah directed them to the small conference table in the corner of her office. No sooner were they all seated than Mitch arrived.

Susannah's heart did one of those peculiar somersaults. He took the seat next to Paige.

"I didn't know this was going to be a formal meeting," she said coolly.

Paige fiddled with her pearls. "I'm the one who asked Mitch to be here. Look, Susannah, I'm sorry about this, but—"

"It's my fault," Paul Clemens interrupted. "Paige and I had a long talk yesterday and I asked her to set this up."

Susannah clasped her hands on the table. "Paul, you've been a friend for a long time, but if you're here in any sort of official capacity for FBT, I'm going to need one of our attorneys present."

"I'm retired, Susannah, although I still sit on the board. Let's just say I'm here in an unofficially official capacity."

"Hear him out, Suze," Paige said. "This is pretty important."

Susannah reluctantly agreed, and Paul began to outline the crisis FBT had been thrust into since the public revelations about Cal Theroux. The fact that a man who had been the chairman of FBT would soon have a prison term hanging over his head had made everything incredibly difficult. The more Susannah listened, the more alarmed she became. She had known that FBT was in trouble, but she had no idea their problems ran so deep. The giant corporation was, quite literally, on the verge of collapse.

Paul finished speaking, and she gazed at him with dismay. "I hope both of you understand that none of us at SysVal wanted to damage FBT. Our problem was with Cal, not the company."

"You've made that very clear in your public statements, and we all appreciate it," Paul replied. "But the fact is, the public perceives us as the bad guys in black hats, while you're Snow White. Companies don't want to do business with us anymore. It's as if we're tainted, and they're moving toward our competitors in droves. We've discontinued the Falcon 101, but that's had little effect. The price of our stock has become a sick joke. Every division of the corporation is in jeopardy."

Paige looked up from the pattern she had been tracing on the table with the tip of her finger. "Suze, this is my fault. I'm hopeless at managing my stock. When I attend FBT business meetings, my mind wanders; everything is so boring that I can't keep my thoughts focused. I never have the slightest idea how I'm supposed to vote. That's why I gave my proxy to Cal. And look what that led to."

"You didn't intend to hurt the company," Susannah said.

"But she did hurt it," Clemens interjected. "And neither

475

Paige nor I want that to happen again. FBT has nearly three hundred thousand employees. Entire communities depend upon us. Many of the small towns where we have plants couldn't continue to exist if we closed down. And we're losing, Susannah. Everything is slipping away."

Paige leaned forward. "I want to give you my permanent proxy, Susannah. I want you to vote my shares."

"Paige, I appreciate the vote of confidence, and I want to help you, but that's one thing I can't do. It would be a direct conflict of interest. My board of directors would never permit it."

"They would if you resigned," Paul said quietly. "If you left SysVal, put your own shares in trust, and took over as chairman and CEO of FBT."

Susannah sat stunned. They wanted her to take control of one of the biggest corporations in the United States, to take her father's old position. A hand grasped hers under the table and squeezed. The solid comfort of that big hand steadied her.

Paul studied her with great seriousness. "FBT must regain moral credibility if it's to survive. Right now, you're the only one who can give it back to us."

Susannah shook her head. "I'm sorry. Truly I am. I'll help you any other way I can, but leaving SysVal is absolutely out of the question."

For the first time since he had come in to join them, Mitch spoke. "Susannah needs a few days. Let her have some time to think it over."

"I don't want time, I—"

"I don't think a few days will hurt," he said smoothly.

She wasn't going to get into an argument with Mitch in front of Paul Clemens, and so she nodded. "Very well. A few days." But even as she spoke, she knew that nothing in the world would make her leave SysVal.

She had no sooner gotten home that night than Mitch appeared at her door. He was still wearing his business suit, and he hadn't even loosened his necktie. As much as she had been anticipating this moment, now that it had come, she wanted to postpone it. The past month had been nerve-wracking, but as she stared at him standing on her doorstep, she finally admitted to herself that she had loved that primitive feeling of being sexually stalked by the man she loved.

How could the reality ever match the expectation? Mitch would be a good lover, but in her heart of hearts, she didn't believe that he would be a great one. He was too neat, too proper. As she gazed into his face, her stomach began to feel queasy. What if she shocked him? What if he liked women who were more restrained in the bedroom?

"I—I'm sorry," she stammered. "I can't invite you in. I've got a bad headache."

"You've got a yellow streak," he replied.

She slammed the door on him and went into the living room, where her hands trembled as she snatched up a magazine she had no intention of reading from the glass-topped coffee table. Why did she have to be such a sex maniac? As passionately as she felt about him, she would never be able to hold herself back. When he found out what she was really like, he would probably run from the house in terror. Maybe he'd send her a memo. FROM: Mitchell Blaine TO: Susannah Faulconer SUBJECT: Inappropriate Bedroom Conduct . . .

He walked into the living room and pocketed the key she had given him when she'd moved into her new home in mid-August.

"I want that key back," she said.

"No, you don't."

She stared at the lushly printed draperies Paige had picked out for her. She loved him so much and she wanted everything to be perfect, but this was real life, not a fairy tale. Remembering that they had something other than sex to discuss, she took a seat on the couch. At least she could postpone the inevitable a bit longer. "I'm not leaving SysVal."

"I don't think you have a lot of choice, Susannah."

"Don't say that!"

He sat down next to her and leaned back into the soft cushions. How could he be so relaxed when she was so uptight? "Somehow I can't picture you living the rest of your life with the fate of three hundred thousand people on your conscience," he said. "Not to mention all those small towns."

"I don't belong at FBT. It's old and stodgy and conservative."

"True. And it's been badly mismanaged ever since your father's death."

"You know as well as I do that they only want me as a figurehead. They'll expect me to use Paige's proxy as a rubber stamp for the majority opinion. Those men don't have the slightest intention of giving me any real power."

Mitch chuckled. "And aren't you going to have a wonderful time showing them the error of their ways?"

She switched tactics. "I don't have a college degree."

"I've got three of them. You want one?"

She tried another path. "I want to have a baby."

His face softened. "Do you? That's great. That is really great. I hoped so, but we haven't talked about it."

"We haven't talked about anything!" She jumped up from the couch. "Don't you understand? The president of SysVal can definitely be pregnant. At SysVal anything is possible. But can you honestly, in your wildest imagination, see the chairman of FBT breastfeeding through a board meeting?"

"Not the old FBT." He smiled, rising to stand next to her. "But the new FBT? The one with an updated product line, a streamlined management structure. The one with on-premises child care. Ah, Susannah . . ."

For a moment they let the vision sweep over them. It was a vision of a new corporation, one with a strong moral center and a commitment to the world it served. A corporation for the twenty-first century.

He took her hand. "You're thirty-two now, practically an old lady, and I'm thirty-eight. SysVal is a company for kids. We have so many talented people working for us that we barely know what to do with them. Let's get out of their way and let them run with it for a while."

"We both can't just walk out. That's impossible. And I'm not going to FBT without you. Our relationship aside, you're the best marketing man in the business."

"I'll stay at SysVal until the new team is in place and the board members' nerves have steadied. Then I'll join you."

He tilted up her chin with his fingers, and his eyes were soft with the depth of his feelings for her. "I love you, Susannah. Oh, God, I love you so much. All those years, watching you married to Sam. Sometimes I thought I was going crazy."

"I know, Mitch. Oh, my darling, I love you, too."

He dipped his head. A warm, hard mouth settled over hers. His big hands splayed over her back, ran up along her spine, tangled in her hair. His mouth was open, his kiss deep and aggressive. It was a man's kiss, a kiss that gave as well as took. Her breasts crushed flat against his chest as he pulled her closer. She accepted his tongue and gave him her own while she wrapped her foot around the leg of his trousers. He clasped her head between his big hands. It felt so right to be kissing him, so perfect to be in this solid, respectable man's arms. Oh, yes, she had been absolutely right to put little boys behind her.

His hand slid down over her breast. "Time's up, sweetheart," he said hoarsely. "I've been going crazy. I can't wait any longer."

At the touch of his hand on her breast, her nervousness came back in a rush. He was a good kisser, but kissing was only part of it. "Mitch, I'm not sure . . ."

He drew back and studied her for an agonizingly long moment. Then he tilted his head toward the hallway. "Upstairs, Susannah," he said quietly.

He didn't realize how important this was. He didn't understand that what happened next—or didn't happen— could put a shadow over everything. "Mitch, we may have some difficulty adjusting to—"

"Now."

She spun around and stalked away from him, marching toward the front staircase as if he held a gun at her back. Sometimes she hated engineers. She really did. Her shoes slapped on the carpeted treads. Since her fears weren't quantifiable, Mitch simply refused to recognize them. Everything had to be rational. The man didn't have one speck of intuitive power in his entire body.

She stomped into the bedroom and kicked off her heels. She could hear him behind her, moving at his customary unhurried pace, as if he were on his way to a staff meeting. As he came into the bedroom, she whirled around. "If this is a disaster, don't you dare blame me!"

He stared down at the carpet and shook his head. "I was

going to try to be a nice guy about this, but I can see that's not going to work." He lifted his head and glared at her. "Get out of those clothes, Susannah."

She was so tightly strung that her temper snapped. "You go to hell!"

"That does it." He reached for his necktie and yanked at the knot. "I was going to be a nice guy. Not come on too strong. A little moonlight. A few roses." He tossed his tie down on her pretty bedroom chair and threw his suit coat on top of it. Standing there in his shirt-sleeves, he splayed his hands on his hips and let his eyes roam over her as if she were a slave girl placed before him for his inspection. "Apparently, I have to remind you that you've been bought and paid for."

Her heart jumped into her throat. Oh, Lord, he was playing with her. The game wasn't over. A surge of love and desire rushed through her as she realized that he understood how she felt after all. Her tension dissolved. She lifted her chin and pursed her lips in disapproval. "I was not bought."

"Money exchanged hands," he said flatly, stripping off his shirt. "You were bought. Now get out of those clothes so I can get you warmed up."

The man had no shame. She walked over to the bed and slid down on it. Then she drew her legs beneath her and gave him her most smoldering look. "No need to warm up something that's already hot."

For a moment she thought she had him.

He recovered quickly.

"Coming from you, that kind of comment doesn't surprise me at all." His undershirt joined his shirt in a pile on the floor. She swallowed hard at the sight of his chest, already anticipating how it would feel beneath her hands. He kicked off his wing tips and removed his socks. "You may fool other people, Susannah, but don't forget that I have three college degrees and I'm not so easily misled. Beneath that prim exterior of yours, you like it wild. And that's exactly how you're going to get it." In one strong motion, he whipped his belt from the loops of his trousers and snapped it in the air. "You're going to get it wild."

Oh, Lord . . . And she had been afraid that he wouldn't be able to keep up with her.

"Get up on your knees and take that dress off right now," he ordered.

Yes, sir. Oh, yes, my very dear sir. She scrambled to her knees and began working feverishly at her buttons. While she worked, he actually had the nerve to slide the length of the belt back and forth in his hand. The sparkle in his eyes almost ruined the effect, but it was still wonderfully menacing, and she was going to kill him if he laughed. Imagine being tied to this incredible man for the next forty years. Her lover, her friend, the other half of herself.

Still, she knew it wasn't good for him to get too full of himself—especially after everything she'd let him get away with these past few weeks. She had a little surprise in store for Mr. Macho. No stuffed shirt in a pinstriped suit was going to call her prim and get away with it.

Opening the last of the buttons, she stripped the dress over her head, revealing the deliciously naughty undergarments she had put on that morning in a fit of nervous anticipation—the soft peach demi-bra and panties, the matching garter belt and stockings.

Mitch's black leather belt fell to the carpet. "That's more like it," he said huskily. He didn't take his eyes off her as he pulled down his trousers.

Susannah swept her gaze along his muscular thighs and then burst out laughing. Mitch was wearing the tiniest pair of black zebra-striped briefs she had ever seen on a man.

She fell back into the pillows and hooted. "How long have you been wearing underwear like that?"

"For a while."

"Do you mean to tell me that during all those endless presentations we've sat through together, all those boring budget sessions, you've been wearing underwear like that?"

"I could ask the same question." He lowered himself to the bed beside her and lightly snapped a peach-colored garter.

She wrapped her arms around his neck and slid her fingers into his hair, pulling him down beside her. "Sometimes I don't wear anything at all," she whispered.

He groaned and gathered her into his arms. His mouth opened over hers as he gave her a ferocious, demanding kiss. Before long, their naughty underwear dropped to the floor.

As they explored the secrets of each other's bodies, their skin grew sleek with sweat. But they had waited so long for this moment that neither wanted it to end too soon, and they prolonged it with gentle warfare.

"You'd better be good," he growled.

"They don't come any better."

"We'll see about that."

Each fought for supremacy—first one rolled on top, and then the other. She bit his shoulder; he retaliated with a nip at the curve of her bottom. She entangled him in the covers and ran from the bedroom. He caught her on the stairs and tossed her over his shoulder to carry her back. Their behavior was disgraceful, woefully inappropriate for people in their positions, but no one was around to point that fact out to them.

He dumped her on the bed and sprawled on top of her, catching handfuls of her hair in his fists. She arched her back and penetrated his mouth with her tongue. His hands roamed her body and found its secrets.

When they could stand their fierce love play no longer, she opened her legs and he cradled himself between them. As he poised to enter her, she looked up at him with her soft eyes.

"This is forever, isn't it, Mitch?"

All the laughter, all the mischief faded. He gazed down at her kiss-bruised mouth, and his face was young and tender with the depth of his emotion. "Oh, my love. My sweet, sweet love. This is till the end of the world."

They weren't children. They had lived through other loves and other lives, and so they knew the gift of their joining was precious. He entered her aggressively, possessing her with the boldness of a man who could only find happiness with a woman of daring spirit. She accepted him fearlessly, filled with the wild joy of a soul that had found its mate. Their bodies fit together as if they had been designed on the day of their creation to make a perfect match. And when they cried out at the very end, they were still gazing into each other's eyes.

EPILOGUE

● ●

The Northern California weather was chill and crisp the January morning Susannah took her place as Chairman of the Board and Chief Executive Officer of Falcon Business Technologies. She wore her most conservative gray suit, her lowest black pumps, her simplest earrings. The only other piece of jewelry she permitted herself was the heavy gold wedding ring on her left hand. It was a beautiful piece of jewelry, but the number of large diamonds that sparkled in the band made it a bit flashy for FBT tastes.

A small group of men greeted her at the entrance of the Castle. "Welcome to FBT, Mrs. Blaine."

"Good to have you on board."

"Wonderful to meet you, Mrs. Blaine."

"Ms. Faulconer," she said. "But please call me Susannah."

They beamed their pleasure at her—a dozen dark-suited executives who knew that her sister's proxy had given her control of the corporation's largest single block of stock. She searched their ranks for the sight of a female face, but then remembered that women at FBT rarely rose above the ranks of middle management.

The men were gracious tour guides, leading her through the building as if she had never been there. They chatted as they escorted her along the hushed hallways and into richly carpeted offices. They opened doors and cupped her elbow to guide her.

"We've planned a long orientation period for you, Susannah."

"No need to hit you with too much at the beginning."

"We have a complete staff set up to advise you. They'll answer any of your questions . . ."

". . . explain our policies."

". . . direct you so you don't misinterpret any of our procedures."

"They'll keep things running smoothly so you won't be bothered with too many details."

"We thought it best if you concentrated on public relations for the foreseeable future."

"Holding press conferences."

"Giving interviews."

"Being a woman, I'm certain you'll want to do some redecorating."

"Your assistants have a list of the charitable functions we'd like you and Mr. Blaine to attend in the next few weeks. Quite important."

She smiled her cool, inscrutable smile and envisioned the executive dining room as it would look when it was transformed into an employees' child care center. The precious speck of life already growing inside her would be one of its very first customers.

She desperately wished Mitch were with her today, but it would be at least six more months before they could turn SysVal over to that brilliant band they'd chosen to lead their young company into a mature, profitable adulthood. She was going to miss working with him. By the time he came on board at FBT, her pregnancy would be advanced. She smiled as she envisioned the macho strut that was going to put in his walk—the first man in history to impregnate the CEO of Falcon Business Technologies.

Her head lifted ever so slightly as the building's loud-speaker system emitted three gentle chimes. "Mr. Ames to security," a soft voice announced. She tried to imagine that voice warning of a Japanese invasion in the parking lot.

She endured another hour of polite admonitions and

veiled commands before she excused herself and headed to the offices of the chairman. As she walked into the reception area, an army of identically clad assistants snapped to attention. They began picking up leather folders and legal pads. And as they walked forward, their mouths moved.

"Mrs. Blaine, if I could brief you on your agenda for the week . . ."

"Mrs. Blaine, we've scheduled your first press conference for—"

She held up her hand. "My name is Faulconer. You may call me Susannah. And the next person who says a word to me will—I swear to God—be given permanent responsibility for cleaning out every coffeepot in this building."

Turning her back on all of them, she walked into the private office of the chairman of FBT and shut the door.

With the exception of the many sprays of flowers from well-wishers, the office looked much as it had when her father had occupied it. She toured the room slowly, touching familiar objects—the bookcases, side chairs, a brass lamp. The gold and blue draperies drawn back from the great wall of windows were exact reproductions of the ones she remembered. Her father's huge desk with its polished malachite top still dominated the room. The bronze FBT falcon hung on the wall behind it, its wings spread wide to encompass the globe on which it perched.

The awesome scope of the task she had set out for herself swept over her. "Oh, Daddy, what am I doing here?"

But her father wasn't talking to her today. Maybe he knew what she had in mind.

To steady herself, she began opening the cards propped in the various flower arrangements. One was from Paige and Yank. They were converting the old guest house at Falcon Hill into a state-of-the-art laboratory for Yank. He had decided to work independently, dividing his time between projects for SysVal, Sam, and whoever else managed to capture his imagination. It amused Susannah to watch the man who had once been so involved in his work that a nuclear explosion couldn't distract him now shoot up his head at the faintest echo of Paige's footsteps. She could only imagine what he would be like when they had a child.

A dozen roses had arrived from Mitch's children. Their

thoughtfulness touched her, even though she suspected their father had been behind it. Still, they were wonderful kids, and the cheerful acceptance with which they had greeted her marriage to their father had been a blessing.

Angela had sent a splashy display of carnations, snapdragons, and daisies. So far, she was the only one Susannah and Mitch had told about their baby, and she had immediately announced that the child was to call her "Na Na."

"Not 'Granny,'" she had insisted, adjusting the silver-studded sleeves on her new red leather jacket. "I'm too young for that. But 'Na Na' has a nice ring."

Mitch and Susannah were touched by Angela's offer. Both suspected she would prove to be a first-rate grandmother, regardless of what she chose to call herself.

Susannah's eyes teared as she read the card from her former mother-in-law. "You'll always be my daughter. Knock 'em dead, kiddo!"

She walked over to the malachite desk, and after a moment's hesitation, took her place in the great leather chair that had once belonged to her father. The panel of switches that controlled the FBT fountains was still there. She jotted down a note to have it removed. That sort of power held no interest for her.

As she pushed her notepad aside, she spotted a small package wrapped in silver foil. It couldn't be from Mitch; his present had been on her night table when she had awakened that morning. While he had looked on, she had unwrapped a week's supply of naughty black underwear imprinted with the FBT logo.

"Dress for success," Mitch had said, and then he'd kissed her until she could hardly breathe and dragged her into the shower, where they'd made love.

After turning the silver box about in her hand, she opened the envelope that accompanied it and pulled out the card. In big block letters were the words REMEMBER YOUR ROOTS. It was signed, "Sam."

Inside the package she found a small gold charm, a perfect replica of the Blaze. She cupped it in her hand and told herself that a wise executive understood changes couldn't be made overnight. Adjustments had to be implemented slowly. Upheaval threatened people, made them feel insecure.

The wise executive understood the value of tact and patience.

And then she gazed about the spacious office and remembered that this was the place where her father had humiliated Sam.

"You were wrong, Daddy," she whispered. "You should have listened to him."

Taking the charm with her, she got up from the desk and went over to investigate the walnut cabinets. In one of them, she found the equipment that tied the executive office into the building's loudspeaker system. In the next cabinet was the elaborate stereo system that Cal had installed. She pulled a tape she had brought with her from her purse and slipped it into the cassette deck.

Looking down at the little Blaze charm in her hand, she smiled to herself and whispered, "This one's for the kids in the garage." She picked up the microphone and switched on FBT's loudspeaker system.

"Listen up, everybody. This is Susannah Faulconer speaking. Beginning in exactly one hour, my door is open. Everybody in this company who wants to talk to me, start lining up. Rank doesn't count. First come, first served. My door stays open until we're done. And you'd better be ready to strut your stuff, because starting right now, I'm throwing this corporation into chaos. All official policies are suspended. All normal procedures are up for grabs. We're going to rediscover who we are. And when we're done—if we're very smart and very lucky—we'll be ready to dazzle the world." And then she hit the button on the cassette recorder.

While the hallowed halls of FBT filled with the music of the Rolling Stones, she settled back at her desk, propped up her feet, and waited for the screams to start.

AUTHOR'S NOTE

This novel is based upon fact: the events surrounding the birth of the personal computer industry. These events, as well as the people, corporations, and organizations which were involved, serve as the factual foundation upon which my fictional drama takes place. My fictional characters are not intended to resemble real people, and any interplay my characters have with real persons and actual corporations is entirely a product of my imagination.

Of the many books and articles I have read to research this novel, the most useful was Steven Levy's fascinating book *Hackers: Heroes of the Computer Revolution*. Also useful were *Fire in the Valley: The Making of the Personal Computer,* by Paul Freiberger and Michael Swaine; *Silicon Valley Fever,* by Everett M. Rogers and Judith K. Larsen; *The Ultimate Entrepreneur: The Story of Ken Olsen and Digital Equipment Corporation,* by Glenn Rifkin and George Harrar; and *Charged Bodies: People, Power and Paradox in Silicon Valley,* by Thomas Mahon.

Readers interested in the rich and fascinating history of the Apple Computer Corporation would enjoy Michael Moritz's excellent *The Little Kingdom,* as well as John Sculley's *Odyssey,* a work that I consider one of the most intriguing books published in the last decade—a business book that has all the page-turning qualities of best-selling fiction. I would like to thank all of these authors for fueling my imagination and giving me so much of the valuable background for this novel.

I am deeply indebted to my trio of technical advisors: Dan Winkler, Gerald Vaughan, and Bill Phillips. Any errors in this book are entirely my responsibility. The three of them did their best with me.

I would also like to express my heartfelt appreciation to the wonderful people at IBM and Apple Computer, Inc., who so patiently answered my questions. Thanks also to Mary Pershall, Richard Phillips, John Titus, and DeDe Eschenburg for their helpful contributions.

And to the people at Pocket Books—you're the best! A special thanks to my editor, Claire Zion, who believed in this project from the beginning and never lost sight of the vision, not even when I did. Steven Axelrod, you have truly been a blessing. And I will forever be grateful to Linda Barlow, who encouraged me to write *Hot Shot* and whose extensive contributions to the final draft were critical.

Thanks, Lyd, for helping me learn what sisters are all about. Ty and Zach, be your best.

Susan Elizabeth Phillips
Naperville, Illinois